THE KIL

Ian St Ja... millionaire at the age of thirty, when the merchant bank backing his enterprises suddenly collapsed and took his business with it. In the years afterwards he started a management consultancy and later turned it into a small investment house. In 1977 he retired to write full time. His earlier novels include *The Balfour Conspiracy* and *Winner Harris*. Married, with three children, he and his family live in Ireland.

Available in Fontana by the same author

The Balfour Conspiracy
Winner Harris

IAN ST JAMES

The Killing
Anniversary

FONTANA/Collins

First published 1984 by William Heinemann Ltd

A continental edition first issued
in Fontana Paperbacks 1985
This edition first issued in
Fontana Paperbacks 1985

Copyright © Ian St James 1984

Made and printed in Great Britain by
William Collins Sons & Co. Ltd, Glasgow

CONDITIONS OF SALE
This book is sold subject to the condition
that it shall not, by way of trade or otherwise,
be lent, re-sold, hired out or otherwise circulated
without the publisher's prior consent in any form of
binding or cover other than that in which it is
published and without a similar condition
including this condition being imposed
on the subsequent purchaser

With love and thanks to my daughter Karen,
who helped type the first manuscript
. . . and the second . . . the third . . . fourth and the fifth.

PROLOGUE

When I began to write the story of my father's life I thought it would be easy. I had access to his old business records, copies of letters, press clippings, all the material I needed. Not only that but I knew a great many of his friends. But then I discovered a side of his life which had been hidden from me. The more I delved the more I found out, until a kind of pattern emerged which linked his life to the lives of other people. I thought it was coincidence at first, but that theory died as more facts were unearthed. I spent months in London, New York, Dublin, Paris, Belfast, even Nairobi – always searching to uncover the tracks. The revelations astonished me. My father had been involved in a feud which stretched back to his boyhood – a feud which touched the lives of a great many people. It smouldered over the years – spluttered, died down and flared up again – but it never went out. It was always there, if not always apparent. It was forever the link between the Connors and the Averdales, the O'Briens and the Riordans – a link that endured relentlessly – until THE KILLING ANNIVERSARY.

BOOK ONE

CHAPTER ONE

Finola Connors took to her bed. She did so wearily. For weeks she had suffered a sapping loss of energy. Everything was an effort, even simple things like carrying water up from the stand pump two flights down in the street. In days past she had done that a dozen times without catching her breath . . . now she counted every step and rested on every landing . . . and only half filled the buckets instead of slopping them to the brim as in the old days.

The good old days, she thought, shifting her bloated body uncomfortably. Times had been hard, but weren't they always. She sighed as her mind drifted back. So much had happened in this room, this one entire room for the two of them, when families of ten and twelve lived and slept in rooms no bigger in the next street. It had troubled her once. She had felt guilty – all this space when Dublin's slums were the worst in Europe. But hadn't Michael Collins explained it, the day she and Pat had moved in nine years ago. ''Tis not for you lovebirds,' he had said, waving a hand at the room, 'but for the whole of Ireland.' How right he had been. The meetings had started the very first week – not a day passed without one of them wanting to come in. She had seen them all in this room – Padraic Pearse and James Connolly, Eamon de Valera and dozens more. Some of their talk went beyond her, but she had watched and listened, and helped Pat where she could . . . guiding decisions with her sound common sense. Nine years? Had it really been that long? So many hours of excited crack with young patriots. Boys some of them, they had made her feel old. Erskine Childers always joking, Mick Mallin smiling, Dev serious, Cathal Brugha with a scowl on his face.

A sudden contraction made her cry out. She went rigid, paralysed by fear. Her eyes focused on the crucifix over the door. The agonies of childbirth were nothing new to Finola Connors – she had been six times pregnant before, only to birth a still-born child every time.

The spasm passed. She panted with relief and wiped beads of sweat from her hairline. How long, she asked, how long since the last contraction – how long until the next? Without a clock she was unable to judge. But sure there was plenty of time. Time for her sister to arrive, time even for Pat to be pacing the landing. She smiled as she remembered telling Pat that the baby was at least ten days away. Wasn't it for the best – best for a great lump like Pat to be well away at a time like this.

She cast about for fresh thoughts to keep her mind off the pain. Her gaze settled on the fireside chair. Joseph Plunkett's chair. He always sat there in the old days. Him with his long hair and rings on his fingers, and his never-ending talk. He used to say Ireland had a standing army of a hundred thousand poets. Pat would go red in the face and say it's a hundred thousand soldiers we need, *soldiers* not bloody poets! Her eyes shone at the memory. 'This room,' she said aloud, 'sure wasn't Mick right. Hasn't this room played a part in birthing a new Ireland.'

But another spasm struck fear into her heart and made her writhe on the bed. 'Soon,' she whispered, 'Brigid had better come soon. *Someone* had better come soon.' Even the sound of Pat's step on the landing would be welcome.

But Pat was in Mulligan's Bar, talking about the events of the day.

'What happened then, Pat?' someone encouraged.

Pat waited until those furthest away edged closer. Then loudly he said, 'Lord Fitzalan himself was there. Lord Fitzalan – His Britannic Majesty's representative in Dublin, the last Viceroy of all Ireland.'

'The last at last,' shouted the crowd at the bar.

'Lord Fitzalan himself,' Pat repeated, 'standing there with his hand held out. "I'm glad to see you, Mr Collins," says he, and Michael Collins shook the hand, "Like hell you are," says he, with a grin a mile wide.'

Hoots of laughter gave way to howls of triumph. At the end of the mahogany counter an old man tucked a fiddle under his chin and began to play the ballad of Kevin Barry. Those around him took up the song, Pat joined in too, though he would have been forgiven a sad note in his voice, for Pat had known Kevin Barry. Pat had sent the boy to his death. The summer before last. They had set up an ambush in King Street and killed a soldier. Young Barry had been captured and court-martialled. The IRA claimed he should be treated as a prisoner of war – but the British hanged him as a murderer.

The men roared the song, shouting with pride. Pat shouted too, but he wondered how many would have met death with the courage of that eighteen-year-old medical student. He pushed the thought aside. It was a sour note on a night like this. Tonight was for celebrating a new Ireland, free of the British at last. Next to him Danny Hoey was ordering up another round of drinks, while along the bar his cousin Eamon was recounting his role in the Easter Rising. 'Sure now,' he was saying, 'wasn't it then it all started? Wasn't it then we lit the lamp of freedom for all Ireland?'

But Eamon was a poor story-teller and was shouted down – while Pat was plagued from all sides to tell the same tale – as if there was a man there who hadn't heard it before. But no man loves a story better than an Irishman, and Pat had the gifts of a shanachie. Just the sound of his voice carried men back to their boyhoods, when the arrival of a story-teller would turn a whole village upside down with excitement. Extra turf would be thrown on the fire while they settled down to hear of Robert Emmet and Daniel O'Connell . . . and of the Fenian Risings and so many things. But all agreed that no man alive told the Easter Rising like Pat Connors, and for sure there was no better tale to tell in Ireland on 21 January 1922.

Pat began slowly. It was a close-run thing, he reminded them. Eoin MacNeil nearly called the whole thing off – especially when Casement was arrested – but Darlin' Padraic Pearse had insisted they go on. Pearse and Connolly had carried it through – without them the Rising would have gone the way of all the others – brave talk with no more substance than a whiff of smoke. But on that Easter Monday morning Pearse and Connolly marched their men out of Liberty Hall and down Sackville Street to the General Post Office. And moments later it was

Commandant-General Pearse who stood between the massive pillars at the front of the building. 'Irishmen and Irishwomen,' he shouted, 'Ireland, through us, summons her children to her flag and strikes for freedom.'

And sure enough a flag appeared on the roof of the GPO – the traditional green flag with the gold harp, but 'Irish Republic' had been embroidered across this one in gold silk. Then another flag was run up, a strange new flag, a tricolour of green and white and orange. Green for Ireland, orange for the Orange brothers in the north, and white for peace between the two.

Elsewhere in the city other rebels moved into position. Daly took over the Four Courts. John Connolly occupied City Hall. Sean Heuston's men marched into the Mendicity Institution . . . and Eamon de Valera took a force to occupy Boland's Flour Mills, overlooking the roads from Kingstown.

In the space of two hours, Dublin, second city of the British Empire, had effectively fallen to a handful of Irish rebels – with barely a shot being fired.

Years later Irishmen would ask, 'Where were you in 1916?' – and Pat Connors was one of the lucky ones. 'In the GPO,' he would answer, 'along with Pearse and Connolly and other brave men.'

'Tell us about the Lancers, Pat,' someone prompted, fearing Pat might miss some of the story.

Pat sipped his stout. It began quietly, he remembered. They erected barricades in the Post Office. Then, late in the afternoon, a group of Lancers appeared at the end of the street. The setting sun glinted on spurs and brass buttons. A light breeze tugged at the Lancers' pennants as they rode down Sackville Street. Suddenly rifle fire blazed from the GPO. Four Lancers lay dead on the cobblestones. The Easter killings had started.

Some Lancers escaped, and tore off to spread the news. Military commanders were stunned. It was hours before they flashed the news to England by naval telegraph . . . and gave the order for the six thousand British soldiers in Ireland to grab their arms and march upon Dublin.

On the Wednesday the British brought a gunboat up the Liffey and began to shell Liberty Hall. And the Sherwood

Foresters landed at Kingstown – only for their march on the city to be stopped at Mount Street bridge by a detachment of Dev's men sent from Boland's Mill. Time and again the Foresters moved forward, to be driven back by the Volunteers.

But British strategy inside the city was unfolding. Rebel positions were encircled, and then reduced to rubble by artillery fire. The gunboat on the river switched aim to the GPO. Field cannons started pounding from the end of Sackville Street. Machine-guns added their own deadly chatter . . . until the word went round . . . the GPO was doomed . . . it was merely a matter of time.

Shells ripped the crumbling fabric of the GPO for the rest of the day – but still the rebels held out. Thursday was the same. The boom of the gunboat's cannon, the snarl of artillery and crackle of machine-guns – all met by sporadic rifle fire from the Volunteers. Their flags still flew above them, and men scrambled amid the rubble to take up fresh positions. The badly injured were carried away to some hospital by women Volunteers – flames soared high into the sky, bathing the whole city in a scarlet glow. Fire swept through Dominick Street to the north and Abbey Street to the south . . . but still the guns pounded.

Finally Connolly made the decision to move. He led a group into Abbey Street, where they blasted their way into the *Independent* building. That done, he returned for the rest of his men. A ricochet bullet smashed through his ankle. In agony, under fire all the way, he dragged himself down the alley between Abbey Street and Princess Street, and hauled himself back into the Post Office.

The battle raged on through the hours of darkness. The gunboat boomed, the artillery never stopped. A red glare lit the sky. Great scarlet showers of sparks soared with each shell burst . . . but still the rebels fought on.

When Friday dawned nobody noticed – the grey morning light was imperceptible beneath the pall of greasy smoke. The men in the GPO clung on but elsewhere the battle was turning against them. Dev's detachment on the city boundary had finally fallen to the advancing Foresters. The British were across the canal at last . . .

Fires swept the Post Office. The roof collapsed. Bullets

whined everywhere. Connolly was carried to the front of the building, to direct operations from a stretcher. Michael Collins and Magistrate O'Rahilly were despatched to find alternative headquarters. They led a dash down Henry Street, awash with machine-gun fire. O'Rahilly fell, as did others on his heels. Collins got through almost alone. Another escape route had to be found. They tried Moore Street. Everyone made a run from the Post Office – with Connolly carried on his stretcher. They holed up in a grocer's shop, firing from every window as the British charged after them. Nearby was a pub, already in flames. The publican emerged from his door, leading his family under a white flag – a terrified huddle of people who barely reached the corner before being scythed down by bullets.

Inside the grocer's the rebels worked furiously – knocking through one wall, then another, until emerging in a fishmonger's shop in Great Britain Street. Exhausted, wounded, dazed – they erected barricades, then picked over their ammunition like misers counting gold. The British covered every movement with a blanket of fire. The fall of darkness brought little relief. The British infiltrated positions on all sides – denying the rebels chance to sleep or rest, or even tend the wounded.

They held a conference the next morning – with Connolly propped against a wall, wincing with agony. It didn't take long to accept the inevitable. They had no choice but to surrender. Elizabeth O'Farrell, a Volunteer Nurse, was sent carrying a white flag to the British . . . and, at 3.30 p.m. on Saturday 29 April, Pearse, wearing his Volunteer uniform with its Boer War slouch hat, ceremoniously handed his sword to Brigadier General Lowe on the steps of the burnt-out Post Office. The 1916 Rising was over.

In Mulligan's Bar, Pat Connors took a long swig of his beer. Nobody had spoken since he started, for nobody interrupts a shanachie. Even now the bar remained silent. They watched and waited for the rest of the story. Finally Pat burped softly and resumed his tale, lowering his voice to an undertone of reverence.

The executions began four days later. Pearse was the first. At his court-martial he said, 'When I was a child I

14

went down on my knees and promised God I would devote my life to free my country. I have kept my promise.'

Then the British shot him.

Thomas MacDonagh told his court-martial, ''Tis sweet and glorious to die for one's country. I am proud to die for Ireland, my glorious Fatherland.'

Then the British shot him.

A priest took a beautiful girl into Joseph Plunkett's cell and performed a marriage ceremony by the light of a candle. The girl was allowed ten minutes alone with Plunkett – then the British shot him.

Daly and Michael O'Hanrahan were executed at the same time. Poor Willie Pearse was court-martialled seemingly for no other reason than being Padraic's brother. Then the British shot him too.

James MacBride was executed on the fifth of May. Ceant was shot on the eighth – along with Mallin, Heuston and Colbert.

James Connolly was court-martialled in a chair, unable to stand on his shattered ankle. Earlier a surgeon had shared a few words with him while applying a splint to his broken bones. 'I'm wasting my time,' he told Connolly, 'they will shoot you for sure.'

'Oh, you think so?'

'I'm sure of it.'

'Why?'

'Can they buy you?'

'No.'

'Can they frighten you?'

'No.'

'Will you promise to be a good boy in future?'

'No.'

'Then they can do nothing but shoot you.'

'Oh, sure don't I recognize that,' said Connolly cheerfully. And minutes later he was joking with his wife and daughter. 'Do you know, Lily, a man came into the Post Office to buy a stamp. "Go away," says we, "we're fighting the British." "Oh," says he. "Is that the case? Sure it's a fine bloody revolution when a man can't even buy a stamp at the Post Office."'

Then the British shot him, sitting in his chair because he

was unable to stand. Sean MacDermott was executed along with him. Fifteen brave men were executed in ten days. Later an Irishwoman wrote, 'It was like watching a stream of blood coming from under a closed door.'

And so it was, Pat remembered – but Ireland would never be the same. The centre of Dublin lay in ruins. More than thirteen hundred people were killed or wounded during Easter week. The Rising had been put down, but Padraic Pearse had been right – a blood sacrifice had been needed and one had been given. So that now, on 21 January 1922, the British had sounded the last retreat from Dublin Castle – the British were going at last!

Three miles from Mulligan's Bar, in the cluttered room on Ammet Street, close to the Quays in Dublin's dockland, Finola Connors cried out with pain. Contractions racked her body. She jerked convulsively on the bed. Beads of sweat rose on her forehead to break into rivulets on the sodden pillow. Strength drained from her like sand through an hour-glass.

The spasm passed. Her lips moved in prayer as she turned towards the window. The night blackness glinted back from a gap in the curtains. She imagined the brooding bulk of the Guinness Brewery at the end of the street, with its chimneys that never stopped churning, and the all-pervading smell of yeast and malt which came with the soot. How many times had she stood at that window waiting for Pat? How many hours, weeks, months of her life had been spent looking down into that mean little street? She knew its scenes by heart – men selling potatoes from handcarts; ragged children with white, pinched faces, soldiers searching for hidden arms – and sometimes Pat himself, striding along with his shoulders back, as if he owned Dublin itself.

Her eyes brightened. They always did when she thought of Pat – even now, even during the last year when she had watched him change and been frightened by his new ways and adopted harshness. He was still her Pat underneath, still the same strong, gentle boy who had courted her. But her eyes darkened as she remembered his coldness at times, his callousness when he spoke of killing informers.

16

'We're at war, Finola,' he would say, 'and wars are won by killing people – it's the way things are.'

Her gaze strayed to the crucifix above the door, but even three decades of the rosary failed to erase the picture which haunted her. The body of a girl, no more than eighteen – her head shaved, tarred and feathered, then killed. Finola had known her, they had almost been friends. There had been no harm in her, just a young girl out for a bit of fun, who saw no harm in going out with a British soldier. Now she was dead and Finola's heart ached at the memory of her.

She had lost Pat to Mick Collins, that was the truth. But if so, she only partly resented it. She did not dislike Mick – how could she dislike anyone with his charm. She was no different to the rest of them, ready to agree to anything after an hour in his company. She had been proud at first, proud that Pat was one of Mick's most trusted men, proud when Mick asked Pat's advice . . . but the killings had sickened her. Black and Tans were one thing, but the killing of Irishmen and women was something else again. Killed on suspicion of being British informers.

A sudden stab of pain emptied her mind. She clutched herself and cried out – and was writhing on the bed when Brigid arrived, complete with Dary and Cooey, her two eldest.

One look took Brigid to the bed. She placed a hand on her sister's brow, while casting a quick look around the room. Then she despatched the children down to the street to fill the water buckets.

'And where's himself at a time like this?' Brigid wanted to know.

Finola sighed with relief as the pain subsided, but a few seconds passed before she had strength to answer. Even then her voice was weak, 'Sure won't he be working for Ireland somewhere. With Mick Collins like enough, or waiting–'

'It's my place he should have been, fetching me an hour ago. I suppose he was working for Ireland when he got you in this state, was he?'

Finola raised a faint smile, 'Sure doesn't he think it's a week away. Would you want him under your feet –'

Brigid's snort could have meant anything.

'It's my seventh time,' Finola said weakly.

'And don't you forget it. The seventh is the lucky one and everyone knows it. Sure won't you soon be nursing the strongest baby boy you ever set eyes on.'

'Did you know Pat was the seventh too?'

'I did not,' Brigid said with a surprised smile. 'The seventh son of a seventh son! Did you think of that? Sure won't he be the king of all Ireland one day – ' Words died in her throat as another contraction made Finola writhe on the bed. Brigid moved quickly to provide what comfort she could. Finola's clutching fingers clamped tight to her hand. Yet how tight was tight? Every ounce of Finola's strength was in that grip, but Brigid knew she could shake free if she wanted. If Finola was as weak as that now . . . Brigid shied away from the thought. She waited until the spasm was over, then drew a chair up to the bed. 'It'll be a long night by the look of you,' she sighed, rummaging in her basket, 'and you'll be needing some comfort before it's over.' She withdrew the bottle of Cork Gin from her bag with a flourish.

Finola looked greedily at the full bottle. She drank little as a rule, no more than a glass of stout with Pat on high days and holidays. But if it helped ease this terrible pain . . .

A few of them were singing *The Soldier's Song* in Mulligan's Bar, but they were off in a corner. The other men clustered around Pat, trying to persuade him to continue. Men under the spell of a shanachie no more left a tale unfinished than gave up drink for Lent.

But Pat was in two minds. He had given his word to wait for a message from his man, but that was hours ago. It should have been delivered by now. He glanced at the clock and felt a sudden uneasiness, as if something were wrong. But that was absurd . . . for *anything* to be wrong today, today of *all* days . . . with the British leaving Dublin Castle at last. Yet as he stared at the clock a nagging worry gnawed at his mind.

'Tell us about prison,' someone pleaded.

'What's that?' Pat asked absently.

'When you were in Mountjoy. After the Rising.'

Pat looked hard, as if seeing the questioner for the first time. A young man, no more than eighteen. He looked at the others. His cousin Eamon was his own age, thirty-six, whereas old Flynn the fiddler was the far side of sixty and O'Rourke was nearly as old. But the rest were younger – *young* men, little more than boys. Dear God, that's all they'd have been in 1916 – just boys.

Pat resigned himself to telling the tale. Maybe it was for the best. If he had to wait, talking would stop him worrying – a man can't fret for the morning when recalling last night – and it *seemed* like last night.

The British turned Dublin upside down after the Rising – searched the city from end to end, street after street, a house at a time. Three thousand people were carted off to jail – some were sent over the water to a special internment camp in Wales – but Pat and Eamon were incarcerated in Dublin, and were still there when the British Prime Minister came to inspect the jail four weeks later.

'Not that High and Mighty Mr Asquith stayed long,' Pat remembered with a grin, 'but you could see he was worried sick. He had a face like yesterday's rhubarb.'

Pat and Eamon were soon released, and by Christmas Michael Collins was home from Wales with the rest of the boys. Mick really went to work then, not that he had been idle in the internment camp, picking his men and explaining what he wanted when they got back to Ireland. Even so, 1917 progressed quietly – Dev got out of Dartmoor in time to win the East Clare By-election for Sinn Fein, the new Republican Party, in June – and then, in September, Thomas Ashe died.

Thomas had been in the Rising, alongside Pat and Eamon. He was released at the end of serving his time, but was re-arrested in August for giving 'a speech calculated to cause disaffection'. Well, most people thought it was a ridiculous charge and on Thursday 20 September Ashe went on hunger strike. Four days later, after being forcibly fed by the British, Ashe died in the Mater Hospital.

Collins organized a funeral fit for a saint. *Nine thousand* Volunteers escorted the coffin through the streets. Down the Dublin Quays went the cortege, and up O'Connell Street packed out with crowds. Fianna Boy Scouts sounded the Last Post at the Glasnevin Cemetery, then the armed escort fired volleys into the air. There was no oration at the graveside. Collins wouldn't allow it. After the volley he simply announced, 'Nothing additional needs to be said. That volley is the only proper speech to make over the grave of a dead Fenian.'

The whole country wept. Sean O'Casey wrote a ballad, and the hymn which Thomas Ashe himself composed was sung all over the place, not just in church but in pubs and on street corners. People flocked to join Sinn Fein, yet while all this was happening thousands of Irishmen were in Flanders, fighting the Great War for the British. Of course they had volunteered, but when Lloyd George wanted to *conscript* Irishmen in 1918 . . . well that was different. Even the church spoke out against it, and at the General Election in December Sinn Fein swept the south like fire through tinder. Seventy-three seats they won to the Westminster Parliament. Not that the newly elected members could go because half were locked up in British jails for speeches 'calculated to cause disaffection'. So those who were free boycotted Westminster and set up their own parliament in Dublin. The Dail they called it, and Dev was elected President.

The British really saw red. The Dail was declared illegal and twenty thousand people were arrested in the first six months of 1919. Cabinet ministers went on the run and conducted their business from hole-in-the-corner offices all over Dublin. British detectives from G Division started lifting Republicans faster than a dog picking up fleas – at least they did until Mick Collins put his Squad to work. Pat Connors was in the Squad. They shot three detectives dead before Christmas. Then the British brought a top man down from Belfast, Detective Inspector Redmond – but the Squad took care of him in January. After that dozens of men resigned from the Royal Irish Constabulary for fear of the Squad – so the British recruited the Black and Tans.

They were butchers. Whole lorryloads would roar into a village. Out they would jump, firing shots in the air and ordering men and women from their homes, lining them up against a wall, young and old, the sick included – to be questioned and searched. No raid ever ended without a dozen people being beaten senseless with rifle butts – and more often than not the Tans set fire to the village as they left, as a 'final warning'.

In Mulligan's Bar Pat Connors paused to sip from his jar. Men around him remained predictably silent. Even the youngest remembered the Black and Tans. Everyone knew of villages and towns burned to the ground – Balbriggan, Lahich, Meath, Mallow . . . and Cork of course . . . the Black and Tans went berserk in Cork. And with the burnings came the killings, all over Ireland.

By autumn 1920 Dublin was an armed citadel, shut down at night under curfew. Civilians were not allowed out from eight in the evening until five the next morning. All night long tanks and armoured cars careened through the streets. Citizens were pulled from their beds and taken off to suffer God knows what torture at the local barracks.

Ireland groaned under the lash. Ireland wept. Ireland prayed – and might have succumbed but for the will of one man. It seemed at times that only Mick Collins stood between the British and total subjugation. And Collins was enough.

Pat remembered the shop in Abbey Street. 'We turned it into a painters and decorators. George Moreland's we called it, because it sounded Jewish and Protestant at the same time. We acted the part too – all dressed up in overalls, pretending to be busy with paint pots and things.'

Abbey Street was but a minute from Dublin Castle, so it was easy enough to nip out for a gun battle with the G men and be back in overalls in no time. Daily ambushes took place all over the city. Collins took risks which made Pat's hair stand on end. Every man in the Squad worried about Collins. The military were offering ten thousand pounds for him, dead or alive, but still he cycled around the city like a village postman without a care in the world. First he was at Moreland's organizing the Squad, then off to another fake business. To the Irish he became a living legend – to the British the devil incarnate. The British wanted Collins killed off, and the sooner the better. So a group of army officers met in Cairo to plan the destruction of Collins and all that he stood for – and in October the Cairo Gang arrived in Dublin.

They drifted into the city in ones and twos – and by the end of the week had taken up lodgings all over the city. Then they went to work, always at night, emerging like vampires when curfew fell. Dressed in civilian clothes they swooped everywhere, dragging suspects from their beds and carrying them off to bare barrack rooms for interrogation. One by one those associated with Collins were identified. It was time for the killings to begin.

Men with English accents burst into a room at the Exchange Hotel in Parliament Street. There they murdered John Lynch, a Kilmallock businessman. It was a mistake. The Cairo Gang sought *Liam* Lynch, the leader of the West Cork Brigade of the IRA. Liam escaped and raised the alarm.

Collins struck back. His spies reached everywhere, even into the Castle itself. By 21 November he was ready. At first light that morning men from the Squad fanned through Dublin. Some went to Mount Street. Two men lodged at No. 38, a Lieutenant Aimes and a Lieutenant Bennett. Both were serving officers in the British Army – yet neither was attached to a regiment stationed in Dublin. They had no obvious duties, no apparent reason to be in Ireland at all. Both were secret members of the Cairo Gang . . . and at nine that morning they were dragged from their beds and shot dead.

Simultaneously a visit was paid to a house at 119 Lower Baggot Street where lodged a certain Captain Baggelley, the very same man who had murdered John Lynch. At precisely nine o'clock he too was pulled from his bed and shot. The same fate befell his best friend, Captain Newbury, a few doors away at No. 92 Lower Baggot Street.

Elsewhere, on their way back from mass, a dozen young men walked briskly to No. 28 Pembroke Street. A maid answered the door. The men pushed past. They consulted their watches. 'It's to be done at nine o'clock,' Collins had told them. And at nine it *was* done – with a vengeance. Some of the Cairo Gang refused to come out of their rooms. Others were shot as they opened their doors. Two agents were killed on the landing, already running with blood.

Visits were made right across Dublin. Some of the Cairo

Gang were staying at the Gresham Hotel – they were shot too, some in front of their wives.

The game was up for the Cairo Gang. Anxious men could be seen leaving their lodgings all over Dublin – hurrying towards the Castle with their baggage. Mick Collins had drawn blood. But the day had just started. When news of the morning's events spread, the Black and Tans took to the streets intent on revenge . . . and they took it in full that afternoon.

A football match was being played at Croke Park. The army was searching the crowd for arms – and the Black and Tans joined in. Half an hour later they mounted a machine-gun and opened fire into the crowd. People panicked and ran on to the field. The firing continued. An old man was sawn in half. A young boy fell screaming. Dead and wounded were all over the pitch. Finally the army intervened and a handful of brave British soldiers drove the Black and Tans back to prevent a massacre. As it was twelve people were killed and seventy badly injured. Ireland had suffered its first *Bloody Sunday* of the twentieth century.

In the cramped room on Ammet Street Brigid O'Hara was out of her depth. Faced with a breech birth and a haemorrhaging patient, she sent Dary racing for a doctor. Meanwhile she did all she could – while Finola uttered piercing cries and garbled prayers. She called for Pat again and again as her back arched and her legs splayed wide on the blood-soaked sheet. Brigid bent over her, wiping sweat from the tear-stained face until Finola's wild thrashing subsided. Now her limbs jerked with each successive convulsion as if pulled by unseen strings . . . but her strength faded as the blood seeped out of her.

Cooey, aged seven, sat in the corner, hands clamped over her ears, eyes clenched shut in her frightened face, wishing for the hundredth time she had gone with Dary to find a doctor. She had wanted to go, pleaded . . . but her mother had refused – 'Sure now, Cooey, you stay where you are – I'll maybe have a need for you later.' Need me for what, Cooey asked herself, not daring to question, not wanting to know, not wanting to hear the screams from the bed . . . just wanting to be gone from this room.

The group in the corner of Mulligan's Bar was giving out with rebel songs, while at the counter Pat continued his story.

Bloody Sunday set a torch to Ireland. Ambushes became commonplace in Dublin – and fighting was even more ferocious outside the city. Flying columns of IRA men waylaid lorryloads of Black and Tans on country roads. Death stalked the land twenty-four hours a day. The *Irish Times* mourned – 'The whole country runs with blood. Unless the fighting is stopped every prospect of a political settlement will perish and our children will inherit a wilderness.'

But who would stop the killings? Who could obtain a settlement? Ulstermen in the north didn't want a settlement – at least not the one advocated by Mick Collins. Protestant Ulstermen would fight to retain their links with Britain – they were British and proud of it.

At Westminster Lloyd George struggled to find a formula acceptable to all sides. King George V made a speech – 'I appeal to all Irishmen . . . to forgive and forget, and to join in making for the land they love a new era of peace . . . in which the Irish people, north and south, under one Parliament or two . . . work together in common love of Ireland.'

Pat Connors rubbed his jaw reflectively. It had not been easy, accepting the idea of a truce. He remembered the arguments – 'We've won nothing yet. The British still rule Ireland. Let's get on with the fight.' But fight with what? Few knew it – certainly not the British government – but the IRA was desperately short of arms and ammunition. According to Mick Collins they were within three weeks of defeat, and not just for want of bullets – loyal men were almost as scarce. Many had been arrested, tortured, put to death. Pat had lost friends by the score – and Mick's closest friend, Dick McKee, had been murdered in the guardroom of Dublin Castle on the eve of Bloody Sunday. Aye, a truce was sorely needed . . . so in July one was declared. After two and a half years of bloodshed, peace descended on Ireland. Leather-gaitered IRA men came down from the hills and mixed freely with Black and Tans in Grafton Street. Ireland sighed with relief.

General Smuts, the South African Prime Minister, came to Dublin as an intermediary seeking a formula for negotiations. Dev faced a devil of a job. Sinn Fein was split down the middle – some wanted a Republic at once, nothing else would do, but others were prepared to obtain independence in stages – and when Smuts floated the idea of Dominion status, making Ireland like his own South Africa or Canada or Australia, the idea caught on. Dev said if Dominion status were offered he would do his best to persuade his colleagues to accept it – and Dominion status *was* offered, when Dev went to London to meet Lloyd George a month later. But it was Dominion status with a difference . . . six counties in the north would be excluded . . . not, as Lloyd George was quick to point out, due to any British imperial wishes, but simply because Ulster Unionists insisted on remaining British. Dev said bluntly: it was all or nothing – and that was the impasse. Negotiations broke down. Dev returned to Dublin, and Lloyd George threatened to end the truce.

But the truce held. Dev and Lloyd George maintained an uneasy contact, and after much haggling the Irish were invited to London again. This time Dev stayed in Dublin and Arthur Griffith and Michael Collins led the delegation. The conference dragged on for weeks, bogged down again and again by the two issues of the Crown and Ulster. The hardline Republicans wanted Republic status now – Australians and Canadians and the like could please themselves – but Ireland could hardly be a Republic if their leaders still swore allegiance to the British Crown. And as for Ulster – well, one look at a map was proof that it was part of Ireland – so of course it had to be included.

The talks droned on through October to November and into December. The Ulster leaders, meeting Lloyd George separately, refused to have anything to do with the south. Ulster was British and insisted on remaining so. Then Lloyd George, as ingenious as a cartload of monkeys, came up with a compromise – two parliaments, one north and one south, with a boundary in between fixed according to the wishes of the inhabitants. Collins thought about it. The gains would outweigh the losses. They would get *most* of what they wanted . . .

The talks gathered pace. Collins and Griffith argued long and hard. Membership of the British 'Empire' was ruled out . . . but membership of a 'Commonwealth' was accepted. Words were played with, clauses altered . . . until finally there seemed nothing left to argue about. Twenty-six of Ireland's thirty-two counties had won the freedom to govern themselves. The name of the new state in the south became the very last issue – the word 'Republic' was anathema to British ears – but even that was resolved by the adoption of *Saorstat* meaning Free State. The conference had lasted eight weeks – now, at last, the talks were over. The Treaty between Great Britain and the new Irish Free State was signed . . . and the first details appeared in Dublin's newspapers that evening.

Finola screamed. Brigid winced as fingernails dug into the flesh of her upper arms. Instinctively she glanced down to see the effect of this latest contraction – only to blanch at the sight of even more blood seeping across the soiled sheet. Not seeping, *gushing*, spurting crimson red as from an open artery. She hid her terrified expression by lowering her face on to the pillow next to Finola's matted hair. She kissed Finola briefly, then pulled away and turned quickly to the small girl in the corner – 'Cooey! Outside – on the landing this minute!'

Cooey's eyes sprang open. Her mother's fear was obvious. Cooey bolted from the room. Brigid hurried after her, closing the door on Finola's screams. 'Find Dary,' Brigid said urgently, 'try Doc Rafferty's in Meardon Street first – that's where he should be. If not . . . if not . . .' She pushed a hand through her hair, carrying a smear of Finola's blood across her forehead. She cast round desperately for other ideas. Dary was a good, sensible child, he'd be waiting on Rafferty as like as not, or seeking him out if he was off somewhere else. 'If not,' Brigid repeated helplessly, 'well *someone* at Rafferty's will be knowing.' She pushed the girl along the landing, propelling her by her shoulders. 'Get the doctor back *here* now, Cooey, you understand that? Get the doctor here – then go looking for himself as fast as your legs will carry you.'

'But where? Where will he be? Where will I be finding Uncle Pat?'

Brigid groaned. Pat Connors might be anywhere, in a pub probably, arguing his head off for the rights of Irishmen while the very life ebbed from the girl he married. 'Try Mulligan's,' she suggested urgently. 'If he's not there like as not they'll know where to find him.' She gave the girl a final push towards the top of the stairs: 'And run Cooey, run all the way.'

The girl's feet clattered on the steps, one hand sliding down banisters as high as her shoulders. She reached the half landing when she heard her mother calling after her. 'And after himself fetch Father Murphy,' Brigid shouted, leaning out from the balustrade, 'and hurry now, Cooey, run all the way.'

'Mick Collins is a fuckin' traitor,' shouted the big man in the corner of Mulligan's Bar, 'a traitor to all Ireland.'

Conversation stopped dead. The sudden silence was deafening. All eyes swivelled to Pat Connors who froze with a glass midway to his lips.

The man advanced from the corner, shaking himself free of restraining hands. 'Collins sold out, says I. The British still rule the north.'

Pat lowered his drink and stared coldly. 'You're drunk,' he said quietly. 'Any more of that and it's outside you'll be, flat on your back.'

But the man ignored the warning. He pushed Danny Hoey aside and stuck a finger under Pat's nose. 'Collins sold out,' he repeated.

Pat tried to stifle his temper. He would never forget meeting Mick on his return from London. The newspapers were full of the Treaty. Mick slumped into the car as if he hadn't slept in a month. 'What are they saying about me?' he had asked, bone-tired. Pat had answered loyally, 'They are saying what's good enough for Mick Collins is good enough for them.' Mick had grunted and looked out of the window. 'You know, Pat, when I signed that Treaty it felt like signing my own death warrant. There will be trouble, mark my words, but we got the best deal we could. It gives us freedom to achieve freedom for the whole of Ireland. It's a big step forward, we must make people see that.'

The man spat on the floor. 'That's what I think of Mick Collins.'

Pat growled a warning, 'You'll not repeat that in my hearing. Mick and the others got the best deal they could – better than anyone would have thought –'

'Says Collins. But I say different and there's plenty who see it my way.'

'You were there, I suppose?' Danny Hoey asked sarcastically. 'Standing up to Lloyd George an' Churchill and the like –'

It was as far as he got. The big man turned and hit all in one movement. Danny's head went back like a chicken with a broken neck. Then Pat slammed his fist into the big man's stomach. Within a second every man there was throwing a punch. Mulligan himself scrambled over the bar and took a flying leap at the big man's friends as they charged from the corner. Eamon grabbed a man by the hair and bounced his head on the counter. The whole place erupted in uproar. Pat Connors was the target – the big man and two others took after him like dogs at a rabbit. Not that Pat reacted like a rabbit. He caught one such a blow that the man's feet lifted from the floor and he flew backwards over a table. Then Pat went down himself, with the big man swinging a boot. Danny Hoey, still groggy from that initial blow, barged into the big fellow and knocked him off balance. Pat rolled on to one knee, then catapulted forward into the big man's middle. Over they went, knocking chairs and tables aside, in and out of men's legs, swearing and grunting and gouging . . .

The big man staggered backwards through the street doors. Pat went after him. Down they went, with the others emptying out on to the pavement to watch them battle it out. Pat was getting the better of it when a small boy broke through the ragged cordon of men. 'Uncle Pat! Uncle Pat!' the boy shouted breathlessly. The onlookers grabbed him, pulling him back – but the boy squirmed away, as quick a a fish. '*Uncle Pat!*' he screamed, his small chest heaving. But Pat's head was full of his own stertorous breathing and the shouts of the crowd. '*Uncle Pat!*' screamed the boy.

Then Pat heard. He glanced sideways, surprised to see the child so close. In that split second the big man lunged, looping his hands round Pat's neck and locking until his knuckles shone white in the lamplight. Pat's face jerked down to meet the big man's head with a sickening thud. One, two, three awful head butts. Those nearby heard Pat's nose break under the very first blow. The big man butted again. Pat reeled under the onslaught. Again the big man's head smashed into Pat's face . . . and again, until the big man no longer had the strength to hold Pat upright. Pat hit the gutter like a sack of potatoes.

'Uncle Pat! Uncle Pat!' The small boy was on his knees. Tears streamed down his face. His narrow shoulders jerked as he sobbed. Mulligan swooped and lifted him clear. Someone ran out from the pub carrying the slops bucket. Guinness-scented water stung Pat back to life. He cursed, then opened one eye in his broken face as Danny probed with a handkerchief. Mulligan returned, barely able to hold the child who wriggled like an eel. Finally the boy broke free and threw himself down in the gutter at Pat's side. 'Uncle Pat!' he gasped, still sobbing for breath. 'Please – the Mammy says you're to come right away. Doc Rafferty's there, an' Father Murphy . . . and . . . oh, Uncle Pat!'

CHAPTER TWO

Few in Ammet Street had a good word for Pat Connors when it came to the death of his wife. Even those who forgave his absence from Finola's death-bed could find no excuse for his subsequent behaviour.

The stories they told were true enough. Of how Pat came home that night, smelling like a brewery, with one eye closed and a gash as deep as the Liffey in his head. The room overflowing with people – Brigid of course, clutching the newborn baby to her breast, the surgeon, Father Murphy and at least a dozen others. The keening and wailing could be heard all over the street. Pat strode in and fell to his knees, grasping Finola's lifeless hand in his own.

He stayed there fully five minutes according to some, crouched silently, without a word, a cry or a murmur. When Father Murphy tried to comfort him Pat pushed him away. Brigid showed him the child, but Pat wasn't having that either. Instead he stood up and turned on his heel. His feet pounded the stairs and a moment later he was out in the street, swallowed up in the darkness.

They searched all night. Brigid's husband, Tomas, led men and boys up and down the Quays until dawn, fearing that Pat had thrown himself into the Liffey. In the morning Father Murphy and others looked all over – they even sent word to Mick Collins himself, who dropped what he was doing and rushed down to Ammet Street with the Dail at his heels. The neighbours never saw the like in all the years they lived there.

The wake when it came was the strangest imaginable . . . with the women keening as usual, but half the men absent looking for Pat. Mick Collins himself came to the funeral, all dressed up in his new Free State uniform. Dev and Cathal Brugha came too – though it was no secret they were at Mick's throat over the Treaty. In Pat's absence, Tomas led the mourners, with Brigid beside him carrying the newborn child swathed in a white blanket. The rain held off, which was a miracle. The coffin was lowered into the ground and earth thrown over it. Father Murphy stepped forward, but Mick Collins brushed him aside. Instead of words Mick drew his revolver and fired a salute over the grave.

Then, out of nowhere, Pat Connors appeared. Some claimed after to have seen him watching from the cover of the juniper trees. Maybe they did, but the first most saw was when he pushed his way to the front of the mourners. Mick Collins was still over the grave, a haze of smoke rising from his revolver. He thrust the pistol away and stretched out to clasp Pat to his chest, but Pat held him at bay as he stared down at the loose earth. He was drawn and tired-looking, in need of a shave and attention to his bruised face – but no tears wet his eyes. Instead he bore a look of disbelief – the expression he might have worn if confronted by a barefaced lie.

Father Murphy whispered, 'Glory be to the Father and

30

the Son and the Holy Ghost,' and might have gone on in the same vein but for the look on Pat's face, which clearly said that was a lie too. How he did it without saying a word nobody knew, nobody cared either, they were too shocked at Pat's meaning.

Pat turned away. He pushed past Cathal Brugha as if the man weren't there. Brigid called after him, afraid he was leaving – 'Pat, it's your son I have in my arms.' He switched his gaze to the bundle in the blanket, staring as if he had never seen a baby before. People held their breath, hoping that sight of the infant might ease the shock from his eyes. But not a bit of it. Instead he shook his head, then pushed through the onlookers to walk across to the low wall surrounding the churchyard. It was broken in part, and freshly delivered stones waited on the ground for re-building. Pat stooped and gathered the largest into his arms. He retraced his steps to the grave, where he dropped to his knees and gently laid the stones into place over the broken earth. Father Murphy stepped forward, but Pat pushed him away and started back to the broken wall and the heap of loose stones.

'Pat,' Mick called softly, 'I've a mind to give a hand with that, if you'll let me.'

Pat might have been looking at a stranger. Nobody would have believed the two men were close. Finally Pat's shoulders heaved into a shrug of indifference – and he turned away to gather more stones. Mick followed him silently – and after him went Dev and Cathal Brugha and every man there – like an army of ants, fetching and carrying from the wall to the grave. The cairn grew higher and higher. Pat pushed now and then to check it for balance. Nobody spoke. The work progressed to the sound of stone clinking on stone – with the primitive melody of women keening in the background, and men's breath rasping as they strained under the weight of the stones.

It was soon finished. Standing four feet high and five square the cairn was solidly built. Pat rested his hands on stones a third the way down. When he pushed, veins like whipcord stood out from his neck. The cairn stood firm. Pat stepped back. A sob escaped his lips. Then he stepped back again until he was beyond the mourners and close to the juniper trees. Never once did his gaze leave the cairn. Mick Collins turned, as did the others. The scene resembled a tableau with everyone watching Pat stare at the cairn. But it seemed wrong to scrutinize a man grieving over his dead wife – so after a moment all eyes looked back to the cairn – and in those few brief seconds Pat Connors vanished.

The gathering broke up after that. Dev and Brugha hurried off for a meeting with their political friends. Tomas and Brigid led some of the others back to the empty room on Ammet Street. There was no talk as to what would happen to Finola's baby, it was just accepted that Brigid would care for him until Pat turned up – that was the talk, Pat and his astonishing behaviour. Where had he gone and how long for – those were the questions. Some wanted to mount another search, but Tomas was against it – 'Leave him be,' was his verdict. 'Won't we lock up here and go home. Pat knows where we live well enough, he'll turn up when he's ready.'

But weeks were to pass before Pat showed himself, and those days were a mess. Ireland was torn apart by the Treaty. Dev walked out of the Dail in protest, and with him went Erskine Childers, Cathal Brugha, Austin Stack, and even Robert Barton who had signed the Treaty in London along with Mick Collins. Even Ernie O'Malley – one of Mick's most trusted organizers – denounced the Treaty and all that it stood for. The oath of allegiance was the sticking point – that clause in the Treaty which compelled Irishmen in the Dail to swear allegiance to the British monarch as head of the Commonwealth. Dan Breen spoke for many when he said it made the Treaty 'the negation of everything I ever fought for . . . I'll never be compelled to give allegiance to a foreign king.'

Mick and the others struggled on. Arthur Griffith formed an administration which ratified the Treaty by sixty-four votes to fifty-seven – supported outside the Dail by the Church and business, along with the unions and most of the public – all of whom were sick to the back teeth with the killings. But a large part of the IRA was against it, so there was no telling what would happen. One thing was sure, more trouble was coming, and Mick Collins, beset by problems, missed Pat Connors more keenly than ever before.

As for Pat, he walked fair across Ireland. Finola's death had broken him. Shunning company, he took to the hills and walked. Nothing made sense any more, not God, not the Catholic Church, not Mick Collins, not a Free Ireland, not anything. He was lost. As lost as yesterday, lost as truth in the mouth of a liar. They were all liars – all the bloody priests, the bishops, the Pope – the whole fucking lot of them. There was no God – or, if so, God was a ghoul.

Pat's fists clenched and unclenched as he walked. He kicked the turf and banged into stone walls as if to knock them aside. He walked until he dropped – to wake at dawn ready to walk again. He seemed oblivious of the rain, or the mist, or the pale sun which occasionally pierced the scudding grey clouds. Constant damp ate into his joints and brought cramp to his muscles, but he felt no physical pain. He lived in his mind. He experienced no emotion at all for much of the time, save that of anger. A deep burning anger, born of betrayal. What he valued most had been put to the sword. Someone would pay for that – the betrayers would pay – when Pat identified them.

He ate nothing for two days – then, on the third, bought some bread on the outskirts of a village. He walked quickly away from the startled shopkeeper, eating as he went. His travels were without plan. He cared not where he went. Only solitude mattered. The need to think lay heavy upon him. He stuck to the hills, avoiding villages, shunning contact with anyone.

He walked westwards, but lacked a clear idea of his whereabouts. Not that it mattered. Not that anything mattered now – for anger gradually gave way to despair. He kept going because it occupied his mind with minor decisions – which path to take, which wall to climb, when and where to cross a river. And walking kept him alive, for he was soaked to the skin, and to stop might mean never starting again. So he pressed on, driving himself, taunting his aching body while jeering his past beliefs, cursing God, the Church and all humanity.

Late on the fourth day he reached the outskirts of Sligo. He had not been there before and was ignorant of the history of the place. Not that he cared. From an overlooking hilltop he saw the town straddling a river as it flowed into the sea. He paused, sniffing the salt air. Suddenly his pulse quickened. In the bay was an island, isolated, remote, cut off. He caught his breath. Perhaps it was his mood, but the very desolation of the island drew him. Without knowing why he knew he was going there. His journey would end on that speck of land surrounded by the cold waters of the Atlantic. He peered again into the fading light. But was it surrounded by water? A kind of causeway seemed to link it to land on the far side. He walked a hundred yards and stared again. Rain, finer than mist, filtered the scene, blurring outlines. He strained his eyes, still uncertain – but the mere suggestion of a causeway was enough to quicken his pace. He could not explain the compulsion which drew him – he just knew that he wanted to get on to that island.

It took an hour to reach the far side of the bay. He clambered down the cliff to the water's edge. Gulls swooped and screamed around him. Waves, shoulder-high, smashed into a promontory, drenching him with spume-tipped water which left seaweed in his hair. Sand and shale tugged at his feet. A buffeting wind, full of the pungent ocean, took his breath away – but the causeway stood before him like the entrance to a secret place.

Pat never hesitated. He plunged down the beach and started across, skidding on weed-covered rocks and cursing aloud as the very force of the water threatened to knock him over. Inexplicably, he felt excited. The sense of space, of sky and sea, of the strong, raw power of nature, was overwhelming. Gulls screamed alarmingly as they dived past his head, beating their wings, as if to drive him back. Pat roared defiance, but his shouts drowned amid the crashing waves and the rising howl of the wind. Then he stumbled. Suddenly he was down. Water swirled to his elbows and covered his haunches. Above him the sky darkened and the heavens opened up. Rain fell in a drenching downpour, while on all sides the sea spat and hissed as the tide raced in.

For some moments he lacked the strength to rise – just clinging to the rocks below the water absorbed his strength. The shocks of the past days, lack of food, the effort of walking a hundred miles and more, all tore at his failing energy. Total exhaustion was near. He managed a half step forward, only to be swept over by an onrushing wave. He spluttered to the surface, cutting his hand on an outcrop of rock. Driving rain reduced visibility to a few yards, but one searching glance over his shoulder said it was hopeless to go back – he was cut off by the rising tide.

He struggled forward, pulling himself up, only to fall once again. He crawled and stumbled – somehow he made it to the shore. He collapsed on the beach and let the rain beat down on him. It was thirty minutes before he regained enough strength to move. He groaned with fatigue. Every muscle ached. His very bones seemed bruised and tender.

Time lost all meaning. How long it took to stumble upon the abandoned cabin was an unanswerable question. It seemed hours as he scrambled about in the pitch black, fighting the howling gale to stay upright, teeth chattering, eyes screwed into slits against the blinding rain. It *seemed* hours, but it may have been less – he was just thankful to find shelter. The door was barely held by a hinge, panes were missing from the window, but it was a blessed sanctuary on such a wild night. He stumbled about the single room like a blind man, with outstretched hands, shivering uncontrollably. He fell against a table in one corner and under it found some rags. In the hearth he discovered some old newspapers. Sacks caked with dried mud were heaped in another corner. Painfully he stripped off his clothes and rubbed himself raw with the sacks – and when his skin burned all over and his circulation was restored, he wrapped himself into the sacks and crawled under the table. For the first time in four days he was too exhausted to think, too crushed to demand answers to the questions which plagued him. The wind howled through the roof timbers and tore at the door – but Pat Connors slept soundly at last.

Meanwhile Pat's friends in Dublin prayed for his safety, but people feared the worst as the days passed.

Dublin itself was like a powder keg on the end of a slow fuse. An uneasy peace prevailed, but no matter how persuasive Mick Collins was in the Dail, *real* power lay with the soldiers of the IRA – and they were split down the middle, with units pro- or anti- the Treaty according to the views of their commanders.

Fights broke out wherever men argued about the Treaty. No pub was safe for a man with strong views. And everyone knew Pat's views. A theory took root that he had got drunk after the funeral and become involved in a fight. He was handy with his fists but what if he had been outnumbered? Or what if – as was happening more and more – some of the anti-Treaty IRA had come looking for him with a revolver? Many a man with plenty to say had got himself shot, or had just disappeared. Which is what people thought had happened to Pat.

When Pat awoke, daylight streamed through the window. Gulls circled high in a washed-out sky. The familiar sound of their cries took him back to the Quays and the room on Ammet Street. Suddenly it all came back – Finola was dead! Like a blow as he recovered consciousness. Finola was *dead*! He groaned and rolled over, wishing he were dead too. Suddenly a noise caught his ear. A tiny sound. Hairs prickled on his neck. Fighting the British had given him a sense of survival. He *knew* he was being watched. Someone was in the room! Memories of last night scrambled through his mind. He had been alone, alone in the sea, on the shore, in this wreck of a cabin. But he was not alone now.

He remained motionless for a long moment – then moved fast, rolling over to make a moving target. He glimpsed a kaleidoscope of images – floor, window, sky, walls, door – until he came to rest in the centre of the room.

A boy stood just inside the door, a youngster, no more than twelve, with a mass of red hair above frightened eyes. Pat laughed, but the sound emerged muddled, between a groan and a sigh of relief. The boy jumped like a startled hare and fled, his footsteps scrambling over the shale outside.

Pat listened to the sounds fade into the distance, then grunted and heaved himself upright. His swollen ankle throbbed painfully as he carried his wet clothes to the broken window, where he hung them to dry. He took his

36

boots to the door and flung them out into the wintry sunshine. The sea was less than thirty yards away, but it was different from last night – still grey and speckled with foam, but this sea lapped the shore like a tabby cat at a bowl of milk. This sea threatened no one.

Hours later, Pat went for a walk, his clothes still damp and his boots white from salt water. Five days of stubble scratched his chin and a scab had formed across the cut on his forehead. He limped badly, favouring his left foot. Meeting him would have made anyone jump. But Pat met nobody.

The island was larger than he had imagined. Inhabited too, to his disappointment. Smoke rose from a huddle of cottages. Deliberately Pat walked in the opposite direction. He wandered. Perhaps his mind wandered too. His thoughts always started and finished with Finola, but they ranged far and wide in between. Why? Why had she let him think her time was a week away? He could have helped, done something, fetched aid. Why had she not confided in him? And why had she been taken from him? That was the biggest why of all.

He sat on a huge boulder staring out at the Atlantic as if seeking answers from all that space. Overhead wheeling flights of plover called plaintively. Pat stared, sometimes sightlessly, sometimes registering a shift of light or a changing cloud pattern. Then he trudged back to the cabin, for no other reason than the wind had turned cold.

He discovered some potatoes in one of the sacks. His matches had dried and he lit a fire of driftwood. He found some turf and roasted the potatoes. Night fell. The wind was up again, not as rough as last night, but enough to rattle loose boards in the roof. Suddenly he heard a different sound. Footsteps. Someone was approaching the cabin. He turned towards the door. He wondered if it were the boy again, but these steps were heavier, the steps of a man. They paused outside. Pat had wedged the door shut against the wind, opening it would need a good kick. Then came the knock, three taps delivered to the door by somebody's knuckles.

'Go away,' Pat shouted.

A delay while Pat's response sank home. Then a man's

voice, 'I come in peace.'

'Then go the same way. I'll not trouble you, whoever you are.'

Another pause, 'I came to offer help.'

'It's not help I'm wanting, just peace and quiet. Is that asking too much, for God's sake?'

The longest pause of all. Then, 'Nothing is too much to ask for His sake. Are you a Catholic, my son?'

Pat groaned aloud. *A priest!* Wouldn't you know it – they clung like leeches to the body of Ireland. There was no escaping them. Even here, stuck half into the sea, even here comes a priest, interfering . . .

The priest misinterpreted Pat's groan. 'A Protestant then?'

Pat's frustration echoed in his bitter laugh, 'I'm nothing – nothing, do you hear? Now leave me be, get away from my door.'

'No man is nothing in the sight of God.' The answer came swiftly this time.

'Bollocks!' Pat sprang to his feet and wrenched open the door. The priest stood before him, a silver cross on a chain catching the light from the fire. He looked up unflinchingly, viewing Pat's broken face with shrewd grey eyes. Pat raised his arms in a gesture of helplessness. 'There's nothing for you here, Father. Can't you understand that? Go away and leave me in peace.'

By way of answer the priest proffered a blanket which he carried folded over one arm. 'I thought you might be cold, my son. Nights here are wild at times.'

'I am not cold.'

'Then won't I be leaving it anyway,' said the priest, stepping over the threshold. 'You might be glad of it later.'

Pat turned away.

The priest rubbed his hands over the fire. 'You've turf then.' His gaze wandered round the hearth, 'And tatties. Ah well, you're dry and warm and fed, that's a mercy.'

Pat stared into the fire. Inwardly he railed. He almost got up and left. Only the splatter of rain on the broken window kept him at the fireside – that and the thought of crossing that sea again at night. He wondered if the priest lived on the island. He had not seen a church. Pat sighed. Wasn't there a cluster of cottages, a dozen perhaps. But even one cottage meant people and people were never left in peace for long without some priest interfering.

'I saw you on Saint Patrick's Chair this afternoon,' said the priest, dropping to his haunches. 'Did you make your wish?'

Despite himself, Pat risked a sideways glance of enquiry.

'That grey boulder with two ledges like steps. It's called Saint Patrick's Wishing Chair. Legend says the Saint himself cast it there.'

Pat remembered, the granite rock *had* been shaped like a chair.

Unexpectedly the priest chuckled, 'You're allowed one wish a year. People swear by it. People with troubles mainly.' His quizzical gaze rested on Pat's face. 'They sit in the chair and wish their afflictions away. It's harmless enough.'

Pat poked the fire with a stick.

'Well then,' the priest straightened up, joints creaking. He rubbed the small of his back with one hand. 'So long as you're comfortable . . .'

Pat broke the stick in half and tossed both parts on to the fire.

'I'll be along then,' said the priest moving to the door. 'Have a good night. God bless you, my son.'

Pat listened to the footsteps crunch away into the distance, then he rose to shut the door. After which he turned in for the night. For a while he huddled on the floor with a sack over his legs – until, when the fire had died and the temperature fell, he collected the blanket from the table. 'It's only a blanket,' he muttered. 'A man made it for another man to use. That's all.' And having settled that in his mind, Pat fell asleep.

Others were trying to settle matters in Dublin. Nobody could say what would happen. It was one thing for Childers and de Valera to speak out against the Treaty, but another matter entirely when Tom Barry and Liam Lynch clamoured for an armed uprising. The situation went from bad to worse. People went about their business as best they could, but tension increased every day.

Not that Brigid concerned herself with politics. She was too busy caring for the new baby. And Father Murphy had raised the matter of the christening. Tomas had protested about that, 'We've no right. Pat will be back soon. It should be left for him.' But Tomas was overruled. Besides it seemed that only Tomas believed Pat was still alive – Tomas was the only one who thought Pat *would* return.

So the child was christened Sean Connors. That was the first time the world heard the name. Not that the world was listening. Just Tomas and Brigid, with their own children clustered around Father Murphy.

Pat remained in that broken-down cabin for days. When it was raining he stayed indoors, when it was dry he fished with a line and hooks found in the cabin. And for an hour most afternoons he sat in the Wishing Chair, glaring balefully across the grey waters at the gulls and the fishing boats. Pat's presence on the island was ignored. Only the priest came to see him. The priest came every night, and brought a gift every time.

On the second visit it was a kettle and tea and sugar. As soon as Pat heard footsteps he guessed it was the priest. Outside was dark, wet and windy – how the priest ever saw his way was a source of amazement. 'Bloody cat's eyes,' Pat growled under his breath.

'Well, Father,' he glowered, opening the door. 'What brings you this time?'

The priest held the kettle as if it were a lamp lighting the way. 'Concern,' he answered succinctly, crossing the threshold.

It was warm in the cabin. Pat had tacked sacking across the broken window to stop the draught. The fire crackled in the grate and lit the scene with a flickering light. Pat wedged the door shut and the priest set to work brewing the tea. Steam rose from his cassock as he busied himself in front of the fire. Pat couldn't resist a grim smile. 'You look like a vision of hell – all that steam and the flames behind you.'

The priest smiled, 'And doesn't that make a fine start for conversation. Better than last night, you had me thinking you were a deaf mute by the end of it.'

But there was little *conversation* that night. The priest was left to do most of the talking. And talk he did. Pat found out where they were for a start. Coney Island – a spit of land on the edge of the ocean. Sailing west the next land is America, three thousand miles away. The name means 'island of rabbits' in the Irish, and Pat remembered seeing many of them among the dunes. 'Once upon a time,' said the priest in the manner of all shanachies, 'a hundred people lived on Coney. Not even the great famine culled the numbers. The potato blight didn't harm the fish, you know. But now it's less than thirty still living here, and don't more leave every year.'

Pat listened, he could hardly do otherwise, sitting there, supping the priest's tea. But he took care not to offer any encouragement. If the priest was dismayed he showed no sign of it. He stayed for an hour on the second night and then let himself out. Pat remained brooding into the fire, not looking up to say goodbye or thanks for the tea or anything – not a word. Then, when the priest's footsteps were swallowed up by the wind and the sea, Pat wedged the door shut, rolled into his blanket and tried to sleep. But sleep came harder now. His body was rested. Fresh air and the bracing wind had blown the cobwebs from his mind . . . and thoughts of Finola tormented him.

The battle with the priest began two evenings later. The old man came earlier than usual, this time bringing soda bread and fresh milk. And he was an *old* man, with thin grey hair as soft as a baby's and eyes full of cleverness. Eyes which betray you, my friend, Pat thought. Too alert, too watchful, too knowing to be the eyes of the simple man you pretend to be.

Later, when Pat looked back, he could never quite place when the conversation turned to God and matters of faith. Perhaps such concerns were always on the priest's mind and so never far from his lips. Or perhaps the priest watched and waited until he could turn the talk with sly cunning. However it was done, it was suddenly there between them – as enticing as a partly clad woman bent on seduction. Neither could turn his back on it. Pat hated it, and the priest was consumed by it. They fought to convince each other with equal vigour but in contrasting styles – Pat

41

angry, bitter, stubborn – the priest nimble, cool, polished. Like two fighters – one slugging his weight, mixing it – the other boxing, dancing back, jabbing and counter-punching.

'Sure I'm a Catholic,' Pat roared, trapped into an admission, 'an official Catholic. When the British threw me in jail and asked my religion I'm a Catholic. A legal Catholic, that's all. It meant little then and nothing now.'

'You have suffered a great hurt, my son. It's written in your face. But rejecting God, trying to hate God, will do nothing for you. Only loving God –'

'There is no God! Will you listen! You blather on, you don't listen, that's the trouble with priests. A man can make a life without God –'

'Without love? Without compassion?'

'Sure will you stop stealing what's not yours. Love isn't Christian. Or compassion. Weren't cavemen crying with compassion long before Christ –'

'But not before God, my son.'

And later . . . when the priest talked of sin . . . Pat exploded, 'Do you know what I think? I think half the sins you go on about are invented. Sure now, wouldn't the bloody priests starve if they relied on the really sinful . . . on murderers an' the like. But murderers don't go to church, so the priests invent all these little sins so that the poor gullible bastards go down on their knees to pray for forgiveness. Most of them have nothing to be forgiven, nothing to be ashamed about, but they are made to *feel* ashamed, so they pay money to the churches and the poxy priests inside them!'

'I am here to help, my son, not to condemn –'

'Liar! You're here to put me back on my knees. Well you're wasting your time, Father. I'll beg forgiveness from no man and no God, never again!'

And later still, when Pat demanded to be left in peace, the priest said, 'This is the place God sent me –'

'You volunteered fast enough. You sniffed me out like a bloodhound –'

And yet later still . . . Pat more furious than ever, *No! I've seen people live by your rules. They are fool's rules. There are better rules, there *must* be.'

42

They argued for hours. When the priest left he was visibly shaken from the encounter. So was Pat, whose anguished blasphemous shouts echoed round the cabin for hours.

Inevitably, perhaps their encounter was less savage the next evening. Each approached the other warily, conscious of the divide between them. Pat's blind rage had exhausted itself, but he was no less determined.

Against him stood the priest, practised in the art of argument. He arrived at seven that evening, carrying a half-sized bottle of whisky.

Pat smiled grimly, 'Are we to indulge the sins of the flesh then, Father?'

The priest chuckled, 'Days like this threaten every joint in a man's body with arthritis. Doesn't a bottle this size show moderation? I've found a spoonful a powerful help against the damp.'

'A spoonful?'

'Or two,' chuckled the priest.

They spent the next three hours together. The time passed easily to begin with – the priest had charm, and Pat was too much of a shanachie not to enjoy accounts of local folklore. But the second half of the evening was a test of will power. The old priest was as sharp as a blade about matters of faith. Pat remained resolute. He kept his temper, but was no less dogmatic in his denial of God. And he refused to disclose why he was there, what had sent him walking blindly across the countryside. It was a stalemate, but they parted without bitterness, although the priest was puzzled and thoughtful. Whereas Pat was still lost. Even while arguing his face bore an expression of hurt bemusement, like a child who had been punished without knowing why.

He had another bad night, not violent but as restless as ever, tormenting himself with memories of Finola. His mind overflowed with his past unkindness, his cruel lack of thought. Guilt racked him – guilt at his worthlessness compared to her goodness, guilt for being alive when she was dead.

The weather was foul in the morning. Rain, steady and impenetrable, grey and depressing. He sat in the doorway and glowered, knowing it was set for the day.

The priest wore fisherman's oilskins that evening. He brought some fruit, four green apples in a soggy paper bag. They drank the rest of the whisky and talked. But Pat was so morose and unresponsive that the priest left early, feeling frustrated and worried – frustrated that he had failed to connect with the man's mind, worried that the man might do away with himself.

Another day. A white sky, high up and far away, without cloud for once. Not much wind. Pat waited until mid-morning, then walked down the curling green road to sit in the Wishing Chair.

An hour passed. Pat hardly moved. Above him a crack of blue appeared in the sky – a thin stream of blue widening to a river, then a lake, then the whole sky was blue. It was like watching a stage. The Wishing Chair might have been the front row of the stalls. Pat caught his breath. The scene was transformed. Sand dunes turned gold, bare branches of trees were no longer grey but orange and brown. The sea came alive with a million dancing points of light, until it hurt just to look. His eyes smarted. His hands rose to shield out the glare. He was almost blinded, the scene was blurred – and only when his hands met tears did he realize he was weeping. He buried his face in his arms and sobbed uncontrollably. The dam had burst. After twelve long days. It was a release, like a head of steam blowing a safety valve.

He never knew how long he wept, but finally he felt a great tranquillity, a sense of peace. The loneliness remained . . . he would feel the loss every day of his life. Future pleasures would be muted compared to those of the past, victories would never be so sweet, defeats would be harder to sustain . . . but he had a life, if he chose to live it . . .

Suddenly his mind filled with a picture he had previously rejected. He saw himself at Finola's graveside. Mick Collins was there . . . and Dev and countless other old friends. Brigid stepped forward, carrying a bundle wrapped in a blanket. 'Pat,' she had called, 'it's your son I have in my arms.'

'A son?' he whispered, only half believing, 'Finola, did

you leave me a son?' He choked, remembering how many times she had looked forward to a child, especially a son. But was it true? He made himself think back to that dreadful night – to the room on Ammet Street. All those people. Finola on the bed. He concentrated on Brigid, standing there with a tiny baby at her breast. Brigid was always nursing a baby. Brigid's fertility made Finola feel her own lack more keenly. But he hadn't thought . . . or he *had* thought . . . then at the graveside, Brigid had said, 'Pat, it's your son I have in my arms.'

'I have a son,' he said quietly. Suddenly he knew it was true. He shouted, '*We* have a son!'

A dozen thoughts struck him at once. The day, when Finola . . . when his son was born. The British had left Dublin that day. His son would be the first of a new breed of Irishmen – freeborn, free of the British after eight hundred years. His son was the first, the very first! And another thing – it was Finola's seventh time pregnant. She had delivered a seventh son to a seventh son! My God, the boy would be a genius. The first freeborn Irishman, the seventh son of a seventh son – both together. And *my* son, Pat exulted . . .

He knew he would go back to Dublin in the morning. He felt embarrassed. He had never run away from anything before. Yet he hadn't so much run away as been drawn to the island, as if it held a secret for him. What it was eluded him. He thought about it all afternoon. He had brooded on the meaning of life for days. He concentrated as never before . . . and then it came to him . . . the secret he would pass on to his son.

The priest found Pat in a changed mood that evening. Instead of doubt he found a certainty, an acceptance of life quite different from his own but every bit as sure. For Pat had at least glimpsed what he was searching for, even if he was to spend the rest of his life defining it.

The two men talked as old friends – but then men who argue as they had either become friends or enemies. Pat was glad – 'Sure now, would you ever think the day would come when someone would abuse you as I have? 'Tis powerful sorry I am for the way I've spoken at times.' He grinned, a real grin, free of bitterness for the first time since

Finola died. 'I'll tell you something, Father. Anyone ever speaks to you like that again, you let me know. I'll break his bloody neck.'

But the priest was sad. 'I failed you, my son. I tried, but I failed.'

Pat rested a hand on the priest's shoulder. 'You know, Father, when the British were about to shoot Connolly, a surgeon asked him to forgive his executioners. And Connolly said, "I pray for all brave men who do their duty according to their lights." Father, you did your duty like the brave man you are. Sure I'll always be grateful for that.'

The priest made a final effort, 'I shall be in church when you go in the morning, my son. Will you come to mass?'

Pat hesitated. Then he shook his head. 'I know you'll not understand, Father, but a man ought to be able to make a life without your God, and without turning into the Devil. If I intend to try wouldn't it be an insult to set foot in your church? And I never insult a friend.' He brightened, struck by a sudden thought, 'It's one of my rules, Father – never insult a friend – one of the rules I'll live by.'

At the crack of dawn next day Pat was back on Saint Patrick's Wishing Chair, casting a last look out to sea. Then, when the tide went out, he crossed to the mainland. He found the old British barracks quite easily. 'I want to telephone Michael Collins himself in Dublin,' he told the astonished IRA commander.

They locked him in the cells until the call came through.

Mick Collins roared down the line. 'Where in God's name have you been? Haven't I enough on my plate without worrying myself sick over you?'

'Sure you're lucky. I've had damn all on my plate for days. Will you tell them to give me a decent meal before sending me home?'

CHAPTER THREE

Mick Collins greeted Pat with open arms when they met in Dublin. The two men closeted themselves together for days, while Pat learned what had happened in his absence.

The anti-Treaty faction of the IRA had organized itself into a separate force and its new leader, Rory O'Connor, had called a press conference to repudiate the IRA's allegiance to the Dail. A reporter asked – 'Are we to take it that you want a military dictatorship then?'

'You can take it any way you want,' came the answer – and there seemed no other way to take it when Rory O'Connor's new independent IRA marched into the courts of justice in the Four Courts and took possession.

Pat was blunt in his advice to Mick, 'You can't let them get away with it. Give me a squad of men and I'll flush them out by midnight.'

But Mick was loath to set Irishmen to kill Irishmen. Besides he was worried sick about something else. The new Prime Minister of the north had flatly refused to consider any boundary rearrangement which might reduce the size of Ulster. Mick had banked on the Boundary Commission awarding the new Free State the best part of three counties. Without that he would never have signed the Treaty. Now people were saying he had sold out – *him*, Mick Collins of all people! Pat had never seen him so angry, nor so close to despair.

Collins was besieged by problems. In the south he had the anti-Treaty faction to worry about, while in the north Prime Minister Craig sanctioned the death penalty for the possession of arms. Craig went even further by appointing Sir Henry Wilson, arch-enemy of Irish nationalism, to set up a para-military force, the A and B Specials. Twenty-five thousand Orangemen joined up to preserve the six-county state of Northern Ireland. Ulster's Catholics went in fear of their lives and sought help from the only source available – the IRA. And as the prospects of an effective Boundary

Commission receded, Mick Collins sent guns to the border, irrespective of whether the IRA units were for or against the Treaty.

Pat Connors protested, 'Mick, they'll use those guns on us one day.'

'In God's name, what else can I do? Let our people be slaughtered?'

The shadow of the gun covered Ireland once more. Violence spread through the south like a cancer. Post offices were robbed, trains were held up, isolated villages were forced to pay 'taxes' to support soldiers of the anti-Treaty IRA.

Collins worked like a demon, but the issues seemed irreconcilable. Dev and his supporters would have nothing to do with the oath of allegiance, nor would they accept a divided Ireland. Mick argued furiously – 'Australians swear the oath, Canadians, South Africans, every politician in the Commonwealth. Does it make them less free? Does it hamper the way they run their affairs? Sure it doesn't matter a damn!' And as for Ulster, 'Help make the Boundary Commission work and we'll get the best part of three counties. Sure, what will they be left with? They'll have to fall in line with us in the end.'

Dev remained unconvinced, but the two factions of the IRA were on the verge of open civil war, so *something* had to be done. Dev and Collins called for an election. The country would vote on the Treaty . . . and, on 16 June, the Irish Free State went to the polls for the first time.

Pat took a couple of days off after polling day. He had worked non-stop for five months. By the middle of June he was exhausted. He slumped into his bed at Ammet Street and slept the clock round, his first such sleep – deep and undisturbed – since that night in January when he had scrambled ashore on Coney Island.

Pat had gone directly to Brigid's place on his return from Sligo. His haggard looks had startled her. She had stared at the scar on his forehead and the dark circles beneath his eyes. 'I've seen better-looking faces eating hay,' she said, before bursting into tears. Tomas had mashed some tea after that, while Brigid dried her eyes and fetched the baby.

48

'What's he called?' asked Pat, taking the bundle on to his knee.

'Sure will you listen to him,' Brigid exclaimed. 'And shouldn't he be telling us. But it's Sean, that's the name Finola always wanted in a boy.'

Pat stared at his son, whose answering gaze was so bold that Pat burst out laughing, 'He doesn't think much of me, does he?'

'And why should he?' Brigid demanded, taking the baby back and holding him to her shoulder. 'Where were you when you were needed?'

'In the Post Office,' Pat said with a rueful smile, 'with Pearse and Connolly and other brave men.'

He meant it as a joke, or at least an apology. But Brigid's nerves were too stretched for levity. 'Here's your new Ireland, Pat Connors,' she snapped, holding the baby in front of him. 'That's what it's about. Babies and young ones growing up with food in their bellies. Not men murdering each other . . . and fighting and killing . . .' she choked and dissolved into tears, then ran from the room with the baby in her arms.

Pat rose to go after her, but Tomas waved him back to his chair, 'Let her be. Tears are better out than in. She's been this way ever since . . .' he squinted at Pat, 'ever since Finola passed on. She's not over it yet.'

After that the two men talked for a while, with Tomas pausing every so often to relight his pipe. Tomas was deceptive, Pat reflected, easily underestimated – he was not a leader but nor was he easily led. Tomas was – well, just Tomas. Happy enough to listen to anyone – but he went his own quiet way.

They agreed the baby would stay with Brigid, and Pat would visit when he could. After that, Pat rarely more than slept at Ammet Street. He worked from dawn to dusk for Mick Collins, and spent a few hours on a Sunday at Brigid's with his son. The baby fascinated him. He couldn't stop looking at it. Even while it slept Pat marvelled at the beauty in that tiny face. It wasn't just that the child was beautiful and would be a good-looking boy – Pat took that for granted. Most leaders had a certain physical appeal, so *of course* young Sean would grow into a fine figure of a man

– but Pat's ambitions soared to a much higher plane and at times his secret thoughts made him seethe with excitement.

So after working all hours to polling day and refreshed by his sleep, Pat rose and hurried round to Brigid's place – where he spent an enjoyable day playing with his son. But a few hours of peace and quiet were enough for Pat. Assured of his son's well-being he was anxious to be off – and when a messenger arrived from Mick Collins, Pat was pleased – even though the urgent summons concerned an event that threatened to shake London and Dublin to their very foundations.

It seemed that Sir Henry Wilson, having established new security measures in the north, had returned to London. On that particular day he had unveiled a memorial to the men of the Great Western Railway who had fallen in the Great War. That done he took a taxi to his house on the corner of Eaton Square, and there – on the steps of his own home – he was shot down by two gunmen, both of whom were chased and arrested by the police.

Events were chaotic after that. The two gunmen admitted to being members of the IRA. But which IRA? For now there were two – those who supported the Treaty, and those who were against it. Impressed by Mick's struggle to implement the Treaty, the British Government assumed that the assassins belonged to Rory O'Connor's rebel IRA. In fact Dunne and O'Sullivan, the two men arrested, had acted on their own initiative but, as Pat Connors well knew, Wilson's execution had been ordered months before by no less than Mick Collins himself. Westminster's reaction was a rare stroke of luck, funny enough to bring a smile even to Mick's troubled face – at least in private. In public he poured scorn on any suggestion that the men had been sent by *either* faction of the IRA. 'Where is the proof?' he demanded, knowing that none would be forthcoming.

Meanwhile Mick held the British Government at bay and prayed for time, time for the election results to come in. And two days later they arrived. Despite everything – despite intimidation from the anti-Treaty forces, despite much heart-searching about the north, despite the conflicting arguments – the Irish people had voted overwhelmingly in favour of the Treaty.

But Mick's celebrations were cut short. British public opinion was in an uproar about the killing of Sir Henry Wilson. Westminster issued an ultimatum. Unless Collins restored law and order – which meant arresting the rebels – the Treaty would be cancelled. Again Mick played for time – but the British were so adamant that after four days and four nights Mick could resist no longer. A note was sent to the rebels in the Four Courts demanding their surrender. No reply was received. At four o'clock in the morning of 28 June, two field guns were mounted on the opposite side of the Liffey – and at seven minutes past Mick Collins gave the order to fire.

Few people knew it, but the Irish Civil War was about to begin.

It took two days to reduce the Four Courts to rubble. Only then did Rory O'Connor surrender. Rebels elsewhere continued to resist. Pat Connors attacked anti-Treaty strongholds all over the city. One incident engraved itself on his memory. A St John's Ambulance man stood at the entrance to a blazing building, begging a small, dark-haired man to surrender. The man refused, instead he brushed the ambulance man aside and charged the Free State lines, firing a Thompson submachine-gun as he ran. At Pat's signal the man was cut down by a hail of bullets. Cautiously Pat moved forward to bend over the body. It was Cathal Brugha. Pat had last seen him at Finola's funeral, standing between Dev and Mick Collins. Pat's heart ached as he looked down into that white face. 'Dear God,' he muttered, almost in tears, 'where will it end?'

But it was just beginning. Sixty people were killed and three hundred injured during eight days of street warfare. July was worse as fighting spread across the country. Old allegiances counted for nothing. Mick sent soldiers into the Grand Hotel at Skerries to arrest Harry Boland, one of his cloest friends. Boland resisted and was shot in the stomach. He died soon afterwards, asking to be buried next to Cathal Brugha. Mick and Pat had lost another old comrade.

Bloody week followed bloody week. Mick cast all other duties aside in favour of his role as Commander-in-Chief of the Free State Army. He threw himself into the campaign. And wherever Mick went Pat was not far behind. By early August, helped by 10,000 rifles sent by their old enemies the British, the Free State forces were getting the upper hand. When they captured Cork, Pat began to speculate on an early end to the fighting. But then came awful news. Arthur Griffith, overworked by running the government in Mick's absence, had collapsed and died. The Free State had lost its first elected leader.

Mick and Pat hurried back to Dublin for the funeral – but as soon as Cosgrave and Kevin O'Higgins were elected leaders of the Dail, Mick was anxious to return to Cork. 'The rest of the country will fall into line if we can restore peace in Kerry and Cork,' he said.

Pat nodded. 'When do we go?'

'Not you. You stay in Dublin in case of trouble here.'

Pat accepted the decision – and when Mick headed south, Pat strolled round to Brigid's place to spend a few precious hours with his son. He was astonished to see how the child had grown, and Tomas and Brigid were delighted to watch his excitement. Sean gurgled contentedly, and everyone enjoyed themselves.

Pat spent the next week checking security arrangements in the city. If Dublin held firm, Mick Collins would settle the rest of the country. Which is what Mick was doing – travelling the length and breadth of County Cork, inspecting his troops. His charm conquered everyone. Invariably he greeted his men with a joke, fashioning their mood until they were receptive to his message. First things first, he told them – restore law and order, then prod the Boundary Commission towards a favourable settlement for the north. 'We'll get a united Ireland, boys – without further bloodshed if we play our cards right.'

After which his convoy was away to the next stop. He travelled in the back of an open Rolls-Royce, flanked by motor-cycle outriders, with an armoured car in front and a Crossley tender behind. It made quite a procession – and the convoy had reached Baelnamblath, on the road from Macroom, when it was ambushed.

Mick was out of the car at the first shot, his revolver in his hand, ducking and weaving across to an outrider who lay wounded on the ground. His troops poured out from the

Crossley and fanned up the hillside, taking what cover they could as they gave answering fire. Gradually the rebels were forced to retreat. Half an hour later the skirmish was as good as over. Gunfire became sporadic. Mick wondered whether to give chase, or to proceed on his journey. He stood up. Then it happened. A sniper's bullet ricocheted and pierced the back of his head. Men dashed to him, but it was too late. Michael Collins was dead. Killed by an Irishman.

In Dublin, Pat refused to believe the news. Mick dead? Mick with his quicksilver tongue. The greatest Irishman ever to draw breath. Dear God, Mick *was* Ireland half the time. Without Mick the British would still be in Dublin Castle. 'Without Mick . . .' Pat repeated blankly, racked by misery. First Finola . . . now Mick Collins too . . . both snatched away within six months of each other . . .

Brigid worried herself sick that Pat would wander off again. She washed and cooked for him, while inventing endless excuses to keep him at her place. Of course Sean was a draw, and although Pat sometimes gazed at the child with unseeing eyes, Brigid was heartened by other occasions when he responded with a sad smile or by sticking a finger out for the boy to grasp.

But Pat was not allowed to brood for long. A week after the funeral he was sought out by Richard Mulcahy, formerly Mick's chief of staff and now a Minister in Cosgrave's government. 'Are you giving up *now*?' Mulcahy demanded. 'Giving up when what Mick fought for is in sight? He would have disowned you for sure!'

Not many spoke to Pat like that – but Mulcahy had supported Mick too, so perhaps that gave him the right. Anyway Pat took it. Only the slow reddening of his face showed his rising temper. Mulcahy gripped his arm and led him away for a quiet talk – and it soon became clear that he was under orders to get Pat back into the fight. And Mulcahy could talk the hind legs off a donkey, so it was no surprise when Pat set his sorrows aside to rejoin the fray. Brigid and Tomas were sorry to see him go, but privately agreed it was for the best. No amount of brooding would bring poor Mick back, and there was something unnatural about Pat when he lapsed into his long silences.

So Pat hugged his son goodbye and went back to war –

and a monstrous bloodbath it turned out to be. Cosgrave's government applied emergency powers every bit as harsh as those employed by the British in the worst days of martial law. The unauthorized possession of a revolver was made punishable by death, and those who scoffed at the idea of Irishmen executing Irishmen were mistaken. Erskine Childers was mistaken. Pat's old ally was arrested while spreading anti-Treaty propaganda, and when searched was found to possess a revolver. The tiny pearl-handled gun had been a gift from Mick Collins himself, but even a pedigree like that failed to save Childers. Following a court-martial, he was taken from his cell and shot at Beggar's Bush barracks.

The rebels hit back. Liam Lynch, leading the anti-Treaty IRA in the south, issued orders to shoot members of the Dail on sight – and a week later Sean Hales, whose own brother commanded a brigade of rebels, was shot dead as he walked to the Dail.

Which provoked the Dail to retaliate – this time through the men in the prisons, men like Rory O'Connor who had led the occupation of the Four Courts. Ever since his arrest O'Connor had awaited trial with the others – but killing members of the Dail changed everything. O'Connor forfeited his life. He and his senior men were woken in their cells and shot without trial.

Old friends were killing each other all over Ireland – and Pat Connors was in the thick of it, hunting out Republicans with single-minded ruthlessness. He rarely wore his captain's uniform, saving it for State occasions and friends' funerals. Instead he toured the country with five trained men, all dressed in civilian clothes. They travelled in two cars with enough guns aboard to stock an armoury – but the weapons were rarely seen by the public. Pat was too clever for that. He would arrive in a village, put up at a pub, and spend the evening talking to the locals. Two of his lieutenants would be with him, while the other three propped up another bar counter down the road – all doing the same thing, buying drinks and waiting for tongues to wag. Men were cautious at first, but as the drink flowed and the night wore on Pat generally found out what he wanted. Early the next morning he moved on – travelling far and fast, before stopping at a different pub in another village to repeat the performance over again. His reasoning was effective. A man nursing a hangover might regret his indiscretions, he might run scared, scared enough to be curious about the inquisitive strangers. However, little could be done if the strangers were gone, and after a day a frightened man would come to forget the wagging of his tongue. But Pat never forgot. He passed some information to the new Criminal Investigation Department in Westland Row, and passed even more to the Free State Army intelligence units – but some information he withheld. Pat was ever mindful of one thing, his need to find the man who shot Mick Collins. Pat wanted that man for himself.

Weeks, months, passed as the civil war ran its bloody course. Both sides committed terrible atrocities. Interrogations were conducted with the aid of a hammer – the castration of prisoners became commonplace – men were tortured until they went mad. Shocked and frightened, the Catholic bishops condemned the Republicans harshly: 'They have caused more damage to Ireland in three months than could be laid to the charge of British rule in as many decades.'

In Kerry, Pat Connors dwelt in the valley of death. His intelligence-gathering missions soon became too well known to be continued. The boot was on the other foot, as units of anti-Treaty IRA sought to capture and kill Pat's small band of men. Mulcahy ordered Pat back to Dublin, but Pat refused, remembering Mick's words – 'The rest of the country will fall into line if we bring peace to Kerry and Cork.' But bringing peace was no easy task, especially when Pat was shot in the leg and two of his men were killed in an ambush.

A month later, Pat struck back. In nine engagements over eight days his squad killed eighteen IRA rebels and wounded a score more. Pat and his men slipped away to the Boggeragh Mountains, to hole up while Pat's leg healed and he planned his next move.

Gradually the Free State forces gained the ascendancy. By the spring of 1923 more than 13,000 Republican prisoners were in jail – many of them wounded, or on hunger strike. In six months the government executed seventy-seven rebels, three times more than the British shot in the two and a half years of the Anglo-Irish War. Even that failed to quell the rebellion, until – after a running fight in the Tipperary mountains – Liam Lynch himself was killed. For the first time since the outbreak of civil war, the rebels faltered. So many of their leaders were dead – Cathal Brugha, Rory O'Connor, Richard Barrett, Erskine Childers – now Liam Lynch too. The only survivor with enough authority to marshal the flagging Republicans was Eamon de Valera, but a month after Lynch was killed it was Dev himself who gave the order to surrender. More than 8000 men came down from the hills. The Irish Civil War was as good as over.

Pat dragged himself home to Dublin. Physically he was much changed. He would never walk again without a limp, but it was more than that. In twenty months or so he had aged ten years. His eyes bore a haunted look. Some memories could never be erased from his mind. He remembered rescuing a man from the rebels – the poor devil had been kicked half to death and his entrails slithered out of his anus as Pat picked him up. He remembered another man, pinned to the floor with six-inch nails through his hands. And the sounds . . . the screams . . . made up a blood-curdling soundtrack that went round and round in Pat's head.

Years later, people pointed out that Sean Connors was a mere baby during the civil war. He could not have been influenced, they said. But his father was influenced, and his father never forgot. Nor did he die before telling Sean all he had seen. There were times in Kerry when Pat nearly gave up . . . without God, without Finola, without Mick Collins . . . but the thought of Sean kept him alive. It was the memory of sitting on Saint Patrick's Wishing Chair as dawn broke on Coney Island, and saying aloud – 'I wish I could write it all down. The magic a man like Mick has. That trick of getting his own way. Sure now, there must be a list of rules somewhere, rules which make some men giants among men. Don't I wish I could put it all down . . . the way some men get power, and how others let it slip through their fingers. Would you imagine that. A set of rules for a man to pass on to his son . . .'

CHAPTER FOUR

Brigid hated politics. She always had. Even before the civil war she had distrusted politicians, and Finola's excited chatter about Irish unity had simply bemused her. Whether the land was ruled by the English or the Irish made no difference as far as Brigid could see. The poor would always be poor, children would still need feeding – politics were an irrelevance. The only politician she had any time for was Pat Connors. She felt a sense of duty towards him – affection too because of the happiness he had given Finola – and the two feelings combined to produce a kind of protectiveness. Odd to feel protective about a giant like Pat Connors, but if ever a man needed watching over it was him. She had been shocked at the sight of him coming back from Kerry. Not just the way he dragged his leg – God knows enough cripples haunted Dublin for that to be common enough – but by the way he had aged.

But, as she said, time heals most wounds – so gradually the old pattern re-established itself. Pat slept in his room on Ammet Street and shared the occasional meal at Brigid's table, but they saw little of him except on Sunday afternoons, when he played with the children or helped Tomas on his vegetable patch. Slowly Pat recovered some of his old self, enough anyway for Brigid to consider him more or less normal. At least he looked as if he slept at nights, and there was a sense of purpose about him again, especially when he looked at young Sean.

The boy was taken to Ammet Street every Saturday afternoon, first carried by Cooey and later as a toddler on the end of Dary's long arm. There he was left for an hour or two, and during those hours on a Saturday father and son forged a bond that was to last all of their lives. Perhaps living apart helped. The relationship might have been different had they seen more of each other. Of course they met at Brigid's when Pat visited, but the atmosphere was different – Sean was one of the family there and Pat took care to pay attention to all of the children. But Saturday afternoons were special – the high spot of Pat's week. Not a visit passed without his heart quickening at the sight of his son. He hugged the boy, delighting in the growth of bone and muscle and never ceasing to marvel that he and Finola had made this child between them. 'Did you see him, Finola?' he would ask her afterwards. 'The size of him. As big as a barn and already as sharp as a knife to go with it.'

Pat often talked to Finola. He treated his room not as a shrine to her but as a telephone box. Sometimes the line was bad and he had trouble hearing her, but they had constant conversations. It was a harmless eccentricity. He had become a self-contained man, but not a lonely one. He ate well, sketchily at home perhaps but he took one or two meals a week at Brigid's place. He drank moderately, but not to excess. Most of all he read, biographies mainly, and English and Irish history, and *all* the newspapers, starting with the *Irish Times* and *Dublin Gazette* in the morning, and not ending a day without the *Independent*, the *Mail*, and the *Herald*. And he had a few visitors, politicians and journalists mainly. During the day he was busy working for the Free State and during the evening, when not at Brigid's or drinking with some politician, he talked to Finola about the rules he was formulating. He wrote them down secretly, hiding his papers beneath the floorboards, so that not even Brigid would come across them when she cleaned up once a week. And on Saturday afternoons, Sean came to see him.

What struck most people about young Sean was his air of assurance. It began with the eyes – Finola's eyes, Pat always thought as he looked at them, bright blue and as clear as a summer sky. The short nose came from Finola too, whereas the square jaw and glossy thick black hair were Pat's – even Pat recognized that. But the smile, when it came, was something else. Pure goodness. 'Born for the church,' Brigid sighed wistfully, though never in Pat's hearing, for Pat's continued absence from mass shamed the whole family. Pat's denial of Catholicism even alarmed his son occasionally – after all, *everyone* went to mass.

'But Da . . . aren't you afraid of eternal damnation?'

58

'What kind of God is that?' Pat snapped, darkening with temper. 'What God creates men to cower like animals? . . .' he broke off, aware of the boy's alarm, knowing he had said too much. 'Oh, leave it alone, son. Sure now, do as Brigid says and you'll come to no harm. We'll talk about it another day. You'll be making me forget what I was going to tell you . . .' and Pat would be away into one of his stories.

As for Sean, he idolized his father – not surprisingly perhaps for Pat Connors was something of a legend in Dublin. They still sang songs about him in the pubs. People still talked of his past . . . the man who had fought in the GPO with Pearse and Connolly . . . the man Mick Collins loved as a brother. The stories lingered on, and Sean liked nothing more than to persuade his father to talk about them. And Pat told the tales with his shanachie's skill, leaving the brutality aside to concentrate on the humour, while the boy hugged himself with glee.

'You've heard about the looting going on while we were in the GPO? Well shops were plundered left and right as people took advantage of the situation. Then along comes a priest, determined to put a stop to such wickedness. Down Parnell Square he goes, huffing and puffing with indignation, till he bumps into a boy your age, loaded down with an armful of boots. "Where did you get those boots, boy?" thunders the priest. The boy looks over his shoulder, but keeps running. "In Earl Street, Father, but you'll have to hurry or they'll all be gone."'

Sean hooted with laughter and begged for more stories. Pat obliged, skilfully weaving fact and fiction, but only so far as it suited his purpose. He never lost sight of his objective, which was to prepare the boy's mind for the rules.

Years later, Sean could never work out exactly when it all started – he was eight or nine – but life was different from that day on. The concept of the rules acquired the importance of a magic inheritance. Precisely what they amounted to Sean could not define – how could he, when his father still held them secret? But to the best of his understanding the rules were a formula known only to very great men. They had made Mick Collins the greatest

Irishman ever to draw breath. One day Sean would be a great man himself . . . if he followed the rules.

'They'll be awful hard to learn, won't they, Da?'

Pat shook his head, 'Hard to follow maybe, but not hard to learn.'

Sean digested that. His eyes narrowed. 'I'll have to die, won't I, Da? They'll end up killing me like they did . . .' He almost said Jaysus Christ but stopped in time, '. . . like they killed Mick Collins.'

Pat laughed, 'Sure, that's nonsense. Mick was the bravest, wisest man I ever set eyes on . . . but even Mick wasn't knowing the whole pack of rules. Maybe nobody gets to learn them all . . . but you'll be knowing a powerful lot more than Mick when we finish. You'll know enough not to get yourself killed.'

Sean appeared neither glad nor sorry about that. Death is irrelevant to the young. Instead he asked, 'When will I be big enough to be told, Da?'

Pat made him stand against the wall to be measured.

'But that's as tall as you are, Da,' Sean cried in dismay.

'Sure, that's when you'll be ready to know *all* the rules . . . but maybe we could start when you're that big.' Pat lowered the mark by fifteen inches. 'Just the smallest rules, wouldn't you say.'

'Will I be that big next year, Da?'

'Next year, the one after,' Pat shrugged. 'Soon enough. Just so long as you don't get too big to walk through that door when we've finished.'

Sean longed for that day more than anything. His father never set a specific date, merely that mark on the wall, and not a Saturday passed without Sean standing beneath it to be measured. He imagined that day a thousand times. 'Will it take long, Da? Will it take you long to teach me the rules?' 'Ten days or so, but you'll spend the rest of your life getting them right.' *Ten days!* Ten days with the Da and nobody else – not Aunt Brigid or Uncle Tomas, or Maureen or Dary . . . 'Will I stay here, Da? Will I sleep here?' His father had stopped him with a wave of his hand. 'We shall go away – to an island I know.' *An island!* Sean had never heard his father speak of an island before. Ten whole days on an island, learning the magic rules . . .

So every Saturday Pat Connors cast his spell over his son. Even when they were apart, Pat found himself thinking about Sean and the need to teach him the rules.

Pat continued to work for the Free State government – acting as security advisor to Mulcahy, a shadowy job which suited him. Had it not been for the changes within himself, or had Mick Collins been at the helm, Pat might have wanted to play a more active role. With Mick in charge Pat would have felt sure the country was on the right course, but Cosgrave's government inspired no such confidence – especially when it came to dealing with the Boundary Commission.

The Prods in the north were as adamant as ever – not an inch of the six counties was to be yielded to the Free State. Craig, the northern Prime Minister, even refused to nominate a man to sit on the Boundary Commission. Dublin seethed, while the British struggled to make good their promise given when the Treaty was signed. Eventually Westminster appointed their own Ulsterman as the north's representative. The Free State nominated Eoin MacNeil, and at last the Commission was in session, under the chairmanship of Mr Justice Feetham, a South African judge who was deemed to be impartial.

The Commission sat for a year. Behind the scenes Pat heard grumbles that MacNeil was getting nowhere, which turned out to be true when Justice Feetham summed up. No recommendation could be made, he felt, which materially affected the political integrity of Northern Ireland. As soon as Pat realized the way of the wind he delivered a blunt warning to Mulcahy. 'Dublin will erupt,' he forecast bitterly. 'Mick would never have signed the bloody Treaty with this as the outcome!'

Cosgrave and O'Higgins rushed over to London, where they renegotiated *another* clause in the Treaty – the one dealing with their obligation to make financial payment for Britain's loss of the south. A deal was struck. The Commission's report would be stifled – the six counties would remain as they were – but Britain would write off the debt owed by the Free State. Cosgrave returned to the Dail in triumph – but Pat Connors was sickened as he listened to the speech. The Republicans in the north had been sold out for a handful of silver.

Such then were the years of Sean's childhood. Even after the civil war they were violent times. Fifteen thousand prisoners were released from internment camps when the fighting officially ceased – but those men never forgot their suffering. Nor did they change their minds about the Treaty, they hated it . . . and Dublin continued to teeter on the brink of violence.

For instance, Sean was only five when Kevin O'Higgins was gunned down in the street. Sean was on his way to mass, with Brigid and the rest of the family. Suddenly a man leapt from a car. He shot another man at point blank range. Miraculously the man seemed only injured – he turned and ran – but two other men appeared, both armed. They fired. The man fell. The killers raced off. It was over in a minute. Only later did Sean realize he had known the dead man, he had met him at Ammet Street, the man had been a friend of his father's.

That was in 1927, the year Dev went back to the Dail. Sean was too young to understand elections, but one memory stayed with him. He had been set upon by a street gang. 'Is your Da for Dev or against him?' demanded the leader, twisting Sean's arm. Then another kid shouted, 'That's Sean Connors – his Da's for the Treaty.' After which they had beaten him up. He limped home to Brigid and asked, 'Is it *bad* to be for the Treaty?'

She washed his face and inspected his cuts. 'Sure it's bad to be for it and bad to be against it. Politics is all bad, don't you forget it.'

'Is the Da a bad man, then?'

'Oh, hark at that. Isn't it one question after another with you.'

Sean had to wait another four years for an answer. His father had been talking politics to him for months by then, so Sean's education was advancing by leaps and bounds. 'Dev shilly-shallied over the Treaty for years,' Pat told him, 'until another General Election, when Dev formed a new party – Fianna Fail he called it, Warriors of Ireland.' Pat smiled at the extravagant title. 'Well, Dev got himself elected and went to the Dail –'

'What about the oath, Da?' Sean interrupted. 'Wouldn't

he have to swear the oath?'

'Aye,' Pat ruffled the boy's hair, pleased with Sean's knowledge. 'Aye, sure he's got to swear the oath an' all. So everyone is on the edge of their seats wondering what will happen. In strides Dev to be met by the clerk of the chamber. "There's a small formality first," says the clerk, "I'll have to be asking you to take the oath." Dev bridles at that, "I'll not swear any oath," says he, and turns on his heel and walks out.'

Sean sat with his chin cupped in his hands, his elbows resting on his knees.

'A month passes,' Pat wrinkled his brow, 'no, maybe more. Anyway, Dev comes back and says to the clerk, "I am not prepared to swear the oath. I am not going to take the oath. I am prepared to put my name down in this book in order to get permission to go into the Dail, but it has no other significance." And with that Dev pushes the bible aside and signs the book which all members of the Dail have to sign. "You must remember," Dev says loudly so everyone can hear, "I am taking no oath." Then he takes his place in the Dail. And don't the rest of his new Fianna Fail party do the very same thing.'

Sean stared, not properly understanding. 'So the clerk called the guards and had them thrown out.'

Pat shook his head, 'No, Dev was in. He had signed the book.'

'But what about the oath?'

Pat scratched his head. 'The Constitution is a bit muddled about that. You see, signing the book and swearing the oath sort of went together. I suppose the truth is nobody knew what to do.' Pat chuckled, 'I bet Dev banked on that all right. And isn't the auld devil still there today.'

'Without swearing the oath?'

'Without swearing the oath,' Pat agreed solemnly.

Sean scowled. 'So all that fighting, Da. What they did . . . your bad leg . . . everything was for nothing. Couldn't Dev have done that to begin with and saved all that killing?'

'Maybe – or maybe Dev never thought of it before.'

Thus another Saturday afternoon drew to a close. But Pat always ended with a story funny enough to send the boy away laughing and looking forward to his next visit. Not that the exchanges were all one-sided. Sean had information of his own to impart. Usually he recounted the events of his week with boisterous excitement, but one day he hesitated. 'You won't be telling on me?' he asked anxiously.

Which Pat took to mean he was to learn something not known to Brigid, or at least which Sean thought was not known. In Pat's experience nothing happened in that household without Brigid learning about it, whether she let on or not. He answered carefully, 'That's a terrible thing to be asking before I know what it is. Couldn't you at least be giving me some kind of clue?'

At which Sean threw caution to the winds and explained about the donkey. That summer he and his cousin Michael had helped out at a farm near Palmerstown. They had given half of their earnings to Brigid, but used the other half to buy a donkey.

'Aunt Brigid knows,' Sean added hurriedly. 'She thinks we're keeping it as a pet.'

'Aye,' Pat nodded. 'An' wasn't I told all about it the other Sunday. She knows you've got the animal up at the farm. So what's the big secret?'

'A pet!' Sean's derision was cutting. 'Wouldn't you think Aunt Brigid would know we're too old for pets?'

Pat regarded his ten-year-old son in silence, then listened intently as Sean's voice fell to a whisper. The donkey had cost two pounds. The cost of its feed and keep were three shillings a week. But Seamus O'Malley was paying them two shillings a day for the hire of the animal!

'Who's Seamus O'Malley?'

Sean was astonished. 'Don't you know Old Seamus? Da, everyone knows Seamus.'

Old Seamus was a knacker who pushed a cart from door to door collecting rubbish and cast-offs. Or at least he used to – now Sean's donkey pulled the cart. Brigid considered Old Seamus to be no fit company for young boys on account of his habit of falling down drunk most nights of the week. Hence the secrecy. Sean hurried on with his explanation. Six days a week at two shillings a day earned twelve shillings a week, less overheads – which meant the capital cost of Charlie the donkey was recouped in just over a month. After which the new enterprise of Sean Connors and Michael O'Hara could look forward to a clear profit of nine shillings a week!

'Suppose Old Seamus doesn't pay?' Pat queried cautiously.

Sean shook his head. 'Don't we make him pay when he brings Charlie back every night? A day in advance, in case he spends it on booze before morning.'

'Suppose he runs off with the donkey?'

Sean hooted with laughter. 'Old Seamus run? He has trouble walking by eight every night.'

'Why wouldn't Old Seamus be buying his own donkey instead of dealing with gombeen men the likes of Michael and you?' asked Pat.

Sean accepted the description without batting an eyelid. Gombeen men were shrewd traders. A gombeen man might own shops and lend money on the side – he might do any manner of things, but they would all earn money.

'Old Seamus never had more than ten shillings in his whole life. He spends it on booze, Da, as fast as he gets it.'

Pat cast a guilty glance at the three bottles of Guinness on his shelf, but Sean was too busy explaining to notice. He and Michael were buying another donkey next week. 'What do you think of that, Da?'

'Does Old Seamus need another donkey?'

'Not Old Seamus – Paddy Cullen who collects down Baggot Street. He needs a donkey.'

'An' will he be paying you two shillings a day too?'

Sean nodded, and hastened on with an explanation which seemed to envisage donkeys forever more. Soon every knacker in Dublin would have a cart pulled by one of Sean's donkeys. Pat interrupted the outpouring to point out that some traders already had donkeys. Some even had horses.

'But there's still plenty of Old Seamuses, Da. I bet Dublin is full of them if you looked hard enough.'

Pat made a final attempt to dampen Sean's ambitions. 'Wouldn't you be better off saving some money? Seems to me you're no better than Old Seamus, spending money as fast as you get it, him on booze and you on donkeys.'

'Wouldn't that be a dreadful waste, Da, locking money up like that. Nearly as bad as Old Seamus boozing his. Mick heard Mr Caffety say that money should work for you – well, nothing works harder than a donkey.'

Sean found his Old Seamuses right enough. Twelve months later he and Michael owned seven donkeys – and a year or so after that the Connors and O'Hara stable boasted thirteen donkeys and one bay gelding. It amazed Pat who could never understand grown men doing business with boys. But Sean looked embarrassed when Pat said as much. 'They're not *doing business*, Da. It's only a few Old Seamuses messing around with a couple of kids.' His embarrassment gave way to a proud smile, 'And we give Aunt Brigid two pounds a week now.'

Pat smiled, remembering when Sean and Michael had delivered their first little bonus. The whole story had come out, Old Seamus and all. But Brigid had to admit that the old man had not driven the boys to drink, and she was more than pleased with the money. The boys spent every spare minute up at Palmerstown. Brigid never had to ask where they were, it was always the stables – stables mind, not just a paddock or a patch of waste ground. Even Charlie, their very first donkey, had been housed in a stable – a crude affair which Sean had built from old packing cases scrounged in the docks, and which he enlarged whenever Charlie had brothers or sisters. The Connors and O'Hara stable was nothing to look at, even Sean admitted that, but at least it was dry, and Sean made it warm by packing mud and straw into the cracks in the woodwork.

People thought the boys were mad to begin with. Local donkeys were thin scraggy beasts whose coats were rough from sleeping out in all weathers – but a Connors and O'Hara donkey could be spotted a mile off. It would have a healthy coat and be wearing a straw hat which Maureen had made. And whoever was using it would be keeping a watchful eye on his charge, knowing that Sean inspected each beast at the end of the day.

One day Pat was in a pub when a man ran in and shouted, 'Eh, Garret, kids out there are tormenting your donkey. It's in a right lather.' And a man down in the bar slopped Guinness over the counter. 'Oh Jaysus,' he groaned as he rushed to the door, 'that Sean will have my hide if anything happens to that beast of his.'

The incident stayed in Pat's mind. He never mentioned it to Sean, nor at the time did he go outside to see what was happening. He was shocked after, telling himself it was a poor father who doesn't protect his son's donkey. Yet there was only one answer. Sean needed neither help nor protection. That man had fairly flown to the door for fear of facing Sean's wrath – that man in his fifties, when Sean was aged twelve at the time.

Years later, when Sean Connors was rich and famous, millions of words were written about his childhood. Rubbish most of them, a mixture of half-truths and lies. Certainly Paul Thompson's *The Power in the Back Room* got it wrong. All that stuff about starving in a Dublin slum and running bare-arsed through the Liberties – Brigid must have spun in her grave. Of course they were poor – living as they did in the tiny terraced house, with Tomas sleeping with the boys and Brigid with the girls, just one room downstairs and a kitchen – but they were *proud* poor. Being poor is a million times different from the childhood Sean was supposed to have had. He was strictly brought up. School with the Christian Brothers and scars on his hands to prove it – prayers seven times a day, confession every Saturday and mass on Sundays. Brigid and Tomas loved him as their own, and Pat Connors would have died for him. Most people who researched Sean's early life spent too much time looking in the yellowing pages of old newspapers. Had they known Sean's parents, or Brigid and Tomas and the rest of the family, maybe fewer lies would have been told. For the truth is that despite Pat's political activities, Sean's boyhood was fairly well regulated – or at least until he was thirteen when everything changed. But even Sean's reaction to that was foreshadowed the year before – when Maureen had the trouble with the Protestant boys.

Maureen was Brigid's youngest, two years older than Sean. Brigid had feared losing her once, the way three others had been lost before their first birthday, but Maureen had survived, plagued by a consumptive cough and a weak constitution. She was not a pretty child, but her plainness was compensated for by the sweetness of her disposition. Her first faltering steps had been taken to fetch something for Tomas, and she seemed to have been running errands ever since. She had watched Brigid's early ministrations of Sean with interest, and by the time she was five Maureen was taking a hand herself – bossing him gently with that straight-faced seriousness which little girls usually reserve for a favourite doll. Sean had responded with good humour, and more than once Brigid had come across them talking with the hushed whispers and solemnity of a mother superior conversing with a bishop.

But the relationship changed over the years. Roles reversed. Sean shot up, and his sturdy frame showed signs of equalling Pat's one day. When he was seven he was a good four inches taller than Maureen, and a year later he was head and shoulders above her. By nine he was even bigger than Michael, Brigid's second boy who was eleven and a half by then.

Sean's size was good and bad news. The bad was that it made him an immediate target. At one time his face seemed permanently bruised from encounters with older boys who recognized a comer when they saw one. Some bloody battles ensued. More than once Sean limped back to Brigid's after a beating, creeping up to the bedroom before facing the family. Maureen helped mend his clothes before Brigid saw them, and her neat stitching helped perpetuate that special closeness which had marked their earlier life.

The good news was that Sean's size and spirit marked him out as a natural leader. Small boys set on by bullies saw Sean as their saviour. Sometimes he was, but he often earned another black eye in the process.

The remarkable thing was that none of this coarsened his manner. That he could be as tough as old boots never stopped him being gentle at times, especially with Brigid's girls, and most especially with Maureen who was not allowed to as much as lift a kettle while Sean was in the kitchen. He would take it from her, still talking or doing whatever, so that his actions passed unnoticed by others. But Brigid noticed. Brigid continued to nurture her dreams of the priesthood, right up to the day when Maureen had the trouble with the Protestant boys. Then the dream died, never to be revived again.

It happened on a Saturday, alongside the canal. The pattern of Saturdays had long been fixed. Sean went to Confession in the morning, on his way to the stables at Palmerstown. His afternoon was spent with Pat whom he would leave at about four-thirty to be back at Brigid's for tea – and then he returned to the stables for another hour in the evening. Brigid's day had a different pattern, but was just as rigid. She and Maureen cleaned the house from top to bottom in the morning, after which Maureen left to go to her own Confession at St Matthew's. Usually Brigid accompanied her to the Percy Street bridge – and while Maureen took the short cut down the canal towpath, Brigid would walk along the opposite bank to meet Tomas on his vegetable patch.

And so it was that Saturday afternoon, when Brigid and Tomas were returning from the vegetable patch, walking slowly down the towpath, him with a hatful of potatoes and her carrying two cabbages big enough to last until Monday.

'There's Maureen now,' Brigid said, looking across the canal.

Maureen had emerged on to the opposite bank, on her way home from St Matt's. Two small boys accompanied her, one with a missal under his arm, all three engaged in animated conversation. Then the Protestant boys struck, leaping from the bushes with blood-curdling whoops to fall upon the startled Catholic children. Maureen screamed with terror while her companions bolted, wriggling and swerving to escape clutching hands. The smallest boy dropped his missal and as he retrieved it the Protestant boys were on to him – one pinning his arms while another punched his face. Somehow the boy broke loose and scrambled clear, perilously close to the edge of the canal – while his friend raced off in the opposite direction. But Maureen was trapped, with the five Protestant boys dancing around her like wild Indians round a totem pole.

'Hey!' Tomas shouted from the opposite bank. 'Hey there – you leave that girl alone this instant.'

But the boys were safe from Tomas. He was a good fifty yards from the Percy Street bridge. They hurled abuse across the muddy water and screamed and jigged around Maureen. She swayed one way, then the other, trying to avoid flailing fists while covering her tear-stained face and screaming in terror. Suddenly she stumbled and lost her balance. She was down – and they were kicking her.

Tomas dropped the potatoes and started for the bridge, while Brigid shrieked across the canal. Then a figure appeared at the end of the towpath. It was Sean, on his way home from Ammet Street. He was twenty yards from the boys, but one glance was enough – Tomas breaking into a run on the far side, Brigid frantically waving, and Maureen being kicked on the ground. Sean charged. One tormentor shouted a warning, two whirled round to meet the challenge. They were as big as Sean and clearly confident of the outcome – but then Sean was amongst them.

Nobody doubted Sean's killer instincts after that day. He took a running jump at the two who swung towards him, cracking his heel into a shin with bone-shattering force, and butting the other boy's face so hard that blood flew everywhere. Then he was at the others, fists lashing, his knee finding a groin, his heel grinding an instep, bobbing and weaving like a prizefighter. Back and forth they fought over Maureen's prone body, until two boys ducked away, clutching bloody faces. A third hopped painfully, rubbing his shin. But the remaining two were made of sterner stuff – one landed a swinging blow that knocked Sean down. He rolled over, escaped a flying boot by a hair's-breadth, and hurled himself head first at his opponent. Down they went, legs and arms everywhere. The fifth boy kicked wildly at Sean, missed, and overbalanced into the canal.

Meanwhile Tomas was half way across the bridge. His shouts brought other people running. A uniformed soldier started down the towpath, with three other men trailing behind. The boy who clambered out of the canal ran away, followed by the lad with the cracked shin. The bloody-nosed youth panted after them, with the fourth boy on his heels. But Sean still pinned one enemy to the ground.

'Sean!' Tomas gasped, 'Sean, it's all right now.'

Sean took no notice. His left hand gripped a handful of the boy's hair, while his right fist hammered again and again into the boy's face.

'Sean!' Maureen wailed, on her knees next to him.

It did no good. Sean's white face was a twisted mask of fury.

'Give over boy,' shouted the soldier, pulling at Sean's shoulders. Sean shrugged him away.

Another man burst past Tomas. 'For God's sake! Stop him!'

It took four men to pull Sean off. Even so he delivered a tremendous parting kick to the youth's ribs. Afterwards one of the men said it was like wrestling with a caged animal.

It was five minutes before the boy on the ground could sit up, ten before he could walk. The soldier called two of the youths back from where they watched twenty yards away. They advanced cautiously, watching Sean all the time.

Maureen sobbed quietly now, as frightened by Sean as by anything else. Her lip was cut and she sucked it noisily between gasping for breath and wiping her eyes.

Sean's eyes glittered like chips of steel. He watched the youths retreat down the towpath. Afterwards one of the men said, 'He was trembling all over, but none of us dared let him go or he'd have been after them again.'

Finally Brigid arrived to hold the sobbing girl in her arms. 'There there, no damage done. Merciful heaven, I've never seen the like.' Whether she meant the attack on her daughter or Sean's counter-attack was not clear.

Not until the wounded youth had reached the bridge did the men loosen their grip on Sean. He pushed them away and took a deep breath, while casting a glare down the towpath. Brigid gave Maureen a quick kiss, and hurried to Sean's side. 'All right, Sean. Sure now, it's all over . . . best forgive and forget.'

He seemed to come out of his trance then. The soldier mistakenly reported afterwards – 'When the Mammy spoke to him he gave her a weak smile. He even had blood on his mouth – I tell you, he tried to rip that kid's throat out with his teeth.' An exaggeration, but they were all shaken. The soldier went on – 'He looked at the Mammy and said, "I'll maybe forgive, we'll see about that, but I'll never forget. Sure I will not, I'll never forget."'

No more would the witnesses forget what they had seen. Death had been seconds away for that boy in the dirt and everyone knew it, including Brigid. There was no mention of the church after that, not as far as Sean was concerned.

Tomas called at Ammet Street later, anxious to explain the full circumstances in case Pat heard the tale elsewhere. When he reached the end of the story, Pat gave a start of excitement, 'What's that you say? When Brigid talked of forgiveness – Sean said *what*?'

Tomas frowned in concentration. He was still upset and liable to muddle things. 'Something like he would maybe forgive, but he'd never forget. I don't recall the exact words . . .'

Pat sucked his breath and rocked back and forth with excitement. 'The rules,' he whispered. 'Forgive if you like, but never forget. God Almighty, the boy has learned one of the rules!'

'Did you say the rules?' Tomas was puzzled.

Pat froze. He gave Tomas a sharp look, 'Sure I said nothing of the kind. What sort of damn fool thing would that be to say?'

So there the matter ended, and Tomas took himself off home shortly afterwards.

But Pat sat staring into the darkness for hours.

CHAPTER FIVE

The following years were full of change for Pat Connors. Almost against his wishes he was drawn to the forefront of Irish politics. Dev's Fianna Fail won the General Election in '33, but they only heightened the tension. The election was rigged. The muscle boys of the officially outlawed IRA had put Dev into office. Pat had evidence of Fianna Fail men voting a hundred times, even five hundred times, using names from half the tombstones in Dublin. Few prosecutions were brought because people were afraid. Some who did speak out were found in back alleys afterwards, dead, with IRA warning notes pinned to their bodies.

They were violent times all over the world. Fascism prowled Europe's grey streets like a marauding jackal. Hitler rose to power in Germany, Moseley formed his squads of Blackshirts in London – while in Dublin General O'Duffy founded the Blueshirts. Duffy had been chief of police until Dev sacked him – so he teamed up with Cosgrave to form a new party – Fine Gael they called it, meaning Tribe of Gaels. Events were predictable after that – in the Dail the Tribe of Gaels clashed with the Warriors of Ireland (Fianna Fail), while on the streets outside their supporters fought even more violently.

Few voices were powerful enough to be heard above the turmoil, but one such belonged to Pat Connors. He abandoned his shadowy role, and stumped the country, from one public meeting to another. 'Is this the Ireland Pearse and Connolly died for?' he demanded. 'Mob rule. Is that what you want? A place where decent people cannot live in peace . . . when men fear an IRA bullet or a Blueshirt knife? Must this island of ours always lust for blood? I say this . . . Ireland needs democratic government . . . deserves democratic government . . . and by God must rise up and *demand* such a government before it is too late.'

But there is little drama in moderation. The offerings of Pat Connors looked dull when compared to the excitement of communist-type revolution, or the glitter of Nazi-style rallies. Acts of violence increased every day. Yet despite such intimidation, or perhaps because of it, Pat Connors applied himself as never before. He was no longer Michael Collins's disciple, he was his own man, shouting his own message, and people were beginning to listen.

For Sean too, they were years of change. He was growing up fast, but had not yet grown up. He knew of his father's widening influence because he heard people talking – he was proud and loved his father more than ever, but he was still just a boy. Every day was a magical adventure.

Weekends were solid with happiness. The magic started first thing after Confession on a Saturday, when he and Michael took themselves off to the stables. Then Sean spent an exciting afternoon with his father before hurrying home to tea and dashing back to the stables for another hour in the evening. Sundays were even better. Sundays were best of all. His first job after mass was to take the donkeys for their weekend bath in the Liffey. That was riotous. A donkey called Merlin was the clown of the stable. Each donkey was a character – talkative Charlie hawed the others to death every night with news of Old Seamus – Garth was greedy and bad-tempered in the mornings – Molly was quiet and shy – and so on. But Merlin was the clown. His favourite trick was splashing the others on a Sunday morning – especially Garth who detested the water. Merlin sidled alongside, giving gentle nudges of encouragement until Garth forgot his fears and relaxed into a paddle. Then Merlin kicked out his legs and rolled over into the water with a tremendous splash. Poor Garth bellowed and screamed with panic – while Merlin hawed with helpless laughter. It happened every Sunday, all the year round, and if Merlin was stopped from soaking Garth he was teasing the others a minute later.

Bathing took all morning, and by the time the donkeys were back in their stables Maureen would have arrived with soda bread and cheese for lunch. In the afternoon Michael and Maureen groomed the donkeys, while Sean mucked out and did the repair work around the stables. After which he washed and went up to the farm to pay another week's rent and to buy feed. That always took time because Farmer O'Flynn was forever trying to add a penny to the price of oats or charge extra for the hay. But he treated Sean with elaborate respect. So did Mrs O'Flynn. It was Mrs O'Flynn who first started to call Sean 'Mr Connors'. She had called him 'that boy' until he was thirteen. 'That boy's back for the donkey feed,' she shouted to her husband from the back door. But one day it changed. She was carrying a pail of water across the yard when he fell into step beside her and took it from her – just took it out of her hands and went on talking like a grown man. Her quick glance of surprise caused her to catch her breath. Of course he was still just a boy, she told herself – but he had a man's way somehow, and a man's manners. And she breathed a little faster when he smiled at her like that. So she had called him 'Mr Connors' from then on, as a sort of joking acknowledgement that he would soon be

74

more than just a boy.

Sean's visits developed into a little ritual after that, but the new arrangements unnerved him to begin with. Especially the first time that Mrs O'Flynn met him at the door and guided him into the kitchen with her hand on his arm. She had walked so close that her body brushed his, and he had tingled all over and gone red in the face without knowing why. She had sat him down and poured him a mug of hot tea. Freshly baked bread was on the table. She spread a slice thick with butter. 'Working the hours you do, Mr Connors,' she smiled, 'sure now, won't you be fading away unless I take you in hand.'

Sean thought it very good of her to address him as Mr Connors. It made him feel grown up. Not as grown up as her of course, even though she was so much younger than her husband, but it narrowed the gap and made it easier to talk to her. And it was pleasing to sit there at the end of the day, especially with her so interested in donkeys and knackers like Old Seamus. After tea she fetched her husband. Sean rose politely as she left the table, and she squeezed past as if the kitchen had shrunk, which was silly really because there had seemed plenty of room earlier. When she came back she told Farmer O'Flynn, 'Tea's in the pot. I had a cup with Mr Connors so I won't stop.' She stood ironing her dress over her hips with her hands. 'Well then, I'll leave you men to your business.' And she gave Sean such a smile that he quite overlooked that she had left without drinking her tea.

He got to know her well. She always made tea on a Sunday and sat chatting before fetching her husband. Invariably she gave Sean a little hug at the door, and somehow things were always spread over the floor so they never could pass each other without a bit of a squeeze.

Maureen grumbled on the way home, 'You were over an hour up at the farm today.'

Sean tried to explain about Mrs O'Flynn being interested in donkeys, but Maureen snorted and refused to listen, so they walked in silence until Michael made a joke or challenged Sean to race the last hundred yards. Then they arrived at Brigid's all out of breath, and Sean's Da was there to greet them, to make the perfect end to a perfect day.

The strange thing was that once Mrs O'Flynn started to address Sean as Mr Connors everyone followed her lead. Farmer O'Flynn took it up and gradually it spread to Old Seamus and the other knackers. Sean liked it when he grew used to it. He called all the men Mister anyway, even Old Seamus, not deferentially but politely enough. Respectful but firm was the best description. He did most things without giving offence, which perhaps was the secret of his modest success . . . he rarely gave offence unless he had to. The men rather liked him. Old Seamus and the others had heard of his temper – even seen it spark once or twice – enough for them to take pains to avoid a repeat performance. But even that was unlikely, because Sean weeded out potential trouble-makers after the first year. So in a way it became almost a status symbol for a knacker to be seen driving a Connors and O'Hara donkey . . . which was perhaps another reason why Sean's business prospered.

And prosper it did – though there was little money about. Most weeks Sean was paying for new donkeys, so he was left with only Brigid's two pounds. But half way through 1935 Sean called a temporary halt to buying more animals. The net income from the stables rocketed to seven pounds a week. True earnings were apparent for the first time. Sean felt like a millionaire, and he and Michael were planning their next move when Maureen fell ill.

Her consumptive condition had worsened since Christmas. The doctor said, 'It's a good summer she needs, plenty of sunshine.' But it had been a poor summer again, and Brigid grew so worried that Maureen was stopped from visiting the stables – and by September Maureen was confined to her bed for days at a time.

Sean had an idea. He discussed it with his father at one of their Saturday afternoon conferences. 'Uncle Tomas has got a brother in California, hasn't he, Da? And another one in Australia? Wouldn't you think Maureen would be better off there?'

'Aye,' said Pat, who had been worrying about the same thing, 'but it's the fare. Tomas was saying the other day – a voyage like that costs money, even if she's met and taken care of at the other end.'

'How much money, Da?'

Pat scratched his head. 'Wouldn't America be cheapest – but if she's to have a penny in her purse when she gets there even that would cost a hundred pounds.'

A hundred pounds! After paying Brigid, Sean was left with five pounds a week. Twenty weeks at five pounds made a hundred. But Sean already had eighteen pounds which he was about to spend on another donkey. A hundred take away eighteen . . . left eighty-two . . . fives into that . . . sixteen and a half. *Maureen could be sailing to America in sixteen and a half weeks!*

The words came out in a rush. Pat listened as calmly as he could with his heart bursting with pride. Then he said, 'But what about Michael? Half the money's his. Here's you throwing it about –'

'Mick will agree,' Sean said promptly.

Pat was bone-tired after a week's political battles, but he insisted on walking round to Brigid's place – where he shut himself away with Brigid and Tomas in the kitchen. Brigid was in tears by the end of it. Nobody could say whether they were tears of sorrow at losing her daughter, tears of joy at the thought of Maureen's improved health, or tears of gratitude for Sean's offer – but tears came in a flood and it was fully fifteen minutes before she recovered enough to be led into the living-room. Even Tomas's eyes were shining, and he kept clearing his throat as if coming down with a bad cold. Then the scheme was announced to the family. Maureen was going to her Uncle Rory in California!

Sean's donkeys had made a dream come true. Not that the boys were allowed to foot the bill entirely – Brigid returned one pound of the two they gave her every week, and Pat chipped in another pound a week . . . but Sean's idea had made it all possible. He and Michael were the heroes of the hour, heroes to the whole family, except to Maureen herself. And she wanted to stay in Dublin.

She said very little that night. Not that she had much chance amid the excitement. Pen and ink were produced for an immediate letter to Uncle Rory, and Uncle Pat promised to see a man who would know about getting a berth. They even worked out her date of sailing. She would be on the high seas for Christmas. Cooey kept saying, 'It's sunny every day in California,' while Dary kept telling Maureen about the oranges. 'You'll be able to pick one whenever you want. They even have orange trees on the streets in California.'

But all Maureen could think of was that they were sending her away. *Sean* was sending her away. She had not asked to go. It would break her heart. Didn't they know that? Didn't they know she loved each and every one of them? Didn't Sean know how much she loved him?

So the evening was a nightmare for Maureen. And it was raining in the morning, so she was kept at home instead of being allowed to go to the stables. She knew she had to speak to Sean alone, to persuade him to keep his money. But privacy was rare in that little house. Moments alone were hard to come by. Sean was only there at meal-times and bed-times, and the whole family was gathered then.

Maureen willed herself better. She even looked better. She was allowed up for an hour on Monday, and the same on Tuesday and Wednesday. But days slipped past without an opportunity for a private talk with Sean. Her anxiety mounted to fever pitch – until, on the Saturday afternoon, she engineered a chance to see him alone. Brigid allowed her to go to Confession – so, muffled up against the damp air, Maureen set out for St Matt's. But she went only as far as the towpath, where she stayed to waylay Sean. Thoughts of the Protestant boys made her tremble. She kept a watchful eye on the opposite bank in case her father should be walking back from his vegetable patch. She paced up and down to keep warm . . . until her breath caught in a flutter as she saw Sean striding towards her on his way home from Ammet Street.

She ran to meet him and clung to his arm. 'Let's not go straight home,' she begged. 'Let's just sit and talk for a while.'

Sean glanced at the darkening sky. He was planning another visit to the stables.

'Please, Sean. We hardly ever have a chance to talk . . .' she forced herself to say the dreaded words, 'and what with me going away soon.'

They sat for a moment on the parapet of the bridge. Sean

78

sensed her mood and began to encourage her, 'Sure you'll love California when you get there. All that sunshine an' all. And Uncle Rory with a big house and doing so well for himself.'

She cared nothing for Uncle Rory or his big house. Her heart simply ached to stay. She struggled to find the right words, but it was hard – people had been going on all week about how lucky she was and how everyone was making a sacrifice for her. The whole street had heard by Monday. Father Murphy declared it a blessing and said Sean was growing up with every Christian virtue intact – thanks to Brigid and no thanks to Sean's Da. And Cooey said it wasn't fair because she was just as sick as Maureen and if Maureen was going, why wasn't she. Whereas the Da kept choking up whenever he looked at her, and gave her an extra hug every day . . . and the Mammy was so proud that one of her children was going to the United States. This one said that and that one said this, until after a week of it Maureen felt bruised and bewildered. Only one thing stayed clear in her mind . . . her love for Sean. And she knew he loved her too, otherwise why would be spend all of this money? He hadn't offered a penny to the others . . . but Sean was sending her away.

She watched him skim a pebble across the canal. 'I'm really a lot stronger than most people think,' she began at last. 'Sure it's just now and then I get poorly. Wouldn't you think everyone gets sick at times.'

'I don't,' Sean answered, matter-of-factly. He turned to her with a smile. 'And neither will you when you get to California. Everyone says the same.'

Suddenly the hopelessness of it all overwhelmed her and she burst into tears. 'Oh Sean, why didn't you tell me first?'

His arm went round her as he tried to explain about telling the Da and everything happening so quickly. Maureen was sniffing and sobbing so hard that she barely heard a word. She wept uncontrollably while Sean muttered helpless words of encouragement. The more she cried the more desperate he became. He clutched wildly for words to comfort her, until finally he blurted out, 'You'll just be sizing the place up for the rest of us, that's all. Sure won't I be over to see you soon enough myself.'

She pulled away. Her blurred eyes searched his face. 'Really?' she said, her voice full of hope. 'Really, Sean? You'll be coming yourself?'

He hesitated. His father wanted him to be a great man in Ireland. There was the business of learning the rules. The Da wouldn't want him running off to America.

'I'll wait for you, Sean,' she said with trembling intensity. 'I'll wait for ever and ever . . . if you promise to come.'

He squirmed, not knowing what to say. Avoiding her eye, he glanced away, searching for inspiration. Then he saw Tomas on the far bank. 'Here comes your Da,' he said with stifled relief. 'Come on, let's go and meet him.'

But she held his arm, 'Promise you'll come for me, Sean. Promise.'

He felt trapped, frightened. Then he remembered one of the rules – such a simple one that he almost laughed. Relief flooded through him. 'Never tell a lie,' Pat had warned him. 'But sometimes the truth can be damaging, so avoid it altogether. Answer a question with one of your own.'

'Promise me, Sean,' Maureen pleaded, 'will you promise to come?'

'Will you promise *me* something?' he countered. 'Will you promise to eat lots and lots of those oranges? So you'll get all those vitamins. Oranges for tea –'

'Sean, I will. I will, I promise.'

'And will you promise to write once a week?'

'I'll write every day,' she answered, her eyes shining.

'And . . . and will you promise to lay out in that lovely warm sun . . . and get brown all over?'

'I'll get as brown as a berry. Oh Sean, I promise!'

'And . . .' Sean laughed, sharing her excitement but for quite different reasons. The rule was working! Actually working. It was so easy . . . once you knew the rules. Maureen was laughing with him now, wiping her tears away. But suddenly her eyes clouded with concern and she was gripping his arm tighter than ever. 'And you're to promise me another thing,' she said fiercely. 'You're to stop seeing that Mrs O'Flynn while I'm away.'

He blushed bright red, caught off guard. 'Sure what's got into you? All I do is go up and pay Farmer O'Flynn –'

'She's a bad woman. I just know she is. I don't want you seeing her again. Promise me. You can send Mick on a Sunday...'

Mercifully Tomas arrived to put an end to the conversation. Sean thought about it later that evening while walking up to Palmerstown. Sure what was the harm of a cup of tea on a Sunday? And Mrs O'Flynn was so interesting. And pretty. And she had a nice laugh ... and ... and he remembered the Sunday before when Mrs O'Flynn had been pouring the tea. She was bending over the table and there was a gap in her dress. He couldn't help looking. Her skin was so smooth that he wanted to stroke it. There was a channel, all peach-coloured shadow beneath the curving white mounds of her breasts. He longed to plunge his hands into her dress ... and was struggling with his feelings when she glanced up and caught the direction of his eyes. But she stayed as she was, leaning forward, her eyes finding his and dragging them away from that gap in her dress. Finally she straightened up with a small laugh of amusement. 'Why, Mr Connors,' she said in her smoky voice, 'I've never seen that look on your face before.' Then she did something to her dress, tightening a button or something, because both her hands were smoothing the material over her bodice, and Sean wished it was his hands on her body instead of her own. And all the while she had watched him with a contemplative look in her eye ... so that he blushed and felt his mouth go dry. But she had not seemed angry or mad with him, in fact the reverse, she acted as though he had pleased her in some way.

Pat went to a funeral in Lucan the following week. Padraic Riddell, a friend for twenty-five years, had been murdered by the IRA. Padraic had worked in Moreland's shop in the old days, and been a member of Mick's Squad. Now he was dead ... shot in the back, with a note pinned to his jacket, IRA WARNING.

Against the advice of his friends, Pat insisted on going to a public meeting after the funeral. He knew he would face a hostile audience ... Lucan had long been a stronghold of the outlawed IRA ... but Pat was so

81

sickened and distressed by Padraic's murder that it would have been a betrayal not to have spoken out. 'To suffer in silence does no good at all,' he told his companions.

The hall was far from silent. It was packed tight with a jeering crowd. Shouts of abuse thundered at Pat as he made his way to the platform. Men shook their fists, while others unfurled an IRA banner. Pat's appeals for order fell on deaf ears, and after ten minutes of bedlam the organizers were ready to abandon the meeting.

'I'll be telling you a story if you'll listen,' Pat bellowed, 'of Pearse and Connolly in the GPO.'

Even mention of bygone heroes failed to gain a response. Pat shouted above the din, 'There were few of us then. God knows never enough to beat the British, and didn't we know it. But that wasn't the point – the point was it was a rallying call for Irish unity.'

A murmur of agreement rose from a section of the crowd. Pat tried to capitalize on it. 'That was nearly twenty years ago,' he shouted. 'But I'll tell you this . . . I was *proud* to have Padraic Riddell beside me then . . . at my side as we faced the English guns. And now Padraic has been murdered . . . shot in the back by an Irish coward –'

Shouts of dissent thundered towards the platform. Someone shouted, 'Shot by the IRA.'

'Aye,' Pat agreed. 'And do you think Pearse and Connolly would have been proud of that? They'd be sick to their stomachs with shame. Them and Mick Collins –'

'Collins sold out. What about the oath?'

'What about it? Hasn't Dev abolished it?' Pat demanded, 'or don't you even read the papers –'

'So what about the north?'

Pat fought to make himself heard above the rising uproar. 'The same . . . a step at a time. The oath's been dealt with . . .'

'No thanks to you! Get out, Connors. We don't want the likes of you . . .' the voice drowned in the baying of the crowd. Suddenly a stone was flung. It was like a signal. Chairs were upended as men rushed the platform. But Pat was as strong as an ox, despite his stiff leg. After an initial skirmish his assailants fell back. Their objective had been accomplished however . . . the meeting was abandoned before it properly started. People spilled through the doors and out into the night, cheering themselves hoarse.

Pat took his bruised face back down the Quays and brooded in his room on Ammet Street. The ugly scene worried him deeply. The political situation was worsening again. 'Dear God,' he sighed as he poured himself a Guinness, 'Mick Collins himself wouldn't have got a hearing tonight.'

The night slipped by, hour after hour, but still Pat sat in his chair seeking a solution. 'There must be a way, somehow . . . they'll *have* to listen to someone.' He ate some cheese with his stout . . . and peered through the window to watch the sky lighten with the promise of dawn. Only then did he unlace his boots and slump on to his bed. Eventually he dozed off into an exhausted restless sleep.

But his eyes had hardly closed when footsteps scurried down the passage and fists hammered on his door. Part of his dream? The wailing outside was an echo of the despair which had haunted his night. A woman's screams finally roused him. He awoke in a sweat, calling out as he struggled upright. Somebody beat and kicked the door. The handle rattled furiously.

'For God's sake –'

'Pat, will you open this door!'

Brigid! A million fears rushed through his mind. He stumbled as he crossed the room. Then the door sprang open and she was beating his chest with her fists and screaming. 'It's your fault! Damn you, Pat Connors. Will you never listen to me!'

She flew at him like a fury, raking his face with her nails. 'Damn you, Pat Connors. Damn you, damn you . . .'

He pulled her hands from his face, 'What in God's name –'

She shouted hysterically – shaking so violently that he could barely hold her. She wore her nightgown beneath her coat. He pulled a blanket from the bed and tried to wrap it around her, but she pushed him away, 'Damn you to hell, Pat Connors. Damn you to hell for what's happened tonight!'

'Will you stop that!' he roared, forcing her into a chair. 'For mercy's sake woman, tell me what's happened.'

'Sean . . .' she gasped, then dissolved into tears, hands at her face as she rocked back and forth.

More footsteps raced up the stairs. Pat swung round just as Dary burst into the room. Pat grabbed his shoulders, 'What in God's name –'

'It's the donkeys,' Dary gasped. 'They're killing the donkeys . . .'

Pat's mind blurred as he struggled to understand. Brigid wailed and sobbed in the chair. Dary bent double in an effort to draw breath. Pat swung the boy off his feet and carried him out to the landing, 'Now tell me . . .'

Dary gulped wildly, 'The Da's gone up there with Sean an' Mick. We had this woman screaming outside an' when the Da went down she wanted Sean –'

'What woman?'

'From the farm,' Dary panted, then turned to hang over the balustrade.

But Pat was no longer listening. Instead he was tying his boots. He stumbled down the stairs with Brigid's sobs and curses still ringing in his ears.

Sean ran all the way, leaving Tomas and Michael far behind. Through the half-light of dawn he raced, his shadow dancing over the Quays, footsteps clattering on the cobbles to echo back from darkened doorways and deserted alleys. Up the hill towards Palmerstown, gasping for breath, running blind, his mind full of the picture of Mrs O'Flynn standing in Brigid's kitchen. He had been stunned, disorientated, dragged half awake from his bed. Mrs O'Flynn there – at Brigid's place – white-faced with her hair all wild, sobbing, 'They're killing the donkeys. We couldn't stop them . . .'

'Wait,' Tomas begged as Sean threw on his clothes. 'We'll get your Da and a few others . . .'

But Sean could not wait.

Maureen appeared at Brigid's elbow, 'Sean wait . . . *please* wait . . .'

But Sean had not waited.

Michael was dressing, 'Give me a minute. Wait for me . . .'

But Sean had waited for no one.

He had plunged out into the darkened street and started to run. He lengthened his stride, he shortened it again up the hill, then lengthened it when he reached the outskirts of Palmerstown. The stitch in his side faded with his second wind. The grey light of a new day sketched the outline of trees across the skyline, and suddenly Sean realized it was raining.

He was half a mile away when he heard it. He charged up the lane towards the farmhouse, his heart full of dread. The braying was pitiful. He knew all of their voices. It was Molly, but Molly as he had never heard her before. Molly in terrible agony. Molly in monstrous pain. Then he rounded the bend and saw the smouldering wreckage of his stables.

He found Molly in the end stall. He had to climb over Garth and Merlin to reach her. She had fallen awkwardly in the corner, prongs from the steel fork so deeply embedded in her neck that the blood-covered tips were through on the other side. Terrible wounds marked the rest of her body. Her soft brown eyes accused him as he appeared in the doorway. The sound of her pitiful braying broke his heart. He knelt before her, not daring to touch the fork for fear of worsening her agony. He felt sick and nearly vomited. Tears stung his eyes and blurred his vision. He sobbed harshly, 'Dear God. Molly, what have they done to you?'

Her liquid brown eyes pleaded with him. He turned and ran, covering his ears with his hands to shut out her cries.

Farmer O'Flynn was slumped at the kitchen table. Sean saw the blood-soaked rag clasped to the old man's head, but little else registered.

'I'm sorry,' O'Flynn began, 'I tried –'

'Have you a gun?' Sean demanded.

The old man's eyes widened in alarm, 'They've gone . . . besides they were too many.'

'Can't you hear Molly?' Sean screamed. 'For God's sake, put an end to her misery.'

O'Flynn tried to stand, but almost passed out. 'Next room,' he said weakly, 'shells are in the drawer . . .'

Sean had already left the kitchen. He had never handled a gun before. He rushed back with the shells and asked the old man to load the rifle. Then he ran back to the stables. His hands were shaking. He distrusted his aim. He rested the muzzle against Molly's ear. Then pulled the trigger.

Tomas arrived as the shot rang out. He was out of breath and terribly afraid. He lurched off in the direction of the shot, fearing something dreadful. And his worst fears were realized as Sean staggered towards him, clutching the rifle and covered in blood. But it was Molly's blood, not Sean's . . . though it took Tomas some time to realize that.

After that everyone arriving fresh to the scene met a vivid first impression. Michael was overcome by the smell – the thick heavy stench of blood and excreta which clung like a cloud of poison gas. He vomited violently, then wandered through the carnage in a state of shock. Every animal had been slaughtered. Part of the stables was burned to the ground.

Even the professional eyes of the *Garda Siochana* – the police – were shocked by the savage brutality.

Pat Connors loomed out of the morning mist to find glassy-eyed men wandering through the debris like victims of shell-shock. He ran to his son and clasped him in his arms, running his hands through the boy's hair and over his face, in a mute gesture of thankfulness to find Sean still in one piece. Father and son clung to each other, sharing their strength. Then Pat held him at arm's length, studying his white face. Gently Pat led him across to the farmhouse, telling him to go inside and wash the blood from his arms and face. But it was an excuse, Pat wanted to spare him further sight of the mutilated carcases.

As Sean walked slowly away Pat turned his attention to the stables. One wall still stood upright at the far end. The message IRA WARNING had been written in red letters three feet high. Pat groaned at the memory of Brigid screaming at him. He touched the lettering, and his finger came away sticky with blood.

When Maeve O'Flynn returned to her farmhouse, her first thoughts were not of her husband . . . a man thirty years older than her . . . but of Sean Connors, a mere boy. She found him alone in the kitchen, standing at the big sink, stripped to the waist. Shirt and jacket were flung over a chair. He was washing his chest with water brought in from the yard.

'They killed the donkeys,' he whispered, shock in every line of his face.

She put a finger to her lips, 'Hush.'

He stared with unseeing eyes. 'They killed the donkeys,' he repeated blankly.

She crossed to the door and locked it – then pulled the curtain across the window, so that only the glow of the turf fire lit the room. She shed her coat and returned to where he stood. The water was barely warm to her touch. She collected the kettle from the hob and emptied it into the sink.

'The donkeys . . .' he whispered.

She soaped the flannel and used it on his chest, massaging warmth into his skin. After which she sought to comfort him in the only way she knew. Her arm slid round his neck to draw his face down to hers. The kiss made her tremble so violently that she fumbled with the buttons on her blouse. She watched his eyes as she guided his hands on to her breasts.

'There, Sean,' she whispered into his hair. 'Isn't that what you wanted on Sunday?'

His muffled reply was lost on her cheek. She let him hold her while she undid his belt. She reached behind him and soaped his back . . . and his chest . . . and his stomach. And when she reached lower Sean Connors was kissing her not with the timidity of a boy, but with the intensity of a man.

CHAPTER SIX

The knackers arrived at eight o'clock. Some were physically sick at the sight. It took them half an hour to recover nerve to face Sean. Each tipped his hat and murmured shocked regrets. ''Tis an act of terrible wickedness, Mr Connors,' said Old Seamus, and he spoke for everyone there.

Pat, talking to the Garda, looked up, expecting to see a man addressing him. Instead he saw his son being spoken to with such respect that Pat was astonished, even more so when the whole line of knackers shuffled past Sean . . . each with his hat in his hands and a crumpled look on his face . . . each conveying condolences to *Mr* Connors. Pat glowed with pride, despite the circumstances. Then the farmhouse door opened and a young woman appeared whom Pat took to be the farmer's wife. Younger than he expected, she looked flushed enough to have just risen from bed. She handed a mug of tea to Sean – and a puzzled Pat tried to identify his son's answering look. The boy's eyes widened with wonder, as if she had performed a miracle instead of making the tea, which Pat dismissed as nonsense, and he was trying to be more precise when the policeman at his side asked what was to be done with the carcases.

Inevitably Sean decided. If it was all right with Farmer O'Flynn he would bury them at the bottom of long meadow. Mrs O'Flynn hurried away to consult her husband, who emerged a moment later with a bandage around his head. Permission was quickly given and the old man shuffled back to the house and into his bed.

The rest of the men spent the whole morning digging a pit deep enough to accommodate the animals, with Pat Connors working harder than any man there. He was consumed by a terrible rage – and anger so violent that just to wield a spade was a relief. He swore continuously, cursing the unknown enemies who had struck in so cowardly a fashion, while searching his mind for a way to make things up to his son. Pat lacked the money to buy some more donkeys. Had he had the cash he would have bought replacements there and then. Poverty weighed heavy on his shoulders for the first time in his life. He had never considered himself poor. His ambitions had been for Ireland, not to amass personal wealth. It came as a shock to realize that Sean had accumulated more assets than Pat had ever known. By Ammet Street standards Sean had been rich – now, Pat thought bitterly, he has nothing, and all for being my son.

So Pat sought to relieve his guilt by shifting more soil than all the knackers put together. And while the men laboured Maeve O'Flynn made endless trips from the farmhouse, carrying mugs of tea. She paused occasionally to share a word with one of the men. Few noticed that she ended each visit standing next to Sean – few that is except for Maureen, and Maureen noticed everything. She had refused to go home. Instead she spent her time collecting wild flowers from the hedgerows and watching Farmer O'Flynn's wife. Twice she asked Mrs O'Flynn about her husband, only for Mrs O'Flynn to answer – 'Oh sure now, won't he survive,' as if it was of no consequence. The girl and the woman exchanged glances, each instinctively aware of the other's hostility. Maureen's heart sank as she glimpsed the curvaceous figure beneath the top coat, and when the woman placed a possessive hand on Sean's shoulder Maureen positively cringed – 'What right has she to touch him like that? Sure there's not an ounce of decency in the whole of her body.' Whereas Maeve O'Flynn was much more composed. She confronted the thin, white-faced girl and noted the gawky, undeveloped figure. 'A child,' she thought dismissively, 'what could a child teach a young bull like Sean Connors?'

As for Sean, he was numb. First the shock of finding Mrs O'Flynn in Brigid's kitchen, then the frantic race to Palmerstown to discover this awful slaughter. His heart ached for Molly. He grieved over Charlie and the others. Never again would Merlin splash everyone on a Sunday. Never again would Molly give him a friendly nuzzle, never . . . he pushed the memories aside, knowing they would reduce him to tears. Instead he concentrated on digging the grave. The pit was three feet wide now, and twice as long. Sean tried to calculate how large it needed to be, but he closed his mind to thoughts of the mutilated bodies. He hurled another spadeful of earth upwards, and caught a glimpse of Maureen across the meadow. The trip to America would have to wait now. They would need to write to Uncle Rory. Sean bent his back and swore he would send Maureen away to the sun one day. He promised himself that. He would raise the money somehow. He paused to catch his breath. Sweat chilled his bare chest, and as he glanced down he saw the smear of dried soap on his belt. He trembled as he remembered the scene in the kitchen, him clinging to Mrs O'Flynn as she washed him down. 'Me kissing her an' holding her body like that, an' her soaping me all over, then her hands at the top of my legs . . .' He had clung to her fiercely. 'Mrs O'Flynn,' he had gasped into her hair, 'you'll send me blind if you do that.' But she had chuckled deep in her throat and held him tighter than ever.

They buried the animals and covered the pit. Maureen spread posies of wild flowers over the broken earth, and fell to her knees to say a short prayer. Sean choked up, stifling his tears, while next to him Michael sniffed loudly. The knackers looked on with sad, stern faces. After which it was time to bid Mrs O'Flynn goodbye. 'Now don't forget,' she told him as they parted, 'you're to come and see me any time, Mr Connors, any time at all.'

The following weeks were full of pain for Sean. He was moody and truculent, and kept a hair trigger on his temper. A wrong word creased his face into a frown, while an indifferent response, or worse – a jesting humorous one – would start a fight. Baiting Sean Connors became a favourite sport along the Quays among young men aged eighteen and upwards, few younger had a taste for it. Sean responded to a taunt like a salmon rising to a fly. Time and again he was carried back to Brigid's beaten half senseless. But the hammerings had no more effect than Brigid's pleas to stay out of trouble – the next day he would be in another fight. Winning seemed not to matter. The stronger the opponent the more Sean relished the battle. Brigid and Tomas – even Pat Connors himself – were in despair, fearing Sean would get himself killed. And then, suddenly, the violence in Sean seemed to burn itself out. It had lasted a month. By which time Sean had fought half the Quays, but even those who thrashed him without mercy had no desire for another confrontation. So Sean was left alone.

Time passed slowly then. The loss of the donkey business left a gaping void in Sean's life. Even the prospect of starting work as a copy-boy on the *Gazette* failed to excite him. How could it? He and Michael had generated an income of seven pounds a week from a part-time venture – the *Gazette* would pay ten shillings for Sean's full-time efforts. The discrepancy looked enormous. He was grateful to his father for getting him the job, but he viewed

90

the meagre financial rewards with misgiving – and the prospect of being called 'boy' after being addressed as 'Mr Connors' really got under his skin. That hurt – once he stopped mourning his beloved animals. He had seemed set to make his way in the world. Now he was starting from scratch.

But eventually his thoughts acquired purpose again. He brooded less and his spirits revived from his crushing loss. The experience had shaken him, but he had learned from it, even if defining *what* was not easy. Then it came to him. He tingled with excitement as he grasped the meaning of his lesson. He wanted to tell somebody, but stopped himself. Only one person would understand. His father – and Sean wasn't quite ready for that. So, some six weeks after burying his donkeys, Sean bought a small notebook and made his first entry.

'The rules of Sean Connors,' he wrote boldly. Then he set the pencil aside and thought, not because he was at a loss but from an anxiety to be precise. A rule might be drawn from a specific experience, but it should cover every eventuality when set down on paper – otherwise it would never serve for the future. For the hundredth time he asked himself how he could have saved his donkeys. Never once did he blame his father. The donkeys had been his responsibility, not his father's. It was his fault, he was to blame – and Sean was determined to do better in future. Thus he thought long and hard before writing that first rule into his book. 'Rule One,' he wrote. 'Assets must be protected at all times.'

He was proud of the word asset. Mr Caffety had used it once when Sean and Michael were in his shop.

'What's asset mean, Mr Caffety?' Sean had asked without hesitation.

Mr Caffety had frowned and scratched his head. 'Sure, you're a boy for questions. Well, an asset is a . . . well a thing you own in business. Like this shop an' everything. I own it. It belongs to me. They're my assets.'

Sean had looked at the assembled merchandise with new eyes – pots and pans, buckets and mops – things he had known all his life, without realizing they were assets.

But protecting Mr Caffety's assets was easy, Sean

reflected when composing his rules. Caffety's shop was boarded up every night, and Mr Caffety lived upstairs and never went out. Protecting *living* assets like donkeys was a lot harder. And even if he had lived over the stables like Mr Caffety above his shop, Sean was honest enough to wonder if he could have saved his animals from the IRA that night. The whole matter needed careful thinking about. Which led to the second rule. Only deal in *protectable* assets. Sean stumbled over the word protectable – spelling it three different ways and even wondering if the word existed – but it expressed what he felt so he printed the version which looked right. Then he hid the book away, delighting in the surprise he would give his father. For Sean still looked forward to that day when his father would teach him the rules. Now he had rules of his own, and the secret knowledge of that filled him with pride.

But not all of Sean's time was spent formulating his rules . . . two other matters occupied his mind. The first was Mrs O'Flynn. He would never forget her taking his hands in hers and cupping them over her breasts. He remembered her silky smooth skin and the way her nipples had hardened under his fingers. But most vividly he remembered her hands on his body . . . the teasing explorations, the rhythmic stroking . . . and that wild, pulsating moment when he had clung to her with all of his strength. He never thought of that without breaking into a sweat. The miracle was he hadn't gone blind. He tested his eyesight every day, peering across the Liffey to read hoardings across the water, relieved to see even the smallest letters as clearly as ever.

He dreamt of going to Palmerstown . . . but what would he say to Farmer O'Flynn? They had no business to discuss, not now. Besides, Sean wondered if he could face the man again, after doing that with his wife. But he longed to see her. He cursed his frustrations aloud. One thing was clear – he had to get some assets again. If Maureen was to see America, and if he was ever to renew his exciting friendship with Mrs O'Flynn, he just had to have assets. But how? How when the *Gazette* would pay him only ten shillings a week?

92

So time passed slowly. Sean composed his rules and daydreamed of Mrs O'Flynn – but another matter occupied his thoughts at least part of the time: the need to find the men who had murdered his donkeys. The Garda were getting nowhere. People were afraid to talk. An IRA warning meant what it said, lay off if you value your life. And Sean had been told to láy off . . . by his father, by Brigid and Tomas, by Father Murphy and just about everyone. But he persevered discreetly, helped by the knackers, now reduced to pushing their own carts through the streets of Dublin. Not that anything came to light – not a face, nor a description – not even the tiniest clue. In fact Sean was no closer to identifying the killers than when he started. But his father was.

Pat Connors had ordered his son to stay out of it, but he felt no such concern for himself. He pulled the city apart. Past favours were called in. He recruited an army of allies, including Duffy's Blueshirts. He persuaded newspaper friends to pass on any likely snippets of information. And he went further. Pat taunted the IRA from every public platform in Dublin. 'Who are these brave men,' he roared, 'whose love of Ireland is so great that they embark upon such heroic deeds? Don't they deserve a medal? After all, it takes guts to creep out at dead of night, armed to the back teeth, ready for battle. And what a battle. Killing donkeys! That's real courage. Come forward I say, don't skulk in the shadows. Won't we be after building you a statue, alongside the likes of Parnell himself.'

Brigid went wild. She had devoted thirteen years of her life to resisting Pat's influence over Sean. She almost died during those awful weeks when the boy dragged himself home all battered and bruised. When Sean was out of earshot she railed furiously at Pat – 'Isn't it enough harm you've done him already? Let it rest before it brings misery down on the lot of us.'

Pat could not let it rest. He spent every waking hour brooding about it . . . and nine weeks later he had a name . . . followed by another the very next day. The information came from informers, but Pat thought no less of it for that. The feeling grew that he was on to something. Both men were known to be sympathetic to the IRA, and both lived just outside Palmerstown. Not only that but the Garda had considered the men as possible suspects in the murder of Padraic Riddell, whose funeral Pat had attended the day the donkeys were killed. The more Pat checked, the more convinced he became. By the end of a week he was sure the men were involved – so on the Friday evening he caught the tram up to Palmerstown, where he supped a pint at the Deadman's Inn.

Most of the bar recognized him. Pat's bulky figure was too well known to pass unnoticed. Some even guessed why he was there. Conversation dropped to a whisper when the two men arrived. Not that Pat seemed to notice. He propped up the counter, talking to the landlord, while watching the men in the mirror as they advanced to the counter. The man nearest Pat froze in his tracks – but the landlord was already pulling their beers so it was too late to withdraw. They took their glasses off to a corner, where they whispered and tried not to look at Pat who turned to stare at them. That was all he did – just stare. Stared over the rim of his glass, or while he wiped his lips with the back of his hand. But Pat *knew* they were the men, and they knew he knew. Guilt sweated from every pore in their faces. They sloshed their pints down and scuttled off almost at once.

Pat ordered another Guinness while casting an eye at the other occupants. More than two men had been involved in the donkey killing, and Pat wanted the lot. Meanwhile he was satisfied to have put the fear of God into two of them. He guessed that even as he stood there the word was being spread.

When his glass was empty Pat grasped his blackthorn stick firmly and crossed to the door. He stood outside for a moment, adjusting his eyes to the darkness, while listening with grim amusement to the hubbub of talk which had broken out in his wake. Then, when he was satisfied that the men were not waiting in ambush, Pat walked slowly back to the Quays. But not to Ammet Street. He had calls to make first.

Tim Finnegan invited him in. Tim had been a colleague in Mick Collins's Squad when they had been the scourge of Dublin Castle. Tim was an old friend and always ready to help.

After which Pat went to Brigid's place to change the arrangements for the following day. For the first time in months he would be unable to meet his son at their regular time. Instead he left word that he would expect Sean at seven in the evening – and then Pat went home to Ammet Street.

He pulled the bed away from the wall, then dropped to his knees to slide a section out from the skirting board. Plunging his arm into the gap he withdrew a heavy object, wrapped in oilskin. He took it to the table. The Smith and Wesson revolver gleamed blue in the light . . .

Saturday morning was crisp and fine. A breeze blew up the estuary to drench the Quays in the scent of the sea. Gulls wheeled and dipped across a colourless sky high above the Liffey. Sean Connors leant on the parapet by the Ha'penny Bridge, idly watching men load casks of Guinness aboard the barge which would carry them down to the big ships at the mouth of the river.

'Were you thinking of throwing yourself in, Mr Connors?' asked a soft voice.

He jumped, and swung round to meet the amused look in her eyes. It was the first time he had seen Maeve O'Flynn dressed up for town. Her smart coat and jaunty hat seemed the height of elegance to him.

Her mouth dimpled into a smile. 'Sure, aren't you a disappointment, with me forever hoping you'd be along to see me.'

Her teeth were the whitest he had ever seen. He felt overcome – how could he explain that he had started out for Palmerstown nine times in as many weeks, only to turn back on every occasion.

'Did you not want to see me again?' she asked.

He blushed. The quick amusement in her eyes heightened his confusion. 'It was not that at all, Mrs O'Flynn.'

'You've been too busy then?'

Not even that. How could he explain that he spent most of his spare time walking the Quays, just looking and thinking. He kept his eyes and ears open for clues about who killed his donkeys, but that was just the half of it. The rest was spent watching people earn a living – scratch a living in most cases, while shrewd gombeen men made deals in the warmth of a dockside pub. Goods moved in and out of the Quays all day, *assets* Sean reminded himself, assets which men wheeled and dealed into fortunes. He tried to calculate profit margins and turnovers . . . while all the time dreaming of when he would have assets of his own again. But how could he explain that to Mrs O'Flynn? Instead he mumbled an enquiry about her husband.

'Oh him,' she tossed her head. 'Haven't I just put him on the train for Cork. Isn't he away 'til Monday and there's me with enough jobs in the yard to wear out an army.'

Maeve O'Flynn's easy words masked her excitement. Secretly she was delighted. She had thought often of Sean – almost every day – and her mind had been full of him as she walked back from the station . . . racking her brains for an excuse to call on him. It would mean facing Maureen again, not to mention her mother . . . and Maeve's instincts warned her to tread warily. But her husband's absence provided an opportunity too good to miss . . . and here Sean was, worshipping her with those big blue eyes, standing there with his tongue hanging out. God, he must have grown another yard already, and weren't his shoulders broader than ever? The boy was a threat to the womanhood of Ireland. Why even a nun would quake at the sight of him. And him so unaware of the trembling he could bring to a poor girl's limbs.

She rested a hand on his arm. 'You'll be as busy as ever I suppose? A strong man like you would clear my yard in no time at all. Whereas for me . . .' she trailed the words off into a silent acceptance of her inadequacies.

But Sean saw no inadequacy and he conveyed his willingness to help in one fumbling sentence.

She squeezed his arm. 'Oh, you're an angel. Will you come up this afternoon then?' Her face fell. 'Sure, I'm forgetting – isn't it Saturdays that you see your Da?'

Sean shook his head, explaining excitedly that he was not expected at Ammet Street until seven, so *this* Saturday was perfect.

'Well isn't that grand. Could you come at two? And after

the jobs won't we have tea together, just as we used to.'

Pat Connors was less than a hundred yards from the Ha'penny Bridge when his son and Mrs O'Flynn were making their arrangements. Not that Pat knew – and even if he had his mind was so full of other things that he was unlikely to have paid attention. For Pat received a *third* name from his anonymous source and was discussing this latest news with Tim Finnegan in Mulligan's Bar. They sat in a corner and argued in whispers.

'Will you listen or won't you?' Tim demanded. 'I tell you this changes everything. You'll be a fool to go through with it now.'

Pat's plan was simple. They would waylay the two men in Palmerstown. Using a borrowed car which Tim would drive, they would arrive at the farm where the men worked as labourers and invite them for a ride. The revolver beneath Pat's jacket would make the invitation irresistible. After which . . . well, Pat had conducted interrogations in Kerry. Within an hour he would have the name of every man involved in killing the donkeys.

Tim squirmed. 'Will you let me explain? Didn't I promise to help? But this changes things. The best help I can give you now is to make you see sense.'

'You said you'd drive, that's all. Won't I do the rest.'

'Didn't I think it was just a couple of louts last night. We'd knock the shit out of them. But now Riordan's involved. *Riordan himself!* You're lucky to be alive, the way you've been shooting your mouth off at meetings. You know that –'

'Ach, I remember Riordan from the old days. All mouth –'

'Will I say it again. If Riordan's involved he'll have word from those two thunderheads by now – but there'll be no shaking in his boots with Riordan. If he thinks you are pinning anything on him he'll not wait for you –'

'And what's that supposed to mean?'

'You know damn well. He'll be on the streets by now, looking for you –'

'And I'll be ready.'

'Jaysus, Joseph and Mary! God bless Finola's soul. How

did she put up with –'

'So you're backing out?'

'I am not. Won't I do anything reasonable? Won't I stay at your side if you want me? Won't I drink and eat with you, watch your back –'

'But you'll not come looking for these two men of mine?'

'I'll not go within a mile of them with Riordan involved. Nor would any man with an ounce of sense. I'll stick by you if he comes looking for you – that's different – but I'll not go looking for trouble meself.'

'Then I'll go alone,' Pat said flatly.

'Will you talk to Mulligan first. Sure he'll tell you the same –'

'I'll talk to no one,' Pat hissed furiously, rising from the table, 'and neither will you. 'Tis a poor day, Tim, that's all I can say – a bloody poor day when a man can't look for help from his friends.'

And with that he left – ignoring Tim's pleas to stay and talk things out – ignoring even Mulligan's wave of farewell.

'You've not listened to a word I've said,' Brigid complained as Sean rose from the table. 'You've not even finished your dinner.'

'Are you feeling all right, Sean?' Maureen asked anxiously.

'Aye, grand,' Sean said, collecting his jacket from the hook on the door, 'it's just I've a bit of a job to do this afternoon.'

Brigid gave him a sharp look. 'Well you be at Ammet Street by seven. I'll not have Pat Connors say you never got his message.'

'Sure won't I be back long before that.'

'Well you make sure. I'll make sure too, because I'll be round there myself to give the place a bit of a clean.' Brigid frowned at him. 'And no fighting now. And don't you forget about that other business either.'

Sean smiled at Maureen as he went out of the door. Poor Aunt Brigid – forever reminding him to stop asking questions about the IRA. She was always worrying, without cause really, Sean thought gloomily. He was getting nowhere, and had almost given up hope of finding out who had killed his donkeys. Not that he would forget. *Forgive if you like, but never forget.* It was one of the rules.

Such were his thoughts as he walked along the Quays – but his mood changed as he started up the hill towards Palmerstown. He pictured Mrs O'Flynn as he had seen her this morning, dressed in her fine wool coat and jaunty hat. God, she was beautiful. The loveliest woman in Ireland. Even her ears were pretty. He had never considered ears before, ears were just ears. But not Mrs O'Flynn's, hers were moulded like sea shells. And her eyes shone all the time like she was enjoying some secret joke. And her smile . . . those lovely white teeth . . . and the way she cocked her head when she looked at him. Sean shook his head in bewilderment. He hoped he would say the right things. Sometimes he got tongue-tied. But she never hurried him, that was another marvellous thing about her.

He had to walk up the lane to reach the farmhouse. He dreaded that. It would be an ordeal. He paused, remembering the last time, that terrible morning when he had raced all the way from the Quays. He had heard Molly from here, that awful pitiful braying which had stabbed his heart. He took a deep breath, then walked as far as the long meadow. It was worse than he thought – it hurt more. How many times had he been up here, bursting with excitement at the prospect of a day with the animals. Now they were dead, buried over there, beneath brown earth already dotted with weeds. It would grass over next spring. Nobody would know what lay under the earth. But he would know, and would never forget.

He looked bleakly across the meadow, then sighed and turned to hurry on to the farm. The yard was tidier than he expected. Enough jobs for an army according to Mrs O'Flynn, and he was wondering what they might be when the door opened. She stood in the entrance. 'That was a terrible look on your face back there,' she said, 'I wanted to cry. I was coming to fetch you.'

She was wearing a dressing-gown, at least Sean supposed it was. The nearest he had ever been to one was standing outside Switzer's windows and wondering who would buy such a useless garment. It seemed senseless to dress twice . . . once into a dressing-gown, then into clothes.

'Well?' she opened the door wider. 'Will you be coming in, Mr Connors?'

He squeezed past into the kitchen. It was steamy inside, not smoky, but thick white steam like dense fog. Condensation ran down the walls and dripped everywhere. Through the haze he managed to make out a galvanized bath-tub propped up by the door. It was still wet, inside and out.

'You're an early bird,' she smiled, 'I'm not even dressed from my bath.'

He fought the urge to look down her cleavage. But where else to look? To stare into her face was rude, but gaps in the dressing-gown made him swallow hard.. . .

'Sit yourself down, Mr Connors. Here, let me take your jacket. What with the oven fire and everything, sure the only way at times is to wear nothing at all.'

It *was* hot. Stifling. Not just warm, but hot, steaming jungle hot. Sean had never been there on bathday before.

She set the jacket across the back of a chair. 'Will you do as you're told and sit down. Then I'll be getting some tea,' she cocked her head, 'or is it Guinness these days, Mr Connors?'

Guinness? He had tried it once and thrown up. He couldn't even stand the smell. 'Tea's fine, Mrs O'Flynn, but wouldn't I be doing the jobs first?'

'You'll do nothing until you tell me where you've been hiding yourself. How long is it since we last had some crack, just the two of us? You must have a hundred things to tell me.'

Sean couldn't think even of one. He watched her fuss with the kettle. The heat was suffocating. Even without his jacket it was unbearable. The thick heavy-knit sweater prickled his skin. His feet itched in his boots. But Mrs O'Flynn seemed to glow. She bloomed. A rose-coloured flush added lustre to her cheeks, and the white kimono tantalized with glimpses of skin which Sean felt sure would be miraculously cool to his touch. If he *dared* touch. God, he remembered when she had let him touch her before. The memory made him sweat all the faster. His body hardened. He crossed his legs in an effort to sit still, while responding to her chatter with nods and shakes of his head.

100

He groaned under his breath, telling himself she would think him a fool unless he said something. She would tire of being polite and throw him out. Swallowing hard he said – 'Will I open the window, Mrs O'Flynn?'

'And let in a draught? Wouldn't I catch my death if you did that?'

The kettle boiled and they had tea, the drinking of which made him sweat all the more. Tea seemed to leak out through every pore in his skin. He was awash with sweat. Rivulets trickled down his chest. The waistband of his trousers turned soggy. He stuck to his chair. But the steamy atmosphere and hot blast from the fire were not the only causes of his discomfort. The kimono was a peep show. Whenever Mrs O'Flynn moved Sean caught a glimpse of heaven. Gaping sleeves revealed slender arms – the neckline showed the curve of her throat and the line of bare shoulders. But enchanting though they were, such views were nothing compared to the thrust of her breasts and the enticing cleft between them – a sight so riveting that Sean forgot his manners and stared. Vivid recollections of his last visit filled his mind – Mrs O'Flynn locking the door and drawing the curtains, shedding her coat and opening her blouse – guiding his hands on to her breasts. 'There Sean,' she had whispered, 'isn't that what you wanted?' Please, *oh please*, let her do it again!

'Why Mr Connors – I do believe you've stopped listening to me.'

His eyes snapped up to meet hers. Something in her look was different. The amused twinkle had gone. Her mood had changed. But changed to what? Her face bore an expectant expression – as if she wanted him to do something.

'I was asking if you liked my new dressing-gown?'

He swallowed. 'It's grand, Mrs O'Flynn. It's the first one I've seen.'

'It's the first one I've owned.' She rose quickly in a graceful blur – to pirouette like a dancer. The skirt flared high and wide. Sean sucked his breath as he glimpsed ankle and calf and thigh.

'I bought it this morning,' she said with a teasing smile, 'after seeing you. Do you know why? Because you make me feel young again. A young girl, in love with life, everything ahead of me – oh, I can't explain, the words won't come but I know how I feel.'

She was still on her toes after the pirouette, her hands smoothing the kimono over her breasts. In response to his compliment she curtsied deeply, folding a leg under her to kneel at his feet. She reached up to twine her fingers in his, then drew his hand down to her lips. Her hair tumbled forward. She kissed his wrist and the back of his hand, his palm and each finger. Sean tingled all over. Then she placed his thumb between her lips and sucked strongly, sliding his thumb in and out of her mouth with a slow, purposeful rhythm. Sean's toes curled. His whole body jerked. Every nerve end throbbed. His other hand reached for her, but she drew away and rose to her feet.

'Weren't we talking about my kimono,' she said breathlessly. 'I want your advice. It's reversible – white one side, peach the other. Which do you like best?'

Suddenly, magically, the sash fell away and the robe opened. She caught the hem and twirled round and round. The only naked woman Sean had seen before was a bronze replica in Phoenix Park, and he had averted his eyes from that because Maureen had been with him. But Maeve O'Flynn was flesh and blood, not bronze – and Sean was alone with her, uninhibited by other people. He was too excited to be embarrassed. Overwhelmed – and astounded by the mass of dark pubic hair which climbed in riotous abundance. She came to him then, pushing his knees apart to smother his face in her breasts. He cupped her buttocks with his hands, and with a shiver of shock glimpsed the kimono as it slipped past on to the floor.

That day lived in Sean's mind for the rest of his life, but details escaped him. Undressing for instance. And moving from the kitchen to the bedroom. One second he was in the chair, nuzzling her breasts, marvelling at the swell of her nipple under his tongue – then they were on the bed. He wanted to feel her all over, wanted to touch, squeeze, explore, admire, give thanks, worship the lush ripeness of her body. But when his hand moved down into her fur she moaned. He pulled away, thinking she was in pain, but she drew his hand back and pushed his fingers deep into those tightly coiled hairs. The experience was too overwhelming to be enjoyed. He was emotionally bewildered, astonished. Shivering with excitement – and then trembling with fear. She burrowed beneath him in a frenzy of movement, raking a leg sideways to hoist him above her. Suddenly he was terrified. Panic choked him. She was writhing like a mad thing, wet with sweat . . . her hands rubbing him, exciting him . . . forever drawing him into the damp mass of fur at the top of her legs. Maureen's words exploded in his mind – 'That Mrs O'Flynn is a bad woman. Wicked, I know she is.' Sean feverish brain erupted. He pulled away and gasped for air. He was trapped between her legs. He tried to sit up. Her knees rose to cross behind his shoulders. Her legs encircled him. He was in shock. He remembered female spiders ate their mates. Oh God, she's biting me now! She'll eat me! Panic! Her hand guided his penis into her. He was being sucked in. He groaned – with pleasure and terror – 'I know you will eat me alive, Mrs O'Flynn, but don't stop now whatever you do!'

Quite unknown to Sean his father was also in Palmerstown, driven there by Eamon Donovon, Pat's cousin who had fought in the Rising.

Pat had called on Eamon after leaving Mulligan's Bar, and although apprehensive Eamon had felt obliged to help an old comrade. So they had driven to Palmerstown in search of the men Pat had identified the previous night. But the men were not to be found. Observation of the farm yielded no sign of them, neither did a tour of the lanes. Eamon left the car to make enquiries at the farm, and returned with the news that the farmer himself was looking for them – 'They never turned up for work this morning, and their cabins are empty.'

Pat swore. 'You know what's happened, Riordan has taken them under cover.'

Eamon nodded. Old IRA tactics – men on the run usually hid out in Kerry or the like, or until the threat to their safety was removed.

Pat cursed again. He had been too clever by half. Not only had he lost the men he was looking for, but now they were ready for him – *Riordan* was ready.

'What will we do?' asked Eamon.

'Drive for a bit. Keep looking. Try the pubs and ask around.'

They spent another hour combing the neighbourhood – with predictable lack of success. Pat considered what he knew about Riordan. They had been comrades in arms against the British. Then they had gone opposite ways. Riordan had led flying columns of anti-Treaty IRA all over the south. These days he was a respectable publican, but rumours lingered on. Some said he was still active in the IRA, and at least one man – Pat's informer – said Riordan was responsible for killing the donkeys. And Pat believed him.

Eamon was getting nervous. 'Wouldn't we better be telling the Garda?'

Pat made a gesture of disgust. He tried to put himself in Riordan's position. It cost money to send men into hiding. Riordan wouldn't like that – not if he were paying. So what would he do? What would Pat do? Finnegan was right. Remove the threat. Riordan would come looking for him – or send some of his men.

'Where next?' Eamon asked.

Pat had an idea. Not much of one, but options were thin on the ground. 'Riordan might know about me,' he said thoughtfully, 'but he doesn't know how much I know about *him*. Not yet anyway.'

Eamon remained silent in the parked car.

'Suppose you were Riordan and I walked into your pub? What would you do?'

Eamon gasped, 'Do you *know* Riordan's pub? Full of his cronies with dogs in their pockets.'

Dogs was old IRA slang for revolvers. Pat shook his head. 'Forget them. You are Riordan, right, and I come up to your bar counter. I lean across and whisper in your ear. I know you were killing the donkeys, says I, and I'm here for a reckoning.'

'But you haven't the proof?' said Eamon nervously.

'You don't know that. You *can't* – not for sure.'

Eamon stared.

'Well,' Pat persisted. 'What would you do?'

'Don't be a damn fool. One of his men would rip a

knife into you before – '

'Then I'll need you there to watch my back. Just like the old days – '

Eamon shook his head. 'I'll not go into Riordan's pub with you. Not by myself. It's bloody crazy. Walking in like – '

'So we'll need help. Who would lend us a hand?'

They thought about that. Eamon bitterly regretted becoming involved, but it was too late to back out. The best he could do was improve the odds. So they talked of men they knew . . . friends . . . men who might hold a grudge against Riordan. Half an hour later they had a list of eight names.

'Will you come, then?' Pat asked.

Eamon squirmed unhappily. 'I'll come . . . if the others join in.'

'Right then,' Pat smiled grimly. 'Let's away and see the first of them.'

Two miles away from where his father sat talking about possible death, Sean Connors – to his surprise – was still very much alive. He basked in sensual pleasure as Maeve O'Flynn's skilful fingers roused him again.

'Is that nice?' she asked coyly as she nibbled his ear.

'Wonderful, Mrs O'Flynn.'

'Did you really think I was after murdering you?' she giggled.

Sean blushed. He could hardly believe what was happening. He glanced to where his hand cupped her plump breast and marvelled at his own accomplishment. It seemed so natural – as if he had been doing it all his life. How stupid to have been afraid, how understandable for her to laugh. Not that he minded now, her soft laughter was as warm as her body. They had made love four times and Sean had already learned the knack of withdrawing from her just before he climaxed.

And Maeve O'Flynn was delighted. Already she was planning further meetings, scheming up ways to arrange her husband's absence more often. She was set to achieve the best of both worlds – an old man to give her security, and a young admirer who could be taught to make love in all the ways she wanted.

She propped herself up on one elbow to look down at him. Her hair tumbled forward. She brushed it back and the flowing movement of her arm lifted her breast so gracefully that the very simplicity of the act made it beautiful. Sean's eyes filled with wonder. Everything about her was beautiful. She caught his expression and smiled. 'Do I take it you are pleased with me, Mr Connors?'

He could think of no suitable reply. Words sounded inadequate. So instead he drew her mouth down to his, while his other hand moved to open her legs.

Tim Finnegan was drinking himself into a stupor in Mulligan's Bar. Pat's parting words corroded his conscience. It was a poor day, Finnegan admitted, a bloody poor day when a man turns yellow on a friend. But Jaysus, I'm fifty-one. When a man gets to my age he stays out of trouble. God Almighty, Pat must be fifty himself. Fifty! And there's him charging round like a wild bear – ready to fight the world – and all for the sake of some donkeys!

But no amount of solitary boozing could resolve Finnegan's problem. Guilt engulfed him. He had let Pat down . . . now Pat was in danger, with maybe a score of Riordan's men out looking for him. Finnegan shuddered. Eventually he could stand it no longer – he called Mulligan over and confessed the whole wretched story. Mulligan was incredulous at first, then disgusted, and finally boiling mad – 'You just let him walk out? Without raising a finger to stop him?'

'I tried! May God strike me dead if I didn't. But once Pat Connors . . .'

Mulligan was no longer listening. Instead he was looking round the bar for help. He needed good men and he needed them fast. He thought quickly . . . Eamon Donovon, Pat's cousin, would help. And Paddy Sullivan was a good man, so was Ulick, his brother. Then there was . . . Mulligan made a list, while at the same time shouting for his son. A boy of twelve ran in from the street. Hurriedly Mulligan rattled off a dozen names and their likely whereabouts. Then he pushed the boy through the door, urging him to get the men back to the bar as quickly as possible.

Finnegan was still babbling, 'I wish to God I'd gone now. That's the honest truth. If anything happens to Pat –'

'Shut your mouth,' Mulligan snapped angrily. Not every man in the bar could be vouched for. Mulligan knew the doubtful ones, and enough were present to add to his worries.

Time passed slowly after that. Behind the bar the hand of the clock seemed to stop. At five-thirty the boy was back, most of his messages delivered. *Most*, but not all – 'Mr Donovon was out, Da. He went out in his car with Mr Connors.'

Brigid, of course, had no suspicion of any of this. As far as she knew Pat Connors was about his business as usual, and young Sean was out earning a few coppers. And Brigid herself had been busy that day – cleaning her house from top to bottom, worrying about Maureen being late back from Confession, and giving Tomas his tea when he arrived home from his vegetable patch. She wished she had cleaned Pat's room on Thursday, her usual day for doing it, but she had been sniffing with a cold all week and not felt up to it. Even now she felt far from well – but a promise was a promise and at least Maureen would come round to Ammet Street to give her a hand.

The door banged and Brigid sighed with relief. Ever since the trouble with the Protestant boys she had felt uneasy about Maureen walking home along the canal. Most weeks Brigid met her, but her cold had put her so far behind this week that nothing had been dealt with in its usual fashion.

'Have you seen Uncle Pat?' Maureen asked as she entered the kitchen. She had been stopped twice on her way home by men looking for Pat Connors. 'Friends of his,' she added hurriedly, seeing Brigid's look of alarm. 'Mr Sullivan was one of them. His brother was with him, you know, Ulick that works in the market.'

'What did he want with Pat?' asked Tomas.

'Just had I seen him,' Maureen shrugged. 'Then wasn't I asked again on the corner by another man.'

Tomas went back to his paper. The sort of life Pat led

people were forever asking after him, wanting favours most of them.

Brigid blew her nose noisily. 'Well, drink your tea then,' she said to Maureen. 'You can tell Pat Connors half the world is out looking for him when you see him at Ammet Street.'

'Is Sean about?' Maureen asked hopefully.

'Sean is not. And didn't he promise to be home by now, with his Da expecting him at seven.'

'He'll maybe go straight there,' Maureen said in Sean's defence. 'Didn't he say he'd see us –'

'In a room covered with dust unless we get a move on,' Brigid said sharply, glancing at the clock. 'Come on, finish your tea, and we'll get round to Ammet Street.'

They were holding a council of war in Mulligan's Bar. Four more of Pat's friends had assembled in answer to Mulligan's summons. Tim Finnegan's story was carefully digested.

'Pat should have told us himself,' Billy Timms said, voicing the general opinion.

Mulligan pulled a face. 'Sure you know what a mulehead he is. Isn't it typical he'd go by himself.'

'But he's not. Eamon is with him – and Finnegan would be if he had any guts.'

'Riordan,' one of the men whispered fearfully. 'Wouldn't you know that bastard would be behind it.'

Billy Timms cut him short. 'So what's happened so far?' he asked Mulligan.

'I sent the Sullivan brothers out looking for him. Then Garret arrived and he went too.'

Timms drummed his fingers on the counter. That was a waste of time, he thought, splitting up the forces in a futile search. Pat and Eamon could be anywhere. Still up at Palmerstown most likely. Timms cursed, thinking Eamon should have known better.

Mulligan read his mind. 'Wouldn't you think Eamon will talk some sense into him. Sure the pair of them could walk in that door any minute.'

But the door from the street remained ominously closed.

Finnegan whispered, 'It's the boy I'm worried about.'

They swung round to stare. Finnegan twitched. He prodded a matchbox along the bar with a nicotine-stained finger. 'It's young Sean I'm thinking of now. Riordan's a vicious devil.'

Others might have dismissed it as the rambling of a man in drink – but Mulligan's eyes narrowed. He pursed his lips in a soft whistle. 'If Riordan got hold of the boy, that would stop Pat dead in his tracks. Finnegan could be right. Riordan might go for the boy. Hasn't he hit Pat through the boy's donkeys already?'

Billy Timms stared. He was shorter than Mulligan and a few years younger – a strong, tough man who worked in the docks. Hard grey eyes looked out from a weather-beaten face. But even his expression showed a flicker of fear. 'Has anyone seen young Sean? What does the boy do with himself these days?'

But nobody knew.

Sean was desperately late. He would have to run all the way to reach Ammet Street by seven. He stood just inside the kitchen door while Maeve O'Flynn kissed him goodbye.

'Here,' she whispered. 'There are nicer ways to say goodbye than this.' She guided his hand under her kimono.

'I must go,' Sean protested. 'Honest, Mrs O'Flynn, I must.'

But she was merely teasing and made no complaint when he pulled away. They had agreed people would worry if Sean failed to keep his appointment. Things would be arranged differently in future. Maeve promised herself that.

'Until tomorrow then,' she whispered.

Sean turned for a last look at her. How could he express himself? It would sound so inadequate to say 'Thanks for a lovely afternoon' to the woman who had changed his whole life.

She smiled and pushed him to the door, 'Go on, away and see your Da . . . and don't be late back here in the morning.'

So he said nothing and left, walking hurriedly down the lane and on to the road. He broke into a trot. He skipped, light-headed with joy. His mind burst with exquisite pictures. Mrs O'Flynn on the bed – under him – on top of him. So many different sensations, so much discovered . . . the most shattering experience of his life, the most exhilarating, the most pleasurable, the most . . .

But he ached. God, he ached! After a mile he ceased to run and contented himself with a brisk walk. Time and again he pictured Mrs O'Flynn. He remembered scene after scene. Then – suddenly, he was struck by a thought. A terrible thought! 'People will know!' He stopped dead in his tracks. 'The Da will find out. Aunt Brigid will know. They will see it on my face. They will know – I must look different. It stands to reason. They will know . . .'

The thought took hold. It was wicked, what he had done. Maureen was right – Mrs O'Flynn *was* a wicked woman. 'Now I'm wicked too,' he moaned. What if the Da finds out? Suppose anyone finds out? 'Mary Mother of God,' he muttered. 'Won't they skin me alive.' Even that mattered less than their shame. He imagined them turning their backs, not meeting his eye, talking among themselves. Aunt Brigid avoiding Father Murphy on the street. Poor Tomas, even more bent than ever. And Maureen! His blood froze. 'Dear God, Maureen will kill herself!'

Suddenly he dreaded going to Ammet Street. His father read him like a book. His father would say, 'Well, son, and what have you been doing?'

'Fucking Mrs O'Flynn, Da – and it was grand!' Sean groaned in horror. 'What have I done – oh Jaysus!'

He walked on, dawdling now, dragging his feet, weighed down by guilt. Even his smell was different. He pushed up a sleeve to sniff his arm. Her musky scent filled his nostrils. 'Like she sprayed me all over. Jaysus, I *smell* different, I look different . . . they will know for sure.'

He stopped at the side of the road. What a terrible secret. But how to keep it a secret? He had never lied to the Da before. Nor to Aunt Brigid or Maureen, or anyone. Not real lies. It was one of the rules. His spirit plunged. Then, like a pinpoint of light at the end of a tunnel, he glimpsed a ray of hope. 'Sometimes to tell the exact truth is damaging,' his father had counselled. 'Answer a question with a question . . .'

Sean's heart pounded. To use the rules against the Da

was the hardest test he could imagine. But he had no choice. 'Oh God,' he prayed, 'let nobody find out. Let nobody find out and . . . and I'll never do that again. Never, never, never. I promise, God, honest I do.'

Even a bargain like that – the sacrificing of so much future pleasure, failed to alleviate Sean's foreboding. His despair deepened at every step. Something awful was about to happen – he just *knew*, something terrible, even worse than losing the donkeys. He walked down the Quays like a pilgrim in the valley of death. The great bulk of Guinness's brewery loomed up on his right. The misty waters of the Liffey swirled dark and sinister on his left. A feeling of doom enveloped him. His earlier euphoria was completely forgotten. He was aware only of a premonition. And it was with that feeling of utter helplessness that Sean shuffled towards Ammet Street.

Mulligan experienced a great wave of relief. Pat Connors had just walked through the door, followed by Eamon Donovon.

'Thank Christ, you are here,' Mulligan shouted, rushing out from his counter.

Pat was astonished. He and Eamon had searched the town, when his friends were all here, assembled and waiting. They knew what had happened, one look told Pat that. Finnegan had talked, that much was clear.

They crowded round. Mulligan returned to his side of the bar and drew a couple of pints. Then the details of the afternoon were told – the futile excursion to Palmerstown, and the growing realization that Riordan was ready and waiting.

'He'll not play cat and mouse with me though,' Pat said, lowering his voice as he told them of his plan to confront Riordan in his own pub.

There was a moment's silence, then Billy Timms said, 'You'll not go there alone.'

'Well then,' Mulligan challenged, 'do I hear you lot hollering to volunteer?'

Embarrassed grins appeared and heads nodded in assent – but Mulligan was not ready to celebrate. He was worried about Sean. Ever since Finnegan had come up with the idea

Mulligan had fretted about it. In a low voice he explained the theory to Pat. Pat went white. Every drop of colour drained from his face. He knew it was possible, *he knew it!* He swore viciously. He had played this all wrong. Old age was making him soft. He had forgotten his cunning. By Christ, if anything happened to young Sean . . .

'Well?' Mulligan asked. 'Where is he, Pat?'

Pat glanced at the clock. Sean was probably at Brigid's place, or on his way to Ammet Street by now. 'Come on,' he said quickly, 'we'll get Sean off the streets before we do anything else.'

Brigid arrived at Ammet Street at twenty to seven, later than she had intended, having been delayed first by Maureen, then by a neighbour wanting to borrow some sugar. 'Always the way,' Brigid sniffed to herself. 'Start late and a hundred things crop up to make you even later.'

Now she was out of breath from walking too fast and irritated by Maureen's chatter. 'Will you save your breath for cleaning that room,' she scolded.

They climbed the stairs, Brigid wheezing with her chesty cold. She hoped Pat was not home yet. She worked quicker with him out of the way. Tomas was the same, forever getting under her feet and complaining he couldn't find things after she had tidied up after him.

'Here, I'll open the door,' said Maureen, holding out her hand.

Brigid fumbled for the key in her bag. She handed it to her daughter and then clutched the balustrade, overcome by momentary giddiness. 'It's just this wretched cold,' she grumbled, 'I'll feel better in the morning.'

Maureen was outside Pat's door. 'That's funny, the key won't turn.'

'Here, let me,' said Brigid, advancing along the landing.

'No, it's turning. It's just stiff, that's all . . .'

Maureen's words died on her lips. The door splintered to matchwood. A flash of light scorched the whole landing. Walls erupted. Masonry tore into fragments. Debris hit the stairs in a great swirling mass, ripping the banisters away with hurricane force. Timbers fell spinning to the lobby below. The uppermost stairs collapsed, leaving a gap to the half landing. People below screamed as ceilings caved in. Outside the street was drenched with splinters of flying glass. The roar and force of the explosion rocked the Quays.

Pat Connors dropped his blackthorn stick and ran the last twenty yards to the corner. A column of oily smoke rose above Ammet Street. Fear rooted him to the spot. He cried, 'Sean! Dear God – Sean!'

Doors opened, people spilled out. Pat heard shouts, screams. He glimpsed shocked faces. Then he was running – 'Sean! Sean! Where are you, Sean?'

A girl had fallen, hit by a shard of flying glass. She crouched, hands at her head, blood oozing between her fingers. Pat skirted her and ran on – 'Sean! Sean!'

A boy got in the way. Pat brushed past and raced into the building – 'Sean!'

He stumbled towards the stairs, blinded by dust and smoke, to clamber over mounds of pulverized plaster. He side-stepped a fall of masonry which plunged down like an avalanche. The handrail had gone – banisters had been torn away. Stairs jutted out like the ledge of a cliff face, ending in mid-air. Pat almost fell over the edge. He scrambled back, cursing with fear. 'Sean!' he roared, peering up into the swirling dust.

'Da! I'm here!'

Pat whirled and lost his footing. He slid and half-fell to the foot of the stairs. His son rushed over, panting and coughing. They fell into each other's arms, sobbing with relief.

Sean had been at the bottom end of Ammet Street when the explosion occurred. He had raced all the way – fearing to find his father's mangled body in the wreckage. For a split second he relaxed, safe in his father's embrace. Then his premonition jolted him rigid. He pulled away and stared into his father's face. 'Maureen and Aunt Brigid! Da, they were coming round to clean your room.'

The dread feeling hit Pat like a hammer. He peered through the dust up to the half landing. The edge of the first floor was dimly visible. It was knee deep in debris.

'Da, would you think – oh no – *NO!*' Sean ran past and began the ascent of the stairs, stumbling to keep his balance.

113

Pat pulled him back. 'Get out, boy. Get out. Leave this to me.'

'But Da, they're up there – I just know – I *know*!'

Sean's premonition. This was his punishment. God's punishment. God's wrath for what had happened that afternoon. Yet it was unfair. Brigid and Maureen hadn't done anything. Brigid and Maureen were the kindest, most wonderful people in the world . . .

'Pat!' shouted a man from the entrance. He emerged into the dim light, shielding his eyes and coughing from the dust. It was Billy Timms. He clambered up to the half landing and he gasped when he saw Sean, 'I went to Brigid's place looking for you. But where's Brigid herself? Tomas said she had come round here –'

The sob torn from Sean sounded inhuman. He rushed at the fallen masonry, heaving great blocks against the wall to build stepping stones to the floor above. Pat and Billy Timms threw themselves into action. Tears smudged Sean's dust-grimed face as he worked. Jagged rubble cut his hands. Panic gave him strength. He moved as much debris as his father. He stood back and shouted Maureen's name. His anxious eyes searched the debris on the upper floor. Below, other people gathered at the foot of the stairs, shouting advice, shifting rubble, and trying to fashion a ladder from the broken balustrade.

Fifteen minutes later Billy Timms hoisted himself painfully up to the floor above. The first thing he saw was a human hand thrust out from the fallen timbers. It was Brigid. Timms knew she was dead as soon as he touched her.

Pat scrambled up the makeshift ladder, with Sean behind him. Pat found Maureen. He pushed Sean away, not wanting the boy to see the mutilated face. 'Billy,' he shouted, despair in his voice, 'get Sean back down below.' When Sean protested Billy Timms thumped him on the point of his chin. The boy's knees buckled, his eyes glazed and he dropped like a felled tree.

Pat was crying. Tears wet his face for the first time since Finola died. He stumbled on, through a gap into his room. He hardly recognized it – the far wall was totally devoid of plaster – bare bricks, broken and cracked, gave it an unfamiliar look – but the skirting board was intact. Pat dropped to his knees and scrambled through the wreckage, digging furiously until his hands closed on the precious notebooks. A tremor shook his body. Much else that was precious had been destroyed that day – but the Connors Rules were intact.

CHAPTER SEVEN

That Saturday marked the end of Sean's boyhood. His ripening maturity accelerated fast after that, especially when his father took him to Coney Island.

Not that Pat left Dublin without resolving his outstanding score with Liam Riordan. Riordan had more to answer for than ever before. The deaths of Brigid and Maureen shattered everyone.

Tomas was a broken man. Brigid had been his life. Without her and Maureen, Tomas withered like a plant pulled from its roots. The rest of the family, weighed down by grief, gathered about him in a shield of loving kindness – Sean too, whom Tomas regarded as an adopted son much of the time, stayed close to the man's side. But Tomas was inconsolable. He withdrew from a world which in any case had never captured his interest. He had created his own world and filled it with Brigid and the children, the church and his vegetable patch. But now Brigid was gone and Tomas wallowed in a well of despair. Even Father Murphy, the aged priest who had known and loved the family for most of their days, even Father Murphy was unable to provide comfort.

The funeral itself, with the coffins closed to hide the mutilated bodies, was a raw, agonizing ordeal so heart-rending that few got through it without breaking down. At the graveside Tomas had to be physically restrained from throwing himself into the open pit. People on all sides keened and wept with unrestrained passion. Heaven was the richer, but the world was the poorer for the passing of

115

Brigid and Maureen – and when their goodness was praised by Father Murphy the poor man choked up and had to be led sobbing from the congregation.

Pat Connors mourned with the rest of them – more so, tormented by the knowledge that Brigid and Maureen had lost their lives because of him. He could not look at Tomas without being swamped by guilt. Yet one man shared that guilt – Liam Riordan. 'I'll kill that bastard before I die,' Pat swore in the room above Mulligan's bar, to which he had moved with the few possessions recovered from Ammet Street.

But there was a matter of equal importance – one which had given meaning and purpose to Pat's existence for almost fourteen years. Sean and the rules! To pass on the accumulated experience of a lifetime. The need to do that kept Pat from Belfast, which is where Riordan was suspected of hiding . . .

Pat locked himself away after the funeral and brooded. He barely slept for making his plans. Then, two days later, he was ready. He went downstairs to the bar for a drink.

'Still no sign of Riordan,' Mulligan reported softly. 'Word is he is hiding out in Belfast.'

Pat scowled. 'He will stay there right enough. At least till the hue and cry dies down. Then he'll come crawling back here. Unless . . .'

Unless what, Mulligan wondered? Pat Connors was not the man to let things rest, but the Garda were helpless as usual, defeated by lack of witnesses and faced by a wall of silence.

But half an hour later Mulligan knew that Riordan would not dare to even come home . . . and Pat Connors was sending him a message to prove it.

Sean forgot Mrs O'Flynn, at least until Wednesday. Then he was sent on an errand down the Quays, and a woman looked at him with such frank appraisal that Mrs O'Flynn burst into his mind. He blushed, while the woman smiled knowingly as if amused by secret thoughts. She knows, he thought in panic, she knows about Mrs O'Flynn and me – what we did – she can see it in my face! He hurried away in an immediate sweat. Maybe women saw things hidden to men? Aunt Brigid would have seen it – and Maureen – they would have seen it and been ashamed. Guilt sharpened his grief. Tears pricked his eyelids. He drew a deep breath, to control his emotion – to cry here, on the Quays, to be *seen* weeping, would be intolerable. But his heart ached for Aunt Brigid. Poor, dear Aunt Brigid. And Maureen – sweet, gentle Maureen whom he would have sent to the sun had she lived . . .

He wandered the Quays for an hour, reluctant to return to the doom-laden atmosphere at Brigid's place. It was his first escape since Sunday, and a relief to get away from the sound of sobbing and the sight of red-rimmed eyes. So he walked – across O'Connell Bridge, past the rebuilt Post Office, then along Abbey Street and beyond the theatre. People on the streets laughed and shouted as if nothing had happened. Yet Sean's whole world had turned upside down.

Eventually he retraced his steps to the Quays, walking over the familiar cobblestones, to become absorbed in watching the usual hustle and bustle. The sight took him out of himself. Soon he was caught up in his game of watching people earn their daily bread. No matter what else happened, the gombeen men went on wheeling and dealing. He sighed, and suddenly itched to be among them, pitting his wits against theirs in the never-ending game of building a fortune. Just seeing them made him feel better. He sucked in a great lungful of air to rid himself of his depression, and partly succeeded, but it would close in again, he knew that, it would close in again when he returned to Brigid's place.

So why return? The question so stunned him that he stopped in his tracks. But why – the question ought to be asked – why return at all? So much had changed, his whole life . . . He would have to leave one day, so why not today? The idea took his breath away. His mind blurred with the consequences – suppose he *did* leave – where would he go?

He would live with his father. Why not? They would find somewhere together. How much better than just seeing each other on a Saturday. His spirits rose at the prospect of living in an adult world, full of his father's friends, politicians, newspapermen, all arguing their heads off as they put the country to rights. But would his father agree? Suppose his father *preferred* to live alone. Sean went cold. His mind clouded with doubt. He argued back and forth. He could not stay with Tomas forever. But what was expected of him?

The idea buzzed round in his head until he could think of nothing else. He decided against returning to Brigid's. Instead he changed direction and made for Mulligan's Bar, rehearsing his arguments as he walked, screwing up his courage to face his father.

Pat Connors was finalizing plans of his own. He sat in the room above Mulligan's Bar and discussed details with the Sullivan brothers and Eamon Donovon.

'Right then,' he said. 'That wraps it up. Don't forget, leave the woman to me.'

'What about Riordan's son? If he tries to interfere –'

'A son?' Pat said in surprise. 'I never knew Riordan had a son?'

Eamon nodded. 'About the same age as Sean. Maybe a year or so older.'

Pat's mouth tightened. 'Riordan's son gets treated the same as Riordan's wife. I'll deal with the pair of them.'

'What about the Garda?' Eamon asked.

'Fixed,' was Pat's only comment. He had spent the morning with the Garda. Most of the senior police officers were old friends. Many had fought the British with Pat. Several owed him their lives. Today they would repay past favours.

Paddy Sullivan rubbed his hand across his chin. The light was dim in the room, but alcohol had bronzed and polished Paddy's face until it shone like a copper kettle. 'You want us at Riordan's pub at three-thirty, right?'

Pat nodded. He checked the safety catch on his revolver, then slipped the weapon into a holster beneath his jacket.

Eamon was about to say something when the door opened. Mulligan poked his head into the room. 'Your boy is downstairs, Pat. Shall I send him up?'

Ulick Sullivan swore and pointed to the crate of explosives in the middle of the room. 'We'll want to hide that first.'

But Pat shook his head. It was time Sean learnt what went on in the world – no point in teaching him the rules then denying him chance to see them used. 'Sean's coming with us,' he announced bluntly, 'so he may as well come up now.'

They all protested, Mulligan included – but Pat was adamant. So after arguing for ten minutes, Mulligan led Eamon and the Sullivan boys back down to the bar. 'Right, Sean,' Mulligan jerked his head, 'you can go up now.'

Sean took a deep breath. He rehearsed his arguments one last time, then climbed the stairs, little suspecting that his own idea was about to be swamped by a far more momentous one.

By half past three Billy Timms and Tim Finnegan had been in Riordan's pub for an hour. Not that they were drinking heavily – two pints each, barely enough to quench Finnegan's thirst – but it was hardly a social occasion. They were there to count the house, in particular identify potential heroes – those who might rush to Mrs Riordan's aid when the trouble started. Hopefully nobody would know about the trouble until afterwards – and afterwards would be too late.

It was a large bar, and crowded. Riordan was not the biggest gombeen man in town, but far from the smallest. He owned a butcher's and a draper's as well. 'If only he had stayed out of politics,' Finnegan mused, 'he'd have a lot to be thankful for.'

Billy Timms grunted. Every publican in Dublin was in politics, one way or another – even Mulligan, though Mulligan was all right. Timms watched four men in the corner, all of whom bore the mark of Riordan's bully boys. As for the rest of the crowd . . . his gaze wandered, pausing here and there to examine the bulges in men's jackets, wondering if they hid a revolver. Timms slid his hand into his own pocket and caressed the cold steel of his gun.

Finnegan muttered, 'Three-thirty. Where in God's name is Sullivan?'

Exactly at that moment the street door opened and Ulick Sullivan entered carrying a can of paint and some brushes. He wedged the door back as Paddy arrived with a step

119

ladder. Both men were dressed in overalls and were quite obviously ready for work. Paddy bumped and barged his way across the crowded bar, knocking at least three people with the ladder. 'Watch what you're doing,' a man shouted angrily. Paddy swung round to answer and delivered a nasty blow to another set of shins.

Billy Timms hid a smile. Like old times, he thought, remembering the decorating business in Abbey Street. Mick Collins himself couldn't have done better.

The barman rushed round to investigate – 'What the hell are you doing?'

'And what does it look like?' Paddy answered, bumping into a table. 'Aren't we here to paint the place on Mr Riordan's orders.'

'Sure nobody told me,' snapped he barman. He would have protested further but Ulick asked him to hold a can of paint. Danny Hoey came through the door, staggering under the weight of a full set of ladders. Wind and rain blew in from the street – a newspaper swirled in at knee height. 'Shut that bloody door,' someone shouted. Danny snapped back – 'Will you wait till I get inside. Besides, there's a lot more to come yet.'

Billy Timms' nod of approval was almost imperceptible. Even so he continued to watch the men in the corner – especially when one of them placed a hand on Paddy's shoulder. Paddy won't like that, Billy thought, just as Finnegan nudged his knee. Billy looked across to the door. Pat Connors stood in the opening with Sean a pace behind him. Billy cursed. Sean's involvement was something new. He studied the boy and breathed a small sigh of relief. Sean's face lacked colour, but apart from that he looked steady enough.

'Take your hands off me!' roared Paddy Sullivan. There was a scuffle at the bar. Everyone turned to watch. If they hadn't, Ulick would have dropped a can of paint – or Finnegan would have started an argument – or Paddy would have created another diversion. And while people were distracted Billy Timms watched Pat Connors and his son walk across to the private rooms at the back of the bar. Billy watched, but nobody else did – they were too busy arguing with Paddy Sullivan and the rest of the 'painters'.

Pat's revolver was in his hand as he went through the door. The small room was empty. An open door opposite revealed the foot of a staircase in the passage. 'Lock the door,' Pat said over his shoulder. Sean bolted the door to the bar, just as a woman came down the stairs and into the room. Pat reached her before she could cry out, his gun arm encircling her neck and his left hand clamping over her mouth – 'Listen, Mrs Riordan, and listen carefully.'

The petrified woman went rigid with fright. There was very little struggle. She was middle-aged with pepper-and-salt hair, and dressed in a grubby smock.

'Do as I say and you'll not get hurt,' Pat hissed in her ear. She rolled her eyes and nodded her head.

'Get rid of those people in the bar,' Pat said. 'You are closing for alterations. Do exactly as I say and you'll not be hurt, but *exactly* – understand?'

She shuddered as the muzzle of the gun pressed into her neck. Pat repeated his instructions – then he released her. She fell forward, grabbing a chair for support, gasping and retching as if about to be sick.

Suddenly footsteps sounded on the stairs, then in the passage. A boy hurried in. His eyes widened as he saw them. Pat moved with astonishing speed, looping an arm round the boy's throat and jabbing the revolver into his face. The woman's hands flew to her mouth to stifle her words – 'Oh God . . . no –'

'Shut up,' Pat snarled, tightening his grip on the boy.

The woman whimpered. She seemed about to fall on her knees to beg for mercy. Sean's instinct was horror. He stepped forward, wanting to reassure her, wanting to help – until he remembered Aunt Brigid and Maureen, and what his father had said in the room above Mulligan's Bar. He remembered what he must do and steeled himself to do it. He risked a sideways glance at the boy. He knew him – not well, but he had seen him around. Older than me, Sean thought, but I'm as big as him. The boy squirmed in Pat's grip, twisting until the revolver prodded his eye. The woman continued to plead – 'Please – not him – *please* –'

'Call the barman,' Pat interrupted. 'Tell him to close up.

The painters outside are ready to start work. Say you forgot to tell him before – right?'

She was too frightened to understand. Her eyes fixed on her son, 'Please –'

'God Almighty! Do as you're told!'

She shuddered as if Pat had slapped her. Pat snarled, 'I'll break his bloody neck unless you do as you're told!'

The woman cast another beseeching look at her son, before turning and walking like a sleepwalker across the room. Sean stood beside her, unbolting the door, he opened it a crack. The noisy argument was continuing in the bar. The woman placed a hand on the wall to support herself, drew a deep breath and called to the barman. Her voice was weak. She called again, drawing on her strength. Eventually the man came to the door. She issued her instructions. He protested. She insisted, panic adding stridency to her voice. Grumbling the barman went away. Sean sighed with relief. As he closed and bolted the door, the woman fell against the wall, sobbing with released tension. Sean turned away, and unlooped the rope from around his waist.

'We are tying you up,' Pat told the boy. 'A precaution, that's all. Behave and you'll be all right.'

Pat released him and the boy collapsed into a chair – bent double by a paroxysm of coughing and gasping for breath. Sean moved swiftly to bind the boy's feet – then moved behind the chair to tie his wrists. The boy twisted round, his eyes blazing. Sean quelled the tiniest flicker of fear. He worked on the knots and had just finished when a muffled knock announced that Billy Timms was asking to be let in from the bar.

Timms took the scene in at a glance. 'Okay in front,' he said, 'everyone is clearing out. Tim is locking up. Paddy is dealing with the barman.'

Pat nodded, then turned to his son – 'Open the back door.'

Sean went into the passage and found the back door. A Garda stood on the step, a very senior Garda judging by the badges of rank on his cap and epaulettes. He nodded at Sean, and led the way briskly back to the room.

Mrs Riordan was sitting on the arm of the chair next to

her son. She gaped at the uniform. Hope flared in her eyes. But it died a second later.

'Mrs Riordan,' the Garda said without ceremony. 'I have a warrant for your husband's arrest in connection with the murders of Brigid and Maureen O'Hara –'

'No,' she gasped and shook her head. 'No . . . not Liam –'

'If you know of his whereabouts it is your duty to inform me,' he continued. 'I must also warn you that warrants may be issued to arrest you and your son for conspiracy –'

'My God! What are you saying –'

'I expect to have such warrants by six this evening, in which case I shall arrest you both,' he paused. 'If I can find you, of course.'

Bewilderment was written all over her face. 'What does he mean?' she was asking herself. The whole world had gone mad. She cast an imploring look at Pat, searching for an explanation. But Pat's expression remained blank – and the policeman was already marching out to the passage and through the back door.

Ulick arrived from the bar, weighed down by two heavy cans, one in each hand. He went out to the passage, then clumped up the stairs, leaving a strong smell of petrol in his wake.

'Mrs Riordan,' Pat said evenly, 'you've ten minutes to pack to escape arrest. You and your son are catching the five o'clock train to Belfast.'

'Belfast?' The boy found his tongue. 'What about this place? Who will look after things? The Da will go mad if –'

'Tell him in Belfast,' Pat said with indifference. He turned to the woman, 'Time is passing. You have *less* than ten minutes now.'

She stared around the room, a dazed look on her face. Shock befuddled her mind. She couldn't think, couldn't *believe* what was happening. Blank unseeing eyes sought familiar objects, trying to focus on reality. But reality had been supplanted by nightmare. Arrest? The five o'clock train to Belfast? This was her home. What would she take, what would she leave, what could be sent for later? A moan of despair escaped her lips. Her total helplessness was

123

pitiful. Sean turned away, unable to watch.

'Nine minutes left,' Pat said so coldly that his son shivered.

'I'll help you pack upstairs,' Billy Timms said not unkindly.

'Pack?' she echoed blankly, as he took her arm and led her from the room.

Paddy Sullivan came in from the bar. He nodded to Pat. 'Everything is fixed in the cellar. Time is short though.'

Pat slid his revolver into its holster. 'What about the street outside?'

'Being dealt with,' was all Paddy said as he went back to the bar.

Ulick returned from upstairs, sprinkling petrol from a can. 'Upstairs is drenched in the stuff,' he told Pat on his way through to the bar.

Suddenly the boy screamed. 'You're going to burn us alive! You're going to *murder us* –'

Pat knocked him almost out of the chair. 'I warned you. Start shouting and I'll gag you.'

The boy burst into tears – and was still sniffing when his mother returned. She dropped her suitcase and rushed to his side. Panic gave her courage. She screamed at Pat – 'You're burning us out. Damn you for your cruelty. Damn you! Damn you . . .' She collapsed in a flood of tears, her arms around her son.

'Time is running out,' was Pat's only response.

Sean looked at his father in horror. He would never have believed this cold remorseless anger. Billy Timms struggled into the room with a canvas bag stuffed with clothes. Mrs Riordan sobbed and shrieked, 'Mary, Mother of God! Will you stop! I can't think! I need more time.'

The boy interrupted, 'Get the money. The Da will want the money.'

She swayed to her feet, sobbing, peering furtively through her fingers, as if afraid of Pat hearing.

But Pat had heard. 'We are not thieves,' he said with icy contempt. 'There's not a man here who would touch a penny.'

She whirled round to the sideboard and wrenched open a door. Papers, letters and old newspapers tumbled out.

She stumbled under the weight of a heavy box.

'Here,' Billy Timms bent to open the suitcase. 'Put that in here.'

'Is that it then?' Pat demanded.

The woman's last reserves of pride and self-respect crumbled. She flung herself at Pat's feet and grovelled – tugging his trousers as a supplicant might the robes of a bishop. She begged for more time. She offered him the cashbox. She wailed and wept, but Pat ignored her. 'Loosen that hobble, Sean,' he said, pointing to the boy.

Sean obeyed and a minute later the whole party was making for the back door.

Two motor cars reversed up the alley. Mrs Riordan was bundled into one, flanked by Billy Timms and Pat Connors. Sean climbed into the front, next to the driver, and watched the Sullivans guide Liam Riordan's son into the second car. Then they were away, passing a Garda at the bottom of the alley, who touched his cap when he saw Pat.

They circled the block and came out fifty yards from the pub. The normally busy street was almost deserted. Men dressed in overalls had roped off a section round the pub. Ladders stood against the wall as if work was about to commence – but nobody was working. Instead the men stood beyond the ropes, looking expectantly towards the pub. Suddenly a muffled explosion shook the whole building. Window panes shattered and burst on to the street. A great sheet of flame belched up from the bar. Tongues of fire and sooty black smoke licked out through one of the broken windows.

Mrs Riordan sobbed uncontrollably, 'Twenty-one years. We lived there twenty-one years. Worked, saved . . . God, what is to become of us now?'

'Twenty-one years,' repeated Pat. 'That's a long time. Longer than the life of my niece. She was only sixteen – *sixteen* – when your husband murdered her.'

'No! Not a girl – Liam wouldn't –'

'He's a murdering bastard. A killer of women and girls . . . and *donkeys*!'

Fire swept through the pub with the speed of light. Smoke swirled upwards, caught by the wind. Inside the building orange-tipped flames spat and crackled in every room. Outside the very air shimmered in the heat haze.

They drove round the corner and arrived just in time to see the front of Riordan's butcher's shop erupt into shards of splintered glass. Then a whump of flame preceded a cloud of dense black smoke. A moment later that building too was engulfed in fire.

The draper's shop was already ablaze when they reached it. Garda were barring entry to the street. The two cars halted on the corner to give the occupants a good view of the destruction – then they moved off, as sedate as a funeral procession.

Mrs Riordan wept all the.way to the station. Her misery tugged at Sean's conscience. He felt confused, sickened by events. Nothing said above Mulligan's Bar had fully prepared him. He was horrified. Yet unable to stifle other emotions – respect, and a tingling thrill that his father had delivered such a terrible punishment. Rough justice, harsh, brutal – yet justice of a kind. But the punishment was not over.

'Give your husband a message from me,' Pat Connors shouted above the woman's sobs. 'He's finished in Dublin. I've wiped out his businesses – and if he ever sets foot here the Garda will arrest him for murder.'

Tears fell even faster. The sobs grew louder. A sound cracked like a whiplash. Sean shut his eyes and bit his lip. Another crack, as Pat slapped her again. 'Look at me, damn you,' he roared. 'You're looking at a widow-maker. Tell him that. And tell him to watch his back – because some day soon I'm coming to Belfast to kill him!'

The car stopped in the station forecourt. Sean kept his eyes front, afraid to look over his shoulder. The woman whimpered until a back door opened and Pat heaved himself out on to the pavement. The other car drew up alongside, and the Riordan boy emerged from the back seat. The rope had been removed from his wrists. He was made to carry the canvas bag and the suitcase as the procession set off down the platform. Seats had been reserved on the train. Pat Connors handed tickets to Mrs Riordan, and repeated his warnings to her, perhaps for the boy's benefit.

It was a minute before five o'clock.

'Goodbye, Mrs Riordan,' Pat said, as he handed her up into the carriage. 'You should pray that you never see me again.'

The boy clambered up after her. He heaved the cases on to the luggage rack, after which he turned to lower the window. He was trembling and white-faced, but his eyes blazed at Sean. 'I'll kill you for this one day,' he hissed. 'Bloody well kill you. You remember my name, Matt Riordan. It will take you to your grave.' Then he spat through the lowered window into Sean's face.

Sean had no time to retaliate. The window slammed shut. A guard blew a whistle, the engine shuffled its wheels – and the train was moving. The boy curled his lip as he stared down into Sean's eyes – and the next minute he had gone.

Sean could *feel* the hatred as much as he felt the saliva running down his cheek.

'Here,' his father held out a handkerchief. Sean wiped the spittle away, and turned to follow them back to the car. They drove off slowly. Sean sat in a daze, the terrible events vivid in his mind. So much had happened, so quickly . . . Mrs Riordan's misery, the boy's hatred, the violent destruction . . . Suddenly he recalled Billy Timms coming into the room at the pub and saying – 'Paddy is dealing with the barman.'

'What happened to the barman, Da?'

His father was in front next to the driver. 'Tell him, Billy,' he said.

Billy Timms would rather not, that was clear from his face . . . but Pat's tone brooked no argument. 'We chained him down in the cellar. Paddy set the explosives around him.'

Sean clenched his fists and drew a deep breath. He pictured the man struggling to free himself . . . minutes ticking away . . . seconds . . .

'He was the one who set the explosives in Ammet Street,' his father said. 'We found out that much.'

An icy chill slid up Sean's spine. He closed his eyes to blot out the picture of the cellar, but the explosion echoed in his mind. He saw the scene outside the pub . . . watched

127

glass cascade from the windows of the butcher's shop . . . and saw the oily smoke rising above Riordan's draper's. Most of all he remembered the hate in Matt Riordan's eyes – 'I'll kill you for this . . . remember my name, Matt Riordan . . . it will take you to your grave.' Sean shuddered. He was afraid, but he was aware of something else. He was learning the rules.

Next morning Sean said goodbye to Tomas and the family. Of course he would see them again, when he came back from the magic island with his father, but the relationship would never be the same. Sean sensed it when Tomas hugged him goodbye – and Michael looked as sad as the grave when he shook hands.

The morning papers were vivid with photographs of the gutted pub. Tomas was almost sure Pat was involved, but he said nothing. He might have, had he known Sean had been part of it – Tomas would have been appalled by that – but Sean held his tongue.

So Pat Connors and his son left for Coney Island. Each wore strong boots and carried an oilskin cape against the weather. Both sagged slightly under the weight of their rucksacks. Pat walked with the aid of the blackthorn stick he had used since the civil war, and if the prospect of walking several hundred miles daunted him, not a flicker of concern showed on his face. He would never undertake a more important journey. Fourteen years had been spent in its preparation. Not for a moment did he doubt the rightness of what he was doing. Nor did he question Sean's ability to learn, the boy's quick mind delighted him. Pat's only worry was about his own abilities as a teacher. The importance of what he had to convey made him question his own competence. But he felt sure the timing was right. It was right to remove Sean from Dublin . . . right to give him something to think about, to take his mind off grieving for Brigid and Maureen.

As for Sean, so much had happened that it was hard to absorb. Not that he would admit that to his father. So he walked proudly at his father's side, matching his stride, vowing to keep pace no matter how far or fast they went.

They talked as they walked – easy talk, without restraint,

more like friends than father and son. And Pat, keyed up to start, began immediately. Not that Sean recognized it as a lesson. Pat's way of teaching was quite different to that of the Christian Brothers. Pat told stories . . . funny stories, sad stories, inspiring stories . . . tales which captured Sean's interest so completely that he passed the lane leading up to the O'Flynns' farm without even noticing.

Pat's theme was history and the men who made it. And he had an uncomfortable respect for the truth – enough, for instance, to admit that the 1916 Rising had not been universally popular. Many Irishmen had hated it. When British reinforcements landed at Kingstown they were met by Irish women bringing tea and biscuits. And afterwards – when the rebellion was quashed – few in the crowd cheered as they watched Michael Collins and the others marched down to the docks under escort. Most had cursed and flung rotten vegetables. Even when the men returned, less than a handful of people greeted them. Most turned their backs. Employers shut their doors. Shopkeepers refused credit . . .

Pat chuckled, 'You'd never know now. The men who took part are counted as heroes. It's been made to look like a popular rising, but the truth is we sometimes got better handling from British soldiers than from the Irish.'

There was no bitterness in Pat's voice – resentment would have defeated his objective. He sought to show what the world was *really* like – not what it should be, nor what it might one day become. 'Know it for what it is, Sean. Know men for what they are. Know that and you can deal with every man in it.'

They ate at a farmhouse that night and slept in a barn, to be up at dawn and on the road again. Pat recalled his earlier journey to Sligo, when Finola had died birthing Sean. He had stormed across the countryside, black with rage and bleak with heartache. Now it was different. They walked at a leisurely pace and made frequent stops to shelter from the rain or admire a view. And Pat talked nonstop, and – to his surprise – without consulting his notebooks. He counted those as his most precious possessions. He had been terrified of losing them in Ammet Street. But now he was unfolding his rules he found that he knew them too well to need written words.

Sean listened and questioned, and sought to crystallize his father's experiences into black and white solutions. His father restrained him. When Sean flatly condemned all Irishmen who had failed to rally to the flag in 1916, Pat shook his head. 'The Irish are no better than anyone else. Most people keep their heads down when things are uncertain. They wait 'til it's safe. Only when an issue is decided will they venture an opinion.' He chuckled, 'And then most of them go along with whoever is winning.'

Pat stopped by a stone wall. The land fell away, dipping into a valley. On the far side sheep were circumventing a stream, perhaps looking for a crossing. Pat pointed – 'See those sheep, seven of them following the other one. They will follow him anywhere. Not because he knows where he is going, but because it saves them thinking for themselves – if they can think, which the poor dumb creatures probably can't. Are you contemptuous of them too?'

'But Da, they're just sheep –'

'Are you contemptuous?'

'Well no . . . I mean, you can't have contempt . . . it's the way they are.'

'Exactly,' Pat grinned. 'It's the way most people are too. So why be contemptuous of people but not sheep?'

'But people should have minds of their own –'

'Should?' Pat cocked his head. 'Sure there you go again. Changing the world. But you'll not change it that way. You are starting all wrong. Assuming things which aren't true, assuming people think for themselves. They don't as a rule, not most people. They just follow the crowd and don't you forget it.'

And Sean never did.

They reached Sligo on the fourth or fifth day, Sean lost track of time – time and places were less important than his father's talk, which was as well perhaps because Coney Island disappointed them. The surrounding cliffs loomed larger in Pat's memory than in reality. Nor was the sea so rough, or the island as mysterious. Sean was disappointed too – unrealistically he had imagined a tropical island, with the sun blazing down from a brilliant sky. Coney Island was not like that. But Saint Patrick's Wishing Chair and the

130

tumbledown cabin were still there – so father and son spent a couple of days on Coney Island, walking, talking, arguing, laughing and enjoying each other's company.

Perhaps memories of the priest turned Pat's mind to Catholicism and the power it holds over the Irish. He recounted his reservations, not aggressively but with the patience of a man who has tried a medicine and found it not to cure his ills. He was only bitter when it came to the church's ambivalence towards Irish Republicanism. He remembered the Bishop's pastoral which condemned the Republican oath in such outright terms that unrepentant Republicans were refused confession by many priests. He told of devout men going to the firing squad having been refused communion, and of men who died without the Viaticum. 'The church can't make up its mind,' he said, and to prove his point told stories of other men at confession with other priests – 'I stole, Father' 'What did you steal, my son?' 'Explosives, Father' 'For use in Ireland, my son?' 'No Father, for use against the British in England' 'Oh well, that's all right my son' said the priest, happily giving the IRA men absolution.

Sean frowned. 'You're confusing me, Da.'

Pat laughed. 'The church gets confused about things which are none of its business.'

'Everything is the business of the church,' Sean declared doggedly.

Pat was delighted – 'Sure, Brigid would be proud of you – and that's nothing to be ashamed of for she was a grand woman right enough.'

'But even you go to mass again now,' Sean persisted. Pat scowled. It was true, he had returned to the fold. He had kicked against it for years, until finally he was trapped by his blossoming political career. A man could no more hold elected office in Ireland without going to mass than he could fly through the air.

'There are times you have to balance what you want,' he said sorrowfully. 'Going to mass does me no harm, even if I want to throw up at times. It is expedient Sean, and that's something I want to talk about. Sometimes a man has to eat shit. It goes against the grain, you holler and scream, but sometimes you have to accept something unpalatable

131

to get what you want.'

It was a hard lesson for a boy to learn from his father. Perhaps Pat's uncompromising language made it harder. But he illustrated his point with a whole string of stories to get his meaning across . . . until Sean grudgingly admitted the word 'expediency' to his vocabulary.

Generally Pat trod carefully in shaping his son's thinking, always careful to avoid confrontation, indeed demonstrating a rule in the process – 'Direct confrontation is the first impulse of fools and the last choice of wise men. But when it is unavoidable, strike hard. Strike to kill.'

Which prompted Sean to voice his worry, 'Will you really go to Belfast, Da, to kill Liam Riordan?'

'If I don't, I reckon he'll come looking for me, sooner or later.'

'He might not. He might stay in Belfast like you told him to.'

'Then he will have got away with murder. He will have murdered Brigid and Maureen and got off scot-free. Is that what you want?'

Sean struggled for an answer. Of course he wanted Riordan punished. The man should suffer the wrath of God – he *would* suffer the wrath of God – but Sean was afraid for his father. His father was the one permanent rock in Sean's life – if anything ever happened – he shrank from the idea. Slowly, in faltering words, he tried to express himself.

Pat heard him out, letting love respond without a display of sentimentality which would have embarrassed them both. Then he said, 'I must do it, Sean. It's part of the rules I live by. I wouldn't be me if I ran away from it. But I'll strike a bargain with you. Liam Riordan can have a stay of execution, as long as he stays out of Dublin.'

Which was how it was left. Sean was pleased, but his dreams that night were interrupted by a thin-faced boy with furious eyes – 'I'll kill you for this, remember my name – Matt Riordan – it will take you to your grave.'

They left Coney Island the next day. Back on the mainland they stayed a while on the beautiful shores of Lough Gill. Each day was different. No plan was rigid. Once a week they stayed at a pub and soaked in a hot bath,

132

but other than that they slept in barns, or farms, or cabins. Irish hospitality was plentiful and although Pat paid for whatever food and lodging they received, it cost little. By day they fished for trout or salmon, or walked and climbed hills – but always they talked. They talked and talked and talked.

Pat described every man he had ever known – the weak and the powerful, the brave and the cowardly, the famous and nonentities. He dissected character, analysed behaviour, commented on ambitions – but always with the purpose of showing Sean men as they are. He talked of greed and lust, pride and vanity, power and corruption. He invented situations and placed his characters in them with the skill of a playwright – then asked Sean to define how each man might react under stress, testing his understanding while apparently playing a game. And time and again Sean delighted him with explanations as clear as they were convincing. They talked mainly of the Irish. Of men like Charles Stewart Parnell, whose demands for Home Rule for Ireland had dominated British parliamentary life in the eighteen-eighties. Of Parnell's rise to power, and his subsequent fall after the greatest sexual scandal ever known in politics. They talked of Eoin MacNeil, Connolly and Pearse – of Collins and de Valera. And throughout it all Pat sought to demonstrate how some men gravitated to power while others were shoved aside. How some men led, while most followed.

They talked of the Irish language, which many wanted to become the dominant tongue in Ireland. Pat was uncertain – 'It's part of our heritage all right – but half the world speaks English. Future generations won't thank us if we stick them with a language only used on this island. Wouldn't you think we are insular enough, without that?'

Pat talked of 'the black rules'. Not everything could be achieved by adhering to such simple principles as 'a promise given is a promise kept', or 'preserve your reputation as you would your life'. Pat unveiled another set of rules. At times, Sean was told, it pays to cheat!

Perhaps that was the hardest lesson of all, because it tarnished his image of his father, and jarred against Brigid's upbringing. But Tomas and Brigid would not have

133

survived five minutes in the power struggles which Pat described – as his son recognized. Despite which Sean clung to many of his childhood values, and resisted his father's arguments. Not that Pat was dismayed by that – it was not his intention to turn his son into a scoundrel, but merely to teach him the pragmatism of power . . . to show there were times to turn all other rules on their heads. To lie was unacceptable generally, but occasionally huge objectives could be won by use of the BIG LIE. To cheat, even to murder, had been the way of powerful men through the ages, and Pat quoted historical references by the score. Not that they sounded historical. Pat made them come alive. Sean saw the characters as flesh and blood, he suffered their setbacks and rejoiced at their triumphs. Set in the context of their sprawling lives, the occasional BIG LIE seemed almost acceptable – Sean could see no way to avoid it.

It was a huge experience for Sean. The concepts embodied in his father's rules were awe-inspiring. Pat moved on with his shanachie's skill . . . drawing examples and parallels, creating imagined case-histories which put his characters into impossible situations. 'Get out of that,' he challenged – and time and again Sean did. Sean enjoyed it . . . but it was only a game. He could not imagine a real life situation in which he would be so ruthless – until he remembered Matt Riordan. 'I'll bloody well kill you,' Matt Riordan had hissed. Sean whispered under his breath – 'Someday you'll try, but now I'll be ready for you.'

So the lessons ended. By the end of four weeks Pat had realized his dream. He cast his mind back to Saint Patrick's Wishing Chair on that morning so long ago – 'I wish I could write it all down,' he had cried to the wind. 'There must be a list of rules somewhere, that makes a man a giant among the rest of us. If only a man could set the rules down – what a gift to leave to a son.'

He rummaged through his rucksack and withdrew his precious notebooks, wrapped in oilskin for protection. He handed the package to Sean, who turned it over and over in his hands. It had been his dream too, a dream come true. He tingled with excitement. Knowledge was wealth and here was an asset beyond price. Words failed him.

Gratitude, love, respect – emotions coursed through him. He opened his arms and embraced his father in a great hug of joy. Pat ruffled his son's hair. Neither said a word because at that moment neither could speak. Pat thought to warn the boy to guard the notebooks and keep them secret, but decided against it – a gift was a gift, to be cherished or not by whoever received it. Pat knew Sean would cherish the rules for the rest of his life.

A minute later Pat delivered his final judgement. 'Never ask for advice,' he said. 'Never ask any man, especially me, for I've written down all I can tell you. It's all there – in the rules – if you look hard enough.'

So they turned for home. It took four days to walk back to Dublin, and conversation lagged for the first time. Having delivered his blueprint for a life, Pat felt drained and exhausted. Now his left leg dragged badly and he leaned heavily on his stick. But it was a comfortable silence. Sean slowed his pace in unspoken recognition of his father's difficulties – and kept such an eye on him that their roles seemed to reverse – as if Sean was the man now, with every decision to take.

The night before they reached Dublin, he dreamt of Mrs O'Flynn. He awoke with a groan, unwilling to drag himself away from images of her soft rounded body. He wondered whether to tell his father? He felt so close to him. The rules gave them so many shared secrets, but he hesitated. He remembered the story of Charles Stewart Parnell, whose affair with a married woman had ruined him. And he recalled his father's contempt. That decided Sean. To disappoint his father was unthinkable, so he pushed all thoughts of Mrs O'Flynn aside.

In the same way he decided to keep his own rules to himself. They seemed puny compared with the real thing. And different. Yet they *did* have a purpose, Sean thought stubbornly, they dealt with the acquisition of assets – whereas his father's rules concerned political power. But a rich man was as powerful as a politician, more so at times. And a politician without money was surely at the mercy of the gombeen men, and gombeen men struck hard bargains. The ideal, Sean concluded, was to be a rich politician – and so to have need for both sets of rules.

On their last morning, they made an early start and reached Palmerstown by noon. This time Sean did glance up the lane to the farm, but it was merely a quick turn of his head, taken without breaking his stride. Decisions about Mrs O'Flynn would wait for another day. Meanwhile father and son walked steadily down the hill and along the Quays. Sean looked about with fresh eyes. Things were the same, and yet different. Houses looked smaller, the Liffey less wide, labourers not so muscular, and gombeen men less prosperous. Yet the scene had changed less than Sean himself. He walked with his head high and his bold blue eyes meeting the look of all and sundry. The weather had bronzed his face to emphasize the white evenness of his teeth. His thick black hair needed cutting and swept over his ears to add width to his face. Never had he felt fitter or more certain of himself – which was as well – for his brimming self-confidence was tested to the full within minutes of arriving in Dublin.

They entered Mulligan's Bar together, Pat's bulkier figure a half pace ahead . . . and Sean was barely inside the door when Mulligan's loud voice stopped him in his tracks.

'Thank God, you're here,' Mulligan shouted, rushing out from his counter to grip Pat's hand. 'We've been searching the town for you.'

'You knew I was away –'

'Aye, but not forever. St Patrick himself wouldn't believe the performance we've had here this morning.'

'What performance?'

'That woman. Up at the farm. O'Flynn's wife. Didn't she come in here two hours ago, screaming for Mr Connors –'

Sean's stomach turned over. 'Mrs O'Flynn? What's happened?'

Mulligan turned to him for the first time – 'Brace yourself boy. I know he was a friend of yours. But he's dead. Old Farmer O'Flynn is dead!'

CHAPTER EIGHT

Afterwards Sean remembered them as the happiest days of his life. By the end of his first month on the *Gazette* he was head over heels in love with newspapers. Accessibility to the famous made Sean tingle with excitement. It was that which attracted him, not the prospect of professional advancement. The editor's chair held no appeal for Sean Connors, as the then incumbent Dinny Macaffety was quick to find out. Macaffety made a fearsome first impression – a bull-necked, red-faced, whiskey-smelling giant, with a voice like a foghorn – slumped behind the avalanche of papers which cluttered his desk. Hooded eyes surveyed Sean through a haze of cigarette smoke – 'So you're the donkey boy,' Macaffety barked at their first meeting.

Sean made what he hoped was a suitable reply.

'I'd know you anywhere,' Macaffety growled. 'You're the spitting image of your father. And you've a touch of his temper I'm told.'

Sean admitted he could be hasty at times.

'Well my temper will blister your arse!' Macaffety said, pounding his chest to cause a cloud of cigarette ash to rise from his lapels. 'Remember that before you raise your voice in this office.' He snorted and rose from his chair, to cross to the window where he stared down into the street. 'I hire and fire. Nobody tells me otherwise, got that?' He turned, looking larger than ever with the grey light of a Dublin morning behind him. 'There's a queue a mile long for good jobs in this city. You know that, I suppose?'

Sean nodded.

'I could have the pick of Trinity College if I wanted,' Macaffety continued. 'Educated young men, older and wiser than you.'

Sean said nothing.

'Yet I have to take you. *Have to!* Never set eyes on you until now, but I have to take you. And for why? Because

137

of Pat Connors, God help me,' Macaffety sounded disgusted. He collapsed back into his chair, ran a hand through his grey mane and fixed Sean with a brooding look. 'I ought to have my head examined. Wouldn't you think I need a doctor?'

Sean hesitated, 'Would it be because the Da's your friend, Mr Macaffety? You're doing him a favour, maybe?' He waited for a response, but when none came he added, 'I'll do my best not to let you down, Mr Macaffety.'

'And I'll never give you the chance,' Macaffety rapped back, but his interest sharpened, 'So – you know all about favours, do you?'

Repaying favours was one of the rules, but Sean decided against saying so. Instead he said, 'The Da says it's the mark of a big man to repay favours. It's something I've been brought up with.'

Macaffety tilted back in his chair and gave the boy his full attention. Boy was wrong, he thought, his editor's judgement automatically substituting 'young man' and then 'hungry young man'. But hungry for what? He examined what he knew about young Sean Connors. The donkey business was legend, so were the fights – but both were the action of a *doer*, not a watcher. Reporters and writers were watchers of men, not men of action themselves. The contradiction provoked a question, 'What makes you think you will make a newspaperman?'

Sean met the stare without flinching – 'Everyone says I'm forever asking questions. Wouldn't that be a help, Mr Macaffety?'

'Only if you know the answers.'

'The Da says I'll learn them from you, if I watch hard enough.'

Macaffety felt the first twinge of uneasiness. Staff on the *Gazette* went in fear of him. Not that he sought to frighten them – he shouted a lot, and swore and cursed when things went wrong, but that was only to be expected – the lilylivered lot should stand up for themselves in Macaffety's opinion. People walked all over you if you let them. Nobody walked over Macaffety. Nor men like Pat Connors. And they wouldn't walk over Pat's son if Macaffety judged right. But that was no reason to go easy on the lad, in fact the reverse, rough him up a bit, see what he was made of. 'So your Da has been filling your head with grand ideas, has he? No doubt he said you'll be sitting in this chair one day.'

Sean was genuinely surprised. 'No sir, he never told me that.'

'You thought of it yourself, I suppose?' Macaffety's voice took on an edge.

Sean considered, but shook his head. 'No sir, but I don't think I'd like to be editor.'

Macaffety was surprised. 'Oh? So you'll be a reporter the rest of your life?'

The conversation had taken an unexpected shift. Sean sensed he was creating a poor impression, but the situation worsened as he lost his composure. 'No, I don't think I'd like that either, Mr Macaffety.'

'Then in God's name, why are you wasting my time?'

Sean floundered, red-faced. He gulped, and words fell from his lips like falling bricks, 'I think I'd like to own a paper one day.'

'*Own one!*' Macaffety's eyes popped as he started to laugh. 'Own a paper? Have you the slightest idea what it costs?'

Sean's misery deepened. His first morning was all turning sour. He had not known what to expect. Mr Macaffety was supposed to be his father's friend, yet he was baiting and jeering like an enemy. But instead of turning into despair, misery sparked off Sean's temper. 'No, I don't know what a paper would cost, but the Da says Dev spent more than fifty thousand starting the *Irish News* and that's not half such a good paper as the *Gazette*, so I reckon I will need more than that.'

Macaffety stopped laughing. It was funny, damn funny he told himself – but the lad had answered back, despite his embarrassment. No one else on the *Gazette* would have done that. Macaffety frowned, 'And where will you find more than fifty thousand pounds?' he demanded.

'I'm not ready to buy a paper yet, Mr Macaffety, so I don't need the money right now.'

Macaffety stared. Years later he claimed he made up his mind about Sean at that moment. The boy had answered so calmly, without conceit, but with a sureness which quite belied his discomfort. Macaffety was impressed – but he could not resist turning the knife – so when he summoned an assistant a few minutes later, he introduced Sean with a flourish – 'This is Mr Connors. He's going to own the *Gazette* one day, meanwhile he has consented to work here as a copy-boy. Take him away and show him his duties.'

The story was too good to stifle. Everyone on the *Gazette* knew it by the end of the day. The *News* and the *Times* had heard it by Friday. Sean was painfully aware of being a laughing stock, but he suffered the jokes with a grin, more concerned for his father's reputation than his own. Yet the incident did him no harm. Almost overnight every paper in Dublin had heard of Sean Connors, and though people laughed most were careful about what they said, perhaps for fear of Pat Connors. The jokes prompted Sean to write a new rule into his book. Never reveal a dream to anyone. And he made himself a promise – that he *would* buy the *Gazette* one day.

Meanwhile Pat Connors's star was rising in the Dail. Cosgrave, leading the Fine Gael parliamentary opposition, was no match for Dev, though it must be admitted that Dev had few equals in the whole of Ireland. But Pat's spirited speeches won such wide acclaim that he was elevated to the front rank of Fine Gael politicians. A supporting player for years, he seemed to be moving to centre stage. In fact his views were in such demand that first the *Times*, then the *Independent* and even the *Gazette* – irrespective of whether they were for or against Dev – published articles by Pat Connors. Pat's fees began to mount up, so much so that he and Sean left the rooms above Mulligan's Bar and took a small house in Ballsbridge – which was to become Pat's home for the rest of his days. It also became the meeting place for politicians and journalists – and on Saturday nights in particular, the downstairs rooms buzzed with political gossip, or erupted into gales of laughter at one of Pat's more scurrilous stories.

Sean basked in the atmosphere. He was thrilled – an entire house, just for him and his father, with a woman coming in to cook and to clean. That was exciting itself, but Sean could hardly contain himself when it became clear that the leading figures in Dublin were to become regular guests. He listened to conversations with rapt attention, soaking them up like a sponge. He analysed what men said, determined to discern their true meaning. Visitors' pronouncements were measured against the secret yardstick of the rules, and time and again Sean found other meanings to their words – self-justification for their actions, self-interest disguised as philanthropy. None of which dismayed him, on the contrary it confirmed the underlying truths in his father's rules – know men for what they are, not what they would have you believe. It was as if the month spent tramping the countryside had been his classroom, and now the house in Ballsbridge was a testing ground.

Initially Pat's guests accepted Sean as a courtesy to their host. It was Sean's home and up to him if he chose to spend his free time gossiping about politics. So Sean was tolerated. But attitudes changed after a few months. Nobody commented outright on Sean's growing maturity, but gradually his opinions became known – and in every case because he was asked. Guests would say – 'What do you think, young Sean?' – and he would tell them, diffidently at first, but with growing confidence as he forgot what they might think of him and concentrated on what he was saying. His common sense shone through, that gift inherited from his mother which mixed so well with his developing shanachie's skill that most listeners were nodding as he finished. 'Not bad,' they would say. 'In fact I said much the same thing myself, only this morning.' So Sean was accepted, and within a year men could be heard saying – 'Wait until Saturday night – Pat and young Sean will have something to say about this.'

It was the same at the *Gazette*. Life was difficult at first. When Macaffety joked everyone laughed – so Sean was the butt of much humour. But after a while the laughter died away, to be replaced by respect, quite simply because Sean Connors was the best copy-boy the *Gazette* had ever had. He was everywhere at once – jobs were done a sight more quickly by Sean than anyone else – paste was mixed, messages run, tea made, beers collected from the pub next door, pencils sharpened, typewriters cleaned – nothing was too much trouble, no job unworthy of his best endeavour. And he was always there – starting earlier than he had to, and only finishing when he could walk home in the early hours clutching the new day's issue of the *Gazette*. Such energy would have been remarkable anywhere, in Dublin it was phenomenal. Even Dinny Macaffety was heard to growl – 'Sure I get dizzy just watching him. God help us if he does buy the place – we'll be run to shadows inside of a week.'

Only on Saturday did Sean rest. It was his one day off from the *Gazette*. But even then he was busy, though not always in the way people imagined – for on Saturdays Sean went to Palmerstown to help the Widow O'Flynn.

People accepted it. Ever since Farmer O'Flynn's heart attack – the day Mrs O'Flynn arrived in Mulligan's Bar searching for Sean when he returned from Coney Island with his father. He had dashed upstairs to comfort her, where she fell round his neck and sobbed all over him. Then, white-faced and shaking, she had walked down on his arm and he had driven her donkey-cart back to the farm. After which he had taken over . . . arranged the funeral and everything. 'Like a grown-up son,' said the gossips, 'the poor woman has got her troubles right enough, but it's a blessing to have that young man to lean on.' And the Widow O'Flynn had demurely agreed.

After the funeral Sean went to the bank and listened to an account of her comfortable finances. The farm labourers were told they could stay on without fear of not being paid – and every Saturday morning Sean inspected their work and dealt with their wages. The farm ticked over. Farmer O'Flynn would have done better, for Sean was no farmer – but he made sure no money was lost.

He went directly to the farm in the early hours of every Saturday morning, leaving the *Gazette* at past midnight to tramp the lonely miles up to Palmerstown. 'I may as well, Da. Milking starts at six in the morning. If I come home first I'll have to leave at five.'

'But where will you sleep?'

'There's a loft in the barn. The Widow O'Flynn has put a bed there for me. It's cosy enough.'

Which was true. The explanation was accepted by all.

Sean made sure of that – every Saturday morning the labourers arrived to find him descending the ladder from the loft. Tired as death he looked, as well he might, having dragged himself from the Widow's warm bed an hour before. But the world saw nothing of that. All the world saw was a young man selflessly doing his duty by a dead friend. 'He sticks at it,' said the gossips – and the Widow O'Flynn demurely agreed.

Apprenticeship years, Sean called them afterwards – learning politics, learning newspapers, learning how to please a lady in bed. Sometimes he wondered which was the most important, even which was the most enjoyable – for although Maeve O'Flynn was an imaginative teacher, so was Dinny Macaffety. Sean had been at the *Gazette* just over a year when he was summoned to Macaffety's office one day. 'Sit down, *Mr* Connors,' Macaffety barked.

Sean ticked through his jobs that morning, wondering which had caused dissatisfaction. In between running messages and a dozen other tasks he had worked the front counter for an hour, accepting death notices and wedding announcements. He groaned at the thought of mixing them up – 'Mr and Mrs Flagherty are pleased to announce the engagement of their daughter Bernadette to Tim Feegan, aged eighty-eight, who died on Tuesday with a smile on his face.'

'I've been thinking,' Macaffety scowled. 'No man should own a newspaper without being a reporter first. Wouldn't you say so, Mr Connors?'

Sean's mouth went dry. A reporter! Reporters earned three pounds a week and expenses on top. Reporters had a chance to build assets.

Macaffety tilted back in his chair and scratched his stomach. 'Well, as you are still with us – filling in time before going on to better things no doubt – I thought we'd maybe ask you to do a bit of reporting. That's if you've a mind to oblige, of course –'

'That's wonderful, Mr Macaffety. Tremendous –'

'Only if you can *do* it. You think you're ready to write a news story yet?'

'News stories – features – headlines –'

'My God!' Macaffety threw up his hands. 'Wouldn't you

143

know I'm redundant. This tired old hack who served his time in London's Fleet Street –'

'Ready to learn. That's what I meant, Mr Macaffety. Ready to learn how to –'

'Will you please not interrupt!' Macaffety slapped his hands over his ears and peered mock fearfully across his desk. 'Your mouth has shut so I take it you've stopped talking. Now will you *listen* for a while. If you understand that nod your head, then maybe this business of teaching you might start.'

Sean nodded vigorously and remained silent as Macaffety rose and shambled across to a filing cabinet. He poured himself a whiskey, returned the bottle to the drawer, slumped back behind his desk, and started. It was rare for Dinny Macaffety to deliver a lecture on newspapers, but compulsive listening when he did. Sean sat glued to his seat. Newspapers were food and drink to Macaffety, life itself – printer's ink ran in his veins and his heart beat to the clacking of the litho-machines. At one point he growled at Sean, 'You've got something. I don't know what is it yet, nor do you I suspect. I doubt you will ever make a really *great* newspaperman, you don't want it badly enough. You've an itch to do something with your life though, and that's commendable. But if you're to go about Dublin as a *Gazette* reporter you will at least be competent, or you'll answer to me. You understand that much, don't you?'

Macaffety did not wait for an answer – 'Being a newspaperman is the best training for life there is, so you'll get that out of it. It will open your eyes. You'll learn twice as much as you write. You'll find out who owns who among the gombeen men, who *owes* whom – who can't pay his bills, and the ins and outs of every crooked deal in town. You'll watch the politicians, which should be easy for you, but you will find out a hell of a lot more than who's sucking up to your father in Fine Gael. You can watch Dev for me, and that takes some doing. You'll learn who's running the IRA this week and who is trying to take over, and keep quiet about both if you value your knee-caps. You'll hush-up abortions for fear of the bishops. And when a bride's waist is thicker than it should be you will turn a blind eye.

You'll keep regular at mass every Sunday, along with the rest of us . . .' he paused to smile wolfishly across the desk, 'even your Da has to suffer that. Besides, it's not such a hardship for watchers of men like us. That's when you see them for the hypocritical bunch of bastards they are – all standing up for the good father when they've spent the week stealing and drinking, or shoving their hands up the skirts of other men's wives. Yes, sir, you will learn a lot working for me.'

So Dinny Macaffety delivered his lecture, a strange mixture of newspaper lore and philosophy, each wedded so close to the other that separating them was impossible. Not that Sean tried. He was too absorbed, but he jumped when Macaffety mentioned the rules. 'There are precious few rules in this business. But you'll learn to live by some. Never write what you don't know to be true. Never write what isn't clear in your mind – don't even start unless it is. Don't rat on your sources, don't ever do that. Anyone asks you to reveal a source, you send him to hell – including me, and I'll ask often enough, but you keep a tight mouth if you want to work here. There's not a lot else. Don't take cheap gifts. Don't be bought. And don't kiss any man's arse – not that you've shown an inclination to do that.'

All of which happened about eighteen months after Sean returned from Coney Island with his father. At sixteen, but looking older, Sean Connors was a junior reporter on the *Gazette*, earning two pounds ten shillings a week. During the early hours of a Saturday morning he made love to his mistress – and late on a Saturday night he rubbed shoulders with the power clique of Ireland. Life was perfect, or would have been but for two things. First was the Riordans. True, they stayed away from Dublin, but Sean feared their return. He still had nightmares in which he saw Matt Riordan's white face in the darkness. But most of all Sean worried about Tomas. No matter how busy they were, both Sean and his father kept in touch with Tomas and the family. Sean visited every week. The family seemed to be falling apart. Tomas had never really recovered from the loss of Brigid and Maureen – Dary and Cooey and the others were making their own, rather unsatisfactory lives, and only Michael seemed to retain his mother's values.

Tomas tried to keep the family together – but without Brigid's devotion to their individual needs the unity of purpose had gone.

So Sean visited out of loyalty, while nursing a secret plan. He had made himself a promise when Brigid and Maureen were killed. He would never be able to repay Brigid for her love – but he could do the one thing she would have wanted, which was to send the family to Australia, something Tomas had always dreamt about. Of course it would be different now, Sean realized, for Tomas to sail into Sydney Harbour without Brigid and Maureen – but at least those children still left to him would be at his side. It would re-unite the family.

Sean wrote to his uncles – Uncle Rory in California and Uncle Mike in Perth. Both replied offering help, but not *enough* help, that was the problem. It cost a fortune to transport five people to Australia, and although both uncles could contribute, Sean was still looking for the enormous sum of five hundred pounds. But how was he to raise it? He could never save it. He might have done once, when the donkeys were working for him, when he had assets – but now, on a salary of two pounds ten shillings a week, it would take years. 'And Tomas will be dead by then,' he told himself sadly.

The Widow O'Flynn had the money, as Sean knew from his knowledge of her financial affairs – and once, when he was more than usually worried about Tomas's failing health, Sean was tempted to ask for a loan. But something warned him against the idea.

Time passed – weeks, months – then an unrelated incident occurred which was to bring the elusive five hundred pounds nearer. In fact it began with the Widow O'Flynn. Sean was in her bed during the early hours of a Saturday morning, warm and snug after making love, when she said – 'I've something exciting to tell you.'

Sean made an effort to rouse himself – 'Haven't I had all the excitement I can stand for a while. Will you let me rest.'

She giggled and poked him in the ribs – 'Stop acting like an old man and listen to me. I'm selling the farm – there now – what do you think of that?'

They made tea and sat on the bed to discuss her news,

146

Maeve O'Flynn clad in that wonderful dressing-gown, and him totally naked. He was not completely surprised, Maeve O'Flynn had married a farmer to escape poverty, not through a love of the land. She had often spoken of her dislike of the farm – it was lonely, she had no company, the life was miserable – especially for a young woman with money in the bank and hot blood in her veins.

'I'm going to open tea-rooms in Dublin,' she announced. 'Doesn't that sound exciting?'

In a way it was a brilliant idea. Maeve O'Flynn lacked business training, but she was shrewdly intelligent and attractive as well. She would surely make a success of some tea-rooms.

'And you are going to help me find the premises. I thought in King Street perhaps, or maybe even Grafton Street itself. Will you start looking on Monday?' she pleaded – and Sean promised he would, adding yet another job to an already overcrowded schedule.

If Sean's life in Dublin was full and exciting, Matt Riordan's life in Belfast was a nightmare. Matt's misery had plumbed the depths since the day the Riordan family home had been destroyed by Pat Connors. Arriving in Belfast had been traumatic. Matt's mother had wept non-stop through the journey. His own nerves were in tatters by the time the train reached Belfast. Matt had never been north before. His father had been born there, in a tiny terraced house near the Falls Road – which was where they went from the station, to be given an uncertain welcome by Matt's grandmother. She had wept at their story and grown angry, pulling her hair and beating herself with shrivelled red fists. Matt had been hard-pressed to think straight, what with his grandmother keening and his mother shrieking. He had ached for his father, even though he would be accused of standing by when he should have stopped the Connors gang singlehanded – but he was ready to face even that for a chance to talk things over with a man instead of two wailing women. But Matt's father was away. He was mostly away, Matt found out, on secret business for the IRA. It was a fearful blow. Matt had buoyed himself up throughout that awful day with the thought of reaching

147

his father. His father would know what to do. His father would take some terrible revenge. But when Matt arrived in Belfast his father was not to be found. And worse was to follow. After a traumatic day came a terrifying night. They went to bed early, simply because they had nothing left to say to each other. Matt slept in the narrow cot sometimes used by his father, while the two women camped down in the only other bedroom. Matt tossed and turned, his mind alive with the day's events. The only scene which restored some spark of pride was when he had spat into Sean Connors's face . . . at least he would be able to tell his father about that.

Then, at about an hour after midnight, eerie sounds filled the street outside – a growing chorus of screams and high-pitched keening. The cry 'M-u-r-derr-eh' was repeated over and over again. It rose to a crescendo, accompanied by the metallic banging of what sounded like every pot and pan in Belfast. Matt flew to the window. It *was* pots and pans; women were rushing from doors all down the street, to beat the walls and kerbstones with pots and pans and dustbin lids. Suddenly two trucks rounded the corner and skidded to a halt. Armed men leapt out and rushed into the houses, knocking people aside, kicking doors open, charging up stairs . . . *charging up the stairs in Matt's house!* Two men crashed into his room, waving guns and ordering him against the wall.

The mattress was torn from the cot and ripped open. Floorboards were lifted. Then they saw the suitcase behind the door – the suitcase Matt had brought from Dublin. 'No!' he screamed as they wrenched open the cashbox. A rifle butt caught him full in the face. His mouth filled with blood, choking him. He staggered, then flung himself at his attackers. They beat him senseless. They might have kicked him to death but for his mother who wrapped herself round one man's leg and clung on like a leech. Seventy houses were raided that night in a search for hidden arms. None were found, but when the B Specials drove away an hour later, the Riordans' life savings went with them.

Liam Riordan arrived at dawn to find his wife and mother tending his son. He listened with incredulity to the catalogue of disaster. To be wiped out – to be wiped out in a day! Everything gone, home, businesses, and now their savings too! He swore. He swore revenge, swore with anger, swore at God, swore at the British and the black-hearted Prod bastards who had beaten his son senseless. In temper he struck his wife so hard that she fell and cut her head. He swore at his mother who whimpered in a corner. He seethed and ranted. Then he left, stopping just long enough to throw some coins at his wife, enough money to feed them for a few days, and pausing to promise that one day they would take their revenge – on Pat Connors for a start, and then every murdering Prod bastard in Ireland.

That was Matt Riordan's introduction to Belfast. He learned much about the city in the following years, but little to his liking. He thought it black and ugly compared to Dublin, the buildings less grand, the streets half as wide and the squares not so gracious. There were even parts where Matt feared to tread – Donegal Road, Sandy Row, Newtonards Road – and the Shankill of course – no Catholic set foot in the Shankill without a dozen mates ready for trouble. Unless Matt was on a specific errand he stayed close to home – in the Catholic ghetto which stretched from the Lower Falls up to Lenadoon, flanked by the Springfield Road one side and Andersonstown on the other. Later Matt was to visit other Catholic families in the Short Strand, or up by the New Lodge Road, but in his early days he only relaxed in the relative security of his grandmother's house, located as it was in the middle of the largest Catholic ghetto in Belfast.

He made friends – being beaten up by the B Specials on his very first night gave him immediate fame. Boys of his own age visited to sit at his bedside and commiserate about his bruises. They exchanged backgrounds, each intrigued by the other's accent. The Belfast boys gasped when they learned what had happened to Matt in Dublin. What shocked them most was that the outrage had been perpetrated by Catholics. They would have dismissed that had not Matt's grandmother sworn the story was true. Even so, it was hard to believe that no black-hearted Prod bastard was involved.

Matt waited for his father to return. It was all he could

do, just wait. Each day his body ached a bit less, while his hatred for the Connors festered more. He wondered if his father was already back in Dublin, making the Connors rebuild the Riordan home a brick at a time. Certainly his father would extract a terrible revenge. Matt was sure about that.

Then, on the eleventh day, his father returned, but not in the way Matt had expected. It was early in the morning, at just after dawn. Matt woke with a start to find a man with a revolver standing at the window in the bedroom. Then Matt's father entered the room, carrying a Webley pistol which he slid into his belt. 'Get up,' he whispered, 'and keep quiet – we don't want the whole street knowing we're here.'

Downstairs his mother poured hot water over the tea. Men took up positions around the house, one in Matt's room overlooking the street, another guarding the back door. Matt's grandmother took them a cup of tea. Matt's father sat at the kitchen table with two other men, to whom he seemed to defer, which surprised Matt who had never seen his father show respect to any man. Another chair was drawn up to the table and Matt was told to sit down. His mother sat against the wall behind him. Matt looked expectantly at his father – but it was the man in the middle who opened the proceedings. 'This is a court of enquiry,' he said quietly, 'conducted by officers of the IRA. We wish to learn of the events which made you homeless. You have nothing to fear by telling the truth. Do you understand that?'

Matt said he did and looked at his father for encouragement. They made him tell them the whole story. His mother broke down and started to sob, but a sharp word from his father ended that. Mostly it was Matt telling them what had happened in Dublin. Everything was written down. When it was over Matt was asked to swear it was true and sign his name at the foot of every page. His mother signed too and was asked if she had anything to add, but she shook her head and said Matt had remembered everything – as if he would ever forget.

The quietly-spoken man looked Matt in the eye. 'This is all we can do for the time being. You won't like it any more than your father does, but that is the way it must be for now. There is too much at stake elsewhere –'

'At stake?' Matt interrupted, forgetting they were armed, forgetting he had been frightened earlier. 'What do you mean *at stake*?'

'Shut up!' his father shouted, then lowered his voice. 'Shut up, for God's sake.'

The quietly-spoken man stared at Matt. 'There's no time for explanation. Your father has other work to attend to – work of the highest importance. You should be proud of him. Nothing is more urgent than the work he has in hand now.'

Matt could barely believe it. He swung back to his father. The Connors were going to get away with it? Just because this man said so.

'Enough!' his father hissed, throwing a warning look. He tapped the notes on the table. 'This is a death warrant for Connors. Just think of that. Every man in this room is wanted both sides of the border – they risked their lives to get this statement. You bite your tongue and ponder on that!'

Matt was lost for an answer. He had no time for one anyway because his father was talking past him to his mother – 'I'm going away, maybe for a long time. Money will be sent here, and this is where you will stay. You're to make no attempt to go back to Dublin until I return –'

'How long? How long will you –'

'God knows. A year maybe – maybe even –'

Sudden footsteps sounded on the stairs. A man rushed in, 'Quick. There's a patrol at the end of the street.'

Guns appeared in every hand as the men dashed out of the back door. Matt's grandmother fell to her knees and began to pray. Matt's mother wept, Matt himself sat in a state of shock. The wailing erupted outside – 'M-u-r-derr-eh' – accompanied by the beating of pots and pans. Shouts were heard in the far distance. Matt flinched for the sound of a shot. But no shots were fired. The IRA men escaped. The Royal Ulster Constabulary rushed up and down the street, and went away. Another day had started in Belfast.

After that, days dragged into weeks and weeks to months, time lost all meaning for Matt. It was ages before his surroundings meant much. But neighbours called every day and gradually their talk got through to him. He was appalled when it did – he was bitter about his own circumstances, but his past had been spent in paradise compared to the lives of his new friends. Most of their fathers were unemployed, some drawing Poor Relief, others drawing nothing – disqualified from official help by some rule or other, and kept from the workhouse only by the charity of friends. Even Poor Relief was a pittance – thirty shillings a week, irrespective of maybe ten mouths to feed and nine shillings and eight pence of that went on the rent. Matt had never known real hunger, not the aching gut-gnawing emptiness to which his new friends were accustomed. It was a way of life for them, sometimes a way of death. Officially 70,000 men were unemployed in Belfast, but Matt soon learned the real figure was over a hundred thousand, and almost all were Catholics – which was not surprising when he discovered that the bastard Prods kept the jobs for themselves. The Government took care not to employ Catholics. The Minister of Agriculture, Sir Basil Brooke, even gave speeches about it – 'Roman Catholics are endeavouring to get in everywhere . . . I recommend those people who are Loyalists not to employ Catholics, ninety-nine per cent of whom are disloyal . . .'

Of course there were protests. Catholics organized hunger marches – whole families were starving, something had to be done. But marches were declared illegal by the Government. Assemblies were broken up by baton-charging B Specials and RUC men. Yet the Government withdrew the order when the Orangemen wanted to march to commemorate the Battle of the Boyne – confirming what was already apparent, Catholics were second-class citizens to be set on at every opportunity. Riots occurred almost every day after that. Curfew was imposed at night. The RUC moved with massive strength into the Falls, armed with rifles and backed up with armoured cars mounted with machine-guns. Catholics erected barricades and cut deep trenches into the roads to hinder the movement of vehicles – and up went the cry again, 'M-u-r-derr-eh' to alert the people of the ghettoes to yet another raid.

Some Protestants wanted the total annihilation of all

Catholics. The United Protestant League declared its object as being – 'Neither to talk with, nor walk with, neither to buy nor sell, borrow nor lend, take nor give, nor have any dealings with Catholics, nor for employers to employ them, nor employees to work for them . . .'

Matt recoiled from the Protestant hatred. His mother shrivelled to a shadow of her former self. In Dublin she had been a woman of some standing. She had carried authority in Riordan's businesses. Money was not plentiful but she had never gone short. But in Belfast she lived in her mother-in-law's house, used her mother-in-law's things, felt her mother-in-law's tongue. True, Liam Riordan sent money for their keep, but a lodger was a lodger all the world over. The grim bleakness of life in the ghetto appalled her, the regular raids sapped her spirit. She wept for her lost life in Dublin. She ceased to live, she merely existed.

Meanwhile, Matt searched for work. His eighteenth birthday fell during that first year, fell being an appropriate word for it can hardly be said to have been celebrated. Matt was a trained butcher and had worked in his father's shop. He could also run a bar, tap barrels, and do any number of useful things – and what he couldn't do he could learn, for Matt Riordan was neither lazy nor stupid. It seemed inconceivable that he would fail to find *some* kind of work. At least it did to begin with. Matt tried everywhere, even that bastion of the Protestant working class, the shipyards. The foreman was so amazed that he laughed, but when Matt persisted the man's good humour faded and he called a gang of riveters to teach the boy some manners. The beating left Matt aching for days. It was the same at the ropeworks and the linen mills. Matt toured the meat market, hawking his skill as a butcher, but to no avail. Protestants would not employ him, and the few Catholic businesses were family concerns, barely able to support father and sons. Matt tried the pubs for work as a barman – only to meet the same story. He tried the docks, the railway, the construction industry – big firms, little firms – he applied to them all, but apart from an odd day's work as a casual labourer, Matt found no employment at all. By the end of the first year he had accepted the inevitable –

153

that it was well nigh impossible for a Catholic to obtain regular work in Belfast.

The Catholic Church denounced the situation. People flocked to mass, penitent in their confessions, and ardent with their prayers. Matt went too – but more and more his thoughts turned away from the Hereafter to the problems of *now*. Now was his misery, now was his hour of aching discontent.

So Matt brooded and smouldered. He watched his mother age ten years in twenty-four months. He compared the happiness of his boyhood with that of his new life . . . and cursed his father for remaining absent on IRA business. Sometimes Matt succumbed to total despair. The black mood only lifted when his thoughts turned to Pat Connors, the man who had deprived him of so much. Resentment beat the anvil of hate, deprivation fuelled a furnace of bitterness. Matt craved revenge as others craved food and drink. Time and again he promised himself – 'One day I'll get my own back . . . one fine day!' And Matt lived for that day.

Sean Connors thought less and less about Matt Riordan with the passing of time. Why should he? – Riordan was in the past, it was the present which consumed Sean, every exciting moment of it.

He would have claimed to know Dublin well before he had started as a reporter, but after twelve months pounding the streets for the *Gazette* he *really* knew the city – and the people. It was impossible to walk fifty yards without being hailed by someone he knew – whether Old Seamus pushing his barrow, or one of Dev's Ministers. Of course his job helped him become well known, and being the only son of Pat Connors did him no harm – but those were not the only reasons. His size made him stand out, six foot tall and still growing; broad-shouldered, slim-hipped – and his looks helped. Maeve O'Flynn was not the only girl attracted by Sean's thick black hair and deep blue eyes. But mostly people liked his manner and his way of getting things done.

Word soon spread that he was looking for a shop, though very few people knew he was acting for Maeve O'Flynn, for the simple reason that Sean kept that information to himself. He planned to tell the world when he was ready.

Meanwhile he had taken to meeting people in Bewley's Café in Westmoreland Street, partly because it was convenient to talk over a cup of coffee, and partly to gauge the takings. Bewley's was *the* place. If the Widow O'Flynn was to succeed she would have to outshine Bewley's. So Sean watched and counted, and in fact it was in Bewley's that he first met Jim Tully, the financier. Tully had been in the IRA in the old days, along with Pat Connors, and although the link had never been strong it was enough to interest Tully in meeting Pat's son – especially when Sean's enquiries for a shop reached Tully's ears.

Sean had never met a better dressed man. Tully was about forty-five, his dark hair still glossy, his eyes keen and a smile always at the edge of his lips. He joked all the time and flattered outrageously – so much so that the corner booth at which they were seated soon became the focus of curious eyes. Not that Tully worried about that – instead he paused occasionally to turn in his seat and bow slightly, as if acknowledging silent applause. But his voice fell to a confidential whisper when it was time to talk business. 'Now about this shop,' he said. 'They tell me you plan to buy the town, lock, stock and barrel.'

Sean grinned, 'And they tell me you've already bought it.'

Tully's delighted roar threatened to bring the roof down. Sean laughed too. Talking to Tully was like being warmed by a fire. But the fire had burned others, or so Sean had been told. Tully's big plunge into property had been in the twenties. Until then many of Dublin's businesses and grand houses had been owned by Protestants, some of whom were sorely troubled by the sectarianism preached by Catholic politicians. Tully had played on their fears. 'Who knows what will happen? The way Austin Stack talks you'll be needing the blessing of the Pope himself just to own a brick wall.' Many Protestants had sold up there and then. Most who remained withdrew from public life and quietly minded their own business. Meanwhile Jim Tully acquired some fine freeholds . . . at very advantageous prices. How much his reputation as a former IRA gunman influenced negotiations was something people speculated about – and those who did hinted at a far darker side to Tully's character than the one being displayed in Bewley's Café.

'Now weren't they right about you,' Tully beamed across the table. '"Jim", they said, "leave that young Sean Connors alone. He's too smart for you, he'll have the best of a deal in no time at all."'

Sean doubted that, but he was flattered and since two of Tully's sites sounded promising, they arranged to meet again the following week. That dealt with, Sean left Bewley's to hurry to his next appointment, and in the rush of the day forgot all about Jim Tully.

The *Gazette* office buzzed with the usual hum of activity when Sean returned at five o'clock. He started work immediately on the one good story he had dragged from the day, and had almost finished when he received an unexpected summons to go to the editor's office.

Dinny Macaffety stood with his back to the room, staring down into the street. He held a whiskey in one hand and a cigarette in the other. He was in shirt sleeves as usual, but his shoulders were slumped uncharacteristically. 'Lord Bowley is dead,' he said without turning round. 'You hear that, young Connors? Lord Bowley is dead, God rest his immortal soul.'

Sean had never met Lord Bowley, but he knew who he was. Lord Bowley was the proprietor of the *Gazette* – or at least *had been* – lock, stock and barrel as Jim Tully would say. Not that he played any part in running the paper, living in Africa as he did. He had gone there years before – on a visit at first – then he had returned and sold up: the big house at Dalkey, twelve thousand acres of land, thirty miles of coastline, everything – everything except the *Gazette*. 'I know I'm a sentimental old fool,' he had told Macaffety, 'but the *Gazette* is part of history, and a man shouldn't sell history.' He had rambled on about the opportunities in Africa until Dinny Macaffety had sweated out the question 'What happens to the *Gazette*, sir?' Lord Bowley had been startled. 'Why, didn't I say? You run it, Dinny. God knows you've been doing that for years anyway – me being away won't make a ha'p'orth of difference.'

So to all intents and purposes the *Gazette* had become

Dinny Macaffety's paper. A new book-keeper had been appointed, a local solicitor joined the board – a copy of the paper was posted to Lord Bowley each evening, a modest dividend went his way every twelve months – but Lord Bowley had not inspected his one remaining investment in Ireland for ten years. He was happy in his new life and so was his son, who had long since confirmed to Macaffety that the arrangements would stand in the unhappy event of anything happening to his father. Now the unhappiest event of all had occurred . . . Lord Bowley was dead.

'I'm very sorry to hear that, Mr Macaffety,' Sean said. 'The Da said he was a fine man, and I know you thought the same.'

'And his son,' Macaffety whispered to the window-pane, 'his son is dead too. They were both killed in a train crash.'

Sean felt uncomfortable. He couldn't really share Macaffety's grief. Lord Bowley was just a name to him, a portrait in the boardroom, a photograph in the back issues. But he hated to see Macaffety like this. Macaffety the raging tyrant was someone he had learned to cope with . . . even to like . . . but this . . .

'The paper's finished,' Macaffety said mournfully. 'Bloody well done for. It will never be the same again.' The last words slurred together – 'neverbethesameagain'. Suddenly Sean realized the significance of Macaffety's earlier comments – *His son is dead too*. So who owns the *Gazette* now, Sean wondered? Macaffety turned and slumped back into his chair. His red face was more flushed than usual, making the pouches beneath his eyes swollen and bruised. Pain and anger marked his expression. He fumbled through the papers on his desk until he found what he was looking for. 'Some damn lawyer in Nairobi,' he muttered, then read aloud. 'As Lord Bowley's only son and heir died with him in this tragic accident, the entire estate now passes to his Lordship's cousin, Lord Averdale in Ulster. Naturally he has been informed of this bequest and we are awaiting instructions. However, knowing of your long and happy association with Lord Bowley, we felt it our duty . . .' Macaffety snorted and crumpled the letter into a ball. He looked directly at Sean for the first time. 'It's all over, sonny. A new broom will sweep the *Gazette*, and some of us will be swept straight out of the door.'

Sean shifted his weight on to his other leg and remained silent.

'You'll convey my apologies to your father,' Macaffety said, tossing the rolled-up letter into a wastepaper basket. 'There was no way I could foresee something like this.'

Sean's expression must have betrayed bewilderment because Macaffety barked – 'My God, you don't know what I'm talking about, do you? And you're a smart young reporter, supposed to know everything happening in Ireland. You've not even heard of Lord Averdale, I suppose?'

'No, Mr Macaffety.'

'God help us,' Macaffety swallowed a mouthful of whiskey, then sucked his lips. 'You'll have gathered he's a Prod, I suppose, a real dyed-in-the-wool Orangeman. He'll be another like Lord Brooke, wouldn't employ a Catholic to save his life. I tell you, within a month this paper will be so Unionist that the *Times* will look like a radical broadsheet. We'll be preaching the gospel according to Westminster again. How does that prospect strike you?'

Sean tried to answer but Macaffety overrode him. 'We're out,' he said, pointing a finger. 'I'm out because of fifteen years of editorials complaining about the British in Ireland. And you're out for being your father's son. Averdale will have his own people in here. He'll not want young Jackeens from the Quays. He'll want educated young Prods straight out of Trinity. We'll have the Protestant Ascendancy all over again.'

Sean finally found his voice, 'Am I being fired, Mr Macaffety?'

Macaffety threw his hands in the air. 'I'm telling you what to expect, that's all. Ask your Da, he'll tell you the same. If you've the sense I think you have you'll look around and see what else you can find. Understand?'

Sean heard, which wasn't quite the same as understanding. His dismay deepened. Life at the *Gazette* was all he could imagine, all he *wanted* – especially now everything was so settled. He enjoyed living in Ballsbridge, he enjoyed the Widow O'Flynn, and looked forward to seeing her more often when she got her tea-rooms. Now to be told it was all over . . .

'Send Pat Andrews up, will you?' Macaffety said, by way of dismissal.

Sean turned blindly for the door. It's so unfair, he thought bitterly. Then he pushed the self-pity aside. After all, it was the way of the world. A man without assets was like a cork on the sea, swept one way, then another. I must get some assets, he vowed. Then I can be my own man, free of all others. But Sean's determination was touched with envy. Some people were born lucky, he thought. Imagine inheriting a newspaper! This Lord Averdale was probably rich already. Assets go to assets, Sean mourned, the rich get richer. He returned to his desk and sat deep in thought – but in particular he wondered what manner of man Lord Averdale might be.

Lord Averdale was a proud man, and with good reason – the history of his family was largely that of Ulster, and, as Lord Averdale frequently asserted, no man could have a more illustrious history than that. The Averdale record stood for itself and anyone with the temerity to question it was likely to hear a recital of events from 1610 onwards from his Lordship himself.

Sixteen ten when the first Averdale set foot in Ireland. Damn all happened before that – just a lot of Irish chieftains beating hell out of each other. That's how the Plantation came into being – it was the only way to bring peace to the place. The Plantation was a high-risk business though, which is why the City of London became involved. Hard-headed businessmen were needed to settle a place like Ulster. So City businessmen formed the Honourable Irish Society of 1610 and took on the job of civilizing Derry. First thing they did was to change the name to Londonderry – then they divided the land between themselves and sold it off to Scottish and English settlers – not to the Irish of course, who had no money, besides that shiftless lot caused the mess in the first place. The Crown kept ten per cent of the land – rough hillsides for the most part – and rented that out to the Irish, who had no choice but to take it.

More than 13,000 settlers came in after 1610. They faced

159

a hard life – not just to establish decent farms, though that was hard enough, but in keeping the Irish at bay. Catholic Gaelic mobs slaughtered thousands of innocent Protestant settlers in 1641. Samuel Averdale's own wife was dragged from her bed and murdered hideously, and so were dozens of her friends in a year of terror which only ended when Cromwell brought his army over to restore order. But no Protestant ever forgot what happened in 1641 – no more than they would forget what happened in Londonderry forty years later, when the Catholics rose again.

James III was King of England then – a *Catholic* King replacing a *Protestant* Protector. Not that James ruled for long. In 1688 came news of revolution in England – the *Protestant* William of Orange was winning his fight for the throne. But the situation in Londonderry was already critical by then, as Gaelic Catholics ran riot – and tension increased tenfold when King James sent Lord Antrim's Redshanks, a *Catholic* regiment, to garrison the city. The people of Londonderry were appalled – already surrounded by hostile Catholics, now the King sent more of the Papist devils! But the King was the King, and had to be obeyed. So with fear in their hearts, the Protestant citizens of Londonderry resigned themselves to complying with the King's wishes, when suddenly the unexpected happened. A gang of thirteen apprentice boys seized the keys of the city and slammed the gates on Lord Antrim's Redshanks. The siege of Londonderry was about to begin – a siege which intensified some months later when King James himself arrived at the gates and was refused entrance. William of Orange sent troops to relieve the city, but his ships arrived at the mouth of the Foyle to find that the besieging army had blocked the river with a wooden boom. The ships could proceed no further. Loaded with desperately needed supplies, heartbreakingly close to the city walls they anchored and waited.

Inside the city, 30,000 Protestants were starving to death. Dogs, cats, mice, even candles became a familiar diet – until supplies even of those ran out. Deaths mounted, sickness spread, and with it fear of the plague. Antrim's besieging army delivered their terms for ending the siege – and received the famous reply – 'No Surrender!'

160

defiant words which live forever in the hearts of all Irishmen – Protestant and Catholic alike.

More ships arrived from William of Orange – but the boom across the river held. The situation within the city grew ever more desperate – until, on 28 July 1689, the ships ran the gauntlet. Defying the massed batteries of the besieging army's shore-mounted guns, the ships sailed for Londonderry. They smashed the boom. Shore batteries blazed furiously, but the ships sailed on, replying with cannon and musket from every plank above the water-line. The shore batteries roared again and again. Still the ships came on, staggering when hit, some ablaze from stem to stern, but still afloat – until they reached the quay below the city. The siege of Londonderry was over at last.

Samuel Averdale died that night. For him the rescue came too late. He starved to death, dying with cheers ringing in his ears, clasped in the arms of his eldest son, Hugh. Ulster had claimed the second of its Averdales.

The raising of the siege led to the eventual defeat of King James in Ireland. Landing at Carrickfergus the following year, William of Orange won a huge victory at the Battle of the Boyne, then routed the remaining Catholic forces at Aughrim. The triumph of Protestant over Catholic was complete. Orange conquered Green and never forgot it.

CHAPTER NINE

'Aye, Dinny's right if you ask me,' Pat Connors said when he heard about Lord Averdale. 'The *Gazette* will never be the same.'

Sean wanted to ask for advice. To be out of work now, just when everything was going so well! But to ask for advice, even from his father, was against the rules.

He worked harder than ever at the *Gazette*, treasuring every moment, fearful it might be the last. He tried to ignore the atmosphere – the whole place had changed. The spark had gone from Dinny Macaffety. Once the very air had been charged with Macaffety's determination to run the best paper in Ireland – now the door to the editor's office remained closed, and the man behind it sat in resigned apathy.

News of the paper's change of ownership was all over Dublin, spread further after the memorial service held for Lord Bowley and his son. Even the Widow O'Flynn spoke about it – 'They say the new owner is a Protestant, connected with the government in the north. They say he'll make changes.'

Sean feigned indifference. It was a technique he was practising. If something troubled him he refused to talk about it. It could worry him sick but there was no point in discussing it if the rules forbade him to ask advice. It was a hard trick when he was so worried, but one he was determined to master.

'Sure now,' Maeve O'Flynn continued, 'most people are worried to death. Most people who work at the *Gazette* I mean.'

'People worry too much,' he answered.

She smiled, seeing through his act but thinking no less of him for that. Indeed she was pleased, awarding herself at least some of the credit for his growing self-confidence.

'Sure you're a cool one,' she said. 'Sometimes I think there's ice in your veins.'

Hardly that, he thought, watching her across the kitchen table. Her beauty still captivated him. They had been discussing some premises owned by Jim Tully and even now the excitement showed on her flushed cheeks. He watched her play with the top button of her dress, a teasing signal that she was ready for bed. He remembered the first time she had opened her blouse and drawn his hands on to her breasts – remembered the shock of excitement, the sensual arousal, and his fear of the unknown. But he knew now – and the knowing made her even more exciting.

Maeve O'Flynn's nimble fingers undid the buttons of her bodice. There was no hurry, the night lay before them, a delicious banquet to be savoured. She rose and crossed the room to sit on his lap, arranging herself carefully to avoid his thrusting hardness. His hand moved under the fabric to cup a breast. God, she had waited all day for that . . . all week really . . . to be held, fondled, stroked.

162

They adjourned to bed, him carrying her from the kitchen as easily as she might have lifted a pillow. And at five o'clock he left her, dressing himself in the dark before turning to kiss her goodbye. She would sleep late, whereas he would yawn his way down from the barn loft to greet the labourers in an hour's time.

It was cold in the barn – too cold to sleep. Sean shivered and wrapped a blanket over his shoulders. His mind drifted pleasurably back over the night, but as dawn broke his thoughts turned to the new day – bringing a reminder that some of yesterday's worries remained unresolved. He was no nearer to Tomas's five hundred pounds, and Tomas slumped deeper into despondent old age every week. Tomas would die soon, poor devil, simply fade away before Sean could repay his debt of gratitude. Sean cursed his luck. If only he had some assets. Then he could send Tomas and the family to Australia. Assets were the key to everything. Given assets he wouldn't worry about his future at the *Gazette*. Given assets . . . Jaysus, he thought angrily, hadn't that actually happened to this Lord Averdale – he *had* been given assets. 'I should have been born a Lord,' Sean said aloud to the empty barn. He wondered what it was like, to be pampered by servants, to have every whim obeyed, to live in a huge house in Ulster. Sean had never been to Ulster, not even to Belfast. Suddenly he shuddered. The cold, he told himself – but it was a lie. Belfast reminded him of Matt Riordan. The thin white face leapt out of the darkness. Instinctively Sean raised his hand to wipe the imagined spittle from his cheek. He shuddered again. He generally did when he thought of Matt Riordan.

Matt Riordan's life had taken on new meaning. A succession of events had led him to reach certain conclusions. What astounded him was his previous ignorance. He was appalled at the time he had wasted. He grew angry with his past foolishness. But the past was over, and now Matt's life had a purpose.

He had been born at the beginning of the Anglo-Irish war, but despite two uncles killed by the British and his father's long absences from home, the drama of the

163

struggle had never registered with Matt. He had been his mother's baby and then a mother's boy. She had devoted her life to him . . . easily done with his father away so often, first fighting the British, then the Free Staters. Matt had grown up without him, not missing him, in fact the opposite – he had resented his father's homecomings because they absorbed his mother's time. Only when he left did she relax and put things to rights – with Matt at the centre of her life and her performing her proper function, which was to dance attendance on him from dawn to dusk and beyond if it suited him.

All of which had lasted until Matt was twelve. His father began to spend more time at home then. That was when the rows started – vicious arguments between his father and mother which ended with his father thrashing her to within an inch of her life – or so it seemed to Matt as he listened to her screams and rushed to her aid – then it was his turn to take a beating. His father had taken a belt and leathered Matt so badly that he was laid up for a week. Time and again after that Matt pitted his puny strength against that of his father. Matt was mauled badly every time – until eventually he learned to cover his ears when his parents quarrelled rather than face another whipping. That was how Matt learned to hate. The ability to hate is like any other, it can be developed with practice . . . and Matt got plenty of practice early in life.

It had been a hard time for Matt. He had avoided his father as much as possible, detesting his coarse ways and the dominant air. Men in the pub were watchful of Liam Riordan. Of course Matt knew why – the reasons were bound up with the IRA. His father had fought the British and then the Staters in the Civil War, his father held rank and led men into battle, his father had been a commander of brilliance, according to some. But nothing associated with his father found favour in Matt's eyes. To him his father's past was a source of secret contempt, and in the same way that Matt scorned his father he scorned the IRA.

He knew that his parents' quarrels were mostly about him. His mother wanted him to be a doctor – his father said the boy was to work in the family business. Of course his father's wishes prevailed. They had opened the butcher's shop by then, and Matt was to be an apprentice butcher. The matter was decided, all arguments ceased.

To begin with Matt was revolted at the prospect of handling animal carcases for the rest of his life, but after a while that ceased to have importance, far outweighed by the rest of the job, which mainly consisted of serving in the shop. Matt enjoyed that. He enjoyed meeting people – women mostly – and exchanging a joke from behind the counter. Perhaps them being women helped, after all Matt's childhood had not given him much experience of men. Not that there was anything sexual about it, Matt saw them as customers first and women a long way second, but he relaxed and related to them in a way that they liked. Certainly they were always pleased to have a crack with him as he chopped up their orders. Matt became popular. He forgot his mother's ambitions and concentrated instead on becoming the best butcher in Dublin. The shop gave good value and business improved, a fact which did not escape Liam Riordan's notice.

Then one of the barmen fell ill and Matt took a turn in the pub. There too he was a success. Customers found Matt a sight less intimidating than his father. A man never felt the need to prove himself with Matt, whereas with his Da . . . So the bar takings rose steadily, another fact which did not go unnoticed by Liam Riordan.

Gradually the relationship changed between father and son. They were not friends, but at least they ceased to fight. The atmosphere improved in the home, with less to argue about. Matt's mother ran the drapery and when not engaged there she took to sketching local scenes around Dublin. People laughed at first – as she hurried back from mass on a Sunday to take a stool and sketchbook down to the canal. But some of her work was quite good, good enough anyway for people to pay modest sums for . . . which was another thing noticed by Liam Riordan.

He was a strange man, even his friends admitted that. 'Made of granite,' they said. Liam Riordan could no more settle to a life of business than he could swim the Irish Channel. Making money, despite his natural aptitude for it, was a poor substitute for the thrill of fighting for Ireland, or perhaps even *dying* for Ireland. Unlike his son, the lives of individuals were of no interest to Liam Riordan, it was the future of 'the people' which mattered. 'The people' should be free of British tyranny. 'The people' should be free of those Prod bastards in the north. So every once in a while Liam Riordan went missing on IRA business. It was the way he was, always had been and always would be.

Matt stayed out of it. His contempt for the IRA never faltered. He made his own plans for the future – one day he would inherit his father's businesses and expand from there, first into another butcher's shop, then into a whole string of them.

But then the future vanished. Tomorrow's life was destroyed, wiped out – Pat Connors murdered it. Pat Connors and that son of his!

And so to Belfast and a succession of shocks. First the kicking handed out by the B Specials, then the fruitless search for work and the degrading misery of rejection. He hated his life . . . watching his mother wither into an old woman . . . forever cursing his father's failure to exact revenge on Pat Connors. Matt's cup of bitterness overflowed. The grinding poverty of the Falls registered only as background to his despair. Belfast was a black hole from which he must escape. But escape how? Without money, without help – escape was impossible. That conclusion numbed him for weeks. It was Belfast or death, and though one seemed as bad as the other at times, Matt chose Belfast. It was his first step to recovery.

After that people helped. Little by little friendships began to matter. Matt cared nothing for 'the people', that great abstract of his father's, but he was affected by the sufferings around him. It upset him to see pinched-faced kids growing up with rickets. It was a worry to hear men talk of thieving as the only way they could provide for their families. He was outraged when a neighbour's boy was so badly beaten by a gang of Prods that the poor child was crippled for life. Slowly Matt became part of the community and felt better for becoming so – listening to other people's troubles eased his own bitterness. And just as Dublin housewives had once warmed to him in the butcher's shop, so did the women of the Falls Road . . . and so too did the men. Matt Riordan was a sympathetic listener. People began to respect his opinions. Yet he was nothing to look at. Of average height, thin and wiry, stronger than he looked but that wasn't saying much . . . hair a mousey brown . . . dark grey eyes. But he liked people and it showed.

It was therefore inevitable that Matt's latent talent for leadership attracted the attention of the IRA . . . and in particular that of Ferdy Malloy, since it was Ferdy who called every week with money sent from Matt's father. At least that was how the payments were described – in fact the money was not *sent* at all, Liam Riordan had merely arranged for sums to be delivered to his wife at regular intervals – but it appealed to Ferdy's romantic nature to pretend that although Liam Riordan was far from home his thoughts were forever with his loved ones. Matt and his mother knew better.

Ferdy Malloy took some getting used to. Matt was dismissive at first, seeing merely the caricature which Malloy presented to the world – a man who had lost the use of one eye, dressed in an old flannel suit under an oversized raincoat, dragging his left leg in a limp. Ferdy's disabilities should have made him conspicuous but the extraordinary thing was that he seemed to materialize out of thin air. One moment a man was alone, then Ferdy was beside him. Only afterwards could the faint shuffling sound of the limp be remembered, and afterwards was too late for some men to remember anything.

Ferdy had sensed Matt's dislike and been intrigued to discover its reasons – after all Matt might have starved but for the money Ferdy delivered. There had to be a reason, Ferdy said to himself, and set out to find it. His first surprise came when he mentioned the IRA. Matt's face clenched like a fist . . . which intrigued Ferdy all the more. Why does the boy react like that, when his own father is revered as an IRA hero? So Ferdy probed. Not that it sounded like an inquisition, Ferdy was too skilful for that. He rarely even asked a question. Instead he developed a habit of bringing tit-bits of news whenever he called, so that after a while he became the fount of much knowledge. He even encouraged questions for which he had no immediate answer – 'Sure won't I have to find out about that,' he

167

would say, 'I'll have the answer next time I'm here.' And he did. Ferdy never hurried and was endlessly patient – why not, he thought wryly, sure I'm not going anywhere . . . and neither is Matt Riordan.

Such then was Matt's indoctrination, though it was months before it became obvious. Mostly he and Ferdy talked of current conditions in Belfast, or of England where Ferdy had lived for a number of years, or even of faraway places like Russia and America . . . which was how Matt learned of the international dimensions of the IRA . . .

'Take Russia for instance,' Ferdy said airily. 'Joe Stalin received a delegation from the IRA in 1925. Pa Murray and Sean Russell went over and met Stalin himself. We got some guns but only a few, Pat Murray reckoned they didn't have any to spare, but they made a lot of excuses to avoid saying so.'

Most of the guns came from America, and the extent of Irish influence in the United States astonished Matt. 'And why not?' Ferdy demanded. 'Sure the place is half Irish, didn't you know that? You'll never guess the number of Irishmen over there. Come on now, have a guess.' And when Matt suggested a figure Ferdy clapped his hands in triumph. 'You're wrong by a mile. You'll be amazed when I tell you. Twenty million. There are *twenty million* living Americans with Irish blood in their veins. There now, and what do you think about that?'

Ferdy went on – 'There are Irish Societies all across the States, and don't they hate the British as much as we do. More in some cases. But they get a bit muddled at times, what with them being so far away an' all – so we have to send someone over to straighten them out.'

Then came a revelation. Ferdy gave a sly grin, 'That's where your Da is now, did you know that? Over in America getting us more guns and ammunition.'

So *that* was the important mission. Matt remembered the quietly spoken man that morning. 'You should be proud of your father,' he had said. Well Matt was not proud – Matt found the whole thing contemptible. Wasn't that typical, him rushing off to America, talking about 'the people' while his own wife and son suffered in Belfast. Pat Connors was the bloody enemy, not the British. But Matt stifled his rage and encouraged Ferdy to talk more about America.

Matt learned a lot that day – for instance that Eamon de Valera himself had been born in the United States. 'Didn't you know that? That's what saved his life after the Easter Rising. The British would have shot him along with Connolly and Pearse and the others. The Clann saved him. They got a copy of Dev's baptismal certificate from St Agnes Church in New York and took it to President Wilson himself, and the President got on to his Ambassador in London to tell the British to back off.' Ferdy nodded knowledgeably. 'The Clann saved Dev's life – reckon he should remember that now and then.'

The Clann was the Clann na Gael of course, even Matt knew that . . . the most powerful group of Irishmen outside, or perhaps even inside, Ireland. The Clann had collected millions of dollars in 1920 for the Irish Victory Fund. The Clann had smuggled arms and money into Ireland for generations. But the Clann had been confused by the Treaty of 1920. Americans had switched off then, believing that the establishing of the Irish Free State had solved the Irish problem. 'That's why your Da is there now,' Ferdy said cheerfully, 'telling them about these bastard Prods. Your Da will make them see sense, don't you worry.'

When Matt seemed reluctant to discuss his father, Ferdy pursued the matter. 'You maybe don't understand your Da. I've known him for years and he's a great man, believe me.'

Matt snapped that there was nothing great about a man who sailed off to America without looking after his wife. Ferdy shook his head. 'Ach, it's a different set of priorities your Da has. It puts me in mind of when he organized the hunger strike in Mountjoy. Did you ever hear about that?'

Matt shook his head and Ferdy told him the story. 'We got taken by the British in 1920, beginning of April it was. Anyway a whole lot of us get bundled into Mountjoy jail, me included, slammed into a cell, frightened out of my wits. Next morning the cells get opened up and we found ourselves in the exercise ring. Just down from the north I was, an' green as a cabbage. Then a man lines us up and gives us a speech. We're prisoners of war, says he, and

169

should be treated as such but the governor won't have it – so we're going on hunger strike, the whole lot of us. Well that was the start of it, but this man was fair and proper – he says we should each consider the consequences and anyone can back out without it being held against him.' Ferdy paused to shake his head. 'I was scared stiff. I wondered how long I could hold out on a hunger strike. Maybe everyone wondered the same – but this man had a way with him. I tell you he was like a superman, strong, commanding – you felt he could do anything. We were mesmerized. So of course nobody backs out and the hunger strike starts.'

Matt guessed that the man was his father but said nothing to interrupt.

'I was hungry enough to eat old boots,' Ferdy remembered. 'Every meal I ever had came back to haunt me. But after about four days I stopped thinking about food, or at least stopped thinking so much. Every now and then someone down the block would start singing. "The West's Awake" or "The Felons of our Land", songs like that, and we'd all join in to keep our spirits up. The warders weren't bad either – they told us thousands of people had gathered outside the gates, all saying the rosary for our welfare – an' there was talk of a nationwide strike, and then rumours started flying around that we might be released. Well that cheered us up and kept us going, and after ten days the miracle happened – the British gave in. We were all taken off to the Mater Hospital, driven through crowds of people all jumping for joy – and when we got there the doctors and nurses and nuns all showered us with gifts and greetings and . . .' Ferdy broke off in his excitement, 'I remember now – there was even a bishop – that was the first time I kissed an episcopal ring. Anyway the hospital was all decked out with flowers, and we had a special breakfast of porridge and fruit, and two days after that the British released the lot of us. A hundred men, the biggest hunger strike in history. There, what do you think of that?'

But before Matt could answer Ferdy hurried on with the rest of the story. 'I didn't find out till after, but the British in Dublin Castle got so worried about the General Strike and the thousands outside the prison, that they had offered concessions earlier on. They had even offered political status. But your Da turned them down flat. Said it was too late. He'd got them going by then, so he said he'd settle for nothing less than the release of all prisoners. So he got us all out. Is it any wonder I say he's a great man?'

Slowly and carefully, Ferdy Malloy built a bridge between father and son. It was months before Matt realized what was happening, and by then other forces were at work. Belfast itself, as much as Ferdy's sly words, drove Matt into the arms of the IRA. Every day Matt saw examples of discrimination which made his blood boil. Every night a neighbour delivered another tale of woe. And every week friends had their homes smashed by ruthless squads of B Specials in their ceaseless hunt for hidden arms. Yet Matt's earlier hatred of his father was so strong that he refused to believe his father's way could be right . . . or at least that was the way of things until Matt got a job – and that changed everything.

Finding work had been a miracle. A big engineering company opened a small factory about three miles away from its main works, and a hundred men were taken on as labourers. Matt rushed back to his grandmother's house with news of his job, delirious with excitement. The pay was meagre, four pounds four shillings for a forty-four-hour week – but there was talk of overtime so Matt would end up with more than that. And even four pounds four shillings meant money in Matt's pocket – *his* money, which came neither from his father nor the IRA. After three years in the north Matt had something to celebrate at last! He could hardly believe his luck. A job, a wonderful, marvellous job. He barely slept that night for excitement. As it was he was up before six, washed and dressed, with a small packet of sandwiches in his pocket, ready to go.

He was outside the factory at seven-thirty, and inside half an hour later, with the factory hooter still buzzing in his ears. He worked like a Trojan. No matter what he was asked to lift, he lifted it – whatever he was told to carry, he carried. It was heavy, monotonous work and the English foreman was a slave driver, but Matt sweated and groaned cheerfully through the day. He returned to the little house in the Falls exhausted that night – exhausted but triumphant. The neighbours gathered to greet him, as delighted as he was – if Matt can find work, they seemed to say, there's hope for the rest of us.

The next day was harder. Matt's muscles had recovered little of their strength. His whole body ached. But he gritted his teeth and some of the stiffness eased as the day wore on. I'll get used to it, he told himself, just give me time and a better diet maybe. When the day ended he slumped back to the Falls and went directly to bed, too exhausted to tell his friends about his day at the factory.

His third day went easier. He paced himself, conserving energy, resting now and then, but getting through his work to the satisfaction of the foreman, which was all that mattered. And Friday started well. Matt woke refreshed – when he stretched he felt the elasticity back in his muscles – the soreness was less painful. He hurried to the factory, where the day passed without incident – except for one curious thing. Half way through the afternoon the foreman paused for a word. 'You're to go to the office when the whistle blows. Okay? Don't forget now, there's a good lad.'

The foreman was a tough Yorkshireman whose accent was sometimes too thick for Matt to understand. He ran after him – 'The office? Me, why – what's it about?'

The man shrugged and took a step away.

'My work is all right, isn't it?' Matt asked anxiously.

'Aye lad, there's nowt wrong with your work,' said the man as he hurried away.

Matt worried for the rest of the afternoon. What could the office want? At six o'clock he went to find out. He was not alone, about twenty men gathered in the corridor, each with a worried frown on his face. Someone knocked on the door and was told to wait. Several men lit cigarettes, while others nervously watched the clock over the door. At ten past six a man came out. Matt had never seen him before – a burly man with untidy black hair, wearing a crumpled but obviously expensive grey suit. 'My name is O'Brien,' he announced, 'I'm Lord Averdale's General Manager.'

Lord Averdale owned the factory, Matt had heard mention of that.

'There's been a bit of a mistake,' O'Brien said briskly, 'I'm sorry but these things happen with a new factory and inexperienced staff. The truth is there's no work for you men here.'

Several men started talking at once. O'Brien waved them down – 'I said I'm sorry, that's an end to it. You'll not lose out though, you'll all be paid for a full week, even though you're finishing tonight . . .'

Matt missed the rest of his words. A mistake? The foreman had vouched for his work. How could there be a *mistake*?

The office doors were fully opened now. Matt saw other men behind a trestle table. Names were called, and men filed forward to collect their wages. Two workmen became angry and started to abuse O'Brien. Quickly half a dozen men moved from behind the table and hurried the protesting workmen down the corridor. Money appeared in Matt's hand. He counted it, then he too felt a hand on his elbow as he was steered towards the exit.

'Hey you,' one of the dismissed workmen grabbed his arm. 'You're Liam Riordan's son, aren't you?'

Matt stared into the man's face without seeing him. Regular work, that's what he thought he had got, regular work. Now he was finished – after four days.

'Listen to me,' said the man shaking Matt's shoulders. 'What's wrong with you anyway? Are you Riordan or aren't you?'

'Yes,' Matt admitted blankly, 'I'm Riordan.'

'By Christ you're a poor bloody swap for your old man. Where is he? Where's Liam Riordan? We need his kind for this.'

Half a dozen of the dismissed men crowded round, all talking at once.

'That bastard Averdale,' someone said. 'You bet it was a mistake. The mistake was letting that English foreman take us on . . . Averdale's usual Orange bastards would have known better. Down Croppies down! That's all they understand.'

'What do you mean?' Matt asked, coming out of his daze.

'What do you think? It's bloody obvious. You heard O'Brien going on about inexperienced staff. That foreman's only been in Belfast two weeks. Not long enough to tell a Prod from a – '

'He knows now. He'll not make that mistake again –'

'Not and work for that bastard Averdale –'

'O'Brien's as bad. O'Brien's worse if you ask me.'

Suddenly Matt knew it was true. Every one of the Catholics had been sacked. He felt sick as he listened to the angry talk. There *was* work. Regular work. New men would be taken on in the morning – but none would be Catholics.

'There must be something . . .' he began helplessly, only to be interrupted by a shout from the factory steps. O'Brien was shouting at them – 'Get out of the gates. Away to your homes now – I'll not have a disturbance.'

A disturbance? They had only been talking. They stood a few yards inside the factory gates, a small group of nine men, just talking – and here was O'Brien bawling about a disturbance!

'Away with you,' O'Brien bellowed. 'If you're not away this minute, I'll throw you out.'

They might have gone but for that. Two of the men had already turned towards the gates. But O'Brien's words infuriated them. They were all sick with disappointment, and tired after a hard day's work. Most were married and faced the heartache of hungry wives and children when they reached home. Frustration boiled into anger. The man next to Matt growled like a dog, low in his throat. Others swung round – then someone stepped forward and before they knew it they were all walking back to the factory. 'Come on then, O'Brien,' someone shouted. 'Throw me out if you can.'

'Get back,' O'Brien roared, 'get out of this yard.'

Suddenly the doors behind O'Brien burst open and other men appeared – too many for Matt to count and moving in a rush. Down the steps they charged, shouting and yelling, clubs and staves held high above their heads. Matt sensed men scatter on either side. Boots clattered on the cobbles as they raced back to the gates. Matt ran too – but surprise rooted him to the spot for a split second. Besides he had to turn – the men on the steps were already running full pelt. They caught him within twenty yards. Most of the dismissed men were caught within thirty yards. None reached the gates.

Matt and the rest fought – but they were outnumbered and fists and boots were no match for clubs. Matt threw one man off, before a wooden stave split his head open. His knees buckled and he dropped like a sack of potatoes.

They kicked him for an hour – or so it seemed. Matt never knew how many men did it. It felt like hundreds. Once, above the cries and screams around him, he heard O'Brien bellowing, 'That's enough – get them through the gates.' Matt *thought* he heard that, before he lost consciousness.

Running water revived him – a thin trickle of water. He opened his eyes to find himself face down in the gutter. Water was running into the drain. It was raining. He could hear voices, women's voices, men groaning, a woman weeping. It was dark, night-time, he had no idea of the hour. A street lamp cast a dim light. He tried to move but a sharp pain made him cry out. Then hands moved gently on his shoulders, turning him to slide something under his head as a pillow. He felt desperately tired. He closed his eyes.

The next he knew he was being carried over a threshold into a house. He heard a woman say, 'For God's sake go easy on him.' She sounded close to tears, but when he saw her she was nobody he knew – a total stranger. His head hurt, so did everything else – but his head hurt the worst. They lowered him on to the floor in front of a fire. He shivered then – he had not shivered outside in the rain, but he couldn't stop once he was in front of that fire. The woman wrapped him in a blanket. A man groaned elsewhere in the room. Matt closed his eyes and tried to stop trembling. Then he dozed off again.

When he roused himself he was propped against the wall. The same blanket covered his shoulders. A man squatted down to speak to him – 'You've come back to us then. That's the spirit. Try not to move, I've just sewn your head back together.'

The doctor spent half an hour with him. Matt caught phrases like 'two cracked ribs – fractured ankle – dislocated wrist – bloody miracle he's still alive'. He saw the woman again, the one who had helped to bring him in. She was sitting on the floor, holding a cup to a man's lips. The man's hands were bulky with bandages. He caught Matt staring and managed a cheerful wink. Another man lay in front of the fire, propped on one elbow, smoking a cigarette. He looked quite normal apart from the bandages around his head.

'Try not to move,' the doctor was saying, 'I'll be back in a minute.'

The woman rose as the doctor crossed the room. She pointed to Matt. The doctor nodded and hurried away. The woman smiled and brought Matt some tea. 'I've no sugar, I'm afraid, but it's hot and strong if you'd like some.'

Matt sipped a mouthful and accepted a cigarette. One drag made his head spin. He handed it back. 'I don't think I can walk,' he said. 'Would it be possible to sleep here tonight? I could pay, there's money in my pocket –'

Tears filled her eyes and she was saying something in a soft, comforting voice when Matt spied Ferdy Malloy entering the room. 'Ferdy!' Matt called, but the sound came out as a croak. Then Ferdy was limping over, dressed in his oversized raincoat as usual, anxiety etched into every line of his face. Matt felt so much better just for seeing him – seeing a familiar face. Then the woman burst into tears, thrust the cigarette into Ferdy's hand and hurried from the room.

Ferdy said – 'Eh, Matt? Upsetting the ladies – that's not like you.'

It took Ferdy a while to sit on the floor, his crippled left leg made things awkward, but he managed eventually. 'Christ,' he said, 'you look bloody awful. The doctor's coming back in a minute. Feeling rotten, eh?'

Matt tried to nod, but pain shot through his head.

Ferdy waved to a man in the corner: 'Right, Tim – I'll be over directly.'

Furniture had been pushed into bay windows, all jumbled up. Men were stretched out everywhere. Matt counted them. Four, no five of the men he had worked with. One was putting coal on the fire.

'What happened to the others?' Matt asked.

'Rinty McGuinness is next door. The bastards broke his legs. And the doctor is upstairs with O'Malley – God knows what's the matter with him.'

How odd, he thought, Ferdy knows all their names but I don't. I worked with them but the only one I got close to was Micky Nealson. Matt looked round the room but failed to find him – 'There was another lad with us,' he said to Ferdy, 'Mick Nealson. What happened to him?'

Ferdy stared with his one good eye for a long moment. 'He's dead,' he said flatly, 'Micky Nealson is dead. The bastards murdered him.'

Quite suddenly Matt was weeping. He caught a blurred glimpse of others crossing themselves, he supposed he crossed himself too – but all he really saw was Mick Nealson's face, laughing with excitement the day they were taken on.

Ferdy clambered to his feet and went over to talk to another man until Matt recovered. When he came back Matt said – 'Christ, we were only trying to work. That's all, Ferdy, I swear to God that's all we were doing.'

Ferdy nodded sadly, 'I know, I know son. Don't take on so.'

Matt could hardly speak. He was choked up at first, but when the awful injustice seeped into his mind he became angry. Shaking with temper he turned to Ferdy. 'I met a man once, with my father, the last time I saw him. I dunno who he was but he must have been important to give the Da orders. He spoke very quietly. A hard-eyed sort of man. Ferdy, you *must* know who I mean?'

Ferdy shrugged, 'Perhaps.'

'Take me to him, will you, Ferdy. As soon as I can walk. Will you take me?'

Ferdy stared with his one good eye. He searched Matt's face for a full minute. Then he said, 'Aye, I'll take you. I reckon you're ready.'

Matt Riordan was not the only one for whom the name Lord Averdale had significance – Sean Connors was also concerned, though he tried not to show it. Outwardly his career continued much as before – Sean was diligent, conscientious and hard-working. Not that Macaffety seemed to notice – he was too concerned about the *Gazette*'s change of ownership. A letter had arrived from

Lord Averdale's General Manager, a man named O'Brien. Curt and to the point, it had acknowledged the transfer of the late Lord Bowley's estate and requested copies of past balance sheets . . . and ended with the ominous note that Macaffety was to continue as before . . . for the time being.

Then came an extraordinary meeting, or rather a meeting with an extraordinary man. Sean tingled with excitement when his father mentioned that the man might visit them. Certainly there was the chance of a meeting. After all the man was coming to Dublin for informal talks with political leaders . . . which really meant Dev and a couple of ministers . . . . but *this* man had a reputation for wanting to meet all shades of opinion . . . and where better to hear the voice of Fine Gael than the small house in Ballsbridge?

Sean looked him up in the archives at the *Gazette* . . . not expecting to find much, the filed clippings were notoriously deficient on overseas dignitaries, even when – as in this case – they were United States ambassadors of Irish extraction. To his surprise Sean found a file six inches thick. He was gripped from the first page. Not just because the man was of Irish descent – other Irishmen had found fame and fortune in the United States – but because of the diversity of the man's activities. The range was breathtaking. Every page of clippings showed a different aspect . . . businessman, movie-magnate, banker, politician, diplomat . . . the list seemed endless. Here he was pictured with an actress . . . here with some New York bankers . . . there with Winston Churchill . . . there with Roosevelt . . . and over the page with Cardinal O'Connell of Boston.

Sean's imagination stalled. This man had achieved the impossible – this man who dined at the White House in Washington, at 10 Downing Street in London and who spent weekends at Windsor with the King and Queen of England. This man who had started with so little and who now was so rich.

So the imminent arrival in Dublin of the United States Ambassador to the Court of St James gave Sean much to look forward to – especially when he studied the man's record.

In the event their meeting was brief. Ambassador Joseph P. Kennedy rationed his time, but he did accept an invitation to the house in Ballsbridge – on the understanding that he brought his son Joe Jnr, and stay only for an hour.

So began Sean Connors's lifelong friendship with the Kennedy family. Not that anything took place that evening which gave any hint of what was to come. There was hardly time for Sean to be involved in sustained conversation, he never even had a chance to ask a question, though he answered a few.

'So you're the son of Pat Connors,' said the Ambassador shaking hands.

Sean tried to hide his disappointment. He had expected so much, whereas this man looked so *ordinary*. Untidily dressed in a baggy grey suit, his tie knotted clumsily, friendly blue eyes peering out from behind thick glasses.

'Yes, sir,' Sean replied nervously. 'May I welcome you to Ireland and to our home?'

'Why thank you. And I believe you're working already – as a reporter – is that right?'

'Yes, sir, with the *Dublin Gazette*.'

The Ambassador smiled broadly. 'Well I want your word on something right now, young man. Anything said tonight is off the record. Is that understood?'

Sean was accustomed to hearing confidences in his father's house and shocked at the suggestion that he would ever reveal them. But the Ambassador's friendliness removed the sting from his words, and he chuckled as he introduced his son. 'Sean, I'd like you to meet Joe Junior. He's delighted you're here because he'll have someone his age to talk to while I chunter on with the rest of the greybeards.' The Ambassador threw his head back and laughed so heartily that the others joined in. Afterwards Sean realized that the Ambassador's readiness to laugh was part of his charm – in fact Sean's most lasting memories of Joe Kennedy were of him slapping his thigh like a threshing machine while roaring with laughter. Just like Jim Tully in so many ways – except Jim dressed a lot smarter.

The gathering was quite small, at the Ambassador's request, so that just seven people sat down in the parlour that evening. Joe Junior was older than Sean, but his smile reflected his father's good humour. They greeted each other affably but said little – both too anxious to follow the conversation going on between their fathers. The talk ranged far and wide – Ireland, the border, the north, England and America. And Germany, of course, the Ambassador said quite a lot about Germany. 'There's going to be war,' he said at one stage, 'the signs get clearer every day. War in Europe, all over again, but this time . . .' he wagged a finger, 'this time nobody will drag America in – not Chamberlain, nor Hitler, nor Churchill . . . *nobody!*'

Later he gave his reasons: 'The United States seeks no territory, makes no demands, utters no threats. We just want to be left in peace to develop our land of opportunity. And I tell you this . . . opportunities *are there* . . . waiting to be grasped by men willing to work.' The fingers of one hand closed slowly into a fist. 'We don't want our young men slaughtered in another senseless European war. We want them at home, developing the country – and leaders throughout the world should want the same thing.' He brightened, then smiled broadly, 'That's why I was so pleased to hear Mr de Valera yesterday – speaking out in favour of neutrality. I know you gentlemen are in opposition, but I take it you go along on that?'

Pat Connors assured him that Fine Gael was as anti-war as anyone, but pointed out that the United States was better placed to stay out of a conflict in Europe. 'Winston Churchill wants our ports. If he seizes them we'll be attacked by Germany anyway. Sure now, there's precious little we can do about that,' he paused slyly, 'unless America guarantees our neutrality. Now that might be different . . .'

But the Ambassador was not to be drawn. He turned the implied question aside and moved on to other things. Sean hung upon every word, straining over the Ambassador's unfamiliar accent. (For years afterwards Sean believed that America's principal seat of learning was located at 'Hahvad'.) The talk of war was not surprising . . . many people were speculating on such dangers in 1938 . . . yet a thrill of excitement ran up Sean's back at the Ambassador's insistence that war was inevitable.

The visit was soon over, and the Ambassador and his son were shaking hands goodbye. 'I take it you will follow your father into politics,' the Ambassador beamed at Sean. He turned to the rest of the party: 'Gentlemen – we need a photograph – Joe Kennedy Junior, future President of the United States, seen here shaking hands with Sean Connors, future Taoiseach of Ireland.' There was a good deal of laughter as the two young men shook hands, their faces flushed under embarrassed grins. Then it was over and the Kennedys had gone.

Sean told the Widow O'Flynn about it the following afternoon. He went up to the farm on the excuse of mending a broken sash-cord and afterwards they had tea together as usual.

'He's wrong,' she said when Sean recounted the details. 'The Ambassador is wrong – you'll never be Taoiseach, Sean, never in a million years.' His disappointment was so obvious that she laughed and moved round the table to sit on his lap. 'Don't feel so bad about it, you'll do lots of other important things.'

Sean was nettled and it sounded in his voice: 'Oh, and you can tell the future, can you?'

'Enough to know Ireland won't hold you.' She nuzzled his ear. 'Not for much longer anyway.'

'So where will I go?' asked Sean.

'Oh . . . all over I guess. Sure won't I be picking up newspapers to see Gloria Swanson on *your* arm instead of Ambassador Kennedy's.'

'But I want *you* on my arm.'

He might have slapped her for the effect it had.

She sat bolt upright, her hands on his shoulders as she stared into his face. 'God bless you, Sean Connors, but I think you really mean that.'

'Of course . . .' he began, startled by her quick tears. She clung to him for a long moment, then pushed him away, to stand up and reach for her handkerchief. 'Oh dear,' she said after blowing her nose, 'you are never to say that again, Sean Connors, do you hear now?'

He was bewildered. Tears were so unlike her. Her lively teasing smile was so much part of her as her soft brown hair. He reached up and drew her back on his lap. 'What in God's name was that about?'

'About you being a boy instead of a man.'

His protest drowned in her embrace, but she caught his hand as it plunged under her skirt: 'Listen to me first! Will you stop that, Sean Connors, and listen a minute?' Something in her voice made him obey. 'I'm twenty-eight and you've yet to see your seventeenth birthday,' she said sternly. 'Let me see now . . . that means when *you* are twenty-eight I'll be forty. Sweet Mary, can you imagine? Forty years old! When you're in your prime I'll be an old crone.'

'Whatever's wrong . . .?' he began.

'You are, saying a thing like that. Wrong even to think it, God help us, wouldn't another woman be taking advantage of you?'

Then came the lecture. Sean failed to understand at first, couldn't get the drift of her meaning . . .

'I forget your age at times,' she said, stroking his face. 'You've learned too fast for my own good. But we've suited each other, wouldn't you say –'

'We *are* suited –'

'We are *now*, but not forever . . . there was never a future, my darling. Hush . . .' she put a finger to his lips, 'let me finish before I bawl my eyes out. Sean, you've far to go . . . it's written in your eyes . . . but you've to be careful who you take with you. And it cannot be me . . . it never could . . .' She swept past his protest by raising her voice. 'It's not just we're differently aged, though isn't that enough to bring you to your senses . . . but . . . but I could never keep pace. I'd pull you down instead of helping you up. We'd end up hating each other and I couldn't stand that . . . this way you'll remember me with love in your heart. I was your very first woman, nobody else can ever be that, no matter how much you love them . . .' she blinked back her tears, 'and I'll remember you for the life you brought back to me . . . and the tenderness –'

'But I love you.'

'You *think* you do –'

'I do –'

She put a finger to his lips. He caught her hand: 'Are you

sending me away?' he demanded. 'Are you saying we're finished?'

'Not yet . . . but soon, you'll be wanting to move on and I'll not stand in your way.'

Sean's bewilderment grew. He had not intended to propose marriage but the prospect of losing her frightened him. Suddenly he remembered something. Earlier in the week they had visited some shop premises with Jim Tully. Tully had been captivated – entranced by her looks and trim figure. And her tongue had been as quick as his, so the afternoon had passed amidst gales of laughter. Tully had flattered outrageously . . . and now?

'It's Tully, isn't it?' Sean challenged, on fire with jealousy.

'It's you we are talking about –'

'It *is* Tully –'

'I'm your woman, not his –'

'Not much longer by the sound of it.'

'I'll be your woman as long as you want me. But never your wife.'

The certainty of her words brooked no contradiction. He felt more confused than ever. He *liked* escorting her out in public. Dressed for town the Widow O'Flynn turned men's heads wherever they went. Admiring glances sped her way. Sean had been proud when he caught the envious gleam in men's eyes. He wanted to say, yes she's mine, isn't she beautiful! And now this? He couldn't understand it. He repeated her words angrily: 'So you'll be my woman as long as I want you. And then what? What happens if I finish with you?'

'Sean, this was always to be the outcome. You mustn't –'

'So what happens to you?'

'Does it matter?' She slid to the floor at his knees and looked up at him. 'It's the boy who's hurt now, but the man will thank me later. Oh, Sean, don't you *see* – you come here talking of ambassadors – I wouldn't know how to behave in half the places you'll go in your life, and I'll not have you ashamed of me. Nor will I cripple your future –'

'What happens to *you*?' Sean repeated through clenched teeth.

'I suppose I'll marry again. Maybe you're right – I'll marry Jim Tully.'

Shock took his breath away. They were both trembling, staring at each other, her begging him to understand, him hurt and confused.

'So you won't marry me because of my future, but Tully's different. Doesn't he have a future?'

She managed a faint smile: 'Jim Tully is a likeable rogue who's done well for himself. But he's twenty years older than me. I'll always be a young girl to him, don't you see? And he's made his world *here*. I can cope here . . . but I'll never make out where you're going –'

'Will I tell you again! I'm not going anywhere.'

And so it went on for another half hour, until Sean stormed from the farmhouse in temper. He walked as far as the Quays, furiously angry, desperately jealous, bitterly hurt. His world was collapsing. First trouble at the *Gazette* – now trouble with the Widow O'Flynn! He swore aloud. Doesn't it all boil down to assets every time. This Lord Averdale gets the *Gazette* – now Jim Tully walks off with the Widow O'Flynn! He chose not to think about how she had begged him to stay. He forgot her words of endearment. He put her tearstained face behind him. He just hurt. He hurt all over, not even a kicking could have hurt more.

He was fifty yards past Mulligan's Bar before he realized it. He whirled round and retraced his steps.

'I'll have a whiskey,' he told Mulligan.

Mulligan stared. Sean Connors had never so much as touched a glass of Guinness in all the years he had known him.

'Whiskey,' Sean repeated.

He emptied the glass in three gasping gulps. His throat caught fire, his stomach kicked, his eyes smarted, his legs twitched and he nearly died coughing – but he stood his ground. 'Another,' he gasped.

By the time Mulligan's son had found Pat and brought him, Sean Connors was swaying like a tree in the wind. He examined his fourth whiskey with a dreamy expression on his face. Then he was sick. Pat and Mulligan got him out to the street, where Sean heaved into the gutter. He sat down at the roadside and wearily contemplated the wreckage of his world.

Pat had been worried stiff about the Widow O'Flynn but he had held his tongue – not to do so would have been a breach of the rules. Besides it was just Pat's intuition. He prayed to be wrong. The church would crucify the pair of them if there was any truth in Pat's suspicions. The Dublin of 1938 was no different from Parnell's about matters of sexual scandal.

Mulligan helped to stand the boy upright, then Pat took him home.

After putting his son to bed, Pat chuckled on his way downstairs: 'Finola,' he whispered, 'would I have been right about that woman all along? God help the pair of them. Maybe it's over now and he can count himself lucky.'

Sean felt anything but lucky the following morning. His head throbbed and his mouth tasted muckier than the bottom of the Liffey. Even three cups of strong tea failed to revive him properly. He shuffled off to the *Gazette* like an old man. Once there he slumped behind his desk and was sitting with his head on his hands when Dinny Macaffety came into the office. 'You've heard then?' Macaffety barked, and realized his mistake when Sean responded with a blank look. 'Well why else would you sit there like a dead duck in a thunderstorm. You'd better look a lot livelier when his Lordship arrives. Do you hear me – Lord Averdale himself will be here in ten days' time!'

Sean groaned. That was all he needed. Another rich man to thwart his ambitions. Go to hell he thought, Lord Averdale can go to hell for all I care . . . and by Christ if he interferes with me I'll do everything possible to hasten his journey!

CHAPTER TEN

Nine generations of Averdales had built an empire in Ulster. So many died defending it that the Ulsterman's cry of 'No surrender' might have been set in the family's coat of arms – but it was hardly necessary. Just as birds were known to fly, so the people of Ulster had learned what to expect from the Averdales. Three hundred years leave an indelible mark.

Samuel was the first, starving to death in besieged Londonderry in 1668. But he left a son who left another, and each generation prospered. So much so that George, Samuel's great-grandson, inherited fifty thousand acres when he came of age. Not that George was content, George took the family into business by helping to found the Belfast linen industry.

Then came more of the Troubles. Catholics banded together under the United Irishmen banner, causing Protestants to retaliate by forming the Orange Order. Events were predictable after that. Protestant landlords formed part-time yeomanry and routed mobs of United Irishmen from one end of Ulster to the other. But there were casualties. George Averdale was one, and his son Thomas another, both killed defending their lands in Armagh from a rioting band of United Irishmen. Luckily for the Averdales, and some say for Ulster, young Andrew survived.

Andrew was a titan. It was Andrew who lobbied Westminster to make Ireland part of the United Kingdom, a mission which succeeded in 1798 with the Act of Union. Ulster, along with the rest of the land, was incorporated into the United Kingdom of Great Britain and Ireland – with representatives elected to the House of Commons. Trade restrictions were lifted. Belfast boomed. The population jumped from 20,000 in 1801 to 100,000 in 1851, and 350,000 by the end of the century. Steam power helped birth the biggest shipyards ever seen. Belfast claimed the largest linen thread company in existence – and the investments of the Averdale family flourished as never before.

Of course there were problems; Parnell and his Home Rule Party for one – damn fellow should have known better as a Protestant. As the then Lord Averdale said, 'Home Rule means ruin. It will resurrect trade barriers . . . tariffs will be slapped on Belfast products. What will happen to Averdale investments then?' And what would become of the 350,000 citizens of Belfast who were dependent on businesses owned by men like the Averdales? Ulster businessmen formed an alliance with the Conservative Party at Westminster designed to stop Parnell at all costs . . . and in Ulster recruits flocked to the Orange Order like bees round a honey pot. Ulster's leading families had *made* Belfast – they refused to hand it over to a bunch of Croppies who would ruin it in a generation. Consequently they would employ nobody not loyal to the Union. Orange foremen were told to recruit only Orange workers. By 1866 Harland and Wolff the shipbuilders employed only 225 Catholic Nationalists out of 3000 men – and Harlands were typical.

The Averdales fought hard. They had much to fight for – by 1907 the whole of Ireland exported twenty million pounds' worth of manufactured goods – ninety-five per cent of which originated in Belfast, with a good proportion finding its way back into the Averdale businesses.

Parnell was stopped, but others climbed on to the Home Rule bandwagon. Ulster still resisted – Edward Carson threatened to establish a Provisional government in Ulster if the Home Rule Bill was passed. Four hundred thousand people marched through Belfast in his support. Yet in the south, agitation for Home Rule continued, and at Westminster weak politicians prevaricated. Ulstermen were spurred to defend themselves as never before. The Ulster Volunteer Force was formed, and armed in 1914 when 25,000 rifles and half a million rounds of ammunition were landed secretly at Larne. Ulstermen were ready – and in the nick of time for during Easter 1916 a band of rebels seized the Dublin Post Office and declared a Republic. But Ulster stood firm.

After that, well, viewed from Belfast, the south went mad. First a rebel parliament in Dublin under that maniac de Valera, then the Anglo-Irish war and the Black and Tans. Ulster stayed out of it. Union meant what it said . . . union with the United Kingdom. Devious schemes cooked up by Lloyd George designed to bring peace to the south seemed a poor offering compared to total union. But the hard-headed men of Belfast began to suspect it was Lloyd George or nothing. As Lord Averdale said at the time – 'We want union continued for the *whole* of Ireland. We never asked for one parliament in Dublin and another one here – but if Lloyd George forces us to have one we must use it to protect ourselves.' Which is what happened – and when the new Belfast Parliament met for the first time, on 7 June 1921, the leading families of Ulster divided the jobs up among themselves.

Sir James Craig, the whiskey millionaire, was made Prime Minister. Hugh Pollock, the flour importer, became Minister of Finance. John Andrews became Minister of Labour – the same Andrews who was on the board of the Belfast Ropeworks, *and* the Belfast & County Down Railway, *and* chairman of his family's linen business. Some of the toughest businessmen in Europe had got themselves a country.

One name was conspicuously absent – Lord Averdale. The reason was simple. Old Joshua Averdale was dying and, on that very same day, 7 June 1921, gasped his last breath. He had seen much in his lifetime – the blossoming of the British Empire, the growth of industrial Belfast, a world war fought to end all such wars, in which his eldest son Robert was killed. The shock of that finished his mother . . . Lady Averdale died three months after receiving the news. She had adored Robert, everyone had – golden, dashing Robert, destined for so much. The Empire needed such men. A whole generation lost. Now the Averdale fortune would be left in trust for young Mark, who in 1921 was only eleven years old.

So when old Joshua died no Averdale stood ready to take his place. For the first time in three hundred years the chain of command had been broken. An Averdale son would not be taught about power by his father. That task would be performed by others – and perform it they did, though rarely in a way which suited young Mark. He was the despair of the select preparatory school in the London suburb of Dulwich, and the larger but equally exclusive establishment on the Thames known as Eton School threw him out on his sixteenth birthday. Schoolmasters decided that he needed firmer control than they could provide, and the suggestion that he be put down on Dartmoor in His Majesty's Prison was made with only the faintest of smiles.

He was born at Brackenburn, the huge family mansion outside Belfast, with its sweeping views across Lough Neagh and five thousand acres for a back garden. Lady Averdale, having discharged her responsibility of delivering another son, promptly handed him over to Nanny who, with the help of a nightnurse, took good care of him. After which Mark's infanthood was unexceptional – although there was one incident which, in retrospect, demonstrated two aspects of his character with piercing clarity – his stubbornness, and his love of possessions.

He was five at the time, and playing with some toy soldiers in the nursery. They were expensive reproductions of the armies of Wellington and Napoleon and although much of the intricate craftsmanship went over the boy's head he was captivated by the tiny figure of Napoleon. That too was a pointer for the future – Mark's knack with a collector's item – for the model was a connoisseur's piece if ever there was one and the boy singled it out from the moment he saw it. So much so that with Mark behind him Napoleon *won* the Battle of Waterloo time after time.

None of which was known to old Joshua Averdale who stopped at the nursery one day and became intrigued by the armies spread across the floor. To his eye something was wrong. He started to shift the pieces around. Then he picked up Napoleon. Mark uttered a strangled cry and tried to snatch it back. His father was too quick for him. Mark flew at his father – forgetting fear, ignoring Nanny's shrill warning. Old Joshua tried to brush him away – but Mark grabbed the hand holding Napoleon and bit – sinking teeth into flesh and hanging on like a bull-terrier. Not until Napoleon fell to the ground did Mark let go, despite the blows raining down on his head. He was thrashed an hour

189

later, bent over a chair while his father wielded the cane with his undamaged hand. Mark screamed and was sent to bed – but then came the mystery. Old Joshua was determined to confiscate Napoleon, but Napoleon could not be found. Napoleon was *never* to be found. Mark had hidden him and no amount of further punishment persuaded him to reveal the whereabouts of the piece. In the fullness of time the matter was forgotten, but apart from Mark nobody ever set eyes on Napoleon again.

A similar incident occurred at the Dulwich school four years later. Mark was not popular. His Ulster accent caused amusement and the constant teasing probably did amount to provocation – but Mark's retaliatory actions were indefensible. As when his stamp album went missing. The boy who borrowed it returned it intact an hour later – but Mark's outrage was fearful – and his action of holding the boy's head down the lavatory while classmates urinated over him was too much for the school. Mark was expelled the same day.

It was the same at Eton. The school's considerable disciplinary system broke its back on him. He established the still unequalled record of being beaten more often than any boy in the school's history. Academically he was a failure, taking an interest only in art and history, ignoring everything else. Socially he was the leader of the most troublesome group in school, but apart from a boy called Ashendon and a handful of others he was ostracized – a matter about which he seemed supremely indifferent. He was a non-event on the famous playing fields and achieved distinction only as a cross-country runner, where his stamina was such that he outran even the oldest boys in the school.

Of course his parents were long since dead by then, so responsibility for the boy rested with his four harassed guardians. Initially they drew some comfort from his prowess as a cross-country runner, seeing in it such qualities as courage and persistence which they hoped might be repeated elsewhere . . . but they waited in vain. Mark Averdale reserved his determination for a few special things of his own choosing . . . as the world was to find out.

Mark celebrated his sixteenth birthday by holding a midnight picnic on the river. Hampers from Fortnum's guaranteed an excellent feast, but as well as food it was subsequently discovered that the seven boys consumed four bottles of vintage champagne and two of Haig's Dimple. Who suggested the nude bathing was never revealed, not even by the coroner's inquest – all that established was death by accidental drowning of young Peter Marsden. By then, however, Mark Averdale had already been expelled.

What to do with him – that was the question. No other school would take him. A university career was out of the question. Even the army was doubtful – Sandhurst was sounded out, but they refused with positive firmness. For a year a succession of tutors were engaged in the thankless task of furthering Mark's education. All of them failed, although the last did achieve some insight into Mark's character. In his letter of resignation to the guardians, Mr Harvey MacPherson, a Scots educator of very good reputation, wrote:

'The boy is far from stupid. I caught him on the raw last week by condemning his intellect. Indeed I went so far as to say that he lacked a sufficiently retentive memory to attain any level of scholastic achievement. (Not something I would normally say to a pupil but Mark's refusal to study riled me more than usual that day.) He gave no reply at the time but the day before yesterday presented me with a copy of Othello. *Then he sat down in front of me and wrote the entire play out from memory, including stage directions and scene setting. The exercise took him four hours during which time he barely paused, and then only to ask for more paper. When he finished he said perhaps I would like to check his work for accuracy, then he left my room and I did not see him until the following morning.*

Of course I checked the work thoroughly and with the exception of two spelling errors, it was totally accurate. It may interest you to know that there are fifteen thousand words of dialogue in Othello, *and the stage directions in my edition account for another seven hundred. (I can vouch for this since I counted the words myself.) I must tell you that I consider Mark's achievement to be quite remarkable – the equal of which I have not come across in fifteen years of teaching.*

Naturally yesterday morning I complimented him. In fact we discussed the work, enough to establish that as well as learning the lines he fully understood every aspect of the play. I apologized for my ill-judged criticism of his intellect and went on to plead, as persuasively as possible, that he take a greater interest in his studies. He refused point blank. He said he had memorized the play simply to refute my criticism, but that his attitude towards traditional theories of education had not changed one bit.

Then came an even more disturbing incident. I was saying it was my duty to provide him with an education which would help when he assumed responsibility for the House of Averdale. He smiled at that and said he already had everything necessary. He rolled up one sleeve and took out a pocket-knife and, before I could stop him, cut a deep incision in his forearm. I was appalled by the blood, but he remained icy calm. "Averdale blood", he said, then tapped the knife blade, "and cold steel to keep the Croppies down. That's what made the Averdale fortune, and that's what will keep it."

Doctor Lawton's medical report is attached and you will be relieved to note that no permanent damage was suffered – although nine stitches were sewn into the boy's arm – but I must confess the incident upset me profoundly. (Incidentally, you may be unfamiliar with the term, but "Croppies" denotes Catholics over here.)

The letter concluded with various platitudes. The kind Mr MacPherson even managed to find something good to say about the boy, praising his obvious iron will and courage and adding, surprisingly perhaps, that Mark had an eye for beautiful things – '*In particular*,' MacPherson wrote, '*the boy has a well developed interest in painting and can speak quite knowledgeably about every canvas in Brackenburn. In fact I am something of a student myself, and I remembered reading that Rouen's famous painting* Women Bathing *was owned by the Averdale family, so naturally I was hoping to see it at Brackenburn, since quite apart from its reputation as one of the most sensual paintings in the world it is commonly regarded as Rouen's masterpiece. But the painting was neither in the gallery nor the Long Room, and when I enquired the servants told me that Master Mark had removed it to his bedroom. As a matter of fact I asked Mark if I might view it, but was refused in a manner which I can only describe as curt. I mention this not because of my small disappointment, but as a sidelight on Mark's character. Some things he will share with nobody. Of course the painting is his to do with what he likes – but his possessiveness amounts to an obsession at times.'*

In London, the guardians – now reduced to three by the death of one of their number – were at their wits' end. They had served Joshua Averdale in various capacities in his lifetime, but the task he set from his grave seemed impossible. MacPherson's letter was read and re-read. The incident involving Rouen's painting was not the first indication of Mark's possessiveness – but Averdales *were* possessive, even if, to the guardians' knowledge, no one before Mark had taken erotic paintings into their bedrooms. What to do with the boy? Finally they hit upon Africa. Lord Bowley, the late Lord Averdale's cousin, had settled there. He was a widower with a son of Mark's age – perhaps he would take the boy for a while?

Mark accepted the suggestion – leaving Brackenburn was a wrench but the great house would not be his unfettered until his twenty-first birthday. And if he stayed, no doubt the guardians would appoint another tutor. So, two weeks after his seventeenth birthday, he sailed from Southampton to Africa – where he remained for more than three years.

Lord Bowley was well known for his shrewd judgement. He harnessed Mark's restlessness by making him work the Bowley estates – a tract so vast that a man could ride the boundary all day and not get back to his starting point. He sought to curb Mark's possessiveness by restricting him to little more than his horse, a rifle, a knife and a bed. And best of all he gave his son Percy to Mark as a companion. Percy was older by six months, a strong, easy-going boy with his father's gift for man-management, but who was growing restless without company of his own age. Mark's arrival suited all three of them. Lord Bowley worked the boys hard and they responded – so much so that at the end of eighteen months Lord Bowley sent the boys on holiday. 'You've worked damn hard and I'm grateful, but it's time you took a break. Go and see Africa. Look at it before it all changes, before they civilize the place. Take a year if you like, two youngsters your age, time you had an adventure before you settle down.'

So they went, taking Mbejobi, Lord Bowley's most trusted servant, with them. They saw Africa – spending fifteen months trekking from one coast and back again. They slept rough, stalked elephant, shot lion, ate wildebeest, got bitten by snakes, waded rivers, climbed mountains and damn near killed themselves – but Mark remembered the sheer exhilaration of those days for the rest of his life. Mark celebrated his nineteenth birthday in Nairobi's most exclusive brothel, not leaving his bed for a week. Percy won three hundred pounds in a Jo'burg card game and lost it at knife-point afterwards. Mark squandered fifty pounds at the Cape Town races. Percy got roaring drunk in Port Elizabeth's most exclusive bordello. They were thrown out of Mozambique. But they saw Africa – from the magical sunset over Kilimanjaro to the spray half a mile high above the Victoria Falls.

Lord Bowley inspected them keenly when they returned. 'Well, you both look healthy enough. If I didn't know better I'd think you'd led decently upright lives. No doubt you'll swear you've not touched a drop of whiskey, or taken any bad women to bed – or done any of the other normal, healthy, disgusting things I expected of you.'

They spent a week recounting their adventures, and the old man seemed to enjoy the hearing as much as they had enjoyed the doing. Lord Bowley, Mark decided, was the wisest man in the world.

Most nights they slumped on the verandah, resting aching muscles after a hard day, drinking whiskey, and generally feeling pleasantly tired. Sometimes they talked of Ireland. 'I miss it at times,' the old man admitted, 'but I had to get out. De Valera is destroying it. Ireland's no place for a Lord now, not in the south anyway. Maybe it was nothing but a poor place to start with, but a man as narrow and blinkered as de Valera will ruin it for sure.' He snorted contemptuously. 'Freedom! He'll give 'em

194

freedom all right, freedom to starve!'

'And the north?' Mark asked anxiously.

'The north's all right if you remember one thing,' Lord Bowley wagged a finger, 'you're under siege. You've seen the mess in the south. They'll do the same for Ulster if you let them. Be firm, stand up for yourselves, nobody else will if you don't. And watch those English politicians – some of them couldn't hold tight to a brass washer. They'll give it away one day if you let them – but you're British and you insist on your rights.'

Lord Bowley was proud to be British and proud of the Empire. 'The British invest,' he said, warming to his theme, 'time, money, men, know-how – of course they want a return on their capital, why not, but they build a country up, not milk it dry like some of these other buggers. And take the Commonwealth – another great development. When people are ready to run their own affairs they should do so. Perfectly right. That's what de Valera should have gone for, *full* membership of the Commonwealth, with all the benefits of trade and investment. Now he's half in and half out. He's not trusted, so nobody invests tuppence in Ireland – and all because of a crack-pot idea of becoming a republic like America. There's no comparison – America's rich in resources while Ireland needs all the help it can get. I'll tell you, had this Commonwealth idea been around in 1776 America wouldn't be a republic – they'd be inside the Commonwealth, growing rich behind a wall of preferential tariffs.'

So, beneath Africa's velvet skies, Mark learned much the same brand of politics as his father would have taught. Enemies of Unionism would get the same reply from Mark as first fell from the lips of another Averdale at the Siege of Londonderry – 'No surrender!' It was in his blood, and nothing learned from Lord Bowley contradicted his most cherished convictions.

Thus the guardians raised an Averdale after all – and the two who were still alive to greet Mark's ship at Southampton were more than pleased with the young man they met. He was tall and lean, with sun-bleached fair hair and healthy bronzed skin. Africa had performed a

195

metamorphosis, turning a troublesome boy into an attractive young man – an attractive *rich* young man, for although the trustees had failed to expand the Averdale empire at least they had kept it intact. Which was why, five weeks before his twenty-first birthday, Mark Averdale was in England . . . to claim his inheritance.

Mark was still an Averdale. He proved it at Southampton. Crates of possessions stretched from one end of the quay to the other. Trophies by the ton. Skins, antlers, the head of a brindled gnu, elephant tusks, zebra hides – the list seemed endless. Overwhelmed Customs officers organized a special examination shed, but their inspection was casual by comparison. Mark went through everything with a fine tooth comb and only when he was satisfied that it was complete did he pass it for onward shipment to Brackenburn. What was his was his . . . and God help anyone who failed to respect his property.

In London he stayed at his family's house in Belgrave Square and his guardians and trustees called to discuss the Averdale investments. They were considerable. The company which bore Mark's name – Averdale Engineering – was but a small part of his inheritance. Indirectly he owned fifteen per cent of Belfast's linen industry, nineteen per cent of the shipyards, five per cent of all whiskey distilled in the Province, and a scattering of holdings in any number of businesses. In addition to which he owned a house in London, three farms in Ulster, and of course Brackenburn. But sole control of this empire was not his for another four years – the family investments would be supervised by trustees until Mark's twenty-fifth birthday – 'apprenticeship years', Joshua Averdale had called them in his will.

Mark was undismayed. He had plans of his own. Meanwhile his income was substantial and, most importantly, he had Brackenburn. Brackenburn drew him. He still remembered pining for the great house while at school. Even in Africa he had been homesick at times. So the minute Mark finished with the guardians and trustees he left London and journeyed to Ulster.

Brackenburn! Even in a country blessed with great houses, Andrew Averdale's mansion was exceptional.

Nothing rivalled it in Ulster, and although the south had some fine houses, few equalled Brackenburn. In England it was surpassed by Blenheim Palace in Oxford and Castle Howard in Yorkshire, but only just – indeed it closely resembled Castle Howard. It was smaller but not by much, where Castle Howard was 600 feet long, Brackenburn was 500; where the Great Hall at Castle Howard was 34 feet square, Brackenburn's was 30 – but both were crowned by a dome and flanked by staircases. Both houses had curved arcades connecting the main building to a kitchen block on one side and a stable block the other – and both had wide paved terraces on their southern elevations, backed by a gracious portico surmounted by a pediment. But in Brackenburn's Long Room the alabaster Corinthian columns rose twenty-five feet to a ceiling far finer than anything at Castle Howard. And Brackenburn's entrance was more impressive. No, it mattered not that it was a shade smaller than Castle Howard, to Mark's eye Brackenburn was the most magnificent house in the world. And it was his!

So he returned in the summer of '31 and all through that autumn the leading families of Ulster trekked out to Brackenburn to pay their respects. Many did so warily. Joshua had been dead ten years, and hard-headed businessmen are not in the habit of keeping seats warm for other men's sons. The order had changed. Joshua had left a vacuum and those who had filled it were anxious to assess what effect this new Averdale would have on the affairs of the Province.

It took a while to find out. Initially Mark was too busy building a pavilion for his African collection to have much time for Belfast society. But he received callers in a proper manner and accepted invitations to various functions, so that by the end of a year most people had formed an opinion of him. Socially he was at the pinnacle, Ulster's most eligible bachelor, possessing an arrogant charm and enough dry wit to give a good account of himself at a dinner table. He was tall, wore his clothes well – and of course he was rich. But, Mark was amused to note, he was thought of as a political lightweight and a non-event in business. Both judgements were oversimplifications. Mark was a

Unionist. His political views reflected those expressed by Lord Bowley, with one significant difference, Lord Bowley in Mark's opinion had run away – Mark never would. Ulster was British and would remain so. No bloody Fenian would ever sit in Brackenburn. Averdales and Ulster belonged to each other and God help the man who tried to separate them. Mark's views were so obvious to himself that he rarely bothered to express them.

Similarly with business. Mark knew others had gained ground, but he had no intention of devoting his life to commerce. Business was a means to an end, and the end was to generate wealth – it was the deployment of that wealth which fascinated Mark. He planned to spend a lot of money, so *of course* business was important, but what was needed, Mark decided, was a first-class general manager with Mark breathing down his neck. That would keep the Averdale investments up to scratch and leave Mark free to devote himself to the more important things of life. And he had long since decided upon those.

He was a collector. It had started with Napoleon, that tiny toy figure from the nursery, then it had been stamps, not until he was thrown out of Eton did it become works of art. It was then he had discovered Rouen's *Women Bathing* in the gallery at Brackenburn. Of course it had been there for years, Mark had played in the gallery as a child but had never looked at the canvases properly. Colours and shapes had registered but few of the subjects. Then he had arrived back from Eton in disgrace and everything changed. For the first time he sensed the great house was his. Old Joshua was five years buried by then, and Mark's mother no more than a memory – he was the new master and the house seemed to know it. He inspected rooms he had never set foot in, he visited the kitchen block, saw the bakehouse and the dairy – he found two bedrooms above the chapel which had never been used. He counted the books in the library. He moved his things into the main bedroom, bathed for the first time in the great marble tub which stood resplendent in his dressing-room. In short he made himself at home and the house seemed to respond. Every day it revealed a new or forgotten treasure, and eventually it led him to the gallery.

Rouen's masterpiece was fifty years old then. When first unveiled in Paris it had provoked an outburst of indignation not known since Gautier's *Mademoiselle de Maupin*. What caused the uproar was not so much the subject matter, four female nude figures grouped around a tiled pool, but the manner of the painting's execution. There was no doubt that Rouen was a master of the female form, that was as certain as his love of women, for he was a notorious letch. Paris was not shocked by that. Nor that Rouen's nudes were so voluptuous that few men could look at them dispassionately. Rouen's nudes were not paint on canvas – they came alive in the most glorious detail. Every curve evoked a response, every buttock invited the clasp of both hands, a man's palm would itch to feel the weight of a breast, milky white thighs demanded to be parted. When he looked at a Rouen nude a man could feel the texture of her skin, taste her nipple in his mouth, smell her hair and all but possess her. But that too Paris had come to expect by 1887 and every one of the figures in *Women Bathing* did credit to the artist's reputation. All were breathtakingly desirable – but this time there was a difference. It began with the way they were looking at each other. The figure on the left reclined at the side of the pool, one foot idly dipping into the water as she gazed at a companion. It was that look, that seductive glance delivered from beneath lowered eyelashes, a faint flush on her cheeks, her lips slightly parted. An invitation. No man could mistake it. The body language of every other figure took on new meaning. The knowing half-smile of the reclining figure, the way her raised thigh mockingly concealed her womanhood – and the response it aroused in the other girl, one arm outstretched, nipples erect, eyes alive with anticipation. And the two other figures were gazing at each other with unmistakable longing. Rouen had portrayed four lesbians! And this a decade before Oscar Wilde described Huysmans's *A rebours* as a parade of the sins of the world – and almost two decades before Beardsley illustrated *Salome*. The Paris of 1887 was shocked. 'Here indeed,' in the words of Verlaine, 'decadence shimmered in purple and gold.'

The painting had a startling effect on the sixteen-year-old Mark Averdale. The girl at the poolside mesmerized him. No woman had ever looked at him like that but he had no doubt about her meaning. And her eyes seemed to look directly back at him, to send an electric shock up his spine. He drank in every inch of her, from her flame red hair to the polished pink toenails. She was the most beautiful thing he had ever seen. She was perfect, flawless, unique. He grew giddy when he imagined his hands on her body, his lips on hers – and he grew giddier still when he imagined pushing that coyly placed thigh aside. To possess her! To have her as his own! A man would be a king to own such a beauty.

Rouen's painting was moved to the master bedroom and few nights passed without Mark playing with himself as he stared at the girl with the red hair. He christened her Kate for no reason he could think of – and night after night Kate's name was on his lips as his seed spurted into his hand.

Then came his first sexual experiences, taken in a dozen brothels across Africa. Some of the girls were white, others were brown, some were freshly pretty and others so experienced that they coaxed unforgettable sensations from his body – but none were as beautiful as Kate. It was always her name he called at the moment of climax, and when he opened his eyes he was forever disappointed not to find Kate beneath him. Even later, when he returned to Brackenburn at the age of twenty-one, Kate's beauty remained untarnished. Reading and experience had taught him the true meaning of Rouen's painting, but he rejected it as a cruel joke played by the artist on his model. It was impossible to believe that a girl so beautiful could be a lesbian.

By then Mark had become a dedicated collector. More than wild game trophies had been acquired in Africa – endless bazaars had been raided for the ivories and wood-carvings which emptied from the crates into Brackenburn. The erotica disappeared into Mark's bedroom, but the bulk of the collection was housed in the new pavilion which Mark had built over the bakehouse.

Mark saw his place in history. The name Averdale would become synonymous with art. He would create a great collection, arrange exhibitions – loan paintings to the Tate in London, the Louvre in Paris and the Met in New York. The Averdale name would become internationally famous. But some paintings would be kept for himself. Some works would be his alone. He would not share Kate's beauty with anyone.

By 1932 Mark's African Pavilion was completed. He had settled as far into Belfast society as he wanted to go – and by 1933 his income had taken him to sale rooms all over Europe. Brackenburn was turned into a treasure house. Not a room lacked something exceptional – a Poussin, a Caravaggio, a Palmer, a sketch by Braque, a Chippendale secretaire, a bronze by Greuze – the list was endless as the effect was pleasing, for without doubt Mark had a very good eye. And just as his possessions multiplied around the house so too did the collection of private art in his bedroom. Erotica abounded – but Mark never found anything more sensual than Rouen's painting. Nothing aroused him as did that figure reclining by the pool. Kate was perfect, flawless, unique.

But Mark sought other things during those years, not hurriedly for a collector never hurries when choosing anything, but he planned to have them by his twenty-fifth birthday when sole control of the Averdale fortune would be his. The first was a wife and the second was a general manager. Brackenburn needed a mistress to supervise the staff. Running the great house took more time than Mark could spare – and a wife was needed to produce Averdale sons. The need for a general manager was equally obvious. Mark was spending to the hilt. His investments would need to yield every penny if his plans for the Averdale Foundation were to mature – and a general manager would help find the money.

So in 1935 – during precisely the week that Matt Riordan arrived in Belfast and Sean Connors set out across Ireland with his father – Mark Averdale married Dorothy Manners, eldest daughter of Sir Walter Manners, the local Unionist MP. Manners too was a rich man, not in the Averdale class but he farmed a useful acreage. His daughter had been raised partly in Ireland and partly in England, as is the way with the Anglo-Irish. Ireland had taught her to ride and England had taught her to read.

She was neither plain nor pretty. In a good light and dressed in clothes which suited her she could look attractive, but at other times her prominent teeth lent a distinctly horsey cast to her face. But she had good skin and rich brown hair, and a reasonable figure which looked best in the jodhpurs she wore for at least part of each day. Dorothy was an expert horsewoman, quite knowledgeable enough to advise her father when he took her racing. She was too practical to be really feminine and tended to be impatient with her younger sisters who giggled about the young men who took them dancing. Truthfully Dorothy was surprised by Lord Averdale's attentions – surprised, flattered and impressed – especially when she was shown over Brackenburn. After that she worked at it – reading huge tomes on art and antiques – so that before the courtship was over she could talk quite knowledgeably about Brackenburn's treasures. She would never be an expert but then she never sought to be, feeling much safer by prefacing her opinions with, 'Mark is the real connoisseur, of course, but I do rather like this . . .'

The wedding night was adequate. Dorothy tried hard. By the time Mark came to her room she had doused herself with so much cologne that she reeked like a scent factory. Then she removed her nightdress and submitted to his fondling with such enthusiasm that she fondled him back – causing him to come in her hand, which created a delay of half an hour until he recovered. And when she did get him inside her, at the second attempt, his stiffness seemed to subside at every second. Eventually she mounted him and rode as hard as she would her bay gelding. He enjoyed that. His knees lifted, his hands clasped her buttocks, and with her heavy breasts bouncing madly in his face he urged her on with such cries of encouragement that she might have been leading the field in a point-to-point. Even his climax reminded her of a horse race, with Mark crying, 'Whoa . . . oh God . . . whoa!' She went to sleep with the satisfied feeling of having done her job well.

When she awoke in the morning he had returned to his room. She was surprised but not dismayed, in fact she was rather pleased. She rang for tea and read the *Telegraph*, then bathed and dressed and went down to join him. He kissed her cheek and after breakfast they spent a pleasant day exploring Brackenburn. Of course Mark knew its history by heart, but it was still new enough for Dorothy to want to learn more. And so began the pattern of their days together.

Mark visited her room seven times in the first month. She blessed the man who had taught her to ride, 'Squeeze with the knees,' he had told her, 'that's how to make him respond.' How right, she thought. But she was not unhappy. If the sex act failed to excite at least it did not nauseate. She could take it or leave it and began to suspect it would be left more often than taken in the years ahead. Meanwhile she was mistress of Brackenburn which meant a great deal to her. The great house needed an exceptional hostess and Dorothy felt quite up to the challenge. Belfast society held no fears for her. She planned to hold court, but was shrewd enough to move slowly – changes should appear to be of his making, not hers. So to begin with she contented herself with mastering the running of Brackenburn, a considerable task in itself since there were twenty-two indoor and nine outside staff to be organized. But Dorothy coped so well that by 1936, within a year of her wedding day, Brackenburn functioned more smoothly than at any time in its history.

Mark was pleased too – Dorothy's presence at Brackenburn had transformed his existence. The grounds looked perfect whatever the season, and the house itself was immaculate. Of course there was the matter of sex, but then Mark had never looked on Dorothy as a sex object. That was not her function. It would be unfair to expect her to rouse him to the same fever pitch as an African whore, or to provide the excitement of Molly Oakes, his mistress in London. Molly was superb. But even so, despite such discreetly taken pleasures, Mark's sexual desires were only partially satisfied. The truth was he was seeking perfection, chasing a dream – a dream of a willowy, milk-skinned woman with flame red hair. He was looking for Kate. No matter that his bedroom was now crammed with erotica, it was always Rouen's painting which drew his eye – and not a week passed without him spending one night masturbating while gazing upon Kate's artful expression. It was the way she looked back, that knowing look which inflamed him. He talked to her, using every foul gutter word he could put his tongue to, but still she smiled as her eyes seduced him. She was perfect, flawless, unique.

Dorothy never set foot in Mark's rooms. Once, during her first month at Brackenburn she had gone thinking to inspect the work of the housemaids, but the rooms had been locked. The housekeeper explained that maids were not allowed in the master's rooms for fear of damaging his treasures. Dorothy thought that absurd. The maids cleaned everywhere else, besides how were the rooms kept clean? Apparently Jenkins, the master's valet, did everything necessary. Dorothy raised the matter with Mark . . . but Mark grew quite angry . . .

Apart from that incident, they were superficially happy. Certainly they never quarrelled, Dorothy made sure there was nothing to quarrel about. The house was organized to perfection. Mark's treasures were cared for – household accounts were maintained with an auditor's vigilance, and twice a month Dorothy rode Mark in bed with the vibrant energy she displayed on Pegasus, her hunter.

But Mark still lacked a general manager. His guardians liked the idea, seeing only wisdom in placing an experienced businessman at Mark's elbow. They put forward various candidates but Mark turned them all down, sensing that none possessed the ruthlessness which would be necessary to screw every ha'penny out of the Averdale investments. Nineteen-thirty-six and '37 were busy years. Mark tried to split himself in two, supervising his investments while adding to his art collection. It was impossible. He found himself at board meetings when he wanted to be at Christie's in London – or in a Paris sale room instead of dealing with business in Ulster. He grew more desperate with every passing month – and then he found Eoin O'Brien.

They were such opposites that it was difficult to imagine them having anything in common. Mark was tall, fair-haired and long-chinned; O'Brien was short, dark and granite-jawed. At twenty-seven Mark affected an air of assured calm. At forty-five O'Brien attacked life with both hands. Yet physical differences cloaked similarities. Both were Ulster Protestants, with all the stubbornness of the breed, both were greedy for possessions, and both could be ruthless in getting them. And they were to share something even more important than that.

O'Brien owned a small engineering company, tiny by Averdale standards, employing only a hundred men, but it provided O'Brien with an excellent livelihood – enough for him to own a smart house in Belfast's most exclusive suburb. There he lived with his wife and two children, a prosperous upright pillar of the community. He read the lesson in church, presided over his Orange Lodge, and was a local committee man of the Unionist Party. Eoin O'Brien was considered a coming man, perhaps with a future in politics. But his ambitions were much more basic than that. O'Brien wanted a fortune, perhaps as large as Averdale's, and he had promised himself to have it before he died. Already his company supplied Averdale Engineering with components, and although he hardly mixed in the same circles he had met Averdale a number of times. His next step was an invitation to Brackenburn: get that he told himself, and he would be on his way. And in 1938 O'Brien received such an invitation – but for reasons he never knew, nor would have suspected in a thousand years.

It had begun in Liverpool. Mark was on his way home from London where he had purchased an exquisite Moreau for eight hundred guineas. The auction had been so competitive that he had almost lost it, but he had clung on, determined to have the Moreau, and he had – but at twice the price he had expected to pay.

He had stayed in London overnight, at the house in St John's Wood, where Molly Oakes was so sympathetic about the price he had paid to indulge one passion that he quite overlooked what it cost to satisfy another. Then he caught the morning train to Liverpool, where he took a cab from Lime Street to the Adelphi Hotel, intending to lunch before boarding the mid-afternoon ferry to Belfast. After a drink in the Steve Donaghue Bar, he adjourned to the dining-room for a solitary meal – and it was there that he got the shock of his life. He was just about to order when he glanced towards the door, for no other reason than the man at the next table had turned and Mark had followed his gaze. He gasped aloud. The menu fell from his hands. His heart stopped. Colour drained from his face. A woman was standing just inside the door, her head turned towards the lobby as if waiting for someone. Even from fifteen yards away there was no mistaking that flame red hair or the alabaster whiteness of her skin. *It was Kate!* The girl in Rouen's painting.

'Is anything the matter, sir?' asked the waiter at Mark's elbow.

Mark sat rigid. He had worshipped too long at the altar of Rouen's genius to be mistaken. It *was* Kate. Her height, her slim grace, the angle of head, the long eyelashes. Suddenly she turned and looked directly at him. Green eyes met his. Deep emerald-green eyes, just like in the painting. She blushed. Colour suffused her cheeks until they bloomed like a peach – exactly the shade Rouen had captured.

'Sir?' The waiter poured a glass of water from the carafe on the table.

The woman turned and walked out.

Mark rose unsteadily. He crossed to the door, leaving his papers, ignoring the worried head waiter. Kate! He tried to call her name but the sound emerged as a dry croak. He reached the door in a daze and was just about to go through when she returned. A man followed her, apologizing for keeping her waiting, a dark-haired bulky sort of man. Then they all bumped into each other.

'Why, Lord Averdale,' exclaimed the man.

It was O'Brien, Eoin O'Brien.

Mark tried to pull himself together but he was still trembling when they shook hands.

'May I present my wife,' O'Brien was saying, 'Sheila, this is Lord Averdale.'

Sheila? The name was wrong – Sheila was a horrible, meaningless, blasphemy of a name. But close up Mark was even more bewitched. The resemblance was uncanny. The same shy half smile, the familiar lowered lashes, the identical white pillar of her throat. Her name was Kate, not Sheila!

They lunched together. Not that Mark ate much, his

206

appetite deserted him. But he drank, consuming an entire bottle of claret while O'Brien and his wife shared a bottle of hock, with O'Brien drinking three-quarters of that. It was O'Brien who did most of the talking, prattling on about his business.

Mark tried not to stare. He was shocked, both by the resemblance and tiny differences. She was older. Rouen's nymph was no more than nineteen, this woman was in her late twenties. And Mark was stupidly surprised when she spoke not in French but in a musically soft brogue. But her eyes, her throat, her hair, her nose . . . all were identical. She was his. What right had O'Brien to have found her, to have married her . . .

Mark couldn't decide if he wanted the meal to end, or go on forever. O'Brien ought not to have been there. Had it just been the two of them . . . Mark's head swam. But he knew one thing – he had to possess her. Suddenly Rouen's painting was not enough, not now, not when he had seen her in the flesh.

They parted and went their separate ways, the O'Briens to London, Mark back to Ulster and Brackenburn. That night Dorothy was made to submit to variants of the sex act she had never dreamt possible – but even with his eyes closed Mark could not sustain the pretence that it was Kate. He returned to his rooms, bitterly vengeful. It was monstrous for O'Brien to possess such a vision . . . the man lacked breeding, he was a crude, fumbling artisan with no artistic feelings . . . it was wrong, wrong, wrong . . .

By morning Mark's plans were made . . . and ten weeks later they bore fruit.

Mark himself received Eoin O'Brien when he made his worried appearance at the Averdale offices. It was their first meeting since their chance encounter in Liverpool. O'Brien was already very different – he had been buoyant and confident then, but now – no matter how hard he tried to disguise his feelings – he was anxious and nervous. Mark sat him in a comfortable chair, suggested a glass of Madeira and offered him a choice of cigars.

O'Brien came straight to the point, 'It's a favour I'm asking, Lord Averdale. Nine weeks ago your company cancelled its business with me. I'd like you to reconsider your decision.'

Mark seemed surprised. He had no idea, he said, the matter had escaped his notice . . . he would look into it. O'Brien was left nursing his glass and his hopes while Mark went to investigate. He returned clutching a sheaf of papers. 'I'm sorry O'Brien, but apparently we get similar components from Germany at a much keener price,' Mark shrugged. 'Of course, I had no idea, but under the circumstances my people could hardly have done anything else. The difference is quite considerable. I'm most awfully sorry.'

O'Brien blinked. He had heard the story elsewhere. German manufacturers were causing havoc all over Europe. Even so, O'Brien had examined his costings, studied his methods of manufacture – his own outfit was highly efficient, even if he said it himself. Too efficient to be beaten by some bloody Krauts who had to climb over a tariff wall to get it.

'May I ask how different?' he said bluntly.

Mark seemed shocked, almost embarrassed, but he consulted his papers. 'Well, it's a bit unethical,' he said doubtfully, 'on the other hand I'd rather deal with a fellow Ulsterman than a Jerry any day. But the truth will hurt, they're cheaper by a mile. Thirty-five per cent actually.'

There was no doubting O'Brien's dismay. He had steeled himself to drop seven, even ten per cent – but thirty-five per cent was impossible. That was below cost. It defied logic – nobody could make a profit at that price – nobody! His normally agile mind was lost for an explanation, which was not surprising for he would never have guessed the truth – that Mark Averdale's London bank paid the Germans a forty per cent subsidy on everything shipped into Belfast.

'Look here,' Mark was the picture of concern, 'I'd tell my people to switch back to you if it were five per cent . . . but well, I'm sure you see my position.'

O'Brien crept back to his office like a whipped dog. He felt grateful to Lord Averdale, it had been good of the man to see him in the first place and he had been damned decent to reveal that German price. In fact the meeting had ended with the hint of an invitation to Brackenburn. O'Brien had hankered for ages after that – but it was ironic for it to come now, when he was facing ruin and disgrace. The collapse had been so sudden. Ten weeks ago he had been on top of the world. Then Averdale's had cancelled their contract, bad enough when their business was twenty per cent of O'Brien's turnover – but even worse had followed. Three other customers had transferred to the Germans. Suddenly O'Brien was operating at a loss. Half his plant lay idle. He had surplus capacity, surplus labour. Men had been laid off, good men, skilled machinists most of them . . . but even a reduced payroll had not returned him to profit. His overheads were too heavy for his smaller volume of business. And now his bankers were fidgeting . . . . he would need to find smaller premises, much smaller . . . either that or beat those Germans. But thirty-five per cent!

He summoned his auditors and within a week sat contemplating an updated financial statement. The company was barely solvent. If it collapsed, some assets would fall short of book value. O'Brien stared ruin in the face. He thought of his wife and children . . . the Chamber of Commerce, the Lodge, the Club . . . and shuddered. It seemed so bloody unfair when he had worked so hard.

Then, the very next day, something remarkable happened. God is never far away in time of trouble and it seemed to O'Brien that God Himself had intervened on his behalf. He had taken his wife to lunch at the Queen's Hotel, as he did once a week, and that day was her twenty-eighth birthday so it was special. Not that O'Brien felt like celebrating but he hated to disappoint her. Something will turn up he told himself . . . and then it did, in the shape of Lord Averdale.

Averdale was in the hotel lobby, not the dining-room, indeed Lord Averdale rarely dined there. So when the doors opened and O'Brien glimpsed Lord Averdale outside he was surprised enough to mention it to his wife. 'There's Lord Averdale,' he said, rising hastily, 'I'll ask him to join us for a brandy. To toast your health on your birthday.'

He would not have presumed three months previously, but the chance meeting in Liverpool, the courtesy extended in Averdale's office, and the hint of an invitation to Brackenburn all combined to give O'Brien confidence – and his fleeting fear of a public snub faded as he saw Averdale's smile of recognition. But Averdale was not alone. He introduced his companion as a Mr Ashendon, then listened politely to the invitation to join the O'Briens for a brandy. 'You too, Mr Ashendon,' O'Brien said hurriedly. 'Just for a birthday drink.'

So the invitation was accepted. At the table Mark graciously toasted Mrs O'Brien, then finished his brandy and rose to leave. Ashendon protested, 'It's my turn. Surely you'll allow me to order another round to toast such an elegant lady?' But Averdale declined. 'I'm sorry but I'm late already,' he said to Ashendon, 'but you stay. We've finished our business.' Then he was gone, leaving the O'Briens with an unexpected guest at their table.

Not until he was seated in the back of his Rolls-Royce did Mark's heart stop pounding. He breathed a sigh of relief as the driver nudged the car into Queen Street's traffic. He congratulated himself, really it had been remarkably easy, even if his hands did shake as he reached for a cigarette. Seeing her again did that – to be *that* close, to touch her hand, to look into her eyes when proposing that toast, to smell her scent! His head swam.

Of course he had seen her since Liverpool, quite often, more than she ever knew. Muffled in a greatcoat with the collar turned up, he had shuffled past her house on many a morning. He had watched her wave the boy off to school. He had watched her return from visiting friends. He had watched her leave once a week to have lunch with O'Brien at the Queen's. He had watched her so many times – and always with the same aroused excitement.

Mark's nights were tortured by thoughts of her in O'Brien's arms. Even Rouen's masterpiece seemed to mock . . . that knowing look in Kate's eyes acquired a new meaning . . . look at me, she seemed to say, look and lust, desire and dream, want and crave as much as you like . . . but only Eoin O'Brien will plunder my body. '*No*,' Mark had cried, 'no, you are mine, mine, mine!' But Kate had just smiled her artful smile.

Then one day Mark saw her daughter. Even at six she

210

was beautiful. She walked at her nanny's side, head erect, chin tilted, confident, as graceful as a gazelle. Her resemblance to her mother was striking, almost uncanny. The same vibrant red hair, pearl-white skin and huge green eyes too large for her face. And the name . . . Mark had been within yards when the nanny had called, 'Kathleen, it's time we were home.' *Kathleen!* How many Kathleens were not called Kate? The name escaped his lips before he could stop himself – 'Kate' he had said aloud. The child looked at him, startled, eyes widening to golden-flecked pools of deep green. Then the nanny had taken the girl's hand and hurried away. He had stared after them. Kate! Three generations. This child, the mother, and the girl in the painting. His heart pounded. The mother was flawed, O'Brien's thick-fingered engineer's hands had fumbled all over her body, O'Brien had planted his seed in her belly . . . Mark still desired her, but his pleasure was diminished by that knowledge. *But the child!* Only a true collector has the patience to wait.

He sighed and stared at the back of his chauffeur's head. Now it was up to Ashendon who was being paid too well to fail. The Rolls purred through the outskirts of Belfast and set off for Brackenburn, where Mark would pace the floor until Ashendon phoned . . .

At the Queen's Hotel Ashendon's charm was having a devastating effect on Sheila O'Brien, but then Ashendon's practised smile had weakened the resolve of ladies all over Europe. He and Mark Averdale had been friends ever since they were thrown out of Eton, after that party on the river – since when Ashendon had squandered his inheritance and now lived on his wits. And he lived well . . . though never on the grand scale he described. The rich palace he talked of in Rome was in fact a modest apartment, his flat in Paris was a borrowed room, and the villa in Capri was total invention, as were his art galleries in Rome and Venice, Paris and Milan. But it made a fine story and Sheila O'Brien, who knew London and Edinburgh but nowhere 'on the continent', could almost see the blue skies and feel the sun when Ashendon lapsed into excited Italian.

Eoin O'Brien was also impressed, besides it was doing

his reputation a power of good to be seen in animated conversation with Lord Averdale's friend. But Ashendon's way of looking at his wife was beginning to get on O'Brien's nerves. From the moment he sat down the man had stared at her . . . Sheila had noticed it too, she could hardly not notice! God in Heaven, the man might be stinking rich but he had no bloody manners.

But then Ashendon apologized. 'I'm most terribly sorry for staring,' he said, 'but the resemblance is truly remarkable. Please let me explain.'

He told them about an artist who had lived in Paris and painted his favourite model time and again, so much so that she had become famous. Even now her portrait hung in the Louvre. And Mrs O'Brien, Ashendon assured them, was so like her that even Rouen, the painter, would have been hard put to tell them apart.

The O'Briens were mollified . . . but Ashendon was merely baiting the trap. 'I'm not exaggerating,' he laughed, 'in fact I can prove it. Come and have tea in my rooms, I'll show you a photograph.'

Sheila was too intrigued to resist, and although O'Brien was conscience-struck about returning to his office he sensed that the luncheon had turned into something of an occasion. Besides Ashendon clinched it with an intriguing remark. 'It's too public here,' he said, lowering his voice, 'but, well, Mrs O'Brien's likeness could be worth a great deal of money.'

Upstairs in his suite, Ashendon ordered tea. Then he opened a red suitcase. Sheila watched with mounting curiosity. Meeting Ashendon was quite an adventure for a doctor's daughter from Antrim, who despite her looks had led a very sheltered life . . . O'Brien had married her when she was just seventeen, so life had been a matter of exchanging her father's house for his. Since when she had been a dutiful wife, and had given birth to two adorable children. O'Brien dressed her well, her house was as smart as her neighbours', they holidayed in London and Scotland, and by her own provincial standards she lacked for nothing. She was quietly happy and it showed in her face.

Which was why Ashendon thought Mark Averdale was

wrong to compare her with Rouen's famous model. Even in *Looking Glass*, a reproduction of which Ashendon took him his suitcase, there was a difference. Rouen's girl exuded sexuality, whereas Sheila O'Brien glowed with femininity – the two were not always the same. Rouen's nymph seduced by arching an eyebrow, the very idea of seduction might shock Mrs O'Brien to the core. And yet ... Ashendon glanced from the coloured photograph in his hands to the woman ... and yet? Who could tell what she might look like if properly aroused? Perhaps if she were taken out of her stuffy bourgeois environment ... perhaps she could be taught ... perhaps even as Rouen had taught his model ... was that what Mark Averdale had in mind?

Ashendon waited until the maid had delivered the tea tray. He left Rouen's painting face down on the table while handing other reproductions to the O'Briens, talking non-stop about style and technique to impress them with his expertise. When the maid left Ashendon could delay no longer. He prepared the ground with care. 'The resemblance will strike you immediately,' he said to O'Brien, 'ignore the obvious similarities such as the red hair and green eyes ... look at the bone structure ... the high sculptured cheekbones, the width of the forehead ... why even the *hands* are those of your wife.'

Hands were the last thing O'Brien looked at when he saw the picture. The girl was completely naked. Nude! Totally! She lay on a couch, one arm raised to hold a looking glass, the other smoothing her hair as she admired herself. Quite, quite nude!

O'Brien went brick red. The paper shook in his hands.

'See what I mean about the cheekbones,' Ashendon said smoothly.

O'Brien swallowed hard, 'Dammit, I had no idea – '

'Oh, do let me see,' Sheila O'Brien could restrain herself no longer. She rose quickly, bewildered by her husband's reaction. O'Brien tried to turn the paper away, but her hands had already grasped an edge.

'Oh,' she said, and then again, 'Oh.'

Spots of colour marked her cheeks. She caught her breath, but her gaze remained fixed on the painting. She took in every inch of the figure on the couch, from the perfectly formed breasts to the slender waist, the rounded buttocks and the long, long thighs . . . and the look in the girl's eye. 'Oh,' she said again in a whisper.

But Ashendon heard the pride in her voice.

'We must go,' O'Brien announced, rising to his feet. 'Sheila . . .'

But Sheila was still gazing at the reproduction in her hands. 'You know,' she said thoughtfully, 'wouldn't you think she's even more like Kathleen?'

'*Our* Kathleen?' O'Brien was shocked even further. 'Our *daughter* –'

'Wouldn't you think so? When she grows up I mean?'

'You have a daughter?' Ashendon's note of pretended surprise was just right.

'And a son,' she smiled, but her eyes stayed on the painting.

'Amazing,' Ashendon said. He looked at the tea tray as if seeing it for the first time. 'Ah, tea. You promised to stay for some tea.'

O'Brien took some persuading but his wife had returned to the sofa, the reproduction still in her hands. The next moment the most amazing thing happened. She copied the pose of the girl in the painting – holding the paper to match the angle of the looking glass, while patting her hair with her other hand. She tilted her chin to the right angle, then she looked at Ashendon. He went cold. Hairs rose on the back of his neck. It was the *same look* – the same smouldering look.

Ashendon took a deep breath and began talking to O'Brien. By his own standards he was fumbling, thoroughly unnerved by that look – but he told the prepared story as best he could, of the rich art collector in Rome who worshipped at Rouen's shrine and who would pay a fortune for new works based upon Rouen's famous model.

'You mean fakes?' O'Brien asked, intrigued despite himself.

'Certainly not. He would commission Italy's greatest painters and sculptors . . . perhaps Vitelli, even Orsinni, I don't know . . . but I suspect he would pay hundreds of pounds to the model –'

'To pose like that?' O'Brien was horrified. 'Are you suggesting –'

'Simply saying –'

'But the implication –'

'I'm sorry, but sometimes those of us who devote our lives to art forget how some people react. An artist's eye –'

'The implication,' O'Brien persisted.

Ashendon begged forgiveness. 'I mean no offence, quite the contrary. To rank alongside the Mona Lisa even . . .' he shook his head, his expression eloquent. 'Imagine your wife and daughter, immortalized in –'

'*My daughter!* She's six years old!'

'But has inherited her mother's extraordinary beauty,' Ashendon broke off and hurried to the case. 'Look,' he sorted through his photographs, 'let me show you something. Take this as an example.' The picture was Prud'hon's *Venus and Adonis*, two nude figures seated on a grassy mound, embracing – while in the foreground a naked boy-child romped with a pet dog. Prud'hon's idealized romantic love was lost on O'Brien. All he saw was the woman's snow-white flesh, the fair curls of pubic hair . . .

Besides his wife was saying, 'Not Kathleen without clothes. I wouldn't allow that. It's different for a grown woman, but a child . . .'

Ashendon knew he had won. She would do it.

He put his suggestions with consummate skill. Perhaps he could arrange a London studio . . . if the artists would not travel from Rome they might settle for photographs, taken by an expert, from every conceivable angle . . . and of course the sculptors would want exact measurements . . .

A faint blush appeared on Sheila O'Brien's face.

Ashendon hurried on . . . it might be possible to photograph the child in a party dress, Ashendon would do his best to persuade them . . .

Eoin O'Brien was in a daze. He would never have believed it an hour before. Even now, actually to allow his wife . . . he looked at her, wanting her to say it was out of the question. But her eyes were on Rouen's painting and apart from the colour in her cheeks she might have been oblivious of the conversation. Incredulously O'Brien heard himself speak. 'How much?' he asked. He was actually asking *how much*! He heard his own voice without believing it. 'You were talking about hundreds of pounds?'

Ashendon waved a hand, 'There is much to organize first, but if it happened, well the photographer would need several sessions . . . perhaps three, each of two hours . . . I can't say exactly . . . possibly five hundred pounds each session.'

Fifteen hundred pounds! O'Brien remembered his auditor's statement. Fifteen hundred would restore him to solvency. He could pay his creditors. Money alone would not beat this German competition, but it would buy time . . .

Ashendon coughed and looked suddenly embarrassed, 'There is a condition I must make. Well, if I help bring this about . . . you must be discreet. For instance, Lord Averdale is a client of mine. If he thought I had taken advantage of a chance introduction . . .'

O'Brien shuddered. Of course secrecy was essential – not that the matter would be taken any further – after all it was just an idea, wasn't it? But Ashendon knew better than that, and when he bade the O'Briens farewell he stressed he would be leaving Belfast in the morning. If they wished him to pursue the matter . . .

O'Brien confessed his business problems to his wife that night. She was not completely surprised, he had been edgy for weeks. 'I would have kept quiet,' O'Brien said miserably, 'but this fellow Ashendon's idea . . .'

Strangely she did not really mind, in fact she was secretly excited. Ashendon's face had revealed too much. His lust had been recognized to stir feelings in her that were exciting and frightening at the same time. She wondered what it would be like, taking her clothes off, posing nude. Beads of sweat had broken out on Ashendon's brow when she had looked at him like that. She wondered if the photographer would sweat? She hoped so, she would try to make him sweat . . . but it would be so much easier if Eoin wasn't there.

216

Ashendon was finishing breakfast when O'Brien called at the Queen's the next morning. They adjourned upstairs to the suite, where his bags were already packed.

'Absolute secrecy,' O'Brien insisted. 'My wife's reputation . . . and mine too . . .'

'We are mutually dependent. Should Lord Averdale ever find out –'

But O'Brien had worried about that overnight. 'Suppose he sees a statue of my wife. He travels too, you know. In Rome perhaps. He would recognize –'

'Only Rouen's famous model. Your wife's likeness is already well known in the art world. Don't you see, her unique similarity is a total disguise.'

Ashendon promised to cable his Italian collector from London and let O'Brien know the outcome as soon as possible. Hopefully everything could be arranged in a month. O'Brien said goodbye and hurried to his office. A month? He was pleased, his mail that morning emphasized how hard his creditors were pressing. Fifteen hundred pounds would sort them out. Which left the problem of the German competition – but when Lord Averdale telephoned and suggested lunch, Eoin O'Brien began to hope for a solution even to that problem.

Mark Averdale, however, had something quite different on his mind, and after a passable meal at the Union Club he came to the point with unusual directness. 'I need a general manager to run my business affairs,' he said, 'but finding the right man has been the very devil. The Belfast people I've interviewed haven't the experience, and those over from the mainland don't know enough about Ulster. But after we bumped into each other yesterday, well . . . I began to think of you for the job.'

O'Brien was taken aback. He had been wondering what had prompted the invitation . . . but this?

'Why not?' Mark chuckled. 'You're an Ulsterman. A practical businessman. Frankly the more I think about the idea the more I like it.'

When O'Brien pointed out he was in business already, Mark skilfully avoided the obvious but made the point obliquely. 'I know how successful you've been in the past, but today . . .' he shrugged, 'who can tell how long this slump will last. In my opinion, only the very large concerns will survive.'

O'Brien saw a glimmer of hope. Fifteen hundred pounds from Ashendon would prop his business up for a while longer, but the future was still bleak with this German competition. But if Averdale wanted him, Averdale might buy his business to get him.

'I might at that,' Mark agreed when the idea was put forward. 'We could slot it into Averdale Engineering very nicely. Suppose I buy it for the value of the assets, plus three years' profits for goodwill. That sounds fair, doesn't it?'

It did sound fair for a business that was solvent – but O'Brien's was not. The current loss had wiped out the profits for the past two years and asset value would not pay the creditors. But asset value plus Ashendon's fifteen hundred might just be enough . . .

'I want you to understand what I'm offering,' Mark smiled. 'Sole charge of my investment portfolio. First the engineering company, then supervision of my holdings elsewhere. You would be answerable only to me. You must realize, O'Brien, this offer is worth a great deal of money.'

Mark told him exactly how much money – first the salary, more than O'Brien had been able to take out of his own business even in a very good year – and then the bonus. The bonus was the *real* money, a hundred pounds for every thousand he could squeeze out of Averdale profits. Ten per cent of Lord Averdale's additional wealth. O'Brien would quadruple his income.

O'Brien saw more than a glimmer of hope, he saw the answer to his prayers. A lifeline, a chance to escape from his difficulties not only with honour, but to a secure and lucrative future.

'Look,' Averdale said briskly, 'I won't beat about. I'm in a hurry to make this appointment. Sleep on it by all means, but I can't give you longer. There's a man over from Liverpool to see me tomorrow who fits the bill on paper. I'll have to chance him if you're still undecided . . .'

O'Brien told his wife that night. She suggested he tell Lord Averdale about the current loss. 'After all, it's the first time and . . .'

But that would not do. Averdale was unlikely to trust his

investments to a man whose own business was insolvent . . . in fact he might cancel his offer entirely.

It all turned on making O'Brien solvent again. It all hung on that fifteen hundred pounds from Ashendon.

And O'Brien had just explained that when Ashendon himself had telephoned from London. He'd said, 'I think it's on, I think my people in Rome will settle for photographs taken in a studio.'

'When? When would they want to . . . to do it?'

'Oh, as soon as I can arrange everything. Inside a month, I'd say.'

O'Brien breathed a sigh of relief. But then Ashendon added a qualification, 'Oh, just one other thing. I tried them on the idea of your daughter in a dress. No good, I'm afraid. Artists want the bone structure, you see, so I'm afraid both models must be nude.'

O'Brien winced – but with salvation so close only one answer was possible, 'I'll arrange it,' he said thickly.

The next morning he signed contracts with Lord Averdale, including one which guaranteed his company to be solvent. The gamble was on. He had taken the plunge. And Lord Averdale set him to work immediately. 'Look, I'm sorry to start you off with a nasty one, but some fool English foreman took some Croppies on over at the new works. Damn fellow doesn't understand how things work here. But you'd better sort it out before we have real trouble.'

And so Mark Averdale at last engaged a general manager who would screw every last ha'penny from the Averdale investments. He was pleased, especially with the firm way O'Brien had sorted out that business of employing Croppies at the new factory. True, the men had rioted instead of going peacefully, but O'Brien could hardly be blamed for that. So Mark Averdale had every cause for satisfaction.

He allowed three weeks to elapse before he raised the matter of O'Brien's business. 'My people say it's quite solvent, so long as all of your customers pay. These people Brown & Company seem a bit slow. They're still outstanding with fifteen hundred pounds, you know.'

O'Brien knew full well. Brown & Company were a

figment of his imagination. He had raised a fictitious invoice to balance his books – in order to guarantee solvency. Ashendon's fifteen hundred pounds would be substituted as soon as it came to hand. But it was still *not to hand* . . . and three weeks had passed.

'Browns will pay,' O'Brien said hurriedly, 'I know they will.'

O'Brien was hectically busy for the rest of the day but the matter stayed on his mind, a nagging worry which tied knots in his stomach. In fact he was feverish with worry by the time Ashendon telephoned that evening.

'I know, old boy,' Ashendon said smoothly, 'I've had the devil of a time setting everything up. But all's well now. Four weeks' time, the studio is booked, the photographer has been approved by my people in Rome – everything's ready.'

Four weeks! More delay. O'Brien steadied his hand as he wrote down the address of the studio in Chelsea.

'Just one more thing,' Ashendon went on, 'the sculptor wants very detailed measurements. Down to the last centimetre. You might warn your wife . . . tell her to expect a certain amount of, well, man-handling so to speak.'

CHAPTER ELEVEN

The great house of Brackenburn and the Falls Road were not far apart, less than twenty miles as the crow flies – but twenty might have been a thousand in 1938 – they were in different worlds.

Belfast had become a battle-ground for Matt Riordan. The beating inflicted by O'Brien's thugs had turned him into a soldier. There was no chance of compensation for his injuries – the men dismissed from Averdale's lacked independent witnesses, whereas O'Brien had lined up a dozen clerks who swore blind that the Croppies had started the trouble. The RUC even told Mick Nealson's young widow that he would have faced charges for incitement had he lived.

Matt blazed at the injustice and complained bitterly to Ferdy Malloy, but there was little Ferdy could do – in fact there was little *anyone* could do – not just about the Averdale riot but about the whole rotten mess. The system was stacked against them. Catholics were frustrated at every turn. Seventeen years after partition Protestant Unionists ruled from Stormont more firmly than ever. Ulster had become a one-party state. While many Catholics had no vote at all, many Protestants had several. That was monstrous enough but it was the clever re-arrangement of electoral boundaries which really kept the Unionists in power. Even in Derry where Catholics outnumbered Protestants two to one, gerrymandering was enough to return the Unionists time after time. Nationalists lost heart. Local elections were foregone conclusions, so the bulk of the seats went uncontested. And without the ballot box little was left for the Catholics. Even the working class lacked solidarity. In England trade unions were uniting workers against employers, but in Belfast Protestants were ready to attack any Catholic who claimed a job . . . as Matt had found out.

In the ghettoes, Catholics went hungry by day, and in fear of their lives by night – but some fought back. Pockets of resistance flared around the city. Matt sought them out – limping to meetings with the aid of a stick, often wincing in pain from his strapped-up ribs. Ferdy Malloy took him to Queen Street, near the docks. Catholic Queen Street was parallel to Protestant Frederick Street, and a series of intersections ran between the two, all of which turned into shooting galleries at times. Anyone crossing the inter-connecting streets was as likely to be hit by a Catholic bullet coming up as a Protestant bullet going down. But Ferdy went via 'the tunnel' – a route developed by housewives concerned more with safety than privacy – which tracked in and out of people's houses and back-yards. More than once an occupant was interrupted having a stand-up bath in a galvanized tub – but Ferdy simply introduced Matt as 'one of the boys' and passed on to the next house.

'One of the boys' meant the IRA and in the weeks following the Averdale riot Matt met Jimmy Steele, Mick Traynor, Hugh McAteer and dozens of others . . . all of whom welcomed him warmly. The name Riordan opened doors. Almost every man told a story of Liam Riordan and showed obvious pleasure in meeting his son. Their hero-worship embarrassed Matt. He felt confused, guilty about his past attitude towards his father, but although he said little the repeated eulogies hastened his reassessment of the world.

Ireland as one country was beyond Matt's memory. He had grown up with partition – but some of the men he talked to were of his father's generation. They remembered the dreams of their youth. Many wore the *Fainne* in their lapels, a small ring denoting them to be Irish speakers. They were so disappointed with Matt's lack of that language that he vowed to learn it as quickly as possible. It was from these older men that Matt got the flavour of days gone by – when the people of Ireland had united against the British Empire. Pride shone in their eyes as they described one exhilarating adventure after another. Their spirit had seemed indomitable in 1916. Men had followed their leaders with unquestioning loyalty. Whatever Dev said, or Cathal Brugha, or Erskine Childers – no matter who said what it was right. Unity! Unity to achieve freedom.

Listening to their emotion-choked voices it was easy for Matt to understand what had drawn his father into the movement. And for the first time he understood the bitterness. The Treaty had been a betrayal. To have fought so hard and at such a terrible cost . . . then to be sold out . . . to be sold out by friends and comrades, fellow Irishmen . . . seemed like the end of the world. It *was* the end of the IRA – the IRA as it was – the Civil War saw to that, with men like Collins and Brugha going opposite ways. The IRA had been torn asunder, along with the whole country.

The men wearing the *Fainne* made their disgust obvious. The Civil War had decimated the IRA. The pre-1921 IRA had ceased to exist. The leaders of the new Free State had abandoned the goal of a united Ireland – Dev and Cosgrave disagreed on many things, but both Fianna Fail and Fine Gael supported the new constitution in the south. But Matt's new friends had kept faith – their vision was unchanged, they still dreamt of a united Ireland, free of the British at last. Anyone who thought otherwise was their enemy – be he Craig in Stormont or de Valera in Dublin. The very concept of two Prime Ministers in separate parliaments was repugnant. 'And so it should be to all Irishmen,' one said bitterly, 'especially men like Pat Connors and that rat pack in Dublin.'

A veil lifted from Matt's eyes. Most of the men knew Pat Connors. He had been one of their leaders in the old days . . . but the old days were over . . . now he was their enemy. Suddenly Matt saw things so clearly that he almost cried with joy. He hated Pat Connors, so did these men. He hated Averdale, and these men did too. It was like coming home. He no longer felt so alone, so threatened. He could strike back – with these friends of his father's.

Matt's respect for his father had been growing for weeks – grudgingly at first, he had hated too long for it to be otherwise. But he *understood* his father now, understood how traitors like Pat Connors had caused such bitterness, understood and sympathized because he felt the same way. Matt's feelings had gone full circle. Once upon a time his father's opinion didn't matter a damn, but it did now. He was proud of his father now, and wanted the feeling reciprocated. Like father like son, people would say, but Matt had a lot to do before that. First he had to acquire rank and standing within the IRA – and he was determined to achieve that before his father returned to Belfast.

The discipline surprised him. Men did what they were told, obeyed orders, even Liam Riordan who had wanted to rush back to Dublin to take revenge on Pat Connors – but the IRA had insisted otherwise. The trip to America was too important . . . it had been planned for months . . . it *had* to take place, and as the Riordan name was respected over there he stood the greatest chance of success. And he *had* succeeded, which was why he had been sent on to Canada, and from there to Spain. Which was why he was now in Germany.

'Germany?' Matt gasped.

'They helped us in 1916. They sent arms and there's hope they will send some now. There's another war coming. This one could finish the British Empire once and for all.'

So much depended on his father. Matt could no longer stifle his pride, especially when Liam Riordan's work in the United States began to pay dividends. Fifty-five rifles were smuggled into Belfast via Liverpool. A crate of vehicle spares arrived from Detroit – but instead of tractor parts the IRA men unpacked sixteen Thompson machine-guns and sixty thousand rounds of ammunition. Twenty revolvers came in from Amsterdam. Fifteen more rifles reached them from Madrid . . .

Matt dedicated his life to the IRA after that. He was taught to shoot and handle explosives, and spent a weekend in the Sperrin Mountains learning much more – codes and signals used by the RUC, how to organize an ambush, how to read a map. Back in Belfast he helped develop a lamp signalling system for use against the night-time skirmishes of the Murder Gang. After a while routes throughout the Falls and Short Strand blinked with red and green lights after dusk – green for all clear and red for alert, as IRA men signalled from one corner to another. And it worked – time and time again flashing red lights resulted in the Murder Gang being driven off. But one night it failed. One night a lamp remained green when it should have flashed red – and the Murder Gang penetrated a safe zone to claim another victim.

Matt was summoned to the subsequent IRA court-martial – not as an offender or even a witness, but to perform his duty if punishment was awarded. Miley O'Faolin's lamp had remained green when another fifty yards away had flashed red for ten minutes. But Miley had been eating his supper. Gunfire had him scrambling back to his window vantage point – but too late for the man dying on the ground, and too late to save Miley from a court-martial. He was found guilty and sentenced. Bullets were to be put through both of his knees. Miley's Counsel appealed while Matt paced up and down outside. He felt sick, his hands sweated . . . he had wounded a B Special a week before but that was different, that was the enemy . . . but to cripple a friend! He prayed that the sentence would be set aside. Other offenders had been beaten with batons, or overdosed with castor oil . . . knee-capping was rare. But a man had died because of Miley's bloody

224

supper . . . a man had *died*!

The sentence was reduced. Only one of Miley's legs was to be shattered by a bullet. They dragged him outside to the yard and held him over a milk churn. Matt fired from less than four feet away. He spewed up afterwards, and woke that night bathed in sweat, with Miley's terrible screaming in his ears. But he had obeyed orders. Discipline was essential. His father would be proud.

Perhaps it was Matt's unquestioning obedience which led to him being given an early command – or perhaps the name Riordan was enough. But whatever the reason his chance came a week later. The IRA was to mount an offensive – reprisals were to be taken against Belfast industrialists for their discriminatory employment practices. An example was to be made. Matt could hardly believe his luck. A chance for revenge . . . less than six months after being beaten senseless by Averdale's thugs! Not that Averdale was mentioned in the briefing – Matt was simply told to prepare a plan for striking a prime target, and to present his ideas within seven days.

He thought of nothing else. Time and again he walked past the Averdale factory, noting security precautions, gauging distances, calculating the effect of bomb blast. But he abandoned the idea . . . the nearby houses were too close . . . Matt had memories of being carried across the threshold of one such house after being kicked half to death. He remembered a woman's kindness, her tears and words of comfort . . . and he could not do it. He dared not risk hurting her. But it *had* to be Averdale, one way or another . . .

Then he read something in that morning's *Belfast Telegraph*. Beneath a photograph of Brackenburn ran the headline – '*Another art treasure for Lord Averdale*'.

'*After one of the most fiercely contested auctions ever held in Sotheby's famous sale rooms, Constable's* Willow Trees, *widely regarded as being one of the finest examples of English landscape painting, was purchased by Lord Averdale for the record sum of eleven hundred guineas. Among those bidding against Lord Averdale were several representatives of foreign art galleries – including Mr*

Isadore Newton of the Carnegie Museum of Fine Arts in New York and Herr Heinrich Hoffman of Berlin. Commenting afterwards, a joyous Lord Averdale said he was greatly relieved to have saved this treasure for Great Britain. His Lordship also confirmed that Willow Trees *will shortly occupy pride of place in Brackenburn's Long Room, which together with the gallery at Brackenburn now houses the most important art collection in Northern Ireland . . .'*

Eleven hundred guineas for a painting! It seemed blasphemous to Matt. Kids were starving in the Falls. His own mother was sick. Poverty marked every house for miles around, yet eleven hundred guineas had been paid for a painting. And Holy Christ, just look at that house! It was bigger than the ships being built in the yards. Outrage left Matt feeling ashamed – ashamed for any man who could turn his back on the sick and needy to indulge himself in an . . . an *irrelevance*. Matt turned back to the photograph of Brackenburn. He had never seen it before. It was a palace, as long as a street, taller than a church . . .

He was still shaking with anger and disgust half an hour later when he went in search of Ferdy Malloy. He wielded the rolled-up *Telegraph* like a club in his hand. But Matt had made up his mind about one thing. The search for a target was over.

Lord Averdale was quite unaware of Matt Riordan's existence. Elsewhere to inhabit the same city might create common interests – paths might cross to establish some contact, even a nodding acquaintanceship – but not in Belfast. The division between 'the haves' and 'the have nots' was unbridgeable. If Mark Averdale thought of the Falls Road at all it was with a shudder of distaste. It was a festering seed-bed of revolution, a reminder of the need for B Specials and a strong RUC. But in fact thoughts of the Falls rarely crossed Mark Averdale's mind – especially at a time when he was so immersed in other matters.

Had Lord Bowley's death occurred earlier Mark might have gone to Africa to settle the estate himself – as it was, by the time the news reached Brackenburn Mark's encounter with Sheila O'Brien had changed the course of his life. Not that he was unaffected by the news, he was genuinely upset, in many ways the Bowleys were the closest thing to a real family he had known. The tragedy jolted him – but life goes on, and brings with it the need to make decisions about all manner of things – which in Mark's case now included the Bowley estate. However his anxiety was settled by the lawyers in Nairobi who wrote to say that the estates could be run by a contract manager for the time being . . . and of course there was no urgency about the newspaper in Dublin, which had more or less run itself for years. So with everything in abeyance Mark's thoughts turned greedily back to Sheila O'Brien.

Seeing her filled him with an exquisite mixture of pain and pleasure. It was tantalizing, so near and yet so far. Hunched in his greatcoat on the park bench near her home, he devoured her with his eyes. The urge to confront her was sometimes so compelling that he had to cling to the wooden slats to stop himself from rushing up to her. Once he was terrified that she had recognized him. He jumped up and hurried away, with yet another picture of her in his mind. He was a walking camera – he had only to close his eyes to see her – in her white coat or a favourite green woollen suit – but always dressed. He ached to see her as Rouen had painted her. Every night he stared at the painting in his room and every night reached the same conclusion – that Rouen's nymph and Sheila O'Brien and her child were somehow three generations of the same woman. And she was *his* woman. She had been since he was sixteen. He had hidden her in his room then, safe from other men's eyes. He had worshipped her ever since. But he longed to make sure the resemblance was total – that it extended beyond hair and eyes and alabaster white skin.

The chance reunion with Ashendon had been a stroke of good fortune which Mark had seized with both hands, but he would have achieved his objective without Ashendon. Single-minded ruthlessness was an Averdale trait.

Finding a photographer's studio in Chelsea had been easy, but finding one which suited his purpose had taken more time. Kate would be his for six precious hours. He would gaze on her nakedness as Rouen had looked on his nymph all those years ago — but there would be a difference. Where Rouen's genius had worked on canvas, Mark would record on film . . . and although Rouen possessed the skill of a master, Mark had the thoroughness of an Averdale. His camera probe would be total . . . every angle, every inch, every half inch would be photographed. It would be the most comprehensive study of the female form ever undertaken — and for that Mark needed a very special photographer.

Humphrey Leonard had not wanted the job. His initial reaction was to dismiss the man as a freak. Half way through their second meeting he almost asked the man to leave the studio. But the fee made Leonard reconsider. It was a great deal of money. So much so that he agreed to ponder the technical problems involved and give Mark an answer the following day.

So Mark made a third visit to the studio and listened carefully as Leonard outlined his proposals. The construction work would be considerable . . . the technical difficulties profound . . . the cost even higher than originally supposed — but yes, the project was possible! Mark parted with a large sum of money and returned to Ulster.

Some weeks later he telephoned Leonard, using the assumed name of Montgomery. 'Yes,' Leonard confirmed, 'the construction is finished. When you are ready I will hire a model and we can have a dummy run.'

Mark travelled back to London. He was growing tired of the capital. The talk at his club was mostly of impending war, which Mark dismissed as depressing nonsense. It was inconceivable that a politician as experienced as Chamberlain would be troubled by an upstart like Hitler. Besides, with the French as our allies Germany would not embark on expansion in Europe. So, having expressed his views to all and sundry, Mark fortified himself with a large brandy and then took a cab to Chelsea.

The interior of the studio had been rebuilt. Mark was astonished. He began to appreciate the technical problems which Leonard had been set to master. They had been mastered, there was no doubt of that — Mark was thrilled with the result, and even more thrilled with what he saw through the scaffolding – a naked girl, reclining on a green chaise-longue. She was beautiful. Her long black tresses hung loose over her shoulder, tips of hair brushed one breast. Mark stared through the glass and silver slats of the custom-built apparatus and was reminded of a precious jewel set in a casket. But this jewel was flawed compared with Kate. Her face relied on youth for its vitality, Kate's bone structure would survive the years. This girl's legs were sweetly curved, but Kate's were longer and more graceful. This girl was obvious, whereas Kate was subtle and mysterious. Mark registered each difference with a little glow of satisfaction, pleased that even the most sought-after model in London was less beautiful than Kate. But then Kate was perfect. Flawless. Unique.

Mark's approval of Leonard's arrangements set the wheels in motion, and it was on the following evening that Ashendon had telephoned Eoin O'Brien. 'The studio is booked . . . a month's time . . . you might warn your wife . . . tell her to expect a certain amount of man-handling, so to speak . . .'

Mark made good use of the month. He stimulated O'Brien's anxieties – underlining in countless ways that O'Brien could only preserve his presence at the hub of things by collecting the fifteen hundred pounds due from 'Brown & Company'. The money *had* to come through. O'Brien was never allowed to forget it . . . as in turn O'Brien never allowed his wife to forget the importance of her approaching visit to the photographer's studio. And Mark increased the pressure by heaping ever more responsibilities on O'Brien. At no time did the man disappoint him. O'Brien had the constitution of an ox – working all hours in a superhuman effort to master every aspect of Mark's investments. Mark was delighted. He had hired the best general manager in Ulster who was quickly beginning to feel indispensable. Mark was glad – it would make it harder for O'Brien to ask for a week's leave in order to accompany his wife to London. Mark had plans of his own for that week which he had no intention of allowing O'Brien to complicate – so on the Wednesday of the third week he delivered his bombshell. Even then he disguised it too sweetly for O'Brien even to notice.

'I'm making you managing director of the engineering company,' Mark announced, 'and I've arranged for you to join the board at the yard.' He smiled as he added another carrot. 'Of course you will be entitled to director's fees as well as your salary. It will give you another eight hundred a year.'

O'Brien was jubilant. Hard work had earned a dividend already. He flushed a quick glow of gratitude to the man on the other side of the desk – but then came the catch. 'I'll be away next week,' Lord Averdale said. 'In Dublin mostly, sorting this newspaper out. But I have every confidence you'll deputize for me here.'

What could O'Brien say? His mouth opened but no words came out. Next week? What would Sheila say? But he could hardly ask for time off – not now.

He bought some flowers on the way home. He told Sheila it was to celebrate his new appointments, but of course it was nothing of the sort, and after dinner he broke the rest of his news – that she would have to go to London without him. He cast around in his mind for a suitable chaperone but knew it was hopeless. Nobody would understand. Even their closest friends would be shocked. O'Brien was shocked himself if he let his mind dwell on it ... Good God, how had it all come about?

O'Brien left the worst part until last – breaking the news that Kathleen too would have to pose nude. Sheila reacted with predictable indignation – for her child to appear in a party dress would be fun, but undressed – besides how would she explain it? Kathleen would tell people afterwards. Their guilty secret would be revealed ... but even for that O'Brien had worked out an answer. Twice in the recent past Kathleen had been examined by the doctor, and each time she had been required to strip off. So why not again? After all, it was a medical examination in a way – the sculptors were interested in bone structure.

Sheila accepted there was no other alternative, but it sullied her pleasure. Taking Kathleen was an inhibiting nuisance – but Ashendon promised it would be for only ten minutes of one session – after that Sheila could relax and enjoy herself. She was greatly pleased that her husband would be absent. Ever since seeing that look in Ashendon's eye she had sensed a pleasurable excitement. Not a day passed without her rehearsing the pose adopted by the model in *The Looking Glass*, practising the heavy-eyed look of seduction and the languid pose. She knew she could do it.

In Dublin Sean Connors was recovering from his upset with the Widow O'Flynn. Years later he counted her as one of the luckiest things ever to happen to him, but at the time he took it hard. He was scratchy and ill-tempered for days following that Sunday visit to the farm. Male pride had taken a knock and he was at a loss to know how to deal with it. He felt so confused – it was not so much that he wanted to marry the Widow O'Flynn as the misery caused by the prospect of losing her. Finally, after days of wretchedness, he divided a piece of paper into two columns and wrote 'For' at the top of one and 'Against' at the top of the other. Then he tried to crystallize his thoughts. It was far from easy. Under 'For' he wrote 'because I'm in love with her' but defining what that meant defeated him. So after struggling for half an hour he turned to the opposite column, and met with a surprise. Reasons 'Against' flew from his pen – starting with those she had given herself, that he was barely seventeen and she was twenty-eight, and by the time he was that age she would be forty. Nobody stayed young forever. He groaned aloud. 'Saggy tits,' he whispered, 'suppose she gets saggy tits?' It was an obscenity to imagine her like that – but it *could* happen. And big thick ankles and a gut bigger than half the boozers in Mulligan's Bar. He shuddered again. And at twenty-eight he was bound to be as horny as ever. Wouldn't he just die of frustration?

The list grew as if the pen had a mind of its own. He was in no position to support a wife . . . what would the Da say? Da would go mad! Men would laugh, women would snicker. And dear old Tomas . . . it would break his heart . . . Sean felt sure of that without knowing why.

The page looked one-sided when he finished. So much for love, he thought wryly, knowing he had half-joked himself into a mood of acceptance. Even so, he admitted, if I loved her enough none of these reasons would matter . . . but they did and he knew it. He tore the paper into shreds and sat thinking about Maeve O'Flynn – 'I'll be your woman as long as you want me,' she had said, 'but never your wife.' He was touched by that. 'She must think a lot of me to say that – and to make a man like Jim Tully wait.'

He clung to the thought, but after a while was unhappy even with that. It was wrong. His love might be less strong than he had imagined, but . . . well, he was fond of her. Too fond to take advantage. 'This way you'll remember me with love in your heart,' she had said – and there *was* love in his heart. Besides he even liked Jim Tully. After which . . . it was not easy, pangs of jealousy interfered with good intentions . . . but at last he decided, and acted the same day, burning his boats in case he changed his mind in the morning. He wrote to her, apologizing for his behaviour on the Sunday and saying she had been right about everything. And he went a step further, promising to see Jim Tully about premises for her tea-rooms. Which is what happened on the Thursday – when Tully took him to lunch at The Bailey in Duke Street.

Sean had explained his problem by the end of the meal. 'So that's it,' he summed up, 'I've done my best to help out, dealing with the labourers on a Saturday morning and so on, but . . . well, it seems to me that you'll be able to help the Widow O'Flynn more than I can.'

Tully's eyes gleamed. 'Sure wouldn't it be a pleasure. And you'd like me to take over this weekend – is that what you mean?'

The changing of the guard. Sean seethed with mixed-up emotions. He had endured agonies of heartache, but to his surprise most of the pain had already passed. It was like a weight lifting from his shoulders. Suddenly he felt free – as free as a boy tending donkeys. His life was his own again – he had nothing to hide from his father or anyone else.

Not that Tully was easily fooled. 'You're a good man as a friend,' he said with a quizzical look. 'Everyone says you've been good to the Widow O'Flynn right enough. I'm the same – a good friend and a bloody bad enemy. It's a favour I owe you and we'll leave it at that – but if there's anything you want in this town you come to me first. Do

I have your word on that Sean Connors?'

So that was that. Sean was racked with jealousy again on the Friday night and the Saturday morning, but he stayed away from the farm, and it was not until Monday that he learned the outcome – when a letter arrived at the office. It was postmarked Saturday, and the Widow O'Flynn had written:

Dear Sean,
I don't know if I'm pleased or angry. You learn new tricks faster than a puppy, but sure didn't you always. Your letter hurt. I cried all night. Except that – well most of it was what I was trying to tell you myself. Would you believe here's the two of us trying to be kind to each other and inflicting more pain than mortal enemies. But some of the things you wrote were nice – I kept your letter and read it every day. I'll never forget you, Sean.

Jim Tully arrived yesterday and came again this morning to see to the men – so he delivered your message without really knowing it, which is what you meant him to do all along. He's nice but he's not you, Sean, and I wish he would stop talking about you – he thinks the world of you, did you know that?

I'm not one for letter writing so I'll end now. I meant all the things I said last Sunday – don't forget, Sean, you are always welcome.
Maeve O'Flynn.

It was the first and only letter she ever wrote to him. The invitation in the final line made him tremble. Had the telephone been installed at the farm he would have called her there and then, and no doubt have visited her that night. But the farm lacked a telephone, and right at that moment Dinny Macaffety was bellowing – so Sean stuffed the letter into his pocket and hurried along to the editor's office.

Dinny looked like a waxworks dummy. His freshly barbered mane was smooth and slick with pomade, the scent of which was drowned by the smell of mothballs from his best suit. He cast a hasty look at Sean. 'We look like something out of Switzer's window. God save us but

233

someone will buy the pair of us before we cross Stephen's Green.'

Sean too wore his new suit. In fact everyone at the *Gazette* looked smarter than usual, and the office itself shone like a new pin – as well it should after Dinny's efforts of the past week. For it was the day of Lord Averdale's visit and Dinny's clean-up had only stopped short at rebuilding the place. Every exterior wall had been painted, floors had been waxed, desks cleaned, brasses rubbed, windows polished to a gleam, until now – at nine-fifteen on Monday morning – the *Gazette* was ready for inspection.

Dinny sighed at his litter-free desk, 'I'll never find a thing again and that's the God's honest truth.'

Mr Daly joined them. He was the solicitor appointed when Lord Bowley went to Africa. Dinny once said that the only paper Daly knew anything about was the one he wiped his arse on. 'A mealy-mouthed pontificating little weasel,' was Dinny's description. Daly stood five feet tall, with bent shoulders and a narrow, pointed face which twitched in nervous anticipation of the editor's every word.

'Did you phone the Shelbourne?' Dinny barked at him.

'I did, and his Lordship's at breakfast. We're expected at ten o'clock.'

Dinny grunted. 'We'll take ourselves round now. He'll never expect a Croppy to be early. It might give us some advantage. God knows we'll need it.'

The plan was simple enough. After collecting Lord Averdale from the Shelbourne Hotel Dinny would conduct him on a grand tour round the *Gazette*. Mr Daly would be on hand to answer any legal queries, and Sean was to follow in their footsteps as a personal assistant, making notes of any matters Dinny dictated. Then back to the Shelbourne for lunch (Sean was unsure whether he was invited to that), after which his Lordship would be leaving for London. But even simple plans sometimes go wrong – and Dinny Macaffety's plan went terribly wrong.

They were at the top of the steps leading to the ground floor when Dinny suddenly stopped. He felt in his pocket for something – then half turned – changed his mind, swung back to the stairs – and missed his footing. He went down like a ton of coal – and by the time Sean had brushed Daly aside, Dinny was crumpled into a heap at the foot of the stone steps, with his left leg bent under him. Sean leapt the last four steps and propped the dazed editor up in his arms – 'Get back to the office, Mr Daly – send someone down to give me a hand.'

Dinny's face was grubby grey, like a dirty shirt. He coughed and groaned, then opened his eyes – 'Dear God, you had no call to do that, boy. This Prod bastard will have me thrown out anyway.'

Sean blushed scarlet – 'I didn't do it, Mr Macaffety –'

'Sure don't I know that,' Dinny chuckled gruffly, then he yelped with pain, 'God Almighty, don't touch my leg!'

Sean's hand withdrew as if from hot coals. He guessed the leg was broken. A clatter of footsteps above drew his attention. Daly was returning with help.

'We'll carry him between us,' Daly was saying, 'take him back upstairs –'

'No,' Sean said with sudden authority, 'he's not to be moved until the ambulance gets here. We'll have to keep him warm. Give me your coat, Mr Daly.'

Sean wrapped the coat around Dinny Macaffety's extra large frame and tucked it under where possible. And ten minutes later the ambulance arrived.

'Just a minute, Sean,' Macaffety said as the stretcher men lifted him. Sean looked into the putty-coloured face. Macaffety grimaced with pain. 'Get yourself round to the Shelbourne with Daly. Explain what happened, then take over – give the tour as best you can. But Sean, you do the talking, eh – don't leave it to that weasel.'

'I'll do that, Mr Macaffety, and I'll come round to the hospital as soon as he's gone.'

But Dinny Macaffety was past caring. His eyes screwed up in pain and he swore lustily at the stretcher-bearers.

Sean turned from the departing ambulance and set off towards Stephen's Green with Daly at his heels. His nerve might have cracked given more time. The new owner's visit was beginning to exceed Sean's gloomiest expectations. Suppose he couldn't answer this Lord Averdale's questions? Daly would be useless. Dinny had been nervous, but at least he could have coped.

They climbed the steps and entered the Shelbourne, to

find Lord Averdale pacing the lobby. Paddy the doorman pointed him out. Sean was surprised. He had expected an older man, with a big military moustache, like Lord Kitchener. But the man who awaited them was young, less than thirty, with fair hair and an impatient frown on his face.

Sean was so unsure about shaking hands that he waved his hands in front of him like a blind man feeling the way. He fumbled through the introductions and excuses, unnerved by the coolly critical gaze. At his side Daly nodded and mumbled confirmation of the accident.

'All very unfortunate,' Lord Averdale said eventually. He extracted a gold hunter from his waistcoat, 'Worse than that – it's annoying. I'm due in London this evening. I can't possibly delay my departure.'

Sean bit back an impulse to say that Dinny had nearly killed himself. Instead he said, 'Mr Macaffety's broken his leg, sir. He'll be in hospital a good while.'

Lord Averdale seemed unconcerned about that. He said 'yes' and nodded in an abstracted way, then turned to Daly – 'You're the legal man, aren't you?'

Daly admitted he was, which seemed to please. Lord Averdale. 'Good,' he said, 'then you'll do just as well as Macaffety.' Which struck Sean as a monstrous insult – there was no comparison between Daly and Dinny Macaffety. Things were going from bad to worse, and plunged to new depths when Sean repeated Dinny's invitation to inspect the offices. Lord Averdale flatly refused – 'No, I don't think that's necessary. Besides . . .' he paused to consult his watch again, 'it would suit me to get this over with. There's an earlier connection to London – a flight you know – I might catch that if I hurry.'

So they had coffee in the Shelbourne. Sean knew it was all going wrong . . . but what could he do? At one point he was almost dismissed, when Lord Averdale said – 'I don't think I need to detain you, er . . . Connors . . . I want to discuss a legal matter.'

But Daly saved him. 'Perhaps he ought to stay. After all, well, technically I know nothing about newspapers.'

'Neither do I, that's the whole point. I don't want to either, especially down here.'

Lord Averdale's shrug of indifference suggested that Sean could stay if he wished, so they adjourned to a corner table where a waiter served coffee from a silver tray.

'I want to sell,' Lord Averdale said flatly, 'I want to sell the *Gazette* as quickly as possible.'

Sell? Nobody had thought of that. All the talk had been about changes . . . but for the paper to be sold?

Sean was picturing Dinny's face. The *Gazette* was Dinny's life. Sean's too in a way. They might have coped with some changes . . . but for the paper to be sold?

'I'll make my position perfectly clear,' Lord Averdale said to Daly. 'I'm well aware of Lord Bowley's regard for Macaffety, so I'm ready to make him an offer. If he can raise the money – perhaps with friends and associates – he can have the paper for the price of its assets. If he can't, or doesn't want to . . .' Lord Averdale shrugged, 'I'll offer the property on the open market. I'll get more that way no doubt, but there's no guarantee that new owners will share Lord Bowley's opinion of the management. Macaffety will have to take his chance, but it's up to him. I can't be fairer than that.'

Daly's only response was a blank stare.

'It's a very good offer,' Lord Averdale said sharply, 'I'd have thought, well, say you and Macaffety between you . . . you'd see your money back in three years . . . nothing wrong with that is there?'

Daly roused himself enough to say it was perfectly fair – but then came another shock.

'You've got until Friday,' Lord Averdale summed up. 'I shall be back from London by then. Net asset value as per the last balance sheet. Fix it up and we'll complete on Friday, there's a good chap. Otherwise I'm afraid I shall have to arrange a sale on the open market –'

'Friday?' Daly's astonishment got the better of him. 'You don't mean *this* Friday?'

'I most certainly do. I'm a busy man. You've got the chance of a bargain, and bargains don't last for ever, you know.'

Sean could contain himself no longer. 'But please, sir – Mr Macaffety will still be in hospital –'

'That's unfortunate, I agree, but it's no fault of mine.'

237

Lord Averdale consulted his watch again, 'Now gentlemen, if you will excuse me . . .'

Mark Averdale was well pleased with himself. Lord Bowley would have approved of giving Macaffety a chance to buy the *Gazette*. True, the timing was tight but that was up to Macaffety – Mark had given him first option. Mark was well used to making investment decisions quickly – within seconds at an auction – so to allow someone the best part of a week was generous in his opinion. He made no allowances for differing circumstances, but then he made few allowances for anyone – it was up to other people to look after their own affairs. Mark had his own priorities. Sheila O'Brien was due at the Chelsea studio tomorrow, and Mark had no intention of delaying in Dublin.

Even the flight to Croydon was exciting. It was Mark's first experience of flying and he found it stimulating. Not that he needed a stimulant – he had been in a fever of impatience for days. Whenever he closed his eyes he saw Sheila and Kathleen O'Brien naked in Leonard's studio. His ambition was about to be realized. He tingled with anticipation. Every hour took him nearer to verification of his discovery. Soon he would have proof that the beauty once captured on canvas had been miraculously re-created and was his to enjoy – his *to possess*! He had spent his last hour at Brackenburn talking to the girl in the painting. 'Soon Kate,' he had whispered – and the girl had smiled back from the pool.

But the mood in London, when he arrived late on that Monday afternoon, was depressing. The capital was dreary with rumours of war. The talk at the club was all about Hitler and Czechoslovakia, or France and the Maginot Line. There was no gaiety, no sense of expectation – in fact the reverse. Men at the club looked surprised, even shocked at Mark's sparkling eyes and flushed face. They seemed to be dreading tomorrow and Mark could hardly wait. Eventually he took himself off to St John's Wood where he drank champagne with Molly Oakes before taking her to bed. But even the pleasure of sexual intercourse with an imaginative partner left him dissatisfied. True, she was beautiful – but Kate would be better . . .

Sean Connors also spent a restless night, but for very different reasons. He sat in the kitchen of the small house in Ballsbridge, drinking tea and studying columns of figures. It had been a long and a worrying day.

Daly had been less than helpful at the office. The *Gazette* was to be sold and that was an end to it – neither Daly nor Macaffety could raise enough money.

'And how much money is that?' Sean had asked – which was how the argument started. According to Daly such confidential matters were no business of a junior reporter, which was perhaps true, except that Sean was due at the hospital to report to Dinny Macaffety. 'Just so long as Mr Macaffety knows,' Sean had shrugged. 'If he starts asking for figures and things . . . well, wouldn't you think he'll want a *full* report?'

The prospect of Macaffety's wrath was too much for Daly. He sealed the balance sheets into an envelope and marked it 'Private and Confidential'.

Sean said not a word. He simply took the large envelope under his arm and left for the hospital – where he found Dinny Macaffety nursing a leg in plaster, and the rest of the hospital reeling from the editor's temper.

Nor did his temper improve when Sean made his report. Dinny's face darkened, 'Friday? *This* Friday? We've no chance of raising the money by then.'

Later, when the initial shock had worn off, Dinny was even more pessimistic. 'It could be a year on Friday for all the good it would do. Where would the likes of me be finding that kind of money?'

'What kind of money, Mr Macaffety?'

'Sure it's all there, isn't it? Give me that envelope.'

So they studied the figures together. Not that Dinny knew how to interpret them – 'How the devil would I know that?' he snapped in exasperation at one stage. 'Do you think I'm a damn book-keeper? Words are my business, not numbers.'

Even so Sean thought he could work out the value of net assets. If he was right they amounted to thirty-two thousand, five hundred pounds. It was a staggering amount of money.

Dinny seemed to lose interest after that – lose heart – he was no businessman. Ever since the death of the Bowleys he had clung to the slender hope that things might remain as they were – with him running the paper for an absentee owner. He had wanted it so much that he had almost convinced himself it was possible . . .

Sean did his best to encourage him – 'Whoever buys it will want you as editor, Mr Macaffety. They're *bound* to – everyone says you're the best editor in Dublin.'

'Whoever buys it will run things their way. I'm too old to learn new tricks. It won't work and I know it. There's no sense in kidding myself.'

Even the prospect of borrowing the money seemed hopeless. 'How much did you reckon it was?' Dinny demanded. 'Over thirty thousand pounds. Nobody in their right senses would lend me that. No, Sean, it's to be sold over my head and there's damn all I can do about it.'

Sean fell silent for a while, then he asked – 'Would you mind if I showed these balance sheets to a friend of mine?'

Dinny shrugged, 'After Friday they'll be public knowledge anyway.'

Conversation dried up after that. Dinny seemed disinclined to talk, and all Sean wanted was to find a quiet corner and study the figures. He left as soon as he could. Macaffety called after him – 'Better get yourself back to the office. Paddy Egan will want all the help he can get.'

But Sean went home. His father was out and Sean had the house to himself. He spent the rest of the afternoon combing through the balance sheets. At the back of his mind lurked the vague idea of showing them to Jim Tully, but first Sean wanted to understand them himself. And that proved difficult. For a start the total value of all assets was nearly sixty thousand pounds – but total assets, he discovered, were very different from net assets. In fact there were all sorts of assets – current assets, circulating assets – Sean's brow crinkled in concentration. Finally he made sense of at least part of it – enough to realize that he had been right to deduct all liabilities from all assets, and thus arrive at the value of net assets which Lord Averdale wanted – the amazing sum of thirty-two thousand, five hundred pounds.

When Pat Connors arrived home they ate the meal of cold meat left out for them by Mrs McGuffin – then Pat left for a political meeting and Sean went back to his figures. It was then that he made his discovery. He was looking at the list of fixed assets, marvelling that plant and machinery were worth an astonishing fifteen thousand pounds, when he stopped. The line above said – Freehold property . . . £5000. Sean had passed it earlier, his interest captured by more dramatic figures – but as soon as he looked back he knew it was wrong. It had to be if it meant the *Gazette*'s offices. The *Gazette* occupied a very large building. The offices ran to four floors, and the print shop occupied the entire basement. If the truth was known they had too much space, spreading themselves all over the place. And a corner site in O'Connell Street was worth more than five thousand pounds. Sean knew that from his attempts to find tea-rooms for Maeve O'Flynn. But what did it mean? Audited balance sheets couldn't be wrong – could they?

It was eight o'clock when he returned to the hospital. He slipped the half bottle of whiskey from under his jacket and into Dinny's hand, and then asked about the office building.

Dinny shrugged, 'Lord Bowley's family have owned that site for generations. He owned the building and he owned the paper. It was all his money.'

'But why does the balance sheet say five thousand?'

'Sure, how would I know? It didn't matter a damn. I just told you, he owned the building before the paper ever started. What would be the point of him charging the paper more – he'd only be paying himself. I suppose some sort of nominal value had to be put down to suit the auditors.'

'But it's worth *more* than that –'

'Is it now?' Dinny flushed with temper. 'So you'll be telling your new friend Lord Averdale, I suppose? Ach, what does it matter. It's not something for the likes of us to bother about.'

But it did bother Sean. It bothered him so much that he could hardly sleep that night. The full potential of his idea eluded him – but one thing seemed clear. If he could pull

241

it off he would make the five hundred pounds he needed to send Tomas and the family to Australia.

Sean Connors and Mark Averdale were not the only ones restless that night – in Belfast Matt Riordan was sleepless too. His had been a long day also, most of it spent well away from the Falls Road, amid the gorse and heather which grew so abundantly on the hills above Brackenburn.

The destruction of Brackenburn had been approved by the IRA. There was still much to do, Matt would go back there tomorrow and again on Wednesday – but his plan had been accepted. The hard-eyed men who wore the *Fainne* had awarded Matt his first command.

Matt had argued powerfully at the secret meeting. Some men had wanted a more political target, a member of Craig's cabinet was suggested, but Matt would have none of it. It was what Lord Averdale stood for that was important, what he represented . . . three hundred years of repression . . . the Averdales had helped found the Orange Order . . . helped bring about the Act of Union . . . and had been foremost in their refusal to employ Catholics . . .

He had sat down not to thunderous applause but at least to grim-faced agreement. Matt was proving himself a Riordan after all. And at the end of the meeting he was rewarded with some very exciting news. His father was coming home and could be back in Ireland by the weekend. Matt hugged himself at the prospect. He would raze Brackenburn to the ground on Friday, meet his father on Saturday . . . and on Sunday they would plan their revenge on the rest of their enemies . . . men like Pat Connors and that son of his.

CHAPTER TWELVE

On the Tuesday morning Mark chose to ignore the newspapers, which were black with headlines about the Sudetenland and Hitler's intentions. Instead he went for a walk in St James's Park. Talk of war seemed unreal on the day his dream was to be fulfilled. War was ugly, brutal – it had no place in Mark's world.

It was a pleasant morning for a stroll. The photographic session would not start until three o'clock, and Mark knew his excitement would become intolerable unless he paced himself. Waiting would be unbearable if he thought of Kate. But walking in the park proved an unsatisfactory solution. Too many girls were clad in thin summer frocks – gusts of wind caught hemlines and swirled silks upwards, revealing shapely knees and gossamer-clad legs, and in one case thighs right up to the girl's undergarments. Mark took himself off to the Ritz for coffee.

The morning passed slowly. He walked up Bond Street, pausing to look in the galleries but making a conscious effort to avoid all paintings of the female form, naked or otherwise. At noon he took a cab to the Savoy, intending to lunch in the Grill – but even that plan suffered drawbacks. The Savoy overflowed with well-groomed women whose musical voices distracted him. Mark examined them all with frank appraisal. He did not classify even one as beautiful – least of all the famous American actress who sat surrounded by business managers and agents, and who several times smiled in his direction. Mark smiled back, straight into her eyes, in a way which pleased her – but she would have been less charmed to know that he thought her eyes too small and her mouth too wide – and that the sophisticated veneer masked a quite ordinary woman. Not a beauty. Not within a million miles of Kate.

It seemed strange to think that Kate and her child were somewhere in this vast city. He had ceased to think of them as Sheila and Kathleen O'Brien – they were Kate – the three generations inspired by Rouen. They – she – belonged to him, formed part of his existence. Odd to think they might not understand that – he was so dominated by thoughts of them that it seemed inconceivable they might not be obsessed in the same way. Perhaps they were – perhaps the young mother at least was conscious of the bonds which drew them together. Perhaps she yearned to be free of O'Brien. 'Soon Kate,' Mark whispered, 'very soon now.' He smiled – and the American actress smiled back at him.

He called at his London bank *en route* for Chelsea and cashed a cheque for the five hundred pounds needed for the first session. Then he sat back in the cab and watched the world go by. But the street scenes bored him and he closed his eyes to anticipate the pleasures ahead. Kate seemed close enough to touch when he did that, she might have been beside him. In some extraordinary way his whole life seemed to have been spent travelling to this meeting – ever since fleeing from Eton and returning to Brackenburn to find Rouen's nymph waiting at the poolside. He had hungered for her ever since – and here he was, in a London taxi-cab, on his way to meet her.

Leonard's studio had two entrances. Harlington Row was the proper address but by arrangement Mark entered the Monk Street door and squeezed past cardboard cartons and down a narrow passageway. The time was twenty minutes past two and 'Mrs Williams' and her child were due very shortly.

Leonard greeted his client affably. He was a neat, sharp-featured little man, dressed in a black sweater and corduroy trousers, who feigned indifference as he accepted the five hundred pounds to be paid to the model. Inwardly he seethed with curiosity. The best model in London would pose for fifty pounds. To pay ten times the rate seemed evidence of insanity – but it made things intriguing. Like other master photographers, Leonard was a student of human nature – and a good one, he had photographed the rich and the famous, the beautiful and the ugly. Many interesting people had passed through Leonard's studio, but none fascinated him as much as the man he knew as 'Mr Montgomery'. His clothes, his upper-class accent, his

244

mannerisms were no different from a dozen of Leonard's more affluent clients . . . and yet the man was prepared to go to these extraordinary lengths to photograph a young woman.

The two men talked for a few minutes, or rather Leonard talked, explaining the steps taken to comply with his client's instructions. A small changing room had been converted into a nursery, complete with dolls and a teddy bear, which is where Leonard's receptionist would amuse the child while her mother was in the studio. The child would be photographed first . . . that would be completed in fifteen minutes . . . after which the main session would begin. Mark glanced at his watch. Half an hour, that was all . . . half an hour, then it would happen. What he was to see would determine the rest of his life . . . and her life, their lives . . . the two Kates, mother and daughter. His mouth was dry with excitement, speech was impossible – he merely nodded his approval and turned away, accepting Leonard's suggestion that he make himself comfortable in the studio. He passed through the heavy sound-proofed doors without a word, leaving the photographer hovering at the back of the reception office, glancing at the clock as he waited the arrival of the young mother and child.

No monarch embarking on the rites of coronation ever experienced a greater surge of anticipation than Mark as he surveyed the studio. It was perfect. In the middle of the room the specially built cage blazed with the radiance of a polished diamond – a score of struts and steel and glass crossmembers bounced splinters of brilliant white light back at the arc lamps. The cage seemed larger when unoccupied and set higher from the floor – but Mark realized it was an optical illusion as he walked beneath it. The floor of the cage was exactly six and a half feet above the ground – Mark's head almost brushed the underside – and the size was a perfect twelve-foot cube. Mounted on all six surfaces of the cage the sixteen cameras focused their hungry eyes inwards to the very centre of the cube – to where the green chaise-longue reclined on its gilt frame. Soon Kate would lie there, as deliciously naked as she had been for Rouen – but whereas the great French artist had viewed her from only one angle and through one set of

245

eyes, Mark's sixteen eyes would peer from every conceivable vantage point – from all four walls, from the ceiling, and from the very floor of the cage itself.

Smiling with pleasure Mark climbed the gantry which ran around three sides and across the top of the cage. He peered joyously through the viewfinders of various cameras. The fourth side of the cube was set into the wall – and it was from the door in that wall that Kate would emerge into the brilliantly lit cube. The cube was all she would see. The rest of the studio lay in total darkness – a black, secret, impenetrable world. A man could stand right up to the bars but the light from the arc lamps made him invisible. Kate would be like a fly trapped in a bottle.

Breathing heavily Mark climbed down the gantry and crossed the floor to a chair. He felt hot and sticky from being so close to the lamps. He loosened his tie and removed his jacket, then fumbled for a cigarette with shaking hands. His fingers were clammy, he tasted his own sweat on the cigarette . . .

Not long to wait . . .

It seemed an age before the door opened. The child stood framed in the entrance, blinking against the blinding dazzle. Leonard's voice reassured her from the surrounding darkness. She raised an arm, shielding her face from the light, then took a tentative step forward like a bather testing the sea. Leonard's warm brown voice gentled her with encouragement. The girl responded by turning towards his voice. She looked so vulnerable. Mark's heart leapt with an urge to protect her – but he steeled himself to remain silent. He sat taut with nervous anticipation. The child was nervous too. Hesitant and uncertain. Wide green eyes, too big for her face, her head cocked at an angle as she listened to Leonard. The photographer encouraged her in a gentle, half-teasing way until some of the strain went out of her face. Her expression softened. At Leonard's suggestion she took the doll, clutched tight to her bare chest, across to the chaise-longue and sat down, placing the doll next to her with the watchful tenderness of a governess. She laughed aloud at something Leonard said, then answered in a cool clear voice. For a few minutes they talked back and forth. She turned and adjusted the doll's stance to an upright position. Leonard joked, using his skill to play a game and the child relaxed with trusting naturalness. She removed the doll's slippers and pulled the miniature frock down over the china feet. 'There,' she laughed. 'Now we're both undressed.' Leonard rewarded her with a rich chuckle and she giggled back, pleased with herself, excited by the whole adventure, more and more relaxed.

But Mark could not relax. He was under too much strain. The warm rapport between photographer and subject developed to his exclusion. He could neither participate nor enjoy. The charm of what he saw completely escaped him – he missed what a father might see, and what Leonard *did* see – a child, brimming with life, revelling in an opportunity to show off without parental restraint. Mark missed it because he was looking for something else. He was looking for Kate . . . and wondering how on earth he could tell whether this small girl would grow up into Rouen's vision of beauty. Instead of enjoying his eyes searched for deformities, for scars, for evidence that she would *not* be Kate. He looked for flaws, but found none. The child was perfectly proportioned . . . her legs strong, her back straight, her shoulders sloped at an enchanting angle. She had grace too, in every movement. But was she Kate? Her skin was magnolia white, her hair the colour of fire, her green eyes were flecked with gold . . . but Mark was in a fever of doubt. He had been so *sure* that he would be able to tell. Now, faced with the moment of truth . . . he was uncertain. He almost sobbed with frustration. In her Belfast park, fully dressed, she had seemed older . . . clothes had given her an air . . . added maturity . . . but now, years had been stripped away along with her frock. He would have to wait an eternity to find out. *Was she Kate?* Where was the absolute *proof*?

He listened to Leonard's coaxing and watched the girl pirouette across the brilliantly lit cube . . . and still he doubted. Hunched in his chair, gnawing his lip, tense-faced in the darkness – the impossibility of it all finally came to him. There could be no *proof* – just indications, all positive – yet only the years would tell whether she would grow up to be Kate.

Suddenly Mark gripped the arm of the chair. Of course there was proof! This was Kate the child, soon he would see Kate the mother – *she* was his proof, his living proof.

Leonard was finishing. With the doll in her arms the girl moved to the door, smiling impishly out into the darkness. The door opened and closed behind her. Mark passed a hand across his damp forehead. He closed his eyes, sick with apprehension. He buried his head in his hands and prayed – and was still praying when he heard the click of the door. *She was there!* All he had to do was look up. Mark sat rigid, unable to move . . . paralysed with fear. How many years had he waited for this? He was soaked in sweat, his shirt clung to him. His heart pounded, the roof of his mouth felt as dry as sand. Every ounce of willpower was needed to move his muscles. Slowly, somehow, he forced himself upright in the chair. He opened his eyes.

She had adopted the pose of Rouen's model in *The Looking Glass*. Hours of study had gone into that position. She had practised so often that to recline naked on a chaise-longue was as natural as breathing. Warmth from the lamps relaxed her body. Leonard's soothing voice from the darkness eased her nervousness. She raised the small looking glass and patted her hair with the other hand. Then moved her hips, stretched one long leg to its full extent – and held the pose.

Mark choked, 'Kate! Oh thank God – Kate!'

The hoarse whisper snapped her head round. Her eyes widened with alarm, she held her breath – like a startled deer. Silence – then Leonard's warm tones reassured her again. She hesitated, still straining for the sound of a second voice – but she heard only the photographer. After a long moment she relaxed, and went back into the pose.

Mark's heart pounded. She *was* the nymph from the pool! But never had Rouen captured so much fire in her hair. Nor caught the delicious contrast of milk white skin and the pink tips of her breasts, or the ripe curved fullness of the breasts themselves. And when she moved the faintest suggestion of muscular ripple showed in her legs . . . legs like a dancer from the ballet . . . slender, tiny ankles, but the grace and power in her calves drew the eye to the perfect roundness of the knee and the long, exquisitely shaped thigh. And the arch of her neck, the white pillar of throat, the clean line of jaw below full sensuous lips . . . all were perfect. She turned and looked out into the darkness, her long heavy lids half lowered against the dazzle of light . . . and when she did her green eyes seemed to bore through Mark's skull.

Leonard's voice caressed her from the darkness, altering the pose, suggesting a mood . . . 'You are waking from sleep, stretch slowly, luxuriously like a cat . . . that's right, turn on one side, knees bent just a little, then s-t-r-e-t-c-h . . . beautiful . . . now wide awake . . . that's lovely . . . just wonderful . . . raise your right arm just a little . . .'

The girl moved so gracefully that the dreamlike quality of the scene persisted. Yet it was *real* . . . happening . . . the dream had come true! Rouen's model had come to life and was even more beautiful than in her paintings. Now she was walking across the cage, pausing, turning, pausing again in answer to Leonard's directions. The sheer grace of her stance took Mark's breath away. For a long sweaty second he stayed stuck to his chair, then – slowly – he rose and crossed to stand beneath the cage. Bathed in the uncompromising glare of light, Sheila O'Brien walked up and down, pausing, turning, walking again. As she passed directly overhead the probing eye of Mark's camera swept over the moving swell of her calf muscles to the alabaster pillars of her thighs and the trembling twitch of her buttocks. Click went the camera. She spread her legs and reached high with her arms. Click went the camera directly beneath her. Mark climbed the gantry on to the roof of the cage. She reclined on the chaise-longue. Click went the camera. She turned on to her stomach. Click. She rose and crossed her gilded cage. Click, click, click . . .

Sean Connors should have been exhausted. He had risen at six and not stopped all day. So much had happened in so short a time that he had to pinch himself to make sure it was true.

He had been at Brigid's place by six-thirty that morning, rousing Michael from his bed. All Michael was told was that Sean needed his help at the *Gazette* – explanations would have to wait until later. By nine o'clock they had measured the basement and the ground floor – using a ball of twine and calling measurements to each other like proper surveyors. O'Toole, the night-editor, raised merry hell, but Sean lied in his teeth by saying he was doing a job for Mr Macaffety – then, at ten o'clock, Daly arrived and wanted to know what was going on – and Sean gave him the same answer.

By eleven they had measured the whole building, and fifteen minutes later were in Bewley's Café, waiting for Jim Tully. Sean checked and double checked his figures. Michael was pestering to know what was going on. Sean almost told him that if everything worked out they would make enough money to send Tomas to Australia – but stopped and instead pored over his notebook, concentrating like mad. He had the concept clear in his mind, but some of the details refused to slot into place – and time ran out then because Jim Tully arrived.

Sean thanked him for meeting at such short notice, introduced Michael, and then plunged straight in – 'I've found a site for the tea-rooms,' he said proudly, 'the best site in Dublin.'

Jim Tully betrayed a mixture of surprise and disappointment. Surprise because the Widow O'Flynn had agreed on some premises in Henry Street – and disappointment because Sean had promised to relinquish his role as her custodian. There was even a third reason for concern. Property was Tully's business. He knew every pile of stones in town. To hear Sean boast of 'the best site in Dublin' was enough to subdue Tully's famous charm – but he disguised his misgivings by asking for the address of this marvellous discovery.

Sean told him and waited. Tully carried a street map in his hand. He worked it out within ten seconds. 'Why – that's the *Gazette*!'

'Ssh!' Sean threw a hurried glance around the restaurant. He concentrated, knowing that Tully would pick up the slightest nuance if it rang untrue. 'It's like this, Mr Tully,' he began carefully, 'the building is larger than we need. We could give up some of the ground floor for tea-rooms and let the whole top floor for offices. That would leave us the basement, half the ground floor and the two floors above.

We could function fine with that – and the rest of the space could earn a rental income.'

It was Tully's turn to glance over his shoulder. He smiled and shook his head in mock admiration. 'Wouldn't anyone think you'd been in the property business all your life to listen to you. Next you'll be talking of cost per square foot and amortizing over ten years.'

Sean was unsure about amortizing, but if it meant a buyer recovering his outlay over ten years, Sean could do better than that. For answer he opened his notebook – 'That's the total square footage, Mr Tully, and overleaf is a floor by floor diagram of the whole building.'

Tully tried to conceal his surprise by poring over the figures.

'It's a very fine building, isn't it, Mr Tully?'

Tully looked up. 'What in God's name is this all about?'

'Wouldn't you say it's one of the best buildings in Dublin?' Sean persisted.

Tully flushed. 'Will you stop going on about it. It's not the Four Courts, or the Customs House, or the Taj Mahal – it's a bloody good office building and you're right about the ground floor – shops or a café make more sense than what's been done with it so far.'

Sean lowered his voice. 'It's to be auctioned, Mr Tully, but nobody knows yet.'

Tully blinked several times, but his jowled face failed to conceal his surprise – or his excitement. Of course he had heard of Lord Bowley's death, but that was a while ago . . . 'Auctioned?' he echoed softly.

'But nobody knows yet. I thought you'd be interested. I could show you over the premises today if –'

'What does Dinny Macaffety say about this?'

'Dinny is in hospital. I'm . . . well, helping out . . . but no one is to know.'

Tully's narrowed eyes strayed to Michael, 'And where do you come in?'

'He's helping out too,' Sean said quickly.

Tully's instincts warned him to be careful . . . but the *Gazette* was a very fine property on a good site . . . he sensed a bargain.

251

'I know the price they'd settle for, Mr Tully,' Sean whispered.

Tully's shrewd eyes gleamed. So that was it. Sean wanted paying for his information. Well, fair enough – good information was worth paying for – if it was *right*. Tully had done a dozen deals on a similar basis. Suddenly Sean's secretive attitude made sense. Tully bobbed his head in approval. 'Good lad, Sean,' he said. 'You mean they'll scrub the auction if –'

'They get the right price,' Sean finished for him.

Tully rocked back in his chair. Meeting Sean Connors had been a stroke of luck – first the Widow O'Flynn, now inside information on the biggest property deal in years. His eyes crinkled into a smile. 'Sure you're a coming man, Sean Connors. Didn't I say that the day we met.'

'So are you interested, Mr Tully?'

Tully reassured himself with another look round the restaurant. 'I might be, if it's not a king's ransom. Their price might be too high – some people have inflated ideas, you know –'

'If you tell me what figure you would offer,' Sean said carefully, 'I could find out if it would be acceptable.'

Tully twitched.

Sean read his mind. 'I'll tell you if your price is too high, as well as if it's too low.'

Tully still fidgeted. 'Price would depend on a lot of things. What kind of lease would the *Gazette* want, for instance. Then there's the cost of altering the ground floor. There's a lot of questions need answering first.'

Sean had answers for some. The hours spent studying the *Gazette*'s P&L accounts told him what rent the newspaper could afford – and Tully already knew that the Widow O'Flynn would pay five hundred a year for the right site. Even so Sean stalled by suggesting that Tully view the building for himself – and the sooner the better.

Jim Tully smiled. 'I was in and out of that building when the Christian Brothers were tanning your backside.'

'Mr Macaffety's just had the whole place painted.'

Tully's eyes gleamed. 'So that's why he did that. To make it look smart for a buyer. Well I'll tell you Sean, a real property man isn't fooled by a coat of paint. He looks for reliable tenants –'

'Like the *Gazette* – and the Widow O'Flynn.'

Tully shrugged. 'She might not like it.'

'With an O'Connell Street frontage?'

Tully accepted the point. An O'Connell Street front was worth more than five hundred a year. He was about to say so when Sean interrupted, 'I want her to have it at that price, Mr Tully. She's a friend of mine.'

Tully stared until the heat rose in Sean's face, but blushing or not he stared right back – 'Just like you're a friend too, Mr Tully. I wouldn't be here unless this was good for you too.'

'Friendship should be a two-way street, Sean,' Tully said with obvious meaning.

Sean nodded, apparently accepting the bait – 'If anything comes of this . . . well, I'd like you to pay Michael a commission of five hundred pounds,' he said, not daring to look at Michael.

Tully's hooded eyes were suddenly expressionless. Privately he thought it made sense for Sean to remove himself from involvement – which explained O'Hara's presence. But five hundred pounds was a hell of a lot for young Sean to be talking about. Tully creased his brow. 'It might be arranged, but first you'd better tell me how much they want for the building. If that figure is too high we are all wasting our time.'

Sean heard the edge in Tully's voice. The fencing was over and Sean knew it. He was terrified of losing the advantage. Tully was so much more experienced . . . Sean was afraid to disclose his hand . . . he *liked* Jim Tully and he thought Tully liked him . . . but so much was involved . . . he was so near to the biggest chance of his life . . .

'Well?' Tully persisted softly.

Sean tried another tack, 'If I told you what rent the *Gazette* would pay, could you tell me what you would bid for the building?' He went cold at the flicker of annoyance in Tully's eyes. It was going wrong . . . he was risking Tully's friendship . . . everything was turning sour . . . but he had to be *sure*.

'Wouldn't you think that's the long way round?' Tully

253

asked icily. 'After all, I've agreed to pay your friend here his commission.'

Sean was miserably unsure of himself. 'Three thousand five hundred a year,' he blurted out, 'that's what the *Gazette* will pay.'

Tully was surprised. The *Gazette* would pay the same rate for office space as Maeve O'Flynn would for tea-rooms. She would be paying under the market price, and the *Gazette* would pay over.

Sean finished with a rush, 'You'll get another five hundred for the top floor. What with that and us, and the Widow O'Flynn – that's four and a half thousand you'd get every year.'

Tully scratched his head. 'Ten-year leases?' he asked.

Sean nodded, white-faced and intent.

Tully considered. The property would fetch fifty thousand at auction – maybe fifty-five, even sixty. He glanced over his shoulder again. 'I'll pay thirty-five thousand,' he said quietly, 'if the *Gazette* and the Widow O'Flynn agree those rentals on a ten-year lease, with an eight per cent rise at the end of three years.'

Sean's head whirled. His breath caught in his throat. It was a deal . . . a marvellous, fantastic, wonderful deal! The rest of his idea fell into place like pieces in a puzzle. Excitement brought the colour back to his face. He felt like shouting. Instead he took a deep breath and concentrated on keeping a steady voice. 'That's too high, Mr Tully, you can get it for less.'

Tully's eyes popped. *Less?* He could hardly believe it. '*Less?* Are you sure? How much less? Would they take thirty?'

'Up a bit – half way,' Sean's eyes mirrored his excitement.

'Thirty-two and a half?' Tully reached across to grab Sean's hand. 'Are you sure? You could get that price, and those leases – all for thirty-two and a half?'

'If Michael gets his commission.'

'Hell, you've just saved me five times that. You could have asked for a bigger commission, and not told me –'

'No point in being greedy,' Sean grinned, 'I've got what I want, besides . . . well, like I said, you're my friend, Mr

Tully, I want you to be pleased with the deal . . . for ever and all time.'

If Tully thought that was a strange thing to say he gave no sign of it. He was too elated.

But Sean had one last condition – 'It will have to be completed on Friday, Mr Tully. If it isn't, the whole deal is off.'

Tully was shaken, but agreed it could be done – if he hurried. He left shortly afterwards. If money was to be on the table by Friday he had much to do . . . talks with his banker . . . a meeting with his lawyer . . .

Michael was awe-struck. 'Five hundred pounds,' he whispered, 'Jaysus, Mary and Joseph – you've made *five hundred pounds*!'

But Sean had made much more than that. Not that he told Michael – but he did explain what the five hundred pounds was to be used for. Michael's eyes moistened as he listened. The whole family in Australia – who would have believed it.

After that, Sean seemed to be dashing all over Dublin for the rest of the day. First he went to the hospital – but even Dinny was only told a fraction of the story. Sean clung on to his real secret. He left a mystified Dinny with a promise – 'Just trust me, Mr Macaffety, and you'll be the editor of the *Gazette* for the rest of your life.'

Then Sean went in search of his father – and spent most of the afternoon waiting for Pat Connors to emerge from a Dail committee meeting. Pat thought it was some kind of joke to begin with – he listened with mounting incredulity. He neither understood nor believed it. What was more he questioned its honesty. But Sean repeated it again and again until Pat got the gist of it – though the fundamental point of how Sean could sell a building which did not belong to him still escaped Pat.

'That's why I need the best lawyer in Dublin, Da,' Sean insisted, red-faced with excitement, 'I'm *sure* it can be done if we're quick about it.'

With some misgivings Pat introduced his son to Senator O'Keefe who, apart from his political commitments in Dail Eireann, was one of the most able lawyers in the Four Courts.

By seven o'clock that evening Sean was sitting in the Senator's chambers explaining his requirements. The old Senator was more than surprised, he was staggered. But Sean argued with dogged tenacity – so much so that after an hour the Senator had to concede that the idea *might* have some merit. It was ingenious, he admitted . . . some of Sean's reasoning was awry . . . but . . . well if the sequence of events was rearranged . . .

Which was how, at ten o'clock that night, Sean came to be intoxicated. Not drunk, despite the glass of whiskey in his hand, but definitely and positively high. He walked – no, he *floated* from room to room in the small house at Ballsbridge, waiting for his father to come home. He climbed the stairs, paced the landing – too excited to sit down – he walked back down to the hall, made a circuit of the kitchen and returned to the living-room. He laughed aloud. Once he burst into song. He raised his glass and toasted the future – his future, *their* future, each and every one of them. To Tomas and the family, who would go to Australia. To Maeve O'Flynn, who would have the best tea-rooms in Dublin. To Dinny Macaffety who would edit the *Gazette* for the rest of his life. To Jim Tully who had won a bargain . . .

'And all because of me!' Sean shouted at the empty house. He chuckled aloud. Even Lord Averdale would get what he wanted – net asset price for the *Gazette*. Sean hugged himself, knowing that he had kept the best prize for himself. Ownership of the *Gazette* – lock, stock and barrel!

Two nights later Lord Averdale was also toasting the future. After three wonderful afternoons in Leonard's studio Mark was beside himself with joy. He had *seen* Kate, alive – in both of her guises, Kate the woman and Kate the child. And he had the pictures to prove it. He sat alone in the drawing-room of his Belgrave Square house surrounded by photographs – enlarged, coloured, black and white – photographs of her body, photographs of her face – the entire room was a montage of Kate.

He had lost his nerve at the studio. He had intended to climb into the cage. Leonard would pose her as Justice, blindfolded, eyes masked and scales in her hand, just like the statue in London. Then Mark would measure her, his hands would rove over her body . . . but he had called it off at the last moment. What if the mask should slip, what if she recognized him . . . the plan was madness, conceived by a mind gripped by an obsession . . . the risk was too great . . .

But Mark's agile brain was still busy . . .

He would send O'Brien to Africa to deal with the Bowley estates. Any suggestion of his wife accompanying him would be vetoed on the grounds of . . . of it being too dangerous for a woman . . . the heat, disease, wild animals . . . besides she might not want to go. After all she had children to consider and O'Brien's trip would be of at least three months' duration. Mark smiled . . . a lot could happen in three months.

He went early to bed, knowing he had to rise at dawn to travel to Croydon and thence to Dublin. Dublin was a nuisance. A waste of time when he wanted to get back to Belfast as soon as he could. He wondered how O'Brien would take the news of Africa? O'Brien would have news of his own, of course – *Brown & Company* would have settled their account – the fifteen hundred pounds would have arrived. Mark chuckled at the prospect of his own money being returned to him.

Matt Riordan was also drinking whiskey – but in very different circumstances. He was sheltering under some trees. A bitter wind howled through the branches to scatter rain on the men waiting below. Matt swore softly and pulled his collar even tighter, before passing the half-sized bottle to Ferdy. 'Do you see anything?' he asked for the tenth time.

'An' me with one blind eye? What chance have I?'

Matt smiled grimly, blind eye or not Ferdy Malloy had a knack of seeing more than most full-sighted men. The six men huddled close together under the elm trees, peering anxiously out into the night. Even the ditch six yards away was barely visible, let alone the lane – but it was there, just beyond a low stone wall, the lane which led down to Brackenburn a mile and a half away.

'I'm going back,' Matt said. 'Give them another five minutes – then I'm going back.'

Ferdy shivered in his wet clothes, fumbling in his pocket for cigarettes. 'Anyone got a light?'

'No! You'll not strike matches—'

'Relax, for Christ's sake. The Devil himself would stay abed on a night like this. Sure a smoke will settle your nerves.'

Ferdy walked deeper into the thicket to light the cigarette. He cupped his hands round the glowing tip. After two draws he returned and handed it to Matt. Nobody spoke for a while. The rain lashed down harder than ever, thudding into the ground beyond the trees, splattering into ever-widening puddles at their feet. Water gurgled and splashed over stones in the ditch. Swirling gusts of wind tore at the branches of the trees, bending them first one way then another. The sky was black – no moon, no stars, thick cloud brushing the hillside to obscure every scrap of light.

'I'm bloody freezing—'

'Shut up,' Matt snapped, straining to hear above the wind crashing through the foliage. Nothing – no signal – just the wild sounds of the night.

They had worked in pairs. Four teams of two. It had taken Matt and Ferdy less than thirty minutes to set the incendiary devices in the old bakehouse. They had been there and back in an hour. One team had returned before them and the next arrived ten minutes later. Explosives had been set in the conservatory and at the back of the chapel. But the fourth team, working on the stables, had *not* returned -- and the men under the trees had been waiting an hour.

Matt gnawed his lip. At eighteen he was the youngest man there, but he was in charge. His first mission, and now something had gone wrong! He cursed under his breath. To delay longer would imperil everyone – they had to move soon or miss a lift back to Belfast in the farm lorries delivering to the markets. They *had* to go. But a good commander never abandons his men, even just two of his men.

'Are you ready, Ferdy?'

'Aye, let's get back down the hill to look for them. Anything's better than waiting. Come on, while I can still move.'

258

Matt sent the other four men back up the hill first – to the safety of the lorries bound for Belfast. Then Matt went – edging sideways towards the ditch. The impenetrable darkness was made even worse by the lashing rain. Matt sank ankle-deep into the ditch and gasped with the shock of freezing water. Not that Ferdy heard, the howl of the wind through the trees was deafening. He stumbled in after, and they both rose cursing on the other side.

Hugging the stone wall they progressed fifty yards from the trees. Around the turn the road straightened to run down to Brackenburn a mile away. Not that they could see the house – not now, it had barely been visible earlier. But the bend led the road off the exposed hillside and into shelter, away from the buffeting of the wind. Gratefully Matt called a rest . . . and a moment later heard voices.

It was the Duffy brothers – the fourth team – on the far side of the wall, no more than a couple of yards away. Matt recognized a voice saying – 'I'll never make it, Luke.' Then Matt was over the wall with Ferdy scrambling after him. Luke Duffy uttered a surprised curse and swung round, but Matt was on to him by them. Duffy's yell changed to a cry of recognition.

It took a minute to hear their story. Danny Duffy had fallen from the stable roof. He had landed on a water butt, cracking his back and hurting his leg. Luke had virtually carried him up the hill, quite a feat considering Danny was so much bigger.

The leg was a mess, Matt's probing fingers told him that. They made a crude splint from a fallen branch and used the belt from Ferdy's raincoat as a binding. After which they gave Danny what was left of the whiskey, and propped him upright – with Matt under one shoulder and Luke the other – and set off. It was hard going, especially when they reached the bend in the lane and were caught by the wind. 'We finished the job though, Matt,' Danny said between clenched teeth, 'we set the charges all right.'

The rain eased off as they neared the pick-up point. Luke's ankles had given out by then and Matt was taking Danny's entire weight. Sweat poured down his face. He was exhausted but triumphant, even wryly amused: they made a pretty poor IRA column – one man with a busted leg, another with a sprained ankle, Ferdy with his one blind eye, and Matt on his knees. But they had done their job. Liam Riordan would be proud. Matt's face split into a tired grin of triumph as dawn streaked the hillside and the farm lorries came down to meet them.

Sean Connors greeted the dawn with excitement too. He had slept, but only fitfully, he was too anxious for the day to begin. He brewed some tea and took a cup to his father, then fidgeted for an hour, dressing in his good suit of Donegal tweed and tweaking his tie into shape.

Michael arrived at eight o'clock, also dressed in his Sunday best. Sean briefed him thoroughly and sent him away, knowing that Michael would do everything asked of him. Then Senator O'Keefe called. Pat Connors was up by then, so the three of them sat round the kitchen table, with the Senator doing most of the talking while Sean poured some fresh tea.

Senator O'Keefe had performed miracles of negotiation with the man at the bank, but nobody had proved harder to convince than Pat Connors himself. Even then, at nine in the morning, Pat sat uneasy and withdrawn, not sharing the excitement of the others. It was not that he was disappointed, or fearful of the bank selling his home over his head if things went wrong, or fearful that a scandal would ruin him in the Dail – though those considerations had crossed his mind. It was more that he wondered what would happen if things went *right*. If this wild scheme worked Sean would be wealthy . . . and the wealthy saw the world differently. What would happen to the boy then? Would it go to his head? Would he be ashamed of his upbringing . . . even worse, would he abandon the rules?

Sean had no such worries. To his mind financial independence could only strengthen a political career. If his father disagreed there was nothing Sean could do – except prove him wrong.

By nine-thirty they were at the bank, being ushered into the manager's office with a flourish. Everything was prepared. Pat Connors had to sign because his son was a minor and under age – but it was Sean who took the bank draft. He stared at the piece of paper, feeling slightly disappointed. Only the figures were impressive – thirty-two thousand, five hundred pounds, payable to Lord Averdale.

The banker stressed that he would certainly seize the small house in Ballsbridge if anything went wrong – even though its value was only a fraction of the loan. 'But we would have to start somewhere,' he said sternly. 'Frankly this is a most unusual business. I don't mind telling you that if it wasn't for Senator O'Keefe's confidence . . .'

They left as soon as they could . . . and made for the Shelbourne, where Senator O'Keefe had reserved a small meeting room. 'Less formal than my chambers and I believe Lord Averdale has already declined to visit the *Gazette*.'

Sean fairly tingled with excitement.

Mr Daly was waiting at the Shelbourne, with Michael O'Hara and Dinny Macaffety. Dinny grinned ruefully at his plastered leg and raised a crutch in greeting. He was visibly nervous, still unsure about what was happening.

Senator O'Keefe took over. The document extracted from his case looked much more impressive than the bank draft in Sean's pocket. 'This is a service contract,' O'Keefe announced, looking at Dinny. 'Ten years as editor of the *Gazette*. How would that suit you?'

Dinny thought he was hearing things. He had lived with the threat of dismissal, now he was being offered the *Gazette* for the rest of his working life. Words formed and re-formed on his lips before tumbling out – 'I don't understand. Has Lord Averdale reconsidered? I mean I thought –'

Senator O'Keefe smiled. 'This contract is with the new proprietor. You see, we expect a change of ownership to be finalized this morning – and the paper must be sure of its editor.'

Dinny stared helplessly. 'New proprietor? Well who's that? Sure now, he'll be wanting to see me first –'

'He knows your work well,' said the silver-haired Senator. 'A meeting is unnecessary, besides clause three gives you total editorial freedom. You won't have problems with the new proprietor, I feel confident of that.'

Dinny's expression was too much for Sean who inspected the patterned carpet with sudden interest. It reaffirmed his

261

belief – that a man with assets can perform more good than a politician any day of the week. He wondered what his father was thinking.

Senator O'Keefe continued, 'May I suggest that you study the contract over coffee in the lounge. Mr Daly, I wonder, since you are here, perhaps you would give Mr Macaffety the benefit of your expert opinion?'

It was done with such courtesy that neither Daly nor Dinny took it as a dismissal. Pat Connors opened the door and Daly led the way out, with Dinny following on his crutches, the look of bewilderment still on his face.

Sean breathed a small sigh of relief. So far so good, but his fingers remained tightly crossed. They waited in silence, not daring to tempt fate with another rehearsal. Sean pretended a nonchalance that he did not feel by looking out of the window. He felt sick with apprehension.

Then, at last, Lord Averdale arrived. Michael announced him at the door and ushered him in with the gravity of a butler – he even helped him off with his coat and offered to take his bags out to the hall. Lord Averdale seemed happy to release one case but he preferred to keep the other, which was large and flat, like cases artists use for transporting their sketches.

Sean made the introductions as completely as he knew how, careful to give each man his proper title . . . *Lord* Averdale, *Senator* O'Keefe, and my father *Teachta Daile* Connors.

Senator O'Keefe rose to the occasion perfectly. He was no stranger to the British aristocracy. 'Castle Irish' they used to call them in Dublin, Irishmen who mixed so freely with the Imperial administration that they became more British than the British. Those days were long gone and it had taken the wily Senator years to recover his political standing – but he still remembered how to behave. He handled everything, from offering Lord Averdale biscuits with his glass of Madeira, to a brief explanation of the contract – 'This is such a simple business that it's barely a couple of clauses. One sheet of paper. Merely that you convey the *Gazette* in its entirety for the value of the net assets shown on the balance sheet . . . er, thirty-two thousand, five hundred pounds.'

Lord Averdale's eyes flicked down the page. With surprise he looked sharply at Sean – 'Am I to understand that *you* are the purchaser?'

Sean blushed to the roots of his hair. Senator O'Keefe rescued him quickly. 'Mr Daly told me your Lordship's instructions,' he said, 'that the *Gazette* should be offered to Mr Macaffety and his associates. Well, the sum was rather more than Mr Macaffety could afford, but his associate Mr Connors has been with the paper some considerable time.'

'You have the money?' Lord Averdale interrupted, still looking at Sean.

'Yes, sir.' Sean produced the bank draft and handed it over. 'My father arranged it this morning . . . in preference to a cheque, sir.'

Lord Averdale's surprise was obvious. He looked from the draft to Pat Connors and then back to the draft. Then he returned to the contract. 'This man . . . er, Macaffety. What happens to him?'

'Oh, he stays, sir,' Sean blurted out. 'That's taken care of.'

'Oh is it?'

Sean blushed again, aware of the frown on the Senator's face. Nobody spoke after that. Sean wanted to say something – anything to break the silence – but a warning look from the silver-haired lawyer froze him into obedience.

Then Michael knocked on the door and came in. He looked at the Senator – 'You asked me to check on the times of the Belfast trains, sir, in case Lord Averdale wanted to know. Well, there's one in forty minutes and another at three this afternoon.'

'Thank you, O'Hara,' said O'Keefe grandly. He turned back to the table and addressed Mark. 'I hope you will honour us by staying to lunch?'

Sean watched in admiration. It was the ultimate bluff. He remembered the Senator's earlier assessment – 'Everything must be ready but we mustn't rush him . . . we'll invite him to lunch . . . he won't accept, don't fret yourself about that . . . he'll not want to socialize with the likes of us . . . but it will take the pressure off, you'll see.'

Sean stood up, his heart pounding as he played his part. 'Hadn't I better book a table now?'

Lord Averdale pored over the contract.

Senator O'Keefe said, 'Aye do that, Sean, will you – and bring a wine list back with you. Perhaps Lord Averdale would choose?'

But Lord Averdale was reaching for the ink stand on the table – 'Thank you but no, I must get back to Belfast. Let's get this over and done with.'

Sean struggled to hide his relief. It had worked. Just as the Senator had said it would. But hell would break out if it hadn't – Jim Tully was due in half an hour. The extent of the gamble took Sean's breath away, not from fear but sheer excitement.

Everyone signed both copies of the contract – Mark Averdale and Sean as principals, Senator O'Keefe as witness and Pat Connors as guarantor to the act of a minor. Sean's hand shook. His signature was different from usual, but legal for all that.

'I'm sure Lord Bowley would have approved of our arrangement,' Lord Averdale said. He folded the bank draft into his pocket and rose to his feet.

'Good luck, sir,' Sean said in a burst, excitement getting the better of him, 'I'm sure we'll meet again.'

'Oh, I doubt that,' Lord Averdale said coldly, on his way to the door, the large flat case in his hand, 'I doubt that very much.'

Then they were alone . . . Sean Connors and his father . . . with the door closing behind Senator O'Keefe as he led Lord Averdale out to the lobby.

Sean looked at the contract with dazed eyes – 'We did it, Da,' he whispered, 'Da – we did it! We just bought the *Gazette*!'

The atmosphere in that little room was still charged with excitement half an hour later. Senator O'Keefe had ordered drinks to be set up on the sideboard and was filling their glasses with the gusto of a man in Mulligan's Bar. 'To you, Sean,' he said, raising his glass, 'to the new owner of the *Dublin Gazette*.'

But there remained one hurdle, as Pat Connors pointed out – 'We'll be without a roof over our heads unless we pay the bank back.' Then – for the very first time – Pat suddenly understood the whole deal. It dawned on him. He gaped for a second, then burst out laughing. 'Would you believe it but I've just worked it all out!' He laughed so hard that the Senator joined in, and Sean gave a whoop of joy which tinkled the bottles on the sideboard . . . and he was still laughing and pacing the room like a demented tiger when Tully walked in, with his solicitor Keaton on his heels.

'Be God it's a wake,' Tully said cheerfully, shaking hands all round. 'If you'd told me before I'd have brought a bottle.'

'Just so long as you've brought your cheque book,' Sean beamed happily.

They settled into their chairs, each with a glass. Senator O'Keefe brought the meeting to order – 'Not that this will take long,' he said with a quick look at Tully, 'I think Mr Keaton and I agreed everything yesterday.'

'That we did,' Keaton agreed. 'Including the leases. If you've got the title deeds, we've got the money. All we need now is Lord Averdale himself to sign the contracts.'

Pat Connors burst out laughing, unable to restrain himself. It was not what was planned. Senator O'Keefe had wanted to lead up to it. Sean had wanted that too. But Tully's face was almost as good. He stared incredulously at the tears on Pat's cheeks. It took minutes to restore order, and even longer to convince Tully that Lord Averdale's signature was no longer necessary.

'*You* own it?' Jim Tully gasped at Sean. 'You bought the *Gazette*? Everything . . . the paper, the printing plant . . . you own the building . . .'

They had to inspect the contract which conveyed title to Sean. The Senator stuck a piece of paper over the price paid and stood over Keaton while the man read it, prepared to swoop if the man tried to cheat.

Jim Tully could not work it out. He knew Pat Connors lacked the finance . . . so how . . . how had Sean raised the cash? Not that it mattered – Tully wanted the building, and the *Gazette* as a tenant. Then he realized something. 'You could have charged more,' he said in astonishment to Sean. 'I offered thirty-five thousand and you let me drop two and a half. You cheated yourself.'

'Did I cheat *you*? That's the important thing, Jim Tully. Didn't you get what you wanted, and didn't I do you a favour?'

It was beyond Tully's experience. He signed his cheque for thirty-two thousand, five hundred pounds. Then the contracts – the Senator and Keaton were busy for five minutes, passing papers back and forth . . .

And so it was concluded.

Sean passed the cheque to his father. 'Thanks, Da, thanks for the loan, and thanks for trusting me.'

Pat could not answer for the lump in his throat.

But the excitement was far from over, even then. Michael was summoned to receive the magic five hundred pounds from Jim Tully – and then Dinny came in. His eyes widened. 'By God I might have known it was you, Jim Tully. Well, it's a very fair contract you've written me, Mr Daly's approved every word of it. Hard man you may be but you've been very generous to me and I'll not forget it. God bless you for it. The *Gazette*'s in good hands now right enough, with you as owner and me as editor, we'll drive the *Times* off the streets, indeed we will.'

The room erupted – Dinny was led to a chair and a glass pushed into his hand. 'You're talking to the wrong man, Dinny,' Tully said, delighted to reveal the secret. 'Young Sean's your new boss, not me.'

It took Sean half an hour to extricate himself. The noise was deafening. Jim Tully sent for the Widow O'Flynn and ordered a champagne luncheon for everyone. The celebration looked set for the rest of the day. Sean was as excited as everyone else – but just for a moment he wanted to be alone. He retreated to the only place he could think of – the toilets downstairs, where he shut himself in a cubicle. He buried his face in his hands and let the events of that wonderful morning flow through his mind. At one point he had owed the bank the dizzying sum of thirty-two and a half thousand. Him, Sean Connors, who had never seen money like that in his life. The debt was paid off now, with Jim Tully's cheque. He owed the bank not a penny, and what was left was his, that was the staggering thing to contemplate. He withdrew the balance sheets from an inside pocket and pencilled in the alterations. Even after deleting the book value of the building, he was left with a fortune. Net assets worth twenty-seven thousand pounds. *His* net assets. He turned to the profit and loss account. Paying rent to Jim Tully would add to the running costs, but even after adding that to the overheads it left a profit of seven thousand pounds. Seven thousand a year . . . for the rest of his life! But Sean knew it was just the start.

Mark Averdale was also reflecting on the morning's events. He sat in the first-class dining car on the Belfast train, still recovering from his surprise. He had not known what to expect . . . the truth was he had been so busy with his plans to send O'Brien to Africa that the *Gazette* had barely entered his mind. The reception at the Shelbourne had completely wrong-footed him. He had half expected them to haggle, or ask for time to pay . . . but nothing of the sort. The contract was perfectly adequate and who could argue with a bank draft?

He shrugged. It was for the best. The *Gazette* had been dealt with, he had been paid. Damn funny people though, especially the new proprietor, he couldn't have been more than about twenty, blushing like a girl all the time. And that business at the end – 'Good luck to you, sir, I'm sure we'll meet again'. Bloody cheek. Typical Croppy – treat them civilly and next thing you know they're up to the big house for dinner.

Mark snorted and put the matter out of his mind. He had better things to think about. First thing to do was go to the office and see O'Brien. Tell him about Africa, but get him used to the idea. Once that was dealt with . . . away home to Brackenburn. He sighed with pleasurable anticipation. He always did when he thought of the great house. But tonight would be special. Tonight he would hang the photographs next to Rouen's painting, tonight would be devoted to Kate. Kate and Brackenburn, the two most important things in his life. He sighed again . . . yes it would be good to get home.

But Brackenburn, even at that moment, was a crumbling inferno. The west wing was ablaze. The chapel roof had already collapsed. Tongues of flame licked upwards through the charred rafters. Blistering heat compelled the fire-fighters to abandon that end of the building. Now all efforts were concentrated on preserving the central core and the east wing, including the famous great hall. And while firemen fought to save the fabric of the house, other men – Brackenburn's servants, RUC men, farm labourers, Averdale employees – stripped the great mansion of its contents. Furniture was dragged from the ground floor on to the paved terraces by a score of men who shielded their faces from the scorching heat and shouted above the crackling roar. The two local fire tenders were completely overwhelmed by the blaze, even now men worked feverishly with extra pumps to bring gallons of water up from Lough Neagh.

Smoke-blackened and hoarse-voiced, Eoin O'Brien stood on a cart near the entrance to the stable block, directing a line of men staggering under the weight of chairs and tables and cabinets. A rough shelter of tarpaulins lashed to an outside wall gave the area the appearance of a bazaar, especially at one end where rolled carpets and rugs were dumped unceremoniously across tea chests of silver. Alongside the rose garden twenty men laboured to erect a marquee which would provide a more secure shelter. Meanwhile O'Brien utilized whatever came to hand. Tireless himself, he bellowed at others, constantly exhorting men to work faster. Like refugees fleeing in the face of an enemy, the would-be saviours of Brackenburn's treasures trudged wearily into the stable yard, caught their breath and turned back to the house.

Closer to the raging flames in the west stood the Fire Chief, directing men as they fell back in an organized retreat to the great hall. Hoses snaked up the steps and through the stone balustrades, carrying gallon after gallon of water into the house. The main staircase was completely engulfed by fire. The upper floors had been abandoned. Below that the Long Room itself was threatened.

Across the lawn fifty yards away, the pink and white summerhouse had been converted into a first-aid post. A tub of butter from the kitchens stood on a table, much of it already used for the treatment of burns. Housemaids were busy tearing linen sheets into strips for use as bandages, while in a corner Lady Dorothy Averdale tried to calm the hysterical niece of the head gardener . . .

All told – counting servants and staff, RUC, firemen, farm labourers and neighbours – more than a hundred people toiled furiously to save Brackenburn. Above them the bruised sky, swollen with clouds, turned black with smoke as the huge pall rose ever upwards.

The warning had been telephoned to the Averdale offices at eleven o'clock. 'You've half an hour to clear the big house before it goes up in flames. And remember, next time you kill a man like Mick Nealson the IRA will kill you.'

The name Nealson had meant nothing to O'Brien. He thought first of his own house, but that was absurd . . . big house meant only one thing in Ireland, *the* big house . . . the house of the master. *Brackenburn!*

It took O'Brien five precious minutes to convince the RUC. Even then the small police station at Bellpicken, three miles from Brackenburn, was not alerted until eleven twenty-five.

Not until he was half way to Brackenburn in a police car did O'Brien question the telephone call. The caller had asked for Lord Averdale, but had settled for O'Brien quickly enough. O'Brien's mind had been on other things – a scheme to reduce costs in the shipyard – anticipating his wife's return from London that evening. He would not have spoken to the caller, had the man not stressed it was a matter of life and death. Then O'Brien remembered the name – Nealson – the man killed at the factory gates? That was Mick Nealson. O'Brien urged the driver to go faster, fearing the worst. His fears were confirmed as they rounded the hilltop above the great house. A thick plume of smoke was already high in the sky, fed by flames as tall as the house itself.

Now, two hours later, the battle was at its peak. Much had already been lost – the chapel was so much smoking rubble, the kitchen block completely destroyed, the conservatory no longer existed. The much treasured African Pavilion above the bakehouse had gone. But much of the east wing remained – the Long Room, the gallery, the library, salons and rooms all extending towards the stable block – all endangered, but still standing. And while firemen battled in the great hall to hold the flames at bay, a long line of other men, coughing against the swirling smoke, worked desperately to clear the east wing of its contents.

The stable block had become store-house and operations room. O'Brien worked unceasingly, dashing from one point to another, shouting above the crackle of fire like a general at the front.

Across the lawn Dorothy emerged from the summerhouse, still shaking from her efforts to calm the gardener's niece. The girl and her uncle had been outside the conservatory when the explosion occurred. Shards of flying glass had slashed the old man to ribbons, it seemed certain he had lost the use of one eye.

Dorothy tried to collect herself with a few deep breaths – but hot, acrid air burned her lungs and made her cough. Her eyes smarted, she dabbed at them impatiently, only to smear another speck of soot across her face. She could hardly bring herself to look at the house, especially the gaunt, gutted skeleton of the west wing. Beyond that firemen bravely fought the furious blaze in the great hall, and dimly on the far side she could just make out three or four men carrying paintings. Dense, drifting smoke obscured her vision. Shock dulled her comprehension until she realized they must have reached the gallery. A great clod of a labourer was trailing two canvases behind him, bouncing the frames down the terrace steps. She saw another man with three precious vases crunched together in his arms. Dorothy set off across the lawn for the stable block.

Minutes later she had taken charge, freeing O'Brien for work in the house. Two men set a Gainsborough down into a bed of urine-stinking straw. Dorothy draped a sack around the edges of the frame and turned to supervise the handling of a favourite Turner . . .

And then it happened. Badly jolted when Duffy fell from the stable roof earlier, the crude timing mechanism of the IRA bomb had slipped by three hours. At two-thirty it exploded. The blast drove the walls of the stable block outwards with an ear-splitting roar. Masonry, roof-timbers, stone lintels, slates, erupted into a suffocating mountain of pulverized mortar. Tremors of shock ran the entire length of the house – right through to the great hall, knocking the blazing staircase completely clear of the walls and half way to the doors. The smoke-filled gallery suffered an earthquake. Shelves in the library gave way, dumping thousands of books on to a floor made sodden by water seeping under the doors. Outside, along the northern elevation, Corinthian pillars snapped like matchsticks to displace the vast curved stone pediment with a thunderous roar. The great house of Brackenburn writhed in its death-throes like an enormous mythical animal racked with convulsions.

Eoin O'Brien went momentarily deaf. He saw men scream, but heard only a thundering in his ears. Twice his escape from the gallery was blocked by falling masonry. He slipped once and twisted his knee so badly that he cried out in pain. Somehow he dragged himself through the door and out on to the terrace.

Survivors scrambled away from the house. They ran down the lawns, casting terrified looks over their shoulders, as if expecting the house to reach out and pull them back. They shouted to each other and pointed at their ears, indicating deafness. Firemen deserted their posts and servants abandoned their master's property.

Not everyone survived. Twenty minutes later, when O'Brien rallied the group on the lawn and restored their courage, they tore at the wreckage with bare hands, desperate to release those trapped under the rubble. But the stable block yielded only victims. Corpse after corpse was revealed. Eight bodies in all, seven men and one woman . . .

Black Friday. A great house destroyed, eight Protestants killed – and Ulster had claimed another Averdale. Lady Dorothy was dead.

CHAPTER THIRTEEN

At four o'clock that Friday afternoon – just as Mark Averdale's train pulled into Belfast, and Sean's luncheon party ended at the Shelbourne Hotel – a delivery van drew to a halt in a quiet road in the Dublin suburb of Rathfarnham. The van had circled the streets for such a long time that the driver might have been searching for an address – but in fact he knew the address perfectly well. He was making sure the house was not under surveillance. His passenger – a grey-haired, heavily built man of about fifty, wearing an American-made suit under his raincoat – sighed his relief. He was tired. A hunted look marked his expression, as well it might for a thousand to one chance had almost caused his arrest earlier that day. He had been recognized when he landed at Cork. He had escaped by the skin of his teeth and rendezvoused with the van – but his face was already on the front page of the evening newspapers, above the caption – 'Liam Riordan, seen back in Ireland.'

As the van drew away, Riordan slipped through the gate and walked briskly to the back door. Rory Quinn opened it almost immediately – 'Be God, get yourself in. The whole country is looking for you. There's your picture in the papers.'

So 'Granite' Liam Riordan returned to Ireland. It was an ironic situation. He had been an honoured guest in Germany, but in Ireland – for whose freedom he had fought all of his life – he was hunted like an animal, and he was greatly relieved to reach the IRA 'safe house'. There were few such havens left. Dev's detectives were everywhere. The IRA had become badly fragmented, its central organization had virtually collapsed. IRA men languished in Kilmainham Jail, and those still free fought each other for control of what was once a national movement. Much needed to be done to restore unity. Which was why Liam Riordan had come home.

His return sounded a rallying-call. Local commanders began to assemble from all over the country. Grim-faced men, each with a revolver under his jacket, came from Galway, Cork, Belfast and Limerick – and they came to the house in Rathfarnham. It took them two days to congregate, and the meeting began on the third – with lookouts posted in the gardens and on every street corner for a mile around.

Liam Riordan got straight to his report. 'It's hard in the States now,' he confessed. 'They don't know who tó believe, what with Dev telling them one thing and us saying another.'

Riordan had persevered, travelling the country, trying to persuade senators and congressmen to intervene with Britain over Northern Ireland. And he had raised some money for arms, never as much as he hoped for, but every man in that room had benefited as they gratefully admitted. Despite that it was a glum report – 'Dev's still got a big following, especially in New York. They think he's a bloody hero.'

The men chorused their disgust. Their account of Dev's wrongdoings would have gone on longer, but they were anxious to hear the rest of Riordan's news. He tried to end on a more cheerful note by recalling a Clann na Gael meeting on New York's 25th Street – 'They had some idea of sending an aeroplane over to bomb the House of Commons in London. It wouldn't have the petrol to get back across the Atlantic, so the idea was to crash-land it on the French coast.'

That particular idea had been abandoned, but it had led to an alternative plan – 'They're dead scared we will start another civil war here in the south,' Riordan told them, 'so we've got to take the fight out of Ireland. The idea is for a bombing campaign in England itself. We'll explode bombs in London and Birmingham and all over – what about that?'

The idea took hold. They agreed to return to it later, after Riordan had told them about Germany. 'Sure there's all the arms in the world there,' he said, 'the whole bloody country is one big arsenal.' He reported on his meetings with Foreign Minister Ribbentrop and Admiral Canaris, head of the Abwehr – 'Ribbentrop is a lying bastard. To listen to him there's no chance of a war. He says that with a straight face when you can't move in Berlin for bumping into a uniform. Canaris is a professional though . . . if there is a war, Canaris will help, I'm sure about that.'

'How will he help?'

'With arms – men too maybe, if we have a go at the north.'

It was late afternoon when they finished discussing America and Germany. No one considered the news good. Clearly they would get little immediate help from the outside world in their war with the British – let alone for their fight against the Irish government. And events within Ireland itself were just as gloomy. Dev had gained the upper hand in the south, and Craig's RUC was as relentless as ever north of the border. The only success in months had been the destruction of Brackenburn.

Liam Riordan was absolutely staggered by the news. Matt? His own son? Typically he had not enquired about his family – not asked for news of his mother, or his wife, or his son – everything was secondary to the fight for Ireland. Nothing could have astonished him more. But there was no mistaking his pride – especially when Jimmy Traynor confirmed that Matt had actually *led* the raid. 'He's a chip off the old block, Liam,' Traynor finished. 'You wait until you see him.' Liam Riordan sat shaking his head in delighted surprise.

It was a cheering interlude in a catalogue of setbacks – but when the story had been celebrated it was time to get back to business. Liam Riordan picked up the idea of a bombing campaign in England. 'The average Englishman doesn't give a damn about Ireland. But he'll take notice when we start blowing bloody great holes in Birmingham and Manchester and the like. There'll be such a public outcry that Parliament will have to do something.'

The plan was deadly in its simplicity. Groups of men would be trained in the use of explosives and sent to different towns in England. By December they would be ready to launch a co-ordinated bombing attack on prime targets. The British government would be told – 'Get out of Northern Ireland – or else . . .'

Training centres were designated – two in the south, Killiney Castle, just outside Dublin, and a hall in St Stephen's Green – and in the north Jimmy Traynor suggested some disused farm cottages near Keady in County Armagh. 'Less than a mile from the border.'

'Why not somewhere in Belfast?'

'Are you kidding? That Brackenburn business has stirred up a real hornets' nest. You can't move without being searched by B Specials.'

So by eight o'clock the bombing campaign was agreed upon, and the meeting was over. The men began to disperse, leaving the house in ones and twos, until finally only Liam Riordan and Rory Quinn remained. They opened a back window to let in some fresh air. Riordan was tired but satisfied. December would bring a badly needed IRA initiative. Headlines for the cause would be captured around the world – and all without endangering Irish lives. It was a very good plan indeed.

When the plan was explained to Matt Riordan two days later in Belfast, he thought it was brilliant – 'Wouldn't you think someone would have come up with this before?'

Traynor laughed. 'I told your Da you'd be in charge of things at Keady. That pleased him nearly as much as Brackenburn.'

Matt blushed. He gave Traynor a quick, sly look – 'He really was pleased then?'

Traynor told him again. 'Some of the men in that room have known Liam Riordan for twenty years without seeing him smile. But he grinned and grinned about Brackenburn. He was too proud to hide it.'

Matt felt giddy with elation. His father was *proud* of him! It was a wonderful feeling. 'When is he coming north?' he asked eagerly.

'When everything is set up in Dublin. He'll have to tread carefully though, the place is alive with Dev's detectives, all looking for him.'

Matt was struck by a sudden thought – 'He's not going after Connors is he? I want to be there –'

'Don't worry about that – he'll have no time for Connors just yet, he'll have his work cut out training men for this

275

bombing campaign. Connors will have to wait until later.'

Matt was reassured. He was excited about the bombing campaign – he saw himself blowing up bridges and BBC transmitter masts at dead of night all over England. But he could never forget leaning out of that carriage that day to spit in the face of Sean Connors. One day, he vowed, the Riordans and the Connors will have a reckoning – and now that his father was back in Ireland that day would be soon.

'You're to get down to Keady in the morning,' Traynor said. 'You'll be safer out of Belfast anyway. Besides, everything must be organized for your Da when he gets up here –'

'So when will he be here?'

'When he can,' Traynor said sharply, 'the end of the month most likely. It won't be easy – he is being hunted from pillar to post.'

They stared at each other, then Matt grinned. 'He'll be all right. Everything will be all right. I can feel it in my bones. Don't worry, they'll never catch him in Dublin.'

But Liam Riordan nearly was caught in Dublin just a few days later – when Gardai raided the house in Rathfarnham. He would have been caught had he been there, but as luck had it he had been delayed overnight at Killiney Castle, so the dawn raid trapped only Rory Quinn in bed with his wife. Both were arrested and although neither would talk, a search of the house revealed some damning evidence. The makings of explosives were found in the basement – potassium chloride, iron oxide, and a half gallon drum of sulphuric acid. Then came another discovery – a grey jacket with a New York tailor's label, and a notebook in one pocket listing Irish-Americans living in Boston – and, most damning of all, an envelope addressed to Liam Riordan.

'He's been staying there all right,' detectives told Pat Connors later. 'Quinn won't talk, nor will his wife – but we think Riordan is still somewhere in Dublin.'

The hunt had been going on for more than a week. Informers had been visited, addresses were being watched – but Riordan had slipped through the net.

Sean was as worried as his father – but not just about Liam Riordan. Sean's first week as owner of the *Gazette* had turned sour. Dinny had acted strangely – not on the day of the deal – he had been overjoyed then. Champagne in one hand and his service contract in the other, he had given speech after speech – 'Be God, I remember the first day I met Sean – him standing in front of my desk . . . "No" says he, "I don't want your job Mr Macaffety, I think I'd like to *own* the paper!"'

Sean would never forget that marvellous meal . . . surrounded by friends. . . . Jim Tully laughing, the Widow O'Flynn misty with tears, Michael choked up about the five hundred pounds . . . and the Da choking on one of Jim Tully's cigars. It had been a wonderful day.

But problems had arisen the next morning.

Sean had arrived at the office early, flushed with excitement. The gloomy atmosphere which had enveloped the *Gazette* would be dispelled. They all had a future again. He went straight to the notice-board in the general office to find out which assignments had been allocated to him by O'Toole, the night editor. The place felt like home again – more than ever when he heard Dinny bellowing from the editor's office. Then Dinny appeared in the newsroom, hopping from desk to desk, swinging his plastered leg like a balance – 'Morning, Mr Connors – could you step into my office for a minute.'

Sean was surprised – the duty roster said he was to go directly to the RDS to cover the agricultural show. But he did as he was told and as he waited in the editor's office he overheard Dinny outside, rearranging work schedules – 'Mac, you can take the Rotary. And Jimmy old son, there's dinner for you at the Gresham tonight, Dev is singing for his supper at the Wolfe Tone dinner.'

A moment later Dinny was back, slamming the door behind him – 'Wouldn't you think they'd laugh themselves sick on the *Times*. There's the new owner of the *Gazette*, running around like a junior reporter. And what the hell would I be doing when you creep back after missing a story? Could I kick your arse like the old days? How in God's name could I do that?'

Dinny went on like that for another half hour – by the

end of which time Sean's bewilderment had turned to shock. He began to realize that he no longer had a job on the *Gazette*.

Dinny threw up his hands in exasperation – 'You are no longer a humble reporter. You're the *owner* Sean. I was wondering . . . would you care to take over the editorial? After all, it is the proprietor's right.'

Sean went white. Dinny's editorials were famous. His fierce broadsides were read out in the Dail. Dinny's no-holds-barred tub thumping had given the *Gazette* its circulation.

'I couldn't do that, Mr Macaffety, I haven't the experience . . . besides you write the best editorials in Ireland.'

The more they talked, the plainer the issue became. There was no avoiding it. What was Sean going to *do* with the paper, now that he owned it? In the excitement of creating the deal he had not thought of that. He had imagined things as before. But the changed circumstances gradually registered as Dinny emphasized point after point.

Finally Sean drew a deep breath and asked – 'Do you think you could teach me to be a newspaper proprietor, Mr Macaffety?'

Macaffety's head went back in a roar of laughter. 'Do you know, that's the one thing I can't. Isn't it the only thing I've never been – a newspaper proprietor. But it is a very good life, Sean. Days at the races, travel around Europe. You go to the opera in London and cross the Atlantic on the *Queen Mary*. By God, it's the life of Old Riley, you'll love every minute.'

Their laughter eased the awkwardness, but the problem was still there to be resolved. Dinny scratched his chin. 'You know,' he said after a while, 'this needs thinking about. Isn't that the trouble? You set the world on its arse and nobody's had chance to catch their breath. Would you do me a favour? Would you take a week off? That's what Lord Bowley would do, so maybe taking a leaf out of his book will help. He was a grand man, Sean. He had a rule. Every day he spent an hour by himself, just thinking. He told me about it, wanted me to do it. I never caught the habit, but for an hour a day he sat quietly thinking . . . about his life, what he wanted for himself and his son . . . what his friends might do, and his enemies . . . things like that. And I never saw him caught out, not once. He was always ready, no matter what.'

Macaffety paused to prop his plastered leg up on a chair beside his desk. 'I'm trying to advise you as Lord Bowley would. It was his paper, Sean, he'd want you to do your best by it. I think he would say an hour a day isn't enough. This is too big. It happened too fast. I think he'd say take a week off to think things over before you do anything.'

Dinny sat smiling, waiting for an answer. It was good advice and Sean knew it. Dinny always gave good advice. And half an hour later Sean was outside on the street, with a whole week ahead of him to ponder his future.

The unexpected freedom felt strange. He strolled the streets for an hour, trying to concentrate, but not really knowing what to do with himself. He paused at Green's bookshop, browsing through the book-laden tables set out across the pavement. He had read a good deal that year, encouraged by his father and Dinny. It was one of his father's rules. 'Read about famous men,' his father had urged during their walk across Ireland, 'learn how they dealt with problems.' Which was all very well, Sean reflected, but nothing in the biographies of Pitt and Gladstone and the like seemed to have the slightest relevance to his life.

Then came the most extraordinary stroke of luck – or chance – or fate, Sean could never explain it. After all, at the time, his perusal of those old books could not have been more casual. He flicked a page here and there – most of his mind was still back at the *Gazette* and on Dinny's advice. Certainly there was nothing eye-catching about the book. Its blue cover was stained with ink on one side and the fly leaf was torn. But he bought it for sixpence and carried it off to Bewley's to read.

Sean read that book twice, that day. He read it again the next morning, and again the day after. It was the most extraordinary story he had ever read – the life and times of Alfred Charles William Harmsworth – who had been born in Dublin, at Chapelizod, half way to Palmerstown.

Not that he had lived there for long. 'The Troubles' had frightened his mother so much that they had moved to England, to Hampstead in London. At school young Alfred had run the magazine and been taught chemistry by H. G. Wells, one of whose books Sean had since read. But it was what happened to Alfred when he left school that excited Sean. Using a borrowed five hundred pounds Harmsworth had founded a magazine called *Answers*, and then a picture paper called *Comic Cuts*. *Comic Cuts* alone earned profits of £25,000 a year, and with those profits Harmsworth bought the London *Evening News*, which itself showed a profit of £14,000 by the end of twelve months. Harmsworth went on to found the *Daily Mail* – then, in 1908, he bought *The Times*, the most famous paper in London. Harmsworth grew rich, very wealthy indeed – and he became Lord Northcliffe when King Edward created him a baronet. And Lord Northcliffe became powerful. In fact one line in the book drew Sean's eye like no other . . . 'In the heyday of his newspaper empire, Lord Northcliffe as good as ruled England.'

Sean was mesmerized. As good as ruled England – and England with a King and an Empire, a Parliament and a Prime Minister – yet the man who had built assets ruled them all! Exactly what Sean wanted to tell his father when they had walked back from Coney Island.

It was an astonishing discovery, vindication too in a way. Sean compared himself to Harmsworth, diffidently, laughing at his audacity. Yet there were similarities. Both born in Dublin for a start, and although Harmsworth's London school may have provided a fine education, Sean had been taught the rules by his father. And while Harmsworth had run his school magazine, Sean had learnt about business with his donkeys. He had done more . . . he had had his first woman, he had bought the *Gazette* – and all by the age of seventeen!

Then Sean stumbled upon the most curious link of all. A shiver ran up his spine. Harmsworth had died the year Sean was born. Coincidence . . . and yet . . . Sean's blood tingled at the wild thought . . . had his love of newspapers been somehow passed down from one Irish-born to another? His heart leapt at the idea of living a life such as

280

Harmsworth's . . . yet why not . . . he had started already . . . he knew newspapers . . . *and* he had been taught the rules by his father. Why not indeed? But to emulate Harmsworth he would have to do as Harmsworth did . . . and cross the water to London.

Maeve O'Flynn's prediction rang in his ears, 'Ireland won't hold you. You'll go far, Sean Connors, and I'll not stand in your way.'

Every night that week Sean tried to talk to his father, but Pat Connors was busier than ever. He had taken to carrying a gun again. Sean knew why of course . . . the hunt for Liam Riordan. Had Pat betrayed the slightest fear, Sean would have felt selfish about thinking of his own ambitions – but Pat treated the matter of Riordan with total contempt.

'Riordan,' he said, when Sean finally cornered him late on the Friday evening, 'aye, he's around, but don't you worry about that. What puzzles me is why he's come back. He knows me of old. He knows I meant it about killing him. I'll shoot the bastard stone dead if I set eyes on him. *And* I'll have the law on my side. There's every Garda in Dublin looking for him, and he'll be knowing it. So why come back to face odds like that, that's what I'd like to know.'

'He's a fool,' Pat continued, 'living in the past. Riordan and his big mouth, always going on about the people – "I speak for the people," shouts Riordan. Maybe he did once, but not any more. I reckon to know what the people want a damn sight better than Riordan – and they don't want more bloodshed, which is what they'll get if they listen to the likes of Liam Riordan.'

He paused to throw more turf on the fire. 'Does he think he's alone in wanting one Ireland? My God, no man wants that more than me. But fighting's not the way. Mick Collins must spin in his grave. To think he nearly had it, all those years back, before the British wriggled out of the Boundary Commission. Sure, Mick never would have let them get away with it. That's what the likes of Riordan did for Ireland – murdered the man we needed most.'

Sean waited, knowing his father would continue.

'He's up to something right enough,' Pat said into the fire. 'There's been a few meetings up at Rathfarnham, plotting the devil knows what. But we'll catch him, don't worry yourself.' He grinned and turned to face his son. 'Still, that's enough about Riordan. What have you been doing? I bumped into Dinny this evening and he says you've been taking time off.'

So Sean told him about the week to think things out.

'Well, it's Friday,' Pat said. 'What decisions have you reached?'

Sean wanted to say he was going to England. He burned to talk about Alfred Harmsworth. He wanted his father to read the book for himself. There was so much to talk about. But Sean's words died in his throat. How could he even *think* of going away when Liam Riordan was still loose? Suppose he went to London and something terrible happened to his father? Sean couldn't risk that. So he smiled and shook his head.

'There's an idea at the back of my mind, but I'm not ready to talk about it yet. Let's give it a bit more time.'

Time, thought Sean, as he went up to bed – time for the Gardai to take care of Riordan.

A week later the Gardai were still hunting for Liam Riordan – and north of the border the RUC were turning Belfast inside out in the search for the murderers of Lady Averdale.

The razing of Brackenburn set off the biggest manhunt in years. Not a night passed without B Specials careering through the Falls, searching and questioning. The city was pulled apart. In Stormont, Prime Minister Craig faced mounting pressure to re-introduce internment. Newspapers demanded the proclaiming of a state of emergency. 'If an Averdale can be murdered,' ran the argument, 'no Protestant in Ulster is safe.'

Tension increased daily. Small incidents threatened to erupt into mob violence. A policeman conducting interviews in the Short Strand was pelted with bricks. A man was knifed during an argument about the British Royal Family. Catholics and Protestants alike scurried about their business, keeping to their own neighbourhoods as much as possible. The weather was unseasonally warm.

Belfast sweltered in an Indian summer and waited for the storm to break.

Meanwhile the RUC investigations took a step forward. Working closely with Eoin O'Brien, detectives pursued a theory about the warning telephone message. 'Remember,' the caller had threatened, 'next time you kill a man like Mick Nealson, the IRA will kill you.' RUC questioning started with Nealson's relatives and friends, then expanded to every one of the forty-two Catholics dismissed from Averdale's. Thirty-six had watertight alibis. Which narrowed the search down to five – three of whom seemed to have vanished entirely.

At seven o'clock one morning, RUC detectives raided a small house in the Falls and dragged two women from their beds. One was taken downstairs for questioning. She was forty-nine years old and had been in poor health for over a year. Her name was Mary Riordan – wife of Liam, and mother of Matt.

For such a frail woman, Mary Riordan resisted bravely. She was quite ignorant about Matt's involvement, but she had watched him become close to Ferdy Malloy. She had been powerless to prevent it. More nights than not she cried herself to sleep, yearning for the old days in Dublin when Matt was a boy. Left alone she might have made him into a doctor. He would have saved lives, not taken them. But Liam had returned – and Pat Connors had followed him – to send them to this hell-hole in the Falls and to Matt's terrible beating outside the gates of that factory. That was when he changed. He was never the same after that.

'America,' she lied, in answer to their questions. 'My son is in America with his father.'

The questions came faster . . . when did he go . . . where was he living . . .

'You're a liar, Mary Riordan! A fucking Fenian whore of a liar!'

The house was searched. Her meagre possessions were flung all over the floor. Upstairs floorboards were ripped from the joists.

'When did you last see your son? How long have you lived here? Where does your money come from? How do you support yourself? Your son is a murdering bastard!'

'America,' she wailed, 'my son's in America with his Da.'

'Liar! Liam Riordan is in Dublin. Even his own kind are hunting him.'

Then came the newspapers – Dublin newspapers, with Liam's face all over the front page. She told herself it was a trick, Liam *was* in America . . .

Questions poured over her in a deluge . . . some quick, some sly, some brutal . . . and all the time 'Your son is a murdering bastard!'

After five hours of merciless bullying something happened to Mary Riordan's brain. She lost the power of speech. She rocked back and forth in her chair, whimpering like a beaten animal, her tear-stained face as clenched as a fist. She had told them nothing, for there was little she could tell – and by noon that day she could not tell anyone anything at all. She had resisted beyond her endurance. Her eyes glittered with an insane gleam as she leapt from her chair to snatch two crayon drawings down from the mantelpiece. She gathered them to her lap, smoothing the paper over her knees, heedless of the men's questions, aware of only one thing – the sketches she had made of Matt while he lay recovering from the injuries inflicted outside Averdale's factory.

It took the four detectives thirty minutes to realize what had happened. An ambulance was summoned. They took the drawings away from her, tearing the corner of one as they prised it loose from her fingers. Then she was sedated and rushed to the asylum.

She died after five days – a small, shabby death, unnoticed by the world – but the death of Mary Riordan was as much part of the Irish tragedy as that of Dorothy Averdale – and those others who, a few days later, went to their graves.

No man looked closer to the grave than Mark Averdale. His face was gaunt and drawn. Dark circles beneath his eyes added to his haggard expression. He had lived in his father-in-law's house since the destruction of Brackenburn, but he could stay no longer – he had to escape from the weeping of Dorothy's mother, and Sir Henry's angry ranting. In Mark's opinion, the Manners had lost a daughter, but he had lost far more than a wife.

The initial shock had shattered him. He had only left the house once, and that to attend the funeral, a nightmare from which he escaped as soon as he could, to flee back to his darkened rooms.

In an odd way he had mourned Dorothy – giving her credit for being a good wife; efficient with the staff, frugal with expenses – unexciting in bed perhaps, but at least she had tried, which was more than most wives did, or so he had heard at the club.

But more than Dorothy he mourned the loss of Brackenburn – that great mansion which had been his birthright. Everything was gone . . . the Averdale collection . . . his African pavilion . . . Not an hour passed without the memory of some lost treasure taunting him – a Van Gogh, a Poussin, Constable's *Willow Trees*, portraits by Doré – all overshadowed by the loss of Rouen's masterpiece. To have lost the nymph by the poolside was the cruellest blow of all.

He sought solace from the photographs. He thanked God for them. They were his link. Kate had gone, but still she lived. Here was her golden red hair, her flashing green eyes and alabaster white skin . . . her breasts, her arms, her long, long thighs. Just by being there she helped him survive. The nymph by the poolside had gone, but Kate the young mother was still his to possess.

The prospect of that gave him strength. Not during the first week when he was physically sick, nor the second when he was too angry to think straight, but after fifteen days mostly spent alone in his room Mark Averdale began to apply his agile brain to the business of living. Which is when he sent for Eoin O'Brien.

They met in Sir Henry's study. Mark listened grimly to a recital of all that had happened since Black Friday.

O'Brien pulled a handbill from his pocket. 'The RUC are looking for a man called Riordan. He was employed at the factory, he was one of the Croppies I fired.'

Mark studied the charcoal sketches printed on the Wanted poster. He listened carefully to O'Brien's account of the interrogation of the mother, and the past IRA activities of the father.

'Vermin,' Mark scowled, 'vermin, the whole bloody family.'

'These posters are outside every police station in Ulster,' O'Brien said. 'The Chief Constable assures me –'

'Offer a reward. Five thousand pounds, for information which leads to his capture. Get our own posters printed. Croppies will shop their own mothers for the right price.'

O'Brien made a note and might have replied, but Mark was warming to his theme. 'Let the press know – I want that reward headline news. Then get on to the Prime Minister's office – thank him for his wreaths, and ask if he'll see me tomorrow afternoon . . .'

Mark dictated orders for another hour, combing through O'Brien's report to identify priorities. O'Brien was a thorough man himself, but honest enough to doubt his ability to match Lord Averdale's efficiency. It was a revealing glimpse of the steel which usually lay cloaked beneath an air of casualness.

Eoin O'Brien sensed much the same thing the following morning, when he accompanied Lord Averdale on an inspection visit to Brackenburn. They sat in the back of the Averdale Rolls-Royce and O'Brien did his best to answer an endless stream of questions. He confirmed that the architects and insurance evaluators would be at the house, together with Donaghue, Lord Averdale's broker. Mark nodded approval, then tried not to wince as the gutted ruins loomed into sight.

Brackenburn! His heart lurched as he looked at the burnt-out shell. Part of the great hall was still standing – but little else. He watched the architects poke about in the rubble, talking in funereal voices of restoration. God, what was left to restore! How could a drawing by Sickert be *restored*, or a Daumier cartoon, or a sketch by Braque. Such treasures were irrecoverable . . . priceless possessions, lost forever. He raised his eyes to the roofless outline of the upper floor, where the nymph by the poolside had adorned a wall. He shuddered, then turned away, unable to look any longer. By God, someone would pay!

O'Brien blanched as he saw Averdale's face, empty of colour save for the eyes which blazed bright with hatred.

It forebode a difficult day. Many would incur Averdale's wrath before it was over – and O'Brien's resolve not to be among them strengthened ten minutes later. Lord Averdale erupted furiously at Donaghue. The broker had remarked that the insurers were in some difficulty about arranging compensation, destruction had been caused by civil disturbance – so negotiations with the government were necessary. It sounded like the thin edge of the wedge. Mark Averdale exploded with temper. Not one of the men gathered around the Rolls-Royce was left in any doubt – an Averdale had suffered loss – Averdales *were* paid – and God help any man who failed to discharge his responsibilities. The impact of the rebuke was reinforced by Mark Averdale's venomous language. Donaghue could not have been lashed more viciously with a horsewhip.

When Mark Averdale finished he turned on his heel. 'Come on, O'Brien. We'll leave these gentlemen to their duties.'

He stepped into the car, while O'Brien rushed to the other side. Then they departed, leaving some of the most respected professional men in Belfast gaping after them. A myth was destroyed in that instant. People had said that the current Lord Averdale, obsessed as he was with works of art, lacked the ruthlessness of his father. It was Donaghue who put it into words – 'By Christ, they're all the same. Scratch an Averdale and there's a tiger under the skin.'

Which were O'Brien's thoughts too, not that he expressed them, in fact he had no time to express anything. 'Look here, O'Brien,' Lord Averdale said, 'this man Riordan and his IRA rabble might make another attack. They might even attack you. After all, they associate you with Nealson's death. Not your fault, but you can't reason with vermin like Riordan.'

O'Brien said he had no fear for himself – which was exactly what Mark Averdale had anticipated. 'That's not the point. I never doubted your courage for a minute. But you have a wife and children, O'Brien. After what's happened I really do feel a responsibility to protect them.'

Mark Averdale unveiled his carefully made plans. The O'Briens would move to the country, just for a few weeks – 'My guess is the trouble will blow over once this Riordan

287

is behind bars, but until then . . .' The Averdale estate at Keady covered a thousand acres, and the big house could be made ready by the morning. Their whereabouts would be kept quiet of course . . . naturally the Prime Minister would be told, and the Chief Constable . . . 'but the fewer people the better. And your wife will adore Keady, so will your children. The Brackenburn staff will be there to see to their comfort. There is a separate wing I can use, so apart from that your wife can have the run of the house.'

O'Brien sat in bemused silence as the rest of the details were explained. Lord Averdale was seeing the Prime Minister later to arrange for a special squad of armed men to patrol the grounds. House staff would be placed entirely at Mrs O'Brien's disposal – and although O'Brien would have to stay in Belfast during the week – 'Naturally you must come down for weekends. I shall base myself there for a bit anyway,' Mark Averdale concluded, 'to make sure that everything is in order.'

O'Brien was being treated as a friend, not an employee. He was glad to be on Lord Averdale's side – the man might be ruthless with enemies, but he took good care of his friends. Not only that, but for a man still grieving his own loss to show such consideration for others was quite remarkable in O'Brien's opinion. So he responded with gratitude – and although he did not really consider his family to be in danger, he had to agree that every precaution should be taken.

So, at eleven o'clock the following morning, a convoy drew away from the O'Brien house. The first and the fourth of the motor cars contained armed RUC men on special duties. The second, laden with cases, carried young Kathleen O'Brien, her brother Timothy, and their nanny Meg Flint. The third vehicle was so full of cases that there was barely room for Sheila O'Brien. She managed a harassed wave to her husband, then tried to make herself comfortable. Her first reaction to this evacuation had been to call it a needless upheaval – but when it was suggested that the children might be in danger, she had echoed Lord Averdale – 'every care should be taken.'

Even so, it was with very mixed feelings that Sheila O'Brien set out on the journey to Keady.

Liam Riordan, on tne very same morning, was also travelling to Keady, though he was making the journey in very different style. Gone were his smart American clothes. Instead he wore a dirty shirt, torn tweed jacket, patched trousers and broken-down boots. The skin on his face and hands had been darkened with dye to give him a weather-beaten look, and three days of grey stubble bristled on his chin. The old trilby on his head was moth-eaten and shabby. But despite his derelict appearance Liam Riordan was a happy man. He had slipped the man-hunt in Dublin and was running free. After three long, wearying years he was on his way home.

Sitting on the buckboard of an ancient caravan, the paint of which had faded until only patches showed on the woodwork, he flicked the reins at the skinny mare between the shafts.

Next to him on the buckboard sat Ferdy Malloy, that shadowy linkman who flitted back and forth across the border like a crippled moth, forever carrying messages from one IRA commander to another. Yet even for Ferdy this mission was unique – bringing as he was one Riordan to another, a father to his son.

A large alsatian loped along behind the caravan, roped to the tailboard – a silent animal, unlike the mongrel which ran free, first in front, then behind, circling and yapping like a sheepdog moving its flock.

It was their second day on the road. They planned to reach Carrickmacross by nightfall, some twenty miles from the border. Tomorrow evening they would cross to Keady.

'So let's hear it again,' Liam Riordan said, 'this business at Brackenburn. You say young Matt planned the whole thing?'

Ferdy told the story all over again. Not that he minded, he was proud of Matt too, after all at least some of the credit for Matt's involvement belonged to Ferdy Malloy. So the two men discussed the razing of Brackenburn in infinite detail, both pleased that they had a good story to enjoy during the hours of their journey.

In Dublin behind them, at Killiney Castle and the Green Lodge at St Stephen's Green, training continued for the men who would go to England. Ahead of them, in a row of abandoned cottages near Keady, Matt Riordan was instructing five other young men in the use of explosives. The bombing campaign in England would shortly begin.

That same morning, Sean Connors was being given something of a lecture by Dinny Macaffety – 'Will I say it again Sean? He'll understand fine if you sit down and talk to him. That's all it needs –'

'It's not as easy as that,' Sean said, shaking his head.

'Will I talk to him then?'

Sean sighed. He wished he had not told Dinny about going to London. Dinny had seized the idea – 'That's a wonderful plan, Sean. We'll make you London correspondent for the *Dublin Gazette*.' They had decided that a week ago, and Sean had thought to tell his father that night. He had waited up, but his father had been out with the Gardai until dawn, searching for Liam Riordan. When finally he arrived home, grey with tiredness and frustration, Sean had lacked the heart to mention it. By which time Dinny had written to half of Fleet Street. Now Dinny was receiving replies from friends and ex-colleagues, all of whom promised to keep an eye out for Sean. 'Sure you'll like them fine. The English are grand. It's the bloody British Empire that's so all powerful stinking awful.'

'If only they would catch Riordan,' Sean grumbled. 'I can't leave the Da now, with Riordan still loose and maybe an IRA rising –'

'A rising now is it? And how can that be with half the buggers rotting in Dev's jails?'

Sean stood up and crossed to the office window. 'You know what they're saying out there,' he said, nodding down at the street. 'Riordan's not back for the good of his health. Something's up.'

It was true. Dev's policy of stiff sentences for IRA men had brought a certain calm. The danger of another civil war would always remain, with hundreds of embittered IRA men north and south of the border, but the prospect of a continuing peace had improved. At least it had until Liam Riordan returned to Dublin.

'The Riordans always were a wild bunch,' Dinny said. 'People will have enough sense to ignore them.'

But Sean felt otherwise. Every day detectives reported IRA men missing from their homes, their whereabouts unknown. They were gathering *somewhere*. And every night Pat Connors came home exhausted.

Dinny changed the subject. 'Will we tell him about London tomorrow then? On his birthday?' He rose awkwardly, hampered by his plastered leg, and hobbled across to the new mahogany bookcase. 'I tell you this,' he chuckled, 'I'll not be able to stop myself getting among these books if you leave them here much longer.'

Sean smiled. It was his birthday present for his father, the first expensive gifts he had been able to give him. Dinny had helped choose the books, and they had bought the bookcase in Switzer's. Pat Connors had already accepted his son's invitation to a birthday lunch at The Bailey tomorrow – but the present would come as a complete surprise. Sean crossed the room. 'Do you think he'll really like it, Dinny?'

'Sure he'll be delirious, and why not. Wouldn't any father alive be proud to accept such a gift from his son.'

Sean hoped so. He cherished his father's love. It was the most important thing in his life, far outweighing his plan to go to London, though he struggled to combine the two. The prospect of London excited and saddened him at the same time. Exciting because London was a bigger world . . . but sad because he would be leaving his own world in Dublin. Not that life in Dublin was without change. Brigid's place was no more – Tomas and the family had already left for Liverpool, their departure hastened on Pat Connors's advice – 'Riordan just might try to harm Tomas. After all, this business between us started because of what Riordan did to Tomas's family.' So arrangements were made and Tomas and the family had left on the first stage of their journey to Australia – all except Michael who had opted to remain, and was now working at the *Gazette*.

'Hey,' Dinny said. 'Cheer up. You're standing there like it's the end of the world.'

Sean blinked out of his reverie.

'Will you take yourself off and let me get back to work,'

Dinny continued emphatically. 'The owner might call me by my first name these days, but he'll play merry hell if this paper doesn't get printed.'

Sean met Dinny's grin with a shy one of his own – 'I'll be away then. I'll bring the Da in around midday tomorrow, then we'll all go off to The Bailey for lunch.'

Dinny waved at the bookcase. 'I can't wait to see his face.'

Neither could Sean, but Dinny's remark about the end of the world had disturbed him. It stayed on his mind . . .

CHAPTER FOURTEEN

Matt awoke in the cottage at Keady. He stretched and yawned, luxuriating in the sense of anticipation. Then he rose from the primitive bed. It was cold in the room. He rubbed his hands briskly, stepped into his boots, and clumped across to the window. The morning looked clear. It would be a fine day, Matt decided happily.

'Careful at that window,' warned a voice.

Matt swung round to see Dougan in the doorway. 'By God, there's nothing about,' said Matt. 'Even the rabbits are asleep.'

Dougan had been on watch through the night. He shrugged, 'There's a wet of tea below if you want it.'

The terrace of five cottages was set into a hillside so densely wooded that the buildings were invisible from the lane. Bushes and undergrowth ran wild, so that even the doors opened into brambles and hawthorns. The cottages at either end were in partial collapse, but the three in the middle were habitable. Matt was using one as a store for explosives and the other two for accommodation. Each cottage contained two rooms, one built on top of the other. The IRA men had removed bricks from the interior walls to provide access from one cottage to the next.

Downstairs Matt filled a jamjar with tea and walked into the cottage next door. His eye fell on the newspapers which Jimmy Traynor had delivered yesterday. *'Five thousand pounds reward'* screamed the headline, above a reproduction of a crayon sketch drawn by his mother.

The sketch had worried Matt. The RUC had obviously raided his home. Traynor had promised to call on his mother today to set Matt's mind at rest – so he could only wait anxiously for news. Meanwhile he was pleased about the reward. Not only was Brackenburn to his credit, now there was a reward on his head. He was making a reputation. His father would be impressed.

'Matt,' Dougan hissed through the gap in the wall. 'There's a car just gone down the lane.'

Matt hurried back into the other cottage and joined Dougan at the window. The lane led up to the manor house, less than a mile away. The big house had never presented a problem before – it was left empty most of the year, apart from a housekeeper and a gardener. The IRA had used the cottages five times in ten months without being disturbed. But yesterday a whole party of people had descended on the manor house.

'Someone from the village I think,' Dougan said, watching the car, 'maybe delivering the papers, or groceries perhaps.'

Matt was not willing to take chances – especially today when Ferdy was arriving with his father. 'Put the fire out,' he told one of the others who had gathered at the window, 'in case someone sees smoke from the chimney.'

Dougan groaned. The cottages were cold and damp. It would be chilly without a fire. But he did as he was told. People no longer argued with Matt.

Two hours later, Sheila O'Brien awoke up at the manor house. A maid drew back the curtains. 'It's a grand morning Mam. The children are at their breakfast already. I've brought your tea, and the papers have arrived from the village, so I've set one on your tray. Would you be wanting anything else?'

A drowsy Sheila O'Brien raised herself on one elbow and looked at the unfamiliar bedroom. As her whereabouts registered, she snuggled back under the sheets. So many strange things were happening that a chance to reflect in solitude was not to be missed.

Her mind immediately turned to Lord Averdale, whom she had met yesterday for the first time since his tragic loss.

She had tried to express her condolences, but he brushed them aside – apparently more concerned to show her the house. The procession went from room to room, but diminished in numbers because a servant took Nanny and the children on a different route – and by the time Lord Averdale ushered her into her bedroom she was alarmingly alone with him.

He only stayed a few minutes, to show her the view from the windows. Perhaps he was merely being a good host – yet Sheila O'Brien sensed an undercurrent which she was unable to define. She felt nervous, more than ever when he stood so close to her that she could smell the pomade on his hair, a faintly familiar scent she had encountered elsewhere.

'I've instructed the kitchen about dinner tonight,' he said. 'Naturally I shall leave it to you in future, but I thought on your first day . . . well I hope you don't mind.'

How could she mind? It was his house. She started to express her thanks, but he waved them aside. 'I shall call for you at eight,' he said – and then left, before she could sat that *calling* for her was quite unnecessary.

She spent the afternoon exploring the gardens with the children – and thinking about Lord Averdale. This house was smaller than Brackenburn and lacked architectural distinction, but it was still very large – and in a peculiar way he seemed to be making her Lady of the Manor. Even the servants sensed it, as was obvious from their attitude. It was as if she was to live at Keady permanently, instead of for a few days.

She played with the children for an hour after their tea, then Nanny took them to bed and it was time to prepare for dinner. Her clothes had been pressed ready for her. She bathed and changed, feeling rather nervous and wishing that Eoin were with her.

Lord Averdale knocked on her door precisely at eight o'clock – and offered his arm as they walked down the stairs. She was tantalized by the scent of his pomade. She knew it from somewhere, but couldn't place where . . . not that it mattered, in fact even to be aware of it proved how nervous she was. But her nervousness diminished as the evening progressed . . . he was considerate and amusing and really quite charming. 'You must call me Mark,' he said. 'After all, titles are too formal if we are to live under the same roof.' So she had responded by asking him to call her Sheila – but he surprised her by shaking his head. 'No, I shall call you Kate. That is how I think of you.'

He had refused to explain. 'My secret,' he chuckled, 'at least for the time being.'

His obvious pleasure relaxed her, far more than she would have thought possible. Perhaps being called Kate helped – as if she were acting a part – she was not Sheila O'Brien, married with two children, but a mysterious woman called Kate, mistress of this huge house, with Lord Averdale as an admirer. And he *was* her admirer. She was left in no doubt about that. Admiration was in his every glance. Altogether it was an extraordinary evening – quite different from what she had expected. She was quite light-headed by the end of it, what with the wine and the firelight . . . and his attentiveness.

He had escorted her back up to her bedroom and paused in the doorway, his eyes inspecting the room behind her, as if anxious for her comfort. When he bowed to kiss her hand she had caught the scent of his pomade again as he turned quickly away, wishing her sweet dreams as he went down the stairs.

After such a long and eventful day she had slept soundly through the night – and when the maid roused her with the morning tea it took a while to collect herself.

She reached for the tray on the bedside table. Suddenly she stopped, one hand on the teapot and her eyes on the newspaper. But it was not the headlines about the man-hunt for Matt Riordan which startled her. It was that scent! She could smell it. His scent, Lord Averdale's pomade! Her eyes flew to the door. Closed, as was the door to her dressing-room. She looked wide-eyed around the room – and then relaxed back on to the pillows. It must have lingered from last night, when he had stood at the door, or even from earlier when he had shown her the room. Odd, but she knew it from somewhere. It was distinctive.

Perhaps at Brackenburn, although she had not thought of the great house . . .

She gasped. Suddenly she *knew*! She choked with fright, staring at the chaise-longue across the room. The studio in London! There was no mistaking that scent. It had been strong under the arc lamps. *That* was why it was familiar!

Mark Averdale had already finished his morning tea. He sat in his dressing-gown, admiring the photographs of Kate. He smiled as he returned them to the artist's case. Soon he would have much more than photographs. O'Brien would arrive from Belfast tonight. His presence would deprive Mark of the pleasure of dining with Kate alone, but his presence was necessary. Much was to happen over the weekend. Mark was to announce O'Brien's next important commission – a three-month trip to Africa to settle the Bowley estates. It was another promotion – and O'Brien could travel in confidence, knowing that his wife and family were at Keady. Yes, Mark decided it promised to be a memorable weekend.

Liam Riordan, however, was not in such a good mood. An axle had given way under the ancient caravan and neither he nor Ferdy Malloy could effect a repair. They might have abandoned the caravan but for the five Lee Enfield rifles and the five hundred rounds of ammunition concealed under a heavy tarpaulin. Even so it was tempting to leave the caravan at the side of the lane and walk the rest of the way. The border was only fifteen miles away. But Liam Riordan had spent much effort to get the rifles this far – and Catholic lives depended on them over the border. They had to make an alternative plan.

Finally they unloaded the rifles and concealed them in dense undergrowth a mile outside Castleblayney. Then they walked alongside the mare as it pulled the tilting caravan into the town in search of a blacksmith.

Travellers and tinkers are common in Ireland. Tradition says they are the descendants of those who survived the great famine, when hordes of people roamed the country in search of food. Thousands died on the waysides, their mouths green from eating grass. Those who lived were resourceful enough to forage for themselves. Stealing and scavenging became a way of life – their *only* way of life – but some of their descendants live the same way. So they are greeted with a mixture of sympathy and suspicion – sympathy because 'there but for the love of God go I', and caution because it is well known that tinkers rarely pay for anything.

So when Liam Riordan and Ferdy Malloy brought their caravan to a halt outside the forge in Castleblayney, the blacksmith greeted them with cautious good humour. He inspected the axle and agreed to mend it, if they could pay. Could he see the colour of their money? So they showed him and he worked – and an hour later they were on their way again, back the way they had come to recover the Lee Enfields.

But the blacksmith was puzzled. Never had he known travellers who were unable to mend their own wagons, neither had he met tinkers so ready to part with their money. His suspicions were aroused. And when he went for his lunch an hour later, his suspicions were confirmed. The picture of one of the tinkers was on the front page of his paper. 'Liam Riordan still sought in Dublin' – ran the headline, but the blacksmith knew better. Liam Riordan was eighty miles from Dublin, and close to the border.

Sean was in Dinny Macaffety's office, proposing a toast to his father, when the news came through. The bookcase and fifty new volumes had already been unveiled. Dinny roared with exuberant laughter – 'Did you ever think you'd see a politician lost for words?' he shouted, as pleased as Sean with their surprise. Not that Pat was speechless long, words poured forth in a torrent. He picked up one book after another. 'Dear God, look at this . . . and this . . . Sean, you devil, what can I say? Wouldn't the National Library itself be green with envy.'

He hugged Sean, while Dinny laughed and waved his arms. For a moment Pat was almost in tears. Not because it was the most expensive gift he had ever received – but because of love for his son. 'Dear God, if only Finola were here!'

Then Pat recovered enough to swing round on Dinny,

'Wouldn't you believe he got me here on false pretences – my own son, we'll go to The Bailey says he –'

'We are,' Sean tugged his arm, 'I mean we will – as soon as you've finished Dinny's whiskey.'

Then the Gardai arrived, two inspectors and a man in plain-clothes. For a minute Sean saw no significance in their arrival – not even when they took his father outside for a private word. Nothing could spoil Sean's happiness. From now on, he vowed, we'll do this every year . . . have a party, and I'll be able to give him something he likes. Whatever he likes!

'Wasn't I telling you he'd be delirious?' Dinny laughed. 'Wasn't I right? Did you ever see a happier man?'

But when Pat came back into the room he looked different, the laughter had gone from his face. 'Riordan has been sighted,' he said bluntly. 'On his way to the border by the sound of it.' He spoke directly to Sean, 'I'm sorry, I'll have to go. There'll be no peace in Ireland with him still on the streets.'

Sean was suddenly clammy with sweat. He shivered. The nightmare. He had almost forgotten the thin face, white with hate, leaning down from the carriage window.

'Now?' Sean said blankly. 'You mean you've got to go now? On your birthday?'

Pat managed a wry smile, 'I'll be back tonight. Could you manage dinner instead, do you think?'

'I'm coming with you,' Sean said quickly. He swung round to Dinny, 'Sorry about –'

'No –' Pat started, but Sean cut him short. 'Come on,' he said thickly. 'Let's get this over with.'

One inspector was already making for the stairs. His colleague cast an urgent look at Pat, but Sean brushed him away, almost dragging his father. 'Come on, we've lived with this nightmare long enough.'

A few minutes later they were in the back of a Wolseley saloon, marked all over with Garda insignia. An identical car drew out behind them. It was exactly one o'clock as they began their race to the border.

Pat Connors was too old a warrior to resist the thrill of the hunt. How many times in the old days had he careened along like this, with the enemy sighted at last. He rapped out questions by the score, listening with scowling intensity to an account of the caravan and its occupants. Garda along the border had already been alerted. A detachment of troops from Monaghan was on its way to cordon off the whole area. But the border with Armagh was riddled with a thousand back lanes . . . Riordan could be making for any one of them.

'He'll have guns on board,' Pat guessed correctly. 'Sure why else would he have taken a chance like that. Riordan is carrying a cargo, he *needs* that caravan, otherwise he would have dumped it by now.'

The plain-clothes detective turned from the front seat, 'The smithy saw no sign of guns –'

'Did you imagine he would?' Pat pulled a face. 'Riordan would have dumped them, and gone back after. It's a stroke of luck for us. Fetching them will cost him time, another hour maybe.'

'If it *is* Riordan,' said the driver.

'It's him,' Pat said grimly and braced himself as the car skidded into a bend. 'By God, I swear it's Riordan at last.'

Pat Connors guessed right about Riordan's movements, but he was wrong about one thing. Collecting the hidden arms had cost Riordan more than an hour. Not until three o'clock was the caravan loaded again. Riordan was back on the road, still fifteen miles from the border.

'We'll not go through the town,' Riordan decided. 'Let's skirt east and get round that way.'

Ferdy was doubtful. 'It will take longer.'

Liam Riordan shrugged. 'Time is not the enemy, being recognized is.'

Ferdy thought about that. Going into Castleblayney had been a gamble, but it had paid off. Nobody had challenged them, the caravan was repaired, the precious rifles were under the tarpaulin. But Liam was right to be cautious. 'We could double back if you like,' Ferdy suggested. 'Head for Crossmaglen maybe. It's nearer –'

'No. That's the nearest point on the border. Anyone looking for us would expect us to cross there.'

Ferdy nodded, 'Aye, besides we'd have twenty miles to travel in Armagh if we cross there. Twenty miles of B

Specials instead of Garda who'll look the other way if you ask nicely.'

'Along the barrel of a gun you mean,' Riordan said with a grim smile.

Ferdy shrugged, 'Or with a fistful of money. I've done it both ways.'

Riordan chuckled and slapped the reins across the mare's back. The animal broke into a reluctant trot. The mongrel dog raced ahead, barking with excitement, and Riordan laughed again at the thought of his son waiting at Keady.

Nobody was laughing at Keady Manor. Sheila O'Brien had spent the whole morning trying not to panic. That scent! What did it mean? Eoin would laugh at her. She flinched at his imagined sarcasm. Few Ulstermen dressed their hair with pomade, but in London . . . well, what would you expect? And at a photographer's studio of all places. Eoin would laugh himself silly.

So she had tried to talk herself out of the idea. Even so the worry had lingered. Then she remembered. Lord Averdale (she still couldn't think of him as Mark) had arrived back from Dublin on Black Friday – *Dublin*, not London! He could not possibly have been in the studio.

Oh the relief! Thank goodness she remembered that before making a fool of herself. Eoin might have been angry.

The day improved after that. Part of the morning had been spent with the housekeeper, who seemed determined to treat her as the new Lady of the Manor. Then she had lunched with the children in the nursery, both of whom were full of excited chatter about their morning's explorations. Nanny seemed delighted with Keady as well. She was quickly making herself at home. It seemed that only Sheila had misgivings . . .

She wondered why? Lord Averdale had been charming last night – and her suspicions about his pomade had been absurd. Yet something made her uneasy – something was wrong. She had expected him to be mourning for his wife. Instead he had been witty and entertaining . . .

Finally she decided there was nothing to do but let the weekend run its course. Her doubts would sort themselves out by Sunday. Perhaps Eoin would decide that the emergency in Belfast was less dangerous than he had imagined. Perhaps they could all go home again . . .

The day which had started with such a fright, gradually settled down. After lunch she returned to her room to change into her smartest frock. Eoin had promised to be at Keady for tea – he should arrive about four o'clock. So by three she was ready – her hair shining and her smile radiant. She went in search of the children, anxious that that they too would be tidied up in time for Eoin's arrival. She found Kathleen on the terrace, listening to Nanny reading a story. Apparently Timothy was still exploring the grounds. Mother and daughter linked hands and went to find him together.

But half an hour later, after searching and calling over every inch of the gardens, they had not found Timothy. Stifling her annoyance Sheila O'Brien returned to the house and handed her daughter over to Nanny, with instructions that Kathleen was to be washed and changed without further delay. Then she went through the house, looking for Timothy.

From four-fifteen onwards every servant in the house was looking for the boy. Lord Averdale emerged from his study to ask what the commotion was about. He listened gravely, then went directly to the rooms above the stables which had been converted into a barracks for the armed guards.

By five o'clock the search was on in earnest. Men fanned through the house and grounds in every direction. Four walked down to the wrought-iron gates at the end of the drive, intending to examine the lane outside.

Behind them Sheila O'Brien fought to control her panic. She had been annoyed to begin with – then embarrassed by Lord Averdale's involvement. But by five o'clock – as she walked uncertainly towards the big iron gates – she was terrified that something had happened to Timothy.

A mile from the gates, all work had ceased in the derelict cottages. Matt Riordan had ordered his men into an upstairs room where they talked in nervous whispers. Matt himself stood at the window and watched the boy draw steadily nearer. They had been watching him for nearly an hour – ever since he emerged from the gates. He had not caused immediate alarm, after all the abandoned cottages were almost invisible from the lane. Most people passed by without realizing they were there. So a young lad out for a stroll presented no threat – if he stayed on the lane. But that had not happened. Instead the boy had explored the verge and then advanced deeper into the wood, so that now he was less than ten yards away, and every step brought him closer.

Matt swore under his breath as the boy disappeared behind a tree. He *must* have seen the cottages. What would he do? Ignore them, walk on past, go up the hill and deeper into the wood?

Suddenly the crash of splintering glass sounded downstairs. Matt caught a fleeting glimpse of the boy dodging from one tree to another, his arm still raised from hurling a stone.

'The little bastard,' Dougan hissed. 'That was a window –'

'He's seen us –' Paddy Cullen began in alarm, but Matt stopped him. 'No, relax, it's just a kid throwing stones. He'll go away in a minute.'

It was quiet for a moment. Then footsteps crunched on the gravel beneath the window. Dougan clutched Matt's arm – 'Let me chase him away.'

Matt shook his head and signalled for silence. The men crouched, holding their breath, listening intently. Footsteps progressed to the cottage next door. Matt stifled his alarm. He thought it's only a kid, maybe Dougan's right, if we chase him off that will be an end to it. But the boy had come from the big house. Suppose he went back and said men were camped in the cottages? Suppose the others got curious . . .

Beneath them a door creaked on protesting hinges.

'Jaysus,' Dougan hissed. 'Will you listen to that.'

The boy had entered the cottage next door. He would find the supplies – potassium chloride, two glass carboys of sulphuric acid – he would see the hole in the wall and perhaps climb through. Matt flinched as he remembered leaving two rifles in there! His heart thumped. He wished

302

Ferdy were here – Ferdy always knew what to do – but Ferdy was on the road somewhere, bringing Matt's father over the border.

Next door a tin can fell to the concrete floor with a hollow clang.

'Matt!' Dougan hissed. 'For God's sake, do *something*!'

Every eye turned accusingly on Matt. But what could he do? Dougan was right, they should have chased the boy off and risked the consequences. But now . . . if the boy saw the rifles . . .

'We'll have to hold him,' Matt whispered, horrified by the prospect of keeping the boy captive while they finished their business.

A sudden crash echoed below, followed by a scream of fear.

'Matt, for God's sake –'

Matt was already moving to the door. He raced downstairs, heedless of the noise, and rushed to the opening in the wall. The smell of acid was everywhere. He scrambled into the next cottage. An old table had collapsed, trapping the boy's legs. He lay screaming, clawing the floor in agony. A glass carboy had smashed, drenching his legs with sulphuric acid. Matt splashed through a great puddle. He slipped and flung his hands forward as he fell. He rolled over, wincing with pain as acid burned the flesh of his hands. The boy's screams filled the air.

Matt rose to his knees. With a great heave he pushed the table back then lurched to his feet, dragging the child upright with him. Eyes streamed from the stench of acid. The boy gasped for breath, then doubled into a paroxysm of coughing as he clawed desperately at his legs. Acid hissed on skin and clothes with spirals of vapour. The boy regained his breath and screamed with pain. Matt's cheek smarted from splashed acid. Then Dougan leapt through the opening and began dragging them back into the other cottage.

The boy's screams had to be stopped. Matt did the only thing possible – he swung a punch, but the blow was mistimed – the boy staggered back more frightened than ever. Dougan steadied himself then struck hard. The boy's knees buckled as he fell backwards into Matt's arms.

They removed his shoes and peeled the remains of woollen stockings from his legs. The flesh was horribly ulcerated. Skin bubbled into blisters even as they watched. Fissures of lacerations burned down his calves. One gory ankle was open to the bone.

'Dear God!' whispered Cullen in horror.

Matt's hands were on fire with pain. He splashed cold tea on his fingers and over the boy's legs. The cottages lacked piped water. Earlier they had drawn water from the stream near the lane, then boiled a can over the fire. But now the can was empty in the cold hearth. The boy groaned and whimpered as he returned to consciousness.

'He's in a hell of a mess!' Dougan turned from the boy and looked questioningly at Matt.

Without thinking Matt rubbed his chin with his forearm. He grunted with pain as blisters burst on his skin. They *had* to bathe their wounds. Even so Matt hesitated, guessing the boy's legs needed more than bathing. Urgent medical attention was needed if his legs were to be saved, perhaps if his *life* were to be saved. Holy God, what a mess!

'We'll have to break camp,' Matt said, reaching a decision. 'I'll get this kid down to the brook. Ferdy should be along any minute –'

'Suppose he isn't –'

'He *must* be here soon. I'll douse the boy in the stream, then leave him outside the entrance to the big house –'

'You'll be seen –'

'What else can we do?' Matt snapped desperately. The pain in his hands was unbearable. He swung back to Dougan. 'You come with me. Cullen, take a man with you down to the lane. Stop the first car that comes along. We'll need to get away in a hurry –'

'What about your Da and Ferdy?'

'One of us will have to stay behind. Hide out and wait for them. Come on, bring all the rifles, leave everything else.'

Precisely at that moment Liam Riordan and Ferdy Malloy reached the crossroads up the lane. On the crest of the hill behind could be seen the pursuing Wolseley Garda car.

Keady village lay three miles ahead, with Keady Manor a mile or so to their left. Liam jerked the reins and the mare took the left-hand fork at a trot. Ferdy was shouting – 'We've crossed the border – but Liam the bastards are still coming.'

The caravan rattled and bounced down the lane. Ferdy pointed to a break in the trees a hundred yards ahead. 'Pull off the road there. Quick, whilst we're out of sight. Get under cover, for God's sake!'

Liam lashed the reins across the mare's back.

Ferdy kept his eyes on the break in the trees. The abandoned cottages must be very near. Help would be ready and waiting. Liam Riordan and Ferdy Malloy were almost home!

The police car swooped down the hill. The driver braked hard into the crossroads. The cat and mouse game played in the back lanes of the border country was almost over. Only the half-blind Ferdy Malloy could have avoided the road blocks with such skill. The caravan would have escaped completely but for a chance sighting – even now only one car was left in the hunt.

Pat Connors shouted, 'Don't turn right. I could see that way. They didn't turn right.'

'That's Keady in front. We've *crossed* the border,' the driver swung round to face Pat. 'There will be hell to pay if we show ourselves in Keady.'

Pat stared past the driver. The road into Keady was tree-lined and straight. Surely the caravan would still be in sight?

'Turn left,' he said, gambling. 'Damn and blast, we were almost on top of them. *Turn left!*'

The other policeman turned in his seat – 'Pat, we've crossed the border! The British will–'

'To hell with the British! Turn left. Do as you're told, for God's sake!'

The driver reversed the car, then turned the wheel, indecision in his every movement. Coming towards them from Keady was a smart brown and cream Alvis. It purred to a halt at the junction, with the obvious intention of following them down the lane towards Keady Manor.

'Put your foot down!' Pat roared.

He lowered the side window and raised the Webley revolver from his lap.

Tall trees flanked both sides of the lane. Upper branches met to create a leafy tunnel. The police car gathered speed as it went into the bend.

In the Alvis, Eoin O'Brien was surprised to see a Garda car this side of the border. He wondered if the driver had lost his way, especially as the lane only led to Keady Manor. But O'Brien paid little attention. He had enjoyed the drive down from Belfast and was looking forward to the weekend. It was an auspicious occasion, to be spending a few days with Lord Averdale – their mutual dependence augured well for the future. Despite occasional reservations, O'Brien was pleased with the way things were going. What Lord Averdale needed now was a long trip abroad – plenty of sunshine to help him recover from his recent tragedy. O'Brien nodded to himself. He would raise the matter over the weekend, perhaps suggest that Lord Averdale make an extended trip to the Bowley estates in Africa. Now that would be the very thing. Relaxed and smiling, O'Brien eased his foot from the accelerator and put the big Alvis into the bend.

Sheila O'Brien was far from relaxed. She had heard Timothy's scream of pain and terror from the brook. Now she was running down the lane from the wrought-iron gates. The four B Specials raced ahead of her, two had already left the road and were half-hidden by brambles as they crashed through the undergrowth.

'Timothy!' Sheila O'Brien screamed as she ran.

The caravan bucked and swayed round the bend. Liam Riordan saw the figures running towards him. Ferdy Malloy was already twisting round with a rifle in his hands. The mare's hooves beat on the road, the mongrel yapped, the woman screamed – but the loudest noise was the revving engine of the pursuing Wolseley. Ferdy swung front and pointed – 'Liam, take us off the road. They'll be on us in a minute.'

306

Liam lashed the mare and drove desperately for the break in the trees. The Wolseley rounded the bend. Ferdy raised the rifle and fired. The shot went wide and high. Lurching from the buckboard Ferdy fired again. The car was almost on top of them. The driver wrenched the wheel. The car skidded past, righted itself, then skidded again to straddle the lane in front of the caravan. The terrified mare reared back, struggling to escape the shafts, but the momentum of the caravan drove her straight into the motor car. Her forelegs smashed like matchsticks. The alsatian snarled and struggled to free itself at the back of the caravan.

At the stream Matt dropped the screaming boy into the water. Next to him Dougan pulled a revolver from his jacket. Matt cursed the pain of his blistered hands, then cursed even more his lack of a weapon. Even as he swore the bushes parted to reveal Cullen with a rifle in each hand. Matt winced as his ruined hands closed around the metal. Ten yards to his left another IRA man opened fire at the police car.

Just at that instant the Alvis rounded the bend and ran into the caravan. O'Brien clawed the wheel and missed the alsatian by an inch as the Alvis spun through 180 degrees. O'Brien was flung forward into the windscreen. A four-inch gash opened his forehead. His hands rose to his hairline sticky with blood. He caught a fleeting glimpse of his wife running towards him. Yet when his eyes opened the lane was empty. It took Eoin O'Brien a minute to realize that his car had turned full circle and was facing back towards the crossroads.

Pat Connors was on the running board of the Wolseley when it was shunted by the caravan rammed by the Alvis. He had been shooting at Ferdy Malloy, who was returning fire as he backed into the trees. The impact of the collision sent Pat reeling into the lane, his revolver spinning from his hand.

Liam Riordan had been hit. Clutching his shoulder he jumped from the buckboard and ran for the clearing twenty yards away. It was a mistake. Had he followed Ferdy into the trees Liam Riordan might have lived – but as it was he had seen his son, and was running to meet him.

Matt Riordan, with Dougan beside him, ran into the road to provide covering fire as Liam Riordan stumbled towards them.

Sheila O'Brien was in the centre of the lane when gunfire erupted. She veered left towards the verge, heading for her son screaming in the brook. A yard from cover she was hit by a stray bullet. It pierced her temple to shatter her face and spray blood-covered pieces of bone in every direction.

Two B Specials gave covering fire to their colleagues as they dragged eight-year-old Timothy O'Brien from the stream. The boy, out of his mind with pain and terror, writhed like an eel. As they reached the side of the lane one man stumbled and fell. Timothy O'Brien was thrown to the ground, less than five yards from his dead mother.

Sean Connors was trying to drag his father back to the car. Hampered by his stiff leg Pat had fallen awkwardly. His head had struck the road with a sickening crack. Semiconscious he rose to one knee. 'The gun,' he gasped to his son. 'Sean, get the gun.'

Paddy Cullen ran into the road with the single objective of capturing the Alvis for use as an escape car. A blood-stained driver staggered from the vehicle. Paddy squeezed the trigger of the Thompson submachine-gun and red blotches shot across Eoin O'Brien's jacket. He was flung five yards backwards by the force of the bullets.

Thirty yards away young Timothy O'Brien lay writhing in agony. He screamed as bullets tore his father apart. He screamed unceasingly as hysteria took over. Mistakenly – in a snatched glimpse – he saw his father's killer as a young man with black hair who waved a revolver as he pulled a man towards the Wolseley. Meanwhile other hands dragged Timothy backwards towards the gates of Keady Manor. Gibbering he pointed to the dark-haired man near the police car – but he pointed in vain because B Specials on either side of him blazed a volley of shots at the trees.

After retrieving the revolver from the road Sean struggled to get his father into the relative safety of the Wolseley. Behind him a policeman opened fire. His second shot caught Liam Riordan in the back, the third smashed Riordan's head as he started to fall.

Matt Riordan had almost reached his father when the bullet split Liam Riordan's head open. Matt shot the policeman and watched him tumble backwards into the Wolseley. Then Matt fell to his knees and tried to turn his father over – but Ferdy Malloy was pulling him away. Matt looked up to shout at Ferdy, then froze, words still on his lips. *Connors!* The Connors were *here* – both of them – father and son!

The Alvis slammed to a halt, with Paddy Cullen at the wheel. Hands were pulling Matt into the car. 'No!' he screamed. 'Take the Da!' Ferdy's rifle clubbed into Matt's head. They heaved him into the back seat. Dougan snatched the Thompson and leapt in next to Cullen. Liam Riordan and two other IRA men were left dead on the ground.

Tyres squealed as the Alvis swerved across the road. Dougan blazed away with the Thompson to smash the windscreen of the other car to a million shards of glass. Then the Alvis lurched past towards the crossroads.

Sean was already in the Wolseley with his father. The dead policeman was slumped next to the driver in the front. The driver screamed as the windscreen burst. Sean cried out as splinters cut his face – and cried out again as his father fell forward – 'Da! Are you all right?' Bright red blood fell warm on to Sean's hands. 'Dear God. Da. Da!'

The car leapt forward as the driver slipped the clutch. In the back Sean hugged his father. 'Da! Don't die Da. *Please* don't die!'

They rounded the bend in time to see the Alvis turn north towards Keady. The Wolseley did not give chase. Instead the driver turned south and roared up the hill.

Pat Connors squeezed his son's hand and tried to talk – but his voice died in a gargle of blood.

Behind them – in the lane at Keady – the sounds of the departing engines were barely audible above the howls of the tethered alsatian and the yapping of the mongrel as it emerged from the wood. The crippled mare whinnied piteously.

In an incident which had lasted five minutes, five men

and one woman lay dead. And ten minutes later, Pat Connors, Irish patriot and hero of the 1916 Rising, died also, clutched to his son's chest as the Wolseley raced towards Monaghan.

BOOK TWO

CHAPTER ONE

Sean was devastated by the death of his father. Of course friends rallied round – Dinny, Michael, the Widow O'Flynn – and Dev himself attended the funeral. Ambassador Kennedy wrote from London. Newspapers published eulogies, hundreds of people lavished praise on Pat Connors, but their words failed to comfort his son. Sean was torn first by grief, then the need for revenge. 'That bastard Matt Riordan,' he roared at Dinny one day, 'I'll kill that sod with my bare hands. I'll murder him, Dinny, you see if I don't.'

He would have searched Belfast, had his friend not dissuaded him. 'You'll never find Riordan in a hundred years,' Dinny said, 'let the police hunt him down.'

But the police showed no signs of catching Matt Riordan. Sean mourned and raged and took little interest in anything else, until – some weeks after the Killing at Keady – a group of friends met secretly in Dinny's office. They had kept Sean from Belfast, but his behaviour still worried them. 'If he stays in Dublin he'll drive himself mad,' said Michael.

Senator O'Keefe frowned, Jim Tully sighed, and the Widow O'Flynn dabbed her eyes. It was left to Dinny to resolve matters. 'Wasn't he going to London anyway, before this terrible business. Can you think of anything better? A new place and different faces – wouldn't that be best for the boy?'

It was the best they could think of – so they embarked upon a campaign of hints and suggestions. If Sean guessed, he said nothing about it. Dublin *was* driving him mad. Wherever he looked he saw signs of his father. Eventually he allowed himself to be persuaded to go to London for a few months.

Arrangements were made and early one morning in October, Sean left for London. The Widow O'Flynn thought he was going for good. She clutched his arm as they walked down the quay. 'Will you stand still and give me a good look at you? Besides, wouldn't you think I'm entitled to be kissed goodbye properly?' Her arms encircled his neck and her lips clung to his for such a long time that the true nature of their past relationship must have been obvious to everyone there. Not that she cared. 'You'll write, won't you?' she sobbed. 'Will you promise me that?'

Sean himself was close to tears as the mail-boat pulled away from the dock – especially when Maeve O'Flynn collapsed in Jim Tully's arms. Senator O'Keefe doffed his hat, Dinny raised both arms in salute, and Michael waved and waved from the end of the pier.

The journey was nothing like Sean imagined, but he had always dreamt of his home-coming too, to be greeted by his father as well as his friends. Now his father was dead, killed by the Riordans and the IRA. Sean swore his revenge, knowing as he did so that he would need to become powerful in order to kill Riordan. And power meant assets. He had to find assets in London. Harmsworth had. If he equalled Harmsworth he would be rich and powerful enough to come back and destroy the IRA and Matt Riordan with it. The prospect of that kept him going, bolstered his determination when it wavered, as waver it did during that journey. He wondered what London would be like. Dinny had talked non-stop about Fleet Street, yet London was more than that – London was fame and wealth and power and so many things. But he felt lonely, more alone than at any time in his life.

He travelled light, just one suitcase and a battered copy of *The Life and Times of Alfred Harmsworth* – together with the rules of course, his father's notebooks and his own – along with Dinny's letters of introduction, mere reinforcements to those already posted to pave the way for the new London correspondent of the *Dublin Gazette*. Dinny had said, 'Every Irishman in London will be waiting to buy you a drink in Mooney's Bar by the time you get there.'

But nobody met Sean's train at Paddington. No messages awaited him at his hotel. London seemed vast and unfriendly. He ate dinner alone and went early to bed, his thoughts back in Dublin with the Widow O'Flynn.

The following morning he went directly to the *Daily Mirror*, nervous about meeting the editor who, as a favour to Dinny, had agreed to provide Sean with a desk and a telephone – 'until he sorts himself out.' Geraldine House looked bigger than Christchurch Cathedral, and 'Bart's' reputation was equally daunting. 'The *Daily Mirror* nearly folded three years ago,' Dinny had said, 'then Bart took over as editor and circulation has never stopped rising. The best men in Fleet Street work there now.'

As things turned out, Sean's anxiety about meeting Mr Bartholomew was needless – the encounter was too fleeting to be painful. Bart had time only for a handshake and a pat on the back, before pushing Sean towards a waiting assistant – 'Harry, take care of this young man, he's a friend of a friend. Give him a desk in the League of Nations.'

Which turned out to be a corner of the newsroom used by half a dozen overseas correspondents, all sharing the *Mirror*'s facilities until they 'sorted themselves out'. Sean met an Australian and a Frenchman, and heard mention of others, including an American named Mallon – 'but we only see him once a week.'

It was a bewildering morning. Sean was left to his own devices. People rushed in and out, busy with a hundred things, none of which concerned him – he was not on the *Mirror*'s payroll, he had nothing to do with the paper – Bart had kept his promise about the desk and the telephone, the rest was up to Sean. The implications were terrifying. At the *Gazette* assignments were allocated by Dinny, reporters were told what to do, but correspondents miles from home created their own work schedules. Sean wondered where on earth to begin.

After sitting there all morning, plagued by doubts and shrouded in loneliness, he took himself off to lunch, not because he was hungry but just to escape. He found a pub on the corner, full of animated talk and laughing faces. The atmosphere took him straight back to Mulligan's Bar. He wished he had stayed in Dublin. At that moment he would have given his right arm to be back at the *Gazette*. He drank a glass of beer and ate a sandwich, listened to loud English voices, and felt more unhappy by the minute. Finally he left, wondering whether to return to Geraldine House or to walk right past, perhaps to go down to the river to think things over.

It was then that the accident happened. It was all over in a split second. He was outside Geraldine House when the man in front stepped into the road, looking the wrong way. Sean shouted and grabbed the man's coat. A taxi skidded, mounted the pavement, and almost ran them down. Sean pulled the man clear just in time. They were all shaken – the man in Sean's grasp, the taxi-driver, and Sean himself. Luckily little harm was done – the man's trousers were torn and his knee was bleeding. He clung to Sean while testing his left foot on the ground. 'Ouch,' he grinned, white-faced, 'when will I remember you folks drive on the wrong side of the road?'

Which was how Sean met Freddie Mallon. Not that he knew that immediately. What he saw then was a smartly dressed man with wavy brown hair, making light of his pain while coping with an accident. The taxi-driver was quickly dealt with – profound apologies and a one pound note from the American.

'As for you,' the American said shakily to Sean, 'you about saved my life. I wouldn't know how to pay you for that.'

Sean was more concerned with the man's ability to walk.

'That's okay,' the American jerked his head at Geraldine House, 'I was making for here anyway.'

After which came the introductions, and when Sean helped Mallon upstairs they found they were at adjoining desks. 'That's fate,' Mallon said cheerfully. 'You must be good news, my new lucky charm.' They exchanged grins, then Mallon busied himself with his mail and some messages. Half an hour later, however, he rose with a groan. 'If I don't soak in a hot tub I'll never move again. I'm going home. What are your plans for the rest of the day?'

The truth was that Sean had no plans, none whatsoever. Mallon grinned. 'Tell you what. Come back to my place and tell me about yourself. I owe you a favour, young Connors, and I hate being beholden.'

Sean learned a lot that afternoon, all of it fascinating. Freddie had worked on several New York papers and some on the West Coast. Now he was a thirty-five-year-old success story, writing a weekly column on Europe for syndication to over one hundred American papers. He filed stories from Berlin and Rome, Paris and Vienna. Sean listened with awed respect, then asked, 'But how do you start, making contacts, I mean? Don't you have to get to know a place first, before writing about it?'

Freddie blinked up from his bath-tub, 'What am I – foreign correspondent or travel writer? I report political and social news – not how Venice looks in the moonlight.'

Later, when Freddie was dressed and they were in the sitting-room, each with a glass in his hand, it was Sean's turn to talk. He began diffidently, conscious of his inexperience – but Freddie was a practised interviewer and two hours later Sean was shocked to realize that he had related most of his life history. He had stopped short of his affair with the Widow O'Flynn, and omitted to say he was the *Gazette*'s owner – yet he had talked about everything else, even the Killing at Keady. Of course there were reasons, including three unaccustomed whiskies, but the drink merely helped ease his nervousness. What made him talk was mostly homesickness and self-doubt; he was still mourning his father, he was a stranger in a strange land, unsure of himself – and Freddie Mallon led the conversation with such sympathetic encouragement that at the end of two hours they were laughing like old friends.

They got on so well that Sean was delighted by the suggestion of dinner. He had planned to go in search of Mooney's Bar, but dinner with this sophisticated American seemed a much better idea. Freddie took him to a tiny restaurant in Soho where he made a fuss of introducing Sean to the proprietor – 'Mario, come and meet Sean Connors. He saved my life today. Do me a favour, if he ever comes in here by himself give him the best, will you do that for me?'

After which they dined well. Sean enjoyed every mouthful, even though he was unsure what he was eating. He liked the atmosphere too. The place was full of Freddie's friends. During the evening at least seven people stopped at their table. Sean was introduced to everyone – 'This young man saved my life today.' For the second time in twelve hours 'League of Nations' proved an apt description. Sean met correspondents from four different countries, all of whom wanted Freddie's opinion on the same subject – the possibility of war.

Sean was fascinated, yet he felt miserably out of place. These men were far removed from Dublin reporters. Sean's tweeds looked clumsy next to their smart worsteds. He shuddered as he contrasted his Irish brogue with their cultured voices. What pained him most was his hopeless ignorance. Maybe Alfred Harmsworth had conquered those men, but they were too much for Sean Connors. London, he decided, was not for him. Even the food he was eating carried some fancy Italian name that he could never pronounce.

Yet, self-conscious or not, he tried to follow their conversation. Where yesterday's statesmen had lived in Sean's books, the statesmen of today were part of these men's lives – they spoke of Hitler and Mussolini, and Roosevelt and Stalin as men they had studied. *Mein Kampf* and *Das Kapital* and Roosevelt's New Deal were referred to with a casual fluency which took Sean's breath away. He could only listen and learn – and try to hang on. He *had* to hang on. Too many people would feel let down if he ran away. Maeve O'Flynn and Dinny expected him to conquer the world. Besides, what would his father have said?

Finally, the impromptu dinner party came to an end. Freddie's friends departed and the American ordered a last cup of coffee. He smiled wryly at Sean, 'We live in troubled times. Maybe the best advice I can give you is to get back home to Ireland.'

Sean flushed crimson. Did that mean he was a boy on a man's errand? The imagined slight cut deeply. He blurted out a reply before he could stop himself, 'I've only been in London twenty-four hours, Mr Mallon. I'll know twice as much by this time tomorrow, and seven times more this time next week. I'm a quick learner. Wouldn't you say that's as useful as . . .' he cast around for an example, 'as knowing how to order food in Italian?'

Freddie Mallon looked stunned, then burst out laughing. 'Listen knucklehead, I didn't mean to insult you. I order in Italian because I did it all my life back home. I was brought up that way, there's nothing special to it.'

Sean felt too foolish to apologize. Instead he fidgeted with his coffee cup.

Mallon grinned. 'Okay, stay in London. Don't be so touchy, maybe I was just envious.'

'*Envious?*'

'Sure. When I was your age my paper wouldn't send me eight blocks to cover a ball game, let alone a war in Europe.'

'There's no war here, Mr Mallon.'

'Chamberlain's scrap of paper? Peace in our time and all that crap. Forget it. There'll be war.' Mallon scratched his chin and smiled across the table, 'Relax. I was trying to help, that's all. I know you're smart, your paper wouldn't send you here to fall on your ass, and Bart wouldn't let you in the *Mirror* without checking you out. And your reflexes are quick, otherwise I wouldn't be here. Now I know you've got a temper too – so okay, what else is new?'

Sean covered his embarrassment with a laugh, and he did manage an apology. They talked for a while after that. Sean was enthralled by Freddie's account of Hitler's Germany. Not all of it was new. Even Dublin's papers had carried accounts of Mr Chamberlain's visits to Germany, but people in Ireland thought that the threat of war had receded, a view shared in England as far as Sean could make out. The London *Times* was positive – 'Peace in our time,' promised Mr Chamberlain, and *The Times* echoed him. Freddie Mallon, however, held a quite different view.

When they parted, Freddie said, 'Now don't forget, kid, let me know if there's anything I can do. I eat at Mario's three or four times a week, and you know where I live.'

It was a warming feeling, to have found a friend in this vast city.

Sean spent the next morning at Geraldine House. Freddie was absent, out gathering news in his own incomparable style. Everyone at the *Mirror* spoke highly of him – Sean was intrigued to learn that Freddie even broadcast once a week for CBS. He was quite possibly the best foreign correspondent in the business. 'Wouldn't you think,' Sean mused to himself, 'he'd be the very man to copy if I stay here.'

Staying was still a big if. Geraldine House was as daunting as ever. Everyone was so busy – too busy for a young Paddy straight from the bog. He was homesick for Dublin and as uncertain as ever – but to run away would be the end of a dream. He would never be powerful enough to smash the IRA and Matt Riordan with it. The thought of revenge gave him courage.

He left at noon and walked down the Strand to a tailor's, where he bought a grey flannel suit, a white shirt, grey socks and a maroon necktie. Next door he purchased some black shoes. Then he went to a bookshop for a copy of *Mein Kampf* which he took to his hotel to read. He felt guilty, stretched out on the bed when he should be working, or at least looking for lodgings. Yet, in a way, he was working – working flat out to repair the gaps in his knowledge. And at seven o'clock he took another step forward. Dressed in his new finery, with *Mein Kampf* under his arm, he made his way to Soho in search of Mario's restaurant.

The American was there already, at what was obviously his usual table. He grinned at the new clothes but passed no comment. Instead he waved Sean into a chair and asked about his day. When Sean told him, Freddie was amused but impressed. 'Well,' he said, 'and what did you make of the great leader's book?'

Sean plunged into his list of queries and was asking about Hitler's plan to carve 'living space' out of Bolshevist Russia, when Freddie interrupted, 'Hang on. Here's the very man. Helmut! Over here.'

A tall, broad-shouldered man bore down on their table. 'Freddie! Wonderful to see you. They said you'd be here.'

Freddie introduced Sean with a flourish, 'Meet my young saviour, Sean Connors of the *Dublin Gazette*. Sean, this is an old sparring partner, Helmut von Roon.'

The tall man cast a look of enquiry at Freddie as he shook Sean's hand.

'Sure,' the American grinned. 'He saved my life yesterday. Pull up a chair and I'll tell you about it.'

Sean listened to another highly coloured account of the accident. When it was over von Roon expressed suitable congratulations, before turning back to Freddie, 'I can only stay for one drink. I'm dining with the Websters. You remember, we met them at your Embassy that night.'

Freddie asked to be remembered to the Websters, then turned to Sean. 'Helmut and I used to burn up the Kurfurstendam together. He knows Berlin night-life like I know the back of my hand.'

The German flushed with pleasure, but his question a moment later had nothing to do with nightclubs. 'What is happening in England? I arrived this morning to a war-fevered land. Everyone is talking about war. The papers are full of rubbish about air raids and incendiary bombs and poison gas. Who is the enemy?'

Freddie's eyebrows rose. 'Are you kidding? After listening to General Goering's cosy fireside chats about his invincible air force, people over here are in a muck sweat at the thought of Germans dropping out of the skies –'

'That's ridiculous. In Germany we have no idea to attack anyone. Did not the Fuehrer tell Mr Chamberlain that he has no further territorial claims? It's the socialist press here, whipping up a war scare. Freddie, I assure you, in Germany there is a spirit of peace and goodwill to all men.'

'Unless you're a Jew,' Freddie said bluntly. 'Remember our last night on the Kurfurstendam? Those people smashing Jewish shops –'

'I was ashamed. Did I not say so? We are all ashamed, decent Germans of whom there are many, many millions –'

Freddie nodded. 'Millions of decent Germans who watch their leaders drive those poor devils to suicide, who steal their money –'

'What's got into you?' Von Roon flushed. 'This is beginning to sound like propaganda. The Jews cause difficulties, that's all. Your President Roosevelt will come to recognize the problem in time, believe me. You will have to do something about them in the end –'

'The final solution?' Freddie asked sarcastically, then he flushed too. 'I'm sorry Helmut, that was rude. We had some good times in Berlin, you and I – drink up, let's forget politics for a while.'

Some of the tension faded from the German's face. After a pause he nodded, and turned to Sean with a smile. 'Please accept my apologies too. Freddie is right, we can have too much of politics. After all, things can't be so bad when an Englishman, an American and a German can share a drink –'

'He's a Mick,' Freddie spluttered, 'a Paddy – he *hates* the English.'

Von Roon's confusion sent Freddie into hysterics. The difficult moment was behind them. After that von Roon stayed for half an hour and told so many stories about shared times with Freddie that Sean was sorry to see him go. He waved as von Roon departed and asked Freddie how long he had known him.

'Helmut? God knows. A couple of years. He's a good sort, helped me no end when I first went to Berlin, but he's like the three brass monkeys about Hitler – see no evil, hear no evil, speak no evil. They're all the same over there.'

He expanded on his theories during the rest of the meal. 'The German psyche cries out for a strong leader. It's part of their mythology, this father figure coming out of the forest. You've started *Mein Kampf* – when you've read that there are a dozen other books at my place if you're interested. They might help you understand why perfectly decent people like Helmut von Roon not only tolerate Hitler but deify him.'

Sean struggled to understand. He was reminded of Dinny talking about the English – 'You'll like them, Sean, the English are fine, it's the bloody British Empire that's so hard to stomach.' Maybe Germans suffered blind spots in the same way.

Over coffee they talked of other things, including Sean's need to find lodgings. Freddie thought about it before reaching a conclusion. 'Move in with me. There's plenty of room at Craven Street. We could team up – share a few expenses, swap contacts, that kind of thing. Two wild colonials together. What do you think?'

Of course the arrangement was one-sided. Sean had no contacts to swap, at least not in London. He had Dinny's letters of introduction, but they were to newspapermen most of whom Freddie already knew. Yet Freddie dismissed all protests with a chuckle. 'Okay, you can be my apprentice. I could use some help. Besides you *do* have contacts. Didn't you say Ambassador Kennedy was a friend of yours?'

Sean blushed. He had mentioned the Ambassador's visit to Ballsbridge when talking about his father. He certainly had not claimed personal friendship.

'Maybe I just need you around,' Freddie concluded. 'Didn't I say you were my new good luck charm?'

A delighted Sean moved into the narrow terraced house the next morning. Craven Street was not the most fashionable address in London, but the location -- half way between Fleet Street and the House of Commons -- suited Freddie perfectly. Soho's restaurants lay to the north, and to the south was the Embankment, a fine place for clearing the head after a heavy night. Originally Freddie had shared the comfortable three-storey house with another American -- 'when he went back to the States I just stayed on. I was comfortable, so why move?'

Thus began an enduring friendship, although the relationship was more like tutor and pupil at the outset. Freddie Mallon was an even harder task master than Dinny Macaffety. For weeks Sean worked as a research assistant, digging into the background of stories, checking facts and confirming details. He spent more time in the reading room of the British Museum than at his typewriter. The joke in Fleet Street was that the shrewd American had found some cheap labour and was working 'the Irish Navvy' to death.

Sean didn't mind. Hard work suited him. New experiences left little room for being homesick. Of course his heart still ached, and every night he remembered his father. Before falling asleep Sean recounted the events of his day, whispering into the darkness as if dictating a letter . . . 'Sure now, Da, you'll remember me saying yesterday . . .' and he was away, cataloguing thoughts and worries, hopes and aspirations. Many were about Freddie and his talk of war. On the other hand not all of the American's thoughts were dominated by the spectre of Nazi Germany -- for instance, five minutes of his weekly CBS broadcast *Seven Days in London* were devoted to some of the unusual sights around the capital, and Sean developed a nose for sniffing them out. Consequently every week he delivered a piece from Billingsgate Fish Market, or the

Royal Opera House in Covent Garden, or even Bow Street Police Station – each story illustrative of an English eccentricity. Initially Freddie insisted on checking every detail, but when Sean proved his facts the American was glad to accept them and concentrated instead on filling the rest of his broadcast.

They often dined at Mario's, where they were invariably joined by other members of the overseas press corps – and gradually the restaurant acquired the same talking shop characteristics as the little house in Ballsbridge. Sean gave a similar account of himself – diffident at first, and only voicing an opinion when sure of his facts. It was a hard school, but a good one. And on the other evenings, when Freddie was on a story or out to dinner with friends, Sean ploughed through the books at Craven Street in pursuit of Freddie's theories on Nazi Germany. Much went over his head, but enough stuck to give him a glimmer of understanding when Freddie argued that the roots of Fascism lay in German nineteenth-century Romanticism.

Sometimes they just enjoyed themselves. Despite rumours of war, London remained the dazzling hub of the mighty British Empire, far removed from straight-laced Dublin. Freddie guided his protégé round the nightclubs and late-night drinking spots – and once to a quiet house in Piccadilly where they spent the night with the girls. The Widow O'Flynn had taught Sean well, for the girl expressed more than professional pleasure with his performance. She nibbled his ear when he left. 'Come again,' she whispered, to which he replied, 'Jaysus, I'll not come for a month after that.'

Christmas arrived. Sean would have gone home but for Freddie. Not that the American need have been lonely, he had invitations to a score of country houses. The truth was that he preferred to stay in London. 'You know, Sean,' he confided, 'these grand English country houses scare the shit out of me. All that fresh air in the mornings, and riding to hounds . . . ugh . . . I guess I'm just a city boy.'

They stayed in London and gave a party for the press corps which lasted, on and off, for most of the holiday. In fact Sean's alcoholic haze was just lifting when he met

322

Valerie Hamilton – on the morning before New Year's Eve.

The Hamiltons were Freddie's friends, as were most people Sean met – but the Hamiltons were special. Freddie kept them to himself for a start. He dined at their Eaton Square house and occasionally returned hospitality by taking Mrs Hamilton and Margaret her daughter out to lunch – but Sean was never invited. He didn't mind – just as Freddie was daunted by English country houses so Sean was shy of the people who owned them, and from what he knew of the Hamiltons they were likely to prove very daunting indeed.

They were part of society, less newsworthy than Lady Cunard or Chips Channon, but newsworthy enough. Gossip columnists were as excited about parties at Ashworth, the Hamilton house in Berkshire, as those at Cliveden, home of the Astors. And Augustus John's portrait of Mrs Cynthia Hamilton had created a sensation at the Royal Academy – 'the most sensuous woman in England' he had called her, and most men agreed. She was well over forty in 1938 but had resisted the years so well that she was often mistaken for Margaret, her daughter. They both had chestnut brown hair, dazzling smiles and smoky blue eyes. Margaret was the attraction for Freddie – as Sean knew from Fleet Street gossip and from watching him prepare for an evening with the Hamiltons. 'How do I look?' he would ask, with uncharacteristic lack of confidence. Sean was amazed. The American's self-assurance was usually massive. Sean found it painful to watch. He considered Freddie's handling of the situation grossly inept – but Sean had been spoiled by the Widow O'Flynn. Not all such affairs ran so smoothly, as he was about to find out.

The morning before New Year's Eve was crisp and fine, and Sean rose early, free of a hangover for the first time in days. Mrs Harris, their Cockney char, arrived at nine and began her attack on the chaos created over Christmas.

Freddie went off to Geraldine House and Sean shut himself in 'the office', a tiny room on the second floor next to the sitting-room. Sean worked one day a week in the office, writing his 'London Diary', a big spread which had become a feature in the *Dublin Gazette* – two thousand words which, together with photographs, took up the paper's middle pages every Saturday. The Diary owed a great deal to Freddie. It was Freddie who taught Sean that readers found the private lives of well-known figures much more interesting than their public utterances. That was when Sean learned to dig deep. Sean Connors was the first to reveal that Sir Oswald Mosley was secretly married to Mrs Diana Guinness. And that the King had dined at the home of Lord Baldwin, solely to meet some Labour MPs. And that the Hon. Unity Mitford was spending more and more time with a certain Captain Fitz-Randolph from the German Embassy. Trivial in themselves, yet when interwoven with Sean's political commentary, they portrayed something of the seething whirlpool of life that was London. Certainly Dinny was pleased with the Diary which was winning new readers for the *Gazette* every week.

On the morning before New Year's Eve, Sean was sweating over his column and Mrs Harris had just finished the sitting-room, when the doorbell disturbed them. Mrs Harris had gone up to the bedrooms and Sean could hear her grumbling on the top landing, so he went to the door himself – and found himself looking at Valerie Hamilton.

He knew who she was. The photographs in Freddie's room showed the whole family – George and Cynthia Hamilton, flanked by daughters Margaret and Valerie. The pose made it obvious that Cynthia and Margaret enjoyed being photographed, whereas Valerie, three years younger than Margaret, seemed totally bored. Her eyes were focused upwards, as if pleading for the intervention of Divine Providence, and there was something of that in her expression when Sean opened the door.

'Oh,' she said. Her eyes rounded as she stared at him. A faint touch of colour appeared at her cheeks. 'You must be the Irish Navvy. You couldn't be anyone else. Black hair and bold blue eyes, with that wild untamed look about you. Freddie's description was quite inadequate. I shall tell him. Is he in?'

Sean responded with a red-faced stare. The Irish Navvy nickname had stuck in Fleet Street, but to hear it from this tiny girl was quite startling – as startling as the girl herself. He tried to remember what Freddie had said about her –

that her political views were a bit strong at times, and 'she's not as pretty as Margaret'. Freddie was wrong about that, Sean thought she was beautiful. Swathed in a silver fox fur, Valerie Hamilton looked like a porcelain statue, five feet high with flawless skin and mocking blue eyes. 'I'm Val Hamilton,' she said, offering him a tiny gloved hand.

He came alive with a start, explaining that Freddie was out.

'Then I shall wait,' the porcelain figure announced. 'If he's not back by noon you can stand me lunch. How would that suit you?'

She looked out of place in the sitting-room. The whole house seemed suddenly shabby. Not that Valerie appeared worried. She gazed through the open door to his desk in the office, 'Oh Lord, are you working? Don't let me disturb you. Give me a magazine or something and I'll be as quiet as a mouse.'

It seemed rude to do that, so he pretended his work was finished, persuaded Mrs Harris to make some coffee, and settled down to entertain his unexpected guest. He wondered how to amuse her. He enjoyed the cut and thrust of the talk at Mario's but that was mainly about politics, he could hardly expect Valerie Hamilton to be interested in that. But she proved him wrong almost immediately. 'Are you preparing your readers for war?' she asked. 'Back in Dublin I mean?'

He managed a confused reply, saying that editors shape the news, reporters merely gather it. As for war . . . well, everyone knew de Valera's views on neutrality.

'You mean you'll sit on the fence?' She sounded horrified. 'Surely the Irish won't want Fascism spreading right across Europe?'

He did his best to explain. As a country, Ireland was less than twenty years old. They were free at last, at least in the south. If the rich nations of Europe squabbled, well that had nothing to do with a poor country like Ireland.

It was not an answer which satisfied her. She swamped him with arguments – Mrs Harris came and went with the coffee, but was barely noticed amid the welter of words. Despite the practice Sean had received at Mario's he found himself struggling at times. Valerie Hamilton held strong opinions, about Hitler's Germany and democracy and all sorts of things. She was the most exhilarating girl he had ever met. She argued with a fierce intensity, relieved now and then by a gamin-like grin, as if to remind him it was only a game, an amusement to pass the time until Freddie arrived. But Freddie did not arrive, and when Sean called a truce while he fetched some more coal for the fire, he realized that it was almost noon.

'Look, I could phone if you like,' he suggested. 'If he's not at the *Mirror* they might know where to find him.'

She had moved to the window. Winter sunshine lightened her donkey brown dress to the colour of sand dunes. Her fashionable short curls shone like a halo. She shook her head, 'I'm not in a hurry. Besides, you promised me lunch.'

He felt ten feet tall. He wondered if Mario's was open. Familiarity had shown him the comfortable scruffiness of the place, but at least he was known there, he could make an impression. Yet he couldn't go as he was. He glanced at his baggy trousers and the old Aran sweater. 'I'll go and change. Won't be a minute.'

'Oh no, it's cold out. Can't we eat here? Then if Freddie turns up we'll be ready and waiting.'

He wondered what was left in the larder. Downstairs the front door banged. Freddie, he thought, bitterly disappointed that his time with this wonderful girl was over. But it was Mrs Harris letting herself out. Relieved, he grappled with the problem of lunch. No doubt she would simply ring for the butler at her homes in Eaton Square or Ashworth. Life was different in Craven Street.

She read his mind. 'I'll help, just show me the kitchen. I'm really quite competent.'

Her grin weakened his protest. It was a grin, not a smile, he had been thinking that all morning. A smile was polite and not always sincere, whereas Val's grin was open and honest.

'What would you have had?' she asked. 'By yourself?'

'Cold beef, I think, and there might be some chutney left.'

'Pickled onions?'

He nodded.

'With a glass of beer?'

He nodded again, then burst out laughing. It was absurd to think of her drinking beer. He suddenly felt very happy – and she was laughing too. 'Well, let's have that,' she said. 'We'll reek to high heaven by the time Freddie gets back, but who cares.'

They ate from trays in their laps, sat on either side of the fire – and talked non-stop, although perhaps Val did most of the talking. When she had finished she set the tray aside and prowled round the room, sipping from her glass as she studied the bookshelves. 'You know,' she said, 'I've often imagined this room. It's more comfortable than I expected. I always thought Freddie lived out of a suitcase – rushing off to Berlin at the drop of a swastika. You too, I suppose. My God, I wish I were a man.'

It seemed a most unlikely thing to say. Sean gazed in astonishment, unprepared to believe that she would want to change at all. He even said so, clumsily, fumbling for the right words.

She grinned as she returned to the fireplace. 'How gallant, but I wasn't really fishing, I'm not Margaret you know. She is lovely, lovely and trapped, like my mother. It's just as well they don't want to do anything, men wouldn't let them, they are only allowed to be beautiful. Still, they're happy I suppose, and other people enjoy looking at them.'

Sean was enjoying looking at Valerie.

'What do *I* want to do?' She seemed surprised by his question. 'Oh, the same as now, I suppose, only more of it. Unless this double life turns me into a screaming schizophrenic.'

Which was how Sean learned of her political activities. She worked for the Labour Party three days a week, in the East End – and talked fluently of the poor and the unemployed, and of Labour leaders like Attlee and Greenwood. Sean was unable to conceal his surprise. It seemed so at odds with what he knew of the Hamiltons.

She grinned, 'I know, I'm the black sheep. The family accept it now, but mother is still kicking up about me taking a flat in Shadwell.'

Sean had never been to Shadwell. It was down by the

docks, and Valerie was taking a flat there in January. 'I'll only use it during the week. We have committee meetings which drag on until all hours. I shall still go home at weekends.' She grinned again. 'The experience will be good for me.'

When he asked why, she said, 'Oh, the Labour Party is full of middle-class intellectuals from tree-lined suburbs like Hampstead. They prattle on about the slums, but what do they really *know*? Nothing at first hand. I can't be like that. Being taken seriously in politics is hard enough as it is, my family is well off, I'm young, female, and – well reasonably presentable . . .' Her glance seemed suddenly shy and out of character. 'Well, *you* said I was. So don't you see – I'll never get anywhere if I'm just another armchair philosopher.'

A moment later, while telling him how important it was to cultivate the grass roots in politics, she stopped in mid-sentence. 'Sorry, am I boring you? I do go on, don't I? Everyone says a month in the slums will change my mind about all sorts of things.'

He made a feeble joke about buying her beer and pickles in the East End, and was delighted when she reached for his hand. 'That's a date,' she said, 'Sean Connors, Irish Navvy and Gentleman of Letters, I shall hold you to that.'

They talked of other things for a while, although politics were never far from Val's mind. 'This war will bring changes,' she said at one stage. 'It's a horrible thing to say, but it could be a good thing for the working class. Not even the Tories can send men off to fight without promising them a better life when they return . . . *if* they return.'

'You're positive then – there will be a war?'

Her eyes widened. 'Freddie's certain. I assumed you agreed. I mean, living here, working with –'

'I suppose I do, but –'

'Oh, I forgot, you're going to be neutral, aren't you?'

They laughed, liking each other more every minute – and once Freddie was mentioned he became the subject of conversation. She was obviously fond of him, and Sean was wondering how fond, when she said – 'If only he were less timid.'

'Timid! Freddie?'

'Oh, I know that's not the right word, but how else do you explain the way Americans lose confidence? They're the most awful snobs, besotted by titles. What really worries Freddie is that Margaret will be *Lady* Tylehurst if she marries Bunny. So what? If Margaret wanted a title she could have the pick of the peerage. Can't Freddie see that? He's so knowledgeable about everything else. I just can't understand him. If he *wants* Margaret to marry him, why not ask her – and put everyone out of their misery.'

Sean felt elated, not just for Freddie but because Valerie Hamilton was not interested in him for herself.

She sighed. 'Lord, that was indiscreet. It's just I hate seeing Freddie mooning about. You'd better keep quiet about that. I'd hate to be thought interfering.' She was suddenly anxious, 'You will keep quiet, won't you?'

He was reassuring her when they heard the front door. Freddie's feet pounded up the stairs and along the landing. The door burst open. 'Say, Sean, guess what –' he stopped, gaping at Valerie reclining on the sofa, stockinged feet up on the upholstery, shoes on the floor, the long since discarded fur wrap draped carelessly over the back of a chair. 'Well, I'll be –'

'Damned,' she grinned in welcome. 'Well, guess what? Has war been declared?'

They all started talking at once, with a good deal of laughter thrown in. The atmosphere became that of an impromptu party – and a party was what Valerie had called about. 'There's been a glorious mix-up about tomorrow night. Half the invitations were lost. But you do *know* we expect you at Eaton Square, don't you?'

Freddie looked pleased and startled at the same time. 'Tomorrow?'

'New Year's Eve,' Valerie turned quickly to Sean. 'You too, if you'll come.'

Freddie glanced at Sean. Nothing definite was planned, except a half promise to meet the crowd at Mario's. Freddie accepted for both of them, and Val left shortly afterwards. Later that evening Sean learned a good deal more about the Hamiltons. Valerie's father held strong views on the Irish. Freddie chuckled, 'Most things Irish send him into a spitting temper. It stems from that 1916 business, when he was fighting the Hun in France – he says rebellion in Dublin was a stab in the back, which I suppose it was from his point of view.'

Then why the invitation?

Freddie shrugged, 'That's Val. She's as strong as he is. The whole family fought her on this Labour Party business, but she still went her own way. Now she's going to live in Shadwell,' he grinned. 'God help the East End.'

Sean hesitated, worried about being made unwelcome, even though he knew he wanted to see her again. He kept picturing her grin and hearing her non-stop arguments.

'Don't worry,' Freddie said. 'There'll be a hundred people there. You'll hardly have a chance to thank your host and hostess.'

The following night they went to the Hamiltons' party in Eaton Square – Sean handsome in a borrowed dinner jacket, Freddie as dapper as ever. Not that Sean enjoyed it to begin with, in fact he hated the first hour. It was like his initiation at Mario's all over again. He felt shy and out of place, uneasy to be rubbing shoulders with the obviously wealthy. He could find no point of contact with people who chattered about St Moritz and the Sporting Club in Monte Carlo.

He saw what Val meant about Margaret – she *was* beautiful – tall and graceful, with a radiant smile. Val suffered by comparison in most people's eyes – but not Sean's. That Margaret was as poised as a fashion plate worked against her with Sean. Fashion models terrified him. They were glossy photographs in *Vogue*, pictures not people. In fact the entire glittering house seemed full of bejewelled images instead of flesh and blood characters. Sean wished he had gone to Mario's instead.

It was not until later that he changed his mind. Val spent more time at his side, dazzling in lemon lace, grinning reassurance while muttering outrageous comments about the more pompous guests. Not all were pompous. Val guided him from one group to another, choosing people who interested her and whom she hoped might interest him. And they did. He found himself revising his earlier opinions. He relaxed and began to enjoy himself. He even danced, though only with Valerie. She floated in his arms,

330

and the smell and feel of her excited him more as the evening wore on. Champagne made him light-headed. He glowed with well-being, and when everyone clasped hands to sing Auld Lang Syne at midnight, Sean Connors fairly exulted. This was Harmsworth's London! This was the London he had dreamt of.

'To the Irish Navvy,' Val grinned across the brim of her glass, 'and to 1939. May it be a wonderful year for you.'

How could it be anything else, Sean thought, looking at Valerie. Dance music swirled round and round that grand London house. It was a different world from Dublin. Right at that moment the IRA and men like Matt Riordan were a million miles away.

CHAPTER TWO

In fact, Matt Riordan was less than twelve miles away. While Sean danced in a glittering ballroom, Matt Riordan sat cleaning his gun in a scruffy attic in Kilburn.

Much had happened to Matt since the Killing at Keady. He had holed up for weeks with Ferdy Malloy in the Mountains of Mourne. RUC men and B Specials had combed the length and breadth of Ulster, but had never come within a mile of Matt's hiding place. Only Jimmy Traynor had slipped through the cordons now and then, to bring scraps of information and supplies of food.

It was Jimmy who broke the news that Matt's mother had died after being interrogated. Matt reeled. His father dead, now his mother. He had loved her every day of his life. Matt hated the RUC and B Specials as never before, but most of all he hated Averdale and the Connors. Without the Connors his mother would have stayed in Dublin . . . without Averdale she might at least have remained alive in Belfast . . .

Then, at the end of the first week in the hide-out, Matt learned something else. Traynor arrived, clutching the Dublin papers. Pat Connors was dead! It was all over the front page. 'Killed after an incident at the border . . . died in his son's arms . . . the funeral attended by . . .' Matt read on, only half believing.

'Your Da took that murdering bastard with him,' Traynor said.

It made Matt feel better. The Riordans had killed a Connors between them. But Sean Connors was still alive, and Matt swore he would kill him one day.

Meanwhile the rest of the news was bad. Averdale had doubled the reward for Matt's capture. Traynor described the manhunt. 'The Falls are being torn down brick by brick. We'll have to get you over the border, Matt, as soon as we can.'

He went two weeks later, crossing to Cavan and thence to Kildare. Finally he holed up in Wicklow. That was tempting – with Sean Connors in Dublin, twenty-five miles away. Matt had wanted to go to Dublin there and then. In the end he had accepted his orders, but not until he was promised, 'You'll go to England for this bombing campaign. And when you come back, we'll all go for Connors.'

It was a big step forward. Matt's arch-enemy was now officially designated a target by the IRA.

As for the bombing campaign – a team of twelve was to be sent across the water. They were less well trained than Matt would have liked, but he was used to making the best of imperfect situations. And he wanted to go. His father had devised the plan in New York with Sean Russell – it was fitting for a Riordan to go.

They crossed to the mainland a week before Christmas, taking advantage of the holiday crowds, and once landed made for separate destinations, some to Liverpool, two to Glasgow, three to London, and Matt himself to Birmingham.

He tingled with excitement. Enemy territory at last. He stared from the train window and marvelled at the size of the towns. Snow Hill Station, when he reached it, seemed enormous. Matt swung along the platform, carrying two suitcases in hands which still bore scars from the acid burns suffered at Keady.

After taking half an hour to find the right bus, he arrived at his landlady's house in Solihull at eight in the evening, well pleased to have completed an uneventful journey. But his satisfaction was short-lived.

Scotland Yard had got wind of the operation. Detectives were already watching the houses of well-known Republicans. From behind the net curtains of an upstairs window, Matt's landlady pointed out the raincoated figure in a shop doorway. And the news got worse. IRA men in the Customs Service were risking their necks to smuggle explosives across – but no safe hiding places had been arranged for storing the stuff!

The woman gave Matt some supper. She was clearly uneasy, and he promised to move on as soon as he could.

By Christmas Day, he had moved to Wolverhampton. There too some of his men were being watched. A temporary dump had been established in a builder's yard, but the explosives had to be moved by the end of the week. Matt rented a basement on the city outskirts and spent a worrying afternoon transferring potassium chloride and sulphuric acid in a builder's van.

It was the same everywhere – local commanders in Coventry and Leamington complained about not knowing what was happening. Matt gave them new orders and stiffened their nerve before moving down to London for a meeting with Joe Reynolds of the London Command. Which was why Matt was in Kilburn on New Year's Eve. Not that his visit yielded much – except the conviction that someone had talked. Newspapers were full of Hitler and Germany, with barely a mention of Ireland – yet British police were watching the Irish as never before.

Matt returned to Birmingham on 3 January. He worked fast and as best he could. Most of the Irishmen he met couldn't mend a fuse, let alone make a bomb. Matt took them back to his lodgings and explained what was necessary, then showed them his revolver and threatened to kill them if they betrayed him.

He was racing against time. On 12 January, announcing itself as the rightful government of Ireland, the IRA sent a note to the British Government, demanding that they declare their intention to leave Ireland. The British were given four days to make an announcement – or else.

Matt brought his troops in the Midlands to a state of

readiness. He had performed miracles of organization –
Birmingham was now encircled by twenty-two secret
ammunition dumps – but Matt worried himself sick about
the competence of his men.

On 16 January, when the British Government failed to
respond to the IRA's note, the order was given. The
bombing campaign was about to begin.

Men took appalling risks, riding to assignments on
jolting trams, with gelignite in lunch boxes on their laps.
Others returned to sites to re-set mechanisms which failed
to explode. It was an amateur's war, conducted by young
volunteers who had left school at twelve and emigrated to
labouring jobs in England. Few bore their adopted country
the slightest grudge. Many had learned to *like* the English.
Yet when Matt made appeals to their patriotism, few could
resist.

Three electricity plants in London were blown up, two
in the Midlands, one in Liverpool – and a gas mains in
Glasgow was sent sky high . . .

The British seemed more bemused than alarmed.
Occasionally Matt overheard snatches of conversation –
'What do the bloody Irish want anyway? They've got their
own country now, haven't they?'

Matt longed to tell them about the Falls Road and the
conditions of Catholic people in Belfast. He held his
tongue for fear of betraying his accent. An Irish brogue
rang out like the Angelus amid the nasal Birmingham
twang.

The campaign went on. Every week, every day, an
explosion occurred. Most were paid for by the arrest of an
IRA man. The police were more vigilant than ever. Houses
everywhere were raided by blue-uniformed officers with
search warrants; tons of explosives were flushed down
toilets by men on the run.

As for Matt, little remained now of the gregarious
youngster who had charmed the ladies in his father's
butcher's shop. He had grown into a quiet young man,
close-mouthed and watchful, and had acquired Ferdy's
ability to merge into the background. He could slip
unnoticed into a pub, and slip out again without people
remembering his face. Yet his inner strength was greater

than Ferdy's. It showed in his eyes and the set of his mouth. Where Liam Riordan had been as strong as an iron bar, Matt was like a coiled spring, always wound up and ready to strike.

His was a solitary business. Sometimes loneliness clutched at his heart. He might see a young couple on a bus and envy their closeness. He had never enjoyed a girl's companionship, let alone experienced sexual union. Once, late at night, he was passing a dance hall when the doors sprang open and young people poured into the street. Matt glimpsed red-lipped girls squealing with excitement, and saw the predatory hunger in a boy's eyes. Couples went off in all directions. Just for a second Matt Riordan yearned for their kind of life, pined for their freedom. But the moment passed with the girls' voices on the breeze. He walked quietly away, through the darkened back streets to his lodgings, where he spent an hour cleaning his revolver before climbing lonely to bed.

All through the spring of 1939, Matt Riordan waged his patriotic war, fought against an enemy already girding its loins for a much bigger conflict in Europe. British politicians tried to ignore the wants of a few Irish fanatics -- but public consciousness was aroused as the IRA campaign escalated. A bomb in Manchester killed a twenty-seven-year-old fish porter. Glasgow's water supply was cut off. Electricity pylons around London were wrecked, and in the Midlands Matt Riordan blasted lock gates apart on the Grand Union Canal.

Scotland Yard detectives redoubled their efforts. Raids on Irish-occupied houses became commonplace. By the beginning of June, Matt had changed his lodgings twenty-eight times. More than once police arrived at the front door as Matt vaulted over a back fence. Dozens of his young volunteers were arrested. The tide, always running against the IRA, threatened to flood. Matt fought on, determined to make the British Government bend to his wishes.

The British Government, however, were not the first to react. By 14 June, the Dail in Dublin had had enough. The IRA was declared illegal. De Valera himself gave a speech -- 'No one can have any doubts as to the result of the campaign in England, and no one can think that this

Government has any sympathy with it.' He went on to accuse those involved of misreading Irish history and making no allowance for changed circumstances.

'Circumstances,' Matt sneered when he read the newspaper report. 'They only changed when you turned into a bloody traitor. By Christ, Pat Connors would have been proud of you now.'

British patience was exhausted as well. A month later Westminster enacted the Prevention of Violence Bill, specifically aimed at the IRA. Home Secretary Sir Samuel Hoare told the Commons that sixty-six members of the IRA had been convicted and that thousands of pounds of IRA bombing equipment had been seized.

Matt knew it was true. In fact things were worse – sixty-six men had been convicted but dozens more were under arrest.

IRA men became desperate. Terror campaigns were launched in London. Bombs were detonated in shopping areas. At King's Cross Station an explosion blitzed the left luggage office, crippling a Scots doctor and wounding fifteen people, including his wife.

In Birmingham, Matt Riordan fought to hold his hot-heads in check. He would kill B Specials without turning a hair, but he was against murdering innocent civilians. 'Will you just read the papers, for God's sake! You're turning the people against us. We're not fighting them, we're fighting their government.'

But tempers were up. The rumour was that IRA prisoners were being ill-treated. Irish blood boiled, and the fight was on with a vengeance. More than once Matt brandished his revolver, threatening his poorly trained crew if they disobeyed orders. Tragically, not even Matt's discipline could hold them in check – and on Friday, 25 August, came the worst incident of all. It was Matt's bad luck that it happened in the Midlands.

In Coventry, early in the afternoon, a man cycled into Broadgate and parked his bicycle outside Ashley's shop. At two-thirty the bomb in the bicycle's carrier exploded. Five people were killed, and more than fifty others seriously hurt.

Word reached Matt at four o'clock, just as he was about

336

to leave Wolverhampton. He refused to believe it at first – *sixty people* – five dead, others crippled for life. The savagery stunned him. He had no doubt of the consequences. Word was already on the streets – 'The bloody Irish did it, that murdering bunch of bastards!'

Two hours later Matt was in Birmingham, standing in the shadows at a street corner and watching the house across the road. Police were picking Irishmen up all over the city. Matt had no intention of being taken easily. His hand closed on the revolver in his pocket. Someone was in his room. A shadow passed across the curtain. Someone was in there – waiting for him.

He turned and strolled to the corner. Once round that he quickened his pace. There was nothing much in his room; a battered suitcase, two shirts and some underwear. The police were welcome to that. For sure he was not going back.

Every newspaper placard screamed the same story – 'IRA Bomb Outrage in Coventry' – 'Massive Police Hunt for IRA Killers.'

Matt bought an *Evening Mail* and read it on a park bench. He felt defeated. The campaign was over now, he knew that. Sixty people dead or maimed in one afternoon . . . *sixty*! 'Dear God,' he muttered under his breath, 'the English will never forgive us.'

He had to get back to Dublin. They would have to start all over again. The IRA would never give up, and neither would Matt Riordan. 'But it's a bad day for the auld country, all right,' he whispered, as he rolled up the newspaper. The date caught his eye, 'Aye, the twenty-fifth of August has been a bad day for us.'

CHAPTER THREE

Twenty-fifth August was also a bad day for Sean Connors, which was surprising as it was a Friday and he looked forward to all Fridays, thanks to Val Hamilton. So much had happened in the 237 days that had passed since that New Year's Eve party. He had changed his mind about all manner of things, but not about her – she remained totally fascinating.

The most common theory was that she was a throwback to her suffragette grandmother who had been imprisoned with Christobel Pankhurst – but that theory gained support only because the rest of the Hamiltons were so conspicuously non-political. They were Tory, of course, as major shareholders in Blue Chevron Shipping and a host of other enterprises they could hardly be anything else, but they were *quiet* Tories who contributed to party funds with a minimum of fuss. George, Val's father, spent his life in the City and little was known of him in Fleet Street – his companies made news, not George Hamilton himself. He was thought to have refused a safe Tory seat on the excuse of being too busy. In fact he regarded the House of Commons as a home fit for rogues and charlatans, and was fond of saying that 'Men who can, run their own affairs: those who can't, go into politics and meddle in the affairs of others.'

Freddie, who had met him dozens of times, still found him difficult. 'The trouble is I never know what he's thinking. He keeps most of his opinions to himself, at least he does at Cynthia's parties. God knows why she married him. Of course he lets her have her own way and pays the bills, but scores of men would have done that.'

Valerie's mother was known as Cynthia to everyone – 'Life's too short to be formal,' she told new acquaintances. 'That's why I *adore* Americans. London's too stuffy, I always say. We could do with a positive invasion of people from Boston and Chicago – just to shake us out of our rut.'

Cynthia collected Americans, apparently convinced that all Americans were rich and that Texas was the size of Bloomsbury. 'You're from Houston? *Texas!* How marvellous – you must know the Mastersons. They're such good friends – they were here last year, you know, standing just where you are now.'

She liked American voices, men's voices preferably. 'I could close my eyes and listen to you for hours – no, really, I could. It's all there in your dark brown voice – the wide outdoors and the big blue skies. It makes me go quite weak at the knees.'

Which is what half the men in the room hoped would happen – for Cynthia Hamilton remained a glamorous figure. In 1939 she was exactly the same age as Rose Kennedy, the Ambassador's wife, whom most people considered her only rival as the most elegant woman in London. By universal agreement Cynthia was good to look at, fun to be with, and knew everyone in town. If she was a bit silly at times people merely shrugged, 'That's Cynthia, but she's got a heart of gold.' And she had. For instance she was always introducing the young men at her parties to those who might help their careers. Even Sean, on his fourth visit, was summoned to her side. 'Well,' she smiled, 'since Val seems determined to play Nora Barnacle to your James Joyce I'd better do something about you.' She dragged him across the room. 'Esmond dear, this brilliant young man is in newspapers. Here's your chance to meet him before you go as dotty as your dear father.' Which was how Sean met Esmond Harmsworth, son and heir of Alfred Harmsworth, whose story had inspired Sean to leave Dublin.

Freddie had fallen under her spell. 'She's so darned nice, hurting her would be like drowning kittens. I couldn't do it.' And neither could others. But another thing had happened to Freddie. He'd fallen in love with Margaret.

Margaret was so like her mother that there was no doubting how she would look in later years – her admirers had only to see Cynthia to know that, and since they liked what they saw, Margaret received ten proposals before her twenty-second birthday. She turned them all down, but with such charm that the men loved her all the more –

Margaret's rejections were said to be exquisite emotional experiences in themselves. London watched and waited, curious to see who would capture her. Speculation was mounting about a possible engagement to Lord Tylehurst – when along came Freddie Mallon.

Freddie was different from the others, most of whom were English, titled and wealthy. Freddie was a New Yorker with charm and a growing reputation, but he still had his fortune to make. Even so, Cynthia took to Freddie and that helped, and Margaret liked him enough to encourage him.

That had been the state of play when Valerie Hamilton called at Craven Street on the morning before New Year's Eve. She was attracted to Sean immediately, which was surprising. Val's mind was usually too full of politics to leave much room for young men. There had been a young man of course; Val had quite happily lost her virginity the year before to an intense student from the London School of Economics. The affair had ended almost before it began – broken off by Val with characteristic decisiveness. She had no regrets. She had wanted to experience sex but had expected it to excite her much more than it had – to her mind a good rousing speech by Nye Bevan was a far greater thrill.

Val was the cuckoo in the Hamilton nest, but she'd compensated by learning to amuse her father. She liked the sound of his laughter and provoked it whenever she could. Her incentive was simple, to compete with her more glamorous sister, and she did, though not easily. Both girls had a sense of humour, so both could be amusing at times – but Val tried harder. Margaret rarely led a conversation because her knowledge of most subjects was superficial. Val researched her material – mainly in the arts and politics, because those were the interests of the people around her. After which she entertained her father with sketches of other people's opinions – wildly exaggerated for effect. He was delighted, with both her humour and her knowledge, and often asked before a party: 'Now Val – what's so-and-so going to say this evening?'

The problem was that her research had led to unexpected consequences. The more she read about the size of the world, the more outraged she became. What had started as a search for material became a genuine quest for knowledge. She still parodied people's opinions, but increasingly expressed views of her own – left-wing views, not Communist, thank God, but those of the Fabians and the Labour Party, which were almost as bad.

By the time she was twenty-one she had met Clem Attlee and various Trade Unionists, and was forever attending meetings at Friends House on the Euston Road. She developed a passion for politics, and expressed real concern for the welfare of the working class. She hated poverty and regarded the slums in the East End as a battleground. When it became obvious that she saw them as her personal battleground, her parents grew very alarmed – but by then it was too late.

Val was a strong-willed twenty-two-year-old who might leave home altogether if George put his foot down, and neither he nor Cynthia wanted that. Besides, they were torn – Val was attracting quite a following. Labour Party MPs, including Mr Attlee, spoke highly of her future in politics. The concern felt by her parents became tinged with a perverse kind of pride. Why their daughter had adopted this interest was a puzzle, and her intention to spend a couple of nights in Shadwell every week was horrifying – but what could they do, except hope for a young man to come along and fill her head with quite different ideas.

Then she met Sean. Freddie kept them together. He seized the chance to take Margaret out more often, as part of a foursome which included her sister. By the end of February a once-a-week date for a show and supper was a regular thing. The four young people were seen all over London enjoying themselves.

George Hamilton, however, was not enjoying it. Still undecided about Freddie, he now had Sean Connors to worry about. 'He's Irish, and penniless by the sound of it. No family, no nothing. God Almighty, first this bloody Labour Party nonsense, now this! What's got into the girl?' Cynthia soothed him as best she could. 'Don't worry about it. He's just a friend. Heavens, they're not getting married. It makes life easier for Margaret, that's all – she and

Freddie, Val and this young man. It's nice for the girls to go out together.'

It was nice for the boys too, and years afterwards Sean was to count those days in 1939 as among the best in his life. What made life so exciting was not just the tingling thrill of falling in love, or working with Freddie, or the hustle and bustle of Fleet Street – it was the sum of all of those things. The pace got faster and faster. Freddie Mallon had a lot to do with that: by being taken under his wing Sean acquired more status in Fleet Street than could have been earned by a year's solid work. People assumed that because Freddie was so good at his job 'the Irish Navvy' was good too – an assumption Sean did his best to live up to. He worked like a slave, accepting assignments from Freddie at any time of day or night. And he continued to read as much as he could. When baffled he asked questions, and when the answers were incomprehensible he asked more questions. He read the newspapers, listened to Freddie's broadcasts, studied politicians. London generated a feeling of being at the heart of things and Sean loved it. He even gained standing from his tenuous relationship with Joe Kennedy, the American Ambassador at the Court of St James.

The Kennedys had taken London by storm the year before. Fleet Street was accustomed to pompous Ambassadors, stuffy men, full of their own importance. The Kennedys were nothing like that. They were lively, frank, Catholic, Irish-American – and numerous. 'What a family!' ran a headline, showing a smiling Joe Kennedy and his wife and nine children.

The Ambassador galloped horses on Rotten Row, went to Twickenham for the rugby, Wimbledon for the tennis, Ascot for the Gold Cup and Epsom for the Derby. His sheer energy captured headlines. When the press called at the Embassy, Joe sat with his feet on the desk. 'A newspaperman's life is a difficult one,' he said once. 'Why should I make it harder?' Fleet Street loved him for that.

And the Ambassador's wife was sensational too. 'As slim as a sixteen-year-old,' said one paper. 'As vivacious as a screen star,' said another. People found it impossible to believe she was a forty-seven-year-old mother of nine. *Nine!* 'Makes you believe in the stork,' quipped a headline.

Even when they left London, the Kennedys made news. Most of the family spent the summer on the Riviera. Snippets appeared in the British papers . . . Mrs Kennedy dining at the Eden Roc Casino . . . meeting Elsa Maxwell . . . dining at the American Embassy in Paris, while Ambassador Kennedy hurried back to London to provide moral support for Mr Chamberlain, who was about to embark on his mission to Hitler's Berchtesgaden.

The Prime Minister and the American Ambassador seemed very good friends. Certainly both believed that Herr Hitler could be accommodated. Even after Berchtesgaden, Mr Chamberlain and Ambassador Kennedy agreed that war could be averted, an opinion which seemed justified at the end of September when Chamberlain returned from Munich. True, part of Czechoslovakia had been sacrificed to Germany, but agreement had been reached with Hitler. And when the Prime Minister promised 'peace in our time' most people nodded their heads.

But not all. Duff Cooper resigned as First Lord of the Admiralty, while in the House of Commons, Winston Churchill declared: 'We have sustained a total and unmitigated defeat. £1 was demanded at pistol point. When it was given, £2 was demanded at pistol point. Finally the Dictator consented to take £1.17.6d with the rest in promises of goodwill for the future.'

More and more people were reaching the same conclusion. The *Daily Mirror* warned: 'We know what the Nazi word is worth.'

Yet Ambassador Kennedy continued to say otherwise. In a notable speech on Trafalgar Day, he said, 'Democratic and dictator countries . . . have to live together in the same world, whether we like it or not.'

These words were not well received, and the Ambassador's honeymoon with the British press ended when he returned to the United States for consultations with his President. In New York he told the *Journal American* – 'I feel more strongly than ever . . . that this nation should stay out . . . absolutely out . . . of whatever happens in Europe.' To Associated Press he said, 'Last summer I predicted there would be no war in Europe.

Well, I am going out of the prophet business on 31 December.'

All of this Sean knew when he wrote to the Ambassador at the end of January, reminding him of their meeting in Ballsbridge and asking for an exclusive interview for the *Dublin Gazette*. Sean defended the Ambassador to Freddie, saying that Fleet Street had expected too much. They had treated him as one of their own, but that never made him a Londoner. He was a neutral, and had now said as much.

Freddie disagreed. 'He and I are fellow countrymen, so I shouldn't run him down. But he's wrong about Hitler. Nobody should expect other people to preserve their freedom for them. Hell, we all want freedom. How can you be neutral about that?'

When Sean wrote to Kennedy, Freddie shrugged. 'Okay, go ahead. Ireland will love him anyway, but take my advice – write the piece as his views, not yours. Sooner or later you'll change your mind about neutrality. You won't want Kennedy's opinions hanging round your neck.'

Three days after posting his letter, Sean was delighted to receive a hand-written reply, inviting him to 'call and fix something up'.

Freddie grinned. 'That's Kennedy, as approachable as Santa Claus. Maybe that's why women like him so much. I'll give you another tip – never leave Val in the same room with him. He's got a knack of getting girls into the sheets that makes him the most envied man in New York.'

Sean was shocked. He remembered the balding, untidily dressed man who had visited Ballsbridge. He was an old man. Besides, he was married to a beautiful wife who had borne him nine children. And he was a devout Catholic!

Freddie laughed more than ever. 'Okay, don't believe me – but Gloria Swanson has been his mistress for years. Her and a dozen others.'

Gloria Swanson the actress! Sean refused to credit it – more than ever after his visit to the American Embassy. Joe Kennedy's welcome was as warm as his smile, and wherever Sean looked another Kennedy was beaming back at him. He had already met Joe Jnr in Dublin, but that first meeting at the Embassy was so overwhelming that of the

344

others only Jack and Kathleen registered – Jack because he was so like his older brother, and Kathleen (known as Kick to the family) because she was so pretty.

The Kennedy interview made the front page in the *Dublin Gazette*. Dinny telegraphed his congratulations. Joe Kennedy liked the article too – and after that Sean Connors had direct access to the Ambassador. Not that he abused the privilege, he was too shy for that. But word spread along Fleet Street that Sean had friends in high places.

Sean often bumped into the young Kennedys afterwards – not Rosemary who led a secluded life, or Bobby or Teddy who were mere schoolboys at Gibbs – but Kick was sometimes at a Hamilton party, and Joe Jnr and Jack were often in the gallery at the House of Commons. Nobody worked at the relationship. They were all busy young people with plenty to do who were merely pleased to see each other now and then. They had the rest of their lives to form lasting friendships, and they were all conscious of the speed of events – especially in March, when Hitler tore up the Munich agreement and marched into Prague.

Sean went to Birmingham to report a speech by the Prime Minister. Normally Freddie would have gone, but he was so sick of appeasement that he refused to leave London. 'Maybe I'll get a column out of Churchill or Duff Cooper. God knows, someone needs to stop the rot. One thing's certain, it won't be that old fool Chamberlain.'

The speech at Birmingham, however, caught everyone by surprise. Sean watched carefully as the seventy-year-old Prime Minister rose to his feet. The ovation was thunderous, as it always was in Birmingham. This was Chamberlain's city and had been his father's before him. Old Joe Chamberlain had been the presiding genius over Tariff Reform, that dismantling of trade barriers which had brought prosperity to Birmingham.

Sean's pencil raced over his notebook. The Prime Minister defended his visits to Germany . . . matters should be settled by discussion, not force . . . Hitler had made certain pledges . . . and the Prime Minister had felt obliged to accept such assurances in good faith.

Sean groaned as he imagined Freddie's reaction. Then

– unexpectedly – the Prime Minister struck a new note. He was beginning to doubt the value of Hitler's guarantees. Of the invasion of Prague he asked his audience, 'Is this the end of an old adventure, or the beginning of a new? Is this the last attack upon a small State, or is it the beginning of a new? *Is this, in fact, an attempt to dominate the world by force?*'

There was deep silence, while people wondered what the Prime Minister was leading up to. A minute later he told them, in a voice trembling with emotion. 'There is hardly anything I would not sacrifice for peace. But there is one thing I must except, and that is the liberty we have enjoyed for hundreds of years and will never surrender.'

This was not the voice of appeasement. Chamberlain was drawing a line. Sean tingled with excitement as men leaped to their feet and roared approval. Their cheers lasted for minutes, great rolling waves of sound which bounced from the walls and the rafters. Sean could feel the emotion on all sides. He longed for Freddie's experience, Freddie would write about the revival of the old English spirit, the spirit of the Magna Carta. Freddie would write of the courage of all those countless people in this little old island who had fought for their liberties during a thousand years of trouble and strife. Sean smiled as he looked at faces shining with excitement on all sides. He forced himself to be dispassionate. After all, he was an observer, not a participant. Besides he was an Irishman, with all the mixed feelings the Irish have for the English. And if war did come, Ireland would be neutral.

The Prime Minister was finishing . . . 'No greater mistake could be made than to suppose that . . . this nation . . . will not take part to the utmost of its power in resisting such a challenge.'

Sean worked hard on the train going home. Appeasement is dead, he wrote, which was Dinny's headline when he ran the story in the *Dublin Gazette*. The proof was not slow in coming. A fortnight later Chamberlain told the House of Commons what would happen if Hitler attacked another small State – '. . . in the event of any action which threatened Polish independence . . . His Majesty's Government would feel themselves bound at once to lend the Polish Government all the support in their power . . .'

Sombre news – and the presses were still rolling with that when another sensation burst. Mussolini's Italy had invaded Albania. Greece and Yugoslavia were threatened. The spectre of war was at hand.

There seemed no end to the sensational news. As May ended, Germany and Italy forged their 'Pact of Steel', and as the long summer days fled one after the other the whole of Europe prepared for war. In a despairing bid to retain independence Estonia and Latvia signed non-aggression pacts with Germany. 'Documents of convenience,' sneered the British press, 'which Hitler will destroy when he's ready.' But when would he be ready? The wires hummed with talks of pacts, pacts with new friends, pacts with old enemies, pacts which might, even at the eleventh .hour, stop Nazi Germany. The British Foreign Office despatched an emissary to Moscow. France did the same, for despite distrust of the Bolsheviks the Russian Bear was preferable to the German Jackal. In Moscow Stalin listened . . . and talked . . . and talked some more until, on 22 August, came the most astonishing announcement of all. Yes, Russia would sign a non-aggression pact, not with the British however, nor with France . . . *but with Germany*! Herr Ribbentrop and Comrade Molotov put pen to paper the same day. The fate of the world was sealed.

London seethed. Warning telegrams flashed to the Commonwealth and the Dominions. Twenty-five merchant ships were requisitioned. Twenty-four thousand Air Force reservists were summoned to duty. All leave was stopped for the Fighting Services. Thirty-five trawlers were seconded for mine-sweeping. And on 25 August the British Government proclaimed a formal treaty with Poland, confirming the guarantee already given.

These were just some of the stories which gripped Sean Connors between New Year's Eve and 25 August 1939 . . . a drama unfolding so fast that he and Freddie had to race to keep up. And race they did. They were greedy for news. Anything that promised a good story was grist for the mill. London was the most exciting stage in the world and Sean and Freddie were in the best seats.

347

When unemployed men entered the Savoy and lay down in the lounge as a protest, Freddie and Sean wrote about it. When archaeologist Mortimer Wheeler married a beautiful widow, Freddie and Sean wrote about it – if for no other reason than Mrs Agatha Christie and A. J. P. Taylor were guests at the wedding, as was Augustus John, who beamed satisfaction at the widow who had been his girlfriend for years.

And in June, when there was a dance at the American Embassy for seventeen-year-old Eunice Kennedy's coming out, Sean was there to record it – just as a month later he was on the Kennedys' balcony with Bobby and Teddy, waving good luck as Eunice left to be presented at Buckingham Palace.

London was becoming Sean's town, and he strode around as if he owned the whole city – even Shadwell, although Valerie had kept him waiting until March before she'd invited him to her precious East End.

Shadwell had needed time to accept Valerie Hamilton – what with her fancy clothes and posh voice. 'Do-gooders' were the curse of the East End and people were suspicious. But eventually Val was judged to be different. 'She ain't afraid of nuffink – not 'er, she'll take 'em all on an' give 'em a bleeding good run for their money.'

She lived in Shadwell for part of each week, leaving the East End on a Friday to return to her other life in Eaton Square. They well knew where she lived. 'Going back 'ome for the weekend then. Good luck to you, Miss. See you next week.' Nobody resented her good fortune. There were more bathrooms in Eaton Square than in the whole of Shadwell, but that was never held against her. She despaired at times – wanting other people to share her sense of outrage. How could they *accept* the slums? Even so, she was glad not to be in the Communist Party. Kids in the street sang *Vote, vote, vote for Harry Pollitt* but few of their parents actually did. The East End wanted a better deal, not Russian style revolution. 'Who'll run the country then? Old Ernie from the docks? Cor blimey, we'll be in ruins in no time.'

Val ran two separate lives. She enjoyed them both – departing happily for Shadwell early on Wednesday and returning on Friday in time to bathe and change for the evening. She looked forward to Friday evenings. Freddie and Sean were always entertaining, usually there was a play to look forward to, or a new restaurant to try – it was fun, and increasingly the high spot of her week. But her feelings for Sean grew ever more confused, despite the fact that shared dates with Freddie and Margaret provided a certain protection.

The truth was that when they were dancing at a night-club for instance, and she felt the strength and size of Sean, she grew frightened. People would never believe it, Val Hamilton, that spit of a girl who shouted Labour Party speeches from a soap box at the dock gates – her *frightened*? But she was – especially when he looked at her in a certain way. She knew what he wanted and thought it was unfair. He was asking for more than she wanted to give. He had no right – and yet, she had to admit, there were times – and increasingly often – when she *liked* to be looked at like that. Perhaps she even answered with a smouldering look of her own.

Once, after a Friday night out, she lay in her bed thinking. Her student from the LSE had been frail and slightly built – the smallest boy she could find. She never saw his penis because she had kept her eyes tightly shut, but its size had surprised her. It felt enormous – and that was *him*, a narrow-shouldered little chap, weighing only eight stone. Sean was well over six feet and as broad as a barn! Her hands moved under the bed covers to the top of her legs. Experimentally she slid a finger into herself. She moaned softly and raised her buttocks, unintentionally creating far more pleasure than ever aroused by her student. He had been bigger than her finger. Suppose he had been twice as big – and suppose Sean was twice as big again. Or even bigger?

Panic kept her awake for a long time that night. The next morning she began comparing husbands and wives. Men were usually taller, but never by as much as Sean towered over her. It would be quite out of the question. There was no point in him giving her those knee-trembling looks. Besides it was wrong! They were just friends, would never marry . . . Val's political career would leave no time for

349

marriage anyway. Yet thoughts of those looks and the need which prompted them haunted her – until something happened which left her sweating and trembling, but which made up her mind.

The front window of her flat at Shadwell overlooked the boats in the West Garden Dock, and her bedroom at the back looked down into a yard, beyond which was an alley leading to a five-storeyed tenement. The alley was a nuisance at night, especially when the pub on the corner disgorged its usual quota of half-drunk seamen, each with a girl on his arm. Fights broke out as men disputed their rights to a girl, and more than once the police were called, often with an ambulance not far behind. Val made it a rule to be home by closing time, and she had observed that rule the night she discovered the alley was not used just for fighting.

She had not meant to look. If she had known what she would see she would have avoided it like the plague. The bedroom was in darkness, lit only by light from the other room. Outside the mist rolled in from the river, and she was drawing the thin, unlined curtains when she saw two people in the alley.

One was a huge man with a knitted cap on his head, the other, a woman so tiny she had to stand on tiptoe to kiss him. The girl's coat was undone and his hands were working under it. Her face was upturned and the man laughed, throwing his head back to show strong white teeth. He said something, she answered, and they kissed again. Then she turned away from him and leaned forward over the trashcans in the corner. Her coat and skirt were rucked up to her waist. She wore no underclothes. The cheeks of her buttocks gleamed like moons in the lamp light. His huge hands were spreading her flesh. His penis plunged forward like a spear. He pressed in and in. At the window Val cried aloud, but the sound escaped as a whimper. Below in the alley the man plunged into the girl again until he lifted her up and turned her towards him. She came into his arms, feet off the ground, white legs fastening round his waist, arms clinging to his neck as her lips found his. She might have been a child, except her actions were not childlike. Her legs worked constantly while he responded by driving up into her. Their rhythm continued even as he carried her with one hand under her buttocks while the other opened her blouse. His head ducked to her breast – and still his hips jerked as she writhed in his arms. Suddenly her back arched, her head came clear of his shoulder – she looked directly up to the window – Val *felt* her eyes – but the girl was blind to everything save the sensations of her body. Her mouth opened as if to scream. A second later she went limp. All movement ceased – two statues caught in the moonlight. Slowly, one leg unwrapped itself from around his body, followed by the other a moment later.

Sweat lay in beads across Val's upper lip. Moistness warmed the top of her legs. Trembling, she turned slowly away and went back to the fire in the other room, thinking of what she had seen, the size of that man against that tiny girl.

The next Friday she said to Sean, 'Do you remember promising me beer and pickles in the East End? Well, I'm still waiting.'

Three weeks after that they made love in front of the fire in Val's flat . . . and the East End became a magical place for both of them.

Sean loved Shadwell. So much of it reminded him of his boyhood on the Quays. Streets down to the docks were paved with stone blocks which became slippery in the rain – just like in Dublin. Irish songs were sung in the pubs. Sean even heard *Down by the Glenside*, a sad revolutionary song about the bold Fenian boys. Eyes glistened with stifled emotion, until someone struck up *The Wearing of the Green* and a minute later everyone was stamping and clapping, just like in Mulligan's Bar.

Not that Irish dominated the place. They shared it with native-born Cockneys and Polish Jews, African seamen and Indian Sikhs. The poor of the world lived in Shadwell, but sometimes the Irish took over. When the church of St Mary and St Michael had feast days, the Catholics scrubbed the pavements and put up little altars, draped with lace curtains and bedsheets – sodalities walked in procession, carrying banners and statues and lighted candles . . .

Val learned to see the East End through new eyes. Some

sights still made her angry, the dock gates for instance, surrounded by queues of ragged labourers, with dockers' hooks at their belts, all hoping for work – ten men picked out of forty by the bowler-hatted foreman, the unwanted drifting away, to reassemble at midday, and again the next morning, and again and again in the slim hope of work. Life was hard. Poverty plucked at Val's heart, and it took all of Sean's time to open her eyes to the humour and colour. To his delight Shadwell even had donkeys – at least on Saturday nights when Watney Street was closed to the usual dock traffic. Out came the donkeys, pulling costermongers' barrows. The place came alive. Up went the stalls and the market buzzed with energy. Naphtha flares lit pavements crowded with women in search of a bargain. Men in striped aprons sold cockles and whelks and jellied eels. Hot chestnuts were stoked over braziers on street corners. Cries of *Tuppence a pound pears* mingled with the raucous rendering of *Nellie Dean* from a pub, pierced now and then by shouts of *Late night final* from the newspaper boys. Jack the Banana King swished his machete through bunches of bananas on the corner of Commercial Road. The pungent smell of vinegar wafted from a fish and chip shop. Street cries blended into a cacophony of sounds, all linked together by the haunting, tinkling notes of a street organ.

From April onwards, Shadwell became a lovers' retreat. Most Sunday afternoons saw Sean and Val naked on a rug in front of the fire. Outside the fog rolled in and sirens sounded mournfully as ships dropped down to the sea. Inside was bathed in the flickering light of the fire, the only sounds the soft sighs of lovers – until five o'clock, when the distant clang of the Muffin Man's bell had Sean hurrying into his clothes. Down the stairs he rushed and into the street, often meeting the lamplighter carrying his pole from one gas lamp to another. He would hurry back with muffins to toast on the fire for tea, greeted by a drowsy and still naked Val.

The two cramped rooms acquired a magic all of their own. It was their secret place, and as the weeks passed they schemed and planned to spend more time there together. Val no longer left Shadwell early on Friday afternoons.

Instead she stoked up the fire and waited for Sean, who usually arrived at about four, in time for two glorious hours of lovemaking before they went 'Up West' to meet Freddie and Margaret for dinner. After which Val went home to Eaton Square – but she often escaped back to Shadwell during the weekend for another meeting with Sean.

Little wonder that Sean found that year exhilarating. By the summer it was hard to believe he was the same young man who had arrived in London the previous year, wearing a ginger tweed suit and a worried expression. All that remained from those days was the nickname Irish Navvy, and that was becoming talked about from one end of Fleet Street to the other. Freddie Mallon's protégé had come a long way.

And yet it was not only Freddie's influence. Other people helped mould Sean – Val Hamilton more than anyone. She opened doors, not just to the Hamilton gatherings in Eaton Square, but to Labour Party politicians as well. And events helped . . . the constantly boiling stewpot of political happenings developed a sharpness in Sean which might not have surfaced otherwise. Each was a factor in his growing confidence. Rarely now was he homesick. If he thought of the Widow O'Flynn it was only to hope that she was as happy with Jim Tully as he was with Val. Nor did he often write to Michael or Senator O'Keefe. The Senator sent him a quarterly statement which showed the *Gazette* to be quietly prospering, so with his assets safe and sound Sean was enjoying life. Of course contact with Dinny was regular, they often spoke on the phone – but Sean enquired about life in Dublin less and less. Even the rules were neglected – and he was often too tired at night to whisper to his dead father. In a changing Sean Connors only one thing persisted – that vague feeling of his that somehow the world was coming to an end. It was a premonition which grew stronger , influenced by his friends on the *Mirror* perhaps, who were convinced that war was inevitable. What would happen to Sean's new life then? He was Irish and neutral, but Freddie continued to pour scorn on neutrality. 'Your father fought to win freedom for Ireland. Everyone should fight for their freedom. Think, Sean, think.'

On 25 August, time for thinking ran out. Sean had filed his usual huge quota of stories, many of the political ones gloomy with overtones of war, but some snippets of gossip gave reason for hope. Barbara Hutton, the multimillionairess, had closed her mansion in Regent's Park and moved to Capri. Winston Churchill had left London to holiday in Normandy. Various other politicians were vacationing in Europe. Surely war must be a long way off if the rich and the powerful could do that? And that very morning the pact announced with Poland must stabilize the situation. Or so Sean thought as he left Fleet Street and walked along the Strand to Craven Street, where he worked in his office for a couple of hours, before going for his visit to Val in Shadwell.

But even as Sean worked at Craven Street, news of a quite different story was reaching Fleet Street. The IRA had bombed Coventry! At least five people were dead. Shocked news editors rushed to revise headlines for the afternoon editions – and before Sean began his journey to Shadwell newspaper vans were already delivering the story of the Coventry massacre.

It hit Shadwell at a very bad time. Only that week there had been trouble in the docks. Half the stevedores were Irish, half were native-born Cockneys – and there was barely enough work for a tenth of them. News of the IRA outrage in Coventry set light to a smouldering fuse. Fights broke out in the dockside pubs – 'You come over here, stealing our jobs, killing and murdering, why don't you fuck off back to Ireland!' And Cockney blood boiled over when they were told to fuck off themselves. Soon men were fighting from one end of the West Garden Dock to the other. Outside the Lord Lovat in Dellow Street, two Irishmen were beaten senseless. Elsewhere, an Irish gang chased a man into the Meredith and Drew stables and thrashed him with horse-whips. A broken bottle was jabbed into a man's face outside the City of Dublin Dining Rooms...

Sean knew nothing of this as he walked down Watney Street carrying a bunch of yellow roses. He hated carrying flowers, but the reward was worth it. He pictured Val's pleasure, and the way she would throw her arms around his neck. He could almost taste her lips, and see the look in her eye as she undressed. He sighed with anticipation and quickened his step, only vaguely aware of the sounds of men shouting.

He turned into the alley and ran straight into them. A crowd of dockers had backed two men up against the wall and were beating them mercilessly. Steel flashed as a docker's hook struck sparks from the brick wall. A man fell – six or seven others kicked out at him with their boots. The standing survivor twisted and turned against the wall, denied escape by men on either side.

'Dear God,' Sean gasped. 'Are you killing that poor devil?'

His accent betrayed him. Someone grabbed his arm. 'Christ, here's another Irish bastard!' He was pushed against the wall. Stupidly he thought first of the roses, holding them above his head. A fist cracked into his face. His mouth filled with blood. A steel-tipped boot caught his knee . . . and a moment later Sean was fighting for his life.

He fought in a mist of rage, as he had fought for Maureen alongside the canal, all those years before, or along the Quays when his donkeys were killed. He grabbed one man by the ears and used him as a battering ram. He upended another and smashed his face into the wall. But they were too many for him. They came from all sides – twelve, maybe fifteen men, three of whom lashed out with steel hooks – a flailing mass of half-drunken men on a blood lust.

Three minutes later he was down, felled by a steel hook plunged into his shoulder. Blood blinded him from a gash in his forehead. As he struggled to one knee a boot caught him behind the ear. He sprawled back down across cobblestones red with his blood. He raised his arms to fend off the blows. Again he was kicked down. Dizziness engulfed him. Far off, came the distant sound of police whistles. A steel-shod heel stamped on his fingers. A boot found his stomach, another cracked his head. A kick jarred his spine. He screamed. Dimly he heard the whistles again – and suddenly the men were gone, their fleeing footsteps clattering over the cobblestones.

He lay in his blood and knew he was dying. That phrase 'the end of the world' repeated emptily in his mind. Blood poured into his left eye, blinding him. His right eye throbbed. He was tempted to pass out, oblivion would be welcome. Somehow he forced his left eye open, willing it to focus. A yellow rose lay a yard from his head. Val's favourite colour. His broken hand reached for the flower. The alley looked a mile long, each cobblestone a yard wide. Behind him three crumpled figures lay inert on the ground, ahead the alley was deserted. Hazily he saw the entrance to the yard at the back of Val's building.

He dragged himself, using his one good hand and his right leg. Twice he collapsed. He wondered how he would climb the stairs to Val's place. His breath came in gasps. He was sticky with blood.

She saw him from the window – down by the trashcans, not moving. A crumpled mess of soiled clothes wrapped grotesquely around broken limbs. She screamed, sure he was dead. She screamed again and ran down the stairs, and was screaming hysterically when she reached the yard. Two policemen raced down to the alley. One struggled to hold her back, not wanting her to see what they had done to him. But Val saw.

He almost died in the ambulance. The stretcher bearers thought he had gone. The hospital said he was virtually dead on admission.

Val never left his side. She fought, she begged and pleaded with the hospital staff. She and Freddie arranged for a private room, with a cot in one corner for Val. George and Cynthia Hamilton arrived late that night and implored her to go home. She refused. Her fight was only just beginning.

She fought like a tigress. Something told her she was his lifeline. It was inexplicable so she made no effort to explain. Who would understand? Even Freddie would have disbelieved her if she had said she was willing Sean back to life. She talked to Sean all the time, not out loud, in her mind, saying how much she loved him, telling him over and over and over again, 'I love you Sean, I need you Sean, I love you . . .'

For twenty-four hours he was not expected to live.

For forty-eight hours even partial recovery was doubtful.

For seventy-two hours his condition was critical.

356

Val was there every minute. Twice his eyes flickered but closed immediately. She kissed his broken fingers and sat at his bedside. No words passed her lips. They were all in her mind . . . in her mind she never stopped talking. 'Sean, stay with me Sean . . . I love you, Sean . . .'

Freddie patrolled the corridors, arguing with the doctors.

On the third day Sean's lips twitched, as if with the ghost of a smile. Val burst into tears, and redoubled her soundless efforts – 'Stay with me darling . . . I love you, Sean . . .'

Dinny Macaffety arrived from Dublin that morning.

Senator O'Keefe and Michael O'Hara reached London in the evening.

Freddie put them all up in Craven Street where they spent the night talking about Sean. It was then that Freddie learned that Sean actually *owned* the *Gazette*. Dinny told him the whole story and swore him to secrecy, in return for which Freddie explained about Val Hamilton.

Dinny smiled sadly. 'Wouldn't you think he casts some kind of spell. The finest-looking woman in Dublin is worrying herself sick across the water.' He fell silent for a minute, then chuckled, 'And her engaged to be married.' He turned to the Senator, 'Wouldn't you say Jim Tully's given more money to the church in these last two days than the whole of his life. Sure, there's every good father in Dublin praying for Sean.'

And not just in Dublin. Special Masses were said in Shadwell as the East End came to its senses. Fresh flowers arrived at the hospital every morning. Newspapers published daily bulletins, while Fleet Street colleagues waited and hoped. Ambassador Kennedy telephoned the hospital, and Val's friends in the Labour Party sent even more flowers and messages of goodwill.

Val continued her vigil, white-faced, heavy-eyed, aching with fatigue, but as resolute as ever.

At ten o'clock that night, seventy-seven hours after Sean was admitted to hospital, the miracle happened.

His eyes opened wide, just for a second, but long enough for him to see Val and for the faintest of smiles to touch his lips.

Val's mind talked in letters ten feet high – 'I love you, stay with me, I need you . . .'

'Val,' the tiniest whisper came from his pillow.

Her head went to his pillow. When he spoke every word took an entire breath. 'Will you shut up, woman – and let a man get some sleep.'

He had heard! She had not spoken aloud. Somehow he had heard! Her eyes flooded with tears. She fell to her knees at the bedside, choking, 'Sean, darling . . .'

'Val,' he whispered, then went to sleep.

Terror gripped her. She stumbled outside for a nurse. The nurse's eyes widened as she measured Sean's pulse. 'It's strong,' she said, 'as strong as mine.' They listened to his breathing, deep and regular, not shallow and laboured as before. The nurse fetched a doctor. He expressed amazement, and was astonished even more when Val flung her arms around him, kissing him through her tears.

Freddie arrived half an hour later to find Val in a fever of impatience. 'He's sleeping. I'm going home for a couple of hours. Stay with him, Freddie, don't move from his side, promise – and promise to stay awake . . .'

Freddie pleaded with her to go straight to bed at Eaton Square. Her answer was evasive. He organized her cab and telephoned Cynthia. 'Put her to bed,' he said firmly, 'she's asleep on her feet.'

An hour later the doctor checked Sean's pulse again and expressed bewildered satisfaction – and shook his head when Freddie offered him his heart-felt thanks. 'That wee lassie did more than we did. Don't ask me how, but she did it, we just helped.'

Freddie hoped that the 'wee lassie' was catching up on some sleep. He hoped in vain. At four in the morning Val returned. Freddie was astonished. Doctors and nurses looked on in open disbelief. Val's hair had been rat-tailed and knotted when she left, uncombed in days. Her soiled clothes were the same ones she had been wearing when she had helped lift Sean into the ambulance. Her white, tear-stained face had been hollow-eyed and exhausted. Everyone had agreed she was on the verge of collapse.

She returned radiant. Her face was paler than usual, she

358

still looked a bit strained, but her impish grin was triumphant.

'Sorry Freddie,' she apologized softly. 'My hair took longer than I thought.'

Margaret followed her into the room and saw Freddie's expression. 'Go on, say it, I won't be jealous for once. Doesn't she look lovely?'

Freddie was too overcome to answer. Instead he kissed Val's cheek and turned to leave. She caught his sleeve. 'It's all right, Freddie,' she whispered. 'He's going to get better now, he told me so.'

They left her sitting bolt upright in the chair. When the night nurse looked in Val seemed not to have moved. She held the same pose, her eyes on Sean's face, her lips ready to greet him when he opened his eyes. And when he did – three hours later – the grin on Valerie Hamilton's face outshone all the lights in Piccadilly.

CHAPTER FOUR

Matt Riordan was on the run. Although he was becoming used to it, being on the run in Northern Ireland was a sight easier than evading the manhunt in England after the Coventry massacre. In Ulster, Matt knew dozens of safe houses where Republican sympathizers would provide shelter – in England it was different. After fleeing from Birmingham he had travelled first to Manchester, but of his five contacts there three had already been arrested and the other two were missing. Matt spent the night in an empty tram in the depot, to be awakened at five the next morning by the cleaning staff.

After that he went to Liverpool, where he holed-up for twenty-four hours in the attic of a bakery owned by Ferdy's uncle, Mickey MacGuinness. There he waited for safe passage to Dublin to be organized, but MacGuinness's efforts to make contact with the IRA foundered. Detectives were searching the docks, travellers to Ireland were being scrutinized as never before. MacGuinness was terrified that Matt would be caught on the premises. Finally on the Sunday evening, Matt left, dressed in the new clothes which MacGuinness had provided and carrying an extra fifty pounds in his wallet.

By Monday evening he was in Glasgow, and twenty-four hours later had made contact with Paddy Mullen, the local IRA commander. Mullen himself was under police surveillance so a lengthy meeting in public was out of the question. One brief encounter in a pub was enough. Matt returned to the pub just before closing time and went to the toilets, where he sat in a cubicle until a note was passed under the door. It gave an address in Bothwell Street. 'Go there now' was written underneath. Twenty minutes later Matt walked up Union Street and ten minutes after that he was in the IRA safe house on Bothwell Street.

Paddy Mullen was waiting for him. 'You've got some neck – coming here after what you started down in the Midlands.'

'Will you hold on a minute and I'll tell you about it –'

'Who needs telling! The whole bloody country is going mad –'

'Then get me out. Get me across the water.'

'Just like that? This is nay a fucking booking office for the likes of you!' Mullen glared, red-faced with temper. They sat in an upstairs room, with a man at the window watching the street. Two others were below, guarding the front and back doors. Everyone was jumpy.

Mullen's temper cooled after his initial outburst, but he was as bitter as ever about the effects of the Coventry bombing. 'An Irishman can't cross the street in this city without a copper breathing down his neck. And it's the same all over from what I hear.'

It was. Police surveillance was massive everywhere.

At the end of an hour, Mullen said, 'You can sleep here tonight. Tomorrow we'll have ye aboard a collier for Belfast –'

'That's no good. There's a price on my head –'

'It's Belfast or nothing. Every minute yer here endangers us –'

'I'm to go to Dublin –'

'You're to go to *hell*!' Mullen slapped the table in fury. It was take it or leave it. Mullen wanted Matt out of

Glasgow within twenty-four hours.

Matt pondered his options. Ferdy and the others would help him in Belfast. Perhaps they could resurrect the bombing campaign, against military targets? Perhaps they could have a go at that bastard Averdale? It was tempting – if Matt could reach Ferdy from the collier without being intercepted by some trigger-happy B Special. The only alternative was to get down to London and go to ground in Kilburn. That would be easier, and at least his face wasn't staring down from Wanted Notices everywhere. But London was not Ireland, and most of all Matt wanted to reach Sean Connors in Dublin. It was a prospect he relished – Sean Connors, facing a full IRA trial, with Matt as executioner.

The house grew cold during the hours of darkness. Matt dozed, wrapped in a blanket and slumped in an armchair – and when Wednesday dawned Matt was still weighing possibilities.

By that Wednesday morning, Sean Connors was getting used to hospital. Nobody was forecasting a rapid recovery. His injuries were severe. The wound from the steel hook guaranteed a seven-inch scar down his back. His left leg was broken. His pelvis was fractured, and so were three ribs. Eighteen stitches had been sewn into his right leg. He slept for much of the time, doped against pain – but whenever he awoke, Val was there, freshly groomed and with a grin a mile wide.

Nonetheless, recovery seemed certain by the Wednesday. Sean was taking liquid food. Visitors were allowed – Dinny, Michael, the Senator and Freddie Mallon – all of whom spent a few minutes with him under Val's watchful eye. Even the doctors seemed to defer to Val.

Sean wanted to know *why* – why it happened. Val avoided the issue at first, until eventually she told him about the Coventry massacre, and the backlash in the docks. He was incredulous. It was a shock – another shock to have suffered yet again because of the IRA. The bitter irony brought a wan smile to his face. An even worse shock was to follow.

Val had installed a wireless to amuse him. They listened

to music together, with Val adjusting the volume when he dozed, and they always listened to the news. The political situation in Europe was worse than ever. Hitler grew more bellicose every day. Europe, and the world, continued to teeter on the brink of war. But it was not the European news which caused Sean's relapse – it was an announcement made on Thursday, after the six o'clock news:

'Here is a police message. The police have now named the man believed to have been responsible for last Friday's bomb explosions in Coventry. He is Matthew Riordan, known to be a member of the IRA, and who for some time has been living at 82, Dunster Road, Solihull, Birmingham. Riordan is in his early twenties and was clean shaven when last seen. Height about five feet nine, medium build, light brown hair. Anyone knowing his whereabouts or who think they have seen a man answering to this description should contact their local police station at once. It is emphasized that this man is almost certainly armed . . .'

Sean went rigid. '*Matt Riordan!*' He spat the hated name like a curse. It *was* a curse.

'Sean!' Val flew to his side. 'Sean, darling –'

'Riordan! Fucking Riordan!' He stared at the ceiling, seeing only memories.

'Sean. Darling . . .'

He turned, not seeing her, wiping his face on the pillow to get rid of the spit.

'Sean!'

He saw the lane at Keady . . . the Da, blood everywhere . . . oh Da, what have they done?

'Darling . . .?'

The room flickered in and out of focus. Val bending over him . . . here . . . in this hospital. Broken, swathed in bandages . . . and all because of Matt Riordan!

'Oh my God, Sean, what's the matter . . .'

But he had passed out.

It was an awful night. When he came round they sedated him heavily. Val was beside herself with remorse, blaming herself, frightened by the hatred she had seen in his eyes

362

– the look on his face – and she had never heard him use such language.

Dinny and Michael arrived at eight o'clock to find Sean deeply drugged and Val on the verge of collapse. Dinny took charge, suddenly as authoritative as when in his office. As soon as Val told him about the broadcast Dinny acted. 'You're coming with me,' he told her, 'and you'll *listen* to me if you care for Sean Connors at all!'

He might have slapped her face. She went whiter than ever. Even so, she protested about leaving. Dinny pointed at Michael, 'That boy's known Sean all his life. Do you think he'd let anything happen to him?'

He took her to a restaurant a hundred yards from the hospital. It wasn't much of a place and they made an odd-looking couple – not that Dinny was concerned with appearances. He found a corner table and made her drink some brandy, then he got some hot soup inside her. After which he talked about Sean. She had known about the donkeys, but not what had happened to them. She knew he loved his father, but had not known how his father had died. Dinny told her everything – about Brigid and Maureen and how they were killed – and of Pat's terrible revenge. And of how Sean bought the *Gazette* and sent Tomas and the family to Australia. He talked of the Riordans, both father and son – and he told her all about the Killing at Keady. He talked and talked and talked.

She couldn't stop shaking. Her meal went cold on her plate. Dinny sent it away and persuaded her to have another bowl of hot soup instead. She was steadier after that, even though she was appalled by the terrible violence in Dinny's story.

Finally, after a few deep breaths, she regained control of herself. Her eyes met his, 'You're tremendously proud of him, aren't you?'

He toyed with his glass. 'Sure and why not. There's a woman in Dublin who believes he will conquer the world. And maybe she's right.'

Val's eyes narrowed. 'Is she pretty?'

'Most men think so.'

'Does Sean?'

'Reckon he did, once.'

It was the first Val had heard of a rival. She mustered her courage. 'Does she – did she love him very much?'

Dinny grunted. 'Did, and still does, and always will I reckon. And her getting married an' all.' He smiled kindly across the table. 'But she would have held him back and hadn't she the sense to see it. That's why she let him go. It would have been like caging a skylark.'

Val's hands clenched into tiny fists. 'And me, Mr Macaffety. I'll hold him back too. Is that what you're saying?'

His eyes came up to meet hers and his smile widened. 'Sure now, wouldn't you be the finest skylark a man ever set eyes on.'

She hugged his arm all the way back to the hospital. Michael sat in the bedside chair like a proud sentinel. The doctor was satisfied that his patient would survive the latest shock to his system.

Dinny blushed scarlet when Val kissed him goodbye – after which she shooed everyone out and settled herself next to the bed, to think over what Dinny had told her. 'A different world.' Her eyes brightened a few minutes later and a smile came to her lips. 'Sure now,' she said in a passable imitation of Dinny's brogue, 'wouldn't I be proud of you too? But I'll be wanting to hear all about this Irish colleen when you wake up.'

The following morning, Sean awoke with a temperature. Val kept him quiet all day and the wireless firmly switched off – so it was not until Freddie arrived that she learned the news.

He told her in the corridor, out of Sean's hearing. 'Germany invaded Poland this morning. There's nothing much from Chamberlain yet,' he said as she clutched his arm, 'perhaps peace is still possible.'

She did not share the news with Sean, even the next morning when he looked very much better. Dinny arrived before midday, with Michael and Senator O'Keefe. They were on their way to the station.

'I've a paper to run and a proprietor to keep happy,' Dinny said firmly. 'You are on the mend now, and this nurse of yours will soon have you up and about.'

After Michael and the Senator had said their goodbyes,

Valerie walked them to the hospital gates.

Sean could feel his strength improving. The fever had passed. When Val returned he pleaded in vain to be allowed to listen to the radio. He wondered if her refusal had anything to do with Riordan. She wouldn't even discuss it. The best he got was her promise that he could hear the news tomorrow.

'But tomorrow's Sunday. Nothing ever happens—'

'So don't bother to listen at all. I'm sorry, darling, no more chances.'

He was sedated again in the evening and was asleep when Freddie arrived.

Val went out to the corridor to be brought up to date. 'Everywhere's buzzing with rumours,' Freddie said grimly, 'the trouble is nobody is saying anything very definite. I've been on to Churchill but his lips are sealed. Chamberlain is supposed to be making a broadcast in the morning.'

Sean dreamt vividly that night. Friends flitted through his dreams, all jumbled up. Dinny was drinking stout in the Lord Lovat at Shadwell instead of in Mulligan's Bar. Michael was working for the *Daily Mirror* and not the *Gazette* . . . and Freddie was talking on the telephone, his face wet with tears. Sean's own face felt wet, wet with spit . . . Riordan's spit.

Then he awoke. His surroundings registered. Hospital, bandages, his leg in plaster. It was Sunday, 3 September. Val and Freddie were standing at the far side of the room, listening to the wireless which was barely audible. Sean strained to hear. He recognized Chamberlain's voice, creaking with emotion . . .

'Everything that I have worked for, everything that I hoped for, everything that I have believed in during my public life, has crashed in ruins . . .'

THE WAR! War had begun.

'The end of the world,' Sean whispered, and wondered if it would be.

CHAPTER FIVE

People reacted to the outbreak of war in different ways. Freddie Mallon was triumphant, forecasting that Hitler would get his come-uppance at last. Not everyone was so sanguine. George Hamilton remembered the trenches from World War I and thought it would be a very hard slog. Besides, this time there was German air power to reckon with – Hyde Park was already being turned upside down with air-raid shelters. London might be bombed flat like Madrid. Eaton Square could be reduced to rubble and ashes. But even if that happened and the worst came to the worst, George could never leave London, he had a business to run. So he took a suite in the Dorchester for 'the duration of the war' and closed his house in Eaton Square. He went a step further by offering Ashworth to the Government as a military hospital, together with the use of his two motor cars. 'May as well,' he told Cynthia, 'there'll be damn all petrol in another month.'

George Hamilton's businesslike approach was seen as a shrewd move by others. A steel and concrete structure like the Dorchester stood a better chance of withstanding a *Blitzkrieg* than did London's brick houses. Besides, hotel life was one way of coping with the shortage of servants.

Within weeks the wealthy were flocking to book suites at the Savoy and the Ritz – among them Duff and Diana Cooper, and Charles Sweeney with his beautiful wife.

Among the grand houses closed in London was the Belgrave Square residence of Lord Averdale, who had been a constant visitor to the capital that year. In fact he had spent more time in London than in Belfast, which was perhaps not surprising after the Killing at Keady.

Mark Averdale's face bore lines of suffering which ought not to have been there. After all, he was only twenty-eight. The murder of Sheila O'Brien had devastated him. The burning of Brackenburn had been torture enough, the loss of Rouen's Kate catastrophic – but the loss of the personification of Kate, Kate in the flesh, the Kate he had touched and almost possessed – that was the final blow. Grief tore him apart. He drifted for weeks, miserable and purposeless. All of his plans had involved Kate. Brackenburn would have been restored to former glories and Kate would have reigned as a Queen. Without her, without even Rouen's masterpiece, raising Brackenburn from the ashes seemed pointless.

Bleak-eyed and inconsolable, he had brooded for days. Of course he saw people. He even attended meetings with the RUC, where he had learned with astonishment that the body of Liam Riordan had been found at the roadside at Keady – Liam Riordan, father of Matt! The same Matt Riordan who had destroyed Brackenburn. Hardened police officers blanched. 'I don't just want this Riordan caught,' Mark blazed, 'I want him dead. He's vermin. Understand? Destroy him like vermin. I want to be able to look down on his body and spit on it!'

But Matt Riordan was not to be found.

Fifteen days elapsed before Mark Averdale's tormented mind grasped the one thing that could restore purpose to his life. Kate the young mother was dead – but Kate the child still lived! She and her injured brother had been taken from Keady Manor by their maternal grandparents. Mark vaguely remembered meeting them at the funeral – the man was a doctor, retired, his wife was semi-crippled with arthritis. They had taken the child Kate from under his roof, from under his very nose.

Mark began to function again. Three days later, shaking off the numbness of shock, he called on the grandparents by appointment. With typical thoroughness he had investigated their circumstances before his visit. The doctor was sixty-eight and his wife five years younger. They lived quiet country lives in modest surroundings, without servants except for a girl from the village.

Mark's charm devastated them. He apologized for his behaviour at the funeral. He had been so overcome that to comfort others had been beyond him. He explained how close he had been to Eoin, their son-in-law, and to Sheila, their daughter . . . the three of them had been so full of plans . . . in time the O'Briens would have become wealthy . . .

The grandparents listened misty-eyed as Mark pleaded to be allowed to provide the children with the futures Eoin would have wanted for them. The boy would receive the best education money could buy. The girl would be raised as a young lady. They would live Averdale lives, with all that that implied . . .

The old lady was overwhelmed, but the doctor was cautious. The children were in his charge, Mark's proposals would take them away. Besides, the boy had suffered terrible acid burns, he might be a cripple for life. Mark flinched. He had a horror of illness, the very idea of a cripple made his flesh creep. Nonetheless he had recognized from the outset that it was both children or neither, so he persevered – 'You must visit,' he pointed to the Rolls-Royce outside the window. 'I'll have you collected whenever you wish. Please stay at my homes as my guests.' He paused for emphasis, 'Between us we must do all we can for the children.'

The discussion lasted two hours, with Mark promising to return the following week – 'With my lawyer, who will be helpful to all of us.'

Agreement was reached at the second meeting. The courts would be asked to endorse Mark's appointment as the children's guardian – a mere formality in view of his name and the settlements involved. The elderly doctor had argued tenaciously. Mark was to be responsible for their care and well-being, their education, their moral safety, their upbringing as good Presbyterians, and so much more – more than he had intended. He had not really wanted to be burdened by the boy at all. He shrugged, once the boy was well he could be sent away to school. The most important point, the most wonderful aspect of the whole thing, was his capture of Kate.

Again he pored over his photographs behind locked doors. The pain of seeing Sheila O'Brien's naked loveliness was muted now – his sense of loss was diminished. He gloried again at the thrust of her breasts and the long line of her thighs – glorified in the certain knowledge that another Kate would be his – at last, one day in the future.

Life took on new meaning for Mark Averdale. Six weeks

after the Killing at Keady he travelled to London to engage a nurse for the girl and a tutor for the boy. He conducted the interviews himself and chose with care, examining credentials, verifying references, explaining requirements. Finally he selected a Miss Rose Smith and a Mr Wyndham Williams, who despite his name was Belfast born and well aware of the Averdales.

Mark's plans were now made. The children would live in London, at least for a while, and Mark would visit them frequently. It resolved a number of problems. His most gracious home in Ireland was now Keady Manor, a most unsuitable place for the children after what had happened. Besides there was Riordan to worry about. The RUC had warned – 'The IRA have made you a prime target.' Mark was unafraid for himself – whatever the Averdales were, none were cowards. 'No surrender' was part of their creed. Another Averdale trait asserted itself – 'What we have we shall hold' – and Mark's most precious possession was Kate. Twice he had been robbed of her beauty. It would never happen again. She would be removed to London and safety.

It took Mark two weeks to adjust his business affairs. He compensated for the loss of Eoin O'Brien by dividing his work among others, none of whom were as competent, but with Mark providing tighter control he thought he would manage. He remained in close touch with the RUC and warned them that he would often be away in London – 'Even so, wherever I am, send word when you arrest Riordan. Better still, send word that you've killed him.'

He saw nothing of the children during this time, but made his influence felt by moving the nurse into the grandparents' house and lodging the tutor nearby.

Thus began the new lives of Timothy and Kathleen O'Brien.

Mark moved with unseemly, almost indecent haste. He was worried that Riordan might strike again and that Kate would be harmed, but he found another reason for the grandparents – 'The children's lives have been shattered enough. If they put roots down here, with you, it will be another upheaval to make changes later. There's no telling what harm that could do.'

The doctor agreed that children need a settled routine. To move them to London seemed a big step, but it was taken, and two weeks later the party left Ireland, with Timothy in a wheelchair because of his damaged legs. The tearful grandparents comforted themselves with Mark's parting words – 'Next week the best man in Harley Street will work on those legs.' And a Harley Street specialist did, though his diagnosis differed little from that already given – that in time, with proper exercises, Timothy O'Brien's legs should mend – after a fashion.

Mark cringed at the prospect of sharing his house, indeed part of his life, with a cripple. He wanted the boy packed off to school at the earliest moment, and he gave Wyndham Williams his instructions the very same evening – 'Exercise him until he drops. To hell with his lessons. I'll not be plagued by a snivelling cripple.'

An established tutor might have resigned, but Wyndham Williams was not established. He was a young man with a reputation to make, who needed the cachet of the Averdale name to impress future employers. He had to take what material he was given if he was to become known as a 'moulder of men'. It was a difficult assignment, but he took it on with one condition – that the boy be left completely in his charge, a proviso which Mark Averdale accepted with a sigh of relief.

Wyndham Williams was a clever young man. He suffered no illusions about the difficulties presented by Timothy O'Brien. More than the boy's legs had been damaged. Timothy had worshipped his mother and idolized his father. Now he had nothing – *less* than nothing. Crippled, often in pain, apparently abandoned by his grandparents, uprooted to a strange place by a strange man called Lord Averdale who flinched whenever their eyes met. Timothy O'Brien made a pitiful sight: red-eyed from constant weeping, white-faced from pain and shock, he had nothing to live for.

Williams gambled. He persuaded Tim to talk about the Killing at Keady. He *made* him talk. Time and again Tim was prodded into grisly descriptions. The boy broke down. He wept. He begged not to be forced to relive the worst moments of his life. But Williams was remorseless – 'What happened then – who shot your mother – which man killed your father?' In truth the boy never knew. He described a tall man in the lane, a man with black hair who waved a revolver – but it had all happened so fast. He did not want to talk about it. He wanted to die. He wanted to be with his mother in Heaven.

'And what will you tell her? That you just let it happen? That you didn't love her enough to go after her murderers? You let them escape –'

'I'm not grown-up,' Tim wailed, 'besides . . .' he gestured at his legs.

Williams snorted. 'That wouldn't have stopped Eoin O'Brien. Your father was brave, everyone says so. He would have hated those men so much –'

'I hate them too . . . I can't walk . . .'

'Eoin O'Brien would have made himself walk. Nothing would have stopped him –'

'I can't . . . my legs . . . sometimes I can't even feel . . .'

'You don't feel. That's your trouble. You don't feel love for your parents, you don't feel hate for their killers –'

'You're wrong!' Tim clamped his hands over his ears. 'Please stop saying that –'

Williams would not stop. He went on and on. He sought to arouse emotion – hatred or anger would do – he needed something. He sneered, 'You only feel sorry for yourself. You don't love your Mummy. You don't hate her murderers –'

'I do!' The boy fought his tears. 'I hate those men. You're not fair. You wait till I grow up, I'll show you. I'll get a gun and –'

'From a wheelchair?' Williams jeered.

Tim collapsed into such a torrent of sobbing that even Williams relented. He started to comfort the boy, then stopped, steeling himself for a parting lash. 'Eoin O'Brien wouldn't have cried. Eoin O'Brien would have *walked*!'

The following morning Timothy was found two yards from his bed, where he had collapsed in an effort to walk to the door. Williams ignored the incident. He pretended to be bored with the boy. Instead of lessons he read aloud from a book called *Self Help*. Tim listened, relieved that the tormenting had stopped. Some of the stories interested him – in fact some of the stories were wonderful. Time and again boys had overcome worse misfortunes than his to grow up and become great men. But when Tim showed interest, Mr Williams shook his head. 'Don't be fooled. It took courage to do what they did.' He sighed and stared at Tim. 'If only you had your father's courage. Lord Averdale says Eoin O'Brien was the bravest man ever to walk the streets of Belfast.'

A week later, Tim had a dream. He was in the lane at Keady. The men were there, lying in wait, just as they had lain in wait for his parents. This time, Tim was too quick for them, too brave. He shot them all . . . and walked away . . . *walked* . . . to where his father waited with arms outstretched and a huge smile on his face.

The dream was so vivid that he told Mr Williams about it.

Timothy's treatment began the very next day with a visit to the Seymour Street Baths. He was to be taught to swim. He was terrified. His wasted legs were useless in water. He was sure he would drown when Wyndham Williams carried him to the pool. He clung despairing to his tutor's neck – and clung harder the next morning when they returned to the Baths yet again. With horror Tim learned that they were to come every day – for two hours each morning. His heart sank – but not his body, for his tutor's strong arms were there to keep him afloat – and after a week of splashing and floundering, Tim was astonished to find that he actually enjoyed the Seymour Street Baths. Although he was a long way from swimming, it was fun to be drawn through the water like a fish. And afterwards, when his tutor rubbed him down, it was clear that Wyndham Williams had enjoyed himself too. 'But we'd better do some real work this afternoon, or Lord Averdale will have my blood.'

Real work turned out to mean exercises for his legs, not schoolwork as Tim had imagined. Real work was brutally hard. After two hours, Tim broke down and begged to rest. Mr Williams shrugged, 'Okay, but don't come crying to me when you dream you can walk.'

Tim was too exhausted to respond. He hurt, he hurt all

over. Gratefully he rested. He closed his eyes to relax while Mr Williams read from that same old book by Samuel Smiles – this time when Napoleon was told that the Alps stood in the way of his armies. 'Then there shall be no Alps,' said Napoleon, and he constructed a road. 'Impossible,' Napoleon said, 'is a word only found in the dictionary of fools.'

Tim dozed. Vaguely other stories reached him – Sir Charles Napier, going into battle against 35,000 Belooches with a force of only 2000 men – and driving the Belooches back to defeat. Williams droned on – 'Courage decides the outcome of every battle.' Tim thought of his dream – he had shown courage in his dream.

'Eoin O'Brien would have *made* himself walk,' Wyndham Williams had taunted, 'Eoin O'Brien was brave, everyone says so.'

The son of Eoin O'Brien gathered his strength. Then he started again. Tim exercised for another two hours that day before collapsing. Williams put him to bed and sat for a long time watching him sleep.

After that they developed a routine. Two hours at the Baths in the morning, then home to bed until noon. Two hours of exercise after lunch, then back to bed again. Two more hours in the evening – six hours a day, seven days a week – when the Harley Street specialist had warned that an hour a day was as much as a child could take.

Instinctively, and deliberately, Williams kept the boy and his guardian apart, while feeding their minds with images of each other. With Tim he talked constantly of the history of the Averdales, from the siege of Londonderry on, and of their many bloody battles with the Catholic hordes. Averdales were courageous, honourable and just – their tenacious leadership had kept Northern Ireland in the British Empire. Averdales were also fair-minded men who recognized fine qualities in others. 'That's why Lord Averdale took to your father,' Williams confided. 'He must have told me a hundred times that Eoin O'Brien was the bravest man who ever walked the streets of Belfast.' And Tim's eyes shone even more when he heard of Lord Averdale's efforts to 'bring those murdering Croppies in Keady to heel'. The boy's jaw jutted out as he remembered his dream. Perhaps he would not be alone at all, perhaps Lord Averdale would be at his side? Williams nodded, 'Quite possibly, but remember – Averdales only walk with the brave – and you've still to walk.'

'I'll walk,' Tim said grimly.

Wyndham Williams told a different story at his meetings with Averdale. Never, he said, had he seen a braver boy. Tim O'Brien possessed the courage of a lion cub. Williams stressed the pain and the agony, and the boy's unrelenting determination. 'And I've found out what drives him on,' he said proudly. 'His father was your greatest admirer. He told the boy a dozen times that you were the finest man ever to walk the streets of Belfast.'

Mark was astonished. His own childhood had been sterile, his father had barely spoken to him, let alone held conversations. Williams persisted, 'It's made all the difference. The boy is determined not to let you down. His devotion to you is quite remarkable. If he does walk, that will be the reason.'

At each meeting Mark was told that Timothy was a brave, intelligent little boy who was battling to overcome his disabilities not for himself but to please his benefactor. Touched by such stories, Mark felt guilty about his initial instructions. 'Look, maybe we're overdoing this – ' But Williams thought otherwise, 'It's not us, it's the boy himself. He's got the bit between his teeth and nothing will stop him.'

Mark was taught to believe that his ward possessed unlimited determination. It was not always true. Sometimes Tim gave up. Sometimes he sat on the floor and howled. On black days he knew he would never walk. Williams would study him for a while, then say, 'By the way, guess what Lord Averdale said the other day. "Williams," he said, "it was true about Eoin O'Brien. He was the bravest man I ever met, but I'll tell you something, I think his son will be even braver."'

The boy was in awe of being compared to his father. He wished he could hear such praise directly from his guardian. Tim never saw his guardian. He hardly saw anyone, not even his sister. He lived in this huge house, but except for Mr Williams and the servants, it was like a prison at times. He expressed his frustration. Williams feigned puzzlement. 'I know, I can't understand it. When Lord Averdale was here last week I suggested that he come up to meet you again, but he shook his head. "No," he said, "I'm dying to see him, but if he's anything like his father he'd rather wait until he's fit. I've loads of exciting plans for him then."'

Words rang in Tim's ears . . . *dying to see him* . . . *loads of exciting plans for him then*. They sounded more wonderful than anything Tim could imagine. He dried his tears, screwed up his courage – and returned to his exercises.

So Wyndham Williams kept them apart, while skilfully drawing them together.

Somehow it added to Mark's loneliness. Belfast was a hell of a frustration. His business managers needed constant guidance. The Averdale enterprises were not producing the profits necessary for his art collection. The shipyards were in trouble and the slump showed no sign of ending. Meanwhile he maintained his pressure on the RUC, but in that too he was frustrated. Matt Riordan seemed to have vanished from the face of the earth.

Mark sighed with relief only when he escaped to London twice a month – usually reaching Belgrave Square by four on a Friday afternoon and summoning Rose Smith to his study withing an hour of arriving. The nurse reported on Kate's well-being, before collecting the child from the nursery. Mark inspected her with the worried eyes of a banker examining a doubtful note. Genuine or forgery? The real thing or a passable imitation? How could one tell? Her hair was as red as a sunset, her skin whiter than milk. No blemishes were apparent. She held herself well, with her chin up and her back straight. She moved like a dancer. She sat gracefully. Mark all but took a magnifying glass to her. Then he relaxed as she came into his lap. He was sure he was right.

As for the child, she rather liked preening herself in front of her guardian. Sometimes she sat on his lap and nuzzled him, enjoying the smell of his hair and the feel of his hands on her bare legs. His scent reminded her of when she had taken her clothes off that time. She had enjoyed that experience too, sensing her mother's excitement and sharing it without knowing why.

Kathleen O'Brien had survived the Killing at Keady unscathed. She had not seen the blood-spattered bodies, hence they caused her no nightmares – and when she was told that her parents had gone to Heaven she was mildly pleased – Heaven was a happy place, grandmother said so. One day she would go there too and they would all be together again. Meanwhile her father's absence left her untroubled, and if she missed her mother at times, she missed her old Nanny as much. But Nanny was part of another life, and so much had happened that even she was a fading memory.

Two people were central to her new existence, her guardian and her nurse – and she had the measure of both. She even adapted to her new name of Kate. Why not? A new name for a new life, and since her new life was enjoyable she liked being Kate. Kate could do whatever she wished. Kathleen had been corrected and scolded, but Kate was never reprimanded. Where Kathleen had lived in one house, Kate knew she had several, and all were larger and staffed with servants. And for every dress Kathleen had owned, Kate had a dozen.

She loved Belgrave Square. Living there made her feel like a princess. She *was* a princess – her guardian said so whenever he saw her – 'Ah, here's my little princess!' – and he would watch her with worried eyes while she smiled and walked up and down to show him how tall she had grown. It was part of their game and she played it with zest, twirling and pirouetting on her toes. He laughed and opened his arms to invite her on to his lap. She liked that most of all, to be hugged and squeezed, while watching Rose from beneath lowered eyelids. That was really exciting – the expression on Rose's face. Rose stood by the desk, clasping her hands in an effort to hide her disapproval. Kate would giggle and squirm as her guardian's hands slid under her skirt. Sometimes he squeezed her bottom and she giggled even more, while all the time watching Rose's face. Rose was upset whenever it happened. Rose tried not to watch, but she always did . . . her eyes flicking to the hem of Kate's skirt. Kate caught her every time and screamed with delight. She was a princess having fun with her guardian. Rose was a servant who had to stand and watch. Kate liked to be hugged and petted – but the sense of power pleased her even more.

When Rose was bossy and bad tempered, Kate punished her unmercifully. 'No,' Kate screamed, 'I won't do it. You wait till *he* comes home.' The threat was not to tell tales, Kate was more subtle. She would squirm on his lap until Rose looked positively sick. Once, determined to inflict extra punishment, she had wriggled and shrieked so much that his fingers had caught inside her knickers. He had hurt her then, but Kate had laughed all the louder at Rose. The nurse had been very quiet at bath time that night, and had washed the tops of Kate's legs extra carefully. Kate had been surprised to see the bruises, but remained unrepentant, 'See – I said I'd do it.'

The threat lay between them forever after that. Sometimes Kate wished her guardian would not squeeze her bottom so hard, and sometimes she wondered *why* Rose became so upset – but mostly she was too busy getting her own way. Kate exploited the situation for all it was worth – and within months she was virtually mistress in Belgrave Square. Certainly she always got what she wanted – by fair means or foul.

She spent little time with her brother, although she saw him every day, usually as he returned from the Seymour Street Baths. Timothy was dull, she decided. Besides, Wyndham Williams was so strict that he frightened her. When they were at home she largely ignored them. Instead she plagued Rose to take her walking in the park, or to the zoo, and sometimes to the waxworks at Madame Tussauds. Even as a six-year-old, Kate was fascinated by London.

It was a strange household. Above stairs the occupants lived separate lives – Tim and Wyndham went one way, Kate and Rose Smith another. Rarely did they ever take a meal together, since Tim's exercise times interfered – and although tutor and nurse could have shared a sitting-room, they seldom did. Social contact was minimal. Wyndham Williams had been heard to call Rose Smith 'the worst sort of manhater' though precisely what that meant was a matter of conjecture below stairs, where they tended to despise Rose Smith anyway. Cook said she was spoiling the girl something rotten. 'You'd think it was her own child, the way she acts. No good will come of it, you mark my words.'

Even when Mark Averdale was in London, the household remained divided. 'It's not what I'm used to,' Cook complained to the rest of the staff. 'I'd up and leave except for that dear little boy. It fair breaks my heart what they do to him. Kids need a mother. His Lordship should marry again, that's what. Them kids might have a proper home then.'

But marriage was a long way off for Mark Averdale, at least eleven years by his reckoning. Seventeen was young for a girl to marry, but not unheard of – besides Kate would hardly be marrying a stranger, she would have known him most of her life.

Nineteen forty-nine was when they would marry. He would only be thirty-nine even then – in the prime of his life if he looked after himself. Meanwhile, to comfort himself, his room was now graced with a lifesize bronze of Kate the young mother, fashioned by an eminent sculptor from photographs. The statue was good, Mark knew it was good, almost, he decided, a great work of art. But was it Kate? Rouen's Kate had had a look in her eye, hard to describe but it had been there. It had been in the photographs too. The statue's eyes were guileless and innocent. The sculptor had captured her beauty but missed her soul. Mark could never look at that statue without feeling loss. The burning of Brackenburn and the Killing at Keady had destroyed a uniqueness too elusive for the greatest sculptor in Europe. The spark was missing – extinguished by a bastard Croppie who would die a terrible death if Mark ever set hands on him.

Such then was the pattern of Mark's life. Haunted by memories of what he had lost, he was terrified of harm coming to the young girl who had become an obsession. In Belfast he awoke every morning to the glory of Kate's photographs – and in London to the bronze statue which, despite its limitations, was yet another reminder of the past and a promise of the future. His hands never tired of exploring that cold, unresponsive metal. He knew every crevice and curve, and lived for the day when a flesh and blood Kate would respond to his touch.

Then, as early summer lengthened the days, several events occurred within a few weeks of each other, which changed Mark's routine completely. The first, on 10 May, concerned the boy Timothy, of whom Mark had been hearing more and more from Wyndham Williams. He had wanted to see the child before, but Williams had pleaded for more time. Mark had curbed his impatience. 'Strange,' he admitted, 'I didn't give a damn a few months ago, but now I can't wait to see the little beggar.'

It was not as strange as Mark had imagined. Even the meeting between guardian and ward – when it eventually came – was stage-managed by Williams. Williams left nothing to chance.

It took place on Saturday, 10 May. Nobody would have known it was Lord Averdale's birthday, had Williams not uncovered the date while teaching Tim the history of the Averdales. Williams learned that in March, and it gave him a flash of inspiration. After which he raced against time. Not that anyone knew. Tim was walking on crutches by then, but nobody knew that either. Williams replaced the crutches with stout walking sticks, and increased Tim's exercise periods by an hour every day. And he introduced another project – a handwritten history of the Averdales, laboriously penned on parchment by Tim and set into a leather folder, on the cover of which Tim was to work the Averdale crest.

On Monday 5 May, Williams explained his plan to Tim, and when the boy thought he could do it, Williams shared some of the details with the rest of the household.

Everyone had some idea of what was to take place – but when Mark Averdale arrived on the Friday, little unusual seemed to be happening. The tutor reported that the boy was still making progress.

'Well, when can I see him?' Mark demanded, quite expecting to be asked for more time.

Williams surprised him. 'Perhaps tomorrow afternoon – if that would be convenient.'

Mark felt excited. Williams had so often praised the boy's courage that . . . well, a guardian *should* take an interest.

He lunched at his club on Saturday and returned to Belgrave Square with his head buzzing with talk of war. The situation was serious. The news was bad, but if the Navy strengthened the Fleet it might be good for Belfast . . . the shipyards could be busy again . . . it might bring the slump to an end. Mark was pondering the likelihood of that when Williams entered the study. Mark looked up, 'Good Lord, I'd almost forgotten. Shall we go up and see the boy now?'

'If you wish, sir, but first may I wish you many happy returns of the day?'

Mark was amazed – Williams opened the doors to the hall to reveal the entire staff drawn up in a line, with Kate and her nurse in the centre. The butler stepped forward with a blue box in his hands. 'A small gift, sir, on behalf of the staff – with our congratulations on your birthday.' Kate advanced and curtsied, smiling as only Kate could and shyly offering a package wrapped in silver paper.

Not since Dorothy had been alive had anyone given Mark a gift. He gave few himself. He was not a generous man. His relationships with people, especially staff, were cool and impersonal. Now with twelve people wishing him a happy birthday he felt quite unable to respond. But the proceedings were not over. Williams looked up to the landing.

Heads turned to stifled gasps of surprise. Only Williams and Timothy had known about this. The boy stood at the very end of the landing, leaning on a cane, with a slim leather folder under his arm. With a nervous glance down to the hall, he began to walk towards the top of the stairs. His movements were slow and stiff, painful to watch and painful to make because when a knee buckled awkwardly his hissed intake of breath was heard in the hall below. Cook's hands flew to her mouth. She stepped forward. Williams waved her back. He cast a warning look at the others, but nobody noticed – all eyes were focused on the staircase.

Tim paused at the top, gauging the curved sweep of the stairs. Fifteen steps down to the half landing, and another fifteen from there. He moistened his lips, propped his cane against the balustrade, gripped the banister with both

380

hands, and began to descend. His concentration was total. 'Take it slowly,' Mr Williams had warned, 'get both feet on the same stair, then start off again. Take a stair at a time.'

Watching anxiously, Mark felt confused. He stood with the gifts in his hands, flanked by Kate and Wyndham Williams. The whole thing was unreal, yet there was nothing unreal about the boy on the stairs. He was solid and purposeful, good-looking in a grey flannel suit, the long trousers of which hid the scars on his legs. Nothing like the child Mark remembered. Gone were the red eyes and white, tear-stained face. Instead the boy's cheeks bore a faint flush, his well brushed hair looked healthy and vibrant – an air of determination marked every line of his body. Even so, Mark crossed his fingers.

The grand staircase in Belgrave Square had launched many an elegant entrance, but none so dramatic.

The boy hesitated at the half landing, taking a fresh hold on the leather folder tucked under his arm, while rubbing his thigh with the other hand. His thigh was not troubling him. He was wiping the sweat from his palm and flexing his fingers for a better grip on the banisters before stepping forward again.

Mark found himself counting the stairs, under his breath. One . . . followed by a long pause as the boy's other foot came down . . . two, as the boy's first foot stepped forward again. Timothy never looked up. His eyes focused on his feet, while his left hand edged slowly down the banister, gripping so tightly that his knuckles shone white. Other people were counting. Mark was deaf to their voices at first; until he whispered 'six' and realized they were all saying six. And by the time he said 'ten' people's voices were louder. Cook's hands were clasped and held up to her face. 'Eleven' she called, then gnawed the knuckle of one fist. Beads of sweat stood out on the tutor's face. Beyond him, the butler's usual impassive expression had given way to moist-eyed excitement. 'Twelve!' he shouted triumphantly. Everyone in the hall was willing the boy on. 'Thirteen!' Mark roared amid rising excitement. It was impossible to know if Tim heard. He gave no sign of it. His head remained down-turned as – at last – his first foot reached out and cautiously lowered itself on to the hall carpet. 'Fifteen!' they shouted, and would have rushed forward but for Williams. 'No!' he snapped like a whip crack. It was enough to keep them in their place, but nothing could restrain the outburst of clapping, and the relieved shouts of 'Well done. Oh well done!'

Tim looked up then. His second foot was safely down on the carpet and his left hand locked firmly on to the end of the banister. He smiled shyly – his eyes going straight to Mark Averdale who stood watching from the study doors fifteen yards away.

Mark would have gone forward, but for the touch at his elbow. Williams wanted him to stay. Even so Mark hesitated – and in the same moment the boy began to move.

My God, Mark thought, the boy has left his cane on the landing. With a cane he might do it, but without one . . . Yet Tim had taken three steps, without crutches, or sticks, or anyone at his side to catch him. The smile on his face could not hide the strain – neither could strain mask his courage.

Past conversations with Williams echoed in Mark's ears – 'The boy is determined not to let you down. If he *does* walk, that will be the reason.'

The boy *was* walking. Painfully, awkwardly, favouring his right leg, but walking. His expression was set in a fixed smile and his eyes found Mark's with a message. 'It's not much, but I'll get better at it, you see if I don't.' Like telepathy, Mark thought before dismissing the idea. He didn't believe in telepathy. Even so he had sensed what was in the boy's mind. Mark abhorred public displays of emotion, yet he almost burst with pride. 'His devotion to you is total,' Williams had said – and Mark could see the devotion in the boy's eyes.

Timothy halted in front of his guardian. Triumph outweighed his weariness. His whole face shone with excitement. He proffered the leather folder, 'May I congratulate you on your birthday, sir, and wish you many more to come.'

Life in Belgrave Square was never quite the same after that. The leather folder never meant as much to Mark as his precious photographs – nothing in his life was as important as Kate – but Tim O'Brien won a special place in Mark's affections from that day onwards. Mark came to prize the folder for what it represented, a bond between him and the boy. After that they met for an hour or so whenever Mark was in London and – predisposed to like each other by the cunning Williams – they actually *did* like each other. After all they had much in common, mostly a notable pride in the Averdales, which in turn meant a commitment to the struggle for Ulster.

Mark spent an ever increasing amount of time in London from the beginning of June. Frustration with Belfast was only one of the reasons. Foremost was Kate, of course, Mark was as fascinated as ever by her – but also there was the boy, in whom Mark was now taking a genuine interest. There was also Mark's mistress in St John's Wood. Not a weekend went by without him spending a night in her bed – and finally, there was the ever increasing threat of war.

The brutality of war sickened Mark, but he was realistic enough to realize that it would mean the end of the slump, and perhaps huge profits for him – profits which could be used subsequently to rebuild Brackenburn and establish an unrivalled art collection.

So Mark lobbied government offices for armament contracts and made himself generally conversant with the political situation. The more he learned the more apprehensive he became. This would be a war like no other. London could be destroyed by enemy bombs. So could every city of England. Where then would be a safe hiding place for Kate?

If war came he would send her to the United States. The decision was the most painful and agonizing of his whole life. He searched for alternatives but could find none. His contacts at the War Office were adamant. If war came, the whole of England would be vulnerable to enemy bombing. Not only that, the country would be hard-pressed to repel an invasion.

Mark had a distant relative in Dayton, Ohio, about whom his bankers made discreet enquiries – and when they reported that the relative was comfortably off, Mark wrote to the man, asking if Kate could be given sanctuary 'in the event of war, and of course just for the duration'. The suggestion was accepted immediately.

As summer moved on, Mark Averdale made what arrangements he could. He tried to prepare for every eventuality – until, on 25 August, one event took him by surprise. The IRA exploded a huge bomb in Coventry. Mark was sickened and disgusted, but not unduly alarmed – until the following Tuesday when he was back in Belfast and the RUC telephoned to say Matt Riordan had been involved. Mark was never more frightened in his life. That murdering bastard was in England, within a hundred miles of Kate – maybe even closer, after all he would hardly stay in Coventry. Suppose he fled to London? Suppose he holed up somewhere, waiting for the hue and cry to die down? And suppose he came across Lord Averdale's London address in the telephone directory?

By seven o'clock that evening, a uniformed policeman was posted outside the house in Belgrave Square. By eight Mark was back from Belfast, clutching a dozen copies of the evening paper. The charcoal sketch of Matt Riordan, so lovingly drawn by his mother, stared out from the front page. Every member of the household was given a newspaper. Wide-eyed at their master's agitation, they studied the face of Matt Riordan.

'That man murdered my wife. He razed Brackenburn to the ground. He organized the Killing at Keady. He should be shot on sight like a rabid dog. Memorize that face, for one glimpse of it may be your only chance of staying alive.'

Mark's obvious fear caused panic below stairs. Cook gave notice and refused to spend another night in the house. An upstairs maid left with her. Elsewhere Rose Smith had her bed moved into Kate's room. By noon the following day, *two* uniformed constables guarded the house. Extra locks were fitted. Windows were barred. Mark gave instructions that the children were to be confined to the house – and the house itself was made ready to withstand a siege.

Timothy, strangely, was the only one not alarmed. As soon as he'd seen the newspaper he had recognized Riordan as one of the men who had been at Keady. But Lord Averdale was terribly wrong to blame this man for the killing. Tim knew that was not true. The man in the picture had carried him down to the stream – he had saved Tim's life – and Tim knew it.

He agonized over what he should do. He dared not say a word to contradict his guardian or incur his displeasure. Yet he had to tell someone, and as he prepared for bed he blurted the whole story out to Wyndham Williams.

Williams was immediately on guard. He had seen that the mere mention of Riordan's name sent Averdale into an uncontrollable rage. Williams argued that Tim might be wrong, after all he had been in pain, in shock, half submerged in the stream . . .

'But I'm *not* wrong,' Tim persisted. 'It was this other man, the one with black hair. I told you about him. He was in the lane, with the pistol . . .'

Williams dared not accept that. He had performed a miracle of rehabilitation. Thanks to him the boy had a future with Averdale. But a word spoken in defence of Riordan could destroy the whole relationship. Months of work would be undone. Williams argued and persuaded – it *must* have been Riordan, Riordan was known to be in the IRA, he was known to be a wicked, ruthless man . . .

Williams's argument added to Tim's unhappy confusion. His mind was full of the man with black hair. Finally he could argue no more. Wearily he fell asleep, having promised never to mention the matter again.

Williams breathed a sigh of relief.

Mark Averdale stayed in London until the Thursday, when a management crisis dragged him back to Belfast. Neither Scotland Yard nor the RUC had any news about Riordan. Mark ranted and dictated a blistering letter to *The Times* – but was unable to do anything positive.

The following day Hitler's troops invaded Poland. As Mark journeyed once more to London, he realized that war was now inevitable – and on Sunday, Chamberlain's broadcast had barely finished when the air-raid sirens wailed out over London for the first time.

Mark bundled Kate down to the basement a minute later.

Fate seemed destined to be cruel. All Mark wanted was to look after Kate. He had arranged his life, steeled himself to wait for her to grow up. Now he was faced with war and the terrible decision to send her away.

Rose Smith was summoned to the study after dinner that night. Mark's face was drawn. He was obviously tired and worried. He wished he knew more about the nurse. Something about her worried him. Nothing he could put his finger on, perhaps it was just her lack of femininity. She was so plain, with her mannish short hair and thick horn rim spectacles. Still, he had to admit, her references had been excellent, and Kate seemed happy with her. Even so, Mark disliked conferring so much responsibility on someone about whom he knew so little. But what else could he do?

He told her about America at once – that Kate was to be sent to a relative who lived in a place called Dayton, Ohio. He would like Miss Smith to accompany the child and remain as her nurse for the duration of hostilities. Of course it was a big responsibility, but she would be well rewarded if she gave satisfaction.

She seemed pleased – at least Mark assumed the faintly sneering smile expressed pleasure. She asked when they would go and could she have time to consider it. Mark said a month to the first and gave her twenty-four hours for the second – knowing he would have to find a replacement in a hurry if she refused. After which he dismissed her and poured himself a whisky. She still worried him and he wondered why. Perhaps it was just the pain of sending Kate away – maybe he would feel the same about any nurse. Bleak with foreboding he retired to his room and spent an hour caressing the bronze statue before going to sleep.

The news was common knowledge the next day. Tim wondered if he would be sent to Dayton, Ohio too? He hoped not. War sounded exciting. Besides, he wanted to stay close to his guardian. Then came a shock. Mr Williams was rushing around the house telling everyone that his papers had come through from the RAF. Mr Williams was going to war.

Tim burst into tears and rushed to his room. He had come to trust his tutor. His tutor was his best friend, his only real friend – and now he was going away.

Williams entered the room moments later. 'I don't

believe it,' he said gently. 'Tough Tim in tears.'

Tim was proud enough of the nickname to stop crying – after which Mr Williams lit his pipe and they talked for a long time. 'War changes all sorts of things, old chap,' Williams said, 'but nothing changes friendship. My being away won't alter that, I'll still be thinking about you.' He ruffled Tim's hair. 'Damn nuisance you're not a few years older, a brave feller like you would be made a General in no time.'

Life was changing for everyone. Rose Smith accepted the responsibility of taking Kate to America, and the two of them embarked upon a whirlwind tour of the shops – accompanied everywhere by the bulky figure of a Scotland Yard detective, for Riordan was still on the run and Mark was taking no chances.

Wyndham Williams performed a last act of friendship for Timothy. Having established that the boy would not be sent to America, but taken back to Belfast with Mark Averdale, Williams set about finding his own successor, determined to leave Tim an ally in the house of the Averdales.

September passed in a blur. Mark spent hours at the War Office and the Admiralty. His hunch had been right – war would provide work for Belfast. An extra 13,000 men would be needed in the shipyards, and as many again in the engineering works. And there was talk of Short and Harland's new aircraft works wanting 18,000 more. The slump was over at last.

There was no question of Mark joining the Armed Forces. Belfast's heavy industry would be vital in the coming battle, and there was no telling who would threaten it first – Nazi Germany or the IRA. Sinister rumours were circulating about Eire. De Valera was still preaching neutrality, but how long would that last? The man had devoted his life to attacking the Empire. Once more Northern Ireland was under siege – and once more it was time to cry 'No Surrender!' And time again for an Averdale to stay firmly in Ulster.

Yet – strangely – no bombs fell during those opening weeks of war. Life in London went on as before. Mark hesitated about Kate. He agonized endlessly, even now, with passages booked. But people *were* evacuating, certainly the wealthy and foreign nationals, who were leaving the country in droves. The American Ambassador was pictured waving goodbye to Rose Kennedy as she sailed for America. Mark knew he had to go through with it.

Saying goodbye nearly killed him. After putting Kate aboard her ship in Liverpool, Mark thought his journey back to London would take forever. Finally he reached the sanctuary of his room, where he collapsed in abject misery. His only consolation was that when he saw her next she would be that little bit older – that much nearer to becoming Rouen's nymph at the poolside.

It was time to close the house in Belgrave Square. Kate and Rose Smith had gone to America, Wyndham Williams had gone to the war, and the staff had dispersed in various directions.

Mark Averdale set out to return to Belfast, taking with him young Timothy O'Brien and Mr Tompkins, the boy's new tutor.

Tim left London without regret. His future lay in Ulster. From now on his life would be intertwined with Mark Averdale's. When they boarded the train at Euston, Tim settled into a corner seat and almost sighed with anticipation.

A moment later, Tim's mood was completely shattered. Just as the train began to move, he glanced out of the window. On the platform little more than a yard away, was a newsagent's kiosk. Placards were daubed with a headline – 'Irish journalist leaves hospital.' An *Evening Standard* was clipped in a wire display frame. A big picture almost covered the front page – a picture of a man with an arm in a sling, being helped down some steps. Tim gasped. He strained for a second look. Suddenly he was back at Keady. Gunfire rang out, sharp pains stabbed his legs. It was the man who had been waving the pistol.

Tim craned his neck, staring at the photograph as the train inched slowly past the kiosk. He was sure he was right. It was the same man. The same thick black hair, the same square jaw!

By the time the train had lurched out of the station, Tim

was bathed in sweat. That man was in London. Tim had almost seen his name. If only he had a copy of the *Standard*.

CHAPTER SIX

Matt Riordan was still on the run. He cursed his decision to return to Belfast. Internment had been reintroduced in Northern Ireland. Men were being carted off to prison without proper trial or access to lawyers, even without evidence of a crime – just on suspicion of being members of the IRA. For Matt Riordan, wanted for murder, with a price on his head, Belfast was the most dangerous place in the world.

He remained because he was ordered to remain. He and Ferdy Malloy were among the few senior IRA men still at large. Dozens had been arrested and interned for the duration of the war – incarcerated in the Crumlin Road Jail, or on the prison ship *Al Rawdah*, an old hulk moored off Killyleagh in Strangford Lough.

'They could be in prison for years,' Matt groaned. 'Jaysus, what's being done to get them out?'

Not much, was the answer. Matt was appalled at the way attitudes had changed. Even in the Falls attitudes were different. The war was creating jobs by the thousand. Men were working and earning money. They were putting food on the table and clothes on the kids.

'But you're working to salvage the fuckin' Briti Empire,' Ferdy shouted angrily. 'What about fighting f Ireland?'

'Fuck Ireland. I'll not be spending years rotting on stinking prison ship for lost dreams –'

'They're not lost –'

'They are in Dublin. Dev's as bad as the British. He's sold out –'

'So we'll get rid of Dev –'

'Oh sure, and have Boland in his place? Don't make me laugh.'

Matt was stunned by some of the things happening. IRA

men were even joining the British Army. 'Sure and why not. The pay's bloody good and they'll teach us a trade.'

Matt and Ferdy did all they could, but they were swimming against the tide. One week they stayed upstairs in a pub in the Short Strand and sent word to those friends who were still free. The friends came, never more than two at a time for fear of attracting attention – up the back stairs to tap on the door. Even their whispered identification brought a guarded response. 'Come in with your hands up.' And they entered to find Matt levelling a revolver at them from the far wall. 'If you're armed put it on the bed,' he said softly, 'then sit down and we'll talk.'

It was a reception which nobody liked. Matt just scowled, 'There's more police spies about than maggots on a corpse. Some bloody Judas set Jimmy Traynor up. Otherwise he would never have been taken.'

But they never found the informer.

In October, Matt organized a break-in to the Crumlin, with eight men hidden in a laundry van. Guards had been bribed to let them through the main gates without searching the van. Once inside Matt intended to release Traynor and as many others as possible – then they would fight their way out. Once again, police spies got wind of the plan. The bribed guards were arrested. Matt drove into an ambush. He and his men escaped, but Traynor remained in prison, along with the other internees.

In November, Matt succeeded in smuggling a revolver into the prison hospital. A message was delivered to Traynor, telling him to report sick. The revolver was actually in his hand when guards rushed through the ward and surrounded him. Traynor threatened them with the gun. They laughed, before beating him to his knees with their clubs. The revolver had been unloaded, guards had emptied out the bullets and replaced the gun in its hiding place. Once more someone had talked.

'Dear God,' Matt said weakly, 'there's only you I trust any more, Ferdy, and sometimes I wonder if you talk in your sleep.'

The truth had to be faced. The IRA was beaten in the north.

Half way through December, Matt and Ferdy decided to

go to Dublin. Matt had remained on the run for three months in Belfast, but the strain was telling and he was afraid his luck would run out. Not that he would allow himself to be taken alive. Ferdy had strict orders about that. If arrest ever seemed certain Ferdy would shoot him, and blame the British for his death.

Matt Riordan was now as ready to die for the cause as his father had been before him.

A week before Christmas they crossed the border and went south. Matt travelled happily, and not simply because he was not a wanted man in Dublin. 'Didn't they promise me Connors if I went to England? And didn't I do that for them? So Connors it is.' He shrugged. 'And they can please themselves. If they argue this time, I'll take Connors myself. God knows, I've waited a hell of a time.'

But their reception in Dublin drove such thoughts from Matt's mind. Dublin was as bad as Belfast. Dev was using *The Emergency*, as he was calling the war, to clamp down hard on the IRA. Internment was the policy in the south as well as the north. 'It's civil war all over again,' a man said to Ferdy, 'except this time Dev's got all the guns, and the police and an army.'

Matt and Ferdy had come looking for help. Instead they found the IRA reeling from a succession of blows. Special Branch detectives had arrested scores of men all over Dublin. Of the men who had promised to bring Sean Connors to an IRA court-martial, every single one was now interned on the Curragh. And police spies were as numerous as in Ulster.

Even Matt and Ferdy were treated with suspicion. On arrival they had gone to an IRA safe house in Rathmines, where they had stayed as welcome guests for three days – but on Christmas Eve it became obvious they were prisoners.

Furiously, Matt demanded an explanation.

'We are planning a raid,' he was told. The IRA was to hit the Magazine Fort in Phoenix Park on Christmas Eve. It had been decided that Matt and Ferdy were too unfamiliar with local conditions to take part – and it was best for them not to roam free until the raid was over.

The raid was a colossal success, a coup beyond their

wildest dreams. In the space of two hours, IRA men immobilized the entire garrison and got away with a million rounds of ammunition in thirteen lorries. The news reached the house in Rathmines at ten-thirty when the back door crashed open and a breathless driver rushed in. 'Quick, I'm parked under the trees. Give me a hand, for God's sake.'

It took seven of them an hour to stack three hundred magazine boxes in the basement.

'What a Christmas present!'

Ammunition was being distributed to a hundred hiding places around Dublin.

The IRA had stolen virtually the government's entire stock of ammunition.

Ferdy was beside himself. 'Wouldn't you think the tide's turned at last. God, I can feel it. Matt, we've enough ammo to raise an army.'

Nobody could sleep for excitement. *Over a million rounds!* It was fantastic. By three o'clock in the morning, Ferdy had outlined a scenario for springing every IRA man who was in prison – north and south of the border. By four o'clock they were working out a plan to surround the Stormont parliament, and the Dail in Dublin – simultaneously. By five they were picking men for key positions in a new government. And by six they were too hoarse to talk any longer. They just sat in dazed bemusement with tired smiles on their faces.

'Merry Christmas, Ferdy,' Matt said happily. 'Come on, let's get a few hours' sleep.'

There were nine of them in the house, all drunk with the thrill of success. Matt could not remember when he last felt so happy. Two men were deputed for guard duty, and the others settled down to sleep on the floor.

'What a Christmas,' Ferdy sighed as he dozed off.

The attack, when it came, was so sudden that the guards failed even to fire a warning shot. Before anyone realized what was happening soldiers and police were pouring through every door and window. Matt grabbed a revolver, but was knocked senseless before he could use it. One man escaped: evading outstretched hands he dashed into the garden, where rifle fire tore him apart.

Matt was handcuffed and chained and pulled to his feet. Ferdy was dragged through the front door. All of them were herded into the back of a lorry.

On the way to Mountjoy, they saw the road blocks. Troops swarmed out of every side street. Dublin was under martial law. Not even the British, in all of their years in Ireland, had mounted such a search as was going on in Dublin. All army leave had been cancelled, roads everywhere were blocked, cars and lorries were being stripped to the axles at checkpoints . . .

Ten days later, the government had recovered more than ninety per cent of the stolen ammunition.

The men in the Dail had won the day – even though they had suffered the fright of their lives. The IRA had been defeated again. Many IRA leaders were held pending trial – and Dev and his colleagues were in no mood to be lenient.

On 7 January, the eight men taken alive from the house in Rathmines, including Matt Riordan and Ferdy Malloy, were put on trial. All were found guilty, which was no surprise. The surprise was the savagery of the sentence.

Matt and the men with him were to be committed to prison – for fifteen years!

Matt was led out of the dock, surrounded by guards. Better to have been hanged in Belfast, he thought, than to be imprisoned in Dublin.

CHAPTER SEVEN

By 7 January, Sean Connors had more than recovered from being beaten up in Shadwell, he had capitalized on it. He had been released from the hospital to a hero's welcome in the East End – mainly because he refused to bring charges against the men who had almost killed him.

'I'd have done the same myself,' he told the *Daily Express*, 'if I thought I'd had my hands on those devils from the IRA.'

The *Daily Mirror* reported him as saying, 'The IRA are the scum of the earth.'

By condemning the IRA at every opportunity, he was getting back at Matt Riordan. He became a minor pundit on Irish affairs. Fleet Street had access to him and whenever Ireland cropped up, Sean Connors was good for a comment. It caused problems at times. His views were still those of his father – that Ireland should be united as one country, but by peaceful means, he stressed, not by the use of the gun. Questions on Ireland's neutrality were more difficult. Influenced by Freddie, Sean was beginning to waver – even though he refused to say so in public. Instead he stressed that Ireland was so small and so poor that her involvement was irrelevant – 'Ireland wouldn't make a ha'p'orth of difference.'

Sean's public utterances gave comfort to a number of people. Many Irishmen living in England had suffered backlash from the IRA bombing campaign, and were grateful to Sean for speaking out. A more surprising development was a message from de Valera himself, full of praise for Sean's 'responsible attitude'.

Freddie was impressed. 'Will you look at that. He'll be making you an ambassador next.'

'Like hell. The Da never trusted the man and no more do I.'

Increasingly Sean was used as a sounding board by Irish politicians in their arm's-length dealings with the British Government. It was easily done at Craven Street, which more and more was taking on the atmosphere of an international club – not just a press club either: politicians, minor diplomats and socialites rubbed shoulders with newsmen from a dozen countries.

'We must be crazy,' Freddie said one night, looking at a room full of people. 'We could charge admission for what we've got here. I swear I don't know half of these.'

It had started when Sean left hospital. People came to see how he was and brought their stories with them. After that it just grew. Sean revelled in the atmosphere, which was just like Ballsbridge in the old days. Even in January when he dispensed with his cane, visitors still thronged to Craven Street with grist for Sean's mill.

By February he showed few signs of having been at death's door. He limped slightly but no wounds were visible. Only when he stripped did the scars show, especially the livid one down his back, where the docker's hook had nearly torn the life out of him. He had mended well and soon he and Freddie were as active as ever in their search for stories.

Yet . . . for a country at war, stories of war itself were hard to come by. The British seemed to be playing at it. There were clues everywhere . . . park railings carted off to be turned into munitions, children evacuated from the capital, poisonous snakes in Regent's Park Zoo destroyed for fear they might escape in an air raid . . . but there was little sense of impending disaster. Gas masks were issued, shelters constructed, lights blacked out at night – and yet London went on much as before. The theatres were still open. Freddie and Sean took the Hamilton girls to see young John Gielgud in *The Importance of Being Earnest* and out to supper after, just as they would have before war was declared. Some people thought Chamberlain was right to speculate that the German economy would collapse and sink Hitler with it.

'That's as likely as me swimming the Channel,' Freddie said in disgust. 'When will they realize? I tell you Sean, there's no hope unless the British get rid of Chamberlain and his bunch of appeasers.'

But that seemed unlikely. Besides, not everyone agreed with Freddie. France was secure behind a honeycomb of fortresses which had taken twelve years to build and stretched from the Alps to the Belgian frontier. The Maginot Line was Europe's Great Wall of China. Two million Frenchmen manned the ramparts and Gort's Expeditionary Force stood behind them – 390,000 British soldiers ready to fight on French soil. A German attack could not possibly succeed. 'This war will be a stalemate,' a French journalist told them. 'The gold can stay in the bank, and each Army will remain in its fortress of ferro-concrete.'

'Very cosy,' Freddie said, bluntly disbelieving. 'I spent a lot of time in Germany last year. Nobody there was impressed with the Maginot Line.'

The Americans were calling it 'The Phoney War', and it was easy to see why. Sean was struck by a sense of anticlimax. London had crackled with tension last year, big stories had been easy to come by – but during the spring of 1940 Sean grubbed hard for snippets of news and made every one count.

Freddie coined a joke for his CBS audience – 'It's so quiet here you can hear a Ribbentrop.' By the end of March, however, he was too restless to stay in London. 'I'm going to France. Sean, you take over the CBS microphone. I'll cable the stuff through, use what you can. It will ruin my reputation for me to stay here any longer.'

They threw a party before he left. Margaret Hamilton was among the guests, and there was no mistaking her feelings for Freddie. She had changed since the outbreak of war – become more concerned with events, more like her sister and less like her mother. Parties bored her unless Freddie was there, and with Freddie planning a three-month tour of Europe the question was: 'What will Margaret do?' She could always revive 'the flirtatious five hundred' as Freddie called her former escorts, but the new Margaret was in no mood to do that. Instead, she announced that she had enrolled in the Wrens. 'Why not? I've always liked boats. Who's the best crew at Cowes every year? If I practise on *Samantha* I may even end up on the Admiral's barge.'

Samantha was a river cruiser moored at Staines. George Hamilton had bought it for himself originally, only for Margaret to develop such a passion for boats and to become so expert, that George had made a present of it on her twenty-first birthday.

Her announcement was greeted with cheers and excitement. Freddie, who had known in advance, beamed proudly for the rest of the evening. But Sean repressed a shiver, as if someone had walked on his grave. He looked at Margaret and remembered the glittering parties in Eaton Square. Things *were* changing.

After Freddie left for France, Margaret went down to Staines to mess about on *Samantha* until she heard from the Admiralty. Val visited her when she had a day off from the East End, and returned with comforting reports for George and Cynthia at the Dorchester.

Meanwhile Sean continued to hunt for stories – but hard

news in London was thin on the ground. Ambassador Kennedy returned from another visit to the United States, where he was reported to have told everyone that Germany would crush England in the war, a view he confirmed when Sean called at the Embassy. 'But that's just for publication in Ireland,' Joe Kennedy grinned. 'I'm unpopular enough here as it is.'

Popular or not, Joe Kennedy's assessment seemed justified the very next day – when Hitler invaded Denmark and Norway.

'The Phoney War ended this week,' Sean said in his CBS broadcast, 'when the 20,000 British troops in Norway were routed at Namsos. Now the world awaits London's response.'

London was slow to respond, despite the rising barrage of press criticism. While German troops paraded triumphantly in Oslo and Copenhagen, Chamberlain's government continued to dither. In the House of Commons, however, the mood was changing. On 7 May, Parliament gathered for one of the gravest debates in its history. The atmosphere in the chamber crackled with suspense. By mid-afternoon the Distinguished Strangers Gallery was crammed tight with the ambassadors and ministers of two dozen countries. In the Press Gallery, Sean sensed that hard news was coming at last.

And come it did. Chamberlain survived boos and catcalls from the Labour benches, but then his own supporters turned on him. Leo Amery, former Secretary-of-State, trembled with emotion as he delivered his speech. Concluding with a savage finale borrowed from Oliver Cromwell, he pointed at Chamberlain – 'You have sat there too long . . . depart I say . . . let us have done with you. In the name of God, *go!*'

The debate continued the following day. Speaker after speaker took up Amery's cry. It was left to Herbert Morrison, Val's Labour Party mentor in the East End, to deliver the final attack. His conclusion was a flat ultimatum demanding the resignation of Chamberlain and all who had supported appeasement.

Chamberlain was on his feet, snapping his reply, 'We shall see who is with us and who is against us. I will call on my friends to support me in the lobby!'

Few of them did. Tory backbenchers, many in uniform, filed into the Opposition lobby to vote against the government. At least one officer had tears streaming down his face.

Pale and angry, Chamberlain managed a wan smile as he shuffled from the chamber. The time was 11.10 p.m., Wednesday 8 May.

'Fifty minutes to midnight,' Sean wrote, 'even the English couldn't leave it later than that.'

The news that Winston Churchill had become Prime Minister reached Freddie Mallon in France forty-eight hours later. Exhausted by a day which defied belief, Freddie was too bitter to smile. 'The fools,' he whispered, 'just in time to be too late.'

Freddie had warned them. From the moment he stepped on to French soil he had warned them. Every day his cables to Sean preached the same message – that the French army was a shambles and the British Expeditionary Force not much better. 'Joe Kennedy is right,' he admitted again and again. 'This lot won't hold the Germans for five minutes.'

Morale among French troops was rock bottom. They wanted no part of this war. Their equipment was pitiable. One reserve regiment proposed to tow its guns into battle with tractors, until, at a demonstration for newspapermen, not one tractor would start. Some of the machines had not been repaired in ten years. Freddie saw 1891 rifles, and field rations date-stamped 1920. At Metz a quarter of the infantrymen in the 42nd Division were marching barefoot because their socks had rotted away.

It was the same wherever he went. At Merlebach in the Maginot Line, drunkenness among the troops was so rife that a railway terminal was being used as drying-out rooms – *salles de desethylisation* – to sober up the stupid *poilus*. Officers had no respect for their men and vice versa – discipline was almost non-existent.

The British troops were having the time of their lives. By night, merry on ten francs' worth of wine, they sang the songs of their fathers' war – *It's a long way to Tipperary* and *Pack up your troubles in your old kitbag* – and by day they proposed to fight their fathers' war all over again, from trenches dug on the World War I pattern of six feet deep and four feet six inches wide.

Freddie was appalled. He had seen the slick German army on manoeuvres in 1938. He had written hundreds of column inches about Goering's Luftwaffe. In London he had button-holed politicians, badgered so-called experts, talked on the radio – and been given reassuring answers. After five weeks in France, Freddie felt like the only sighted man in the land of the blind.

General Gort refused to grant him an interview. Commander-in-Chief Maurice Gustave Gamelin had Freddie thrown out of French Army Headquarters. 'Monsieur Mallon' was widely regarded as a trouble-making American journalist whose desire for sensational headlines should be stamped on. In Paris he was summoned to the American Embassy and told in blistering language that complaints had been made.

In despair Freddie searched for other reporters who might corroborate his reports. Paris cafés overflowed with newspapermen, few of whom had been to the Maginot Line.

'What's the point?' they said. 'Nothing will happen up there. It's stalemate. The big story will break here when the diplomats dream up a peace formula. Besides . . . Paris in the spring and all that . . . come on Freddie, have another drink.'

Blazing with temper, Freddie set out to obtain proof of what he had seen in Metz, the shambling apology of an army parading in bare feet with firearms made in the last century. While Sean Connors listened to speeches in the House of Commons, Freddie was touring newspaper offices in search of a photographer. Not one single editor considered the story worthwhile. Finally Freddie found André Sagan, a freelance photographer specializing in fashion work, who was willing to risk imprisonment for photographing military installations and equipment.

'You're safe on all counts,' Freddie said in disgust. 'What we're going to see can't be described as military or even an installation, and they haven't got equipment – that's the whole point!'

After some further haggling, Sagan agreed to make himself available the next day, complete with his Citroën – 'But not until noon, I'm booked for a fashion show in the morning.'

Freddie remained sober that night, though he was tempted to get drunk. Parisians seemed even less concerned about the war than Londoners. A friendly barman gave him the Parisian point of view. 'Why should we fight? We are safe from invasion because of the Maginot Line. Should we fight for the Czechs? Or the Poles? Have you met a Pole? They are animals, ignorant, barely civilized.'

Sagan's fashion show ran late the next day, and it was not until four in the afternoon that he was ready to begin the two hundred mile drive to Metz. 'Perhaps we should leave it until the morning?' he suggested.

Freddie almost had a seizure. Finally Sagan agreed that they should drive as far as Rheims that evening. 'That way,' Freddie said sourly, 'you might be on parade a little earlier in the morning.'

They left Rheims at nine o'clock the next morning, and Freddie was on his way back to Metz, complete with a photographer who promised to swear an affidavit to whatever they witnessed. But not even Freddie was prepared for the sights of that day.

Sagan's Citroën never reached Metz. The roads were choked with traffic, mostly military, hurrying in all directions at once – and the ominous rumble of guns in the distance was unmistakable.

'Where are they holding the manoeuvres?' Sagan shouted to a young French officer.

'Manoeuvres? That's the start of the German offensive.'

The Germans had launched a dawn attack in the Ardennes.

'The Ardennes,' Sagan roared with laughter. 'The Ardennes are impenetrable! Every schoolboy in France knows that.' To him it was a joke. Only Germans would be so stupid. Marshal Pétain himself had described the wooded heights of the Ardennes as 'the best fortification in Europe'. Sagan wagged a finger under Freddie's nose. 'That is why the Maginot Line was never extended beyond Sedan – there was no need.'

400

But the guns had started. Freddie looked at the map on his knees. Sedan was on the Belgian frontier. If the Germans could get through the Ardennes they could swing south and be behind the Maginot Line.

The very suggestion made Sagan erupt with fresh laughter.

Even so, as they drove towards Sedan the boom of artillery grew louder. Sagan's amusement began to fade. Freddie grew more agitated with every mile. Progress was slow, columns of troops marched in ragged files towards the frontier, farm carts impeded army trucks, all was confusion. At Rethel they heard the first rumours. Fort Eben Emael, Belgium's much vaunted stronghold guarding the important city of Liège, had been captured by Germans using a new weapon. Sagan, interpreting rapid-fire French, fumbled for an English translation of gliders.

'Gliders?' Freddie echoed. 'Gliders might even carry troops over your Maginot Line. Did you ever think of that?'

Sagan felt sure that someone in the French Army knew all about gliders.

Freddie scowled in disbelief.

Five kilometres later, Sagan wanted to turn back. They pulled to the side of the road while they argued. Sagan stopped a farmer who had been in Sedan early that morning. The man knew nothing, just that the sound of the guns had become louder and louder, and that there were rumours of German troops pouring into Belgium.

'Through the Ardennes?' Sagan said in disbelief. The farmer shrugged and hurried away.

The road to the frontier was becoming more congested than ever. Sagan insisted that they return to Paris.

Freddie had no choice. Without a vehicle, and an interpreter, what else could he do?

It took them the rest of the day, stopping here and there along the route to beg the latest news from men clustered around wireless sets in open air cafés. Nothing was definite, every statement was contradicted five minutes later, nobody really knew what was happening.

By eleven-thirty that night, Freddie had toured the newspaper offices in Paris. What he heard was frightening. A reconnaissance pilot had flown over the Ardennes and seen blue ribbons of light winding for miles through the woods. The forest was alive with motorized convoys. Reports were reaching Paris of paratroops landing *en masse* all over Belgium . . .

Seven days later Sean was still trying to cope with the stories coming out of France. The speed and ferocity of the German advance had been devastating. Sedan had cracked first, bombed into submission by endless waves of Dorniers and Heinkels. Five hundred pound bombs had ripped through solid concrete. French artillery pieces had been upended like toys. French soldiers had run away. And Rotterdam had been bombed into oblivion by a hundred tons of high explosives. Twenty-five thousand people had been incinerated in the flames and the debris. Holland had surrendered.

London was stunned. The Germans had simply ignored the Maginot Line – outflanked it through the Ardennes. Within seven days they had annihilated two French armies, gained a massive foothold in France and nullified the Allied strategic plan. Already the French First Army and the British Expeditionary Force were in retreat.

Sean's life had taken on a new pattern. Every evening he waited for Freddie to telephone from Paris. Sometimes he waited alone, although generally Val and Margaret were there, Margaret tense and anxious hoping for a word with Freddie when he had finished with Sean. Usually the call came through at nine o'clock, but lines from Paris were so uncertain that it could be at any time.

That night it was at ten. Sean's pencil raced to keep up with Freddie's dictation, the American's voice fading in and out, sometimes lost entirely in a crackle of static.

After the report came the personal news. Freddie had bought a car and was leaving Paris in the morning.

'So God knows when you'll hear from me,' Freddie said cheerfully. 'I've got to get out of Paris. The gloom here is unbelievable. I tried to talk to Reynaud this afternoon and got the usual refusal, but I did see something. I was outside his office on the Quai d'Orsay, out in the corridor. They were burning their own files in the courtyard. Can you believe it? The French Foreign Office!'

'So where will you go?' Sean shouted.

'To find Gort's army . . .' Freddie's voice faded and came back. 'Amiens . . . then on from there . . .' crackle obliterated his voice again, '. . . try to call you, but some of the phones in these villages . . .'

'Hello? Freddie? Are you still there?'

Static masked the reply before the line went dead. Sean rattled the receiver in anger. 'Damn. Sorry, Margaret, but –'

'It's all right,' she turned away. 'How did he sound?'

'Fine, on top of the world.' Sean coaxed his voice into confident tones. 'You know Freddie when he's chasing a story. He said he's moving around so might not call tomorrow night.'

'Oh?' She swung back to stare at him, searching his face.

'French telephones,' he shrugged and grinned. 'Sure now, aren't they even worse than in the auld country.'

They let him work for the next half hour, pounding Freddie's story out on his typewriter. Most of it was a bitter comparison of the machinery of war.

'The French are magnificently equipped,' Sean typed, 'to refight World War I. So is the British Expeditionary Force, while in Belgium, King Leopold is defending his country with horse-drawn cannon that Napoleon might have rejected. Unfortunately nobody told the Germans about this historical pageant, so they have arrived with all the weaponry of modern war. General Gort does not possess a single gun with even half the range of the latest German models. Gort's tanks, mainly "Matildas", carry frail two-pounder guns. The German Mark IVs are faster, more manoeuvrable and infinitely more heavily armed. As for air power . . .'

It was yet another slashing attack on the Allied military command. Sean finished quickly and folded the top copy into his pocket.

They walked round to the *Mirror* together, Sean in the middle with Val on one side and Margaret on the other.

'Where is Freddie going?' Margaret asked as she negotiated the blackout.

'Wasn't I asking that when the line went dead. But he'll

be around, nosing into this and that. Sure don't worry your pretty—'

'And don't waste your Irish blarney on me. Besides, I am *not* worrying.'

She was and they all knew it. And Sean was worried too when they reached the *Mirror*. The first thing they were told was that Brussels had fallen.

'Where's the BEF?' Sean asked.

'Somewhere between Brussels and the sea.'

Even with Freddie's latest report it seemed unbelievable. Gort had an army of nearly 400,000 men.

But Sean could picture only one man, driving across France in the face of that ferocious, unstoppable army.

He delivered Freddie's story which, in exchange for being able to use it themselves, the *Mirror* would immediately transmit to New York – then he and Val took Margaret back to the family's suite in the Dorchester.

As soon as he and Val were alone, Sean told her of Freddie's plans to find Gort's army.

Val understood his worry at once. She tried to comfort him. 'That was before Brussels fell. Freddie must know about that now. The news will have reached Paris. He'll change his plans—'

'No,' Sean shook his head. 'Not Freddie. He'll go chasing the biggest story of his life.'

Finding Gort's army had been easy. Freddie simply drove to Amiens and headed for the sound of the guns. By mid-afternoon he had crossed into Belgium. But progress was slower after that.

It was the people, the refugees – a trickle at first, coming towards him, pushing handcarts, wheeling bicycles laden with goodness knows what strapped over the handlebars. Then it was horse-drawn carts so full of possessions that there was no room on the buckboard and the horse was led by its bridle as everyone walked. Then a queue of such carts, and more bicycles, and pack-horses, and donkeys laden until their knees buckled – and dozens of people, scores of people, then hundreds and hundreds.

They came towards him in a flood, an onrushing tide of desperate humanity. Vehicles of every description, piled high with possessions. When an axle collapsed under an overladen cart, people swarmed around it like ants, heaving and straining to clear the road of obstruction. Families wept as their only remaining earthly goods were dumped into a ditch. And still they kept coming – refugees by the thousand, who cast fearful backward glances, or screamed with fear when a Stuka buzzed overhead.

When Freddie drove into Tourcoing he met British soldiers coming from the other end of the town – motorized patrols, hastily clearing the way for Gort's army hard on their heels. He almost collided with one of Gort's adjutants, the very same man who had thrown him out of BEF Headquarters three weeks before. This time, however, Freddie was given a job. His car was requisitioned for use as an ambulance.

Three men bundled themselves into the back and a young officer, whose left leg ended at the knee, was lifted into the front seat. He grinned cheerfully. 'Bloody cheek, swiping your car. Sorry and all that, but the MO says I'm unfit for boots. My name's Harry Hunt by the way.'

It was Hunt who told Freddie where they were going – 'The general idea is to make a retreat to the coast. The Navy is standing by to pick us up.'

But it was not as easy as that.

Val told Margaret that Freddie had gone in search of the BEF. She was sorry afterwards. 'It seemed the best thing to do,' she said later to Sean, 'I thought she would worry less if she knew Freddie was with the Army.'

But a few days later, German advance troops overran Boulogne and besieged Calais, and everyone feared that the entire Army was lost.

Sean did his best to bolster morale. 'Freddie's not a soldier. He's a non-combatant, an American citizen, a neutral observer –'

'As if neutrality worries the Nazis,' Margaret snapped. 'The Danes were neutral, the Norwegians, Belgians . . .'

Waiting for news was agonizing, and news when it came was invariably bad. The House of Commons listened to one grim announcement after another. The situation seemed bleak indeed, until, outside the Chamber, on the terrace overlooking the Thames and in the tea-rooms and bars, men hushed their voices as they talked of a miracle. There was just an outside chance – a million to one perhaps – but a chance . . .

Sean hurried from one meeting to another, asking questions, probing, searching. He and Freddie were popular in Fleet Street. Most people liked the big Irish Navvy, trusted him with confidences, background for a story . . . and thanks to Dinny's training, Sean had never let them down. And by that summer his contacts spread far beyond Fleet Street. He knew the rich of Eaton Square and the poor of Shadwell, and politicians, civil servants, people who made the wheels go round.

Even so, he unravelled the rumours in fragments. In a dockside pub at Shadwell, old Horace Watson talked of his son who was first mate on the *Maidstone Castle*, a collier which hauled coal from Newcastle down to London. 'Requisitioned by the Navy this morning. Going to Belgium, they think. To pick up refugees, Billy reckons.' Horace shook his head, 'But it's for the BEF if you ask me.'

In a shipping office on Leadenhall Street, a hundred yards from George Hamilton's boardroom, another friend, Tim Davis, confirmed that his company had also had a ship requisitioned. 'Buggered if we expect it back either,' he said, 'especially if it is sent to Dunkirk. Calais would have been all right, but Dunkirk . . .' he pulled a face. 'Right ships' graveyard – the most tortuous twenty-five miles of shoal-ridden coastline in the Channel.'

Jimmy Fox, a senior clerk in the Admiralty, said the same thing. 'I'm still praying we can get into Calais. They'll never get the big stuff into Dunkirk. It would mean small boats ferrying men from the beaches out to the ships. They'd need whalers, lifeboats, motor launches – Christ, they'd never do it with nearly four hundred thousand men to get off.'

Three days later Calais fell to the Germans. The BEF was encircled at Dunkirk. Sean was in the House of Commons when Churchill rose. The green leather benches were packed tight by grey-faced men who listened to Churchill in shocked silence. After a brave fight and an unequal struggle, the Belgians had thrown in their hand,

and the Prime Minister warned – 'The House should prepare itself for hard and heavy tidings . . .'

That could only mean the BEF. Gort's army was done for.

Jimmy Fox was in despair at the Admiralty. Sean overheard him talking to a Rear Admiral. 'Well, how many small boats *do* you want?' the Admiral asked in exasperation, 'a hundred?'

'Look, sir, not a hundred,' Jimmy's voice was tight with emotion. 'Every bloody boat in the country needs to go even to have half a chance.'

Afterwards, alone with Sean, Jimmy confirmed that the Admiralty had compiled a register of small boats only weeks before. 'But they're not using it yet. They're requisitioning trawlers and Christ knows what. It's not trawlers they'll need, it's small boats and the crews to go with them.' He groaned and put his head in his hands, 'It's bloody hopeless.'

Sean left him and went back to Craven Street. The empty house seemed unwelcoming and gloomy. Val had a committee meeting in the East End, war-work of some kind, he knew she would stay in Shadwell overnight. He thought he might go there later, but she would not be home until nearly eleven. He needed to go out. Every room reminded him of Freddie and made him feel guilty.

Eventually he went by bus to Marble Arch and walked down to the Dorchester, with the vague idea of seeing Margaret. She had not been round for a few days. He liked to keep an eye on her, cheer her up, make her laugh when he could. God, he owed Freddie that much. Funny how Margaret had changed. Even before Freddie went to France she had become more thoughtful, less inclined to spend time with her old crowd, in fact she had dropped most of them.

But Margaret was not at the Dorchester. Instead, when Sean announced himself at the desk, Cynthia invited him up for a sherry. Although she was dressed for dinner and as immaculate as ever, she was clearly anxious about something. Sean was nervous himself. He always was with Cynthia, and not just because of his relationship with her daughter. Cynthia Hamilton, more than anyone, represented a privileged world which seemed forever beyond Sean's grasp, no matter how far he climbed from the Quays.

They were quite alone. George had been detained at the office – but Cynthia was not worrying about her husband. 'I'm glad you're here,' she said, 'and it was kind of you to think of Margaret.' Her emphatic use of certain words was muted compared to the way she flayed them at parties. Even so, the habit was still there. 'Margaret is on the *Samantha*. She's taking her up to Greenwich all by herself. I *can't tell you* how frantic I am.'

After that the whole story came out. How the previous evening George had recounted the rumours about the need for small boats, and how Margaret had left for Staines at the crack of dawn.

Cynthia toyed with the stem of her glass. 'George said if the Navy needed small boats they would take them over at Greenwich. I don't know, Margaret's getting so stubborn these days, quite as bad as her sister.' She shot Sean a quick glance, then hurried on, 'What frightens me is her taking the boat further down the estuary. She said she'd telephone when she reached Greenwich. I still haven't heard a word . . .'

Sean took a while to work out the details, but once he had established that Margaret was unlikely to have got beyond Greenwich he agreed to go there at once. It was what Cynthia wanted and she expressed relief at his offer. He finished a second sherry and, promising to telephone her later, hurried out into the evening's gathering gloom. Walking briskly to Green Park Underground, he reflected on the changes being wrought by the war – Cynthia Hamilton living at the Dorchester, worrying about her daughters, one on a boat and the other working in the East End, while husband George stayed over in the City. Changes were happening, and with gathering speed. The British were shaking off their apathy, he thought, and planned to say so in his CBS broadcast and his weekend article for the *Gazette*.

Apathy was the last thing he found at Greenwich. The river was jammed with boats, many moored sideways to form a solid raft stretching into the middle of the Thames. Sean cursed himself for running a fool's errand. It would be impossible to find Margaret on the *Samantha*. Hundreds of people were milling about along the wharfs. But it was astonishingly easy when he started to ask. A river policeman directed him, 'You want to see Captain Wheelan of the Small Boats' Pool. He's got dozens of owners down there at the pilots' office.'

Sean never found Captain Wheelan. He ran into Margaret almost immediately. She was dressed in oilskins and drinking tea from an enamel mug, talking to a group of men wearing duffle coats. She saw Sean as he approached and hurried to meet him. 'Oh thank God you've come. We're off in another ten minutes.'

She had telephoned her mother, learned Sean was on his way, and hoped against hope that he would make it in time. 'The Navy want these boats in Ramsgate by the morning, but they're making the most stupid fuss about me being a woman.' She gave him the mug to hold while she fumbled through her pockets. 'Here, sign this form. It makes you *Samantha*'s owner. Then you can take me as crew.'

The BEF fought down a corridor fifty miles long and fifteen miles wide to reach the thousand-year-old port of Dunkirk. And Dunkirk was a trap, Freddie Mallon was certain of that. Not that he said so, he was too tired to say anything – Second Lieutenant Harry Hunt did the talking for both of them most of the time. In the ten days since their meeting, Freddie had come to regard Hunt as being either certifiably mad or the bravest man in the war. 'The trouble is,' Freddie grumbled, 'my chance of staying alive would be much better with a coward.'

Hunt grinned, 'You're a reporter, aren't you. I'm giving you something to report –'

'To whom? Archangel Gabriel?'

Of course Freddie could have opted out. When they reached Dunkirk that first time from Tourcoing he could have refused to go back for more wounded. But Hunt had pleaded – 'I know we can only bring three men in at a time, but even one would be worthwhile.'

So they had daubed the car with Red Cross markings and Freddie Mallon became an ambulance driver. He worried about Hunt's leg at times. 'If you stayed behind I could bring four men each trip. Did you think about that?'

Hunt was stubborn. 'You've no authority without an officer. You'll run into trouble without me –'

'I'll run into trouble *with* you, that's certain.'

The first week had been bad. Stukas dive-bombed from dawn till dusk, and when bomb-bays were empty they screamed low across the fields to strafe columns of men with machine-gun fire. Gort's troops were powerless to hit back – without anti-aircraft guns, without air cover – they just had to take it.

The British pulled back. Sappers laid mines under bridges and across roads as they evacuated one position after another. Whole villages were devastated. In ruined cottages and gutted barns huddled the now homeless Belgians, who had welcomed the British with open arms two weeks before. Priests had blessed the army as it streamed past on its way to the front. Now the British were in full retreat. Signs of surrender appeared everywhere, white handkerchiefs fluttered on sticks, bedsheets hung from windows, and ashen-faced Belgians watched Gort's army with hostile, bitter eyes.

'Poor devils,' Harry Hunt said. 'They'll end up hating us as much as the Germans.'

If the first week had been bad, the days which followed were hell. The flanks of the corridor were being whittled away. In the south, the 3rd Grenadier Guards and the North Staffs fought desperately to hold a line on the Ypres –Comines Canal. Losses were appalling. The 13,000 strong 2nd Division was reduced to 2500 men. It was the same in the north. Like a hangman's noose the perimeter of the escape route was drawn tighter.

Through it all Freddie and Harry Hunt drove back and forth ferrying wounded men into Dunkirk. At night they slept, when they slept at all, in a field hospital close to the sea-front, where the groans and screams of the maimed almost drowned the thunder of guns. And at dawn came the Stukas, with the whistling scream of their bombs. Every morning was the same, and Hunt's response was the same. As soon as the stump of his leg had been dressed, he strapped on his revolver, and was carried out to the car. 'Come on good shepherd,' he called to Freddie, 'let's round up some stray sheep.'

Finding stray sheep was easy. The British streamed over the countryside in the strangest retreat ever seen. Some came on bicycles, some pushed their wounded in wheelbarrows, a bombardier drove a tractor towing a gun, twenty men journeyed in a Brussels garbage truck, eight more crammed into a taxi. An Artillery sergeant rode a white hunter twenty hands high. They arrived in farm trucks and wagons and on litters drawn by cattle. But most of them walked, stumbling with fatigue on feet misshapen by huge blisters, with blood seeping through the soles of their boots. And they came in their thousands into Dunkirk.

Freddie drove across that battleground every day. The landscape changed. Roads were pockmarked by new craters, short-cuts were blocked by smoking debris, no single route lasted more than one journey. Freddie pulled men out of ditches and dug others from under rubble, while Hunt ordered men to help, sometimes at gun-point. Twice he refused to allow senior officers to commandeer Freddie's car. 'Sorry, sir. You'll have to walk. This vehicle is for wounded men only.' Three times they were strafed by machine-gun fire. Once the car was lifted into the air by an explosion. But they kept going. When the radiator boiled dry they solemnly relieved themselves into a watering can, filled the radiator and drove on. Every day they managed about thirty sorties into that smoking wilderness. Every day their journeys were just that little bit shorter. They were grimly aware of the reason. The advancing Germans were always closer.

The night of 28 May was the worst of all. The day had been horrendous. The Luftwaffe had dropped 30,000 incendiaries and 15,000 high-explosive bombs, and as darkness crept over the land, Hitler's ground forces opened up as never before. All night long their artillery pounded the coast from Dunkirk to La Panne, nine miles away. By morning, black smoke from St Pol's burning oil refineries enveloped the harbour. Flames swept through miles of warehouses. Food stocks were exhausted. Nobody had had fresh water in four days. Only one telephone line remained open to London. One hundred and fifteen acres of docks and five miles of quays had been pulverized into rubble. Corpses of men and women and children littered the streets.

Freddie felt a thousand years old. His bones ached and his face itched beneath its stubble of beard. He watched dawn lighten the sky before he rose wearily from his place on the floor just inside the field hospital. Stiff-limbed he walked to the door. Once outside he sniffed the air and turned his eyes to the sea. Sand dunes heaved like ant hills as thousands of soldiers shivered in the chill air. Those who were awake did as Freddie did – they looked out to sea.

Ships were not easily found on water the colour of gunmetal, especially with a grey sky behind them. They were there though – dark smudges a mile out from the shore. The ships of the Royal Navy. Freddie's eyes probed the morning light to focus on the smaller specks of lifeboats coming into the shore. He sighed with relief. He counted them – ten, eleven, twelve. Better than last night, when he had counted only nine. Rumour said that 7500 men had been lifted from the beaches yesterday. He smiled wryly. 7500 men out of 390,000. It would take more than a month at that rate. Nobody seemed to have figured that out.

Half an hour later the Stukas attacked, but Freddie had left the beach by then. He and Harry Hunt were already a mile out of Dunkirk, driving south on a hair-raising run towards the Ypres–Comines Canal.

They had argued the night before. Harry's leg had racked him with pain, and Freddie had shouted at him. 'For God's sake! It's time you packed up. Get down by the beach. They must take the wounded off first –'

'What about you, Yank?' Hunt had cracked back. 'It's not even your bloody war.'

One last day, they had agreed.

And this was to be it.

The Thames estuary was clogged with small boats. Sean had never seen so many. Wherever he looked he saw boats – all going the same way, down to the sea. But not *out* to sea. They hugged the coastline to slip past the Isle of Sheppey and in again towards Whitstable. 'There's Herne Bay over there,' Margaret pointed.

They had talked all night, with Margaret at the wheel while Sean brewed coffee on a spirit stove in the galley. When dawn rose out of the sea they had waved cheerful good mornings to the crew in the boats on either side. They had talked of the war and of people they knew – and confessed their first impressions of each other.

'You frightened me to death,' Margaret giggled. 'What with that black scowl of yours. I think even Val was a bit daunted to begin with.'

He lacked the courage to admit he had been just as afraid, although his fumbling recollections went part of the way – 'You seemed so . . . so aloof, inaccessible. Too damn good-looking, I suppose. And stinking rich. I didn't know what to say to you.'

'Now we've spent the night together,' she joked in a sad-sounding voice, with her eyes dead ahead as she adjusted the wheel.

It was their first time alone with each other. Each saw the other differently. A barrier had existed before. Margaret's reservations about Sean's relationship with her sister may have remained unspoken, but they had been felt. Just as he had felt sour at times about the way she treated Freddie. Now – after spending twelve hours together in a cramped cockpit, bumping into each other, sharing a dozen small intimacies – the barrier fell away. It was Margaret who breached it. 'You know I've never slept with him,' she said softly. 'That's what I regret. I wish I had Val's courage and wasn't so bloody conventional. God, I've been a little fool. To hell with convention, and to hell with this war. Damn and blast it,' she swore to stifle her tears.

The outburst passed, until a while later, she said in a voice full of strain, 'Why on earth didn't he stay in Paris? Or better still come home two weeks ago.'

Sean provided what reassurances he could. He remembered overhearing a Navy man at Greenwich, 'Didn't he say they've been lifting men off that beach for twenty-four hours already? I bet Freddie's back in London by now, raising hell about me being away with his girl.'

She slid him a quick look of gratitude. 'I suppose there's just a chance –'

'Or maybe he's waiting at Ramsgate,' Sean grinned.

He invented a dozen places where Freddie might be, anywhere and everywhere except the beach at Dunkirk. He made a game of it and laughed so uproariously that she had to join in. The tension eased for a while, but the haunted look stayed in her eyes.

After sailing past Margate and skirting the North Foreland, they sighted Broadstairs and finally Ramsgate itself. The bay was already full of boats, all sorts, hundreds of boats, many built for short-run river work, never designed for the sea. A Navy launch buzzed back and forth, directing newcomers like a collie rounding up sheep. Margaret slowed *Samantha*'s engines to nose between a Thames barge and a sleek cabin cruiser with *Anthony's Mermaid* emblazoned in silver letters on its stern. Sean was glad that Margaret had to concentrate on the boat instead of worrying about Freddie – but the respite was brief. Twenty minutes later they were moored and Margaret was anxious to get ashore in search of news.

They spent all afternoon listening to rumours. Another 17,000 men had been lifted from Dunkirk, making about 25,000 in two days. Margaret looked sick. More than 350,000 men remained trapped on the French coast – and she felt sure that Freddie was among them.

'You don't know that,' Sean kept saying.

'Well where else could he be?'

She telephoned her mother, while Sean contacted the *Mirror* – neither had heard from Freddie. The man at the *Mirror* confirmed that some of the rescued troops had already arrived in London. 'Some of their stories make your blood run cold,' he said in awed tones. 'It must be hell on earth over there.'

The atmosphere in Ramsgate was electric. The town was full of weekend sailors all saying the same thing – 'Let's go across and fetch them ourselves.' But the Navy refused to allow that. The weather held fine. More small boats crammed into the harbour, arriving from points all along the south coast . . .

Sean bumped into Peter Nicholls of the *Express* and Tubby Reynolds of the *Standard*. Both had boats and were waiting to sail if the order was given – and both agreed with Sean and Margaret. They took her for a meal in a pub that

414

evening and told her so – 'Look, the Navy's hemming and hawing about *us*,' Tubby said. 'They certainly wouldn't allow you to go. And as Freddie's friends, neither will we.'

Margaret tried to reason with them. 'Nurses went over on a hospital ship this morning. If they can go, so can I. Besides, I can handle a boat a darn sight better than any of you.'

Peter Nicholls tried to describe what it would be like, relating what he had heard from his office.

Tubby joined in, 'The Navy can't even guarantee we'll get back.'

Margaret looked stricken. She was quiet for a moment, before saying, 'I'm not sure I would want to come back, without Freddie.'

Sean had never seen anyone so determined. Her hands were steady. Her voice calmer than it had been on the *Samantha* earlier.

Nicholls and Reynolds went off to the Small Boats' Pool in search of news, making it quite clear that they expected Sean to force her to see sense. He tried, but Margaret had made up her mind. She was going to find Freddie. 'Even if I can't find him,' she said, 'just the *Samantha* being there increases his chances. You heard that man at Greenwich, they want every small boat they can get.'

'So okay. Send the *Samantha*. You can stay here –'

'And who'll skipper her? You?'

They both knew he lacked the experience. 'I'll find someone –'

'Don't be ridiculous,' she snapped. 'Anyone who knows port from starboard is already involved.'

Her voice softened to a plea. 'Sean, I'm begging you. Tell the Small Boats' Pool that you're taking her across. Once I'm out there in oilskins they won't know I'm not you. Please, Sean, do it for Freddie, if not for me. You don't have to come.'

He sighed hopelessly. If anything happened to her Freddie would hate him forever. If anything happened to Freddie she would hate him. If anything happened to either of them he would blame himself for the rest of his life.

Reynolds returned at that moment. 'They won't let us go tonight. It might be on for tomorrow though, unless the RN makes a dent in the numbers.' He slumped into a chair and looked hard at Sean, 'Well, have you resolved the problem?'

Sean took a deep breath. 'Yes,' he said, without elaborating.

Margaret said nothing at all, and shortly afterwards they wished Reynolds goodnight and left. Ramsgate lay pitch black under a night sky. Not a single light showed in the blackout. She held his hand as they walked through the darkened streets. Half an hour later they were back on *Samantha*.

'Well?' she asked. 'And have we resolved the problem?'

He was about to reply when they heard a deep rumbling in the distance.

'Thunder,' she whispered.

But she was wrong. It was the barrage of the German guns, twenty miles across the water.

The Grenadiers had held the eight-mile front along the Ypres–Comines Canal, at the cost of a thousand dead and three thousand wounded. Freddie closed his eyes to obliterate the past fifteen hours. Deafening explosions denied any chance of sleep. Even to close his eyes was a mistake. Memories revived with searing clarity, sights he would never forget if he lived to be a hundred – which seemed very unlikely.

Dunkirk outdid Dante's Inferno. Shell-shocked men roamed the waterfront, looting, pillaging, raping – even picking dead men's pockets. Some went mad. A man raced through the dunes screaming, 'Lord have mercy on us.' Another, stripped to a loincloth, pranced in circles, raving that he was Mahatma Gandhi. Discipline was non-existent in parts of the town. Defeat and shame bred anarchy. Bands of renegade soldiers, deserted by panic-stricken officers, prowled the streets in a mood of ugly violence. Men with lipstick-smeared faces ransacked shop windows for women's clothes. Many were drunk. Others blundered about, staring with sightless eyes, clutching children's teddy bears while weeping hysterically. Not since Corunna, more than a hundred years before, had a British army fallen back like this – leaving such ruin in its wake.

416

Yet there were others who risked their lives over and over again – men who drove ammunition trucks up to the front line, racing the gauntlet of dive-bombers and shell-fire – and men like Harry Hunt, who seemed not to know the meaning of fear.

Freddie's makeshift ambulance delivered fifty-four wounded men to the beach that day – before the Stuka got them. They were strafed by machine-gun fire and when that failed to stop them, the Stuka climbed high and swept back with the last of his bombs. The car leaped into the air, bucked, turned over and landed on its side. Freddie pulled Harry Hunt to the safety of a stone wall seconds before the wreckage was engulfed by fire.

Both men were shaken, bruised, blackened by smoke – but alive. They remained propped by that wall for at least an hour, smoking the last of Freddie's cigarettes. Neither said much. It was hardly peaceful. A few miles away the artillery pounded incessantly, while Stukas wheeled and screamed down over the harbour like a swarm of angry wasps.

Eventually Harry Hunt roused himself. 'You know Yank,' he said, 'if you had turned left, that pilot would have missed us completely.'

Freddie managed a tired smile. 'That's right, I did it on purpose. Do you think we can go now? Sit on the beach with the others? The idea of a sea cruise is very appealing.'

In ordinary times they would have made an odd sight, but in that place on that day they were just another pair of defeated soldiers. Even Freddie was a soldier from the waist up, wearing a steel helmet and a torn battle-dress blouse. He fashioned a crutch from the timbers of a gutted barn, took one of Hunt's arms over his shoulder, and together they staggered towards the beaches of Dunkirk.

To talk meant shouting over the barrage, and what with the strain of walking, hopping in Hunt's case, they lacked the breath. Freddie prayed he could get Hunt on to a ship, prayed without hope. The beaches were thick with thousands of men. The big ships were too far out. The small boats could never work fast enough. The Germans were closing. It was only a matter of time.

Freddie feared death, but not capture. After all, his

American passport was still in his pocket. And even if Paris fell, surely the American Embassy would still function? Besides, there were men in Berlin who would vouch for him – men who would verify he was a neutral observer, a foreign correspondent. Harry Hunt, on the other hand, would get different treatment.

It took them six hours to reach the waterfront. Hunt was exhausted. Freddie left him being doctored at a field station and went to survey the situation on the beaches. His heart sank. Medical men were working waist deep, hoisting stretchers high over their heads as they struggled to reach the lifeboats. Endless lines of soldiers stretched far out into the water, some of them chest deep, waiting and hoping their turn would come soon. And behind them were the men on the beaches – thousands of men, in long queues as far as the eye could see . . .

By nightfall Freddie and Harry Hunt were dug into the sand dunes. They had not eaten for twenty-four hours, nor had a drink, nor washed their stubbled faces. Freddie had managed to trade his watch for some cigarettes, but had failed to find even a crumb of food.

'You did splendidly,' Hunt said. 'I'd rather smoke than eat anyway.'

They talked the night away. When the thunderous roar of the guns made talking impossible, they just smoked and watched the night sky. Freddie felt amazingly calm. He thanked Hunt for that, Hunt had so much courage that somehow it rubbed off. Even so, it was the longest night of Freddie's life. He found himself talking about Margaret and his hope to marry her after the war, and about life in London, life at Craven Street with young Sean Connors.

'Irish?' Hunt queried. 'Another neutral?'

'Okay, I know, nobody should be neutral about Hitler. Some people just need more time . . .' His words were drowned by a massive explosion. Fifty yards behind them a warehouse gutted by fire finally collapsed.

'Time is running out,' Hunt observed grimly.

And it was. As dawn lit the eastern sky Stukas streaked in to meet it, flying low from the west, howling down to attack the ships crowding the coastline. Within minutes the sky was thick with aircraft. Water spouts shot out of the

418

sea. Men flattened themselves into foxholes.

But Freddie's hopes rose as he counted the ships. More had arrived than ever before. At the east end of the harbour, no fewer than eleven ships had edged in close enough for men to board from a long wooden gangway.

Harry Hunt was shouting and pointing the other way – six more ships were taking on men to the west of the harbour. Within the harbour itself, the inshore waters swarmed with destroyers, their guns blazing defiance at the dive-bombers . . . and even closer to the shore, all sorts of craft were plying furiously back and forth with their human cargoes. The battle, it seemed, was not over yet.

The evacuation went on all day. The harbour was an inferno. Sand quaked with the force of the bombing. Men smothered in foxholes were dug out by friends. Offshore vast columns of water geysered 100 feet high as more bombs screamed down from the Stukas. The destroyer *Grenade* was hit, one bomb falling directly down her funnel, and sailors floundered across decks greasy with blood. Quickly a trawler took the stricken ship in tow, pulling her clear of the harbour entrance before her magazine ignited. A thousand rounds of ammunition went sky high with such violence that nobody could hear the explosion of falling bombs.

Harry Hunt found a new mode of transport. Carried on a stretcher he went up and down the dunes, rallying some men and calming others.

When an hysterical sergeant overturned the stretcher, Freddie Mallon came from nowhere to knock the man cold.

Harry found a soldier from his own unit and after a shouted exchange the man whipped a bugle to his lips and began to play 'Land of Hope and Glory'.

Stukas screamed low over the beaches, strafing columns of men everywhere with murderous machine-gun fire. Soldiers blazed back with the only weapons they had, their rifles. Other men threw themselves on the ground. But most of them simply kept marching, slowly but surely down to the sea. Miraculously Harry Hunt found four more bandsmen. Now the sound of 'Land of Hope and Glory' thundered across the sand dunes, drowned now and then by the staccato chatter of anti-aircraft fire from the destroyers, overwhelmed completely at times by shuddering explosions . . . before, triumphantly, the music soared forth again.

Freddie watched in amazement as Harry Hunt swung round on his stretcher and started to sing, waving his arms like a demented conductor. Above them the sky was black with aircraft. Behind them, German artillery were shelling the town. Harry Hunt was at least three miles up the beach from his one slender chance of rescue, the ships on the east pier – yet he was roaring out 'Land of Hope and Glory' as if he were at the Royal Albert Hall. Bombs were falling like rain. Freddie, who now expected to die, found himself singing at the top of his voice, and, amidst the smoke and noise of that hell on earth, 'Land of Hope and Glory' rang out more defiantly than ever before.

Even as Freddie sang and clung forlornly to the hope of a miracle, the miracle had started. For two whole days boats had been assembling in the small fishing port of Ramsgate. They came from Exeter and Portsmouth, Dover and Colchester, they came down the tidal waters of the Thames and the Test, they came from boatyards all along the south coast – and they were on their way.

'Steer for the sound of the guns,' was the order – and they did.

It was the most incredible armada of small boats the world had ever seen – barges, motor launches, salt-stained trawlers, sleek cabin cruisers, tugs and lifeboats – a massive fleet of a thousand tiny craft. Distant gunfire reverberated over the waves with the thunder of a kettle-drum, as the small boats ploughed through the water with desperate speed.

In the cockpit of *Samantha* Margaret Hamilton shouted with pride as she recognized boats belonging to friends. 'Look,' she screamed at Sean, 'there's Tommy Watkins in *Flying Fish* . . . and look there, that's Betty Marshall's father, that one, *The Hornet*, can you see?'

There were boats on every quarter. Margaret shouted a commentary as she recognized Tom Sopwith's famous racing yacht *Endeavour*, then pointed to the old Isle of

Wight car ferry, the *Wootton*, wallowing through the water behind them.

Still the boats streamed across the Channel. Tubby Reynolds waved from his motor launch, while Sean tried in vain to spot Peter Nicholls aboard his yacht *Newsflash*.

Margaret checked her wheel and took up station between the fishing trawler *Jacinta*, reeking of cod, and the good launch *Count Dracula* which had once belonged to a German admiral.

So they had sailed into Dunkirk. Had Sean imagined anything a tenth as terrible nothing would have induced him to involve Margaret Hamilton. Flames leaped ten thousand feet high and a mile wide from the blitzed oil terminus. Air reeked of cordite and smoke and rancid oil. Terrible sounds floated out of the fog and smoke; klaxons blasted, men screamed and shouted, the guns thundered incessantly, and once, incongruously, Sean thought he heard a snatch of men singing 'Land of Hope and Glory' from a point far down the sands.

'Follow me, *Samantha*,' bellowed a naval rating from a passing launch.

Margaret swung the wheel. Sean glimpsed her face, white and determined under the oilskin pulled down over her head. No time left for talking. They were going in – towards the long piers jutting out into the chill grey water. Sean gasped. Those piers were not piers at all, they were men, thousands of men, standing chest deep in the sea, waiting for the boats.

He lost all sense of time after that. He forgot his vow to protect Margaret, forgot Freddie, forgot everything. He became a machine. As the boat edged in his hand grasped the first soldier and hauled, dragging him in, groaning at the weight of sodden greatcoat and equipment. Other hands gripped the gunnels. Sean heaved them aboard, shouting at them to help their mates still in the water. He pulled another man in, then another and another after him. His arms were almost wrenched loose from their sockets. Then Margaret was turning the boat, gathering speed, and slowing down again as they came alongside one of the ships.

Up the men went, clutching ladders, ropes and hands

thrust down from the rails – with Sean pushing from behind. Then the boat was turning back for the shore and Sean was gathering his strength to start all over again.

He saw faces, fear, wounds, uniforms, rifles – everything was a blur. Only on each journey back, as his chest heaved and he massaged aching muscles, did he risk a quick glance at the miles of beaches, all crawling with men, winding back like serpents over the sandhills and into the mist.

The noise was colossal – the screaming of bombs, crashing anti-aircraft fire from the destroyers, klaxons blaring on ships around them, men in the water shouting for help.

After about four hours the Navy launch returned – 'Everything all right, *Samantha*?' In a reflex action Sean grabbed a man's arms to pull him aboard – it was instinctive, see a face, hear a shout, lean out and pull. The sailor struggled free, 'You're exhausted. Take half an hour out.' He turned, shouting and pointing at Margaret, 'Skipper, pull over by the *Thanet Rose*. Come back as soon as you can.'

They rested because they had to. Margaret, dog-tired by hours of concentration, was drained. They made a hot drink in the galley, shared a bar of chocolate, smoked a cigarette, smiled wanly – and started back. No effort was made to shout above the booming artillery. What was there to say anyway? Neither of them had seen Freddie. Both were frightened, and sickened by the sights they had seen.

Samantha curved away from the *Thanet Rose*. They passed a pinnace manned by teenage Sea Scouts. Behind that, barely visible in the swirling mist, came a Thames barge with russet sails and massive oars. Both boats were low in the water, overladen with their human cargo. Margaret slid expertly past and followed an oyster-dredger from Whitstable back to the beaches of Dunkirk.

Men ashore were trying to help. Sappers in 30-cwt trucks careened down the beach and into the sea until waves washed over the leading vehicles. Other men worked desperately, lashing planks to the truck roofs to fashion jetties twenty yards long. Soon troops were marching three abreast along the rickety gangways in yet another effort to reach the small boats.

Night fell but darkness changed nothing. Men still crowded the jetties and waded deep into the sea. Small boats plied frantically back and forth.

Harry Hunt had restored a sense of discipline to the fifty men clustered around him. By sending out scavenging parties he had even found food and a field cooker. At midnight he and Freddie ate a sausage and tomato served hot into their hands. Further down the beach men were slaughtering French cavalry horses for food.

Predictably, at dawn, the Stukas returned in a last desperate bid to drive the boats from the shore. The crescendo of noise tore eardrums apart. Great plumes of water rose all over the harbour. Skippers aboard small boats fought their wheels to stay on course. Six dive-bombers pounded the old destroyer *Worcester* until she staggered from the harbour in flames. Yet she limped out into the Channel to meet a glorious, unbelievable sight. Swarming over the water towards her came more of England's small boats – barges and yachts, lifeboats and tugs, a powerful cabin cruiser with six dinghies in tow. The impossible rescue was set to continue!

Sean Connors and Margaret Hamilton rested at three-hour intervals, pulling out of the chain for fifteen-minute breaks. Both were on the verge of collapse. Like people in shock, too tired for shouted conversation, too tired to think or to plan. At mid-morning Margaret burst into tears. *Samantha* was almost out of fuel. The tanks held barely enough to continue, let alone get back across the Channel. Sean comforted her while trying to coax a solution from his numbed mind. His head throbbed, his body ached all over.

The Navy provided a tow. *Samantha* went back to the beaches roped behind a launch . . . and returned to the ships . . . and went back to the beaches . . . while all the time Stukas rained death from the skies.

At noon Harry Hunt was on one of the piers constructed by the Sappers. He had lost his crutch and was supported by Freddie Mallon on one side and a Sergeant Major on the other. Freddie could not believe their turn had come – not even when he and Harry fell into a flat-bottomed coal barge with fifty men on top of them. It was not until ten minutes later, when rescued French soldiers heaved Freddie aboard a battle-scarred minesweeper, that Freddie regained his faith in miracles. For the first time in twenty-four hours he dared to think of Margaret Hamilton in London.

Back came the Stukas. The sky was dark with two hundred German planes.

Samantha was sinking. Strafed from stem to stern, she listed sluggishly to starboard, threatening to capsize at every second. Sean, hugging a wounded man upright, fought his way along the crowded deck to where Margaret was jammed tight against the cockpit. Ahead the skipper of the towing launch glanced anxiously over his shoulder as he raced to reach the nearest ship before *Samantha* sank.

'Sean!' Margaret screamed as the deck slid from under her.

He reached her as the sea came to claim them.

'Sean!'

They hit the water together, the wounded man slipping from Sean's grasp.

'Sean!' Margaret spluttered, spitting oily salt water.

The minesweeper *Otter* loomed mountainous above them. Rescued men leapt from the rails to rescue others. Ropes snaked down from fore and aft. Ladders dangled at midships.

Sean got Margaret to a ladder. She had lost her hat. Long hair clung to her skull like a helmet. Hands reached down to grip her wrists.

'Bloody hell, it's a woman,' someone shouted.

Still in the water, Sean turned to search for the wounded soldier. Margaret continued to scream, 'Sean! Where are you, Sean!' A man spluttered to the surface and propelled Sean to the rope ladder – 'We've got the other one,' he shouted. Sean clung to the sodden rope, hoping 'other one' meant the wounded man, but too weary to protest.

Harry Hunt said, 'My God, they've pulled a woman out of the water.'

They craned their necks, but the ship's superstructure blocked their view. Men crammed tight on all sides restricted their movement.

As the *Otter* swung laboriously towards the Channel, the entire panorama of the devastated harbour was put on display. Tongues of orange flame leaped from the

424

warehouses, forking up into the pall of smoke which hung in clouds over the sand dunes. Even above the minesweeper the air reeked of cordite and putrid horseflesh.

The *Otter* turned out to sea, skirting the forest of sunken masts and superstructures at the harbour entrance. Alongside them sailed other vessels – a tug, almost invisible under hordes of men who clung to every inch of her like ants on a jamjar – a yacht, designed for a crew of five and carrying forty – a narrow canal barge which had never before seen the sea – and beyond those were other boats – boats and boats and boats.

So they journeyed back to England, inching into Dover late that afternoon to discover a ships' graveyard. Crippled vessels littered the entire waterfront. But the atmosphere was not that of a graveyard. A frantic army of craftsmen – engineers, carpenters, riveters – worked feverishly in the fading light to repair the damage. And even as the *Otter* came in, another minesweeper sailed out, patches of rough metal showing all over her, battered, unbowed, and seaworthy once more.

An Embarkation officer hailed the Captain of the *Otter* from the quay – 'How many aboard?'

Back went the reply, amplified by a megaphone – 'Five hundred and nine men – and one woman!'

The ripple of astonishment gave way to laughter, and laughter gave way to cheers.

They were home.

Margaret clung to Sean's hand. It seemed unbelievable to be home in one piece, to have come out of that murderous inferno. Yet even as the cheers rang out she could think only of Freddie.

Then she saw him, down on the quay. She was hallucinating surely? The strain, shock . . . The man turned at the bottom of the gangway helping another man, a man with one leg. Freddie? With a face as black as hers and dressed in rags?

She choked on his name, unable to say it aloud. She tugged Sean's hand and whimpered, 'Look, down there. Is it . . .'

The man below glanced up at the *Otter*, narrowing his

eyes as if committing every bullet hole to memory. Suddenly his eyes opened wide. He saw Sean. Then he was shouting and Sean was shouting back . . . and Freddie was fighting his way up the gangway . . .

Laughter and tears, embracing and back-slapping, questions and unfinished sentences – even that was not the end of that incredible day. Val and Cynthia Hamilton had met every ship. George Hamilton himself was on the quay.

Dover went mad. It was a carnival town, with flags and bunting, and 'Well done, BEF' daubed on walls everywhere. Sean and Margaret and Freddie Mallon were part of a miracle. More than 300,000 men had been lifted from the beaches of Dunkirk. Even after the *Otter* other boats sailed in, bringing yet more survivors, to be greeted by brass bands playing 'See the Conquering Heroes Come', and garlands of flowers and singing in the streets.

'Bloody Marvellous!' screamed the headline in the *Daily Mirror*.

'So it was,' Freddie agreed when he could speak.

CHAPTER EIGHT

'We shall defend our island whatever the cost may be. We shall fight on the beaches, we shall fight on the landing grounds . . . in the streets, we shall fight in the hills . . .' The voice from the radio rose to a thunderclap, 'We shall NEVER surrender!'

Kate watched Aunt Eleanor shake her head in a gesture of mute admiration.

'. . . and even if,' Churchill continued, 'which I do not for a moment believe, this Island . . . were subjugated or starving, then our Empire beyond the seas . . . would carry on the struggle . . .'

'I wonder?' Uncle Ned said dryly.

'Sssh,' Aunt Eleanor waved a hand impatiently.

Kate rose from her chair and tiptoed to the door as Churchill thundered '. . . until, in God's time, the New World, with all its power and might . . .'

'He means us,' Uncle Ned pointed an accusing finger at the radio. 'The same old pitch. The British are in a mess and we are expected to pull them out of it.'

Kate closed the door noiselessly. Not that she expected Uncle Ned or Aunt Eleanor to notice – they were too absorbed with the radio and their news. Grown-ups pretended games were for children, but Kate had learned otherwise.

She had learned that lesson during the awful voyage out from England. The ship had pitched about on storm-tossed seas for days. Nazi submarines were rumoured to be tracking them. Yet even those were not the most frightening aspects of that terrible journey. Kate was tormented by the prospects of exile. She was being banished. Tim was being taken to Ulster, but she was being sent away. 'Have I done something wrong?' she asked a dozen times over. 'Am I being punished?'

Never had Kate felt more like an orphan – never more alone in the world. On the second night out from England, she had sobbed for her mother for the first time since the Killing at Keady.

She had tried so hard to please her guardian, only for him to send her away. 'I want my princess to be safe,' he had said. But suppose that were an excuse? Suppose she had not pleased him enough? Suppose it was a punishment?

'Men always punish women,' Rose Smith had sniffed. 'Don't worry. I love you, my darling. I'll look after you for ever and ever.'

Which is when they had played Rose's game in the cabin. Nobody was ever to know about that. It was their secret – a strange, bewildering game which gave Rose so much pleasure that they played it again and again.

Kate had been terrified. She was in her berth, sobbing broken-heartedly – when Rose Smith drew back the bedclothes and climbed in beside her. Next minute Rose was kissing her on the lips . . . and making strange moaning noises . . . 'Rose loves you, my darling . . . come on, do what babies do, suck there.'

Kate butted at the breast like a calf at an udder.

After which they did more peculiar things. Kate did

them to please. She would face goodness knows what in America. She was afraid to face them alone. Besides, orphans had to please, otherwise . . . the 'otherwise' made her shudder. Rose threatened to desert her. If Kate told anyone of their game, she would be abandoned in America and sent to an orphanage. That was a terrifying prospect – so frightening that from that moment on Kate resolved to please everyone as often as possible. It was the only way an orphan could be safe.

Which was much on her mind when the ship eventually docked in New York. They arrived to a battery of flashbulbs, brass bands and Douglas Fairbanks the actor – all lined up to welcome the thirty-five refugee children on the passenger list. Kate's smile adorned the front page of the evening papers – 'Fairbanks greets young English war beauty'. Few readers guessed that the smile concealed a mass of insecurities – nor did the people of Dayton, Ohio, when Kate's photograph beamed at them two days later. 'England's Shirley Temple to live in Dayton' ran the caption in the *Independent*. To the outside world Kate was as poised as she was beautiful – yet beneath the smiling exterior lurked a vast number of misgivings.

Superficially she had no cause for concern. Ned Bleakley was a pillar of Dayton society – owner of the *Independent*, President of the Institute of Fine Arts, Vice-President of the Choral Society – Ned Bleakley was widely respected. He had almost forgotten his distant links with Ulster until Lord Averdale's letter had arrived to remind him. And since the *Independent* had already said by then that refugee children from Europe should be the first beneficiaries of American hospitality, there was no question about providing a home for Kate and her nurse. Ned's house on Hurlingham Drive was large enough to accommodate a dozen refugees, let alone two.

On the other hand, Eleanor had certain misgivings. Childless herself, she lacked any experience of children. She and Ned had their own lives to lead, they were settled and happy . . . a child would be a disturbance . . . even worse, a child might come between them.

Kate had never met two more opposite people – Uncle Ned was tall and thin, and Aunt Eleanor was so short and

428

stout that her hips and torso met without a discernible waist. Her calves disappeared into her shoes without pausing for ankles. Her walk was as stiff-jointed as a doll. Even her face was doll-like, round and fat – and when she laughed she bounced up and down like the Michelin Man.

The house was huge, almost as large as the one in Belgrave Square. Kate and Rose Smith were given their own suite, which included the most luxurious bathroom Kate had ever seen. And Kate adored the rest of the house, especially the big drawing-room with its two grand pianos. Uncle Ned had a billiard-room and a study, and a workshop in the basement – and Aunt Eleanor had her own private sitting-room and a sewing-room, although Kate knew without being told that Aunt Eleanor left the sewing to Mimosa, a huge black woman who spent hours in the basement laundry-room. All the servants were black – Rose said Americans employed only black servants because they were the best. Certainly Kate soon learned to like the ones at 920 Hurlingham Drive, especially Thomas the butler who sometimes took her out for a drive in Uncle Ned's Cadillac.

Right from the outset, Kate was determined to please. She remembered her rule – that an orphan should please in every way possible, as often as possible, because only then was she safe.

The servants were charmed from the very first day – and Uncle Ned was soon singing her praises. Aunt Eleanor was slow to be won over, but once Kate learned not to monopolize Uncle Ned when he returned from his office in the evening, Aunt Eleanor relaxed and positively beamed with approval.

Six weeks after Kate's arrival, Madame Lefarge was appointed as her governess. Kate was to be taught French and the piano, drawing, painting and classical literature. In fact Ned and Eleanor Bleakley were better equipped to teach all of those subjects, except Madame Lefarge's natural language, but Lord Averdale had insisted on a tutor and Madame Lefarge was the best to be found. She was to work with Kate five mornings a week, from nine until twelve-thirty.

As far as Kate was concerned, Madame Lefarge was yet

one more person to please.

Gradually Kate learned what she should do to be liked. Uncle Ned's time with her was restricted to two hours on a Thursday evening (when Aunt Eleanor was at her 'Bundles for Britain' meeting), and an hour or so on Saturday afternoon (while Aunt Eleanor was at the beauty parlour) . . . which was when Kate wrote her 'Appreciation of Literature' essay for Madame Lefarge – who never guessed that it was composed by Uncle Ned. That was Kate's secret with him – their game which nobody knew about, not even Aunt Eleanor.

For the rest of the week, Kate kissed Uncle Ned goodnight, and made sure that she never stayed more than ten minutes when he arrived home from his office in the evenings.

Aunt Eleanor's secret was that she helped Kate with her piano practice – nobody knew about that either, not even Uncle Ned. Aunt Eleanor said – 'Let him think that Madame Lefarge is an excellent teacher.' Kate had agreed, 'It will be our secret, won't it, Aunt Eleanor.'

Madame Lefarge's secrets were many. She wept every day at what the Germans were doing to her homeland – she had very little money and needed every cent she earned teaching Kate, which created a problem, for she had never studied literature and the English classics were beyond her. 'Never mind,' Kate encouraged, 'we shall learn them together. But I wish I could sketch like you.'

So another secret was born. From that day on the sketches which bore Kate's initials in the corner were not drawn by Kate at all. They were the work of Madame Lefarge, who shrugged their secret away – 'Soon you will acquire the knack of the crayon, *ma petite*, then . . . pouff, we shall discard those poor things of mine.'

Uncle Ned was so proud of Kate's sketches that he published them in the *Independent*.

Aunt Eleanor was so pleased with Kate's essays that she read them to her friends.

Madame Lefarge was so impressed with Kate's prowess at the piano that she talked of a genuine musical talent.

Kate was so pleased that they were all so pleased.

So in a hundred small ways, Kate subtly wove her will

into everyday life on Hurlingham Drive. Of course Rose Smith knew some of Kate's secrets, but then Rose Smith had secrets of her own to safeguard when dealing with Kate.

In September 1940, when Kate had been at Hurlingham Drive almost a year, Uncle Ned announced that another visitor was expected. 'Freddie Mallon. We publish his column. He's coming over for a lecture tour.'

'Is that the Mr Mallon on the radio?'

'The very same,' Uncle Ned said proudly.

Even Rose Smith was impressed. Not a week passed without her listening to a programme called *Seven Days in London* which Mr Mallon and another man broadcast. Rose said, 'They make it come so alive. I could almost be back in the old place.'

Kate was losing interest in the old place. Now that she had organized Hurlingham Drive she was beginning to like America. She even used words like automobile and radio without thinking them odd. She wrote to her brother every month, and Rose, acting on instructions, was forever sending photographs of her to her guardian – but Kate rarely felt homesick. After all, where was home? She had left Ulster years ago, and the house in Belgrave Square was now closed.

Kate was beginning to feel safe in America. Mr Mallon's war in Europe seemed a long way away.

Freddie Mallon married Margaret Hamilton twenty-four days after the fall of Dunkirk, a frustrating delay caused by the reading of the banns in church on consecutive Sundays. Freddie was sour about it – 'War quickens the pace of life in other countries, but in dear old England . . .' Even so, so much happened that time passed quickly, even for Freddie. First he and Sean did a CBS special on Dunkirk – by pooling experiences they had the whole story – which they told in an especially extended *Seven Days in London*. The response was instantaneous. The broadcast was hailed throughout the United States as a classic of reporting; Freddie's New York agent signed up more newspapers to take Freddie's column – and, perhaps most important of all, Freddie was invited to give a lecture tour, coast-to-

431

coast across America, giving his views on the war.

Accepting was difficult. He had Margaret to consider and so many Americans were fleeing London that he was afraid of being accused of deserting a sinking ship. 'And it *will* sink,' he said bitterly, 'unless people back home stop listening to Joe Kennedy.'

Ambassador Kennedy's reputation grew worse every day. 'I thought my daffodils were yellow until I met Kennedy,' said a British Foreign Office official. The story was retold all over town. Not only that but Kennedy was rumoured to be as anti-semitic as Hitler – and a third story said that now that his family was back in the States, he was chasing every woman in London.

The Kennedy saga even strained Freddie's close friendship with Sean Connors. 'I tell you, Sean, Hitler doesn't honour neutrality. Neutrality won't save Ireland, or even the States when Hitler gets powerful enough. People who preach neutrality, people like Kennedy, make me sick.'

Sean was shifting his ground, but loyalty stopped him short of condemning Kennedy. He regarded the Ambassador, if not as a friend, at least as someone who was friendly towards him. Privately he was more shocked by Kennedy's womanizing than by his politics, though he remained silent even about that, perhaps because of his relationship with Val Hamilton who was herself the cause of some friction with Freddie.

Freddie disapproved, it was as simple as that – not of their romance, after all he had brought them together, but of their sleeping together. In Freddie's mind sleeping with tarts was one thing, sleeping with a girl whom one respected was another entirely. His sense of propriety was offended. Not that he said anything, neither did Sean, but both were aware of a slight coolness between them. It might have curdled into something worse had less been happening. As it was there was no time to dwell on it – what with the threat of invasion, the wedding, and Freddie's struggle to decide about going to America.

Invasion seemed inevitable, and from what Freddie had seen in France he gave the British little chance of resisting. Dunkirk had created a few euphoric days in London, but it had been a defeat when all was said and done. 'A goddamn rout,' according to Freddie. People felt let down by their leaders. 'Morale gets lower every day,' Freddie observed. Ten million people were too apathetic even to apply for ration books. Half the country still expected the Government to make a deal with Hitler.

'What sort of deal?' Freddie demanded angrily. 'Deals don't work with Hitler. When will everyone realize that?'

On 10 June, a week after Dunkirk fell, Italy declared war on Great Britain and France.

On CBS, Freddie said: 'Mussolini might fairly be described as the jackal of Europe.'

On Friday, 14 June, Hitler's troops marched into Paris. Three days later, eighty-four-year-old Marshal Pétain broadcast from hastily commandeered offices in Bordeaux. 'With a broken heart, I tell you that fighting must cease.'

Freddie snorted, 'An old man with the voice of an old woman is begging for the honour of France. Hitler will make him eat dirt.'

And Hitler did. Four days later, the French leaders were summoned to the same spot in the Forest of Compiègne where Marshal Foch had confronted the beaten Germans at the end of World War I. To underline the humiliation they were made to listen to Hitler's terms in the very same railway coach, Dining Car 2419D, that had been preserved for twenty-two years in a nearby museum.

Britain stood alone.

Ironically, the mood in London began to change. An uncertain light-heartedness made inroads into the gloom. When the marriage took place between Alfred Henry Mallon and Margaret Veronica Hamilton at St Mary's Church, South Kensington, on 27 June, hundreds of Londoners turned out to cheer the bride. 'War or no war,' declared the *Evening Standard*, 'Love will find a way.'

Few people were under more strain at the wedding than the Best Man. Sean had spent most of the preceding three weeks watching Freddie struggle with his decision about the lecture tour. If he went he was to be away for three months, and in three months Hitler's troops might be marching down the Mall. To return might be impossible. Equally if Margaret went to America with him she might never see her family again . . . and if she stayed she might lose Freddie forever.

Freddie was horribly torn. 'Someone needs to tell the people back home. Our ambassadors won't, not Bullit in Paris, nor Kennedy here. Roosevelt says all the right things but does nothing. If I stump the country . . . well, I'm no politician, but hell, I just might make people see sense.'

The fall of France decided him. 'I must go,' he told Margaret that evening, 'and I want you to come with me.'

George and Cynthia were informed first, over dinner at the Dorchester later that night. 'I'll take very good care of her, sir,' Freddie promised, while Margaret comforted her tearful mother.

Sean was told the next morning. He looked stricken at the news.

'It's the right decision,' Freddie said firmly, 'I've looked at all angles and I just might make a difference. You'll handle things fine here, I'm sure of that. You've been carrying too much of the load anyway – what about becoming partners? I'll widen the circulation back home and we'll split fifty-fifty – everything, including the credits, how about that?'

'I'd rather you stayed in London,' Sean blurted out. 'Remember when I first came over, and you took me in like a stray dog? I'd have caught the first boat back to Dublin if I hadn't met you.'

It was too early in the morning to start drinking, but start they did – and by noon they were quite drunk, on whisky and memories, as they remembered back over the two years. As Sean saw it, he owed Freddie too much to accept a partnership. The American had taken over from where Pat Connors and Dinny Macaffety had left off.

Freddie feigned disgust. 'That's the trouble with the Irish. They get so damn sentimental. I'm only going to be gone for three months, for God's sake!'

Sean knew that was not true. He sensed another great change in his life, but defining it defeated him. Even so he was vaguely aware of the irony. He had come to London in search of a fortune, now he was turning down more money than he had ever earned in his life. 'It's this bloody war,' he said bleakly, 'it gives you a new set of values.'

'Sure,' Freddie agreed. 'Everything is different in war.'

Even so, the next day he made Sean sign the partnership agreement. 'Give the money away if it worries you,' were his final words on the matter.

Freddie's last few days in London sped by. Meetings with CBS about Sean taking over *Seven Days in London* – a paralysing drunken orgy of a stag party before the wedding – kissing Margaret while the whole of London looked on – the reception at the Dorchester. After which Freddie and Margaret were gone, to Lisbon and thence to New York by the TWA Clipper.

Sean was overwhelmed with work. Just standing in Freddie's shadow was a full-time job. Freddie's parting advice had been to hire an assistant – 'Find some Mick fresh off the boat. Then work him into the ground.'

Sean had no time even for that . . . and Val Hamilton was as busy as he was. The Labour Party was now part of Churchill's government, and Val's Cockney sparring partner, Herbert Morrison, had become Minister of Supply. The Party stood on its head. Everything they had struggled against was now acceptable. The new Minister of Labour, Ernie Bevin, had spent his life fighting for a forty-hour week, now he told workers to ban strikes and work seven days a week. Clem Attlee pushed an Emergency Powers Bill through the House of Commons which gave the Government more power than ever before. An Englishman's house was no longer his castle; any man with a uniform could enter his house, search it, turn out his lights, send him to bed or take him to jail. As Supply Minister, Herbert Morrison controlled factories and plants, prices and delivery schedules – and Val Hamilton was one of his assistants.

She laughed when Sean teased her about the Party's change of heart. 'I know, but haven't you heard – there's a war on.'

The war now generated constant emergencies, alarms, tensions and strains – and an electric excitement as well. Hours alone were savoured, happiness was snatched at, for who could say what would happen tomorrow? Val was sent all over the country, and was away for days, sometimes weeks at a time. She and Sean had less time together but treasured it more. If Val was in London, gone was the pretence of not sleeping with Sean in Craven Street.

'People *do* talk, you know,' Cynthia Hamilton remonstrated when Val made a rare appearance at the Dorchester.

'Oh?'

'The Bleddows were in on Tuesday, and she must have told everyone in the hotel.'

Val grinned, 'I wonder if she knows her daughter is shacked up with a Polish Colonel in –'

'Your *expressions* –'

'There's a war on. Didn't Shakespeare say something about "Lechery, lechery – still wars and lechery –"'

'He most certainly did *not* say shacked up. Besides you can't condone –'

'No, just enjoy. I'm sorry, I don't mean to shock you, but this is 1940 and there is –'

'A war on,' Cynthia sighed, 'as if one could forget. Not that war makes the slightest difference to the way babies are born.'

'Oh Mother,' Val's eyes widened, 'you don't mean – you and Father – my own parents, well I'm too shocked . . .'

Cynthia chuckled and gave in. She had no defence against Val's high spirits. Few people did. Val had grown in stature and confidence, from a girl to a woman. She worked furiously, believed in her job, was in love and therefore happy – at least for most of the time. Occasionally black moods engulfed her, sometimes she sensed that her country's effort had come too late, and that the German war machine was unstoppable. Even then she made jokes, though only to Sean.

'Darling,' she said one night. 'Come to bed, come to bed now.'

He was working. He had not expected her, it was late, he was to broadcast in the morning from the cramped studio beneath Peter Robinson's in Oxford Circus, his script was unfinished. He sat pounding his typewriter, speaking sentences aloud to practise the feel of them.

'Come on Irishman,' she grinned. 'Make love to me. It might be your last chance. If the Germans come Himmler

436

will seize me as his mistress and you'll never have me again.'

Sean hammered his machine, reading aloud from the script – 'There can be no doubting – correction, there can be no *mistaking* the new mood in Britain –'

She crossed to his chair to nuzzle his neck and stroke the inside of his thigh.

'. . . and the stiffening resolve . . .'

She giggled and reached for his crotch, 'The stiffening other things . . .'

'And, and the aroused . . . Jaysus, Val!'

They went to bed. Two hours later she made some tea and helped him organize his script. The work would be done, it was too important to leave, his work and hers – and yet other needs were important too. Just being in his arms made her feel safe, eased the tension, helped stifle her fears. When they made love she forgot about the blackout and gasmasks and the dire predictions overheard in Herbert Morrison's office. Afterwards it was like being reborn. The black mood lifted, the possibility of invasion receded in her mind. She was her usual self again – confident, courageous and full of talk about 'the new tomorrow'.

'Ernie Bevin is right,' she said. 'This war will change everything. The working class won't be fooled again, not like after the last war. Bevin says –'

'Does Hitler agree?'

'Oh, him –'

'Or even your mother?'

Val grinned, 'Morrison says he'll make her Mayor of Lewisham. She'd be good at it too.'

They laughed and she snuggled against him. 'I don't expect you've seen it yet, but things *are* changing. I go into factories every day. The mood is different, believe me, darling. Production is up, problems are being sorted out – I don't know, but it's as if the people themselves are taking this war over.'

She was right, and Sean had seen it. The mood of defiance had been growing since the fall of France. Only that day a bus conductor had said to Sean, 'Bloody allies, buggering about. We're well rid of them if you ask me. Now it's up to us – and we'll show Hitler.'

Val laughed, 'Isn't that what I said? Chamberlainism is dead, the old school tie is dying, and the future belongs to the working class.'

Sean's column reported the new mood because it was there. He saw examples every day. As men went off to the Army, their women came out from their kitchens to work in factories and offices – to deliver the post, the milk and the bread. Even in London's clubs, waiters had given way to waitresses. Women were in uniform, driving ambulances, directing traffic, sweeping roads – a new breed of women, who wore slacks and went hatless and complained cheerfully about rationing. London became even more cosmopolitan, with streets full of Dutch policemen in black silver-braided uniforms, and de Gaulle's Free French with their black kepis, sharing the pavements with the electric blue uniforms of Dominion pilots. After a while even the sandbagged entrances to restaurants looked as familiar as parks without railings and Piccadilly Circus with Eros obliterated by yet more sandbags. Sean reported the new mood, but he still remembered Dunkirk and asked himself – 'When will the invasion begin?'

The answer was not long in coming. Early August found Sean covering a story just as dramatic as Dunkirk. *Seven Days in London* went out as usual – although now Sean's stories were not gathered in the capital, but in green Sussex valleys and the orchards of Kent. Day after day he craned his neck and watched the dog-fights in the sky . . . watched the dragonfly glint of wings spinning and snarling over the countryside . . . and night after night he scrounged lifts into airfields or bought drinks in nearby pubs, listening to exhausted ground crews talk over the battle. The war in the air was the start of the invasion. Fleet Street was aware of the odds – that the RAF had neither the planes nor the pilots to hold the Luftwaffe back for much longer. Yet every day patched-up Spitfires and battle-scarred Hurricanes rose up to meet the oncoming waves of Stukas and Zerstorers.

The sky became a terrifying place, raining blazing aircraft, shell splinters and parachutes – a huge cauldron of noise, contrails scoring white lines across the blue sky, the air shaking with the whine of engines and cannon fire. Every day, for day after day.

Sean stayed in Sussex and Kent, travelling into London once a week for his broadcast – then, often with John Plum of the *Mirror*, he returned to the chalk hills, or to walk past shopkeepers sweeping broken glass and shrapnel from their doorways.

Sean saw the pride in their faces. Every corner had a newspaper placard, freshly chalked – 'RAF v Germans, 61 for 26 – Close of Play Today, 12 for 0'. Perhaps the claims were exaggerated, but people never admitted that, even to themselves. 'This is our war now,' they seemed to say, 'and we're holding the front line.'

Within a month, Sean knew enough about dog-fights to understand the tactics – and to appreciate the frustrations of some of the pilots. At Manston, for instance, the RAF had to climb into the sky already occupied by the enemy, knowing they would be jumped at 18,000 feet. 'We should pull back to the airfields north of London,' a pilot told Sean, 'and gain height as we fly south. We'd come at Jerry on level terms then. It's so bloody obvious a kid could see it.'

Sean sympathized, but he knew the answer even to that. The top brass were terrified that bombers would get through to London. Large-scale air raids were still unknown. Estimates of possible damage were frightening – some predicted that ten days of intensive bombing would create 200,000 casualties.

So Sean reported the Battle of Britain and felt more part of the war every day. These people were his friends. He was in love with an English girl who made droll jokes about what the Germans would do to her if they landed – jokes he pretended not to hear because he was lost for the right words of comfort. He made his sympathies known in a dozen ways, obliquely, by innuendo – but where Freddie Mallon had said outright, 'America should be fighting this war,' Sean had not said that about Ireland. Ireland remained neutral, by edict of Eamon de Valera and the wishes of most of her people.

Sean was under all sorts of pressures. Ever since being beaten up in Shadwell, he had received callers from Dev's office. An emissary from Eamon de Valera arrived at Craven Street every month. Sean knew why. Freddie's column and the CBS broadcasts commanded a wide following in the United States – and Dev wouldn't want the Americans to get the wrong impression of Irish policy.

He knew Dev's views by heart – that Ireland should stay neutral. He even accepted that with an army of less than 13,000 men, Ireland would be of little use in the war. Yet Ireland could play a part. If the British Royal Navy operated from Irish ports they could protect the life-line of supplies coming from America. German submarines were inflicting crippling losses. One hundred and fifty merchant ships had already been sunk. In June alone 300,000 tons of shipping were torpedoed. Britain's shortages became more severe every day. The sugar ration was cut, butter reduced, tea limited to two ounces per person a week. Newspapers shrank from lack of newsprint, petrol rationing became ever more stringent. Vital materials were drying up. Yet de Valera still refused British shipping the use of Irish waters, or British aircraft the safety of Irish airspace.

Dev's men were not alone in bending Sean's ear. Other men called, men sent by Churchill, men who talked in confidential murmurs. 'It's time for a *united* Ireland to fight this war. What we need is a Council of Defence for all Ireland.'

'A Council of Defence?'

'A cross-border organization that would consider all sorts of things, maybe even ending partition entirely.'

Sean's heart lurched, 'Would the Ulster Government go along with that?'

A shrug. 'They'd buy a common defence policy. Then it would be up to your people to persuade them to go further.'

With hope in his heart, Sean passed the hint back to Dev via his representative, but the Taoiseach was as unyielding as ever. De Valera would rather deal with the devil himself than with Winston Churchill.

The Craven Street crowd, especially some of the American journalists, were at Sean too. Clark Nelson was the most persistent, 'Look kid, let me tell you about political power in the States. The Irish vote counts big.

Places like New York, Philadelphia, Boston – Irish Democrats pull a lot of muscle. Nobody's going to sweet talk them into this war on the side of the Brits except . . .' Nelson wagged a finger, 'maybe a Mick. If *you* tell them neutrality is a dead duck, well I dunno, maybe they'll listen. Why else did Freddie Mallon hand you his empire?'

Was that why Freddie did it? Sean asked himself that question every night. Was Freddie using him? It seemed preposterous – they were such firm friends – Freddie trusted him to do a good job, that was all, and Nelson was jealous . . .

Sean was pulled all ways. What hurt most was the accusation of being bought. Another American told him, 'Back home we treat uppity niggers like you. Give 'em a few trinkets, make a fuss of them. After that they're neither one thing nor another. Can't go back to their own and can't *ever* be one of us. Uncle Toms. That's what happened – the Brits have made you an Uncle Tom Mick.'

The accusation festered. Sean saw himself through the other man's eyes – dressed in English clothes, accustomed to English ways, living in London with an English mistress. Even his accent had changed. After two years with Freddie he sounded faintly American. If he blasphemed he said 'Jesus' more often than 'Jaysus'.

Something had to give. Sean wondered about going to America, perhaps when Freddie came back, *if* Freddie came back. But he would want to take Val with him and she had the same answer for everything – 'Wait until the end of the war.'

Val was in Manchester for the whole of August, working for Herbert Morrison, and Sean was out of London most of the time – watching the Spitfires fight their incredible duels in the sky. Busy, terrifying days – and it was rare for one to end without someone sneering about Ireland in Sean's hearing – 'Bloody Irish, living off the fat of the land. If we go, they go, that's for sure. At least we've got the guts to fight.' One night Sean found himself arguing furiously in defence of de Valera. He wondered what his father would have said. Pat Connors had despised de Valera, but then Pat Connors had positively loathed Churchill.

Sean made up his mind at the end of the month. It was

the hardest decision of his life. He asked nobody's advice. One morning something clicked in his mind and the decision was made. He telephoned Dublin and asked Dinny to come over for a meeting.

Dinny arrived three days later, tired after a difficult journey, and irritable about Dublin's press censorship which sounded even fiercer than London's. Dev was using the Emergency to extend government power over all manner of things. 'Sure there's no telling what he'll do next,' Dinny complained. 'Did you know he's blind now, or as near as dammit. Well, it suits him, he and Frank Aiken and Boland are like the three brass monkeys – Dev sees nothing. Aiken hears nothing, and Boland says not a damn word.'

It was a happy reunion, although as Sean listened to the news from home he wondered if it was 'home' any more. He had never been back, not for a Christmas or a vacation, or even for when the Widow O'Flynn married Jim Tully.

In exchange for the news from Dublin, he told Dinny bits and pieces of war-gossip, and how the south coast was being prepared to face the invasion.

Then he announced his decision. 'We should be in this war, Dinny, and I'm going to say so.'

'Dear God, you've gone out of your mind!' Dinny's face darkened. 'And what do you mean, you're going to say so? Not in print, I hope. Never on the wireless to America –'

They had a furious argument.

Dinny was passionate in his defence of neutrality. 'Sure and why not? Every true Irishman thinks the same. Would you have us fight for Churchill and the British Empire –'

'I'd have us fight Hitler, that's all. To hell with the British Empire –'

They argued for well over an hour.

Dinny talked of the mood in Ireland. 'The country is behind Dev on this. Some of us hate his guts on other things, but not about this. We want no part of a British war –'

'Or a French war? Or a Belgian war –'

'Dear God! Didn't your Da spend his life fighting the buggers –'

442

'And didn't an Irishman kill him?'

'Dublin's still proud of his name. Would you bring shame on it?'

Sean went deathly white.

Dinny put his head in his hands. 'Will you just listen to me? Sean, you've got me so – lookit, I'm sorry I said that about the Da and – God, give me another drink and let's start over again.'

Dinny was too upset to calm down, even after a few more drinks. 'They'll never forgive you, Sean – *never*! Isn't it enough you're fighting the IRA without taking on the whole country? Dev will brand you a souper, a traitor to Ireland –'

'Do you believe that? There are fifty thousand Irishmen in the British Army. Are they traitors too?'

'God help us, they're not on the wireless, shaming Ireland –'

'Shaming? To condemn Fascism –'

'Dublin won't see that. Sean, they'll spit on your name. Will you think of Pat, of all the things he wanted for you, a place in the Dail even. Didn't he always hope –'

'Will you stop bringing the Da in all the time. It's my life, my decision –'

'But his name gets dragged down with you.'

There was a long, painful silence.

Finally Sean shook his head. 'I'm sorry, Dinny. I've my mind made up. Nothing else has changed. I'm as Irish as you about partition or anything else – but this war, Hitler – well, that's different.'

They talked through most of the night, talked not argued, with Dinny almost in tears at times. White-faced and trembling, Sean explained the things he had heard from refugees, what he had learned from his reading and from simply being with Freddie. So much thought had gone into his decision that he was sure it was right.

Dinny saw only the chasm between them, an unbridgeable divide that would keep Sean forever from Ireland. At one point he said, 'When I left home, everyone said I was to bring you back with me, but now,' he shook his head, 'wouldn't it be best if you stay over here. Maybe I can make your friends see what you're at, but Dev and

443

the Dail . . . you know what I mean well enough.'

The reproach cut Sean like a knife. Even the surprise he had prepared would be spoiled, but he went through with it anyway. 'About the *Gazette*, Dinny. I'd like you to buy it. God knows, it's rightfully yours anyway. Pay me so much out of profits every year, whatever you and Senator O'Keefe think fair. I'll never doubt your word on a penny, you know that well enough.'

Even though Dinny accepted the offer and expressed his thanks, the transaction seemed to underline the parting of their paths. They went to bed for a few hours' sleep, both with heavy hearts.

Sean saw him off in the morning – a sad-faced, grey-haired old man who could barely speak when it came to saying goodbye.

Afterwards, shaken and heart-broken, Sean found a Catholic church and sat staring at the stained glass windows for over an hour. It was months since he had attended a Mass. 'Soon I'll be a lapsed Irishman,' he told himself wryly, 'as well as a lapsed Catholic.'

Val remained in Manchester and was still away when Sean broadcast that week's *Seven Days in London*. He was glad. It was his decision, not hers or theirs, but his alone.

It was one of his best broadcasts. Freddie had never allowed guests on *Seven Days* – 'It's my show,' he would say. 'People expect my stories, my way of looking at things.' He had permitted Sean to play a junior role, but Sean's voice had only been heard five minutes at a time when Freddie was in Britain. Freddie was an established broadcaster who could carry the full thirty minutes. Sean lacked that maturity and he knew it. Following his instinct, he had involved other people from his very first solo.

On 1 September he took the process a step further. The programme was a montage – reports of aerial dog-fights taking place 'somewhere over southern England' were interrupted by accounts of other battles, as European refugees spoke of how their own countries had been crushed. Anton Jastrow talked breathlessly of the destruction of Warsaw . . . then Sean was back, describing the duels in the skies above Kent . . . interrupted by Henri van de Criend's heart-breaking account of the bombing of

Rotterdam . . . followed by Sean's vivid description of the grim battle being waged by the RAF. Next came a Frenchman remembering the Stukas swarming over Sedan in May . . . Sean again, with his commentary about now . . . giving way to a Belgian, sweating over memories of being strafed by machine-gun fire. The effect was spine-tingling. *That* was happening then, *this* is happening now. Different voices, European accents, united against a common enemy. The pace of the inserts accelerated as Sean built to a climax. The message was clear. The last-ditch fight over southern England was not a Battle for Britain – but for the whole world.

At the end, immediately after a Stuka's screaming dive and the whistle of bombs – came a pause. In the studio Sean wiped the sweat from his brow and summed up.

'Tonight you have heard a Frenchman, a Pole, a Dane, a Belgian, a Swede, a Norwegian, a Dutchman and an Englishman. They have little in common. In Rotterdam, Henri was a fishmonger. Eiliv is an engineer who built Oslo's roads. André was a gardener in Brussels, and René a policeman in Lyons. Eight men of different nationalities, without common political or religious beliefs – who find themselves united by the need to confront a single enemy. Did they have a choice? Was neutrality a choice? Henri's country is now ruled from Berlin. His country's neutrality was ignored by Hitler, just as Hitler has ignored the neutrality of other countries. Neutrality has ceased to be an option. Indeed a neutral country has less security than one now at war. By not raising an army, it leaves itself vulnerable to Nazi Germany at some future date. And that date will come, in the opinion of the men you have heard tonight.'

Sean drew a deep breath – 'Ten days ago, Prime Minister Churchill paid tribute to the RAF when he said, "Never in the field of human conflict was so much owed to so few." My interpretation was that the Prime Minister meant the British people when he spoke of the many, but now I wonder. Could the many who have reason to be grateful to the RAF include Americans in New York and Irishmen in Dublin? Could those cities, those countries be next? This is Sean Connors, an Irishman in England, bidding you

445

goodnight until the same time next week, when it will be my pleasure to bring you *Seven Days in London*, the weekly news programme from the heart of Great Britain – the country that now stands alone.'

The studio erupted when he finished. Technicians stood on chairs to applaud. His guests crowded round with frenzied enthusiasm. Sean was carried off to a bar to celebrate. He was himself excited. The novelty of broadcasting had never worn off and the technical achievements of his show had been considerable; the quick interplay of stories and accents had worked astonishingly well. It was an advance in technique and he was mastering his craft.

Yet, despite the excitement and the many congratulations, Sean left as soon as he could.

With Val in Manchester, the house in Craven Street was quite empty and Sean felt the need to think. However, the retreat to Craven Street proved a mistake. Ghosts came out of the woodwork. His father was talking about Michael Collins signing the Treaty – 'He knew he was signing his death warrant, but it was the best deal he could get. Sure it was a compromise, at times there's no other choice. It cost Mick his life.'

'Is that what you're saying, Da?' Sean asked aloud. 'It will cost me my life?'

'They called him a traitor, Sean – him, *Mick Collins*, the greatest Irishman ever to draw breath.'

'And me? They'll call me a traitor too?' Sean buried his head in his hands.

A moment later he heard Dinny say, 'Sean, they'll spit on your name. Will you think of the Da . . . what he wanted for you –'

'Shut up!' Sean shouted. 'For God's sake shut up!'

The Widow O'Flynn giggled, 'Sure now, you'll be many things in your life, but you'll never be Taoiseach.'

'Did I ever say I wanted to be?' Sean demanded aloud. 'Did I? Just once? The Da wanted that, not me.'

His eyes filled with tears. He was a little boy again in the tiny room on Ammet Street. His father was teaching him the rules, and he was trying to be brave.

'They'll kill me, Da, won't they. They'll kill me like

446

. . .' he choked on the name Jesus Christ and instead said, 'like they killed Michael Collins.'

But the ghost of his father was gone.

CHAPTER NINE

Sean's broadcast on neutrality, as reported in the Irish newspapers, alerted Matt Riordan to his whereabouts. Until then Matt had assumed that his enemy was still in Dublin. The news that Connors was over the water was disastrous, London was even further from Matt's reach. The only good thing was that the reports of *Seven Days in London* justified Matt's accusations to the hilt. 'Didn't I say he was a treacherous bastard? The proof's there now – for all to see. The pity is someone else might get to him before I do. God in Heaven, I must get out of here!'

But escaping from prison was no easy task.

The IRA was under the heel as never before. De Valera was in the middle of a dangerous game. To the German Ambassador, he stressed he would turn to the British if the Germans invaded – and to the British he promised to call on Germany's help if the British ever set foot in Dublin again. His was a desperate gamble to assert Irish independence once and for all. He was walking a tightrope, and the IRA could jerk the rope out from under him.

Dublin was alive with rumours of German spies linking up with the IRA for an attack on the border. It was certainly possible. Germany had armed the IRA before, in Dev's day, when he was fighting the British in Ireland itself. For the Germans to get together with the IRA again now though would be fatal. Ireland would be in the war whatever Dev did. He had to crush the IRA – and although the widespread arrests after the Magazine Raid had netted hundreds of men, others were still on the loose.

In February, Dev caught some more.

IRA officers of the Western Command were meeting GHQ men in Dublin's Meath Hotel, when suddenly two hundred soldiers surrounded the place and captured the lot. Sixteen more IRA men were thus incarcerated in Mountjoy Jail. Conditions were appalling. The prison was already crammed. The food was disgusting – 'Slops a pig wouldn't eat,' said Ferdy Malloy. Worst of all, traditional IRA privileges were withheld. Men were denied political status, not allowed to work as a unit, nor permitted to elect their own Commanding Officer.

A hunger strike was called.

Dev stood firm.

On 16 April, Tony D'Arcy died, the first hunger striker to die in an Irish prison since the Emergency began.

Dev clamped press censorship in a vice, and continued to refuse to grant political status to the men in the prisons.

On 19 April, Jack McNeela died on hunger strike.

The next day IRA GHQ sent Father O'Hara into the prison with an order – the hunger strike was to be abandoned.

Matt Riordan breathed a sigh of relief. He was as ready to die for Ireland as any man, but he had business to finish first. Ireland's business as well as his own, to rid Ireland of two of her enemies – Connors and Averdale. He would settle with them before he died.

'I'm still a young man,' he told himself. 'I'll get out of here one day.'

Sean would never have believed he and Dinny could have argued so bitterly. True they had patched things up, but the relationship would never be the same. And elsewhere everyone knew about Sean's CBS show, even though it had not been broadcast in Britain. Fleet Street had picked it up, and most of the emaciated papers had carried the story – 'Irish columnist condemns neutrality.'

Perversely Sean resented the fuss. His views did not oblige him to suffer condescending Englishmen with their 'Good show old boy, glad you spoke out at last.' He developed a standard reply, 'Aye, let's beat Hitler together, then we'll throw you out of Ireland once and for all.' It wiped the smile from their faces – 'Funny chap Connors, heart's in the right place of course, but he's damn prickly at times.'

Sean had reason to be prickly. Hundreds of abusive

letters poured into the BBC for forwarding to CBS – and disgruntled Irishmen expressed themselves in other ways – a dozen bricks smashed the front windows at Craven Street one night. Sean nailed boards over the openings and tried to forget the write-ups in the Irish papers saying *'impertinent interference'* . . . *'a treacherous statement, totally unrepresentative of Irish opinion'*. The *Gazette* was the exception – the *Gazette* had published no comment at all.

Even in London, some doors closed against him. Three Irish friends cut him dead, and his telephone call to Ambassador Kennedy met a secretary's frosty response – 'The Ambassador has no statement to make at the moment.'

It hurt.

Every coin has two sides, however, and Freddie's cable of congratulations was not the only one from America – while nearly a third of the calls which had swamped the CBS offices in New York had expressed approval.

Val was delighted, of course. She smiled up from their bed on her first night back from Manchester. 'A call to arms,' she said, opening hers. 'That's how Morrison described your broadcast.'

He rolled into bed beside her.

She grinned. 'I told him we've a lot of fences to mend with the Irish.'

'Is that what you're doing?'

'I'm enjoying my share.'

They made love, slept until noon, and made love again in the afternoon. Val's stay in Manchester had underlined how much they missed each other. Sean wanted this wonderful girl for the rest of his life, but all talk of the future was hushed by her drawing his head down to her breast.

'We'll have the rest of our lives to make plans,' she whispered, 'after the war. All I want now is to be loved, and for you to tell me you love me.'

The next morning they kissed goodbye and went back to their wars – Val north to a factory in Luton, Sean south to the chalk hills of Sussex. They had enjoyed such peace for thirty-six hours that the awfulness of war might have been a bad dream. But it was waiting for them. At Val's factory, old men and young women raced the clock to manufacture the provisions of death – while in Sussex skies boy fighter pilots hurled fragile machines into impossible turns in an effort to kill each other.

Sean limped back into London on Saturday, 7 September, and went directly to Oxford Circus to record his broadcast. He felt tired and strangely irritated, and he wondered why? His script was ready, that was no problem. Then he remembered – he was expected for tea at the Dorchester with Val and her parents. 'Just for an hour,' she had pleaded on the telephone. 'It's weeks since I've seen them.'

He shrugged. George disapproved and Cynthia did too – even though they never said anything. Was it his fault that their daughter refused to get married until after the war?

Seven Days in London went without a hitch, and afterwards Sean spent an hour discussing events with the team in the studio. Everyone drew hope from the past week. Miraculously the RAF seemed to be holding the Luftwaffe. 'Perhaps the worst is over,' someone said cheerfully as Sean left for the Dorchester.

How wrong that was. The worst was about to begin.

At the Dorchester, Sean cursed when the air-raid sirens sounded at five o'clock. He and Val were on the point of leaving, now they would have to make polite conversation until the 'All clear'.

'Have some more tea, George,' Cynthia suggested, her hand on the silver pot.

'I'm awash with the stuff already. I want a proper drink.' George crossed to the sideboard and raised an eyebrow at Sean, 'Whisky?'

Sean accepted and turned back to Cynthia who was planning a party for Somerset Maugham. 'It's on Thursday, you must come, both of you,' she smiled happily as she leafed through her diary. 'There's so much happening this month. David Niven is getting married – have you met him yet? Now when's that . . . ah, here . . . the twenty-second, at the Café de Paris of all places. You know Primula of course. Isn't she *exquisite*. She's the granddaughter of the Marquess of Downshire, you know.'

Cynthia was still prattling on when a buzzing noise interrupted her.

George said it first. 'What the devil's that? Sounds like a million bees.'

Then Val said, 'Oh my God!' and they all rushed to the window.

The sky was black with aircraft, advancing like a swarm of insects, trailing back for miles and miles. Sean, who had spent weeks watching dog-fights, was the first to realize that the planes were bombers. German bombers.

'My God,' Val gasped, 'the Invasion.'

The bombers blotted out the sky. The air throbbed with their engines.

'Where the devil is Fighter Command?' George asked in a strangled voice.

Sean was out on the balcony. There was not a Spitfire in sight, not even a Hurricane. He felt he was dreaming. 'They must be down by the coast – chasing the German fighter escort, then they'll . . .' his voice died amid the first explosion. Dull crumping sounds came from the river.

Val choked, 'The docks! They're bombing the docks.'

Suddenly anti-aircraft guns in the park blazed into life. Black puff balls of flak darkened the sky even more. But the bombers kept coming.

Later that evening the sun seemed to set in two places at once – above Wimbledon in the west and over Poplar in the east. The orange glow in the east lasted longer. The entire skyline was a mass of light – and as the flames blazed, other bombers came to stoke the fire. It went on all night. London was burning.

London never stopped burning after that – at least not for months. The pattern of Sean's life changed yet again. No longer did he hunt for stories amid picturesque villages on the South Downs. The big story was in the capital itself, and the drama of *Seven Days in London* outshone news from all over the world.

Sean went everywhere and saw everything. When he was stopped by officials, or denied access by suspicious civil servants, he used his contacts as never before. Val got him to Herbert Morrison. Peter Plum of the *Express* got him to Beaverbrook, and a whole host of people got him at least close to Churchill.

'But he's Irish,' someone complained in the Prime Minister's office. Churchill snorted, 'So's Brendan.' Brendan Bracken of the *Financial Times* had long been a close friend. 'Come to think of it, Montgomery's Irish, or sort of . . . and so's Alanbrooke.'

Sean won his special privileges. Perhaps his record was known even then. After all he had spoken out against the IRA, and about neutrality, and done what he could to pass messages to de Valera. Perhaps it was because he had sailed to Dunkirk – and of the effect *Seven Days* was having on American public opinion. Whatever the reason, the outcome was the same. Sean Connors took his CBS microphones into every corner of bombed-out London.

He was always there, that's what people said afterwards – with his tin hat and overalls, and a cable running back to his recording van like an umbilical cord. 'You'd have thought he was Chief of Staff,' someone remembered. 'He had special passes for everywhere. I reckon Churchill was behind him – well someone must have been.'

When cumbersome equipment restricted him, Sean gathered stories with an old-fashioned notebook. Afterwards no single fire stood out above all others, at least not in London.

The nights merged into one all-encompassing flame. He remembered intense heat, getting soaked, being icy cold and swallowing hot tea from mobile canteens, before pushing off into the night for still other stories. The Fire Service knew him well. The men were mainly wartime auxiliaries, mostly volunteers. Few had previously tackled a real fire. Londoners had despised them before the Blitz – 'men with guts went into the Army.' The Blitz changed people's opinions. The courage of London's fire-fighters grew into a legend. When they appeared on newsreel screens, entire audiences rose to their feet in spontaneous applause. At dawn, early morning shift workers lined the streets to cheer the raw-eyed heroes as they returned exhausted to their homes. And Sean Connors told the whole world about them.

Life changed for everyone. Every night Londoners burrowed underground into damp shelters and subways.

blown apart. She was there the next day, rescuing a few charred books and other possessions. In fact Val spent most days in the East End. Morrison had switched her duties and given her responsibility for co-ordinating relief services in the docks. She was pleased. The East End was full of her people, they knew her, trusted her, flirted with her, and helped her get the job done. When German bombers destroyed her efforts overnight, she was there again at dawn to start all over again. Sean worried himself sick when she stayed overnight in the East End, but she was quite firm about it – 'Darling, there's so much to do, and I'm on at five in the morning. Besides you'll be out all night – it's you we should worry about.'

They snatched a few words on the telephone every day and spent an afternoon each week at Craven Street making love. Their feeling for each other deepened until it seemed their hearts would burst.

On 13 November, Sean had a letter from Freddie, delivered by the American Embassy. By then bombs had rained down on London for sixty-seven consecutive nights. The storm showed no signs of abating.

'If Joe Kennedy steams this open he will arrest me for treason. I'm working night and day contradicting everything he stands for. Sean, it grieves me to admit it, but a lot of Americans are still against us getting into this war. Opinion here is changing, but slowly. "Seven Days" is helping a lot. Everyone I meet listens to it. My mother has been moved to tears by your words and she is not alone by any means. Did I tell you, you're famous over here. Even the President listens – I was at a reception last Thursday when he told the audience that he tunes in every week!

Which brings me neatly to the point. You've become such a celebrity in America that I think you should take over my lecture tour. Thousands of people would like to shake your hand and get your views on the war. I think it might help especially with you being Irish . . .'

'Well,' Val said, reading the letter, 'fame and fortune await you in New York.'

She sat on the end of the bed, quite naked. When she spoke her voice was artificially bright. 'What am I saying, fame awaits you – Freddie says you're famous already.' She

455

gave him a quick smile, 'I'm pleased for you, darling. It's what you deserve.'

When he reached for her, she avoided him and sighed, 'You must go as soon as you can.'

'Will you go with me?'

Her eyes clouded. 'What a heavenly thought. The two of us, going to America.' She blinked to dispel the dream. 'I'd like that, more than anything, you know that, don't you? But I couldn't, not right now, not yet . . .'

'Then I'm staying too.'

'No. You must go. It's such an opportunity. Besides Freddie says it might help and—'

'We both go or we both stay.'

'That's dreadfully unfair. People depend on me here. I could do nothing in New York. But you must go. You *must*. I'd be glad in a way. You'd be safe. Then when this war's over . . .'

She came to him, scrambling around the bed to throw herself into his arms. 'Darling, we'll have wonderful times, I promise. Oh Sean, I wish I could stay here tonight – but I'll be back again in a few days and . . .'

He kissed her and held her close. They lay in each other's arms for a long time, just talking and stroking each other.

He would never go without her. Finally she accepted his decision. She wept then, and told him the truth, how much she had wanted him to stay, how terrified she had been that he might go. 'I'd crack apart without you. Seeing you gives me strength. I love you so much.'

They made love so tenderly that afterwards Sean wondered if he had dreamt it. Neither of them seemed to move. Her cheeks were flushed, her eyes closed, the rise and fall of her breathing so regular that except for the faint smile she might have been asleep. Then her eyes opened and her long shuddering sigh seemed to last forever.

An hour later the car from Morrison's office arrived to take her to Coventry.

Sean was introduced to the two Ministry officials who would travel with her.

After she had kissed him goodbye, she said, 'I'll be back in five days. Meanwhile stay in the shelters at night and—'

456

He placed a finger against her lips and settled her into the car.

She twisted round as the big Austin rolled down to the Embankment.

For the next hour he fidgeted, imagining her journey to the Midlands. He was glad she was going, if only for a few days. The Midlands were safe. She so desperately needed a break from the bombing. She worked too hard and lived on her nerves more than people realized. If this unexpected job for Morrison hadn't come up, Sean would have insisted that she leave London for a while. He had even spoken to Cynthia about it.

He settled at the typewriter to answer Freddie's letter. He hoped Freddie would understand and agree. The argument with Dinny still haunted him. 'Turning your back on your own people,' Dinny had shouted – and Sean had snarled back, 'Dev's not my people – or the Da's either!'

But who were his people? Freddie was his friend. Val was his mistress. They were the only 'people' he had.

When darkness fell Sean went down to the docks. Bombers came, but not in force. It was a quiet night, the slackest in weeks. He drank a few cups of tea at various fire-watching points, but there was little news to be gathered. Even so, he still felt glad that Val had gone to the Midlands – London was quiet, but Coventry would be quieter. With so little happening he returned to Craven Street and was in bed before one o'clock.

The telephone rang three hours later. 'Sean? Sean, for God's sake wake up.'

He recognized Bob Thompson, a friend in the Fire Service. They had shared a cup of tea earlier.

'Sean, there's a story if you want one. Coventry's been hit. We've had an SOS for two hundred firemen. From what I can make out –'

He dropped the phone, then scrambled after it, praying to have misheard. But he had not been mistaken. It was Coventry.

Thompson said, 'I'm leaving in fifteen minutes. There's room in my car if you want –'

By five o'clock they were racing through the blackout

to the Great North Road. At dawn, they were still twenty miles south of Coventry.

Thompson grumbled bitterly as he drove, 'First easy night in weeks, now this!'

Two other firemen cat-napped in the back seats, resting while they could. Sean had already pieced together what little they knew.

'Same old story,' Thompson complained, 'Jerry had things all his own way. No sign of the RAF. The message we got claimed 30,000 incendiaries were dropped before midnight. *30,000!* Two hundred fires were out of control when we heard. Afterwards the bastards dropped high explosives. It must have been easy – a blaze that size could guide them half way from Hamburg.'

'But if that was before midnight –'

'Phones went, everything went. The place was cut off hours ago. Birmingham called us – they've sent every man they've got. Water's a problem I think – the mains fractured and once that happens –'

'Val's there,' Sean whispered.

Thompson swore. 'Why didn't you – ' he threw Sean a sideways glance. 'You okay? Ah, don't worry, Val's a sensible girl, she'll be all right.'

Few people were all right in Coventry. They drove into a city razed to the ground. Even Thompson, hardened by the London Blitz, blanched at the devastation. The city centre was a pile of rubble, with nothing left standing. Pavements crept out from beneath the debris like broken veins, severed by craters of thick red mud. Twisted steel girders and looped telegraph wires marked what had once been lines of buildings. Smoke rose from still burning fires. Pathetic groups of people fought their way through the wreckage, hoisting timbers and masonry as they searched for survivors.

Sean wandered those devastated streets for hours. He shouted, 'It's all over' into basements and Anderson shelters, then helped survivors climb out, explaining that without power-cables no sirens could sound. He went looking for Val. She would have visited one of the factories. Coventry had dozens, all working round the clock, seven days a week – Vickers Armstrong turning out engines for Blenheim bombers, Hawker-Siddeley delivering engines for Whitleys, Rolls-Royce making for Spitfires, Daimler producing scout cars, nylon parachutes at Courtaulds, rubber tyres at Dunlop . . . Val could have gone to any of them.

He stopped asking questions after a policeman arrested him. When he had properly identified himself, the constable apologized. 'Sorry sir, I thought I detected a trace of an Irish accent. That might have caused you trouble.'

The IRA had bombed Coventry too!

Another lifetime, a different war. How strange that this tired-looking policeman in his torn uniform should remember it. The man managed an exhausted smile, 'Reckon we'll have something else to look back on now.'

Sean accepted some strong tea from a thermos flask and they parted as friends.

The tea helped ease the shock, and when he saw Bob Thompson at ten-thirty he was functioning again. 'Put me to work, Bob. I don't know what to do by myself – you tell me, and I'll do it.'

Thompson got him to the Gulston Road hospital where he worked as a stretcher bearer in an ambulance. Back and forth they went, picking up the maimed and the dying. People flagged them down as if they were a taxi. Sean's stomach turned over whenever they stopped, fearing that the next crippled wreck would be Val. The sights and stories were pitiful. Sometimes the debris was so bad that Sean had to clear a path for the ambulance. They were lost twice when the Coventry-born driver failed to find a single recognizable landmark.

Down torn streets, past gutted houses, around flattened churches, once through a graveyard because the road was impassable. Pangs of hunger were stirred by the juicy aroma of three hundred tons of Sunday joints roasting in a government meat store, still smoking despite the efforts of firemen. The affluent smell of good cigars came from a smouldering tobacconist's. But most smells were of cordite and rubble and death.

By mid-afternoon Sean had still not found Val. Neither had Bob Thompson, nor George Hamilton who arrived just as Thompson was on the point of departing for London.

'You're staying, Sean, are you,' Thompson stated rather than asked.

Sean nodded bleakly.

They worked until dusk, which is when Sean collapsed. Wrapped in George Hamilton's camel hair coat, he dozed in a corner of Gulston Hospital. He slept for only an hour. He knew she was dead when he awoke.

George Hamilton came in and laced a mug of tea with brandy from a hip flask. He passed it to Sean as he talked, 'The rescue teams are still working. She could be anywhere, maybe not even hurt, just helping and too busy to send word.'

Sean remained silent, unable to speak about Val, even to her father.

By noon next day the crippled city was revealed in all its misery. Eight out of every ten buildings had been destroyed or damaged. All twenty-seven vital war plants had been hit. Teams of doctors and nurses were arriving from all over the country to cope with the injured. The death toll rose all the time. Establishing exact numbers was difficult because bodies were still buried beneath tons of debris, or had been blown entirely apart.

Sean helped at the hospital until mid-afternoon, at which time he was replaced by qualified medical orderlies. He was thanked for his efforts and told to go home.

Valerie Hamilton had still not been found.

He wanted to die. His heart had been torn out. 'Oh Val,' he whispered, 'I love you so much.'

George Hamilton found him sitting in the street, apparently watching a man boil a kettle on a still smouldering incendiary bomb. But Sean was staring with unseeing eyes which saw nothing.

'She's gone,' George choked up. He squatted in the dirt and rested a hand on Sean's shoulder.

When Sean looked up, George Hamilton was crying, George Hamilton, who was always so assured, so in control of things, was sitting in the rubble of Coventry weeping.

Sean said nothing. Inside his head he was still talking to her. They were in bed at Craven Street, not making love, just talking softly about how much they loved each other.

George buried his head in his hands. His shoulders heaved as he struggled to talk. 'They only found her arm . . . Oh God, only her arm . . .'

Sean tried not to listen. He closed his eyes and saw her beside him. Gently he kissed her lips. 'I love you,' she whispered back.

'Her ring,' George gulped, '. . . still on her finger.'

Val's opal. A present from a proud father on her twenty-first birthday.

Sean stared at the ring, then closed his eyes again. 'I love you,' she whispered on the breeze which sighed through a trellis-work of broken bricks and twisted iron railings.

A long time later George Hamilton blew his nose noisily and stopped weeping. With a trembling hand he offered Sean a cigarette.

George Hamilton smoked in silence. When the cigarette was finished he cleared his throat. 'I must get back to Cynthia,' he said gently, 'I bumped into a man I know, he'll give us a lift.'

He looked at Sean. 'Come on, son, we're doing no good here. Val would have said, she'd have said, "Don't you know there's a war on?"'

Sean tried to smile, until his mouth twisted and his eyes spilled over with tears.

CHAPTER TEN

8 January, 1942

To my Dear Sister,
Really I'm writing to Uncle Ned and Aunt Eleanor to thank them for my Christmas present which arrived last week (late). It was clever of you to let them know I wanted a slide-rule. American slide-rules are wonderful and every boy in my class wants one now. I only lend mine to my best friend and that upsets the others who say I get more like an Averdale every day. 'What's his is his' they say, as if there was something wrong in that. Anyway, I WANT to be as like an Averdale as I can possibly be.

461

Tell Uncle Ned that I am sorry about his ships getting sunk at Pearl Harbor, but all my friends are pleased that America is now in the war. We are going to win, everyone says so, especially now. And guess what – the first American soldiers coming to Britain will come here to train. Three whole Divisions are arriving soon, it was in the papers. Perhaps some will be from Dayton, Ohio, and will know Uncle Ned and Aunt Eleanor, or even you as you've been there so long.

I am going in for business and politics when I get bigger and the war is over. UNCLE MARK said I can. Did I tell you I call him that now? He said I could at Christmas when we were talking about politics and the war and men's things like that. He said I am just the man to deal with the Croppies. He says having Americans over here will be a good thing because they will see what we have to put up with. He says it's all right for Croppies to be Catholics, he says they can worship the sun for all he cares (he said BLOODY WELL CARES – don't show this to Aunt Eleanor) but it's their disloyalty he can't stand, and neither can I. Do you know there's no rationing down there, but up here even Uncle Mark has to have coupons and things. He says all that Madman de Valera does is complain about the British, but if it wasn't for us he wouldn't have anything. We send him petrol and coal and food and all sorts of things, and all he does is let German spies run around Dublin (and JAPANESE spies, tell Uncle Ned). Uncle Mark says perhaps Americans won't be so keen to send guns to the IRA now that American soldiers will get shot here instead of British Tommies and RUC men.

Uncle Mark says it is two and a half years since we last saw you. It doesn't seem that long because so much has happened and anyway your photographs are everywhere all the time – I can't turn round without seeing you. I said that to Uncle Mark but he said that's not the same, but with you sending photographs every six months at least we all know what you look like.

Oh, and another thing about that Madman de Valera. When he heard American soldiers were coming here he made a big speech in protest. He said he didn't care if the troops were British or American, the north still belongs to him. Uncle Mark went red in the face about that and said *it would serve the south right if we let Hitler bomb Dublin into 'THE BLOODY BOG'. Averdales have been here since 1670 he said, 'not LIKE THAT BLOODY DAGO DE VALERA WHOSE FATHER WAS A MEXICAN BANDIT!' I put that last bit in for Uncle Ned. I bet not many people know that the Madman's father was a Mexican bandit. I thought as Mexico is near you that Uncle Ned might like to put it in his paper.*

I expect you think Uncle Mark swears a lot, and I suppose I shouldn't tell you these things. The trouble is I don't know any things that would interest a girl. I expect I will swear a lot too when I grow up and go in for business and politics. It's the strain I think. Uncle Mark says I will have to deal with English politicians and that lot will make me spit blood. I can swear a bit now but can only spit blood at the dentists or when I have a nose bleed.

Uncle Mark says as soon as the war is over you will come home and live with us. Brackenburn is to be rebuilt and when we grow up you will be the Lady of the House, entertaining me and my business and political friends – at least I think that is what Uncle Mark means. He's a bit vague at times, but I know I'm to go into business and keep the Croppies down – and I know you will be the Grand Lady at the Big House because I heard someone say that he should marry again, and he snapped 'Kate and I will reside at Brackenburn. If I didn't have that to look forward to I'd go mad!' So you see, Uncle Mark's got our futures all mapped out. It cheers me up to know that. I can't wait for this war to end and to grow up, so that I can swear and spit blood and do exciting things.

Must finish my homework now. Don't forget to send me those American comics with your next letter, they're much better than ours.

Your loving brother,
Timothy.

Kate was thinking about the Johnstones when Tim's letter arrived. In fact she had done little else but think about them for three weeks, ever since they met just after Christmas.

Meeting the Johnstones had not worried her – they were

463

just more people to be sent away singing her praises. After playing the role for nearly three years Kate was very well practised. Everyone who visited was impressed, and she still had the household eating out of her hand.

It was a strain at times, trying to please so many people. Kate survived by operating a system of checks and balances – a hint of disapproval here, an extra reward there – but sometimes the system broke down. Especially with Rose Smith. Pleasing Rose had become increasingly strange. Their game had grown more complicated, Rose had become more demanding. Bath time in particular had turned into a ritual for which Rose wore a fluffy towelling robe with nothing on underneath. If Kate refused to play, Rose became very angry – 'You're an ungrateful child. Why should I look after you? I'll leave, then see what your precious Aunt Eleanor does. She'll send you away to an orphanage.'

That was a terrifying threat. The checks and balances had broken down. Kate mended them, she dared not do otherwise, even though bath times became an ordeal from which Kate saw no escape.

Which is how things were, when Kate met the Johnstones.

Linc Johnstone had been born in Dayton, Ohio, and had known Eleanor since his boyhood. He had worked on the *Independent* before joining the State Department – where natural charm had made him as at home in politics as a fish is in water. Washington liked Linc from the minute it set eyes on him. His career had blossomed and he had stayed there, returning to Dayton for only an occasional visit. Which is what he was doing during that Christmas of 1941. Together with his wife and daughter, he was spending a month with his mother, who had a house on Hurlingham Drive. The rumour was that Linc was about to be transferred to the American Embassy in London – and the rumour was true.

He was a man who listened with a flattering intensity. Ned Bleakley said it was like talking to a magnet. 'He fastens on and sucks your words in. Then he changes a few and ten minutes later you're agreeing with him. He never really argues – a man could die waiting to get an argument out of Linc. I like him.'

People liked his wife too. Alison was a good wife to Linc and a devoted mother to Jennifer. In short, the Johnstones presented a fine image to the world. Linc was sandy haired, barrel chested, strong and reliable – Alison was gracefully slim, with fair hair and blue eyes. They were younger than Ned and Eleanor, but worldly wise by comparison – fish who swam in the mainstream of Washington, not the backwaters of Dayton, Ohio.

Alison's one fault – if it was a fault – was that she was not only ambitious for her husband, but for her daughter as well. Few people realized how patchy Alison's own education had been. It was a matter which worried her. She was determined that Jennifer would enjoy better advantages. Jennifer would go to 'a good school in England'. Linc had agreed to that before they had married – boy or girl (they had settled on only one child because of the expense), the child would go to 'a good school in England'.

Of course that was before war broke out in England. Alison had not reckoned on that. Consequently in 1941 Jennifer was at an international school in Washington, much favoured by diplomats, but very second best as far as Alison was concerned.

None of this was known to Kate when she first met the Johnstones – she knew only that they were old friends of the Bleakleys. Kate set out to impress in the same way as she tried to impress all visitors to 920 Hurlingham Drive.

Pleasing Mr Johnstone was easy. He complimented her on her looks, and her playing of the piano, and her fine British accent. He smiled a lot and said he hoped that Kate might become friends with his daughter – 'You're exactly the same age,' he said, 'I'm sure you have a million things in common.'

'They must have,' Aunt Eleanor agreed. 'Why not bring her with you tomorrow.'

Pleasing Mrs Johnstone was more of a challenge. Kate sensed that Mrs Johnstone was not easily taken in by appearances. Kate asked polite questions about Washington and President Roosevelt, and hoped that she was making a good impression.

And she was. Alison was very impressed, and only partly because of her natural fondness for all children. (Linc said she preferred children to adults, and sometimes she had to agree with him.) What also struck Alison was that Kate would make an ideal companion for Jennifer. Not only that, after the war Kate would surely go to a good school in England – perhaps, if the girls became friends, they could go together? The more Alison probed, the more impressed she became. Kate's guardian was *Lord* Averdale, with homes in London and Ulster. He was obviously rich and important. Kate might even inherit a fortune. What a wonderful chance for Jennifer. A friendship made now could change the course of her life . . .

Talking to Mrs Johnstone for so long was causing problems for Kate. When Aunt Eleanor entertained, Kate usually joined the party for tea. Then, after playing a piece on the piano, she made her excuses and left. She rarely stayed as long as an hour. Aunt Eleanor liked to show her off, but Aunt Eleanor liked having Uncle Ned and her friends to herself. Kate had long since known that.

She did try to escape, especially when she saw Aunt Eleanor looking at the clock – the problem was Mrs Johnstone kept asking more questions, and Kate, eager to please, had to answer – but she had been in the drawing-room for nearly two hours.

As the maid left with the tea things, Kate saw her chance. Rose Smith was in the hall. In her panic to escape, Kate said the first thing that entered her head. 'Excuse me, Mrs Johnstone, I think my bath is ready now.'

It was enough. Rose tapped on the door and came in.

Aunt Eleanor's face lit up. 'Ah Rose, there you are. Kate's bath must be ready.'

How could Aunt Eleanor realize the significance of the word bath – or Rose understand that Kate was simply trying to escape from Mrs Johnstone?

Certainly Rose understood nothing. 'Yes Ma'am,' she said, 'the bath is ready.'

And she looked straight at Kate.

Alison stifled a gasp. She stared at the nurse, not believing what she saw. In her thirty-five years she had seen that look only once – after a party in her first year of marriage. She had worn a low-cut dress which had drawn admiring glances from every man there, especially a naval officer with whom she had flirted shamelessly. Linc had become wildly jealous, as she had intended, although the consequences were unforeseen. Back in their apartment he had kissed her with bruising savagery – and undressed her and damn near raped her – and the look on his face had stayed in her mind ever since. That look. Naked lust. The look which had flashed across Rose Smith's face.

Alison felt shocked and then sick. Vaguely she said goodbye to Kate, adding that she would bring Jennifer tomorrow.

It seemed unbelievable that nobody else realized what was going on. When Alison looked at Eleanor all she got was a warm smile. Ned and Linc were already discussing the war.

Alison was so shaken that she could hardly think. She knew what she had seen. It took her ten minutes to recover enough to make an inoffensive remark, managing to express surprise that a girl of ten still had a nurse.

Eleanor sighed. 'Well nobody thought the war would last so long. Lord Averdale sent Rose Smith over with Kate and told her to stay. She makes herself useful, and of course she's devoted to Kate.'

And how, Alison thought.

She said nothing to Linc when they drove back to his mother's house. What was the point? He wouldn't understand the subtleties of the situation, he might not even believe her. Even so, Alison was quite sure of what she had seen. She had heard stories of other nannies. The relationship between nurse and child sometimes became twisted, especially when parental contact was non-existent. And neither Ned nor Eleanor knew the first thing about the complex emotions of a child . . . or the warped mind of a sexual pervert.

Alison was frightened and appalled. Kate might be sexually misdirected for the rest of her life. If so she was beyond Alison's reach. Certainly Jennifer must never be let near her. But perhaps the child saw it only as an extra cuddle at bedtime, or a kiss in the bath, or maybe felt a schoolgirl crush generated by a need for affection – if that were *all*, Alison thought she might cope.

Her motives became muddled. She had been guided by ambition for Jennifer, until in bed that night she experienced such a repugnance for Rose Smith that she flushed hot and cold with anger. Being a nurse was a sacred trust, especially when children were involved. By morning she knew she must do something. She couldn't leave a child in a situation like that – *any* child, let alone a girl the same age as her daughter.

To cap everything, Washington telephoned at breakfast and Linc was instructed to fly to New York that night, next stop London. Alison could have screamed. Linc was not due to go for a month. It was so unfair. Parting would have been a jolt anyway, now, so suddenly, when she needed his advice . . .

Linc telephoned the Bleakleys to say they would not be calling after all.

Eleanor came on the line. 'Why not send your daughter round anyway? It would give you and Alison a couple of hours to yourselves.'

She snatched the phone, 'Eleanor. That's sweet of you, but it's best for the family to be together. I'll call you tomorrow, okay?'

Linc looked surprised and disappointed.

She guessed why. They would be parted for almost a year. 'We can still go to bed,' she said, 'Jennifer can stay downstairs with Grandma for an hour. It's just that I don't want her at the Bleakleys' without me.'

Their afternoon lovemaking was dispirited. Sex seemed a poor proposition to her. It was like eating for the sake of it. Did he think she would forget how to do it? But he expected it, and she loved him, so she tried. She faked a climax and stroked his head on her breast for a long time afterwards.

Then, and she knew it was the wrong thing to do, she knew her timing was bad, but she couldn't help herself . . . she told him about Rose Smith.

Of course he didn't believe her.

'Honey, it's your imagination. I was there too, remember? I didn't see any such thing –'

468

'But what if I'm right –'

'You can't be right!'

'Suppose I am –'

'It's none of our business –'

'Lincoln! I'm talking about a child the same age as our daughter –'

'We can't interfere –'

'Interfere? My God, how can you say such a thing?'

'Alison, you can't be sure. You're over-reacting.'

They were having a row. She could hardly believe it. He was going away in a few hours, and would be gone for a whole year. Germans were bombing hell out of London . . . he might be injured, even killed . . . and here they were having a blazing row about a child she didn't even know existed until yesterday.

'Alison, honey, will you remember one thing. Ned Bleakley is influential in this town. His opinions are –'

'Rubbish when it comes to children. He doesn't know the first thing.'

She was crying and despising her tears. He was as soft about kids as she was really, she knew that, he just had to be convinced. They embraced and kissed and tried to put an end to their quarrel. 'You be very careful,' he whispered, as his last word.

She kissed him hard then, 'And you be careful in London. I really do adore you, Linc Johnstone.'

They dressed and went downstairs to join Jennifer and Linc's mother. He carried his cases into the hall, pretending that he and Alison had spent the last hour and a half packing.

Minutes after that his car arrived from Patterson's Field, and he was kissing the whole family goodbye.

Alison went to bed early and wept, calling herself a bitch for spoiling his last afternoon with an argument. Yet when she fell asleep it was not to a tender dream of reconciliation, but to a nightmare about Rose Smith.

She telephoned Eleanor Bleakley the next morning: 'Jennifer's down in the dumps about Linc going away. I thought I'd take her out to lunch as a treat. It would be such a help if Kate could come. I could pick her up at about twelve . . .'

She took them to the Country Club where they bumped into the golf pro. 'Morning, Mrs Johnstone,' he smiled warmly. 'Are these two young ladies new pupils for me?'

The small joke became important later.

Over the meal, Alison watched the two girls getting to know each other. She breathed a small sigh of relief. Her hunch had been right. Jennifer had been bored with Dayton, and Kate had never had a friend of her own age – both girls were delighted with each other. Even so, Alison felt a pang. Jennifer's pale straw-coloured hair and heart-shaped face were usually admired, but her quite good looks faded next to Kate. Alison reminded herself that most things in life are paid for, and if her suspicions were correct Kate's striking beauty had already brought her a good deal of suffering.

Lunch was an enormous success, and for the next seven days the girls spent a good deal of time together. Alison took them to the cinema, and on outings, and back to the Country Club – where she remembered the golf professional. 'Would you like golf lessons?' she asked. 'After all, you'll want to play in a few years and it's best to start things early.'

Jennifer's eyes rounded. Girls at her school did not start golf until they were thirteen. To start before would be very grown up.

Of course they had to consult Aunt Eleanor, and to comply with Madame Lefarge's timetable of lessons each morning, but everything conspired to throw the two girls together. Jennifer joined Madame Lefarge's morning classes, and every day after lunch Alison took the girls to the Country Club for their golf tuition.

Throughout it all, Alison watched Kate like a hawk.

She even questioned Jennifer.

She was charmed, but not fooled. She saw through many of Kate's stratagems to get her own way. She watched Kate manipulate people at Hurlingham Drive. She even, to a small extent, fathomed Kate's system of checks and balances. Alison was undismayed. She felt she was getting to understand the child. The girl had been alone for half of her life – without parents, separated from her brother, cut off from her grandparents, parted from her guardian.

In a sense she had suffered one shipwreck after another. And Hurlingham Drive was hardly a safe haven. Neither Ned nor Eleanor was what Alison called 'children people', and the rest of the household followed suit, with the single exception of Rose Smith. Alison shuddered. Kate had been fighting to survive.

Three further weeks of observation revealed Kate to be a healthy girl who showed no signs of wanting to indulge in unnatural practices. Alison breathed a heartfelt sigh of relief. Even so, she was worried about being able to keep an eye on the girl for much longer. Jennifer was due to restart school in Washington early in February. It was almost time to leave Dayton and return to the capital.

Which was what Alison was concerned about before the afternoon of 2 February, when everything changed.

Alison and the girls had just returned to the Bleakleys' from the Country Club, where the girls had exhausted themselves with an extra session on the driving range.

'I ache all over,' Jennifer groaned happily. 'I'm going straight back to Grandma Johnstone's to soak in the tub.'

Alison smiled at the pair of them, both flushed and weary and pleased with themselves. It was the way she liked to see them. 'Come on then,' she said, rising from her chair. 'There's no point in me getting comfortable.'

Eleanor and Kate came out to the hall with them, Kate limping dramatically and everyone giggling. Alison felt tremendously pleased, Kate was behaving as a child should, perfectly relaxed and enjoying herself. And Alison was awarding herself some credit for that, when Rose Smith came out of the kitchen door. 'Oh Rose,' Eleanor said. 'Run a bath for our poor tired athlete, will you. She's overdone it today.'

And Alison again saw that look in Rose Smith's eyes.

It was gone in a split second. But Alison had seen it.

Her mind whirled. She felt unable to leave the child, yet what could she do?

She drove back to Grandma Johnstone's house in a daze. That poor child. If anything happened she would never forgive herself. She couldn't accept that it was none of her business. Suppose something like that happened to Jennifer? Wouldn't she hope someone would have the decency to intervene? Oh God! She had to go back, make some excuse to see Kate, be sure the child was safe . . .

Grandma Johnstone opened the door.

Alison blurted out, 'I've left something at Eleanor's. I'll have to get it.' She tried to calm herself by forcing a smile and ruffling Jennifer's hair. 'This one is asleep on her feet. All she wants is a bath and then bed. I won't be long.'

She left and drove the block and a half back to 920 Hurlingham Drive. Her brain stalled. What excuse could she give to Eleanor for returning? Nothing sounded sensible. She couldn't think of one plausible reason. She bit her lip and urged herself to think.

She parked on the road, not the drive, and walked past the front porch to the side door. It was unlocked as usual. She hurried past the kitchen door and into the hall. Up the stairs. Like a thief! Oh God, if I meet Eleanor, what will I say? How will I ever explain . . .

Along the landing. How long since she left – ten minutes, fifteen perhaps. Oh this is awful, not happening, a nightmare. Lincoln would be so furious. These people were his friends, mine too . . .

Kate's sitting-room was empty. The far door was ajar. Alison tiptoed across and peered into the bedroom. Kate was not there. The door to the bathroom was closed. Alison skirted the bed. She listened outside the bathroom – opened the door – and went in.

They were on the floor. Both naked. Kate was on top. Her hand was working like a piston. The nurse was groaning. Her legs were wide apart. She was tugging Kate's head down to her breast.

Alison shrieked. She kicked blindly at Rose Smith's ankle. Kate rolled off, terrified. The nurse gasped and tried to cover herself. Alison attempted to speak but gagged instead. She staggered to the bath and sat on the edge. The nurse scrambled to her feet, pulling a towelling robe up from the floor. Kate stood there screaming hysterically. Alison's hand cracked hard across the child's cheek. Kate gasped, covered her face and began to sob.

Alison could have committed murder. She thanked God afterwards that no weapon presented itself. She stared with hatred and loathing at the nurse, who was moving towards her own room.

'You filthy . . .' Alison screamed. She stopped, taking deep breaths, trying to calm herself. 'Get dressed and –'

'It's my word against yours,' Rose Smith spat back.

Alison was too stunned to answer. She turned to the child, 'Oh God, what are we going to do?'

Sheer terror stopped the flow of Kate's tears. 'Oh please, don't send me to the orphanage, *please*!'

Alison reeled, realizing the threats that had provoked the child's fear. She gasped and spun round to the nurse, only to see the door closing as Rose Smith slammed into her bedroom.

'*Please!*' Kate begged through her tears.

Alison rallied her strength.

'Not the orphanage,' Kate screamed, 'I'll do any-thing –'

'Now listen to me,' Alison grasped Kate's bare shoulders and shook her violently. She stared into the girl's eyes. 'Just answer one question. I'll know if you're telling lies. Did you want to do . . . that . . . what I saw, did you, *did you*?'

'She made me,' Kate burst out. 'She made me do it.'

Alison shook her again, staring hard into Kate's face. She almost sobbed herself. 'God help me, I believe you. But if my Jennifer ever gets into anything like this because of you, may God strike you dead. Do you understand that?'

Kate was too petrified to understand anything.

Alison made her wash her hands and face before bundling her out of the bathroom to her bedroom. Kate could not stop trembling. Alison was shaking herself but she dressed the girl in a nightdress and dressing-gown, then sat her on the bed and talked to her sternly. 'You're to tell no one about this. Not ever. Not even Jennifer. Promise me that and I'll do what I can to help. Break your promise and I'll never have anything to do with you again.'

Kate was sobbing so hard that no answer was possible.

Ten minutes later they went downstairs, leaving Rose Smith still in her room. Alison took Kate to the kitchen and told Melissey to warm up some milk. 'And she's to stay here with you until I fetch her. Let her go to sleep by the fire. Don't talk to her, she's had a nasty shock, just give her warm milk and keep an eye on her.'

After giving Kate a look which warned her to keep quiet, Alison left. Her legs felt wobbly as she walked down the hall to the drawing-room. She heard Ned's voice as she opened the door. She was glad he had arrived home. He was pouring Eleanor a sherry when Alison walked in.

'Alison? I didn't hear the front . . . My God, what's the matter, you're as white as –'

She sat down and asked for a brandy.

Eleanor rose from her chair, concern in every line of her face. 'My dear, what on earth has happened?'

Alison looked at them. Kind, civilized, sane people – but they had let it happen under their very noses. She stifled her temper. 'Ned, you might need a brandy yourself. And pour one for Eleanor.'

She told them what had happened.

Poor Eleanor was lost. She had no knowledge of such things, had never heard the word lesbian let alone some of the other expressions Alison used. But Ned understood. He went grey.

Eleanor whispered, 'You mean that two women would, together . . .'

Ned stared at Alison. 'You *knew* this was going on?'

'Do you think if I had known I'd have let it happen?' Alison snapped angrily. She shrugged helplessly. 'I suspected. Tonight I thought that, well, something might happen . . .'

'Dear God in Heaven,' Ned whispered into his glass.

Eleanor was on the verge of tears. 'I always said we shouldn't have her. You see, we've no experience of children.' She appealed to Alison, 'I never wanted the responsibility . . . but Ned said, well you see he felt obligated to Lord Averdale . . .'

Alison could have screamed. They had not asked a single word about the child! Not asked where she was, how she was – God, how could people be so selfish, so unfeeling!

'We turned the house upside down,' Eleanor said. 'Now this has happened . . .'

Alison's hands tightened into fists on her lap. She sat bolt upright in her chair. 'I thought you were very proud of

474

Kate. After all, she's tried tremendously hard to fit in –'

'Oh she can be sweet,' Eleanor said quickly. 'And pretty –'

'That's the trouble,' Ned burst out. 'She's too damn pretty. I was afraid something like this would happen. Well not exactly like *this*, but, well dammit, that child's so attractive someone was going to get hold of her . . .'

Alison could scarcely believe what she was hearing. 'You make it sound like her fault. She's only a child.'

He flushed the colour of beetroot. 'I know that, but she's too pretty for her own good. I've seen grown men look at her like . . . well, you know what I mean. She'll be trouble all her life.'

Alison wanted to cry. She wished Lincoln were here. She had never missed him so much in the whole of her life.

Nobody spoke for several minutes. Ned poured another drink. Eleanor looked painfully embarrassed and stared at the carpet.

Ned cleared his throat. 'You could have misunderstood the whole thing. I mean, bursting in like that – they could have been fooling around. Sometimes things aren't what they seem.'

Alison stared at him. Rose Smith's words rang in her ears – 'It's your word against mine.' Oh dear God, don't let it come to that.

'Well?' Ned asked. 'What about it? Do you think you could have been mistaken?'

She tried to hide her contempt. 'Shall I draw you a diagram of what they were doing, Ned?'

He flushed his beetroot colour again. Eleanor sucked in her breath and looked more shocked than ever.

Alison wondered how she had ever seen them as friends. All she felt now was contempt, and anger of course, she was beginning to feel very angry indeed.

Ned gave a shaky laugh. 'Well you must have frightened the hell out of them. Reckon they'll never do it again.'

Alison's anger boiled over. She said Ned should send for the Sheriff. If Ned wouldn't press charges, she would. She refused to leave the house while that pervert remained under the same roof as Kate. She said she would write to Lord Averdale and tell him exactly what had happened.

She said all they were thinking about was what people would say about *them*, what their friends would say, the dirty stories people would put around. She said she was ashamed for the pair of them. She said that and a lot more, more than was prudent. She was trembling and in tears when she finished, but she said it. And they said not a word to interrupt.

When she calmed down she realized that she was the only one who could provide a solution. Perhaps because she was the only one who really cared about Kate. Even so the exact arrangements would take a little while to work out.

Eleanor retired to her room, too upset to participate. Alison was relieved to see her go. They would never feel the same about each other again.

Ned went along with everything. Alison left him no choice. It was either do it her way, or listen to her recount all she had seen to the Sheriff.

They went up to Rose Smith's room together. When the nurse claimed to be in bed and refused to answer the door, Alison gave her five minutes to dress and get downstairs. Six minutes later came a tap on the drawing-room door.

Alison did the talking. Rose Smith was dismissed, fired, sacked. She would pack her things and leave the house immediately. It was eight-thirty by the clock on the mantelpiece. If she was ever seen in Dayton again, Alison would report her to the police. If she was discovered to be working as a nurse, or to be in charge of children, Alison would call the authorities. She would receive no reference, merely a cheque for three months' salary. And she was to be gone within the hour.

Alison delivered the ultimatum in a brisk voice which brooked no interruption, but she was terrified the nurse would deny everything and Ned Bleakley would be forced to decide who was telling the truth. So Alison gambled and finished with a lie. 'That child has signed a statement, and when those six pages are read out in court you'll be lucky not to be lynched.'

Rose Smith's defiance died in a split second. Fear shone from every pore of her face. Ned Bleakley's doubts vanished. He held out a cheque, drawn on the Averdale account which provided for Kate.

Rose Smith hesitated, snatched it, then spat at Alison, 'I suppose you'll have her all to yourself now, won't you?'

Alison cried out. She was swinging her arm when Ned caught her hand.

'Get out of my house,' he said, but Rose Smith was already making for the door.

Ned helped a trembling Alison into a chair. 'I could use another drink,' he said, 'what about you?'

She shook her head and asked for coffee instead.

An hour later Rose Smith left 920 Hurlingham Drive and never returned.

Only when the front door banged did Alison take Kate back to her room and put her to bed, telling her to go to sleep and they would talk about things in the morning. But the child was still terrified about being sent to an orphanage.

'No,' Alison said wearily. 'You won't be sent there.'

Then she went downstairs to Ned Bleakley to make sure.

CHAPTER ELEVEN

It was the spring of 1943 before Sean Connors met Freddie Mallon again. Much had happened in the interval. Slowly but surely the tide of war was turning against Nazi Germany and Imperial Japan. The most dramatic headlines were no longer about London, instead other theatres of war made the news. Unfamiliar names in the Middle East and even the Far East were coming to be recognized as easily as Paris or New York. The Germans were retreating from Russia. There was much talk of a second front. An Allied invasion of Europe seemed imminent.

Sean Connors had remained in London throughout. For the first year he told himself he was doing it for Val. Dear Val, who had dreamt of a brave new world – who had loved London so much. Val would have stayed, so Sean stayed in her place. It gave him a reason for existing, which was vital at first. After that, he just lasted it out – immersed in his work, straining to improve his technique, not from professionalism but from a simple determination to get his message across.

Around him, blitzed and battered London was changing. Americans in uniforms had arrived in numbers. The West End contrived a tawdry gaiety. Sean was invited to five parties a night. He went to some, where he talked and drank and smoked his way through the night – but never did he dance or take a pretty girl home. The Irish Navvy became known as the Gaelic Monk.

Freddie Mallon had accepted Sean's wish to remain in London, he even understood and respected the reasons. After which he turned his own energies back to broadcasting in America. In fact, from Pearl Harbor onwards Freddie became part of the war effort. He did a series of shows, some straight news but more and more 'entertainments' from Army camps and Navy depots – broadcasts which were a mixture of quiz games and talent contests and quick-fire patter, all designed to keep the boys in uniform in touch with 'the folks at home'. They were immensely popular. Sponsors queued up for Freddie Mallon. He became a radio phenomenon. And Freddie was shrewd. Just as he owned fifty per cent of Sean's output from London, so he found other young broadcasters to take over shows he had created in the States. By 1943 Freddie Mallon was wealthy, and looking for a new challenge.

Which is what had brought him to London.

He had changed in three years, most noticeably by growing a moustache and a few extra inches round his waist. His hair was thinner, but he looked happy and prosperous. Marriage to Margaret had been an unqualified success – they now had a son and Margaret was expecting again. Freddie's wallet bulged proudly with family snapshots.

By contrast Sean looked leaner, as did most people in London. He was fit enough though, no doubt because he cycled around London every day looking for stories.

Freddie was staggered. 'Cycled? You're not suggesting we get a tandem, I hope.'

It was a warm reunion. They remained closeted in Craven Street for thirty-six hours. What was so exciting was that Freddie planned to stay, at least until the end of the war.

'Item one,' he said cheerfully, 'has got to be the Allied Invasion of Europe. It must come soon. When those boys go I want to be one step behind with the microphone in my hand, all the way to Berlin. We'll do two shows a week, right – call the first *Seven Days at the Front*, all the battles, the real front line stuff – then a Mom and Pop show from farther back, a base hospital, something like that – music and messages to home, and not a dry eye in the house.'

Of course it made sense. Freddie and his agent had already signed contracts with all sorts of people. But that was just the start.

'The next step is when all the Krauts are dead and buried. Then we'll go back to the US of A to a welcome that will blow your hat off. And to more money than you ever dreamed of. What about it, Sean? You've got an audience of millions over there.'

Freddie's enthusiasm was a tonic in battle-scarred London. It was easy to get carried away. Sean was grateful, and yet. Yet what? Sean couldn't say to begin with. He stumbled and mumbled, until Freddie became short-tempered. 'Hell, just spit it out, kid. What's on your mind?'

How could he express himself without sounding ungrateful? And how could he defend something so illogical? But to leave London – Val's London, the London of Alfred Harmsworth, the London he had wanted to conquer – well, it just wouldn't feel right.

Sean struggled with almost forgotten dreams. He talked of gombeen men and the Dublin Quays and the Widow O'Flynn. He even managed a shy smile. 'What with the war and Val and everything, I haven't given anything else much thought. Now you're talking about *after* the war and making a fortune and things. I don't know,' he sighed. 'It's a different set of priorities. I don't want to think –'

'You've got to look ahead –'

'But that far? I'm not even sure I want to make a fortune without Val –'

'You've been living alone too long. It's unnatural –'

'I've been living in London, and I like the place, despite everything. And Harmsworth made his fortune here –'

'Will you listen to me? Harmsworth was yesterday. I'm talking about tomorrow. And tomorrow belongs to the United States of America.'

When Sean looked dubious, Freddie leaned forward in his chair. 'Let me tell you something. This war changed the whole ball game. Four years ago the United States was one of the world's major powers, right – but just one of about eight. Not any longer. Not when this war ends. Forget London, forget the British – the Empire won't exist after the war, and when that goes Britain's influence goes with it.'

'But –'

'But nothing. There's a war boom across the States like nobody's ever seen. We produce half the steel in the world, half the electricity, more than half the oil. National income, wealth, industrial production, all doubled in the last four years. And when this war ends all that production will get turned round to making automobiles and frigidaires and radios. No other country in the world will be able to compete. Everyone will be rebuilding, and with the start we've got, they'll never catch us.'

Freddie could not understand Sean's reservations. 'Is it Dublin?' he suggested. 'Are you homesick for Ireland?'

Sean wondered that himself.

Freddie shook his head. 'Forget it. Don't bury yourself over there whatever you do. De Valera's turned it into the backwater of all time. Ireland's getting a stinking press back home.'

Sean knew that was true, Freddie had sent him the clippings. De Valera's neutrality policy was seen as a threat to American lives. Bad enough that there were unending rumours of German and Japanese spies in Dublin, even worse when the Irish refused to allow the British into their ports, but when de Valera took the same attitude with America . . . 'He's biting the hand that feeds him,' Freddie growled. 'You know we've given him half a million dollars worth of Red Cross supplies. He wanted rifles for his Defence Forces, so the British actually handed him 20,000 of those we sent over for them! He's had the chartering of our cargo ships, access to our wheat, our cotton, our steel. Did you know Churchill even now has invited him to join the Allies? *Even now!* I tell you, the Brits are too soft at times.'

'Hey! I'm Irish, remember –'

'But you're not for de Valera. Come on Sean, you never had a good word for –'

'Maybe, but he's right about the border –'

'Oh really? Well I'm glad about the border. I'm glad American ships can put into Belfast, and American flyers can land in the north of Ireland, and American soldiers can train there. Considering they're risking their lives to save the whole of Ireland –'

'Okay,' Sean held up his hands. 'Don't let's argue . . .'

Freddie sighed, 'I'm sorry Sean, but I had lunch last month with David Gray, he's our Ambassador in Dublin. Some of the things he told me made my blood boil. Gray calls Dev a political racketeer, and that's Gray when he's being polite.'

Sean shrugged and the conversation drifted for a while, until Freddie brought it back to Sean's plans for after the war. 'Has it anything to do with the IRA?' he asked at one point. 'You know, when we first met, you were very bitter. Understandably, after your father and . . . all that.'

Sean felt a sudden twinge of disloyalty. Val's death, the bombing, the war, grinding on day after day had overshadowed everything for so long that he had hardly thought of his father.

'What about that guy what's his name?' Freddie frowned. 'Dinny Macaffety was telling me about him. The family feud –'

'Riordan,' Sean felt himself go cold. 'Matt Riordan.'

'That's right, him –'

'He's in prison.'

Dinny had written about that. Besides Sean still read the Irish papers, even though they were censored. He told Freddie what he knew – that the IRA was in tatters, men were imprisoned all over the place in England and Ireland, north and south of the border. Some men had been hanged, some had been shot, others had starved themselves to death on hunger strike.

Freddie grinned. 'Well that's a relief. I was afraid you were going to devote your life to putting them down. That's what you said once. At least Dev's taken care of the IRA.'

After that they dropped the subject, and in the following weeks rarely returned to it.

Freddie was wrong about the Second Front. The Allies failed to launch an invasion against Europe in 1943. Freddie filled time by broadcasting a series of shows from USAS bases in Britain, and appearing as a guest on *Seven Days in London*. But by November he was yearning for Margaret, home, and a new baby daughter he had yet to set eyes on.

He left before the end of the month, having arranged to record a show on a convoy *en route* to Newfoundland.

'But I'll be back in the spring,' he told Sean. 'We *must* hit the bastards then for Chrissakes! Meanwhile, take care of yourself . . . and start thinking about what we're going to do after the war.'

Sean found it hard to do that. London was being bombed again, this time by Hitler's rockets. The end of the war seemed no nearer to Sean. Besides, the war kept him busy, gave him reasons for existing. He did not want to look too far into the future. What was the point, with no one to share it with?

Sharing was something about which Kate had learned a great deal by November of 1944. She had been in America for more than five years by then, and had known the Johnstones for at least half of that time.

She divided her life in America into two parts – before and after the Johnstones, and there was no doubt which she preferred, even if the second part had started so traumatically.

She would never forget that morning – waking to the knowledge that Rose had gone, and that Mrs Johnstone had caught them together. She guessed people knew, Uncle Ned and Aunt Eleanor *must* know, Rose took orders only from them. She wondered about the servants. She cringed under the bedclothes, not wanting to get up, terrified of facing the household – petrified by thoughts of orphanages and Beadles and Fagin's Kitchens and . . .

Then Mrs Johnstone had tapped on the door, 'It's time you were up, sleepy head.'

Kate had been terrified that Mrs Johnstone would be ready to take her to the orphanage. Instead, Mrs Johnstone had sat on the bed. 'Now we are going to have a talk,' she had said.

Which was how Kate had learned of her future.

Jennifer was to leave her school in Washington, and Madame Lefarge would be her tutor as well as Kate's. They would live in Washington for part of the time, all of them, in the Johnstones' apartment, Madame Lefarge too . . .

Kate could hardly believe her ears.

No one could say how long the arrangement would last – probably until the end of the war, when Jennifer would go to school in England, hopefully, Mrs Johnstone said, to the same school as Kate.

Which is how Kate's new life had commenced.

She had still been stunned by it two days later when they had travelled to Washington, stunned but hugely relieved. Jennifer was delighted, and Kate had never seen Madame Lefarge so happy.

The first year passed in a flash. They did so many things. Aunt Alison took them all over Washington, and farther afield at weekends – taking trips to Chesapeake Bay and to Richmond, where Aunt Alison had friends. And when they returned to Dayton in the summer, Kate was allowed to stay at Grandma Johnstone's house, provided she visited Uncle Ned and Aunt Eleanor twice a week. The arrangements suited everyone. Meanwhile Kate and Jennifer spent every minute together.

When Linc Johnstone returned from London for two months, early in 1943, he found he had virtually acquired another daughter – and that he could hardly move in his Washington apartment for items of female apparel. The arrangement had its advantages. Yvette Lefarge looked after the girls in Washington, while Linc and Alison spent a month in Florida having a second honeymoon. After which the five of them 'did' New York and Chicago before spending Linc's last week in Dayton.

Kate had never been so happy. The Johnstones were so sure of each other, so abundantly loving that it rubbed off.

483

For the first time since the Killing at Keady, Kate felt that she was part of a proper family. They loved her and she loved them back a million times over. Kate felt a sense of belonging at last.

By the time Uncle Linc returned to London, Kate felt she was as much his daughter as was Jennifer. It was the same with Aunt Alison. Kate's whole day seemed to be spent saying 'Aunt Alison would like this' or 'Aunt Alison would like that', until Jennifer shrieked, 'I don't care what Mummy would like, what about doing what *we* want for a change?'

Even Alison had to intervene at times. 'Darling, we're happy to have you with us. Now just relax and be yourself for a while.'

It was just that Kate was so eager to please.

In time, however, she did relax, and life got better and better. In October Aunt Alison received a letter from London saying Uncle Linc was coming home again.

'He's arriving New York on 1 December, and we're all to go there to meet him.'

The excitement was tremendous. They went to New York two days early and stayed in an hotel. Aunt Alison bought Kate and Jennifer entire new outfits. 'Real grown-up clothes at last,' Jennifer squealed, parading up and down in front of a mirror. Then they went to Idlewild airport. Yvette Lefarge looked French and petite. Aunt Alison was positively radiant. Jennifer appeared blonde and mysterious and almost adult. And Kate felt so proud to be part of them.

When Uncle Linc's plane landed they waved and waved until their arms ached. He walked right past, pretending not to see them at all. 'Over here,' they screamed. 'Over here!' He looked astonished. 'I was expecting my middle-aged wife and two schoolgirls. What do I find? The four prettiest chorus girls in New York. Did you hear those soldiers whistle? I tell you, I'm the luckiest man alive.'

And as Kate hugged him she knew she was the luckiest girl.

Christmas 1943 was wonderful, even if Uncle Linc did have to go back to London immediately afterwards. 'Don't worry,' he said, 'the war will be over soon. Then

484

we'll be together again.'

But the war dragged on, although the news got better. The Allies were moving up through Italy. American forces landed in the Marshall Islands. The Russians penetrated a place called Estonia. And then – in June – Kate heard Freddie Mallon on the air. The Allies had landed in Normandy! Not a week passed after that without everyone crowding round the radio to listen to Freddie Mallon's *Seven Days from the Front*.

In August came a day which Kate would never forget. They were at Grandma Johnstone's house in Dayton. Jennifer was on the couch, her blonde head bent over her Grandma's sewing box as she stitched a button on to a blouse. Aunt Alison was at the table, trying to write to Uncle Linc – until the news on the radio made concentration impossible. Grandma Johnstone was in her chair at the fireside, and Kate was sitting next to Yvette, holding her hand.

The Allies had liberated Paris!

Freddie Mallon's voice was hoarse with excitement as he described the scene. The tears in Yvette's eyes brimmed over and slid down her cheeks. Now and then she muffled a sob, and Kate squeezed her hand extra hard. Freddie Mallon was shouting above the noise of people singing the Marseillaise, his voice swamped by sounds of cheering.

Aunt Alison crossed the room to hug Yvette. Kate couldn't speak for the lump in her throat. Grandma Johnstone blew into a handkerchief. Jenny kept her head bent over her sewing box. Paris was free . . . and Yvette Lefarge was so overjoyed that a moment later she broke down and wept uncontrollably.

Every week after that Freddie Mallon delivered another wonderful programme that seemed to hasten the end of the war. In September, Antwerp and Brussels were liberated, and later that month Allied troops were fighting German troops on Reich soil. Elsewhere American troops were pressing Japan. Uncle Linc's letters became more and more positive, he was sure the end was in sight – and he had some momentous news of his own. When peace came, he was to stay in London for at least three more years.

Aunt Alison was jubilant. 'We shall all go to Europe.

You two girls can go to school together. Imagine, you'll be able to spend one vacation with us and the next with Kate's guardian. Won't that be fun?'

Kate could think of nothing so idyllic. In fact she wrote to her guardian about it.

But Mark Averdale was not at all pleased. He replied that he had no intention of losing Kate to a school in England. She would live in Ulster with him. He would build her a palace. Her education would be completed by the best tutors money could buy.

Jennifer did her best to soften the news. 'Don't worry. Your fussy old guardian doesn't know my mother. She's set her mind on us going to school together.'

And Aunt Alison had. She wrote to Linc in London, telling him of Lord Averdale's response. He answered – *'Listen honey, try not to worry. We'll work it out. Kate's a swell kid with a lot going for her. I may be visiting our troops in Belfast before I come home in November. If I get there I'll look this Lord Averdale up. Tell Kate not to worry. We're not beaten yet.'*

When Aunt Alison read the letter out over breakfast, Kate burst into tears and rushed to her bedroom.

She was still weeping when Aunt Alison came in.

'Oh Aunt Alison, can't I choose? I want to be with you and Jennifer and Uncle Linc for the rest of my life. I love you all so much . . .'

Aunt Alison held her close for a long time – 'Leave it to your Uncle Linc, he'll work something out, he always does.'

Kate prayed as never before.

But there had been no news for a month. Even though Uncle Linc had been to Belfast. Now he was on his way home again, and they were once more at Idlewild to greet him.

Mark Averdale had been in London when Linc Johnstone called in Belfast. Deliberately. Mark had no intention of sending Kate to school in England, and saw no point in discussing his plans with anyone except Kate. So Mark had avoided a meeting altogether by travelling to London.

The journey had been tedious. What had taken four

486

hours from Liverpool before the war now took twice as long, travelling in an unheated train, crammed with troops. Mark hated it but it was a journey he made every month, partly for meetings with the Government and partly to see Molly Oakes, his mistress.

Molly was one of the three people who had kept Mark sane during the war. Kate was another of course, her letters and photographs had become treasured possessions. The letters were too short and the photographs inadequate, but they were an ongoing link. On black days he thought the child would never be as beautiful as her mother. On other days he was full of hope that Kate the child would develop into a beauty even lovelier than Rouen's masterpiece. Those days sustained him.

Meanwhile he was satisfied with the boy. Tim O'Brien worked well at school and was streets ahead of his contemporaries in academic subjects. He would never be an athlete, the injuries to his legs had seen to that, but he walked normally and was strong and healthy. Perhaps the most remarkable thing about him was his interest in politics. Studying the history of the Averdales had enabled him to master Ulster history, and that in turn had made him familiar with the growth of industry in the Province. There was no doubt where Tim saw his future. He could already take a set of books to trial balance, and planned to qualify as an accountant as quickly as possible. After which he would move into the Averdale businesses and from there into public life – ambitions which Mark Averdale encouraged.

But Mark could hardly talk to Tim about Kate, in fact only one person knew of his plans for Kate, and that was Molly Oakes who, throughout the grey years of war, continued to provide an oasis of sexual stimulation and satisfaction. When shortages of even basic commodities brought hunger to bombed-out London, Molly Oakes dealt with every black-marketeer for miles around. In a changing world, standards were maintained at her house in St John's Wood.

Molly so indulged Mark's sexual fantasies that he relaxed with her – but rarely with anyone else. He could be charming when he chose, but occasions which warranted charm were few and far between in his opinion. The growing mood of informality, generated by the war, won no approval from Mark Averdale – and when the Americans arrived, he positively shuddered.

American troops, Mark decided, were the last word in sloppiness and uncouth manners. One day he was actually stopped as he left the Unionist Club by a GI who thrust out a hand, 'Put it there, Mac. They tell me you're a real live Lord, for Chrissakes!'

Mark tried to have nothing to do with the Americans. It was difficult at times, with the Government pressing him to host various functions in Belfast. He was coaxed into the US Officers' Club one night, along with a number of other civic dignitaries. A Captain from Omaha, flushed on Irish whiskey, suddenly raised the subject of the IRA. 'I know it's off limits,' he drawled, 'but what the hell, we're all friends here, aren't we?'

The vacuum of horrified silence was filled by the Captain's rambling attack on the British in Ireland. 'Hell, we hate your policy of colonial repression. People should run their own countries, I say.'

Finally Mark could stomach no more. 'And your views on your own country, Captain? You feel you have a stake in America?'

'A stake? I should say so – why my family fought the British at Yorktown – and moved in covered wagons –'

'Yorktown was 1781 wasn't it?' Mark said crisply. 'That's recent history. Nine generations of Averdales have been born in Ulster. My qualifications as an Ulsterman outrank yours as an American by a couple of hundred years. The Red Indians have a more recent claim to your land than any Irishman has to mine. Perhaps when you clear out of North America, I'll think about leaving Ulster. Until then I wish you goodnight.'

Mark stormed out and never set foot in the Officers' Club again.

Americans soldiers and Mark Averdale were like oil and water. He loaned some paintings to the Government once, for an exhibition at Queen's Hall, only to find a Marine sergeant gawking at a Rubens nude, 'Say, Buddy, that's the sweetest piece of ass I ever saw in my life.'

Mark hurried away, enraged that his treasures should be displayed to such uncultured morons.

The Americans were already 'Making the World safe for Democracy'. Mark shuddered. A country without an aristocracy would be unbearable. God alone knew what would become of Britain after the war. Whenever Mark was in London he was plagued by some bloody socialist wielding the power of a Commissar at the Ministry of Supply.

For solace there was only Molly Oakes – and plans for a future with Kate. Until, came a night in November 1944, when Mark was too preoccupied to relax – even with Molly. Linc Johnstone's threatened visit had made Mark think about Kate's schooling. He was determined not to involve her in traditional education, but she would need training in some things . . . .

'It's about Kate's education,' he said. 'The war *must* end next year. Of course she'll have tutors. More important, she'll have me. I'll guide her all the way until we get married, but Molly, I'll want some help from you.'

Molly stroked his hand and kissed the tips of his fingers.

Mark outlined his plans. Marriage to Kate would be the perfect union – but she would be an untutored virgin when she arrived at his bed. He remembered Dorothy's love-making and shuddered.

Kate had to be taught the art of providing sexual happiness. 'It's not entirely unknown, you know,' he said. 'Royalty, people who have the money, Arabs, the Japanese have geisha girls – well, none of them leave it to chance. A girl should be trained, that's what I'm saying.'

The following morning, he left with Molly's agreement to do all that was asked of her. Kate was to be taught by the best tutor money could buy.

That prospect kept Mark cheerful until Christmas. He kept telling himself that the war must end soon. But 1945 opened slowly. Warsaw was captured by Russian troops, but Germans were still ferociously defending the Fatherland.

Mark restrained his impatience as best he could. Privately he began to think the war had been a good thing in some ways. True, Belfast had been bombed, but the city

489

had escaped the blitz suffered by London – and by January 1945 German air raids on Belfast had ceased altogether. Meanwhile every Averdale factory was working flat out, the shipyards were busy, and although profits were controlled, at least there were profits, not losses. The slump was a thing of the past.

So was the IRA. Mark approved of internment. How else could you deal with traitors while fighting a war? Lock them up and throw away the key was Mark's advice, and he was pleased to see it taken.

He knew Matt Riordan was imprisoned on the Curragh. The RUC had told him. He was pleased and displeased at the same time. Pleased that Riordan had been caught, displeased that he had been caught south of the border. Riordan would not have been slammed in prison in Belfast, he would have been hanged by the neck for murder.

January crept into February and then into March. In Europe, Dresden was bombed to ashes and the Allies captured Cologne. In the Far East, the Americans landed on Iwojima, and the Burma Road to China was re-opened. And all the time Mark counted the days until Kate returned.

CHAPTER TWELVE

No one was counting the days more keenly than Matt Riordan. By March 1945 he had been in the Curragh prison camp for four and a half years – ever since Dev had defused Mountjoy by shifting IRA men into other prisons. Poor Ferdy had been sent to Portlaoise. Matt had been relieved at first to be sent to the Curragh – at least the camp was exclusively IRA, except for a few German internees in a separate compound. Besides, a Riordan on the Curragh was part of history. His father had been imprisoned there in the Civil War, twenty-five years before. Dev had been on their side then. Now Dev had locked them up and thrown away the key.

It was the bleakest place on earth. Sometimes Matt

imagined he would spend the rest of his life staring through the barbed wire at the flat plain stretching into the distance. The huts which housed the prisoners were falling apart. Sanitary and kitchen facilities were minimal. The food was slops. Privacy non-existent.

But if the Curragh was bad, Portlaoise was worse. Portlaoise was living death. Matt was tormented by thoughts of Ferdy who had been there since 1940 with six other IRA men. They had been denied political status from the start – ordered to wear prison uniform and obey prison routine. All seven had refused, and the battle had been going on ever since.

The men would not wear prison clothing, so they were left naked. They would not accept mail bearing prison numbers, so they received no letters at all. They were not presentable, so they were denied Mass.

The men were locked in their cells, in solitary confinement, without newspapers, letters, books, without contact with each other, without a chance to talk to a priest or a living soul. They were treated like animals trapped in a burrow. Week after week. Month after month. Year after year. For nearly five years!

Reports smuggled to Matt said that Ferdy was going mad. He raved for hours, screaming about a white horse in his cell. Other prisoners were in a similar state. Matt prayed for their deaths. It was their only escape.

Outside the prisons, the IRA was in tatters. Wives and children went hungry. Girls gave up waiting and married other men. Parents despaired of seeing their sons before they went to their graves.

And inside the prisons, men were left to rot.

On the Curragh, morale was rock bottom. Friction arose between the men from the IRA Northern Command and those from the south. Regional pride sparked off old feuds. Arguments raged about the future of Ireland. The camp was a mess.

Matt tried to create unity, but it was hopeless. Men split into the Grogan faction, the Tadgh Lynch faction, the Pearse Kelly faction, even the Matt Riordan faction. The eight hundred prisoners spent more time fighting each other than trying to escape. News of British reverses in the war were greeted with cheers until, as the years passed and it became plain that 'the auld enemy' was beating Germany, even that unifying factor withered and died.

Matt almost broke in the first year. The prisoners rioted and Matt was identified as a leader. When the riot was quelled, the guards kicked him so badly that walking was impossible for a month. And after that came more beatings, solitary in the Glasshouse, more punishment . . .

He survived. Somehow. After the first year he provoked the guards less often and life was a little less painful. But day after day was the same. Swollen clouds crept over the landscape. Rain splattered into the muddy potholes around the derelict huts. The barbed wire was impenetrable, the guards vigilant, the food abominable. Keeping warm was always a problem, especially for the men with dysentery – and Matt began every morning by picking the lice from his body.

To preserve his sanity he devoted hours each day to remembering the outside world. He dreamed of his boyhood – seeing his mother happy in her drapery and himself in the butcher's shop, laughing and happy and full of plans for the future. All ruined when the Connors burned the shops down. He re-lived that day a thousand times. Just as he re-lived being kicked senseless by Averdale's thugs – and seeing his father shot down in the Killing at Keady. And Eamon de Valera was often on his mind – de Valera who had convinced the people of Ireland that the Curragh was some kind of holiday camp – the same de Valera who was murdering Ferdy, an inch at a time.

Connors, Averdale, de Valera – three men who had turned Matt's life into hell on earth. By the third year on the Curragh his thoughts were exclusively of them. He invented a game in which he brought them to trial. He gloried in the speeches he would deliver, the indictments he would bring, the executions he would carry out. Matt played that game every day of his life. His object was to survive, escape if he could, but if that proved impossible, then to serve out his time with his wits still intact. Then he would take his revenge. That was all that mattered. That was what Matt's life was about.

He acquired a reputation. Hard men gravitated to his

side, recognizing a killer when they saw one. The Matt Riordan faction numbered only eight men – eight, out of eight hundred – but no group was more feared. Each of them had their hate list. Scores would be settled one day, they all knew that, and each would help the other. Meanwhile they watched each other's backs.

Thus they lived out their grim existence until – in March, 1945 – a rumour spread through the camp. The defeat of Germany would bring about the end of the Emergency. Most of the men would be set free. Matt and other long-term prisoners would be transferred back to Mountjoy or Portlaoise – but the men interned for the duration would be given their freedom.

Four men in the Matt Riordan faction were internees. If they were set free, if they were on the outside . . .

Matt began to plan. He discussed his ideas with the others. Clancy Ryan had a few suggestions of his own, so did Joe Costello. McNeela and Blayney went even one better. They had a secret arms dump on the outside . . .

Matt began to count the days until the end of the Emergency.

If time was running out for the Nazi regime, it was also running out for some other people – and on 12 April, it ran out for the President of the United States. The death of Franklin D. Roosevelt shocked everyone.

Freddie Mallon broadcast an emotional tribute from a field hospital set amid the ruins of Cologne . . . 'I have seen men weep today. The very same men who withstood shell-fire with unflinching courage. Some of the toughest soldiers in the world broke down and cried. American soldiers. They wept before straightening their backs, taking a deep breath, and marching on to the front. Let me say this to people back home. In this war your sons and husbands have made me proud to be an American, but never more than today. For it is the American way to show compassion, and Franklin Roosevelt was a compassionate man. History will decide whether he was our greatest President, perhaps even the greatest leader the Free World has known – meanwhile we have all lost a great friend. And not just Americans. One scene today stays in my memory.

A British major, veteran of D Day and countless other battles, paused outside this hospital, where our flag flies at half mast. He saluted and stood there for so long that I couldn't help watching. Then he saw me and came across to shake my hand. He gave an embarrassed grunt. "There are times," he said, "when words are not enough." And, Ladies and Gentlemen across America, this is one of those times. Meanwhile, the mood here in Germany is "Finish the war for F.D.R." Goodnight, and God bless America.'

Two days later in a private letter to Sean Connors in London, Freddie wrote '. . . *what else can be said about Roosevelt's death? It knocked the hell out of everyone here. People are quoting my remark "Finish the war for F.D.R.", but really I only said what was in the hearts of so many men.*'

Other men were dying, and other deaths were revealed. As the Allies swept on across Germany, the world learned with horror of the Nazi extermination camps. Dazed and sickened journalists, scarcely able to believe their own eyes, struggled to describe the most harrowing scenes in history. The whole world flinched at newsreel clips – and so vengeful was the mood, so outraged, that people felt cheated to learn that Hitler had killed himself.

Hitler's death was announced in the Dublin newspapers on 2 May . . . and within hours Eamon de Valera called at the German Embassy . . . to express condolences on behalf of the people of Ireland.

Dinny Macaffety was stunned. He buried his report on Dev's action on an inside page in the *Gazette*, but newspapers elsewhere blazoned the story. Around the globe Ireland was pilloried as a friend of Fascism.

Dinny despaired of Dev's stiff-necked ways, just as he despaired of the censorship. All through the Emergency he had battled for press freedom. When a friend who had joined the Royal Navy was subsequently rescued from a ship sunk in action, Dinny published – 'We are pleased to report that Seamus Cullen is safe and sound after his recent boating accident in the Mediterranean.' The Dail fumed while Dublin laughed, but Dinny lost other battles to Frank Aiken the Censor. Notices of Irishmen killed in action were not allowed to include references to military rank,

494

and once even the second half of the Biblical quotation 'greater love than this no man hath that he lay down his life for his friends' was struck out, for fear that it implied the Irish were friends of the British. Although Dinny grumbled furiously, there was nothing he could do until the Emergency was over.

Finally, miraculously, it was. On Tuesday 8 May 1945, the Allies announced that war with Nazi Germany was officially at an end.

In Dublin, students celebrated by flying the British, American, Russian, French and Irish flags from the roof of Trinity College. Within an hour a crowd had gathered outside the gates, chanting for the removal of all flags except the Irish Tricolour. When the students refused, stones were thrown, and minutes later the mob stormed the University. College Green was a battleground. Eventually police baton-charges broke up the crowd – which then went on the rampage elsewhere, smashing windows at the American Legation, the office of the British representative in Ireland, the Wicklow Hotel and Jammet's restaurant, the last because they were patronized by the British.

'Ah now,' Dinny chuckled, 'things are getting back to normal fast enough.'

The joke brought no smile from Mrs Maeve Tully. Plumper than when Sean had known her, she was still a fine-looking woman. She lunched with Dinny once a month and was forever asking about 'our friend over the water'.

'Will he come back on a visit maybe,' she wondered hopefully, 'now this dreadful war is over at last.'

But Dinny did not know the answer to that.

Professionally the ending of the war in Europe made no immediate difference to Sean. He was as busy as ever. The momentum of work kept him going. *Seven Days in London* went out as usual, describing the scene in the capital. Little had changed in some ways – food was as scarce, rationing was strict, London was still a city of shortages.

Seven years in London had changed Sean Connors. He was still youthfully good-looking, his hair was as black and his blue eyes as keen – but his manner was that of an older man – the inevitable consequence of his experiences and of having few friends his own age. Even Freddie was forty-two at the end of the war.

VE Day was hugely emotional, sad and joyful at the same time. The mood lingered on throughout May. People laughed and wept, offered thanks to the Lord, got drunk, made love, kissed strangers and danced at street parties. Sean reported what he saw and participated to some extent. Yet he made no new friends. He continued to live alone and showed no interest in furthering relationships with any of the girls he met at parties.

He often thought of Margaret. She wrote every month, breathless letters signed 'Your loving sister-in-law'. When he pointed out that she wasn't, she answered, 'I would have been. Anyway, that's how I think of myself when it comes to you.' Her last letter was from San Francisco, where she was staying with friends. She was pining for Freddie, who was now talking of staying in Germany to cover the trials of the Nazi war criminals. 'If he does,' Margaret wrote to Sean, 'I shall try to get back to London and wait for him there.'

Margaret's was not the the only mail from America. So many listeners to CBS wrote that Sean felt he knew America quite well. And Ambassador Kennedy wrote from time to time. People still called him 'Ambassador' even though it was years since he had been replaced in London. Poor Joe had suffered a terrible war. Almost all of his fears had been realized. Joe Jnr had been killed in action. Kick had married Billy Cavendish, who had been killed in the Allied push across Belgium. Jack had been seriously wounded. Yet, although Joe's letters contained much sadness, there was always the invitation too . . . 'Don't forget, when you finally get over to our wonderful country, come and see us . . .'

Everyone was urging Sean to go to America. Freddie was quite determined. 'Let me cover these War Crimes Trials and I'll have finished in Europe. The Japs can't last much longer. Soon it will be glorious peace . . . then, Sean old buddy, we are going home.'

Home? Was home no longer Ireland? Sean supposed not. After all, why go back? There was nothing there but old scores to settle, and Dev had settled most of those for him. The IRA had been crushed. Matt Riordan was rotting in prison.

Matt Riordan was not rotting in prison, even though he was still on the Curragh. The rumours had proved true. Hundreds of men were released at the end of the Emergency. There was even talk that long-term prisoners might be paroled on the promise of good behaviour. Not that Matt was waiting for that.

For two months he had watched the coming and going on the Curragh – more activity in eight weeks than in the preceding five years. Speculation turned into fact. As internees were released, space became available in Mountjoy and Portlaoise for the long-term prisoners. Men were being transferred back, at the rate of about forty a week. The camp on the Curragh was to be closed.

Clancy Ryan had been released on 1 June, and Costello a week later. Blayney and McNeela went out together, on 4 July, and seven days after that Matt had received a letter. It read '. . . *when I got home the family were all well. Best wishes, Rory.*'

The 'family' were the oilskin-wrapped Lee Enfields which Rory McNeela and Blayney had buried the day before Dev's detectives had arrested them in 1940. The weapons had survived in good condition and were ready for use.

Matt permitted himself a grin of satisfaction and settled down to wait.

Clancy Ryan took longer to write, but then Clancy had a lot more to do. His letter, when it came, was from London, not that Clancy had signed it. '*I thought you should know that your cousin died yesterday. He is to be buried in Lymington. He often spoke of you and has left you two hundred pounds in his will. All arrangements have been made. Love, Aunt Clare.*'

When Matt collected his opened letter, the screw sneered, 'Bit of luck today Riordan, but it will be years before you get your hands on that money.'

Matt read the letter in the hut. Interpreting was easy. Clancy had rented them a safe house in England, at a place called Lymington, wherever that was . . . all Matt knew was that it must be near the coast because Clancy's cousin had agreed to take them over in his boat for two hundred pounds. And 'all arrangements have been made' meant that Clancy and Costello had already identified which bank would be knocked over to provide the necessary funds.

For the first time in five years, the sun shone down on the Curragh.

Matt's biggest fear was that he might be separated from the rest of his men still in the camp – Flynn, Bowyer and Casey – or that they might be moved from the camp on different days. They tried to guard against both eventualities by becoming inmates of the same hut, Hut 67. So far the authorities had closed down a hut at a time, moving the prisoners out in separate convoys, using two cars and a closed van. Ten prisoners went out in the van, escorted by the cars. After delivering men to Mountjoy or Portlaoise, the convoy collected the next ten men, and returned twice more to disperse all forty men in the hut. The procedure settled into a routine which Matt studied as if his life depended on it – as in fact it did.

Escape from the Curragh had proved impossible, and neither Mountjoy or Portlaoise would be easy. Matt's best chance, perhaps his only chance, would come during the journey, and on 1 September he knew when that would be.

Costello's contacts in the motor-pool at Mountjoy had proved co-operative. He sent a brief note to Jack Flynn – *'Did you hear Eileen is getting married this month, on the 14th at Clondalkin. She's the second cousin married this year. I know you'll wish her luck.'*

Hut 67 was to be moved on 14 September.

The Matt Riordan faction was to arrange to be in the second convoy.

The ambush would take place at Clondalkin.

Nobody was more relieved to see the end of the war than Mark Averdale, even if he was beginning to think it had been fought for all the wrong reasons. He blamed the new Labour Government. Every day some Cabinet Minister was on his feet talking about the *egalitarian society*. The very expression made Mark fume. What utter rubbish. Men were not equal. They had different talents, conflicting ambitions, unequal resources . . . God Almighty, did nine generations of Averdales fight and die just to be counted as ordinary men? Rank has its privileges, as Mark pointed out. But London was hopeless. Bureaucrats were all over the place like little tin gods . . . all babbling about permits and new regulations. The place had turned communist!

What really drove him mad was trying to arrange passage for Kate across the Atlantic. Even after Japan surrendered in August, world shipping was still hogged by the military. The repatriation of common soldiers was being given priority over First Class fare-paying passengers. Mark cursed and swore at one shipping clerk after another, to no avail.

Then, on 7 September, he received a letter from the United States Embassy in London.

Dear Lord Averdale,

I had hoped to visit with you in Belfast but our itineraries seemed irreconcilable. However I am writing with good news. At ten o'clock this morning I was offered some berths on the S.S. Amsterdam, sailing from New York on the 15th of this month. As I had to give an immediate answer there was no time to contact you, but I hope you will approve of these arrangements. Your ward Kate will arrive Southampton on 20 September. She will travel with my wife and daughter, and Madame Lefarge who as I guess you know has been the girls' tutor for some time . . .

Kate was coming home! In thirteen days! Unbelievable! Kate, at last!

Mark put a call through to the American Embassy, and while he sat waiting he reached for the calendar to put a ring round the date.

Some days later, Sean Connors was similarly circling a date in his calendar. It was a different date, although still in September. His notation also concerned a voyage from America. He read Margaret's letter again.

Dear Sean,

The most marvellous thing happened two hours ago and I cannot write it all down fast enough. I'm coming home. Nobody knows except you, so please let it be a surprise for Freddie and 'those modest folk in the Dorchester' as he calls them. I still can't believe it. This is what happened. A month ago, when I returned to New York from the West Coast, I met some people called the Emersons. I should say re-met them because they came to a party at Eaton Square a million years ago. (Do those days seem a million years away to you too?) Anyway, I was getting out of a cab on Fifth Avenue when suddenly someone said, 'Why, isn't that Margaret Hamilton?' And there were the Emersons, Charles and Paula. I hadn't seen them in years. They didn't even know I was married. Anyway, and this is the point, Charles is in shipping, which is how he came to know 'your distinguished father' as he refers to him. Well, berths across the Atlantic are like gold dust at the moment – but being in the business Charles said he would see what he could do. I hoped like mad of course, but had more or less given up when he called (telephoned) two hours ago with some fantastic news. I sail on the Maid of Orleans, docking in Southampton on the 29th September. What do you think of that?

I still can't believe it. Of course the children are coming too. Can you believe George Jnr is four already? He can't understand it when I say we are all going home, because of course New York is home for him. Me too now I suppose, but you know what I mean.

Sean, would you be a darling and meet me at Southampton? I can't tell you how excited I am, and how much I look forward to seeing you again.

With love as always from your sister-in-law,
Margaret.

On the fourteenth of September, Dinny Macaffety was on the point of leaving the *Gazette*, when his telephone rang. The story made headlines that day. A police convoy had been ambushed at Clondalkin. The attack had turned into a massacre. Four policemen in the escort cars had been killed instantly. The driver of the van carrying prisoners to Mountjoy had been shot dead, and the guard with him was critically injured. The attackers had driven off in the closed van, with the prisoners still inside.

Jennifer Johnstone could believe neither the size of the ship nor their cabin. The S.S. *Amsterdam* was huge, but their cabin was so cramped that it was impossible to imagine four people living in it for five days.

Alison laughed, 'Darling, we only sleep here. Don't worry, you'll soon get used to it. Ask Kate, she's done it all before.'

Yvette prodded an upper bunk. 'Who wants the top deck? Any volunteers? Kate . . . Kate . . . you're shivering . . . is something the matter?'

Kate's shudder was caused by memories of the sea crossing with Rose Smith. She had been afraid of America then. Now she was afraid to go back.

'Kate?' Aunt Alison asked, cocking her head.

'I know,' Yvette said, 'it's the excitement of going home.'

How could Kate make them understand that her home was with them?

Aunt Alison patted her arm. 'Tell you what. You and Jenny go up on deck and have a look round. We won't be long unpacking a few things.'

Minutes later, the two girls were pacing the deck, staring at the New York skyline. 'Goodbye America,' Kate whispered. 'Wonderful, wonderful America.'

'Wonderful wonderful cream cakes, you mean,' Jenny joked, anxious to dispel Kate's gloomy mood. 'And Hershey bars, and milk shakes, and good old T bones. Boy, am I going to miss all that food.'

Kate smiled, 'It will do us good. Look at the size we're getting.'

It was true. Life in the Washington apartment had become one long self-indulgent feast. Both Alison Johnstone and Yvette had a sweet tooth, so Kate and Jenny's diet lacked the discipline a school might have imposed. The girls had grown plump.

'Who cares,' Jenny shrugged, and changed the subject by pointing out buildings along the waterfront.

But Jenny's excited chatter was little more than background to the hubbub of Kate's thoughts. Five days. That was all. Then back to Ulster. Her guardian's last letter was adamant. There would be no school in England for Kate. She would have to say goodbye to her friends. 'Perhaps you can see them occasionally,' Mark Averdale had written, 'but I have been making plans of my own.'

Five days later Lord Averdale was hurrying along the platform at Southampton. He was not in the best of tempers. He had wanted to meet Kate in the Rolls, but petrol rationing denied him that luxury. Then the train had been unheated and crowded and slow. The damn thing even lacked a dining car.

It was only noon and the *Amsterdam* did not dock until four, but trains were so unreliable these days that the nine o'clock from Victoria had been the only one which guaranteed he would be in Southampton on time.

He consoled himself with the prospect of a good lunch at the Doplin. That would relax him. Four hours, and he would see Kate. It was so close he was almost frightened. The last photograph had been a bit blurred . . .

He stopped. The paper-man on the corner was shouting something about Belfast. Mark fumbled for a penny, took the paper and started to read. The next moment it was staring up at him, that hated face, the charcoal sketch of Matt Riordan!

Mark began to shake so violently that holding the paper steady was almost impossible. It took all of his self-control to read the headlines and the opening paragraph of the story . . .

HUNT FOR IRA MEN SPREADS TO BELFAST
Four of the men who escaped from a Dublin prison last week are still at large. All are wanted for multiple murder. Belfast police are believed to be mounting a full scale search of the Falls Road area of the city for Matt Riordan . . .

But Matt Riordan was a long way from Belfast. At that exact moment he was on the deck of Clancy's cousin's boat as it ploughed up the Solent. The choppy sea was made all the more turbulent by the wake of a liner as it passed two hundred yards away on the starboard bow. Matt glared across the water and turned to Jack Flynn at his side, 'If a man must travel across water, that's the way to do it, not in a bucket like this.'

502

Flynn smiled. He was a better sailor than Matt who had been sick in the night. 'Clancy says we're almost there. This place Lymington is just round the next headland –'

'Thank Christ. I can't wait to get back on to dry land.'

Clancy emerged from the wheelhouse. 'Better get below, boys. Don't want to risk you being spotted from the shore.'

Matt groaned. He hated the thought of squeezing his thin frame into that locker. When he did it the first time and heard tarpaulins and God knows what being piled on top, he thought he would never see daylight again. It was like a coffin, like being buried alive.

He gulped his lungs full of air and watched the liner steam on towards Southampton.

'The *Amsterdam*,' Clancy said, watching her through binoculars. 'Reckon that's how your friend Lord Averdale travels, eh Matt? Everything first class.'

'He'll have a fucking first-class funeral,' Matt spat over the side, 'I'll make damn sure of that.'

With which he went below and let them shut him away.

BOOK THREE

CHAPTER ONE

How close they all came to meeting that September. They all passed through the Southampton area – Sean Connors, Matt Riordan and Mark Averdale – they seemed set to collide. But as it happened a difference of a few days kept enemies apart and allowed only the reunion of friends. So the clash never came – nor did it come in what was left of 1945.

Yet that September marked a change in their lives, a dividing line between two phases. Kate O'Brien, for instance, who had spent the five days crossing the Atlantic worrying herself to a frazzle, was almost sick with nerves when the S.S. *Amsterdam* docked at Southampton. Not even the joyous sight of Uncle Linc waiting on the quay quelled the butterflies in her stomach . . . at least not for long.

Uncle Linc was among the first aboard – charging up the companionway to sweep Aunt Alison in his arms. Then he was kissing Jenny and hugging Kate, and squeezing Yvette in such a bear hug that she went red in the face. Everyone was laughing and weeping at once – Kate too, for it was impossible not to share the Johnstones' happiness. But Kate's delight was marred – soon she and the Johnstones would be parted. Soon she would be taken to Ulster by her guardian.

She slipped away from the party and went back to the rails, scanning the dock for sight of Lord Averdale. He was nowhere to be seen, which was worrying in itself, but what worried Kate more was what would happen when he *did* arrive. She wondered if she would recognize him. Six years was a long time, and although she had sent dozens of photographs he had sent none in return.

At five o'clock there was still no sign of him. Then a policeman appeared with the purser. They hurried across to Aunt Alison . . . and a moment later Uncle Linc joined

Kate at the rails. 'Kate honey,' he said, 'there's a policeman here with a message from Lord Averdale . . .'

Lord Averdale did not board the S.S. *Amsterdam* until six o'clock, by which time many of the passengers had disembarked. Mark was feverish with anxiety, partly because he was late but mostly as a result of the afternoon's events. Seeing Riordan on the front page of the *Evening News* had been a tremendous shock. Mark had staggered into a pub and downed a whisky to stop shaking. Riordan! That murdering bastard was back in Belfast on the very day Kate returned from America. After six years . . . six miserable, everlasting years. Mark almost wept with fury and frustration.

Then he had lost his temper. At the nearest police station he'd confounded the desk sergeant by demanding to be put through to Scotland Yard. A furious row had ensued. Mark was almost arrested. Finally a young Inspector, impressed by the Averdale title and intimidated by Mark's manner, took him to CID Headquarters. There Mark ranted on the telephone to Scotland Yard, the RUC, even the Home Office in London – but to little avail. Riordan remained uncaptured and was suspected of being in Belfast. The RUC urged Lord Averdale to take every precaution – 'He's murdered even more men now. He's very dangerous indeed.'

As if Mark Averdale needed to be told that.

'Today,' he muttered through clenched teeth. 'For it to happen *today*!'

At three o'clock a senior CID officer named Briggs took Mark to the police canteen. Lunch had finished. Briggs organized some sandwiches, a pot of strong tea and a half-sized bottle of scotch. They sat at a corner table and Briggs began to talk soothingly of police protection.

'Not for me!' Mark snapped furiously. 'Good God, I'd like nothing more than to meet Riordan face to face.'

Briggs took his time. He was a large-boned man whose ruddy complexion owed less to drink than playing cricket on the village greens of Hampshire. Slow speech and a country burr disguised a shrewd intelligence. He had been hurriedly briefed by the Home Office, enough to know the

506

background – the burning of Brackenburn, the murder of Lady Averdale, the Killing at Keady, and Lord Averdale's hatred of Matt Riordan. Briggs thanked his lucky stars not to be a policeman in Northern Ireland. Privately he felt sympathy for Lord Averdale, but was still anxious to see him on his way – the Hampshire Constabulary had problems enough without becoming involved with Irish terrorists.

As things turned out Briggs had less difficulty than he imagined. By the time Mark sat down in the canteen his shock and anger had subsided. He was visibly shaken but what concerned him most was how this news affected his plans. He glared at Briggs. 'You don't know Riordan. He won't attack me. He'll try to destroy what's mine – my homes, assets, my . . .' he swallowed, 'my possessions.'

'Perhaps the RUC will make an early arrest, sir.'

'And what if they don't? What then? There's a girl arriving from America today. Riordan murdered her parents. He crippled her brother. Would you take her back to Belfast? Would you take that risk?'

Briggs cleared his throat and proffered an answer. 'Well, maybe I'd make other arrangements, just for the time being –'

'Like what? Like sending her *back* to America? Good Christ, she's already been away six years. Am I to spend the rest of my life without her, just because the police are incompetent!'

'Perhaps she could stay with friends, sir? Just for a while. Give the RUC more time –'

'Time,' Mark groaned, his head in his hands.

The conversation continued in that vein for another half hour, with Mark erupting now and then while edging towards the inevitable. Grasping the nettle was painful, but it had to be done. He dared not take Kate back to Belfast if Riordan were there.

It was four o'clock. The *Amsterdam* had docked. Kate would be waiting.

'I'll send a man aboard,' Briggs murmured. 'Say you'll be a little late.'

Mark seemed to have taken root. He had waited six years, but now the time had come he had taken root in a police station, immobile until he reached a decision.

He poured himself another whisky while Briggs left the canteen. The only solution Mark could think of was to send Kate to school with this Johnstone girl. Of course there was Molly Oakes and the house at St John's Wood, but that was to have been a gradual thing . . . besides, Molly had stipulated that Kate must be at least sixteen.

He began to adjust to the idea. At least Kate would be in England. He could visit, half-terms and holidays . . . and perhaps Riordan would be arrested soon.

'I've arranged that, sir,' Briggs said when he returned to the table.

Mark dragged his mind back to the immediate. He began to re-plan his welcome. He must not alarm Kate, whatever he did. Then there were the Johnstones to consider . . . he had planned just to say hello and goodbye, escape as soon as decently possible . . . but now . . . if Kate went to school with their girl, the Johnstones might be important in the future . . . and he was in their debt already.

His nimble brain shook itself free of shock and began to function again. Within an hour it was all organized. Mark booked several suites at the Savoy and arranged that he and Kate, together with the Johnstone party, would be convoyed up to London by a fleet of police cars. Briggs complained about irregularities – but finally the prospect of evacuating potential trouble from his patch was too seductive to resist. He described the exercise as a courtesy extended to visiting VIPs, and hoped the Chief Constable would see it in the same light.

Shortly before six, Mark swept along the Southampton waterfront in a police Wolseley with two others in tow. They stopped alongside the S.S. *Amsterdam* and Mark alighted. He paused at the foot of the gangway and looked up at the rails . . . and then he saw Kate.

Kate was heartbroken at the prospect of being parted from the Johnstones. She was ready to plead, to beg, to do anything rather than go to Ulster. The thought of being torn from dear Aunt Alison and Jenny was completely unbearable.

The reunion with her guardian was as traumatic as she

had expected, especially when he arrived surrounded by policemen. And he seemed so strange – the way he kept staring. Jenny giggled, Kate blushed beetroot, and even Aunt Alison went pink. Then plans were changed in the most astonishing way. Lord Averdale announced that everyone was going up to London together, to stay at the Savoy as his guests.

The Savoy was terribly grand. Kate and Jenny shared a room, and Aunt Alison bustled in to help them dress for dinner – 'Jennifer, you wear your blue, and Kate, slip into that green silk and let me have a look at you.'

The maid was summoned, frocks were sent to be pressed, and Aunt Alison almost expired from excitement. 'He's taken Linc down to the bar for a talk. Kate darling, I think you will be allowed to go to school after all.'

And so she was – it was announced over dinner. Ulster was still recovering from the war – 'Consequently,' Lord Averdale said, 'I think it best if you attend school in England for a while.'

Kate went red with excitement. Jenny hugged her, overjoyed. Uncle Linc grinned from ear to ear. Aunt Alison laughed. But Kate's guardian just stared at her, rather sadly she thought. The girls went to bed early and left the three adults drinking brandy.

Lord Averdale vacated the hotel at eleven o'clock the next morning, but Kate was summoned to his sitting-room first. 'I shall leave Mrs Johnstone to deal with the matter of schools,' he said. 'She seems very capable . . .'

He went on to talk about various things but Kate hardly heard – he was staring so hard that she blushed.

'What's the matter?'

'Nothing, I mean –' she felt her face blazing.

'You've grown,' he said. 'Will you walk up and down for me like you used to? Do you remember, at Belgrave Square . . .'

So she did, feeling utterly foolish, hating herself for blushing so furiously. It was an awful habit which had started quite recently. When anyone looked at her she went quite crimson. Aunt Alison said it was like her spots – 'You'll grow out of it darling, it's just a growing-up stage.' But Kate knew she looked awful – what with her red face and her red hair, her pimply complexion – and she felt as awkward as a carthorse.

'Hmmm,' her guardian sounded disappointed. He looked it too.

Kate stifled her tears. She so wanted to please, especially now, with him allowing her to go to school with Jennifer.

'Yes, well,' he sighed, 'I suppose you are at a difficult age.'

Kate wished the floor would open up and swallow her.

Then two porters arrived to collect some cases, and mercifully Aunt Alison entered as they left. 'May I come in?' she said, stepping through the open door.

Kate flew to her.

'Kate?' said Aunt Alison, giving Lord Averdale a peculiar look.

He left shortly afterwards. Kate dissolved into tears and couldn't stop for an hour. 'He hates me,' she sobbed, 'I could tell . . . and he's been so nice, so kind . . .'

'I'd go red too if someone stared at me like that,' Jenny said loyally. 'It's positively weird.'

But Kate remembered when she had liked to parade in front of him. It had been their game. How pleased he had been then, how obviously disappointed now.

Eventually she responded to their comforting, especially when Uncle Linc said, 'Gee, honey, last night he was saying you're even prettier now than when you went away.'

It was nice to hear but Kate disbelieved him. Something had gone wrong with her lately. Her arms and legs had grown out of proportion. She was ungainly. She woke every morning to find new pimples on her face. Was it any wonder she blushed all the time? She was turning into a freak.

Thankfully she had little time to dwell on herself. Uncle Linc had lived in a bachelor flat 'until my bride arrived'. Now he wanted a house – but finding one in a bombed-out London was not easy. After searching for weeks he had found only two that were possible. The whole family spent the afternoon viewing them. Aunt Alison's disappointment was obvious. Finally she chose the one in Highgate. 'It needs fixing up, but at least it's roomy enough for when we're all together,' she glanced at Kate, 'assuming your guardian doesn't hog you all to himself.'

Kate saw no danger of that. She quite expected him to write saying she had grown so fat and ugly that he never wanted to see her again. She wished they had stayed in America. True, she had got what she wanted – she was going to school with Jenny – but the pain of her guardian's rejection had been mortifying. She disliked this new phase of her life, and it became even more painful the next day – when they went to Victoria Station to put Yvette on the boat train for Paris. Kate had known the little French woman for six years. Now they were to be parted. Everyone wept. Even Uncle Linc kept blowing his nose and saying Yvette must come over and visit . . .

They waved and waved until the train disappeared into the distance.

Schools were a problem. Uncle Linc had investigated schools. 'It's not a walk in the park, Alison honey. Schools got turned upside down in this war along with everything else. Some are still closed, and others – well they're so darned picky you've got to be royalty to get in.'

'Well you *are* a Consul at the American Embassy, and Kate *is* Lord Averdale's ward.'

At least Uncle Linc had found three to choose from. 'One is in Scotland,' he said apologetically, 'but I'm told the Scots are very good educators.'

Aunt Alison had never heard of them. She asked about Roedean and various others, but Uncle Linc shook his head. 'Not a prayer, honey.'

It was yet another difference between pre-war Britain and the austere land to which they had returned, and Aunt Alison said so. The bomb damage frightened her, and the way people *lived* – with everything rationed, and quite ordinary every-day American things unobtainable – 'Honestly Linc, I don't think I'll cope.'

The next day Aunt Alison took the girls to Windsor for an appointment with the headmistress of Glossops.

'What a crazy name,' Jenny complained. 'Imagine being asked where you went to school and saying Glossops. Mummy, you must be joking.'

But Mummy was not – with food rationed just feeding her girls was a worry, at least a school would do that. Post-war England was fast inducing a state of panic.

Glossops turned out to be an Edwardian mansion set in the middle of parkland – situated within the boundaries of adjoining Maidenhead rather than Windsor, an accident of geography which caused the school's eighty maidens some embarrassment with the more loud-mouthed of the local boys.

Miss Jenkins, the Principal, was a tall, thin woman in her late forties who actually used a lorgnette, the first Kate had seen. She and Jenny sat demurely facing the desk while Miss Jenkins raised her eyeglasses in constant inspection.

Glossops, they were told, was not an establishment for the frivolous, nor one for bluestockings. 'We excel at turning out well rounded young ladies,' Miss Jenkins told Aunt Alison. 'Gals from here inevitably marry men in high places – statesmen, industrialists – quite simply, Glossops gals run the best houses in England.'

The school's facilities included a gymnasium, hockey-pitches, stables . . . 'Glossops gals have the best seats in the country' . . . domestic science rooms, a studio with huge north-facing windows, libraries, music rooms . . . Kate and Jenny trudged round on a tour of inspection. Neither liked what they saw. Aunt Alison had promoted the delights of 'a good school in England' for years, but it had been a shadowy concept. The reality – the sight of so many girls wearing the most hideous uniforms – blue serge with box-pleats ('frumps', Jenny whispered) and hats made of felt ('like Al Capone', Kate groaned) filled them with horror.

On the way back to London Jenny said, 'Do we *have* to go to school? It was fun with Yvette –'

'Darling we'll never find another Yvette. Besides you *should* go to school, you'll like it once you've settled in.'

The next morning they travelled to Esher but the school there looked even worse. Jenny said, 'I think we're just too *old* for schools!'

That night they petitioned Uncle Linc but he sided with Aunt Alison. It was Glossops or Esher. The school in Scotland was just too far away for a visit of inspection. With sinking hearts Kate and Jenny chose Glossops.

They started a week later and hated it. Life seemed a muddle to Kate, Glossops was appalling. The only blessing was Jennifer. At night they shared a room with two other girls – Rosemary Danvers-Smythe and Angela Worthington – and by day they struggled with the curriculum. Thanks to six years with Yvette, Kate had the best French accent in school, but other subjects defeated her, especially mathematics. Glossops, Kate decided, was hell. But what lay beyond? One day Jenny would go back to America with Aunt Alison and Uncle Linc . . . and Kate faced a future with a guardian who loathed the very sight of her.

Mark Averdale had been shattered by Kate's appearance. He had tried to disguise his dismay, but he had waited so long and expected so much . . .

After leaving her at the Savoy that day he had returned to his club in despair. By the afternoon he was at St John's Wood telling Molly about it. 'The photographs gave me no idea,' he said bitterly, 'but she's so . . . so gawky. She lacks grace, everything about her is clumsy and awkward . . . and Molly her complexion, her skin is terrible.'

Molly had tried to warn him. Only the week before she had said, 'Girls develop differently. They go through stages – after all, she's not quite fifteen, you mustn't expect . . .'

'I blame the Johnstones,' he was saying, 'Americans have no idea . . .'

It took her the rest of the evening to calm him. She said all the right things. 'Blushing and pimples are part of growing up. She's lost her baby prettiness, that's all. You wanted a woman and you'll get one –'

'I wanted *Kate* –'

'It's the chrysalis stage. Another couple of years and her skin will clear . . .'

Mark was inconsolable. 'I was wrong. I've been a fool. All these years . . . I mean just *look* at my life! All this waiting . . . waiting for Kate, waiting to get that bastard Riordan . . . meanwhile everything is changing, and not for the better if you ask me.'

The following day he travelled back to Ulster, only to be met by yet more bad news. His bank in Nairobi had written again about the Bowley estates. The situation was growing quite critical.

He read their latest letter again and groaned. '*Something must be done. If things continue as they are, you could be faced with the liquidation of the entire Averdale holdings in East Africa.*'

That was frightening. Before the war the Bowley estates had generated profits of sixty thousand a year, net with everything paid. And Mark needed that money for the Averdale Foundation – the great art collection was the only dream left to him. During the war he had added to it, but with the coming of peace he intended to be much more active. The collection would grow at a faster rate – but that would require a great deal of money . . . So Mark Averdale grasped the nettle once more. He would go to Africa himself and salvage the Bowley estates. It had to be done and he had to do it.

Six weeks later he was back at St John's Wood, telling Molly his decision.

She was very sympathetic. 'Poor darling. You are having a wretched time. But it will pass, these things always do. You've just got to learn to have patience.'

Matt Riordan had learned patience on the Curragh. Long years in the bleak prison camp had been hard to endure – but Matt was a survivor. That was clear even in 1945. Just as his misfortunes were clear. Matt Riordan can never be said to have been lucky.

Yet his escape to England went well . . . at least to begin with.

They had landed along the coast from Southampton, and gone directly to the cottage at Lymington. The cottage was perfect, isolated, almost remote, on the edge of the New Forest, a mile out of town. Three bedrooms, a bathroom with a proper catch on the door, two rooms downstairs and a kitchen. Clancy's cousin Bridie had found it. She was in the kitchen when they arrived, ready to serve the best meal Matt had ever tasted. Matt blushed when he looked at her. She was the first woman he had seen in seven years.

Matt awoke early next morning, at just after dawn. Five minutes later he was out in the lane. The sun inched above the treeline to cast warmth on his face. Freedom! He had not dared think of it before, certainly not in Dublin with

Dev's manhunt braying in their cars. Even crossing the water, doubled up in that locker, not knowing what was happening, imagining every noise to be a boarding party . . .

Matt hawked and spat, expelling fear and phlegm together.

He walked a long way without really meaning to, stretching his legs, marvelling at being able to go fifty yards without meeting barbed wire. A breeze carried the scent of the sea. He strolled up the lane and into the woods. Birds sang. A squirrel raced up a tree. Matt watched the tiny animal disappear into the branches. Freedom! He had been locked up so long and seen nothing of nowhere since his escape, moved in a closed van, hidden in an attic out on the Howth peninsula, then the boat trip across . . . Ferdy was dead. Half the bloody world was dead. But Matt Riordan was alive, and Matt Riordan was *free*!

Bridie was in the kitchen when he got back. He felt shy talking to her. She wore a sleeveless dress and when she reached for a saucepan black hair showed beneath her arms. Black hair against firm white flesh.

Clancy came through the door, 'Grand day Matt.' He laughed excitedly, 'Sure aren't they all from now on.'

Flynn came down the stairs, lighting a cigarette. 'Wouldn't you know even a fag tastes better when you're not watching out for some bloody screw.'

And Casey joined them a few minutes later, sniffing appreciatively at the smell of bacon frying in the pan.

'There's only one rasher each,' Bridie warned. 'Wouldn't I feed you better in the auld country.'

'Like they did on the Curragh, you mean? Sure don't worry yourself Bridie, we're living like kings.'

Bridie had done well. There was plenty of food in the larder. She had bought it at different shops in different towns, adding to the store slowly. They had money too, nearly six hundred pounds left from Clancy's bank raids in Dublin – and they were armed. Nobody carried a gun, but six Lee Enfields and five hundred shells were hidden behind the water tank in the loft.

The Matt Riordan Faction was in business.

They spent the morning drinking tea and discussing their

plans. Costello and the others were already in London . . .

'Will you go up to London in the morning then, Matt?' Clancy asked.

Matt nodded. He and Casey would travel together and join up with Costello. Clancy and Flynn would come up the day after, leaving Bridie to mind the house. In London they would all camp down in Kilburn, losing themselves among a hundred thousand Irish in a district where brogue voices were as common as fleas. The Lymington house was to be kept as a safe house – a place to which to retreat if things went wrong.

Bridie went down to the town to buy the newspapers. Only the *Herald* carried the story of their escape from Dublin, but without a picture of Matt, just the rumour that he was suspected of being in Belfast.

Clancy chuckled, 'Won't your man Averdale squirm when he reads that.'

Matt smiled. He planned to make them all sweat. He wondered if Connors knew. Dev certainly knew – Dev had sent his detectives into every pub in Dublin. Eight guards had been killed when Matt Riordan escaped. Dev had stood at eight gravesides, mouthing his usual pious bilge about brave men dying for Ireland. 'We'll be needing those guns up in London,' Casey said. 'They'll be no use at all down here.'

'There's time for that,' Matt said, 'but I don't like the idea of guns in the house. If the police ever search . . .'

'Won't we be burying them? We've still got the oilskins,' Clancy said. 'Wouldn't they be better off buried out the back there for now?'

They picked a spot from the kitchen window and left the job until later. There was plenty of time. They all wanted a few hours to relax. So they spent a happy afternoon lounging around, drinking tea and smoking cigarettes, and laughing and joking. So much so that dusk had settled by the time they remembered the rifles.

Matt took a chair up to the landing. The trapdoor to the loft was set in the ceiling directly above the top stair. Clancy held the chair steady while Matt levered himself up. He fumbled across the rafters to the water tank, then made six journeys with the rifles, passing them down one at a time before returning for the ammunition. The boxes were heavy. Carrying them was awkward, with his head bent under the eaves and his feet edging along the rafters. There were four boxes so he made four journeys, just to be on the safe side.

Three boxes had been lowered into Clancy's waiting hands – then, as Matt stretched down with the fourth, he slipped. He fell head first. Clancy toppled from the chair. Matt plunged past. His back slammed into the balustrade with a sickening crunch. He catapulted over, smashing straight into the banisters. Then he somersaulted downwards, to hit the stone floor below with tremendous force.

Bridie shrieked and ran into the hall.

Clancy staggered like a drunk on the landing.

Flynn emerged from the back room, 'Dear God, what the . . .'

Bridie reached Matt first. He was unconscious. Clancy stumbled down the stairs. He and Bridie turned Matt on to his back. A trickle of blood ran from his nose. 'Mary, Jaysus and Joseph,' Bridie whispered. No bones were broken, Clancy ascertained that by running his hands gently over Matt's body.

But Matt was still unconscious five minutes later, despite the wet towel Bridie pressed to his head, and *still* unconscious ten whole minutes after that. Clancy was outside, checking that Flynn and Casey were burying the arms. Bridie squatted at the foot of the stairs bathing Matt's temple. She worked a pillow beneath his neck, but was afraid to do more . . .

Then Matt groaned and his eyes flickered.

Bridie cried out with relief, 'Thanks be to God. Just you stay still a minute, you hear me, that was a monstrous fall.'

Clancy hurried in through the kitchen door. He dropped down and grabbed Matt's hand. 'Jaysus Matt, you gave us a fright. Rest yourself there a minute. We'll move you upstairs –'

'Clancy?' Matt groaned and stared up at them. 'Is that yourself, Clancy?'

'An' who else would it be – even though you fair brained

me with that box of – '

'Clancy?' Matt squinted at the two faces bent over him, then raised a hand to rub his eyes.

'Don't,' Bridie said quickly, reaching for him, 'don't touch your head. You'll be hurting yourself –'

'I can't see you properly,' Matt whispered. 'Dear God, I can't *see*!'

The next hour was a nightmare. Clancy ripped up a shirt and bandaged Matt's head, not knowing if it was the right or the wrong thing to do. Matt's head was not cut, but the bump on his temple was awesome. The most frightening though was Matt's vision – his *impaired* vision. He saw two and three of everything, all blurred together. No outline was clear, nothing was clear, all was distorted. When he tried to walk he stretched out his hands like a blind man. 'Dear God,' he kept sobbing, 'I can't see, I can't *see*!'

Life seemed to turn sour for everyone from that September. For instance, only a few days after Matt's accident at Lymington Sean Connors was along the coast at Southampton to greet Margaret Mallon when she docked on board the *Maid of Orleans*.

Margaret had missed London painfully. When Freddie had been in New York life was different, but with him away in Germany she had yearned for her family and friends. So when she arrived in Southampton few passengers aboard the *Maid of Orleans* were as excited as Margaret. Sean was hugged and kissed for ten solid minutes. Then he was introduced to young George Mallon and the baby – after which it was all hustle and bustle to get Margaret's trunks organized and on to the London train.

Once in town Sean took Margaret to Craven Street where the house had been cleaned from top to bottom in her honour. Sean had arranged to move out and stay with a friend for the duration of Margaret's visit.

'Oh that's absurd,' she protested. 'Sean, it's your home.'

But he was adamant. 'Freddie will be back from Germany in a few weeks. You'll want the place to yourselves.'

She had no need to ask if Sean's accommodating friend was male – all of Sean's friends were – there had been no woman in Sean's life since Val. It saddened Margaret. Four years was too long to mourn, and while he was not exactly in mourning he had lost his lightheartedness. It was something Margaret planned to change, now she was back in London.

Sean spent an hour or so settling her into Craven Street, and then he left. She kissed him at the door and reminded him of his promise to call early in the morning for her surprise visit to the Dorchester – after which he walked off into the night, making for Tubby's place at Rutland Gate.

It felt strange, leaving Craven Street at eleven at night. It had been home for so long that it had become part of him – but it was part of Freddie too, and Sean felt it was right for Freddie's wife to have the use of it now.

Tubby Reynolds owned a large terrace house which he was trying to convert into seven flats – *trying* being the operative word since he was restricted by shortage of materials and inadequate cash. Sean and Tubby had seen a good deal of each other – in fact Tubby had become Sean's closest friend in Fleet Street since Freddie went away. Their friendship had started during the crossing to Dunkirk and had ripened over the years. Like Freddie, Tubby was older than Sean, forty at the end of the war, but unlike Freddie he was not a dedicated journalist. He once said, 'I think it's a very grubby profession. We're nothing but voyeurs when it comes down to it. Peeping Toms who reveal all for the titillation of our readers.'

He was poring over architects' plans when Sean arrived. 'There's tea in the pot,' he said, barely looking up, 'do you want some?'

And some minutes later Sean was touring the house, clambering over builders' materials with a mug of tea in his hand while Tubby talked excitedly about the money to be made from converting old houses – 'All the large London houses are done for. People can't afford them any more. Skivvies worked for nothing before the war, just to have a job. But that's all changed. Women earning decent wages in factories won't go back to domestic service. Who'll do the housework then? Can you see Cynthia Hamilton on her knees with a dustpan and brush?'

Afterwards Sean went to sleep in a bedroom without a

door. 'Don't worry,' Tubby said, 'that'll be fixed by tomorrow night.'

Actually it took longer, but the door was in place by the end of the week. It was typical of Tubby to underestimate the time jobs took, but despite that the alterations at Rutland Gate moved steadily forward. Tubby continued to work in Fleet Street but devoted every spare hour to supervising his small team of craftsmen. He only employed three. 'All I can afford,' he admitted to Sean, 'what with their wages and the cost of materials I'm flat broke.'

The state of Tubby's finances was well known in Fleet Street. He borrowed from everyone. Every penny went into the house. 'Never mind,' he shrugged, 'I'll make a fortune when it's finished.'

Sean returned most nights to find Tubby waiting to provide a tour of inspection. Sean praised the alterations as enthusiastically as possible, but generally it was late and he was asleep on his feet. Everyone wanted to give Margaret a party, that was the problem, and with Freddie away in Germany Sean was the obvious escort. He enjoyed himself, but successive late nights imposed quite a strain. The pace of his professional life was as fierce as ever. *Seven Days* was more demanding without the continuing drama of war. Stories were varied and took longer to find – but Sean found them, *and* still produced his newspaper columns, five thousand words a week on what was happening in London. He worked long and hard by day, and escorted Margaret everywhere at night – but it was exhausting.

Freddie came back to the surprise of his life. He and Margaret spent a few days 'honeymooning' which gave Sean a rest, but not much – for when the Mallons entertained, Sean was expected as a guest, and when the Mallons were asked out, Sean was invited too. In October, when Freddie returned to Nuremberg for the War Crimes Trials, once again Sean was found all over London escorting Margaret Mallon. Unknown to him she did it deliberately, it was part of her 'resurrect Sean Connors campaign', but inevitably people began to talk. Margaret remained unconcerned. She poured scorn on it – 'Dirty minds will imagine anything. Freddie's never even raised an eyebrow.'

520

Freddie never had cause. Sean made sure of that. His behaviour was irreproachable, but people misread it at times. His fondness for Margaret showed in his eyes. When they went out she took his arm as a matter of course. They danced at nightclubs and sometimes held hands on their way back to their table. People talked . . . but Sean was too absorbed to notice.

Understandably, what with Margaret and a host of other things, the brief mention of Matt Riordan's escape in some of the British press had escaped his attention – but at the end of October a story in the *Mail* set his heart pounding.

IRA IN SMASH AND GRAB RAIDS

Bow Street Magistrates were told this morning that the three men charged with last week's raid on a Leyton jewellers are wanted in Dublin for murder. The men, Jack Flynn, aged 37, Michael Casey, 32, and Clancy Ryan, 36, all members of the IRA, were involved in an escape from a Dublin prison in September following an incident in which eight men died. A fourth man, Matthew Riordan, escaped at the same time and remains uncaptured. He is believed to be in Northern Ireland . . .

Sean's stomach turned over. Months had passed without Riordan entering his mind. Even thoughts of Ireland were rare. Dinny Macaffety had transferred the enormous sum of five thousand pounds to Sean's London bank – the sum settled upon for the *Gazette* – but apart from that Sean's contact with Dinny was spasmodic. He felt guilty at times. He remembered his father's dreams, and his father's death at Keady . . . he remembered his own vows to take revenge on Matt Riordan and the IRA . . . but it all seemed so long ago – before the war, before Val and so many experiences which had changed him. Until seeing that hated name in print. It was like ripping plaster away from a still open wound . . . all the old pain flared up with searing intensity.

But the moment passed. Riordan's whereabouts remained unknown, his name faded from the newspapers. It stayed alive in Sean's mind for a while but as the weeks sped by it faded even there. As usual too much was happening. What with work by day and Margaret's parties by night, November flashed by. Margaret was determined to enjoy herself and to bring Sean alive again in the process – and she did, but it placed Sean under a strain. It wasn't just the late hours. Margaret was a constant reminder of Val. Often Sean's face was touched with sadness. Margaret would say – 'No frowns allowed. Come on, let's dance.' And dance they did, to the growing satisfaction of the gossips. Talk became so widespread that rumours even reached Sean, but when he mentioned them Margaret merely smiled, 'Don't be so ridiculous, you are my brother-in-law.'

They were trying to help each other, but their good intentions nurtured a dreadful seed of destruction. Sean should have remembered how unsure of himself Freddie had been about Margaret in the old days. He should have known Freddie would be jealous – and maybe he did – but what could he do when faced with Margaret's determined efforts to paint the town red? After all, *someone* had to escort her.

Freddie arrived back in London twelve days before Christmas, and he and Sean lunched together the following day. On the surface Freddie was as friendly as ever, but underneath Sean detected a coolness.

'These trials are dragging on forever,' Freddie scowled. 'Maybe I'll take Margaret over to Nuremberg in January.'

Sean had an uncomfortable suspicion that some of the tittle-tattle had reached Freddie's ears in Germany. Of course Sean did what he could – he excused himself from one party, and avoided at least two functions because the Mallons would be there – but that just seemed to add to the gossip. Finally he told himself it was too ridiculous for words, and when Margaret insisted that he attend their party on Christmas Eve he accepted with pleasure. After which Christmas passed happily and the three of them enjoyed themselves. In fact all would have been well – had it not been for New Year's Eve.

Sean hated New Year's Eve. It was seven years since he had danced at Eaton Square, but the very words 'New Year's Eve' evoked a picture of Val in that lemon dress. The passing of time neither dimmed the memory nor dulled

522

the pain, and on that New Year's Eve Sean Connors got drunk – gloriously, hopelessly, pissed-as-a-newt drunk!

Freddie and Margaret found him on the Embankment at four in the morning. They staggered upstairs with him to the sitting-room in Craven Street where they loosened his collar, stripped off his soiled jacket, took away his shoes and flopped him down on a sofa.

'Glory be,' groaned Freddie. 'He weighs a ton. Come on honey, leave him to sleep it off.'

But instead Margaret went to the kitchen and returned with a bowl of warm water. 'I can't leave him like this. You go up if you like, it won't take me a minute to clean him up.'

Her back was to Freddie. She neither saw his expression nor heard him mutter about making coffee. Not that it would have made any difference.

A minute later warm water brought Sean back to life. He groaned and opened his eyes. The first thing he saw was such a vision of beauty that his heart lurched. Her face was inches away. Suddenly his loneliness was too much to bear. Instinctively he reached up with both hands and brought her lips down to his. His grip slid over her shoulders to pull her down on to him. She fell into his arms, pinned to the length of his body . . .

'What the hell!' Freddie roared from the door.

He dropped the coffee things and reached the sofa in two strides, to pull Margaret backwards and on to the floor. After that it was bedlam. Freddie lost control. Sean toppled to the floor in an effort to escape. Margaret screamed and flung herself between them. Freddie grabbed her and slapped her face – 'You bitch! I busted a guy's jaw in Germany when he told me what was happening behind my back –'

'No Freddie. It's not like that,' she sobbed, holding her face. 'Please –'

Sean struggled to his feet – 'Freddie –'

The American turned and swung.

Sean took the punch flush on the chin.

It took Margaret ten minutes to separate them. The baby was shrieking in the bedroom. The nurse ran out on to the landing, struggling into her dressing-gown. Margaret's dress was torn. Sean's eye was cut – and Freddie was sobbing from exertion and jealousy.

Margaret pulled Sean out to the landing, then pushed him downstairs to the front door. 'You'd better go. I've never seen Freddie like this –'

'I gotta apologize. Oh God, I'm so sorry –'

'It's all right. Go now. I'll call you in the morning.'

Then she shut the door in his face. Sean staggered down to the Embankment. A chill wind from the river threatened to cut him in half. His head cleared. Realization hit him like a hammer. He almost wept. 'Oh God, what have I done . . .'

Margaret did not telephone in the morning. At two o'clock in the afternoon Sean went shopping for a huge bouquet of flowers. Then he bought a box of black-market cigars from a tobacconist who had known him for years. He broke the seal and put a note inside to Freddie – 'You two are my dearest friends. How could I insult either of you? Please forgive me.'

From Tubby's house in Rutland Gate he flagged down a taxi and paid the man to deliver the gifts – but an hour later the man returned, unable to obtain an answer from Craven Street.

Sean telephoned. There was no reply. He was expected to dine with the Mallons that night. At eight he dressed for dinner, hoping they would collect him as promised. At ten he went out to a pub and drank his evening meal alone.

The following morning the estate agents who acted for the owners of Craven Street telephoned – 'Mr and Mrs Mallon have left for Germany. The keys are with us, in case you wish to move back into the house.'

Sean said no, he would not move back. After which he tried to find Freddie. He doubted that his friends had left the country already, no matter what the estate agent said, but tracing them was impossible. The Dorchester had no knowledge of them, and Sean was reluctant to ask George and Cynthia.

Ten days later a friend telephoned to say that the Mallons were in Nuremberg.

Sean wrote to Freddie's hotel.

The letter was returned unopened.

524

By the end of January 1946 Sean wondered if he would ever see his friends again. He would do anything for Freddie, and just as much for Margaret. He remembered sailing into hell on earth with her at Dunkirk . . . and being reunited with Freddie in Dover. He remembered . . . and remembered . . . so many things.

Inevitably he spent more time with Tubby Reynolds, sharing the second floor at Rutland Gate – and when Tubby's funds were exhausted, Sean loaned him six hundred pounds to continue the building work. Tubby was grateful but concerned. 'There's no denying I need the money but God knows when you'll see it back. And if you're going to the States with Freddie Mallon –'

But Sean shook his head. 'Don't worry – I have a feeling I'm staying right here.'

CHAPTER TWO

Mark Averdale's decision to go to Africa in 1946 was not taken lightly. He would be away a very long time. The Bowley estates covered thousands of miles. By a quirk of fate the Averdales actually owned even more of Africa than they did of Ulster. When an investment that size goes sour a great deal of time is needed to put it right. Mark harboured no illusions, nor did he overestimate his own competence. His attitude remained constant – he had no interest in business on a day-to-day basis, that was a job for his managers, and if honest men were not to be found in Africa then Mark planned to look closer to home. Plenty of young Englishmen were looking for a future abroad. The British Government was providing finance for thousands of ex-officers to buy farms in Kenya and Rhodesia. White men were flocking to the Dark Continent as never before.

It was as well Mark was encouraged by that, for little else pleased him. Attlee's Labour Government filled him with dread. New taxes were imposed every day. Mark's entire fortune was threatened. The railways had been nationalized, then the coalmines. What next? Suppose the Government seized all agricultural land? What would happen to the thousands of Ulster acres owned by the Averdales? What would Mark be left with – shipyards that were already running down after the war – linen mills producing a product superseded by rayon and cotton – a London house that would cost the earth to re-open!

It was all very worrying and for the first time in years Mark felt unable to console himself with dreams of Kate. No matter what Molly said he could not believe the child would grow up into a beauty. She lacked grace, her skin was bad, she was gauche – there was no magic. His heart ached when he remembered the uncanny resemblance between Kate the young mother and Rouen's model – but that had been a miracle, he had been a fool to expect another. Mark tried to put her out of his mind – but it still hurt, it hurt every night when he dreamt of what might have been.

The one bright spot in Mark's life was young Tim O'Brien, who was everything Mark could have hoped for. The boy was quick to learn and dogged in his application. Mark had never seen such determination. Tim seemed set to master every aspect of the Averdale businesses in Ulster. He was only seventeen but his grasp of commercial affairs was astonishing. Mark had offered him the chance of university, but Tim turned it down flat. 'What I really want is to work as Mr Harris's assistant.'

Harris was Mark's General Manager, and had been for three years. He was competent, but not as able as Eoin O'Brien. Nobody had ever equalled O'Brien's efficiency, but Mark nurtured hopes that one day another O'Brien would surpass even his father's high standards.

'He's a grand little worker, sir,' Harris said. 'I'd be happy to take the lad on.'

'He's as bright as a whistle,' Mark agreed proudly. 'I'm relying on you, work him hard and teach him all you know. He'll carry a lot of responsibility one day.'

So gradually Mark organized his affairs in Ulster to operate in his absence. He met with his bankers, his lawyers, his accountants, and the Unionist Party at Stormont – and said much the same to everyone: 'You'll have to keep an eye on those lunatics at Westminster. Thank God we've our own Government. We can stop the worst of Attlee's stupidities.'

'No surrender,' came the chorus – the time-honoured Ulster rallying cry.

No surrender ran in Mark's blood, and in '46 he felt threatened. His assets were at risk. When asked how long he would be away in Africa, he shrugged. 'All I remember about Bowley's place is it takes three years to turn coffee into a money crop. I'll be home long before then I hope, but I'll not be back until everything's settled.'

And so, in March, Averdale sailed for Mombasa. His last meeting in Belfast was with the RUC to remind them of their search for Matt Riordan.

'Wherever he is now,' they assured him, 'he's not in Belfast, we're damn certain of that.'

But they were wrong. Matt Riordan *was* in Belfast, and had been for some time – and he was *safe* in Belfast, safer than he had been for years.

It all came about following his accident at the house in Lymington. Clancy's cousin, Bridie, had taken over during that long nerve-racking night. While Clancy and the others had argued downstairs, Bridie had sat at Matt's bedside and nursed him through the most frightening hours of his life.

Bridie was barely qualified as a nurse, but working in a Liverpool hospital had taught her not to panic. She had held his hand and reassured him in her calmest voice, while all the time thinking of how to get him to a doctor. There was only one doctor she could trust – her brother Hugh.

'You just sleep,' she said to Matt and then lied, 'I saw this happen to a man in the war. He got over it, with time and good nursing.' She forced herself to laugh, 'And you mightn't know it but I'm the best nurse there is.'

Matt had clung to her hand. 'Will I ever see again, Bridie – *properly* I mean?'

'Och, you'll see fine in a while, but not now. Will you do as your nurse says and get some sleep.'

He was dozing when she left him at dawn. Downstairs Clancy and the others were in the kitchen, worrying themselves to a frazzle, but Bridie was quite positive. 'Either we take him to a hospital, or bring a doctor here. Hugh might help, if I ask him –'

'For mercy's sake have some sense. Besides Hugh's in Belfast –'

'No, he's in London this week . . .' she blurted out.

Clancy scowled and swore violently.

'If I could get to a phone,' Bridie said after a deep breath, 'Hugh *would* help –'

'Bloody Hugh –'

'Hugh's a Ryan,' she snapped. 'The same as us, Clancy. And he's Fergy's big brother!'

Hundreds of Ryans lived in the Ballymurphy district of Belfast. Clancy Ryan had been born there, and Bridie Ryan too, almost in adjoining houses. They had grown up together, them and two of Bridie's brothers. Fergus and Hugh, Clancy and Bridie – inseparable until death. But death had come early for Fergus – he was nine years old when the B Specials had charged into Ballymurphy one day on yet another raid. Fergy had been on the stairs when armed men rushed into the house. Fergy had screamed with fear. He had *not* shouted a warning as was claimed after at the enquiry. He had been going to bed. But some trigger-happy B Special loosed off a shot. The bullet smashed through poor Fergy as if he was made of papier-mâché. He had died in Bridie's arms, with the rest of the family looking on.

Hundreds of Ryans lived in Ballymurphy – and they all hated B Specials.

Clancy and Bridie had stayed in touch after their childhood years, even when he was imprisoned on the Curragh and she was in Liverpool working in a hospital. Her brother Hugh had been with her for a while. He had worked like a dog – day-school, night-school, part-time jobs, shift-work, studying hour after hour to become a doctor.

Once upon a time it had been Fergy and Hugh, Clancy and Bridie – but now it was Clancy and Hugh, with Bridie torn between them. Hugh shunned violence. He still believed in One Ireland. He wanted the Brits out – but not by the IRA killing people.

But early that morning Bridie sat in the kitchen and said – 'Matt's life may be at stake, Clancy. Hugh is never the traitor you make out. He *will* help, I know he will.'

There was no choice. By eight o'clock Bridie was at the call box on the corner, telephoning Hugh in London.

He arrived at noon, driving a borrowed car, using black-market petrol. How he cursed her – 'Didn't you give me your word to stay out of this mess? Didn't you promise!'

He had exchanged dagger looks with Clancy, then gone upstairs to the patient.

'He's a very sick man,' he said when he came down. 'He should be in hospital under observation. God knows, you've wasted enough time already.'

But how could Matt Riordan go to hospital?

'Will you help, Hugh?' asked Bridie. 'Please.'

Hugh groaned and put his head in his hands. Then he swung round on Clancy, 'If I help it's because my duty is to a sick man – and I'll help for Bridie's sake. But I'll do nothing unless I have your word to leave Bridie out of your mad schemes in future.'

What could Clancy do? He had gained Bridie's help by quoting the vow they had made as kids on Fergy's deathbed – 'We swear to devote our lives to freeing Ireland' – and in sense they had, although in different ways. Clancy's way had been with the IRA, for like Matt Riordan Clancy had been on the bombing campaign in England before the war, Clancy had been on the run, and Clancy had suffered at the hands of de Valera.

They were still arguing when Matt shuffled giddily down the stairs.

'Dear God,' Bridie leapt to her feet and sat him in a chair. 'Didn't you promise you'd stay in bed.'

'I wanted to hear the doctor's opinion,' Matt said, white-faced and trembling.

Hugh made a gesture of disgust. 'You need a specialist. My guess is you've suffered some damage to the optic nerve. I can't say if it's temporary or permanent.'

Matt squinted, cocking his head and holding his hands to his eyes like binoculars in an effort to focus. 'I . . . I passed out a couple of times –'

'You should be in hospital,' Hugh snapped. 'I don't

know – you could recover in a few weeks, a few months, or maybe never. You may need an operation.'

It went very quiet after that. A stricken look crossed Clancy's face. Flynn turned pale, Casey looked sick.

'Then I'm no good to anyone,' Matt said softly, 'not like this.'

Hugh softened. 'I didn't say it *was* permanent, I just can't tell, not here –'

'But will you help, Hugh?' said Bridie, and everyone heard the plea in her voice.

Hugh swore and turned to Clancy. 'Do I have your word? You'll no longer badger Bridie to play any part in your murdering schemes?'

Clancy simply said, 'I want Matt to get better.'

Bridie was torn. Hugh was her big brother whom she respected more than any man alive. She was going back to Belfast with him to work in the same hospital and live in the same house . . . but first she had promised to help Clancy.

Clancy made the decision. 'There's no choice, Matt. Hugh's your only chance. Go with him and get better. We'll be waiting when you come back.'

An hour later it was decided. 'It's risky,' Hugh had admitted. 'But his best hope is to be my patient in my hospital. And my hospital is in Belfast.' Belfast! Where Matt Riordan would be hanged for murder!

Hugh had driven them back to London, with Bridie nursing Matt on the back seat. After which they had worked the ration book trick. Bridie had used it before. Patients took their ration books into hospital with them. If a patient died ration books were returned to the Ministry of Food – but sometimes the procedure was overlooked. Sometimes such ration books were sold on the black market – or sometimes used by men on the run.

For Doctor Hugh Ryan obtaining such a ration book from his Irish friends at the London hospital was less than a morning's work – as was acquiring a whole set of blank medical documents. By early evening Matt Riordan had become William Lambert, according to the paperwork in his pockets.

They spent that night in London, actually in the hospital,

530

where Matt was examined by a specialist. Matt's black-outs were thought to be temporary. 'You'll get headaches of course,' said the specialist, 'severe ones I'm afraid, but hopefully they will fade in a few weeks.' But the damage done to Matt's optic nerve was more serious. 'You may need an operation.'

The following morning Hugh Ryan and his sister Bridie, dressed in her nurse's uniform, boarded the Liverpool train with their patient. That evening all three of them crossed on the ferry to Belfast.

Matt Riordan had never been taken into custody by the RUC. No photograph of him existed on their files, no fingerprints, not even a current description. All the RUC had were two charcoal sketches drawn by his mother before the war – and the man who returned to Belfast looked nothing like that.

Seven years on the Curragh had aged Matt badly. His hairline had receded, and the loss of several teeth had made his face thinner. But even those changes were rendered insignificant by the bandages over his eyes, and the white stick in his hand. Not that the RUC constables who watched passengers disembark from the ferry even asked Mr William Lambert for proof of identity. They knew Dr Ryan well and were happy to wave a taxi over for the young nurse as she shepherded her patient down the gangway . . .

He had suffered much pain. The blinding headaches had gone on for weeks. The first operation had failed to correct his double vision – but the second had been successful. 'I'm afraid your eyes will always be weak,' he was told, 'and of course you must wear spectacles, but . . .'

Matt could see. He could see *properly*. He could see the smile on Bridie Ryan's face. He could see the tiredness in Dr Hugh Ryan's eyes after a long day on the wards. And read newspapers well enough to catch his breath when he came across mention of Lord Averdale leaving for Africa.

'There's a better way,' Dr Hugh Ryan told him, during their long arguments about the north. 'There's a better way than with the gun.'

But Matt Riordan could never accept that – not when it

531

came to enemies like Mark Averdale in Africa and Sean Connors in London.

Sean Connors spent much of 1946 hoping for a reconciliation with Freddie Mallon who was still in Germany with Margaret and the children. The Nuremberg Trials dragged on through the summer, revealing successive horrors, until in October came the judgements. Sentences were passed, Goering committed suicide, and the long trials were over at last.

Sean wondered if Freddie and Margaret would return to Craven Street but his hopes were dashed by a chance meeting with George Hamilton. 'They're sailing direct, Le Havre to New York. Cynthia and I are going over for a weekend before they leave. Can I give them a message?'

'Only my love,' Sean said sadly.

It was the closing of a door, behind which lay not only Freddie and Margaret but part of Sean's life. Nine months had passed since that dreadful scene on New Year's Eve, but Sean was still hurt. He might have brooded longer but, as usual with him, events elsewhere demanded his concentration. The first concerned Tubby Reynolds.

Tubby had been falling deeper into debt for months. The flats at Rutland Gate remained unfinished. Time had run out for Tubby. His credit in Fleet Street was exhausted. He owed Sean six hundred pounds, and what was worse – he owed the loan sharks in Soho.

Sean came home one night and found him buried beneath the wreckage of broken furniture. Everything was in pieces – almost including Tubby himself. He was barely conscious. Sean sat him up and swabbed his face, and would have called the police, but Tubby stopped him.

No bones were broken, but Tubby was a mass of bruises. Sean got him to bed, and in the morning the full story of Tubby's debts in Soho came out – 'They beat me up as a warning,' he said painfully, 'but if they don't get their money at the end of the month . . .' He shuddered.

Sean was appalled, not about Soho's money rackets which were common knowledge in Fleet Street, but that Tubby had been stupid enough to become involved. 'I could have lent you another few quid. Why didn't you ask me?'

But Tubby needed more than a few quid. He owed a total of *three thousand pounds*, half of it in Soho, six hundred to Sean, and the rest to various friends in Fleet Street.

Sean had a lunch appointment that day, and CBS interviews kept him busy until early evening, but by the time he returned to Rutland Gate he had made up his mind. He was going into the property business, though not in the way imagined by Tubby Reynolds, whose most fervent hope was that Sean might help pay off the Soho crowd. But then Tubby had no idea of Sean's financial resources, nor of his latent talent for business. He found out about both two days later.

The property had been valued by then. According to a local surveyor it was worth fourteen thousand in its unfinished state. Sean's proposals were very simple. He and Tubby would form a property company into which Tubby would put the freehold of Rutland Gate and Sean would put seven thousand pounds. The company would pay Tubby's creditors in full, leaving itself with four thousand as working capital – which might just be enough to finish the property. The company's shares would be divided sixty per cent to Sean, and forty per cent to Tubby.

'Wait a minute,' Tubby said in dismay, 'I'll be the junior partner. The house is worth fourteen thousand –'

'Eleven, by the time we've paid the creditors –'

'Okay call it eleven. I'm still putting in more than your seven – and you're asking for sixty per cent.'

But Sean was adamant. He gave Tubby a variety of reasons – he had not planned to become involved, he was being hurried into a decision, he would be turning his back on going to America – every reason valid, but there was another he kept to himself. Thanks mostly to the five thousand transferred from Dinny, Sean's bank account stood at seven thousand, one hundred and twenty-eight pounds. He was ready to plunge the lot, but only if he controlled his own destiny – some of Tubby's judgements had proved suspect already.

Tubby was in no position to argue. His very life was at stake if he failed to pay the Soho crowd. He made a half-hearted attempt to reduce Sean's involvement to a straight loan of fifteen hundred, but Sean turned him down flat – 'What about your other creditors? They won't wait for ever. And you'll still need money to finish the place. Come on Tubby, my offer really isn't that hard.'

Which was true and Tubby knew it.

The following morning they went to a solicitor and bought a ready-made company. 'Can we change the name?' Sean asked. The solicitor said they could, subject to the approval of the Company Registrar. 'In that case,' Sean said, 'I'd like to call it the Mallon Property Company, if my partner agrees.'

'Mallon?' Tubby was astonished. 'I thought it was your money. If Freddie is involved I could end up with two partners –'

'He's nothing to do with it. It is my money, but Mallon was a lucky name for me when I came to London, and if I'm staying –'

An hour later the new directors and shareholders of the Mallon Property Company Limited walked down Chancery Lane and into Fleet Street, where they went to El Vino's to toast their future success.

And so began Sean's second venture into business, the third counting the donkey stables of his boyhood. Of course it was a sideline to begin with – Tubby continued to work in Fleet Street, Sean wrote his columns and broadcast for CBS – and in their spare time they slaved away at Rutland Gate. By Christmas the top flat was almost finished, and New Year's Eve saw an event of equal importance. Sean got through it without geting drunk. He and Tubby celebrated with a cup of tea – after painting the top landing.

After that it was hard work. The winter of 1947 was the coldest ever recorded. London shivered in the Big Freeze. Pipes froze, coal stocks fell, the capital almost ground to a halt. But by the end of March two flats were finished and ready for occupation at Rutland Gate. Tubby wanted to sell them outright, except Sean had other ideas – 'Let's lease them, Tubby, we'll make more money in the long run.'

'In the long run we're all dead,' Tubby complained.

But lease them they did. The Mallon Property Company

wrote two seven-year leases (with suitable rent reviews) and in May two happy couples – Mr and Mrs Wynn-Jones, and Mr and Mrs Kent, moved in almost before the ink was dry on their cheques.

Then, that same month, two unrelated events occurred which were to change Sean's future entirely. The first, and most immediately serious, was that CBS reduced *Seven Days* from thirty minutes to fifteen – not through any fault of Sean's, but simply because Americans were less interested in London. More and more Americans had seen the end of the Nuremberg Trials as the conclusion of their business in Europe. They were going home and finding their own US of A to be the most fascinating place on God's earth.

Sean was still digesting the implications of the CBS decision when Michael O'Hara arrived out of the blue with some momentous news from Dublin. Dinny was selling the *Gazette*.

Michael was almost apologetic when he related the story to Sean. 'Sure he's an old feller now, Sean. He's tired out. He's not doing it for the money. He wanted to retire anyway – then this offer came up from another paper and, well, they wanted to buy . . .' Michael shrugged. 'None of us is blaming him.'

It was a shock. Another break with the past, even though Sean had not been as dutiful as he should at staying in touch. Michael told him the rest of the news. Old Senator O'Keefe had retired to Cork six months before, and even Jim Tully was less active . . .

'And Maeve?' Sean asked eagerly. 'How's Maeve?'

'Och, wouldn't you think she's got the secret of eternal youth. She always asks after you whenever I see her.'

Tomas and the rest of the family were happy in Australia. Michael had a wallet full of photographs. Seeing them made Sean feel even worse. Once upon a time the family had meant so much to him – he had loved each and every one of them – but now he was looking at strangers. Even Michael, his dearest boyhood friend, his partner in the donkey business . . . even Michael was from a different world. 'A different world', Val had said that to him once . . .

So it was a bitter-sweet reunion for Sean. He was delighted to see Michael again, but even as they talked he was plagued by his conscience. Bitter-sweet was the right description, he thought – but then everything about Ireland was bitter-sweet. De Valera's dreams of a rural paradise, self-sufficient from the rest of the world, had turned sour. Irishmen were emigrating in greater numbers than ever.

'More are leaving now than since the Famine,' Michael said sourly. 'Me included. Sure I never want to go back'. There's no future in the place, Sean, no future at all.'

Sean remembered his father's dreams and was plunged into gloom. It seemed he had let everyone down, though at least he could help Michael. After a word with Tubby it was agreed that Michael would share the still incomplete second floor at Rutland Gate.

Michael was thirty, a competent journalist having been trained by Dinny, so at long last Sean was able to take the advice Freddie had offered when he had left for America in the war – 'Get yourself an assistant. Find some Mick straight off the boat and work him into the ground.'

During the following weeks Sean took Michael everywhere. Michael was wide-eyed and full of wonder. To a casual observer it seemed that, despite the bomb damage, London was recapturing much of its pre-war gaiety – glittering balls were held at the great stately homes, the young aristocrats around Princess Margaret were constantly headlined as 'the Margaret set' – but Sean Connors was much more than a casual observer. He had learned to dig deep. While splendid dances were taking place at Windsor Castle, the Attlee Government was pushing through such a programme of Anti-Upper-Class legislation that many of the old wealthy were emigrating. Thousands of ancestral acres were sold to pay death duties. Aristocratic owners of stately homes were forced to open their doors to the public simply to pay the rates. It was Val's brave new world, and Sean often wondered what she would have made of it.

Sean worked harder than ever. Determined to hang on to his American audience he took his microphone all over the country. When the *Queen Elizabeth* went aground eight miles from port, Sean persuaded a pilot to smuggle him aboard. That week *Seven Days* carried recordings of Beatrice Lillie and a dozen other celebrities as they waited for the great liner to be refloated. Sean told them, 'You're my first captive audience since the Blitz.'

He struggled to find stories everywhere, but meanwhile he and Michael worked every spare hour with Tubby at Rutland Gate. In September the Mallon Property Company wrote another lease when Major Miles Harding moved into the third floor.

Then Sean was back at Southampton, interviewing Mae West as she arrived on the *Queen Mary*. The Hollywood star wore two-inch false eyelashes and her luggage included 150 dresses. Her show *Diamond Lil* had run three years in America, but the fifty-seven-year-old star was as lively as ever. She told Sean, 'Now I'm going to brighten up dreary old London.'

Dreary old London was changing. Rebuilding was hampered by shortage of materials, but many houses were under repair. And Sean noticed other things as he hunted for stories. Tubby had predicted 'All the large London houses are done for' – and Sean watched it come true. Only two houses in Berkeley Square remained in private hands. Lord Wimborne's 200-year-old house next to the Ritz was sold to the Eagle Star Insurance Company for offices. The Duke of Wellington gave Apsley House to the nation in exchange for a rent-free flat on the top floor. The Duke of Marlborough sold his grand mansion in Kensington Palace Gardens to the French Government. London was changing indeed – and Sean Connors, man of property, began to bless the day he had made his agreement with Tubby.

Sean was even winning his battle to retain American interest in London. Events helped. When a Greek Prince changed his name to Philip Mountbatten and married Princess Elizabeth, Sean and Michael put on an hour-long 'CBS Special' to cover the wedding. The broadcast was a triumph – and it gave Sean an idea which was to earn him a fortune.

Sean's fees for his CBS work and newspaper columns were paid to Freddie's agent in New York. The agent took ten per cent and sent half of the remainder to Freddie – thus

Sean's earnings were reduced by fifty-five per cent. He was paying an agent he had never met, and sharing his income with a partner who ignored him. Sean had allowed the situation to continue in the hope that it might bring about a reconciliation . . . but after almost two years that seemed unlikely . . . and now Sean was paying Michael as well.

The injustice began to irk, especially as he knew Freddie was prospering. Fleet Street gossip was full of praise for the magazine empire Freddie was creating in the States. Besides, that year Sean had received an early Christmas card from Ambassador Kennedy with a note attached: 'Your old partner Freddie Mallon is doing well with his magazines. Of course he's Republican so he gets things all wrong, but I hear he's making a packet.'

That decided Sean. He felt enormously sad to break the link, but Freddie seemed to want it that way. In December Sean formed his second company – The London & Continental News Agency Limited. The 'continental news' was supplied by two freelance journalists who had quit London to work out of Paris and Bonn. By January 1948 he had renegotiated his arrangement with CBS. *Seven Days* was incorporated into their general world coverage, but Sean was to present a series of extended programmes on special events – starting that summer with the first post-war Olympic Games which were to be held in London. Sean's fee income from broadcasting trebled. True, not every paper in the United States renewed their subscriptions to his syndicated columns, but apart from the ten per cent paid to his new agent in New York, the entire income belonged to London & Continental News.

Sean was at last fulfilling the dream which had brought him to London ten years before – he was acquiring some assets. With the sixth flat now let, Rutland Gate was yielding rents of seventeen hundred pounds a year.

'Even so,' Tubby grumbled, 'it will take us years to save enough to buy another property.'

Sean shook his head. 'You find the right place and I'll find the money.'

And Tubby did, he found it in February, in fact he found two adjoining houses for sale in Great Cumberland Place.

After a day spent measuring rooms and testing partition walls he forecast that the gracious old properties could be converted into sixteen flats – 'But one house will cost eighteen thousand, and we might have to pay twenty for the other.'

'Then there's the conversion on top,' Sean said. 'How much will that cost?'

The houses would cost as much again to convert. The Mallon Property Company needed seventy-six thousand pounds in cash!

Sean fairly buzzed with excitement. It was like buying the *Gazette* all over again. He sensed the deal before he could work it out – he just knew it was there. It was the trick with the assets, he told himself, use one lot to buy another . . .

He called on bank after bank. Bankers were cautious. They had never heard of the Mallon Property Company. One pin-striped figure even said to Sean, 'But you are a journalist, Mr Connors. Why not stick to what you know best?'

Sean saw eleven bankers in twelve working days. It was the eleventh who provided the finance – with a few strings attached. The bank would only lend fifty thousand, and to protect their loan wanted a charge on the houses at Great Cumberland Place *and* Rutland Gate. 'Not only that,' the banker smiled at Sean, 'we shall need your personal guarantees. If anything goes wrong you could spend the rest of your lives paying us off.'

Tubby groaned when he heard. 'We're getting deeper into debt. Besides we need *more* than fifty thousand, we worked it out at seventy-six –'

Sean shook his head. 'Seventy-six to complete, but not to start. Even if we pay forty for the houses we'll still have ten thousand for work in progress. And if we live in a couple of rooms in Great Cumberland Place we can let out our flat in Rutland Gate. Rent from that and the others gives us a hundred and sixty a month. That's wages for a few men. Think Tubby, we've just got to phase it through, that's all.'

Tubby was apprehensive and excited at the same time – and quite unprepared for Sean's next suggestion. 'Leave

Fleet Street?' Tubby gaped. 'You mean work full-time in the property business?'

Sean nodded. 'You'll have to if we get Great Cumberland Place. This job will need full-time supervision.'

Tubby frowned. 'I'll need something to live on. That will make a dent in –'

'No,' Sean said firmly. 'London & Continental will cover your wages. We can pay it back from the property company later.'

Finally Tubby agreed. He grinned wryly, 'Just so long as you don't take a wife.'

Sean was a long way from that. There had been no one since Val, and no time to look since teaming up with Tubby. It was different from his partnership with Freddie. Life with Freddie had been fun; parties galore, dressing for dinner, wining and dining with the wealthy. Now Sean rarely attended a party, and when he did it was only for a story. However there was no time to look back – especially when the Mallon Property Company bought the two houses in Great Cumberland Place for thirty-seven thousand pounds.

By the end of April 1948, Sean and Tubby and Michael O'Hara were living in three dusty rooms in Great Cumberland Place – dusty because both houses were covered in pulverized mortar as partition walls were demolished.

Sean and Michael came home every night, changed into old clothes and busied themselves alongside Tubby. They did much of the heavy work themselves, labouring at night so that the skilled men on the payroll would make better progress by day. Never had Sean's nickname the Irish Navvy been more apt.

Yet stories and interviews poured forth from London & Continental News as furiously as ever. When David Niven married a beautiful Swedish model at the Chelsea Registry Office, Michael O'Hara was on hand to record the scene. When a carrot-haired American comedian named Danny Kaye brought the house down at the Palladium, Sean was backstage with a microphone. Gossip and hard news, social and political events, London & Continental News told the world what was happening in London.

Sean's finger was always on the pulse. He tried to look into the future. He wondered what Britain would be like in ten years. The whole world was changing – including the British Empire. The Indian continent had already gone, divided into India and Pakistan to accommodate religious differences – Burma had become an independent republic outside the British Commonwealth, Ceylon had acquired full dominion status – even the African countries wanted greater freedom. Sean interviewed a succession of black Africans as they trudged in and out of the Colonial Office. He remembered Val's old boss, Herbert Morrison, saying – 'Independence for African countries would be like giving a child of ten a latchkey.' Africans were supposedly so unsophisticated that self-rule would not be attained for generations. But when Sean interviewed men like Kwame Nkrumah from the Gold Coast and Jomo Kenyatta from Kenya he wondered how long they would wait.

Meanwhile in Britain itself the Attlee Government pressed on with reforms. Not everyone was pleased. In fact it was Sean Connors who broke the news about Earl Lloyd-George, the fifty-eight-year-old son of the former prime minister. 'I'm leaving England for good,' he told Sean, 'this British Government is the most inefficient since the Stuarts. I'm going to America to seek life, liberty and happiness, which cannot be found in England today.'

One day Sean planned to go to America too . . . but first he would conquer London. Maybe it was no longer Harmsworth's London, it was a city of restrictions and shortages . . . but it remained forever London and was still in many people's eyes the greatest city in the world.

Kate O'Brien was quite sure that London was a great place. She and Jenny adored it and had come to know it well.

To Kate's surprise and Aunt Alison's satisfaction, Glossops had turned out a success. In a sense it offered Kate the best of all worlds . . . school itself, easy access to Aunt Alison at Highgate, and a sanctuary from her guardian. She had been terrified by his reaction to her on her return from the United States. After all he was central to her future, he *controlled* her future. If he disliked her so much . . . she shuddered at the possible consequences.

That apart, life posed few problems. Glossops had lost its terrors by the end of the first term. Kate and Jenny rode, played indifferent tennis but, thanks to the Moraine Country Club, played excellent golf, and generally settled into the school.

With Lord Averdale away in Africa Kate spent half-terms and holidays at Highgate with Aunt Alison . . . which was how the girls discovered London. Aunt Alison took them everywhere . . . films, theatre, the ballet, exhibitions, the Tower, museums and monuments – 'You can't have an opinion on what you don't know,' Aunt Alison said firmly, adding a chuckle, 'and what you don't know won't be worth having an opinion about by the time we finish.'

It was exhausting but fun.

In the spring of 1946, Kate had a wonderful surprise. Her brother Tim called at the school. It was the first time she had seen him since 1939. He wrote in advance, saying he was being sent to London to see Uncle Mark's lawyers, and if he came to Glossops could they meet? Kate gave the letter to Miss Jenkins and explained the circumstances – and Miss Jenkins not only gave her permission to see him but excused her from wearing school uniform.

He was very grown-up, but not so grown-up that he didn't go pink when some of the girls stared at him as he waited in the hall. Then Kate came down and introduced Miss Jenkins who said Kate must be back by six o'clock – after which they went to Windsor for the day, just the two of them.

'We've written eighty letters to each other,' Kate said. 'I counted them.'

She felt nearly as shy and awkward as she had with her guardian – and she blushed beetroot red which was so stupid. He's my brother, she thought – he's the only *real* family I have in the world, yet he's a stranger.

His hair was dark brown, chestnut with auburn tints. He seemed very serious. He walked normally, without any hint of a limp. She almost asked about his bad legs but decided against it.

'Jenny wanted to come,' she told him, 'but Miss Jenkins wouldn't let her.'

542

They walked out of Windsor and along the river for a while. Conversation was so stilted that Kate became tongue-tied at times. Then the rain started and they ran back to the High Street.

'We could go to the British Restaurant if you like,' she said.

The restaurant was awful. They shared a table with an elderly lady and her grandson. The child knocked over a bowl of soup and splashed everyone. The place was so crowded that people walked up and down with their trays waiting for seats.

Kate whispered, 'I've only been here once, with Jenny. It was quite empty –'

'It's always busy on Thursdays,' the grandmother grumbled. 'I'm here every Thursday, it's always the same.'

'Oh,' Tim and Kate said together.

Afterwards they went back to the riverbank and sat in a shelter, staring at the swans. She asked about his accountancy exams and Ulster, and if he knew when their guardian would be back from Africa.

Tim said, 'I think he'll be away for ages. From what I can make out we've been robbed left, right and centre.'

She noticed the 'we'. He used it whenever he spoke of Ulster, very secure in his relationship with their guardian, and quite positive about the future – 'Brackenburn will be rebuilt and we shall all live there.'

'For ever?' she asked. The words hung in the air like a death sentence.

'Well of course, silly,' he said. 'That's always been the plan, for as long as I can remember.'

'But you're seventeen,' she said, blushing furiously, 'I mean, if you were to marry –'

'*Marry?* I don't think Uncle Mark intends either of us to marry.'

'Oh.'

The future seemed more muddled than ever. In one sense she felt relieved. If Tim were always there she might be spared the disapproving looks of her guardian.

He became quite talkative after that, telling her about Ulster – past, present and future. It was her birthplace but it sounded foreign. Uncle Linc had hated Belfast – 'a goddam slagheap', he called it, but she kept that from Tim. Besides Tim was too excited about the future to listen. He expected to be appointed General Manager of Averdale's one day and after that go into politics. He would sit at Stormont and help run the country – 'I might even end up as prime minister,' he said proudly.

'And I'll run Brackenburn. I'll be your housekeeper.'

'Not housekeeper – *hostess*, Kate.'

It sounded very grand. She rather liked the idea until she remembered her guardian's scowl.

Gradually the talk flowed – they were less like strangers, more like pen-friends, she thought – it was impossible to think of him as a real brother – at least it was before he frightened her to death by talking of the Killing at Keady.

Kate was too terrified to take it all in. She had been told that her parents' had died in an accident. But *murdered*! 'How horrible,' she whispered. 'How positively awful . . .'

'The IRA did it,' Tim said grimly. 'Uncle Mark blames a man called Riordan but that's not right. Riordan carried me down to the stream. He saved me in a way. It was another man, big, with jet black hair and fierce blue eyes, I'd know him anywhere. I used to dream about him night after night. By heavens, if I ever get my hands on –'

'Don't,' she pleaded. 'Please don't Tim, it's too awful.'

She trembled, on the verge of tears. He slid an arm round her shoulders – then a wonderful thing happened. She felt really close to him. For the first time in her life having a brother meant something. She poured her heart out after that, overcome by guilt, confessing she had wanted to stay with Aunt Alison for ever, never to come home, never to see him again.

'And it must have been so much worse for you,' she gulped. 'You never even had someone like Aunt Eleanor, let alone Aunt Alison. And you had the war . . . and your bad legs, and that horrible Williams man at Berkeley Square, then Uncle Mark and going back to Ulster where people get shot and killed . . .'

Tears came in a flood, but Tim was patient and kind and comforting.

She held his hand on the bus going back to Glossops, glorying in the knowledge that he was her brother. He was

544

permanent family! And she was so proud of him. No matter what the future held, Tim would be there to face it with her.

Of course she told Jenny – or rather she attempted to – but when it came to retailing Tim's story about her parents Kate found she had shut her ears to so much that all she was left with was Tim's courage under fire. Tim was a hero in her eyes. Even the prospect of living in a rebuilt Brackenburn was different now that she would share it with Tim. In fact she was quite excited, although she was careful not to hurt Jenny's feelings – 'I shall have a suite especially reserved for you and Aunt Alison at Brackenburn – and Uncle Linc too if he can get leave from the Embassy.'

Jenny accepted graciously, though she did have some qualms about going to a place where people killed each other, and which her father had described as 'a goddam slagheap!' However she was pleased to see Kate so happy and wrote to her mother about it.

The school went to Switzerland that first summer, or at least some pupils did, to study in the kitchens of the famous chef Marcel Bonnier. Kate and Jenny enjoyed it and were proud of their diplomas, although as Uncle Linc observed afterwards, 'I don't know when we'll get to taste your cordon bleu cooking, this rationing goes on for ever.'

Meanwhile Kate wrote to Tim every two weeks instead of once a month as before and Tim dutifully answered. He even stopped writing such things as 'I don't know what would interest a girl' and instead simply told her what was happening. He sounded lonely to Kate. His life was all work and no play. Uncle Mark was still in Africa and sounded like staying there for ages – and poor Tim just worked and studied in Belfast.

That Christmas she was able to invite him to Highgate, to spend the holiday with the Johnstones. She was thrilled. The people she loved most in the whole world would be together under the same roof. She looked forward to it for weeks – but was bitterly disappointed when it happened. They all *seemed* to get on, yet somehow there was an undercurrent. Aunt Alison was positively inquisitional at times – 'I can't understand Lord Averdale,' she said. 'He seems to expect you and Kate to live with him for ever.

Surely he realizes young people grow up and want lives of their own. Doesn't he expect you to marry, either of you?'

And when Tim answered, 'Well no, I don't think he does, not when Brackenburn is rebuilt and we all live there', Aunt Alison arched her eyebrows. 'How extraordinary,' she said.

Afterwards Aunt Alison had tried to make amends, by saying, 'It must have been very difficult for him, staying with a houseful of strangers.'

And Uncle Linc said, 'He's certainly a very intelligent young man.'

But they hadn't liked him much and Kate knew it. She vowed never to mix her families again. It saddened her and was a painful warning that she might have to choose between them one day.

After Christmas came the awful winter of '47. Glossops sent half the girls back to Switzerland. 'The Swiss know how to deal with the cold,' Miss Jenkins said in Assembly. The girls were there for six wonderful weeks, during which time they learned to ski. It was exhilarating and exciting, and surprisingly not cold at all.

The year passed – summer spent touring Scotland with Aunt Alison and Uncle Linc, autumn at Glossops and then Christmas again. Tim wrote to say he was spending it with friends in Ulster. Kate felt glad and guilty at the same time. Glad because Yvette Lefarge was coming over from Paris for the holiday, and guilty because she suspected Tim's 'friends' were an excuse to avoid potential embarrassment with the Johnstones at Highgate. But Christmas itself was hugely successful and Kate was overjoyed to see Yvette.

Then back to Glossops and better still another three weeks in Switzerland for the skiing – but this time the trip was marred by an argument, amazingly between Kate and Jenny. Stupidly, idiotically, they fell in love with the same ski instructor. He was tall and bronzed, with thick black hair and vivid blue eyes. The two girls competed shamelessly for his attention. Jenny won by shamming a sprained ankle. Kate steamed with jealousy. Afterwards they laughed, but not at the time. It was the first crack in their relationship, a fracture which was to widen to an unbelievable chasm the next year.

546

They were all growing up. Kate and Jenny were sixteen, and Rosemary a year older. Rosemary was scathing about their lack of boyfriends. Rosemary not only had an admirer in Lincoln, where her people lived, but went out with a soldier called Eric from the Windsor barracks, even though such friendships were strictly forbidden. She met him in a milk-bar in Slough on Saturdays and they went to the cinema. Her stories about what they did after the film was the high spot of the week. When Rosemary undressed on a Saturday night all the girls crowded round to inspect her love bites. The first time Jenny saw them she said – 'Hasn't Eric got any teeth? I can't see the marks.'

Every week Rosemary opened her blouse to reveal a rash of purply blotches. Sometimes she even bore a bite on the inside of each thigh. Eric, she assured them, was very passionate indeed.

Rosemary was saving her virginity for Martin in Lincolnshire because he was stinking rich and wanted to marry her – 'but Eric is so earthy and primitive that I feel like Lady Chatterley with her gamekeeper.'

A reference which passed over Kate's head. She was even more mystified when Angela asked, 'Did you stroke little Herbert or kiss him tonight?'

'Sucked him for hours,' Rosemary said proudly, 'Eric went wild.'

So Glossops was providing a complete education.

And Kate was emerging from her chrysalis stage. Gone now were her pimples and blotchy complexion. Lost too was the habit of blushing whenever anyone spoke to her. A combination of Glossops and Aunt Alison, skiing holidays and exercise, travel and nature, were conspiring to produce a lithe and poised young lady. Perhaps it was inevitable that Miss Broakes, who taught art and drama, was the first to see what the rest of Glossops was coming to realize – that Kate O'Brien was growing into an exceptionally beautiful girl. Kate had developed into Miss Broakes's favourite subject in the art class. 'Just look at this child's eyes,' Miss Broakes would say to her class. 'Aren't they quite the most beautiful you've ever seen?'

Kate had learned to hide her embarrassment, just as she had grown used to posing for the class. The whole process was restoring her self-confidence. How strange, Kate thought to herself, but there was a time when I felt so alone – now I'm surrounded by friends at Glossops and family all over the place – dear Tim in Belfast, Yvette in Paris and the Johnstones at Highgate. It was only when she thought of her guardian in Africa that she worried.

CHAPTER THREE

Mark Averdale's voyage to Africa developed into the most extraordinary journey of his life. Africa had changed him once before, from a callow rebellious youth into a presentable young man – and it was to change him again in ways he would never have imagined.

At the outset he was glad to be going. With his affairs settled in Belfast he felt almost relieved as the ship nosed out from the Mersey and into the Irish Sea. Why not, what was he leaving? He had virtually abandoned his dreams of Kate. Africa would get her out of his system. Certainly it would provide an escape from damn fool politicians at Westminster. The trip was welcome if for that reason alone.

But Mark was not travelling for pleasure. The Bowley estates had to get going again. He needed money. Art treasures were coming on to the market all over Europe. More Nazi loot was unearthed every month. Wealthy collectors were buying as never before. Mark cursed the succession of thieving, incompetent managers who had ruined the Bowley estates – he *needed* that sixty thousand a year.

So as the ship plunged down the coast of Africa and on towards Cape Town, Mark paced the decks and tried to concentrate on great works of art – but Rouen's nymph plagued him as she had most of his life. Every night she disturbed his dreams, and he awoke to re-experience his disappointment with Kate the child. It made him bad-tempered and irritable. Other passengers found him a difficult companion so he was not the only one to breathe a sigh of relief when finally they docked in Mombasa.

Mombasa! The sounds were exactly as he remembered – timeless – the thin, soaring notes of flutes joining the twanging of mandolins – and from somewhere inland the dull, heavy thud of drums. Africa! Mark sucked in the air and felt glad to be back.

Nobody met him. He was not expected. He wanted to get his bearings, find out about things before he descended upon the Bowley estates. He spent three days in Mombasa, listening to the gossip while forming impressions. If the war had been bad for the Bowley estates, it had brought prosperity to some people. Elephant poachers had made a fortune. Mombasa was full of ivory – native poachers and Arab middlemen as far north as Lamu had grown wealthy in the war. But Mark was more concerned with the coffee crop, and he was amazed at the high price it was fetching. One thing struck him forcibly. Kenya was on the verge of a boom. The place seemed full of fresh-faced, pink-kneed farmers in embryo, all eager to get to grips with the parcels of land given to them by a grateful King and Country.

After a few days acclimatizing Mark took the train to Nairobi and began the journey inland.

Nairobi staggered him. It had grown into a city. Once it had been a sprawling shanty-town with a screeching core of Indian commerce. Now buildings were shooting up everywhere – the airport at Eastleigh was even operating international flights. Safaris were starting again – Americans were all over the place talking about making movies – the whole place reeked of prosperity. Yet the Bowley estates had ceased to make money!

Two days later Mark found out why. His discoveries appalled him. The coffee plantations, Lord Bowley's pride and joy, had been allowed to dwindle to a quarter of their former size. The beef herd had been rustled and decimated until the word *herd* was barely appropriate. Wherever he looked he found signs of mismanagement. The Bowley bungalow, a low, thatched, joy of a house, was in complete disrepair. He almost wept when he remembered the blood, sweat and tears which the Bowleys had put into it – all gone to waste. He found the current manager, a man called Llewellyn-Jones, in bed with a Nairobi prostitute who was apparently a permanent guest.

The next three months were a nightmare. Mark threw Llewellyn-Jones out but then found it was not easy to hire a new manager. The good men were buying their own spreads with the help of Government money. And several not-quite-so-good men took one look at the task of rebuilding and turned the job down. Finally Mark engaged a South African, Jan Tatz, who was both desperate and tough enough to accept the challenge.

By the end of 1946 they had stopped some of the rot – but that fell a long way short of restoring the estate to its former glory. Tatz's best estimate was that three years hard work and a sizeable investment would be needed before they saw a penny profit.

It was yet another setback. Mark did not *want* to invest – what with shortages and new taxation his businesses in Ulster were barely profitable. Even if he had the funds available, investing in Africa would be difficult. The Labour Government had now nationalized the Bank of England – currency controls had been introduced – it was no longer possible for a man to use his own money as he saw fit. Yet the same damn fool politicians were as good as giving money to any ex-squadron leader who fancied his hand as a farmer. Mark fumed.

Potentially the Bowley estates were the most valuable part of the Averdale empire – immensely valuable when the Bowleys were killed – but now, milked dry, their worth was questionable. Even if he sold them, or attempted to sell them, in their present state he would realize only a fraction of their true worth.

Finally he struck upon the idea of a partnership. Tatz had no money so he was out of the question – but Kenya had plenty of rich farmers. Mark had met some in Nairobi where he spent some time every week. He was popular in Nairobi. East Africa had long been a happy hunting ground for the British aristocracy, so a new English 'Mi-Lord' was warmly welcomed. Mark was feted like royalty. He dined with the Governor and joined two of the clubs (where everyone knew everyone and each other's business) – and it was at Smith's Club that he first met Jock Standish. Standish owned a spread almost as large as the Bowley estates – the difference being that his was profitable. He was a big, burly man with a ginger moustache who was cheerfully sympathetic about Mark's problems. 'It's the country, old boy. You get robbed blind unless you're careful. Old Bowley must be spinning in his grave.'

They shared a few drinks and a week later bumped into each other again – and when Standish expressed interest in the Bowley estates Mark was more than ready to discuss a partnership. Of course he had heard some of the rumours by then – that Standish could be a bit wild and was something of a gambler – but he had plenty of money and Mark's need for a partner was so urgent that he was ready to talk to anyone.

'Come over for the weekend,' Standish said, 'meet some of the others. I'm sure we'll work something out.'

And so Mark made his first visit to Happy Valley.

It had been famous for years. Lord Bowley had known it, but refused to become part of it, even though it was sometimes referred to as the centre of social life in that part of the White Highlands. It lay between the Aberdares and the town of Gilgil, with its centre nestling along the Wanjohi river which ran down from the mountain of Kipipiri. The landscape was idyllic – a wide grassy valley backed by a leafy, wooded escarpment – but it was not the physical grandeur of the place which drew Mark Averdale, it was Jock Standish and the people who lived there.

The Happy Valley Set became notorious in the twenties when Josslyn Hay and his young wife Idina had entertained at Clouds, a large, thatched mansion with innumerable sitting-rooms and even more bedrooms. Joss Hay was somewhat like Mark Averdale, in fact they had both been at Eton. Joss too was 'asked to leave'. Like Mark, Joss displayed a total disregard for the opinions of others – but it was his wife who added the glitter to the legend of Happy Valley. She had been married twice before Joss and her countless lovers supposedly included Oswald Mosley. She had a perfect figure and her *affaires* had shocked London. Even after her divorce, when she married Joss in 1923, it was hinted that they would be 'unwelcome at Ascot'.

So in 1925 they had settled at Clouds and began to entertain in a manner which was to shape the style of

Happy Valley. Idina received guests naked in her bath, talking animatedly as she bathed, then dressing in front of them while they consumed endless cocktails. By the time dinner was served most of them were in a fair state of intoxication, and after dinner numbered keys were set out on a table so that bedroom partners could be chosen by chance. Idina was only happy if all of her house guests had swapped partners by nightfall.

Joss and Idina were typical – Happy Valley was full of wealthy wanderers, indefatigable pleasure seekers who had grown weary of or been thrown out of other societies. Cocaine was taken like snuff and many were addicted to heroin – people drank, gambled and committed adultery as a matter of course. By 1947 many of the characters who had set the scene in the twenties were no longer there – some had died, by natural or unnatural causes, and others had moved on in their restless quest for amusement – but the style and tone of Happy Valley persisted and lived on in men like Jock Standish.

So when Mark Averdale was invited to spend the weekend at Columns, Standish's vast house on the banks of the Wanjohi, he had a suspicion of what it might be like – but he went, partly out of curiosity but mostly to pursue Standish over the Bowley estates.

On his first visit he arrived at about five on the Friday afternoon, hot and dusty after driving eighty miles in a jeep. He was shown to a guest bungalow by a houseboy, after which he took a cool bath and changed for the evening. Just before seven, he walked over to the main house and joined the other forty or so guests on the verandah, mingling happily with the throng of silks, dinner jackets, bronzed skins, dazzling smiles and glittering jewellery.

Unlike Idina Hay, Marcia Standish did not greet people from her bath. But the warmth of her welcome was as obvious as her figure, splendidly revealed by a low-cut dress. She had brown hair and hazel eyes set into an oval face, which wore an expression of fey innocence. She clung to Mark's arm and led him around, making introductions while providing a bird's eye view of her cleavage. He was impressed. She was a good-looking woman, in fact Happy

Valley seemed blessed by a number of attractive females.

People danced to gramophone music, and talked and laughed and drank – replenishing their glasses from silver trays carried from room to room by the houseboys. As Mark was newly out from 'home' his opinion was sought about 'those bloody socialists who seem determined to ruin what's left of the Empire' – and his views so dove-tailed with theirs that he felt very much at ease by the time dinner was served – more than ever when Marcia Standish slid her hand on to his thigh.

She came to his bungalow later that night, or early in the morning since it was three o'clock before anyone went to bed. 'It's a house rule,' she smiled in the moonlight, 'the hostess gets the pick of the men. Do you mind?'

He did not mind at all. In fact half an hour later he was groaning with pleasure.

But his real introduction to the ways of Happy Valley came when they played cards the following night. 'It's a tradition,' Jock Standish said after dinner. 'Always play on a Saturday night. High stakes mind you. Too rich for some. There's a saying that only the biggest men in Africa play at Jock Standish's table. Right Marcia?'

'Some are bigger than others,' she said, sipping her drink and throwing Mark an innocent look.

Another guest, Vivien Hathaway, laughed in a way which seemed to underline a point, but her meaning was lost on Mark. He felt disappointed. A card game might last a while and he had been hoping for more pleasures in bed with Marcia – but he sensed something else. They were testing his nerve. He watched their expectant expressions, then shrugged. 'Very well, I'm all for tradition.'

'We have a rule,' Standish continued. 'We start at midnight and no man leaves the table until the cock crows – winning or losing. That acceptable?'

Someone cackled 'Cock-a-doodle-doo' in the background.

Mark tried to catch Marcia's eye but she was talking to Harry Jackson, a farmer from the other side of Nairobi with whom she had spent most of the evening. That irked too – Mark wondered if she had been disappointed last night.

George Sidey, another guest, smiled, 'No pressure, Averdale. Nobody's forcing you. Entirely your choice.'

Mark detected the undertone. Resenting the implication that he might back down, he answered coolly, 'Sounds a good idea. Bowley's place has cost me a packet, some of your money might pay for my trip.' And he was still returning Sidey's stare when Audrey Cummings led him off to the verandah. They danced for the next half hour. She was a willowy blonde who moved so rhythmically that he almost forgot Marcia Standish, but the memories of the previous night were too vivid to forget altogether. He looked for her without success until, at ten minutes to midnight, she climbed the steps to the verandah, coming from the direction of the guests' bungalows. Her face was flushed, her eyes bright. Behind her, stepping into the light, came Harry Jackson.

'Poor Marcia,' Audrey Cummings purred. 'One pleasure curtailed by another. She only came back to watch you at the card table.'

'Watch? Won't she play?'

'Not tonight. There will only be five players tonight.'

The card-room was beyond the dining-room at the centre of the house. A log fire blazed in the grate. In the middle of the room was a single table, not small and baize-topped as usual but much larger and draped to the floor with a red chenille cloth. Directly above it shone a single drop lamp, while the rest of the room was left in shadowy firelight.

Cummings was already seated at the table. 'Ah, Lord Averdale. Audrey been looking after you, I hope?'

'Your wife dances splendidly,' Mark answered and was rewarded with a squeeze of his arm.

Most of the guests followed them in, glasses in hand. Music from the verandah drifted in too, faintly audible under the hubbub of talk. Mark sensed a stir of excitement, like the moment before the rise of a theatre curtain. However Audrey was wrong about the number of players, only four chairs were set at the table.

When Mark sat down his knees tangled in the red chenille cloth which was a nuisance because when he reached forward he pulled the cloth with him. Finally he stuck his knees under the table and gathered the cloth in folds across his lap. Once comfortable he became conscious of the table again, which was at least four feet square, much larger than normal for cards – but the extra size was a benefit when Standish began to distribute the chips. Mark studied the stack of polished ivory discs in front of him. 'We've five thousand each,' Standish said. 'Draw more later if you're losing.'

There were indeed only four players – Cummings on Mark's left, Sidey to his right, and Standish himself across the table.

They played poker, not a game in which Mark was experienced, in fact it was banned in his London club. Bridge was considered a gentleman's game, whereas poker was known to lead to all sorts of excesses.

The atmosphere was disconcerting, and Mark winced at the size of the stakes. The lowest valued chips were a hundred pounds. He cursed himself for becoming involved, suspecting the others would play against him. It was the way people packed tight around the table which worried him most. Guests gathered on all sides, crowding as close as around a roulette table. Audrey Cummings was so near that if Mark turned his head his face would be in her cleavage. Her hand rested on his shoulder and her fingers stroked the nape of his neck. Mark glanced up in case Cummings realized what was happening – but Cummings was studying his cards.

Drink flowed as freely as ever. The throng twisted and turned to accept fresh glasses, but no one drew away from the table. Occasional murmurs of excitement accompanied a winning hand, and the soft chatter ebbed and flowed as if in time with the music drifting in from the verandah. It was hot. The heavy air was pungent with cigar smoke and scented bodies – and Audrey Cummings never stopped stroking the nape of Mark's neck.

He concentrated, trying to close his mind to everything but the cards and the faces of the men round the table. Standish's forehead glistened under the lamplight. He was perspiring so freely that Mark could almost taste the strong smell of sweat. And Standish grunted every now and then, and twisted in his seat as if to get more comfortable. Mark played cautiously and won a few hundred in the first hour, mainly from Standish to his surprise.

They were all drinking whisky, Mark included, their glasses recharged by a bottle which dipped in and out of the pool of light at regular intervals. No glass remained empty for long.

During the second hour Standish seemed to be playing more steadily, only betting heavily when he had a strong hand. But Sidey became erratic, plunging recklessly at times, seemingly prepared to lose on the chance that an occasional win would recoup his losses.

As cards came Mark's way he peeked at a corner, then left them face down on the table. The others did the same, as if they too distrusted the audience.

Hands were always visible on the red cloth – toying with whisky glasses, reaching for cigarettes, fingers drumming on the table top, dealing cards, shuffling, cutting, pushing chips forward and collecting chips back.

But Mark was also aware of the other fingers which stroked the back of his neck.

Sidey continued to lose steadily. At two-thirty his chips vanished. In two and a half hours he had lost five thousand pounds. Someone replenished his stock of chips while Standish made a note with a gold pencil. Mark calculated his own loss at less than four hundred. He breathed a sigh of relief, he was coping better than he had expected. Standish was the big winner so far, but Cummings was also ahead.

The music grew louder, the rhythm faster . . . but nobody was dancing on the verandah. The crush of bodies around the card table was as thick as ever. Audrey Cummings seemed to have draped herself over his back, caressing his neck with her lips as well as her fingers. He dared not turn, it was bad enough to meet her husband's eye across the table. Certainly Cummings had become very agitated. He had been playing steadily earlier, now he was reckless. He lost three calls in a row to Mark. Sidey had come back strongly too, he was winning from Cummings – so was Standish, who was sweating less now, even though Mark thought the room had become even warmer.

In the next thirty minutes Mark won three thousand pounds, mostly from Cummings who went completely to

556

pieces. Standish and Sidey won from him too, so that Cummings had to call for more chips. He reached for his drink, shaking so badly that whisky slopped on the cloth. He caught Mark looking at him and managed a glassy-eyed smile in return. Then it was Mark's turn to deal. He was concentrating too hard to dwell on Cummings – the man was probably drunk or upset by his wife's behaviour. Neither reason outweighed Mark's mounting jubilation – he was winning and winning well. They had expected him to lose, he had seen it in their faces – they had not thought him man enough to play their game. It had been a clear challenge. That was why everyone was crowding the table, to witness some gladiatorial test of masculinity.

Mark won another eight hundred, mostly from Standish this time, then – just before four o'clock, he had the most peculiar sensation. He shifted in the chair, thinking he was mistaken. But a moment later he was quite sure. Fingers were stroking the inside of his thighs. He glanced down but saw only the red chenille cloth rucked across his lap . . . yet he could *feel* hands parting his knees.

The room was stifling – he was already sweating. Heat flared through his loins like a million needles. He had an immediate erection.

It was the most exquisitely painful experience of his life. Nimble fingers unbuttoned his fly. Across the table Standish called his bluff on a pair of tens. Mark lost a thousand to Cummings, and then fifteen hundred to Sidey.

Under the table he was exposed. Lips kissed his bare flesh. He could not move for the throng of people on all sides. Music pounded like jungle drums. Fresh logs were thrown on the fire. The crowd seemed more vociferous. Cries of encouragement rang out. Mark lost hand after hand. Standish stared across the table, more impassive than ever.

Mark's head swam. He emptied his glass with a shaking hand. New cards were dealt. He tried to concentrate – then groaned aloud as moist lips closed over his flesh beneath the table. He pushed forward to the very edge of the chair, his legs wide apart and thrust forward.

When his chips ran out he accepted another five thousand without thinking. Thinking was beyond him.

Beneath the table the hands and tongue and lips went on and on, coaxing him to the edge, easing back until he was almost limp, then starting again. On and on. Exquisite torture. Meanwhile cards came and went, Mark gambled and lost, plunging wildly, unable to think.

Confused memories jumbled through his mind. Marcia! It had to be her under the table, committing this most private of acts almost in public, less than inches away from her husband.

Then he saw her across the table – Marcia, as she nibbled her husband's ear. She turned and met his stare. Slowly her lips rounded into an O. She traced the outline with the tip of her tongue. The gesture was unmistakable. *She knew!* Standish knew too! It was in his face, in his eyes. *They all knew!* Realization struck Mark exactly at his moment of climax. He gasped aloud. His heart raced. His shirt was soaked with sweat.

Suddenly people were flapping their arms like wings and shouting crowing noises. 'The cock crows!' Standish roared triumphantly.

Mark's head began to clear. Cummings was helping a willowy blonde out from under the table. His own wife! Mark turned, disorientated, to find Ann Sidey had been stroking his neck all the time. He swung back to see Audrey Cummings kissing Standish on the mouth. She turned to the crowd, took Standish's hand and raised it above his head, 'I give you Jock Standish, still the biggest man at this table,' she smiled wickedly at Mark, 'though it took me a long time to make up my mind.'

Mark lost six thousand pounds – and joined the Happy Valley Set.

'Uncle Mark is having the devil's own job in Africa,' Tim O'Brien wrote to Kate, 'goodness only knows when he'll come home.'

Kate was not unduly concerned. His arrival back in Ulster would only hasten decisions about the future, and she was certainly in no hurry to find out about that.

Life at Glossops had settled down into a happy pattern. Holidays and occasional weekends were spent seeing London with Aunt Alison, there were trips with the school, and school life itself. Kate and Jenny were as close as ever.

Then, that March, Tim wrote saying that he was being sent to London for a week and could spend a weekend at Windsor with her. They would have two whole days together. Kate was thrilled and couldn't wait to tell Jenny – but Jenny was very cool about the whole thing. 'I shall go home,' she said, 'you won't want me around while your precious brother is here.'

'That's not true,' Kate said. She did want her there, she prayed for the two of them to be friends. It seemed vitally important. But Jenny had made up her mind. 'Besides, Daddy says I can go to a grown-up reception at the Embassy. I'm not missing that for anything.'

Kate was disappointed, but the prospect of two whole days with her brother compensated. Miss Jenkins even agreed that Kate could dine at his hotel, providing she was back at Glossops by nine-thirty.

Tim's visit was marvellous. It was even blessed with good weather. They took a boat down the river and talked about Ulster and the Averdale businesses – which is what Tim's conversation was mainly about. Kate didn't mind. She and her brother were together again. She was screwing up her courage to face the fact that really Aunt Alison and Jenny could never be *proper family*. One day they would go back to the States, and Kate would be left behind. It would be the most awful wrench, but it would happen. Meanwhile she had found her brother and they would never be parted again . . . they were two orphans against the world, protected by a rich guardian.

'He's not *that* rich, you know,' Tim said. 'I don't mean he's poor or anything, but, well, business isn't easy these days. The Averdale empire has shrunk. We're having problems in the shipyards, and as for linen – well that's a disaster. I'm hoping he'll salvage some of the fortune in Africa.'

It was the first suggestion of problems. But Tim hinted at more over dinner.

Brackenburn was not being rebuilt. 'The site has been cleared,' Tim said, 'but getting materials is impossible. Besides you need a government permit these days. No work has started, and I don't know when it will.'

Not that it mattered. The Averdales still owned farms on thousands of acres, investments by the score, and the big house in Belgrave Square. 'Perhaps we shall live there,' Kate said, instantly warming to the idea. 'I think I'd like London much more than Ulster.'

Tim thought London unlikely. 'There's a saying in Gibraltar about the Barbary Apes. Something about the apes never leaving while the British rule the island. Well I think the Averdales are the Barbary Apes of Ulster sometimes.'

'And us? The O'Briens?'

He smiled, 'We're as good as Averdales as far as Uncle Mark is concerned – and lucky to be so.'

'I suppose so,' she said thoughtfully, 'but I wonder why?'

'The Killing at Keady, of course. I told you about it. Ever since then we've been treated as family.'

Kate couldn't accept that. Aunt Alison and Uncle Linc treated her as family – but she would never forget her guardian's disappointed expression when she had returned from America.

'Don't worry,' Tim said, 'he was like that with me to begin with. Before I could walk again. But since then he's been very kind. You'll just have to find something to do for him, something very special.'

But Kate could not think of anything she could do which her guardian might especially like.

Kate revelled in those two days. When Tim left for Ulster she felt she really knew him at last . . . really understood him, and loved him as her only *real* family in the world. It was a lovely warming, happy feeling and she was just bursting to tell Jenny about the whole weekend – but Jenny had momentous news of her own. Jenny had fallen in love.

He was an American bomber pilot, aged at least twenty-two, and stationed at Brize Norton in Oxfordshire. Jenny had met him at the Embassy Reception. 'His name is Clayton Wells. Have you ever heard a more manly name? And he thinks I'm eighteen. Well I had my hair up and a slinky new dress, and . . . oh Kate, it was such a marvellous night. We danced six times, did I tell you that? And I'm meeting him again on Saturday.'

Not that Aunt Alison knew. Jenny had arranged to meet Clayton in Slough, in the same way Rosemary met Eric – and so she did. She met him that Saturday, and the one after, and again after that. It became a regular date.

Glossops began to change for Kate then. Previously she and Jenny had shared everything. Now Jenny was either rushing off to meet her Clayton, or mooning around waiting for the next Saturday. Even worse, she told Aunt Alison that she no longer came home for the occasional weekend because she and Kate were entertaining Tim on his visits from Ulster . . . lies which Kate had to corroborate.

'Jenny, why not tell her the truth?' Kate complained.

'Because she wouldn't understand. She'd say I'm too young to be in love. Kate, you *know* she would. As if she could possibly know how I feel.'

While Kate went to France that summer with Glossops, Jenny stayed at Highgate, slipping off on Saturdays to meet Clayton – and when the autumn term commenced Jenny's infatuation was stronger than ever.

It was the end of that brief time when Kate felt surrounded by friends. She and Jenny spent less time together. Visits to Aunt Alison became infrequent – and when they did meet Kate had to lie about time supposedly spent with Jenny and Tim. Kate hadn't seen Uncle Linc in months. Yvette was in Paris – and dear Tim, upon whom she now so heavily relied, was swotting so madly for his accountancy finals that he barely had time to scribble a note.

What made it worse was that all of Kate's other friends at Glossops seemed suddenly to have gone boy crazy. Even Angela had a *fiancé* whose framed photograph sat next to her bed – and all the talk was about the fumbling which went on in the back rows of cinemas.

It was not that Kate disapproved, she was just terrified that people would find out. Especially about Jenny. Aunt Alison would go mad. Kate would be blamed for leading Jenny astray, she just knew she would. Jenny was smothered in more love bites than Rosemary at times – and some were in the most intimate places.

Kate grew increasingly worried. If she were blamed for

what Jenny was doing – well what would her guardian say? And Tim – Tim would be disgusted, she just knew he would.

One day Jenny suggested, 'Why not come to Slough on Saturday? Clayton's got a friend, he's very good-looking, we could make up a foursome.'

But Kate was afraid of being found out.

Word spread that she was stuck up – 'Kate O'Brien acts like a film star. No one outside Hollywood is good enough for her.'

The gossip was right and wrong at the same time. Other girls were understandably envious, for by that autumn seventeen-year-old Kate O'Brien had emerged not just as pretty but glamorous. Other girls possessed a youthful attractiveness, some even promised to become beautiful, but Kate was a beauty already. Everyone at Glossops recognized it except herself. When she looked at Jenny she saw a blue-eyed blonde, whose figure was filling out nicely, who was the dearest friend she had in the world. But when Jenny looked at Kate she saw a poised, shapely redhead with flashing green eyes, a thirty-seven-inch bust and the longest, most shapely legs in Berkshire. Jenny saw a threat. She was relieved when her offer of a foursome was turned down. She never made it again.

The staff recognized Kate's beauty too. Little Miss Broakes went into raptures in the common-room. 'That child has grown remarkably attractive. And she's got a disposition to match. She's always so eager to please. In fact I'd go further, Kate O'Brien is quite perfect in a way. Flawless. Unique.'

Kate knew nothing of what was said in the common-room, nor did she understand the barbed comments which increasingly came her way. Glossops began to turn sour – and now Jenny had taken to sneaking out on Sunday afternoons to see Clayton in Windsor, the gap between the two girls grew ever wider.

Kate turned into herself and became more self-contained. She spent hours in the school library, so many in fact that one day Miss Graham the English mistress accused her of having read every book in the school.

Just when Kate was beginning to accept there was

definitely something odd about her, came her salvation – and appropriately it came through little Miss Broakes.

Glossops was to stage a lavish production of George Bernard Shaw's famous play, *Pygmalion*. And not just Glossops – they were to be joined in the venture by St Edwards, which was *the* school locally for boys, second in status only to Eton. The co-production was to be presented at Christmas. It would run for seven nights to a total audience of several thousand . . . and Kate O'Brien had been selected to play the leading part of Eliza Doolittle.

In the privacy of the staff common-room, Miss Broakes said, 'There was really no other contender. Kate has the looks and the poise, I'm sure she'll be a tremendous success.'

To Kate herself, Miss Broakes warned, 'This will be very, very demanding.'

Kate wrote to Tim that night, with the news that she was to play Eliza in Shaw's play, considered very daring because Eliza actually swore on the stage. And from that day on Kate worked hard. Miss Broakes was right – it *was* tremendously demanding, but Kate relished the challenge. It was a chance to please. A chance to win approval, not just from Miss Broakes but from the rest of the cast – girls from Glossops and boys from St Edwards, including a Mr Coleman, the English master at St Edwards who was very handsome indeed.

Kate threw herself into the part. They rehearsed two evenings a week and all day on Saturdays – and that pleased her too because it removed the temptation to join Jenny and Rosemary in Slough on a Saturday.

Life became more manageable. Kate was coping again. She enjoyed each day as it came and forgot about the future – but then came a letter from Tim which questioned their future in letters seven feet high. Tim's future too, not only hers. Tim was shaken to his core, she could tell from his letter. Neither of them had expected their guardian to do this. '*Never in all the years I've known him,*' Tim wrote, '*has there even been a hint he would do this.*'

Kate was uncertain how to react – but one thing seemed clear, she would never be the grand hostess at Brackenburn now.

CHAPTER FOUR

Mark Averdale had been in Africa a long time by then, more than two years, long enough to have grown tired of the antics of the crowd at Happy Valley. They were a lure to start with – Mark had never met their like before, so some months had to pass until he found their invitations resistible. He and Ashendon had been a bit wild in earlier years, but their escapades were schoolboy pranks compared to what went on in Happy Valley, where the debauchery seemed endless.

Yet, perhaps to his own surprise, it palled after a time. Maybe his Averdale blood saved him. He was as willing as ever to take a pretty woman to bed, but would share her with no one if she really attracted him. And there were a few acts he would not commit, some practices he shrank from, so that he was often on the edge of the crowd. In fact after a while he found himself yearning for the well-ordered arrangements he had established with Molly Oakes – 'Now that,' he told himself, 'is how these things should be conducted.'

But more than recollections of Molly split him away from the Happy Valley Set. Other events helped. Hints were dropped at Government House. The Governor had blacklisted everyone in Happy Valley . . . 'Of course you weren't to know, being new and so forth, but they do let the side down. A word to the wise, eh.'

The trouble was that Standish had promised to help with the Bowley estates, so for a while Mark lingered on at Happy Valley. Few would have guessed he went there in pursuit of a deal. The truth was he worried more every month. He and Tatz had stemmed the losses, but profits were as elusive as ever. Mark *needed* that sixty thousand a year. Without it the Averdale Foundation was doomed. Standish had promised help, even Cummings had come up with a scheme, and Sidey had offered a third, but they all foundered on one point – they all called for Mark to invest a heap of new money.

Mark sought out other people. He spent months in Nairobi, mostly in the bar at the Norfolk or eating cold-buffet luncheons in the vast, old-fashioned dining-room. He liked the place and the people. It was where the *real* Kenya farmers ate and it served good no-nonsense plain food. They sat at every table talking weather and crops and cattle ailments – or moaning about lions stalking their stock, or some bloody Wog stealing their whisky.

They were a hard lot, but by God they knew Kenya. Mark listened for hours. He had no choice. They had something he wanted – they were rich in land and experience, even if they looked to lack as much as a penny. Mark decided that if he wanted a partner he would find one in the Norfolk . . . if he waited long enough. So he sat and listened to these men with their sun-baked faces, who inspected him with faded blue eyes and talked through ragged moustaches. Sometimes their women came too, hastily rouged and powdered, wearing the inevitable ancient tweed skirt, stout stockings and heavy shoes. They were hardheaded folk who dressed plainly at home and made no concessions to the city. They left the smart clothes for their sons and grandsons – and were likely to sniff loudly when they saw African servants wearing tennis shoes, saying it was well known that a Wog couldn't function with shoes on.

Mark had known them, or their like, years earlier when he had grown up with Percy Bowley and his father. They were real old-style Kenya. Settlers who had fought droughts and floods and locusts and rinderpest every day of their lives. They had grown rich in the war. *Everyone* with a farm in Kenya had grown rich in the war – everyone willing to work. The Forces had screamed for endless supplies of beef and wheat – and the farmers had delivered, even those with sons away fighting. 'The trouble with Bowley's place,' they told Mark, 'was no one shifted his arse. Why didn't you get out before?'

Mark would explain about Ulster – about the aircraft factories and the shipyards, as well as the farms which had to be kept going. 'Besides there was a war on, remember, I *couldn't* get here.'

They invited him home and Mark criss-crossed the land, driving a hundred miles over bumpy roads to meet them for drinks. He liked the rough expansiveness of their lives, the shabby spaciousness of the farmhouses, and the warmth of the welcome within them. In truth he liked Kenya – the wild beauty, the infinite landscapes and the long green hills. Enough pioneering Averdale blood ran in his veins for him to enjoy the bracing nip of the evening air in the White Highlands – and the feeling of freedom. There was so much of Ulster in this wild country – if you overlooked the zebra grazing alongside the cattle, or an occasional lion sitting like a big dog at the side of the road.

But Mark could not find a partner. Most of the old settlers were tired and wanted a rest. They had worked hard during the war, now their sons were home they wanted to consolidate – and perhaps have some fun. Few even considered taking on a venture the size and scale of the Bowley estates.

Mark was desperate. He had been in Africa far longer than planned. Every month detailed reports reached him from Ulster. Harris and young Tim O'Brien were coping as well as could be expected, but Mark was anxious to get back.

Standish introduced him to other people, but their suggestions differed little from those put forward by Standish himself. Mark was expected to put up the Bowley estates *and* more capital, which they would manage for half the profits. It was unfair. Mark would risk everything in exchange for their know-how. He refused to deal on that basis . . . but months were passing, he could not stay forever . . . but neither was he willing to be robbed blind.

Then one day at Government House, Ziggy Beck's name was mentioned. He had heard it before, snippets like 'Did you know Ziggy Beck owns sixty per cent of old Tim's place now,' or 'I hear Ziggy Beck has bought the MacLean property.' Enough to indicate she had money, but finding out more proved difficult. People seemed reluctant to talk about her, even at Government House there were shrugs. 'We don't really see much of her. Of course she's always around, she's in Nairobi two days a week, but, well . . . she's not really our type.'

A week later he was in the bar at Smith's when Standish came in. They had a drink in a quiet corner.

'Ziggy Beck?' Standish positively shuddered. 'What on earth do you want with her? She's got a face like a mule. I know she's got the best pair of tits in Kenya, old boy, but no man ever gets near them. She was married to a German spy, a filthy Jew.' He stopped short. 'You're not thinking of doing business with *her*, I hope. People won't speak to you.'

Mark learned more of the story from a Government House official some days later. Apparently Ziggy and Otto Beck had arrived in East Africa in 1938, ostensibly on the run from Nazi persecution in Germany. He was much older than her, people put him at fifty, twice her age. They had money, enough to buy a spread at the far end of Happy Valley, where they reared such good beef that other farmers became envious. In the early days the Becks attended garden parties and other Government House functions – but Otto Beck's accent was so appalling that conversation was difficult, and people disliked his manner which they said was too obliging to be genuine. So after a while the Becks kept themselves to themselves. Various Indian businessmen seemed to visit them, but of course that put the Europeans off even more.

Then came the war, and although the internment policy was a bit muddled old Beck was a German so people felt he should be locked up. There was even talk of his wife being locked up too, but finally she was confined to her farm for the duration. So Beck was carted off to jail, where he died in 1943.

The government official became slightly embarrassed, 'The man did *die*. He wasn't killed or mistreated. Anyone who says so is a bloody liar.'

He stared at Mark for a moment, as if expecting a contradiction. Then he shrugged, 'Well, she just carried on with the business after that. Damn embarrassing really, she blames us for his death of course. We all hoped she would sell up and move on, but she just stayed. And to make matters worse she's a witch commercially. God knows what she doesn't own these days. I wouldn't be surprised if she doesn't have a share in every Wog bazaar from Nairobi to

567

Mombasa. They love her. She speaks Kikuyu better than them, and Swahili, even a smattering of Masai. She treats 'em well, employs doctors, patches them up. Really, I mean in some ways, she's an ideal settler . . .'

'But?'

'She's not one of us. Perhaps we've got a conscience about her. Sounds stupid but there you are. Your friends in Happy Valley hate her. She despises them and they can't stand that.'

It was just a diverting story at the time. Mark was only vaguely interested, especially as he thought he had found a partner by then – a man called Arthur Browning. Mark was getting somewhere at last. Browning was very interested, not just in management but in investing a substantial amount of capital, enough to warrant a full partnership. But then, after ten weeks of detailed negotiations, Browning pulled out. His wife had been taken seriously ill. Her recovery would take careful nursing, and he decided it might be wiser not to take on new responsibilities. It was a fearful blow to Mark Averdale, Browning was the end of the line, his last hope. But then Browning said, 'Why not go and see Ziggy Beck. She's not as bad as she's painted. She's into everything these days. She might be interested.'

Out of sheer desperation, Mark called to see her. She maintained a permanent suite in the Norfolk – part living quarters and part office – where she stayed two days a week to conduct her business in Nairobi. A middle-aged Indian in an alpaca suit ushered Mark through the office to a small sitting-room, where he was left with the promise that Memsahib Beck would join him shortly, and he had just settled into an armchair when she came in.

He had seen her at a distance, but never close up. She was fair-haired, medium height, and firmly well-covered – not fat but strongly built. Her handshake was strong too, brisk and confident. Mark was slightly unnerved. He disliked the idea of the meeting. Business was best conducted with men. To talk business with a woman was an odd thing to do at the best of times, but even worse when she was ostracized by half of the European community, in fact it made him feel decidedly uneasy. He regretted the visit and had just made up his mind to talk in generalities when she broached the subject with indecent abruptness.

'I imagine you've come to see me about the Bowley estates?'

She made no effort to charm and that annoyed him. Women, however plain, should at least try to be charming. If they lacked looks *and* charm they were of no bloody use to anyone, not even themselves.

He waved casually towards the street, 'Well, I just happened to be in –'

'No,' she interrupted.

He stopped in mid-sentence.

She smiled. She had good teeth and her smile drew attention from her square jaw and a nose which seemed too large for her face. Her skin was tanned and healthy. He would never consider her attractive, but she might be presentable with a little more effort. Her clothes – a high-buttoned blouse and a long skirt worn over riding boots – managed to look both casual and businesslike at the same time, feminine but hardly alluring. Yet she had a good figure, strong . . . suddenly he remembered Standish saying, 'She's got the best pair of tits in Kenya, old boy.'

'No,' she said again.

'I beg your pardon?'

'You did not just happen to be in today. You came especially. Standish and his crowd have kept you dangling for months, and now Browning has dropped out. The old-stagers are all too busy swilling pink gins and bouncing grandchildren on their knees – and the latest crop of young farmers haven't the money. Who else could you try? Either you go back to Standish or come here. It must have been difficult but here you are,' she paused, 'even if you brought your prejudices with you.'

There was no rudeness in her voice, she had spoken pleasantly, conversationally almost, but with total confidence.

He felt uncomfortable. 'I've no idea what you mean, Frau Beck –'

Her eyebrows rose. 'I'm not German, no matter what you've heard. As a matter of fact I was born in Copenhagen.'

Her interruptions were disconcerting.

She watched him for a moment, then said, 'Well let's forget prejudices. I admit to a few of my own. Let me save time by telling you what I know.'

And she did. As far as his negotiations went her knowledge was total. She listed every proposal ever put to him *and* his reasons for turning them down. She mentioned every man he had talked business with, as if she read from a dossier. It was very comprehensive, but only took a few minutes. When she finished she smiled. 'You seem surprised?'

He was astonished. 'I don't know where you get your information –'

'How do you suppose I stay alive? Some people detest me here. They'd run me out of Kenya if they could.'

A denial would have lacked conviction, so he said nothing.

She went on, 'In effect you've only had serious talks with two men, Standish and Browning. You were unlucky with Browning, he's honest and not part of the Happy Valley crowd. His reasons for dropping out were quite genuine by the way, if it's any consolation.'

He thought – she's so *damn positive* about things which are none of her business.

'As for friend Standish,' she said with a ghost of a smile, 'he organized a cartel. All very unofficial of course, but every man you negotiated with, except Browning, reported back to Standish. It was very simple. They figured you would have to deal with one of them eventually. They don't care which one – whoever signs contracts will split his profit with the others.'

He was shocked, then angry. He knew it was true as soon as she said it. He cursed himself for a fool and struggled with his temper. 'That's a very serious accusation –'

'I'm just sharing information. It's up to you if you believe me.'

He believed her. She spoke with too much authority to doubt. He tried to calm himself, appear unconcerned. After a long pause he shrugged. 'Perhaps I should give up the idea of a partnership. Maybe I should sell the estates outright.'

570

'The same rules apply. It's the cartel or Browning, and you know his position.'

He felt trapped, almost as angry with her cool manner as with Standish. It was a strain to keep his temper. He hated appearing foolish and naive, especially in front of this infuriating woman. Flushing with embarrassment, he said, 'You seem to have gone to a lot of trouble –'

'On the contrary, I told you before, knowing what goes on keeps me alive.' Her look took on added intensity as she said, 'For instance, I even know what happens at Jock Standish's card table.'

His flush deepened to a brick red.

'I know what he says about my face,' she paused, 'and my figure.'

He looked at her breasts, instinctively, without thinking.

'I see you've heard him on that subject too,' she said with a chilling smile.

Mark Averdale had rarely felt more miserable. He wondered if it was a deliberate attempt to humiliate him. Then, to his intense relief, her frostiness thawed. 'I apologize for embarrassing you, but a real Standish wouldn't have batted an eyelid.' She smiled. 'Perhaps we might do business after all.'

He felt curiously complimented. It would be a relief to talk business, even if she was a woman. 'Very well then,' he said, 'so what about Bowley's place?'

'I'm interested. Why not? There's no better land in East Africa.'

He felt pleased at that and started to outline his ideas about a partnership when she interrupted. 'I'm afraid I have another appointment in five minutes. I'm sorry but I had no idea how long this would take. May I make a suggestion?'

He was too surprised to answer. She had a knack of unbalancing him.

'It's some time since I saw the estate. Why not invite me to lunch tomorrow?'

So he did. On his way to the door he tried to decide on the best way of addressing her. 'Shall we say midday then, Mrs Beck?'

'Call me Ziggy,' she said, shaking his hand briskly, 'yes,

571

I'll be there by noon. Thanks for coming in, Mark.'

He walked to his jeep in a daze. He would have gone for a drink but for the thought of bumping into Standish. His blood boiled about Standish. He would pay him back, he was damn sure about that. Meanwhile his mind was full of the most extraordinary woman he had ever met.

It took nearly two hours to drive back to the Bowley estate. During the journey he analysed the whole meeting. He was ashamed of his own performance. He had allowed her to wrong-foot him every time. Even inviting herself to lunch! That would be all round Nairobi tomorrow night, to her advantage and his detriment. If nothing came of it people would guess – would *know* that Lord Mark Averdale had been rejected by a pariah of society. God what a fool! 'Call me Ziggy,' she had said with a sudden display of oily charm. Of course he made excuses for himself – after all he was unaccustomed to women in business – her approach had been unexpected – he had been surprised. Well tomorrow, he vowed, will be a different matter entirely.

But the following day went very much the same way. She arrived in a dusty Buick driven by the same Indian secretary Mark had seen at the Norfolk. Ziggy Beck was as cool as ever, even dressed in the same style – fresh clothes but cut to the same pattern. He was sure Standish was right about her breasts but her shirt was very discreet. Clothes, however, were the most discreet thing about her – she was alarmingly frank about everything else, and quite scathing about the way the estate had been managed.

In the afternoon they drove over part of the property. Her knowledge was vast. She had only lived in Africa ten years but seemed to have accumulated more understanding than some of the third and fourth generation Kenya farmers in the bar at the Norfolk. Grudgingly he said as much.

'Oh, I'm hopelessly ignorant about a lot of things,' she said. 'Sometimes I think no one will understand Africa – not even them.' She pointed to some natives at the side of the road and made him stop the jeep so she could talk to them. They all seemed to know her, that was Mark's first surprise, quickly followed by a second – their affection for

572

her was quite unmistakable. Mark was accustomed to respect, all Europeans were, but genuine affection was something quite different, even undesirable. She stopped him there for twenty minutes or so, under that blazing sun while she talked and laughed in a Kikuyu which was much too fast and fluent for him to follow.

It irritated him. He thought she was showing off for a start, but it was more than that and he said so. 'It doesn't do to be too friendly,' he muttered as they drove off. 'The Wogs take advantage. They steal everything not nailed down as it is.'

'Oh? Did Standish teach you that too?'

Mark vividly recalled Standish flogging a houseboy for stealing, but decided to keep that information to himself. Instead he shrugged, 'It's a well known fact.'

'It's a well known prejudice,' she corrected sharply.

They travelled in silence for a few minutes after that, but Ziggy Beck was too interested to remain quiet for long. She kept pointing out areas for improvement and talking of the need to diversify into other crops such as pyrethrum and sisal, and on the higher lands, tea. But the steeliness in her eyes earlier stayed in his mind. She was a very determined person, he could hardly think of her as a woman, despite the occasional hints of femininity which her clothes failed to conceal.

Later, back at the bungalow, they discussed the estate further, but when he began to outline what he would require from a partner she stopped him. 'I may have some ideas of my own,' she smiled. 'Surely you can spare me another few meetings? After all you wasted more than a year on Standish and other people.'

He was in a cleft stick. 'How many more meetings?'

'That's hard to say.' She frowned for a moment, then explained, 'I have partnerships all over East Africa. They work because I got to know the people well before we went into business together. We all understand each other. I think that's important.'

They arranged to meet again the very next day, at the Norfolk, 'In my suite if you like,' she said with a smile. 'Nobody need know. I should hate to compromise your reputation.'

He spent the night thinking about her. She was certainly not attractive. Her dogmatic views infuriated him. The trouble was she knew much more than he did – about Africa and Asian merchants, about crops and stock, even about Standish and that other crowd up at Government House. He cursed himself for not taking a firmer line, for allowing her to dictate meetings and agendas – but what could he do – deal with Standish and his bloody cartel?

And so began a series of meetings. They met twice a week, alternately at the Bowley bungalow and the Norfolk. At one stage he suspected she was trying to embarrass him with the European community, but even when he said so she refused to be hurried – 'I think we're progressing quite well,' she said. 'If we do reach agreement I shall be involved in a major investment. You can't expect me to rush into it.'

There was no denying her logic, but Nairobi was buzzing with talk. Mark's one hope was that the rumours might force a better offer out of Standish, but Ziggy Beck had thought of that too – 'If you receive another proposal you will let me know, won't you? I should hate to think I was wasting my time.'

'I'll give you first option until the end of the month,' he said firmly.

She accepted that. They both knew that had she demanded longer he would have had to agree – but it seemed the end of the month suited her too.

Tatz attended many of the meetings. Mark had no choice. Ziggy Beck's questions were too exhaustive and too technical to cope with – even Tatz was lost for answers at times. 'Perhaps you could find out,' Ziggy Beck said, 'before the next meeting.' And Tatz always did, despite the hours of extra work it caused. He once said to Mark, 'I'll be damned if I'll let that woman get the better of me, but I've got to admit – answering her blasted queries has taught me more about the estate than I would have thought possible.'

At other meetings, from which Tatz was absent, Ziggy Beck became slightly less businesslike. Without ever asking a direct question she encouraged Mark to talk about himself – and she told him a good deal of her own history in exchange.

574

Otto, her husband, had been her father's business partner. She had known him most of her life. When her mother died she and her father had moved to Otto's house in Munich, but a year after that her father had died too. She and Otto continued to live under the same roof. 'It was a very proper arrangement. We had a housekeeper and maids. I was a student. He was like an uncle to me.' But Munich was a hotbed of Nazi activity and when Hitler rose to power they moved to Hamburg. 'Otto felt safer there. He was in the timber business and his ships were in and out – he felt if things got too bad we could just sail away. But all the time he was trying to liquidate his assets, a little at a time to avoid suspicion. By Christmas '37 he had moved almost half of his money out, mostly to Denmark. Just in time because the Nazis began to move against the Jews in a terrifying way then. We tried to get out. I could go, I was a Danish citizen with a Danish passport – but Otto being German was blocked. The Danish consul could only help Danes and their relatives – so Otto and I got married. It was his only chance, even then we barely made it . . . the purges began three days after we left . . .'

She puffed on another cigarette. 'We went to Copenhagen, just for a month. Otto was busy collecting what money he had transferred, but Europe terrified him. He knew war was coming, he even foresaw the concentration camps. "Ziggy," he used to say, "Jews will be slaughtered like animals."'

She had wanted to emigrate to America but he distrusted American politicians, many of whom seemed pro-German to him. 'So we came here. He was so pleased. He was like a child. Every day he thanked God for the British. "British justice," he would say, "is the best in the world." He was a Jew but not very orthodox. What he wanted most, his dream, was to become a British Gentleman, and for me to grow into a typical British Lady.'

She smiled, and an uncharacteristic blush touched her cheeks. Then it was gone and the softness went from her voice too. 'We entered the social whirl as they call it, dined with the Governor, watched the polo on Saturdays, all the usual things. He tried so hard to be part of them. But they

575

despised him. To them he was a filthy little yid and I was Shylock's whore. The funny thing was he never saw it. He used to smile and shake his head when I said anything, "It's just their way Ziggy, the British are not like that."'

Later she said, 'I saw it coming, internment I mean. I knew it would happen. Attitudes, derisive remarks, that sort of thing. He wouldn't believe me. I can hear him now, "Ziggy, I'm a Jew. Why in the world would I help Hitler?" So logical. Even when they took him away he was sure it was a mistake. "Don't worry Ziggy, it's a muddle, they'll sort it out."'

She was quiet for so long that Mark felt he had to say something – so he said, 'But there was never any question of ill-treatment, nothing like that.'

'Oh, they gave him two meals a day. Nobody beat him up. Nothing like that. They destroyed his illusion, don't you see? Me casting doubts didn't matter, he was so sure I was wrong, but when his beloved British locked him up for being a German Jew . . .' She shrugged. 'I was allowed to see him ten days before he died. "Ziggy," he said, "thank God you're not one of us. You have a chance for a good life here. I bless the day I brought you to Africa." And ten days later he was dead.'

'You don't mean –'

'Suicide? Oh no, not the way you mean. No, he just stopped living. To his mind I was better off without him. It was his own final solution.'

She told the story very calmly. No tears, no catch in the throat, no heavy emotional pauses. She told it once and never mentioned it again.

On another day, in a different conversation, he asked why she had stayed.

She seemed surprised. 'It's my home. It's the most beautiful spot in the world. Oh no, I shall never leave Africa. I shall die here.' And later she expanded on the subject, 'Of course it will change. The British Raj is finished everywhere, not just in India. You might not like it but it's true.' She smiled, and then laughed softly, 'Instead there will be partnerships. All sorts of partnerships, between black and brown and white – perhaps even Jews. So you see, I'm keen on the principle

576

– but partners have to be right for each other.'

For Mark Averdale the negotiations were an enormous strain. He disagreed with so many of her views. She was a living contradiction of his cherished convictions. Women had no place in business – it was well known they were temperamentally incapable of making commercial decisions. Yet Ziggy Beck *was* in business and took commercial decisions every day, very successfully it seemed, despite the traps laid for her by the European community.

He still found her unattractive. He took comfort from that. It was proof she was not a proper woman at all. More like a man really. Her attitudes, the way she took charge of things, her decisiveness – all very masculine. Yet there were other moments, when she pointed to a view for instance, when she stretched an arm and reminded him that beneath her blouse were 'the best pair of tits in Kenya'.

He had never met anyone like her. He could never properly relax in her company because he was always in two minds about how to treat her. She was not his social equal, she was a person with whom he was trying to do business – with whom he *had* to do business. He had to keep talking, at least until the end of the month.

In a way negotiating with Ziggy Beck added to his problems, certainly it added to his loneliness. He ceased to patronize the Nairobi clubs where most of the talk was about him anyway, and instead tried to keep busy on the estate with Tatz. In the evenings they drank and played cards, but when Mark was invited to dine with the Governor he knew he had to go. He hoped against hope that Ziggy Beck's name wouldn't crop up. It was a forlorn hope. People were too curious, too intrigued. He was circumspect, but when pressed had to admit there was a possibility of doing business with her. 'That's a pity,' someone said, 'she's got her finger in too many pies as it is. Surely there's *someone else*? God knows I hold no brief for Standish and his crowd, but didn't I hear some of them were interested?'

Mark restrained himself from telling them to mind their own business – or from saying if they were that concerned why not help solve his problem. All he wanted was to do a deal and get home. All he wanted was sixty thousand a year from Africa. All he wanted was Ulster and the Averdale Foundation and Molly in bed. Which reminded him, *some* arrangement would have to be made about Kate O'Brien. Perhaps she could go back to the States with the Johnstones? She seemed happy enough with them. His heart ached when he remembered dreams of what might have been – but he tried to dismiss such thoughts as juvenile nonsense. He could almost laugh at a distance – but not quite – it still hurt to picture Kate the young mother and her astonishing resemblance to Rouen's model. But the magic had not passed on to the child. She had failed him. It was best to send her to America and out of his life. He would still have Molly and the Averdale Foundation – if only he could do a deal on the Bowley estates!

The time passed slowly. Three days before the end of the month, Audrey Cummings called to see him. She was alone and arrived at noon. 'I was passing so I thought I'd drop in. We haven't seen much of you lately.'

Audrey Cummings was very pretty. Her honey-coloured skin, sun-bleached hair and willowy figure were hard to resist, especially linked to the memory of her skilful lips and eager tongue. She was a good-looking woman – not the disguised adding machine with whom he had been spending so much of his time.

They had a few drinks on the verandah, but Audrey had called for something more. 'You really are a great disappointment, Mark. Marcia said you were quite wonderful in bed. I must confess I was rather hoping . . .' she smiled, 'Well, I did go to some trouble to introduce myself.'

'I thought you preferred bigger men. Jock Standish, for instance.'

'Oh, don't be silly. The verdict always goes to Jock, it's part of the game.' She smiled. 'But I did give you a lovely time Mark, didn't I?' A husky note crept into her voice, 'And I always say, who needs a card table?'

They spent the afternoon in bed, where she groaned and thrashed about with such abandon that every servant in the bungalow must have heard. Mark was so lost in sensual pleasure that no thought was possible for most of the time

– but just once, as he mounted her again, on her back like a dog on a bitch, their bodies slick with sweat and his hands cupped on her breasts – just once did the red mist of lust clear long enough for him to wonder what it would be like to fondle 'the best pair of tits in Kenya'.

Thoughts of Ziggy Beck returned later, after Audrey Cummings had left. He knew why she had visited – what pillow talk there had been had concerned the Bowley estates, in fact she had said, 'Just think, darling, whenever you come out on a visit I'll be here ready for you, Marcia too if you want her. We'll give you a million times more fun than Shylock's whore.'

To his surprise he resented that. Anyone less a whore than Ziggy Beck was hard to imagine, whereas Audrey was a whore and a very accomplished one – married to a man who had joined Standish in the cartel.

At long last, it was the end of the month. Ziggy Beck was expected for lunch at the bungalow. Mark was nervous all morning. He shouted at the houseboys as if the Governor himself was descending on them – even though he knew Ziggy Beck impressed them more. He wouldn't have believed such devotion a month earlier, now he took it for granted. Just as he knew she would make an offer. Standish and the others hummed and hawed – but she had promised a realistic offer and today she would make it.

He nursed a drink as he waited. She had grown on him, he had to admit. To begin with he had positively disliked her – now he found her assertiveness almost relaxing. At least he knew where he was with her. If she promised to do something she did it – and that was a rare quality. And oddly enough he trusted her, much more than he had ever trusted Standish, even before finding out about the cartel. He would be a lot better off with Ziggy Beck as a partner – he just hoped she could generate sixty thousand a year as his share of the profits.

Her Buick nosed through the gates at noon, driven as usual by the Indian secretary – and a moment later she climbed the steps to the verandah. He walked over to greet her, searching her face for her decision. His guts ached for fear she would say he couldn't expect sixty thousand a year or anything like it. But her smile gave nothing away. She shook hands as briskly as ever – and then, as she sat down, he realized something quite startling. Business apart, he had been pleased to see her, he *was* pleased – in fact he actually quite liked Ziggy Beck.

After a pink gin and a cigarette, she broached the subject of business with her usual directness. 'I'd better tell you now. When you hear my proposal you may withdraw your invitation to lunch.'

His heart sank, and he was trying to maintain what he hoped was a calm expression when she dropped her bomb-shell – 'I can see no prospect of becoming your partner,' she said, 'or of my making an offer for the Bowley estates.'

He could hardly believe her. Dismay welled up within him, followed by anger. She had betrayed him! He had been pleased to see her, but – she had tricked him, more blatantly even than Standish. Colour rushed to his face.

'Please let me finish,' she said. 'I promised an offer and I have one, along different lines perhaps, but only because I understand the situation here better than you.'

He could think of nothing to say. He failed to see where she was leading.

She gave him a quick smile. 'Some people think I already own more than I should. That's why I can't buy outright – and even as a partner they might move –'

'Rubbish. There's no limit to anyone's holding –'

'Not officially. But life can be made awkward in a hundred different ways.'

He remembered his conversation in the Governor's dining-room – the aide who had frowned, 'She's got her finger into too many pies.' He stared, suddenly understanding her caution. They *would* make life awkward. But her decision was a body blow. He tried to counter with reassurances.

'No,' she said, 'I am right, and deep down you must know I'm right.'

His agile mind had never been devoted exclusively to business. His blank face said as much, but he felt angry as well as bemused. 'You've wasted my time then. If that's your opinion –'

'But there is another solution which will benefit you more.'

580

He wondered how he had imagined he knew where he was with her.

'I'll be your tenant,' she said crisply, 'I'll pay you rent. Eighty thousand a year for ten years. How would that suit you?'

His world turned upside down. He stared across the table at the square-jawed, fair-haired, thirty-five-year-old woman and wondered if she were joking. But Ziggy Beck *never* joked about business. *Eighty thousand a year!* For a tenancy?

'There are two conditions,' she said. 'The first is our arrangement is kept strictly secret.'

He could agree to that. He would make a secret deal with the Devil for eighty thousand a year. Images of art galleries and sale rooms rushed through his mind. He would tour Europe – buying, buying, buying . . .

'The second condition,' she said, 'is that we get married.'

Mark Averdale dropped his glass.

M'buta the houseboy appeared at the end of the verandah as if by magic. He glanced nervously at Mark's shocked face, but was encouraged by the presence of Ziggy Beck. He smiled at her warmly, served another pink gin, collected up the broken pieces of crystal with his bare hands, and left noiselessly.

'That's the most preposterous suggestion I've ever heard,' Mark said in a strangled voice. He downed his drink in a gulp and reached for the bottle.

'It is,' she agreed, 'until you think of the mutual benefits.'

'Benefits?' he echoed, still staring at her.

'You get eighty thousand a year. More than you ever thought possible. In addition to which I shall invest in the estate and make it work. At the end of ten years you'll have it all back. It will be yours, free to do what you like with, unfettered by partnership agreements –'

'I can see that but –'

'You're not very gallant. Never mind, I shall make very few demands on you. You said you expected to spend only a few weeks in Africa every year in future – fine, that's all you'll see of me. I have no wish to travel in Europe –'

'I don't understand. Why marriage –'

'Think about it. The estates remain your property and your wife runs them in your absence. Nobody can interfere with that. And I get a lot of protection for all my other interests. Snubbing Ziggy Beck is one thing, offending Lady Averdale is another thing entirely.'

He choked. She planned to make them eat dirt. She would rise from social oblivion to the pinnacle of acceptability. Even the Governor would treat her with care. Ziggy Beck *really expected* to be Lady Averdale! She actually thought he would agree! 'Preposterous,' he muttered, 'I said so before and I'll say so again. The idea is totally preposterous.'

'Had you planned to marry in Ulster?'

His heart lurched. He thought of Kate. All the years he had dreamt of marriage. All the plans to rebuild Brackenburn, he had yearned and schemed . . . but Kate was dead. The magic of the mother had not passed on to the child.

'I don't know,' he said emptily, 'I don't know – I had plans –'

'To rebuild your big house. Well go ahead. I don't want to live in it. And plans for your art collection. You never mentioned a wife.'

He began to realize how much he had told her. He finished his drink and reached for another. 'Madness,' he said, 'complete and utter madness.'

But she stayed for lunch. He could hardly send her away. At one point he said, 'Paying over the odds is an expensive way of becoming my wife.'

She burst out laughing. 'Oh dear, were you going to ask me?' When her amusement subsided she said, 'Don't worry, I'll make this estate pay. Give me three years and it will be yielding over a hundred thousand a year. I'll make a profit over ten years. Meanwhile I shall have acquired some very healthy protection.'

She had an answer for all of his queries. She had thought of everything. For instance she was quite happy to sign a disclaimer to any property rights which might accrue to her as his wife. She neither wanted nor expected to share any part of his life in Europe. She wanted nothing from him, save his name and his company for eight weeks a year.

'Oh, perhaps there is one other thing,' she said, almost as an afterthought, 'a favour really – but while you're in Kenya I'd be glad if you restrained your normal, well your physical, desires. Audrey Cummings this week for instance, something like that might cause me embarrassment.'

He glared. Of course she got it from the houseboys, he told himself, every bloody Wog in Kenya must spy for her . . . and every bazaar. He felt quite drunk. Oddly enough getting drunk seemed the most sensible thing to do. 'And what about *your* physical desires?' he demanded. 'Won't they embarrass me?'

'No, never.'

'What are you then? Some kind of nun?'

She met his stare without flinching. Her name had never been touched by sexual scandal. He knew that but was in no mood to pay compliments. He grunted, 'I assume I do what the hell I like in Europe. Is that it?'

'Of course.'

He leered, 'Well I'd be entitled to conjugal rights in Africa wouldn't I? I woudn't need Audrey Cummings –'

'Our arrangement would be a business transaction. Husband and wife eight weeks a year, a *public* relationship, not private.'

'You mean I don't get into your bed?'

'Why would you want to? I'm not attractive. You're certainly not in love with me, not even fond of me. I don't blame you. I'm merely pointing it out. You'd find no pleasure in my bed, I assure you, so why burden the relationship with a problem?'

'You frigid bitch,' he said, intensely angry.

She rose and replaced her napkin on the table. 'I'm sorry you're annoyed. I need an ally, not a lover. Partners should be friends. It's up to you. I've made my offer. I'll leave you to think it over.'

And she left.

He remained in the bungalow for three days, sometimes sober, often drunk. Whenever he thought of his dilemma he needed a drink, and since he thought of nothing else a bottle was always at hand. Commercially her offer was irresistible – eight hundred thousand pounds over ten years – and without losing ownership. The estates would not only remain intact, they would be enhanced – he had no doubt about that. Meanwhile he would have *eighty thousand a year* – more than his income from farmland in Ulster, more than from the shipyards even in a good year, and far more than from the linen mills.

But to marry her!

How Standish would sneer. Yet . . . and the thought took hold . . . what sweet revenge to set Ziggy Beck up as the social superior of everyone in Happy Valley. They would hate it! He roared with laughter late at night, imagining their faces . . . Ziggy Beck, already richer than them, dining with the Governor, treading a social path from which they were excluded. They might sneer, but they would squirm too.

Even so . . .

Other thoughts took over – thoughts of Ulster, dreams of home. He was sick of Africa. A few months were fine – but two years! He longed for Europe, ached for the art galleries of London and the studios in Paris. Ziggy Beck was his ticket home.

But to marry her!

Yet, would it be so bad? For eight weeks out of every fifty-two and a divorce in ten years. And it solved all his problems in Africa. He trusted her . . . she was reliable . . .

They were married six weeks later. The initial announcement shocked everyone, but people recovered amazingly quickly. Oddly enough it enhanced Lord Averdale's reputation. Shrewd heads began to nod in the clubs. Men reassessed Mark Averdale, even Standish was heard to say, 'He's a damn sight shrewder than we gave him credit for.' Of course the new Lady Averdale received none of the credit, although some people wished they had befriended her before. Even at the Governor's table someone said, 'You know, that Ziggy Averdale is really quite charming. She has such an interesting smile.'

The bride and groom lived at her place, Cutters Lodge, and gave a series of parties and receptions. Everyone went. People accepted invitations out of curiosity, or because of the Averdale name, or because the Governor might be there, or to keep up with the Joneses. They went intrigued, and came away impressed.

Even Jan Tatz, Mark's dour South African manager, was impressed. Suddenly more labour was drafted on to the Bowley estates. Merchants delivered materials and machinery round the clock. The very air hummed with co-operation – and although every penny was counted by a battery of Indian book-keepers, at least money was spent, as distinct from the restricted operation which had existed before. Tatz was brimming with optimism at a meeting with Mark four weeks after the wedding. 'I've been going through the figures again – with this new investment I think we'll hit real paydirt in a couple of years, in fact it wouldn't surprise me to see over a hundred thousand a year.'

It would not surprise Mark either. Ziggy had a habit of keeping her word.

In those four weeks every aspect of their bargain was honoured. He stood beside her at innumerable receptions, holding her hand and easing her path. Nobody from Happy Valley was ever invited, and if Ziggy saw any other enemies among her guests she gave no sign of it – but Mark never doubted she had scores to settle, and would settle in full when it suited her.

Everything went to plan. The secret agreements were signed, Mark collected his first year's rent, wrote to Ulster saying he would soon be home, mentioned his marriage almost in passing – and acted the role of dutiful husband. But the role-playing stopped at the door to her bedroom. Even on their wedding night the threshold was barred, 'We have a business arrangement, remember?'

He had been mildly drunk, mellow enough to be amused – but his view changed with the passing of time. She had changed. She dressed differently, especially when they entertained. Her 'business outfit' was discarded in favour of more glamorous clothes. Her figure was revealed. Her overlarge nose and square jaw seemed less noticeable. Instead Mark was struck by her smile and the amusement found in her eyes – and he was very aware of her body, displayed as it was in a whole series of low-cut gowns.

By the end of six weeks he was sour with frustration. He had been made comfortable at Cutters Lodge. The rambling thatched house was very much in the Kenya style, with guest rooms in one wing and the master suites in another – but his bedroom was separated from hers by bathrooms and dressing-rooms – and her door remained locked against him at night.

'This won't work,' he grumbled one night. 'A man has certain needs –'

'Eight weeks a year,' she reminded him, 'a business arrangement, remember.'

He was damned if he would beg.˙He stifled his anger but it was a strain. In fact the entire relationship was beginning to trouble him. He found himself confused by conflicting emotions. It had never happened before. Dorothy had been a possession, pure and simple, he had owned her. Molly Oakes was an expensive play-thing, bought and paid for. But he could hardly say that about his new wife. The trouble was he *liked* her. Mark had never *liked* a woman before. Worse, he respected her, and to respect a woman was quite foreign to his nature. Yet he found it hard to deny her respect. She was so . . . so honourable.

She kept her agreements with everyone, be they white or black or brown. Consequently, albeit grudgingly, Mark Averdale reminded himself of their 'business arrangement' and schooled himself to keep his side of the bargain.

The night before he left they gave a final dinner for about twenty of the most progressive farmers. Mark's story, prearranged, was that he would be away for some months on business in Ulster. Ziggy would explain his extended absence as and when it suited her.

It was a successful evening for two reasons, the first being the obvious respect in which Ziggy was held by the other farmers. True none of them were 'the Kenya aristocracy', none of their families were alongside that old buccaneer Delamere when he first blazed the British presence across the land, but they all farmed a fair acreage and seemed to know what they were talking about. Ziggy might well have plenty of enemies but she also seemed to have a number of friends.

The other reason concerned Mark Averdale himself. A proposal was made – that while he was in England he should meet Westminster politicians and find out what they were planning for Africa. The idea was widely supported. Mark was flattered and promised to do what he could. People toasted the success of his trip and the evening ended on a convivial note – after which those who were travelling left for their homes, and those who were guests dispersed to their rooms. The host and hostess remained for a moment, knowing it would be another twelve months before they next wished each other goodnight.

Mark poured two final brandies. 'Well,' he said, raising his glass, 'here's to my partner in Africa. To your continued health and prosperity.'

She replied with a toast of her own. 'And to my partner in Europe,' she said, 'a true British gentleman.'

He looked at her sharply, remembering the significance she had attached to the words when she talked of her first husband. But her voice was empty of sarcasm, her smile was genuinely warm. The tribute was meant.

He slept badly that night. He hoped against hope she would come to him, but when dawn broke he was still alone under the mosquito netting. With a dry smile he told himself he should have known better.

Later that morning, he boarded a BOAC aircraft at Eastleigh airport and began the long journey home. Mark was nervous about the very long flight, but it did have an advantage. He could make a two-day stop-over in Rome and still be in Ulster sooner than had he travelled by sea. And with eighty thousand pounds to spend the prospect of Rome's art galleries was too tempting to resist.

The huge plane settled itself after banking low over Mount Kenya. The cabin staff distributed the newspapers and began to serve coffee – and quite by chance Mark's eye fell on a small story in the *Kenya Times* –

Foreign investments curtailed? Rumours grew this week that investments in Kenya by non-British nationals may soon be restricted. Sources at Westminster suggest that the colonial office is concerned about a growing imbalance between British and non-British investment in Africa. Our London correspondent writes – 'various schemes are believed to be under review. One is that investment in Kenya may be restricted to British nationals.

Lord Averdale burst out laughing. Ziggy Beck (he still could not think of her in other terms) had done it again. She *was* a British national, thanks to her recent marriage . . .

His mind dwelt on her for the next few hours. Most of his thoughts were admiring. His ego had recovered from her rejection – he even felt grateful. Sexually Ziggy Beck would be inept. He remembered Dorothy and shuddered. It would have been an embarrassing disaster. 'Why burden the relationship with a problem,' Ziggy had said – and she had been right. She really was a most remarkable woman!

He reviewed his affairs with a certain satisfaction. He had been away much longer than intended, but had salvaged more than he had dreamt possible. Meanwhile young Tim O'Brien had apparently developed splendidly under Harris's tutelage in Ulster. The Averdale fortune had in large part been saved, despite the worst efforts of the Labour Government at home and thieving managers abroad. Mark grinned. No surrender! He was unworried by his marriage of convenience. All thoughts of a *real* marriage had evaporated more than two years before. Of course it still hurt, he had spent too long yearning for Kate for the pain to fade entirely. But he tried not to dwell on it. Instead he looked forward to public triumphs with the Averdale Foundation – and to private pleasures with Molly Oakes.

Three weeks before Christmas 1948 – after an indulgent forty-eight hours in Rome – Mark Averdale came back to the British Isles. His plane landed at Heathrow and he took a cab to his London club, intending to settle himself in and then go directly to St John's Wood. He could hardly wait to see Molly. His suitcases contained presents for her, bought in Nairobi and Rome. In all the years he had known her he had never as much as written her a note. Prudent men did not write letters to their mistresses. It was the way *affaires* were conducted.

But to his surprise an envelope was waiting at his club, marked – 'Not to be forwarded. To be collected by Lord Averdale on his return.' The letter inside contained disastrous news.

Molly had gone to Australia! Sold up and emigrated. She thanked him for the past and wished him well for the future – but she had gone out of his life!

It was a bitter homecoming. London glittered with Christmas decorations. The city was festive with seasonal spirit. Everyone was celebrating . . . but suddenly Mark Averdale felt very much alone.

He went to the bar for a brandy, then had another. He felt . . . betrayed . . . betrayed by a wife in Africa who refused him access to her bed, and a mistress in Australia who should have waited in London. Bloody women! But by Christ he had to have one . . . he had been looking forward to Molly for so long.

Finally he went into Piccadilly and picked up a tart. They spent the night together in a cheap hotel behind St Pancras Station. Mark abused her brutally. In the morning he returned to his club, took a bath and ate an appallingly bad breakfast. He still thought 'bloody women!' In particular 'Bloody Molly!' To make matters worse he had been fond of her. He re-read her letter. Now that the shock of its contents had passed it took on a softer, kinder tone. *'I shall always remember you with fond affection . . . be forever grateful for your kindness . . .'* He lingered over it and realized she had been fond of him too. It made him feel better. He sighed, but he would miss her, that was for sure.

He went for a walk after that, across Green Park to think things out. During the long journey home he had planned to spend more time in London. He would have to if his interests were to be protected – the threat to Ulster lay not in Belfast, just as the threat to the Bowley estates was not to be found in Kenya – the threats were to be found in the same place, at Westminster with this wretched Labour Government. He would take his seat in the House of Lords and defend his interests from there. He had looked forward to that on the journey home . . . it would mean spending more nights with Molly . . . and he had looked forward to that too.

But Molly had gone. He was too sensual a man to do without a woman for long. He brightened. He would make a fresh start. He would find a new mistress, younger, more pliable. That dealt with Molly. The mood of confidence grew. Soon he was full of resolutions. When he went back to Africa he would *demand* his conjugal rights . . . and that would deal with Ziggy Beck. And while he was at it he would deal with Kate O'Brien, arrange a settlement with the Johnstones perhaps . . . and *that* would deal with his adolescent obsession once and for all.

He returned to his club in a better humour. Clear the decks, he told himself. It was almost the end of a year. Start the new year right. And start immediately. He telephoned the American Embassy, hoping to arrange a meeting with this man Lincoln Johnstone ('God, the names these Americans gave themselves – *Lincoln* indeed!') – but then came the first problem. Johnstone was not in the office – 'He's away dealing with a domestic emergency.' Mark asked for the man's home number but was told 'We are not allowed to divulge that sort of information.'

Lord Averdale fumed. Then he had an idea. Telephone this school, Glossops. They would know.

To his surprise the Principal came on the line as soon as he announced himself. She sounded almost feverish – 'Oh Lord Averdale, we thought you were abroad. I'm so glad it's you. I'm afraid we've had something of an emergency . . . yes, concerning your ward, well *indirectly* if you know what I mean . . .'

Mark Averdale did *not* know – and what was worse the stupid woman refused to go into details. He managed to establish that the girl had not been involved in an accident, but Miss Jenkins stopped short at that. What she did say was, 'I do wish we had known you were in London. I should so like to meet you, rather urgently if possible. No, I'd rather not discuss it on the telephone . . .'

Clear the decks, he told himself, deal with it today. So he said to expect him that afternoon and went back to the bar for a drink before lunch – another bad meal, made even worse by listening to an account of the current antics of the Labour Government, after which he called for a taxi and set out for Maidenhead.

It was three o'clock when he reached Glossops. He was curious but not alarmed. Whatever had happened would affect him only slightly. As soon as he got hold of

Johnstone he would settle the girl's future, fairly and properly, but firmly – she would cease to be his concern.

Five minutes later he was shown into the Principal's office – to be greeted by a very agitated Miss Jenkins who had barely introduced herself when another member of staff arrived; 'Ah thank goodness. Lord Averdale, may I present Miss Broakes who was very much involved in this . . . um, this unfortunate incident.'

It took fifteen minutes of humming and hawing before they told him about 'the unfortunate incident'. Apparently the Johnstone girl had got herself pregnant by an American airman. Miss Jenkins walked up and down to control her trembling. 'I can't tell you how shocked we are. In all my years at Glossops . . .' She returned to her desk and reached for her lorgnettes, 'Lord Averdale, I'm sure you can imagine –'

'What about my ward?' he asked bluntly.

Miss Broakes took over. She was nervous but more in control of herself than Miss Jenkins. Apparently Jennifer Johnstone had reported sick two mornings before and the school doctor had pronounced her pregnant by almost three months. Her parents were sent for immediately, but even before they arrived Miss Broakes had pieced the story together. Unknown to the school and without the permission of her parents, Jennifer had been seeing the airman for a very long time. Naturally the Johnstones were distraught, especially Mrs Johnstone – 'I'm afraid she was furious with Kate. You see Kate knew about it from the outset. Not only that but she has . . . well told lies, covering up for Jenny. We had the most distressing scene. Most upsetting.'

'Lying is unforgivable,' Miss Jenkins snapped. 'I've told Kate, absolutely unforgivable!'

Miss Broakes went on to say that Mrs Johnstone as good as accused Kate of leading her daughter astray. Miss Broakes flushed. 'Absolutely without justification in my opinion. Kate has been guilty of telling lies, but girls can be very loyal to their friends – misguided perhaps, but you must see Kate's point of view.'

'Mrs Johnstone didn't,' snapped Miss Jenkins, 'she's forbidden Kate ever to speak to her daughter again and I can't say I blame her – '

'Jenny was Kate's dearest friend,' said Miss Broakes. 'They were like sisters – '

Mark Averdale was bemused. He had not known what to expect. Certainly not this. One thing was clear. The Johnstones sounded in no mood to listen to his suggestion about taking Kate to America. He cursed his own rotten luck. Problems all the way. First Molly, now this.

'Were it not for *Pygmalion*,' Miss Jenkins was saying, 'I would ask you to remove Kate from Glossops immediately, Lord Averdale.'

'*Pygmalion?*' he repeated blankly.

Miss Broakes came to his rescue. Glossops were presenting a joint production of Shaw's play . . . and Kate was playing the leading role. 'We open tomorrow night,' Miss Broakes told him, 'in fact I've just this minute come from a rehearsal. I must get back as soon as possible. Please, Lord Averdale, you must understand – this shocking business has shaken Kate *very, very badly*. I've had the most enormous difficulty with her today. Another upset and goodness knows what will happen to the child.' She turned to Miss Jenkins, 'And without Kate O'Brien we haven't got a play.'

Miss Jenkins was saved the need to reply by the arrival of a maid with a tea tray.

Mark listened as Miss Broakes resumed with an account of the production of *Pygmalion*. 'It runs for a week. It's the principal play of the season in Maidenhead, it even rivals the professional stage in Windsor. We're quite booked out. Four thousand tickets have been sold.' Little Miss Broakes was almost pleading, 'Lord Averdale, whatever you do about Kate, may I ask you to give her at least this week without upsetting her further?'

Mark was stunned. He had no idea what to 'do about Kate'.

Miss Broakes swallowed her tea, 'I must get back to the rehearsal. Would you care to join me in the auditorium, Lord Averdale?' She looked at her watch, 'The curtain should be about to go up for the last act.'

Kate had endured the worst forty-eight hours of her life.

592

Aunt Alison's words still scorched like a searing hot poker. Kate had never known such rejection. She had wept and pleaded, 'I love you, you're my family, please don't do this to me!'

Alison Johnstone had been white-faced with fury. 'You betrayed me! I never want to see you again.'

Kate had been heartbroken. 'What else could I do?' She had wept into Uncle Linc's arms when Aunt Alison took Jenny out to the car. Poor, dear, sweet Uncle Linc, so hurt and bewildered – she had seen the pain in his eyes – but at least he had tried to comfort her. 'There, there, Kate honey. Everyone is too upset right now, things will look different in the morning.'

But when Kate telephoned that morning Aunt Alison had snapped, 'You have been thoroughly deceitful. I want nothing more to do with you.'

'But – ' Kate had started, only to realize that Aunt Alison had hung up.

Miss Jenkins was as bad. 'You reap as you sow. This is the result of your lies. Were it not for this play, and your guardian being abroad . . .'

The single comforting voice in a world gone mad belonged to little Miss Broakes. 'Life is unfair at times, Kate. I'm afraid this is one of those times.'

Life was more than unfair, it was completely unbearable without the Johnstones. Her guardian had washed his hands of her, her brother was too busy, this new Lady Averdale was bound to hate her . . . and now the Johnstones had walked out of her life.

'They are all I had,' she sobbed to Miss Broakes. 'I love them so much . . .'

Dear, kind, little Miss Broakes. She had taken Kate to her room and talked and talked. 'Mrs Johnstone always struck me as a very nice person . . . I'm sure it was just the shock . . . once she gets over it, you'll see . . . give her a week or so and she will forgive you.'

Somehow Kate doubted it – and what would happen then?

'And I'm sure you're wrong about your guardian,' comforted Miss Broakes. 'You must be very precious to him. And then there's your brother, you *know* how much he loves you . . . after all, he visits whenever he can . . .

Meanwhile there was the play.

'Kate, you are the star. Thousands of people are coming to see you. And you're marvellous in the part. Kate, you *must* go through with it. You can't let me down.'

Kate did not want to let Miss Broakes down.

Kate had not wanted to let Jenny down.

Kate had not wanted to let Aunt Alison down, or Uncle Linc, or Miss Jenkins . . . Kate wanted to please, she had always wanted to please.

They had rehearsed twice that day. The morning session was a disaster. Kate found it impossible to concentrate. Aunt Alison kept coming into her mind – and Jenny, poor, sweet, frightened Jenny. 'You've ruined your entire life,' Aunt Alison had screamed at her. 'Only seventeen and you've ruined your life!'

Kate was so wooden and unresponsive that Miss Broakes stopped the rehearsal and took Kate to one side – 'I'd drop you if we had more time. I know you're upset but your performance is hopeless. It's a matter of opinion about your letting Mrs Johnstone down – I'm on your side about that – but if you go on like this you are certainly letting Glossops down, and St Edwards, and Mr Coleman and his boys, and me – and most of all yourself. Come on, Kate – you know the saying – The Show Must Go On – it *must*! Concentrate on Eliza Doolittle. You were word perfect the other day. You are a beautiful actress – the star! Everyone will be so proud of you nothing else will matter. Believe me Kate, I'm *right*.'

Miss Broakes was so positive.

Even Aunt Alison might forgive her if she were a success. And the thought of letting Miss Broakes down, or disappointing Mr Coleman, or Ronnie Blackwood who played Professor Higgins, to imagine that on top of everything else, was completely unbearable.

So Kate poured her heart and soul into the part. Gradually the magic of Shaw's play took over. She forgot about Kate O'Brien and instead became the Cockney waif who was being taught to be a Lady by the eccentric Professor Higgins. In a sense the part was made for her, it touched so many chords in her life. Eliza and Kate were both young girls who wanted to please – both were almost alone in the world – and both faced an uncertain future tied in some strange way to a man old enough to be their father. In fact whenever Kate thought of Professor Higgins she thought of her guardian, she couldn't help herself, even though Ronnie Blackwell was so much younger and nothing like Mark Averdale.

Kate could not be two people at once, and by the end of the session – with help from Miss Broakes and Mr Coleman and the rest of the cast – she was living and breathing as Eliza Doolittle. Every scene was working better. All the months of rehearsing, the hours of coaching from Miss Broakes and Mr Coleman, the friendship of the other people on stage – all combined to help her through the crisis.

Finally came the dress rehearsal when the cast wore costume for the first time. Kate was delighted with her dresses – ragged and tatty for the early scenes, then a magnificent ball-gown for her transformation into a Lady at the beginning of the third act. It was the opening of that act which was giving problems. The curtain rose with Kate alone on the stage, dressed in her new finery, waiting to be inspected by Professor Higgins. First Mr Coleman directed her to be sitting – then he made her walk up and down, as if impatient for the Professor to arrive. But he abandoned that too – 'No, no' he shouted from the front row. 'Sorry Kate, not your fault, but the effect is all wrong. When the curtain rises the audience must be stunned. This is the transformation. You take their breath away. So far they've only seen you in rags. They're on the verge of falling in love with you – so is Higgins – when the curtain goes up they fall all the way. Get it? People must gasp. Suddenly they see you for what you are – the most desirable, the most beautiful girl in the world. We must create some sort of pause, just for a minute, so that every man can just gape at you.'

Of course he was talking about Eliza Doolittle not Kate O'Brien, so Kate found nothing embarrassing in his remarks. But suddenly she had an idea. Even as he was talking the most amazing recollection sprang into her mind. A scene from her childhood, a faint picture which stirred a memory completely forgotten until that moment. Her mother, about whom she had thought a lot since her conversations with Tim . . . she remembered her mother . . . on a chaise-longue . . . admiring her hair in a looking-glass.

'Mr Coleman,' she said hesitantly, 'I have a tiny idea . . . I'm not sure it will work –'

'Anything. I'll try anything. This opening must be perfect.'

They lowered the curtain while Kate explained her suggestion to the stage manager. Bailey, a St Edwards sixth-former, not only liked the idea but wanted to improve upon it. He called down to Mr Coleman, 'Please, sir, can we have half an hour to set this up. I want to try some special effects with the lights –'

Mr Coleman and Miss Broakes went to the staff room for a cup of tea. Most of the others drifted off too, to take their half hour break in the dining-room – but Kate and Bailey worked on. The time was three o'clock.

Exactly at that moment Kate's guardian was being greeted by a nervous Miss Jenkins in her office – and a moment later Miss Broakes was interrupted in the staff room by a summons to the Principal's office.

Mark Averdale insisted he could only stay a few minutes. Certainly he did not want to sit through rehearsals for a wretched school play. Nevertheless he allowed himself to be led into the darkened auditorium. He was still bemused. He wanted to get away from these twittering women – to get back to London and think. Something would have to be done with this wretched girl. Suddenly every light went out and the hall was as black as night.

The curtain rose slowly to show a drawing-room in semi-darkness. The light was so dim that Mark had to strain to see. Slowly certain items focused – bookcases on the right-hand side of the stage, opposite some french windows – and centre stage, at the back, a chaise-longue turned away from the audience.

Mark had not been in a theatre for some time, but the arrangement seemed wrong to him – surely a chaise-longue should be facing outwards . . . but then it moved slowly and

Mark realized it was on a revolving stage.

The lights increased just a fraction. Bookcases moved too . . . the entire room seemed to be turning . . . someone was on the chaise-longue . . . a girl, reclining, a spotlight picked up her ankles and the hemline of her green dress. She came more into view as the stage revolved. Something in her lap flashed in the light . . . a hand-mirror. The rest of the set was in darkness. Just as the chaise-longue reached front centre-stage more spotlights blazed out to focus on the girl. A girl with flame-red hair! Mark went rigid. It was Rouen's *Girl with a Looking Glass*! Right above him. Rouen's nymph – dressed in a shimmering gown of green silk. It *was* Rouen's nymph. The perfectly white skin, the flame-red hair, the arch of her neck, the long languid line of her body. Mark's heart raced. The girl raised the looking-glass in her left hand – then her right hand patted her hair. The pose was held for a fraction of time. She lowered the looking-glass and turned to stare out at the audience. Green eyes met his. The gap was only a few feet, but it was years long. Mark was transported back to a studio in Chelsea before the war. The magic had lived after all!

Coleman leapt to his feet applauding furiously. 'Kate, that's truly adorable. Marvellous . . .'

Miss Broakes was on her feet too – 'Oh Kate, that's just stunning . . . . that's absolutely stunning.'

Lord Averdale sat transfixed, staring up at the stage. Life had slipped through his fingers. What with Riordan, the war, problems on the Bowley estate, troubles in Ulster, this wretched Labour Government . . . fate had conspired against him. But none of that mattered if he had Kate. She had always been what he most wanted – above everything – even above Brackenburn and the Averdale Foundation. 'Oh Kate,' he whispered, 'oh Kate, I abandoned hope. Oh Kate, just eight weeks ago I got married!'

Kate had to pinch herself to believe she had spoken to Mark Averdale as she did. Where had the confidence come from? Earlier that day she would have run a mile. The truth was confused – but Eddie Bailey had already said she looked 'absolutely smashing' on the chaise-longue – and

Ronnie Blackwell had asked her out yet again (the sixth time in four weeks). The boys were good for her morale. They made her feel glamorous. So did Mr Coleman who was forever saying how lucky they were to have such a beautiful leading lady. But Eliza Doolittle was even more important – especially at the beginning of the third act. Eliza had blossomed by then, she had become a confident young lady, capable of twisting Professor Higgins round her little finger – and Kate was submerged in the part. So when Mr Coleman leapt to his feet, and dear little Miss Broakes beamed up at her – well suddenly everything worked. Seeing her guardian was a shock, but his face dispelled her fears instantly – gone was the scowl she had seen at Southampton, to be replaced by a look she remembered from childhood – of admiration, even of awe. When Ronnie Blackwell looked at her his eyes shone like that, so did Eddie Bailey's – so almost before she realized what she was doing she had smiled down from the stage and said, 'Why hello.'

He came to every performance. Miss Broakes even had to change ticket numbers for him to have the same seat in the front row every night. And he sent flowers to her dressing-room, as if she were a *real* actress, which is how she felt for at least some of the time. *Pygmalion* was a gigantic success. Her photograph was in all the local papers. And night after night the audience gasped and applauded at the opening of the third act, when they saw her on the chaise-longue. And every night she took a dozen curtain calls. It was a marvellous week spoiled by only one thing – the absence of the Johnstones.

On the last day of *Pygmalion*, a letter arrived from Jenny, full of news. She and Clayton Wells were to be married! Apparently he had called on Uncle Linc. There had been the most dreadful scene, but it was agreed that the marriage would take place almost at once. The bad news was that they were all leaving for Washington immediately, Clayton Wells included. '*In fact I am mailing this from Victoria as we set off for the boat train. I do wish I could have seen you before we left. Mummy has calmed down a lot, though she says she will never forgive me. Daddy slipped into my room without her knowing last night*

– he says it will take Mummy time. We can't get her to talk about you, though I've tried and tried to explain that you had nothing to do with it, and that you haven't even met Clayton. Daddy says she will get over that too – he says once we get back to Washington she will miss you like mad. Oh Kate, I miss you NOW, without going back to Washington. You won't even be at my wedding! You haven't even met Clayton! Nothing has turned out the way I wanted, but I do love Clayton and I know he loves me. Daddy says that's all that matters – he is being wonderfully kind – and he worries about you too. He knows I'm writing and he sends his love – he will be back in London next March and says he will telephone you at Glossops . . . and of course I shall write to you all the time, and send photos and things . . . but oh Kate, I shall miss you so much.'

The first time Kate read the letter she wept for Jenny. The second time she wept for herself. Poor, muddled Jenny, getting married, having a baby, everything at once – but at least she had Uncle Linc to lean on, and Aunt Alison loved her too much to be angry forever. But Kate's life was empty. The Johnstones had abandoned her.

Pygmalion was her salvation.

Every day was taken up doing something for the show, and once she was on stage in the evening she lost herself in the part of Eliza. The entire week was a blur of conflicting emotions – ecstatic triumph at her curtain calls, but loneliness after – their room seemed empty without Jenny, despite the praise lavished on her by Rosemary and Angela.

Pygmalion came to an end on the Saturday night. They gave their final performance. The boys of St Edwards presented her with an enormous bouquet – and then came a tremendous surprise. Vans arrived from Fortnum and Mason, waiters in dinner jackets seemed to emerge from everywhere – the whole cast was to be given a party in the school dining-room by Lord Averdale. The staff had known for days but had been sworn to secrecy. Miss Jenkins and Miss Broakes were there, looking very grand – and Mr Coleman too, more handsome than ever.

Kate went as Eliza Doolittle, there was no time to change, besides her costume was more glamorous than her own frocks. But that was only part of the reason. Playing her role gave her confidence. Her guardian and Professor Higgins had merged in her mind, so she behaved towards him in the same slightly flirtatious manner as Eliza Doolittle used towards Professor Higgins. He seemed to like it, and it certainly helped her – and other people made allowances for once, they put her behaviour down to excitement, after all she was the star of the show. The two-hour buffet became an extension of her performance, to bring that incredible week to a giddy, glittering, wonderful conclusion.

But reality cannot be held at bay for ever, and at the end of the evening her guardian said, 'I shall stay in Windsor tonight Kate, and tomorrow I'll collect you for lunch. We can spend the afternoon talking about the future.'

She hardly slept a wink. *The future!* How many times had she wondered what was to become of her? How many times had she prayed to stay with the Johnstones? But now the Johnstones had gone . . .

By the Sunday Mark Averdale had recovered from the succession of shocks which had assailed him since his return from Africa. So much had been bad – Molly's defection, the state of the nation, those lunatics in the Labour Party – and naturally the RUC seemed to have allowed that bastard Riordan to vanish from the face of the earth.

The overwhelming discovery was Kate. He had to have her. He knew the instant he saw her. His entire life had been spent waiting for Kate . . .

His marriage to Ziggy Beck was a ghastly mistake. It had seemed expedient, a clever way to resolve a commercial problem worth eight hundred thousand pounds over ten years. But that was before he'd seen Kate . . .

Over lunch on the Sunday he told her, 'I must go to Ulster. Just for two days. Then we shall spend Christmas in London, at the Savoy. There's so much to talk about –'

'Oh, how wonderful. Tim will be thrilled.'

'Not Tim,' he said, 'just us.'

She was a Christmas Princess. They went from one end of

600

Bond Street to the other. He bought her a gift in every salon. In fact he dressed her, making her try this frock and then that – making her walk up and down and swirl her skirts while he sat in the chair and admired her. He seemed as unaware of clothes rationing as everyone else in Bond Street. And the clothes were wonderful – silks and brocades, tulle and taffeta – all wickedly glamorous.

She had her hair cut and shaped in a very adult style. He bought her a diamond clip in Asprey's and a rope of pearls at Mappin and Webb – and back in her suite at the Savoy she changed behind a screen and paraded for him all over again.

All wickedly glamorous.

She guessed what he wanted. She had suspected for days. At the party after *Pygmalion* Rosemary had whispered – 'Now I know why you don't date boys. Your Sugar Daddy wouldn't like it.' Kate had protested, but Rosemary was positive, 'Eric looks like that when he wants to take my knickers down.' Kate's contempt had been icy, 'Lord Averdale has only just remarried.' But Rosemary said that was irrelevant.

By the Sunday Kate was looking for signs, though she had precious little experience – Eddie Bailey had kissed her, Ronnie Blackwell kept touching her, and Mr Coleman's eyes seemed to smoulder whenever he looked at her. Mark Averdale did the lot. He kissed her cheek when he collected her in a car hired for the day, he held her hand over lunch, and his hungry eyes devoured her.

And Kate had thought . . . 'If only Aunt Alison were here . . . or even Jenny, dear sweet PREGNANT Jenny!'

But it was all very proper at the Savoy, separate suites and a kiss on the cheek at bedtime – but his eyes spoke volumes – even seventeen-year-old Kate could see that. She trembled at times. Jenny's pilot must look at her like that . . . and certainly Rosemary got that look from Eric . . . but Rosemary seemed to get by on love-bites . . . Kate doubted Mark Averdale would be interested in biting her, even if she suggested it.

By day they went shopping, or to the Tate and once to the National. Most evenings were spent at the theatre followed by a late supper. He was such an interesting man.

He told her stories about Africa and safaris and big game hunting – and about what Brackenburn had been like in the old days – and he knew so much about art, even more than dear little Miss Broakes.

Of course he was really quite old, about forty she thought, but not 'fat and forty' like the song. He was tall and slim, and he had such an *interesting* face, lined and creased but brown from the African sun. He had suffered a lot. He seemed to have so many enemies, all determined to deprive him of what was rightfully his – like 'those bloody Croppies' in Ireland, or the 'idle, thieving Wogs' in Africa, or that 'bunch of jumped-up clerks in the Labour Government'. Really she felt quite sorry for him . . . and sometimes for his enemies because when he became angry she glimpsed a truly terrifying temper.

When he held her hand she felt none of the magic Jenny had described. 'I just melt,' Jenny had said, Kate neither melted nor flinched, although once when he accidentally brushed her décolletage a stab of excitement drew her stomach muscles together in a way never experienced before.

Every day she blessed *Pygmalion*. Without those months spent learning the role of Eliza Doolittle she could never have coped. The days of Christmas passed like the carol. 'On the first day of Christmas my true love gave to me.' His deluge of gifts became an embarrassment. She wished there was something she could give in return. Then, as she undressed for bed on Christmas night and glimpsed her naked reflection in the mirror, she knew without doubt what she would be asked to give soon. He had been especially affectionate that day. When they danced after dinner he had held her too tightly for her any longer to cling to the lingering pretence that he was merely her guardian.

So much had happened so quickly, but now, now what? He had said nothing about her future.

He did the next day.

He asked her to marry him!

It would be ten whole years before their wedding. He explained in great detail about his 'marriage of commercial convenience' in Africa – and the secret agreement which allowed his new wife to divorce him at the end of ten years.

He talked for a long time. Some words were just a buzz in her ears. Others made no sense at all – 'I love you Kate, I always have, even before you were born.'

There would be no more Glossops, no coming-out, her childhood was over. She would live in London, so would he for most of the time, but obviously they would not live together. He would buy her a small house, she would have an allowance, they would travel, holiday in Europe, to the outside world she would be his ward and his assistant, 'But behind closed doors we shall create a world of our own.'

Her mind reeled.

Brackenburn would not be rebuilt, the Labour Government would not permit the construction of great houses . . . her brother Tim would not know of their private arrangement, her brother Tim would not be told anything until they married in ten years' time. 'Believe me, Kate, I didn't plan it like this. I waited so long . . .'

Aunt Alison was in Washington . . . Kate was alone . . . she was an orphan.

She *did* like this man, he was her future, one way or another. She was frightened, reassured, flattered, excited, all at the same time. He would never hurt her. And she so wanted to please.

So she said yes.

He came to her room that very night. The sensations of lovemaking were not at all as she had imagined. She bled and was sore and uncomfortable . . . and frightened. 'Only seventeen,' Aunt Alison had screamed at Jenny, 'and you've ruined your whole life!'

But Mark seemed to know about everything. The next morning he arranged for her to see a gynaecologist in Harley Street and she was introduced to the mysteries of the Dutch Cap. She almost fainted at the prospect of inserting that enormous round, rubbery object inside herself – it was inconceivable that she would ever get used to it, quite impossible to believe that the sexual act would be anything but abhorrent – but she had no choice, it was part of her new life with Mark. A new life and a new year which were starting together, for it was New Year's Eve and 1949 was about to begin.

CHAPTER FIVE

Sean Connors built a financial empire in the fifties. He enlarged it later during the sixties when his name became known all over the world, but the foundations were laid during ten furious years – from 1949 when he was almost broke, to 1959 when he was a millionaire twice over.

The Mallon Property Company nearly went bust at the beginning of 1949 – surviving by the skin of Sean's teeth and with the help of his bank manager. They were let down by sub-contractors, defeated by planning regulations and plagued by problems – but they clung on and made enough money that year to acquire W. G. Tillet Ltd, a small firm of builders whom Tubby had used on a recent conversion. Old Man Tillet was anxious to retire, but agreed to work another two years to develop his successors – principally his son Brian and a site foreman named Thornton. Tillet's owned a small office in Pont Street so the Mallon Property Company moved in there, and for the first time Tubby Reynolds worked from a 'proper office' instead of the flat in Great Cumberland Place.

Tubby ran the business day to day, but Sean always dealt with the bankers – and it was becoming obvious that a sizeable amount of permanent capital was required for expansion. 'What you really need,' said the bank manager one day, 'is long-term money at a fixed rate of interest. You've got a good business, Sean, why not recruit an outside chairman, someone well known in the City. The right man could raise enough on his reputation, and after that, well I'm damn sure you'll make the right profits.'

Sean knew a dozen men 'well known in the City', but one sprang to mind above all others – George Hamilton, whom he still met occasionally. They always greeted each other warmly. Neither could ever forget sitting in the rubble of Coventry when Val was killed. It created a sad bond – had she lived the two men would have become in-laws – as things were they had become friends, although they met only infrequently.

So Sean went to George and was proud to do so – the Mallon Property Company was a growing concern, Sean was moderately wealthy on paper, and it was an opportunity to prove he would have provided for Val. He hoped George might be interested, but George was much more than that. He was amazed at Sean's involvement in business – he had never heard of the Mallon Property Company. Few people had. The company did not advertise, nor display its name on its buildings. It lacked even an entry in the telephone directory until the acquisition of Tillet's. George was astonished. 'And why Mallon, for heaven's sake? Freddie's not involved is he?'

'Freddie was my best friend,' Sean said simply He once called me his good luck charm. Well he was certainly mine. It just seemed appropriate.'

After which George probed and probed until he learned the details of that fateful New Year's Eve.

'Well I'm blessed,' he said, 'so that's what happened. I've often wondered. I asked Margaret once but she wouldn't discuss it – but she always asks after you when we see them in the States.'

Sean was embarrassed. He had never told anyone, but it was impossible to avoid point-blank questions when he was seeking George's help.

George said, 'It's the most stupid thing ever. I'm surprised at Freddie. Of course you behaved badly, but . . . for heaven's sake, under the circumstances . . .' Suddenly he chuckled, 'Good Lord, half the men in London have made a pass at Cynthia. If I cut them all I wouldn't have a friend left.'

He delved into Sean's accounts like a hungry man starting his dinner. 'First class, Sean,' he pronounced an hour later, 'absolutely first class.' He was as pleased as if he owned the Mallon Property Company himself – or as if they really were father- and son-in-law. Sean was touched. He was too busy to feel lonely, every day was crammed with activity – but now and then he ached for the warmth of a real family, people of his own with whom he could share his triumphs. And his feelings deepened when George suggested they continue their discussion over

605

dinner – at home in Eaton Square.

It was Sean's first visit since before the war. The Square was still elegant – all the 'in' people lived there: Terence Rattigan the playwright, Bob Boothby the Tory MP, the Princess Aly Khan – but the huge mansions had all been converted into apartments. Even George and Cynthia lived in a penthouse occupying a sixth of the original building.

'Plenty large enough,' said George, 'pity I didn't know you were in the business. You could have done the conversions.'

Cynthia, at sixty, was smaller than Sean remembered. Her astonishing looks had faded, but not her vitality. 'Sean! What a delightful surprise! Where have you *been*? It's simply *ages* since I saw you.'

They spent an enjoyable evening together and when Sean offered George the chairmanship of the Mallon Property Company he was flattered by the response – 'I'd be honoured, Sean, honoured and delighted.'

Raising long-term money was not easy, however, even for George Hamilton. The Labour Party was making the business community nervous. But George Hamilton's reputation in the City was rock solid, and six months later he concluded a skilful arrangement. The Mallon Property Company issued two hundred thousand one-pound non-voting Preference Shares at five per cent interest – and George Hamilton's friends subscribed for the lot. 'That's just the start,' he chuckled, 'my people are on standby. They will put up two million the day the Tories win office.'

So Sean had his money for expansion. The two hundred thousand was quickly utilized to buy other properties, and Tubby Reynolds began to compile a secret file ready for a massive leap forward when there was a change of government.

George certainly earned his modest chairman's fee, but he did much more than that – a week before Christmas Sean received a letter . . . from Freddie.

'. . . *when George wrote you had named your property company after me, well Sean I confess it brought a lump to my throat. You've been on my conscience longer than I care to remember. If it means anything I can tell you I regret that*

New Year's Eve more than anything in the whole of my life. Margaret won't talk about it – we tried once but she said, "If I tell you how badly you behaved you will only suspect worse things, but you offended your wife and your best friend so deeply that Sean couldn't be blamed if he never spoke to you again." She said that early on, when we first went to Germany, and those were her last words on the subject. Of course I knew I was wrong. The trouble was when I was out in Nuremberg covering those trials some of the boys kept ragging me about what was going on in London. They dripped away every day about you and Margaret being seen around town, at parties and things – well I guess it got under my skin more than I realized . . .'

The letter was five pages long. Freddie did more than apologize – he invited Sean to visit them in New York and stay as a house guest. And elsewhere in the letter he wrote:

'. . . by the way, George is tremendously impressed with your business. He remembers two penniless news-hounds chasing his daughters before the war – "I was worried then," he admits in his letter, "but I must say our girls had great foresight. Had dear Val been spared I would have been enormously proud of both of our son-in-laws." Sean, I thought you'd like to know about that compliment. Margaret, who is reading this over my shoulder, says she has loved you as a brother-in-law ever since Dunkirk – which makes me feel even worse . . .'

Sean was delighted, flattered and relieved, but could not help thinking that the reconciliation had come too late. Had Freddie answered any of Sean's messages in 1946 he would have packed his bags and joined Freddie and Margaret anywhere in the world. They meant so much to him then. He would happily have been Freddie's junior partner for the rest of his life.

Of course he answered Freddie's letter . . . and Freddie replied . . . so that within a few months they were regular correspondents. The breach had been healed – but deep in Sean's heart he knew things were different. He was no longer Freddie's apprentice. He was his own man now, building his own fortune. Freddie was prospering in New York but Sean intended to do better – in fact he was well along the road to making that point. The property

607

company was expanding and London & Continental News was close behind. They had acquired offices in Fleet Street – and now had staff correspondents in Paris, Bonn, Rome and Zurich, as well as five reporters in London. Sean worked harder than ever. It was hard to say which excited him most, converting old houses or reporting the happenings in the capital – in truth he loved them both. London was as fascinating as ever for Sean – London was still the heart of the Empire – and the Empire was claiming many headlines. There were other big stories of course – UN troops were fighting the Chinese in Korea, Britain and the USA were rearming, and the cold war with Russia got frostier every day. In London itself the Labour Government, burdened by rearmament costs, was trimming social services despite an outcry from its supporters. But there were other stories – stories from the Colonial Office – which made Sean wonder if Britain could maintain the Empire when dealing with so many financial demands. He judged that the average man in the street cared little about the Empire anyway, 'the average man' knew little about it – but some people cared passionately. Empire Loyalists fought in General Elections and a new pressure group called 'Britain in Africa' had emerged, headed by none other than Lord Averdale. Sean was surprised, doubting at first that it was the same Lord Averdale who had sold the *Dublin Gazette* all those years ago – but it was, and by 1951 London & Continental News had quite a file on Lord Averdale's 'Britain in Africa'.

Jimmy Cross maintained the file – Jimmy ran the 'Africa desk' and was Michael O'Hara's right-hand man. So when Sean was curious about Lord Averdale he had everything he needed in his own office – including his own expert to fill in the details. Jimmy Cross related his impressions: – of Averdale's performance in the House of Lords:

'Very forceful, he knows his facts and tears opponents apart.' Of Averdale's holdings in Kenya:

'Vast, I've forgotten how many thousands of acres – but I worked it out once as being the same size as Yorkshire.' Of Averdale's marriage:

'Nobody knows much about her. An old Kenya hand, I think. She seems to run that end of things, while he

608

concentrates on Westminster. Must be a funny sort of a marriage though, with him in London so often.' And of the 'Britain in Africa' campaign:

'As far as I can make out it's financed by the white settlers themselves. They don't have an office. His ward runs it from her flat. And his ward is the most beautiful girl in the world.'

Sean smiled. He had known the most beautiful girl in the world. She was five feet two with eyes of blue. Corn-coloured hair and a complexion so fair. She had died in the Coventry Blitz.

Jimmy flushed, 'I know it's hackneyed, but you should see this girl. She's something else. Averdale's secret weapon, if you ask me. None of the press boys like Averdale much, he's too bloody arrogant – but when this Kate O'Brien takes over at press conferences – well everyone melts. The thing is she's got brains too. She presents a hell of a good argument. Fleet Street eats out of her hand –'

'You too by the sound of it.'

Jimmy hesitated, 'Put it this way. I'm glad I don't have to write bad things about her.'

'And Averdale gets the benefit?' Sean's eyebrows rose. 'I'd hate to think we pull punches because someone has been smart enough to hire a pretty girl to run his front office.'

Jimmy flushed, 'I'd hate that too, Mr Connors, especially when it's not true. I disagree with a lot of Colonial policy and my press clippings prove it, but some of Averdale's schemes make sense. I try to present a balanced view. Africa is a lot more complicated than some people make out – especially in the States, where they seem mesmerized by what goes on at the UN.'

Sean had to agree. African lobbyists at the UN in New York were wiping the floor with the British at propaganda. Sean read the stories without feeling personally involved. His job was to make sure the news was reported without fear or favour – and that was easier said than done once a pretty girl was involved. He made a mental note to ask Michael to go to Averdale's next press conference and check things out. Sean was too busy himself. He was interested in Averdale simply because of their old link through the *Dublin Gazette* – but it was only a casual concern. Certainly his interest was not heightened by the mention of a good-looking female.

Sean rarely gave any girl a second glance. He hardly met any – he continued to live at Great Cumberland Place with Tubby and Michael. Tubby was a forty-five-year-old bachelor and Michael was having a long Irish courtship with a girl still in Dublin. The businesses employed secretaries, but Sean had little contact with them – Tubby hired staff at Mallon and Michael did the same in Fleet Street. Sean actually still typed up his own copy. The truth was he was operating in a man's world and enjoying himself so much that girls had no part to play. There was no *time* for a social life. He even skipped meals unless they had a business connection – breakfast with Tubby, lunch with an architect, dinner with a politician. He was always in a hurry, dashing from one appointment to the next.

Certainly Sean knew hundreds of people. Most of them liked him. They knew he was successful, perhaps even rich, but he never made a show of it. He lived modestly at Great Cumberland Place, in fact years passed before he even bought a car. He spent money, he bought dozens of meals in the Savoy Grill, but ten times out of ten it was to learn something from one of his guests. Nobody minded, it was just the way Sean did things. He seemed to stop getting older. Tubby used to joke that Sean ran so fast that time couldn't keep up with him.

Commercially his next big step came at the end of 1951. He had been thinking about television for some time. Sean judged it to have a tremendous future and although the BBC had a monopoly there was talk of a second channel to be operated by private finance. Sean was convinced that television was a growth industry. A lot of people were frightened by it – film-makers said it would kill the cinema and Fleet Street said newspapers would fail if people could watch news on television. Sean's crystal ball was no better than the next man's – but maybe his intelligence service was.

He wrote to his agents in New York, to Freddie Mallon, to Ambassador Kennedy, to the CBS contacts – everyone he could think of. It seemed to Sean that a second channel would take years to overhaul the BBC's head-start. *If* a second channel *did* start it would need a supply of ready-made programmes to hold an audience, until it could produce them itself. And there was only one source of such programmes – American television.

'Most of it's crap,' Freddie wrote, 'but some of the comedy shows are good. I think the Brits will go for it.'

That was when Sean Connors decided to invest in commercial television. It was a big decision, not just because it meant a financial investment but because of commitment of *time*. Time was always the enemy. There were never enough hours in the day.

Then, in October, something happened which accelerated Sean's plans. The Conservatives won the General Election and promised to end the BBC monopoly. And the Tory victory caused something else to happen – George Hamilton implemented his plan to raise two million pounds for the Mallon Property Company. By the end of November the money was in the bank, and by December Tubby Reynolds was negotiating for a whole string of properties.

Sean's business affairs had never been better. Mallon was especially strong with George as chairman, and Tubby running day-to-day business assisted by Brian Tillet and Jack Thornton. And since Michael O'Hara had a very firm grip on London & Continental, Sean was free to pursue other ambitions.

At last he was going to America – and going in style – first-class aboard the *Queen Elizabeth*. It was the first time Sean had left his beloved London since arriving from Dublin all those years ago – and as he set off on a new venture it seemed only appropriate that he would be sharing that Christmas in New York with Freddie Mallon – the man who had welcomed him to London in 1938.

CHAPTER SIX

By Christmas '51 Kate O'Brien had been Mark Averdale's mistress for three years. Her life had so changed that she could barely recall that day at Glossops when she had looked down from the stage to see him in the front stalls. She had been a girl then . . . by Christmas '51 she was a young woman of twenty who had acquired so much experience that it seemed impossible to believe she had once been so innocent.

In a sense the three years were like layers of paint – the primer had been applied in the first year, then the undercoat, until in year three Kate had emerged shimmering under a veneer of sophistication which was to last the rest of her life.

But it was not always easy. Satisfying Mark Averdale in bed was bewildering to begin with . . . as soon as she became mistress of one position he introduced another, his repertoire seemed endless. She had survived because she wanted to please – so for the most part she had given herself willingly. Mark Averdale left no room for shyness, not in the bedroom. 'How can you be shy?' he would ask as he undressed her. 'Other women have reason to be shy. Who can blame them for hiding their imperfect bodies. But you are the most beautiful woman in the world. Darling Kate, you are perfect, flawless, unique.'

That helped her confidence, but she never grew complacent. In the early days her dependence on him worried her. It was all very well to be told she was the most beautiful woman in the world, but Kate had seen other good-looking girls over all London. Suppose Mark Averdale decided on one of them?

But she stifled occasional doubts and her blossoming confidence enabled her to do most things he asked. He derived so much pleasure from looking at her that to have denied him would have been selfish – so she posed nude while he painted her, posed nude while he photographed her, posed in the bath, posed on the chaise-longue, posed on the bed, posed everywhere – and then came an event which changed their relationship.

It happened at the end of three months. He wanted to make a clay cast of her body. She gritted her teeth, hating the thought of being smothered in clay. In the event the attempt only lasted a few minutes – by the time he had plastered clay over her buttocks he was trembling, and when it came to moulding her breasts desire overcame him completely. He started to make love and they rolled over and over like animals in a mud bath until he spent himself and collapsed exhausted. But when they rested, the clay set and stuck them together. They were joined from the waist to the knees! Rising to their feet was excruciatingly painful. Kate wept with pain and laughter. They edged crab fashion to the bathroom to soak in the bath. She clung to him, shaking helplessly, blinded by tears. Then she realized he was making the most peculiar hee-hawing sound. It was Mark Averdale laughing.

She really liked him from then on. Before she had been in awe, and a little afraid. He was always so serious. Of course he *smiled* at her, but his laughter was different – it was so rare – and she would not have believed he could have laughed at himself, or at their absurd predicament. So, liking him, she relaxed – and that too helped develop her confidence.

For the first year she lived in a little house behind Sloane Square. Mark was having the mansion in Belgrave Square converted. He was keeping the entire house, vast by post-war standards, but he needed room for his art collection and decided that Kate should have a self-contained apartment on the top floor. The separate front door would be obvious to the world, but what would be secret was the elevator from his bedroom to hers.

Time flew. She had a housekeeper and a maid, an adequate allowance, and Mark was forever giving her presents. That summer they spent two weeks in Tangier which was fun, two weeks at Monte Carlo which was very grand – and eight days in Paris. Mark was busy touring the studios, but Kate grabbed the chance to visit Yvette Lefarge. Yvette dined with them on their last night. Of course Yvette *knew*. Kate was a competent actress and might, just might, have fooled her old tutor for a few hours – but Mark's feelings shone from his eyes.

It was the same with everyone they met. Mark's manner was restrained, almost formal at times, but nothing could disguise that look in his eyes. Mark Averdale was besotted and the world knew it.

Kate felt she was meeting *the world* – at least the art world and some of the political world. Mark wove her into the fabric of his life. Within eight months Kate had shared cocktails with Henry Moore at the Leicester Gallery and Barbara Hepworth at the Lefevre – each of whom was considered by their admirers to be the leading sculptor in Britain. Kate enjoyed listening to their talk but was careful with her own comments, fearful of displaying her ignorance. It was the same in artists' studios – she met Topolski in his house at Regent's Park and travelled down to Cookham to visit Stanley Spencer in his tiny house above Cookham Station. She enjoyed the experience, but was cautious in her judgements.

Even with Mark she described her impressions in timid language – finding it hard to explain her reactions to somebody's work. But gradually she developed tastes of her own and found words to justify her selections – which was yet another way in which she gained confidence.

Contact with the political world occurred when Kate visited the House of Lords to hear Mark speak . . . and when she dealt with Ziggy Beck's correspondence. She had quickly learned to think of Ziggy as a friend. Ziggy wrote often, forever enquiring about the views being expressed on Africa by Westminster politicians. Mark himself answered to begin with, but Ziggy's thirst for detail exhausted him. One day Kate suggested – 'Why don't I search the newspapers and clip out anything on Africa? Then I could send her those every month, and you could write a summary. She'd have the whole picture.' Mark leapt at the idea, which had worked so well that even before he returned to Africa that autumn Kate and Ziggy had become regular correspondents.

The aspect of Kate's life which worried her most was her brother. Tim was beginning to suspect, no matter how often she said – 'But this was always the plan, Tim. I remember you saying I would be hostess at Brackenburn, showing off the paintings and things – well the only difference is I'm helping in London.'

'I dunno,' he said, blushing slightly. 'It's the way he looks at you. Kate, you're his *ward* . . . at times I think, well now he's married again it seems odd that Lady Averdale herself isn't running things – '

'She is, in Kenya. Just as you run things in Ulster, and I do what I can here.'

'I suppose so.'

How could she tell him that Ziggy Beck was a business partner, and that Kate herself would be Lady Averdale one day? She firmly believed that. Mark had told her so often. But Tim was a worry. He was the only *real* family she had. And she loved him. She was proud of him. Mark was forever singing his praises – Tim and Mr Harris ran the Averdale businesses in Ulster.

Luckily Mark understood her concern – 'I know it's difficult, darling. I tell you what – I'll go to Ulster alone every month. Only for a few days. You stay in London. God knows there's enough to be done, Ziggy's correspondence is a full-time job. If Tim doesn't see us together, well it might help.'

And it did.

Thus the months flew past. When Mark was away in Ulster, often for more than 'a few days', Kate filled her time in the same way as she would had he been in London – she went to private viewings at the galleries and debates on African affairs at Westminster. The only unusual thing she did was sit through some lectures on *Art and Evolution* at the Conway Hall. Mark certainly would not have done that, but Kate was still soaking up knowledge for her new life. She worked as hard as a conscientious secretary whose boss was away. Heads turned wherever she went, but she kept to herself. She was safe at the galleries, at least from the artists. Since Lord Averdale's patronage was valuable they behaved very properly. Westminster was different – tentative approaches were made by one Peer of the Realm, two MPs and three lobby correspondents – but Kate rebuffed them all with smooth charm. She was, without doubt, becoming more self-assured all the time.

Then it was October and Tim came to stay for a few weeks, while Mark made his first trip back to Kenya . . .

Mark Averdale was never happier. Life had changed for the better and he seemed to change too. Of course basic traits remained – he was as possessive as ever, autocratic and blisteringly rude when he chose . . . yet, imperceptibly and then more noticeably, some of his attitudes altered. But not his desires. His desire for Kate was insatiable. He could never get enough of her. On the Dover train once, *en route* for Paris, after lunching well at the Charing Cross, they had settled into their reserved compartment intending to browse through their magazines – when the sheer beauty of her smile inflamed him. He jammed the door and drew the blinds, and undressed her there and then – and as the train rocked and swayed through the apple orchards of Kent made love to her for so long that they were still naked when the train drew into Dover.

He was the most gentle of lovers with Kate. Once he had imagined Molly Oakes as her tutor, now the idea was abhorrent. The very thought now turned him cold.

When artists wanted to paint her Mark refused – he could not bear the thought. His own efforts frustrated him, he destroyed every canvas. He knew she *should* be painted, he owed it to the world, but nothing would induce him to allow another man to gaze on her naked body. He was a prisoner of the Averdale temperament – Kate was his, and his alone. How could he know she was playing Eliza Doolittle to his Professor Higgins, how could he know she was always so anxious to please? Not that it mattered – Kate was his and their life together was perfect.

Keeping it perfect cost money. The mansion in Belgrave Square drained resources, the art collection devoured cash, travelling abroad was expensive, Kate's allowance, her clothes, the gifts he bought her – all demanded a large income. And Mark *had* a large income, thanks partly to Ziggy Beck in Kenya. His lifestyle was safe – as long as Ziggy was safe.

Even so it was a wrench to leave Kate for his first trip back to Kenya. He blessed the new jet aircraft which

616

reduced the long journey to a few days – but he would still be away a long time. In his luggage were his photographs of Kate – Kate nude on the chaise-longue, Kate on her bed, Kate smiling, Kate serious and Kate sad – which was Mark's own expression as he waved her goodbye from the aircraft as it lumbered out on to the runway at Heathrow.

He dispensed with the optional two-day stop-over in Rome, preferring to go out on the next flight, determined to reach Nairobi as quickly as possible. The sooner he was there the sooner he could fly back. He rehearsed his argument with Ziggy – eight weeks at a time was too much to ask, he had other commitments, surely she would understand? Even as he practised he could hear her reply, 'But Mark, a deal is a deal, surely we have a business arrangement.'

Yet in the event she agreed right away – 'Let's make it twice a year,' she said, 'four weeks at a time. It's a much more sensible arrangement – besides it will make our marriage seem a little less abnormal to the watching world.' Ziggy was forever unpredictable.

He was made welcome at Cutters. Ziggy gave a whole series of dinner parties in his honour – the Governor himself came to one. There was no doubting Ziggy's growing influence. Mark gathered from the gossip that the new Lady Averdale had been very busy that year.

The Bowley estates were a revelation. Endless acres had been given over to the fast money crop of pyrethrum, but coffee had been increased too, tea had been planted on the higher land, sisal had been set down elsewhere, and the wheat fields were an undulating wind-rippled sea of gold. Tatz proudly pointed to one innovation after another.

And Nairobi was astonishing. It was becoming so cosmopolitan. The cobbled courtyard of the old Norfolk was crammed with shiny new cars. The New Stanley had opened a French-style pavement café, full of pink-faced, shiny-nosed tourists who pretended to be locals by screaming 'Bring us another drink, *boy*' to the Wog waiters who rushed around on horny feet.

Kenya was booming . . . and yet Mark detected an undercurrent. He came across Standish in the bar at Smith's Club, holding forth about the Belgian Congo – 'They're giving up, if you ask me. I was there recently and everyone I spoke to was trying to sell up. Land is going for a song, good land that would make a man rich in ten years.'

Belgian territory was nothing to do with British Africa – but British intentions towards the continent were causing concern. Mark was constantly asked about the political mood at Westminster – in particular would the Westminster Government give in to Nkrumah? Everyone was asking that question. Kwame Nkrumah was the black African leader most in the news. Educated in Britain and the United States, he had returned to his native Gold Coast in 1947 and established a national following very quickly. Now his Convention People's Party was pushing for self-rule and Dominion status within the Commonwealth.

Mark always answered along the same lines – 'The Government will buy him off. My guess is they'll give Nkrumah's crowd a few seats in some sort of new national assembly. Real power will stay with the Colonial Office.'

'But will Africans be given the vote?'

Mark had to admit it was possible – 'It doesn't make sense, I agree – nine out of ten Wogs can't even read or write, yet this Labour Government might be daft enough to give them a vote.'

Mark summed up – 'Don't worry. The Gold Coast is a long way from Kenya, and there's fifty other colonies to keep the Colonial Secretary busy. He won't stick his snout in here. I told him a dozen times – leave Kenya to the settlers. Stay off their backs, give 'em a fair deal, and they'll do the rest.'

Which was reassuring as far as it went . . . but Kenya had its own Nkrumah to worry about . . . an agitator named Jomo Kenyatta, whose support had spread from the Kikuyu to other tribes. In fact at the bar in Smith's, Standish said – 'Well Mark, and how do you find this free land of ours? Been to any of Kenyatta's rallies yet – fifty thousand Wogs all jumping up and down for freedom. *Uhuru* they call it.'

It was the first time Mark heard the word. *Uhuru*. Freedom. Oddly enough it reminded him of Lord Bowley, relaxing on the verandah after a hard day, with a glass in his hand, talking about Ireland. 'Freedom,' Lord Bowley had spat the word out, 'De Valera's won them freedom all right, freedom to starve.'

Strange, he thought, for something said then to ring so familiar now.

'Bloody Kenyatta. Should be thrown out of Kenya, or better still strung up.' Standish finished his drink and shouted, '*Boy!* Let's have the same again. Then I'm off back to Columns. I hate Nairobi. The sight of all these bloody Asians getting rich from the tourists makes me throw up.'

It was that very evening that Mark asked Ziggy about Kenyatta – 'This Kenya Africa Union of his – is it anything to worry about?'

She raised her eyebrows and looked at him. 'Yes Mark, I'm afraid *Uhuru* might be. As a matter of fact I'm glad we're without company tonight, there's something I want to talk about.'

Mark had been in Kenya exactly three weeks. Of course he missed Kate but his days had been full and busy – often dinner guests at Cutters stayed overnight, the time had passed amazingly quickly. And, he had to admit, he did *like* Kenya, and he did like Ziggy. Their relationship was different now. He was no longer negotiating with her and that was a relief in itself. Besides, with Kate so fresh in his memory, he was no longer curious about Ziggy in bed. Odd, how she had grown on him. He no longer thought her nose overlarge, or her jaw too square. When he looked at her he just saw Ziggy – and he liked what he saw, *liked* as different from lusted after – *liked* as in respected and, as he had to admit, *liked* as in fond affection.

Of course her shrewd directness still threw him at times. Even the day he arrived, when she met him at Eastleigh, her eyes had twinkled – 'You look tired, Mark, I hope this young ward of yours isn't wearing you out.'

But her smile had been warm. He knew she was pleased to see him – just as, no matter that he missed Kate, he had felt strangely pleased to see her.

So without the worry of trying to out-think her, he relaxed and Ziggy met him half way. Even staying at Cutters was different. Last year Ziggy's guard had been up. All the guests had been white – they were this time too in

619

the main, mostly neighbouring farmers. Mark met again many of the men who had sat down at the farewell dinner a year before – 'Ziggy's political party' as he dubbed them privately. But one evening he had sat down to dinner with an Indian – Ziggy's partner from Mombasa. Nobody else was there, but from the man's familiar nod to the house-boys he had obviously been to Cutters before. His manners were so perfect that Mark had no cause for complaint – though he did go to bed wondering why Ziggy had to do business with such people. But she had thanked him the next morning. 'You were very courteous to Motilal last night. That was nice of you, I'm grateful.' No more was said, yet Mark had the distinct impression of passing some kind of test.

All this and more Mark Averdale knew when he asked her about Jomo Kenyatta – but he had no way of knowing that their talk would shock him so deeply.

'*Uhuru*,' she said, 'is the wrong idea in the wrong place at the wrong time. Nobody's ready for it. The Governor talks of several more generations of Africans being needed before they can run Kenya. Well he's wrong. And Kenyatta talks of *Uhuru* now, or tomorrow at the latest, and he's wrong too. I've told them both but –'

'*Both?* Kenyatta? You've met him?'

'He's been here. He's had dinner here. Twice as a matter of fact.'

'Good Lord!'

Mark was shaken to the core – but unable to stifle a shiver of admiration. Standish and the others at the club cursed Kenyatta's black hide – meanwhile Ziggy actually had the man to dinner.

Her hands swept outwards to embrace the verandah and the gardens beyond. 'You forget. This is my home. Whatever happens I want to know about it. My roots are down deep,' she smiled, 'I'm not ninth generation of anything very important, but I understand how you feel about Brackenburn.'

His heart went out to her. He might have reached for her hand but feared the gesture might be misinterpreted. As it was he was curiously moved. 'Kenyatta,' he said gruffly, 'what's he like?'

'Easily offended.' Her smile widened. 'I told him, black skin or no black skin, Kenya needs me as much as it needs him. I don't think he liked it much.'

'He's a bloody trouble-maker. I'm surprised you allowed him in the house. Standish is all for stringing him up.'

'Yes,' she said dryly, 'Standish would be.'

But the real shocks were just beginning. She talked about *Uhuru* for a while. She was so convinced it was wrong – that it was totally unworkable and impracticable – that Mark relaxed. He thought they were in agreement.

'Don't misunderstand,' she said, reading his expression. 'I said it's wrong, not it won't happen. The persecution of Jews in Germany was wrong but it happened. I know –'

'But what can happen *here*? You don't mean some sort of rising? Good God; the army would be out in no time flat –'

'And then what? Concentration camps? Wogs instead of Jews?'

'Oh for heaven's sake! That's preposterous –'

'You don't vote for Fascism. You wake up one morning and it's there. You mentioned Standish just now – his sort wouldn't stop at one man, they'd string Africans up by the hundred –'

'Well if it's an *uprising*. Dammit, what else can you expect –'

'Not that!' Her face was flushed and suddenly angry. She took a deep breath. 'Sorry. I'm explaining myself badly. Look, you know my views about partnerships – well what Kenya needs is all sorts of partnerships, multi-racial partnerships – and unless we get them the country is doomed.'

After that she talked for an hour, almost non-stop, waving aside his interruptions – driving on to make point after point.

'Don't you see,' she said again and again, 'it's a positive answer to *Uhuru* – unlike the Governor's complacency – and what's more it's the *right* thing to do. The Africans must be given a stake, a worthwhile stake – and we must recognize those poor devils in the Indian community. They're despised by the Europeans and resented by the Africans, yet Kenya couldn't operate without them.

Practically all wholesale and retail trade is in their hands, they provide the skilled workers, electricians, plumbers, clerks –'

'Your ideas go too far. They really won't work –'

'They're the only ideas that *will*! Don't you see – it's this or nothing for the whites. I live here. Africa is like a volcano right now. It's not just the Gold Coast or the Congo – it's everywhere, under the surface, about to erupt – and it will erupt if it's left to men like Standish on one hand, and . . . and to some of the African politicians, who want no more than to be Bwanas themselves, with white men's houses and white men's cars and white men's women!'

The more she talked the more her ideas sounded like a sell-out to Mark – and he said so. 'In Ulster we have a tradition, No Surrender –'

'This is not Ulster and I am not surrendering. No one will shift me from Kenya – it's my home and I'm staying – but I'll give others a bit more in order to live happily with my fellow man – and with my conscience –'

'Wogs aren't *fellow men*! Good God, you talk as if they're rational human beings. They're shiftless and idle, they steal anything not nailed down, they get drunk every chance they get –'

'Have you *seen* the Bowley estates? Who d'you think did that? Tatz by himself?'

Their discussion became heated at times. Ziggy chain-smoked through a pack of cigarettes, Mark drank far more than normal, and their tentative friendship threatened to disintegrate.

But after a dinner which neither of them really ate, they took coffee on the verandah as usual and gradually the tension eased – enough for Mark to say in a placatory voice, 'Well you're on the spot, of course. Your intelligence service has always been first-class – but don't you think you're exaggerating? Listening to you one could almost believe there was some danger. Nobody thinks that – not here in Kenya.'

She smiled rather sadly. 'I grew up in a Jewish household in Germany during the thirties. It taught me to read the signs early.'

'Kenya's a long way from Germany.'

'Is it? It seems increasingly similar to me. There's a very large number of dispossessed, people with nothing, virtually no possessions of any kind who are prey to any glib-tongued agitator who comes along. How do you think Hitler rose to power?'

'Now steady on. That couldn't happen here. It's British territory for a start—'

'And what happens if the British pull out?'

'Out of Africa? You can't be serious. Ziggy, we're not just talking about Kenya . . . for God's sake, there's Egypt, the Sudan, Somaliland, Zanzibar, Uganda, the Rhodesias . . . dammit need I go on? Africa *is* British, at least for the most part. For heaven's sake, some of your ideas . . . I mean really . . . and as for Kenya, well it's just getting off the ground.'

She smiled, 'So is the African.'

He went to bed shortly after – feeling bemused by the whole business. Some of Ziggy's ideas baffled him. He sat on his bed for a while, looking at Kate's photographs and missing her. Then he sighed and turned out the light. But Ziggy's arguments were still buzzing round in his head. Sleep eluded him. He tried for an hour and then gave up. He lit a cigarette and stood at the window smoking – and then he saw her. Suddenly he saw Ziggy's lemon frock deep in the gardens, at least forty yards from the house. He peered into the darkness. It *was* Ziggy – with a white cape wrapped round her shoulders against the chill – walking slowly along the path to the rose garden.

The grounds at Cutters were one of its best features – Ziggy was immensely proud of her gardens – full of great purple jacarandas, ringed by figs and cedars, mottled thorn acacias – and roses. Watering the roses took precedence over everything – guests could be told there was only enough water for a wash, not a bath; cattle could bellow for thirst – but the roses were watered first thing every morning.

She disappeared from his line of vision. He shivered at the window. He wondered if she was meeting someone? The idea was extraordinary, but seeing her like that was extraordinary. But then, twenty minutes later, she returned, walking slowly up to the house. She was quite alone.

He hardly saw her the next day. She went into Nairobi for various meetings and he took himself off to the Bowley estates for a session with Tatz. And that night some more of 'Ziggy's private political party' came to dinner, so there was little private conversation between them.

Perhaps it was the way some of the guests hung on Ziggy's every word which sent Mark to bed in a thoughtful mood – but when he reached his room he started to analyse her various alliances. The smaller farmers seemed to gravitate to her. And she had a better relationship with the Wogs than anyone in Kenya. Then there were these partnerships with various Indian traders – not just in Kenya but Uganda as well. She even had access to the Governor these days . . . and if Kenyatta had visited Cutters how many other black politicians had sat down to dinner? Her network of connections was really enormous. She had spun a web round herself – Mark was part of it too in a way – she had taken his name and nationality, she had encouraged him to become more active at Westminster . . .

Such thoughts kept him awake for so long that eventually, like the night before, he got up for a cigarette. Then he saw her again, in the gardens – coming back this time, walking up to the house from the rose garden, and just as alone as the night before.

He began to wonder – there were guests staying that night – she *could* be on her way back from one of their rooms.

He was shocked, and then angry. Good God, if he had to abstain she could at least do the same. *And* she had given him her word!

His agitation brought all sorts of things to his mind. He remembered Standish calling her husband a German spy. *Had* the man been a spy? Mark had never really thought about it . . .

With one thing and another he had such a restless night that he overslept in the morning. By the time he was up Ziggy had left the house, for the first of her meetings – but she left word to expect her for lunch. He had no plans of his own so he sat around reading the papers and having a few drinks, and – without knowing why – getting more irritable by the minute. Then, at precisely twelve-thirty, her Buick swept up the drive, driven by the Indian as usual, to set her down at the foot of the steps.

She smiled as she came to join him. She wore her usual working-rig of high-necked shirt, long skirt, and riding boots. Her manner was as confident as ever, and although he was accustomed to it he was in such a scratchy mood that he suddenly saw red. 'I think you owe me an explanation,' he snapped.

'Oh?' She sat down, a puzzled, almost hurt look on her face.

He could have bitten his tongue. He wanted to ask what she was doing, creeping around the grounds in the middle of the night – but if he said that it would look as if he was spying.

'What about?' she asked, her gaze firmly fixed on his face.

So he plunged into the other subject which had kept him awake. 'You're getting too involved in politics. All these contacts of yours. I think you're planning some political involvement behind my back. Something like that could be highly embarrassing to me at Westminster.'

Her face seemed to glow slightly, but her skin was too tanned to tell if she blushed – even if she had he would not have known if she blushed from embarrassment or guilt. She did not seem put out, in fact she actually smiled. 'Churchill says everyone in Nairobi is a politician and most of them are leaders of their own parties. But I'm glad you've raised politics – I don't think we finished what we started the other night.'

After which they talked politics for almost three hours. She was very direct, 'I no more believe that the sun will never set on the British Empire than I thought the Third Reich would last a thousand years.' She was not anti-British. 'After all,' she smiled, 'I really *am* a British Lady now, aren't I?' But the Africans had to be given a better deal – 'The white man destroyed a way of life and put nothing in its place. We must either give now or see the whole lot taken away from us. The choice is ours. We can

625

live out our lives in peace here if we help the African, if we teach him scientific farming and modern management – most of all if we give him a *stake*. I'll tell you this, Mark, if Kenya had a middle-class of twenty thousand Africans some of these black politicians would be laughed right out of the country. But as things are the extremists are having a field day sowing the seeds of racial hatred. I've no interest in becoming directly involved in politics, I'm busy enough as it is, but if those seeds take root we shall *all* be involved.'

He disagreed with much of what she said, and told her so, but before the discussion ended she said two things that stayed in his mind – the first because he agreed with it, and the second because it reinforced the affection growing between them.

'Kenya faces two dangers,' she said, 'an African uprising, and I'll do everything I can to stop that – but the other danger is just as great – that some fool Colonial Secretary at Westminster will be stampeded into granting self-rule before the country is ready for it.'

She reached out and put a hand on his arm. 'Both of those dangers threaten our interests. Yours and mine. We're partners, Mark, our futures are bound together. I'll do everything I can here, and I *know* you'll do everything possible in London.'

It was a pledge, an extension of their 'business arrangement', although neither said so in as many words.

Then she said, 'Being Lady Averdale has been very good for me. It's helped a lot this past year. I know I've only got a lease on the name but I shall honour it as long as I use it. Don't worry – I'll try not to cause you embarrassment at Westminster, or anywhere else for that matter.'

Just at that moment a car started up the drive.

'Oh?' Ziggy gave a start of surprise. 'Is that the time? I'm sorry but it's Motilal arriving for a meeting. You stay here, I'll take him down to the office.'

Which she did.

Mark sat thinking after that. He was no longer irritable. The air had been cleared. He felt reassured, and warmly grateful for her comments about the Averdale name. So he relaxed and yawned drowsily. He wondered about going to his room for a nap, but if he slept in the afternoon he would stay awake half the night . . . so instead he went for a stroll in the grounds.

Perhaps he *did* go to the rose garden deliberately. Afterwards he could never be sure – but within ten minutes he found himself on the same path Ziggy had used the previous night. And moments later – at the far end of the rose garden, out of sight of the house – he came across what he thought might be decribed as an arbour. It was a cul-de-sac of lush lawn, flanked by rose bushes, at the far end of which was a single headstone. He read the simple inscription.

Otto Beck
1880–1943

Arranged over the grave were masses of freshly cut roses.

He felt guilty being there. It was a private place. He was a trespasser. For the only time in his life, Mark Averdale felt humble. He hurried away, anxious not to be seen. Yet it had given him a fresh insight into Ziggy Beck – and she was Ziggy *Beck*, the gravestone proved it – she would be Ziggy Beck until the day she died. He breathed a sigh of relief – glad now that he had not tried to demand his conjugal rights. He never would now, he was certain of that.

The last few days flashed by, nothing of importance happened – but one incident occurred which later was seen as a straw in the wind. Paddy Buckland, a farmer from the other side of Nairobi, reported that some of his cattle had been mutilated – 'Thirty animals, hacked about something rotten. I had to slaughter the lot. Some bloody Wog secret society – called Mau Mau or something like that.'

And Ziggy Beck had looked truly worried.

The day before Mark left he went shopping in Nairobi for presents for Kate and, almost to his surprise, bought a very handsome gift for Ziggy as well – a fine jade carving which now looked rather splendid above the fireplace at Cutters.

They parted the firmest of friends. When he kissed her goodbye at the airport he said quite sincerely, 'Take care of yourself, Ziggy, I'll see you in six months.'

She grinned, 'We have a tradition in Kenya – No

627

Surrender. You tell them that at Westminster, from me '

So, for the second time in his life, Mark Averdale left Kenya with a cheque for eighty thousand pounds in his pocket. He was delighted to be on his way back to Kate, but as he waved from the aircraft window he felt a sudden surge of emotion for the stocky, fair-haired woman who waved back.

Ziggy Beck and Kate O'Brien were catalysts of change in Mark Averdale. A stranger *ménage à trois* never existed . . . but there is no doubt it worked and wrought changes in Mark. Who changed him most is impossible to say, both women influenced him, in fact someone said that both women *civilized* him. But as Mark flew back to London he was determined to protect his interests in Kenya . . . his land, his eighty thousand a year, and the woman who now bore the title of Lady Averdale.

As for Kate, her poised confidence really blossomed in the second year. She moved into the completed apartment at Belgrave Square, and if the staff in that huge house ever had their nights disturbed by the mysterious whine of an elevator, they had discretion enough to turn a deaf ear.

Mark Averdale took her on buying trips to the galleries of Rome and Paris, where she again visited her beloved Yvette, and on holiday to Marrakech, which she thought was the dreamiest place in the world. And when, after five months, Mark returned to Kenya again, Tim came over from Ulster to spend the entire four weeks as her companion in London.

It was when Mark returned from his second visit to Kenya that he formed the 'Britain in Africa' movement.

'People must be told what's at stake,' he said to Kate. 'British influence is being undermined right across Africa. God Almighty, the place will go communist if we're not careful. I expect this Labour Government to be hopeless but even some Tories have taken leave of their senses. And as for the Americans . . . they're supposed to be allies but all they do is winge on at the United Nations about democracy in Africa . . . as if that means the first thing to some bloody Wog fresh down from the trees . . .'

From then on Mark's political activities increased – and

Kate's involvement increased with it. She played hostess at luncheon parties which Mark gave for politicians . . . and at least three times a month she circulated at cocktail parties for Empire Loyalists and kindred spirits. But she did more than add decoration, although she obviously did that. Kate and Ziggy between them cobbled together many of the arguments which won Lord Averdale fame at Westminster. It was Ziggy who forwarded facts and figures for Kate to work into speeches and parliamentary questions. And it was Kate who finally persuaded Mark to stop calling Africans Wogs – 'You really must stop using that expression, darling, even to me. If you make it a habit to say African, then, even when you get heated, it will come out as African and not –'

'Bloody Wog,' he grinned.

'They are your partners in Africa,' Kate said firmly.

'Rubbish. Ziggy Beck is my partner and she's as white as I am.'

'And Ziggy *never* calls them Wogs.'

'No,' he admitted, 'but she's about the only person in Kenya who doesn't.'

Kate knew that was true from first-hand contact with Kenyans visiting London. Increasingly Mark's Belgrave Square mansion was becoming Campaign Headquarters for white settlers visiting the capital; first they called at the Colonial Office, then they descended on Mark. Kate spent days entertaining them, showing them the sights and shepherding them round town like a schoolmistress with a crocodile of boisterous pupils. Which is how she felt at times, despite the fact that they were all older than her. She was invariably the only woman and finding things to interest a dozen horny-handed settlers was a constant headache. 'Culture vultures we ain't,' one admitted early one morning, 'I mean all those paintings of Lord Averdale's, well if you've seen one you've seen 'em all, haven't you?' Kate accepted the challenge. She took them to the National and showed them Leonardo's *Virgin on the Rocks*, only to be told that the blue rocks in the background could have been done by a pavement artist. She showed Hals and Gainsborough and Rubens for brushwork, and Chadin for design, and Cosimo Tura for drawing, and the wonderful depth of colour in Titian's *Noli me Tangere*. She amazed herself at the extent of her knowledge – and was gratified by their response – heads nodded, eyes narrowed, arms were crossed in poses of concentration – then she realized they were looking at *her*. 'You're right, Kate,' one man said, glancing at his watch, 'but the most beautiful thing here is about to join us in the pub for a drink.'

She gave up. After that the nearest they got to *culture* was the waxworks at Madame Tussauds, to which Kate had been taken as a child by Rose Smith. But the most popular excursions of all were days at the races, and whenever Kate was forewarned of a pending visit she prayed for fine weather and a meeting at Kempton.

Overall though, she liked them. Most were hard-working farmers who cared passionately for Kenya. 'Hell Kate, we built the country. Without us it would be a dustbowl. Yet to listen to some of the bleeding hearts in London you'd think we never do a day's work. According to them all we do is sit on a tall horse and oversee our lush acres. Good Christ, my old man started in Kenya before the war. He bent his back from morning to midnight. My mother had us kids like a Kikuyu woman. She delivered my brother herself and helped two cows calve the same day. We won that land fair and square, Kate, and we won it by the sweat of our brow – not by beating Wogs half to death. Heck, once upon a time Britain was *proud* of her Colonies – now we're looked on as cut-throats and bandits.'

They were bitterly resentful of attitudes at the Colonial Office. Lord Averdale had become their champion. They would even miss a day at the races to hear him speak in the Lords – 'By God, Kate, didn't he give them stick! He was marvellous. I can't wait to tell them back in Nairobi.'

They were so proud of him, and so grateful. Their feelings spilled over on to Kate, for they never left without giving her a present – 'It's not much Kate, but it's in appreciation of all the work you do for us – and for being so nice.'

So Kate found herself with an ever widening circle of friends. She felt wanted and needed, even important at times – and she loved it. Certainly she was forever trying to help. For instance Mark Averdale was effective at

Westminster, but clumsily inept with the press. One day she heard him berating a journalist from *The Times* – 'Your entire article was a pack of lies from start to finish. Did you make it all up? There wasn't one supportable fact . . .'

Afterwards Kate said, 'Darling, you frightened that poor man to death –'

'He got everything wrong –'

'I know, but he's *still* got it wrong. Shouldn't we try to get him on our side, persuade him to print the facts as we see them –'

'Pariahs! That's all they are. Blasted reporters are the bane of my life.'

After that Kate dealt with reporters – one at a time to begin with. If someone telephoned or called round for an interview, Kate was suddenly 'available' with a typed summary, based on information received from Ziggy. But the situation quickly developed. Once journalists realized they had access to Kate they guarded her jealously. Excuses were made to consult her more often. News was rarely bent, but Kate was invariably given the benefit of the doubt if one existed.

Kate O'Brien was becoming very poised indeed. Raymond styled her hair, Digby Morton designed her clothes, she bought her scent in Paris and her shoes in Rome. If she took it for granted it was only because she knew it was expected of her – Mark wanted her to look her best, he liked her in pretty clothes, even if he liked her out of them more.

She quickly adjusted to the company of men – she had no choice, ninety per cent of the people she met *were* men. Of course a few artists were women, but not many – a few politicians were women, but less than one in fifty – the rest were all men, farmers from Kenya, journalists from Fleet Street, the ministers and under-secretaries from Westminster. It was a man's world.

It was a man's world in Kenya too, a *white man*'s world – and black men were beginning to resent it. There were sporadic outbreaks of violence – crops were burned, cattle were mutilated by gangs who struck in the night. Farmers agitated for greater protection from the police, and the

631

whispers about Mau Mau grew louder. The boom days of Kenya seemed over – farming was limping to a standstill, native workers were either running off into the mountains to join the Mau Mau, or so terrorized by the Mau Mau that they were too frightened to work. Even the professional hunters were suffering, potential clients reading newspapers in New York or London were cancelling safaris left, right and centre . . .

As Mark Averdale made his regular visits he noted the changes. The word *Uhuru* was on everyone's lips. It leapt out from every newspaper. It dominated every conversation. It seemed everywhere, except Cutters Lodge and the Bowley estates – where the big word was *partnership*.

Ziggy was racing against time. In 1951 she launched her most ambitious project. Every family in her employ was given ten acres of land – five they farmed how they pleased, with maize and potatoes, but the remaining five acres were farmed under Ziggy's supervision. While the men laboured at Cutters or on the Bowley estates their families – wives, daughters, all sorts of relatives – tended and weeded, watered and looked after Ziggy's five acres. 'We get the first crop,' she told Mark, 'which is mostly coffee as you can see. In exchange, *when* we get the crop, that's in three years, we hand over title to that patch of land. We're giving the African a *stake*, Mark, a stake in Kenya – and by God it's going to work.'

Not everyone thought so. Standish laughed himself sick. 'You'd think she was dealing with a bunch of clerks in a London suburb. Christ, this is Kenya! And Wogs are Wogs – idle, thieving, dirty, drunken, sacrifice-loving, witch-doctor-dominated Wogs!'

The Governor was uncertain about the whole scheme. 'He said it could create an unfortunate precedent,' Ziggy smiled, 'other big farmers might feel obliged to follow my example.'

'And you said?'

'I hoped he was right.'

Ziggy was planning another step forward. 'I'm going to build a model housing settlement. Look, here are the plans. You see, three-roomed cottages, metal roofs, and central bore holes that will save the women hours of carrying water. Motilal's even working on an irrigation scheme which will feed waste water back to the crops –'

'Motilal?'

'Motilal Gungi, my partner in Mombasa. You met him, remember? His Indian construction outfit is going to build it. Cost price, no profit – as his contribution to a multi-racial society.'

Mark was in Kenya in October when the news came through of a change of government at Westminster. The Conservatives had been returned to office. 'Well that's a relief,' Mark said, 'the Empire is safe with Winston back at Number Ten.'

'I don't know about that,' Ziggy said, 'but Kenya is safe as long as Lord Averdale is at Westminster. You're famous out here now, do you know that?'

It was true. Wherever Mark went in Nairobi men shook his hand for championing their cause at Westminster. His popularity with the settlers deflected some criticism away from Lady Averdale's more 'revolutionary schemes' – while in turn her popularity with the Africans overflowed on to him. Between them Lord and Lady Averdale were becoming the most talked about people in Kenya.

'You know,' he said as she drove him out to Eastleigh to put him once more on the London-bound plane, 'I never dreamt our "business arrangement" would work out like this.'

'You mean you're spending more time on Kenya than you imagined?'

'Well yes, that's true . . . but I didn't mean that.'

'Oh?' She threw him a quick sideways glance, her eyes twinkling. 'You're not still sore about the clauses in fine print?'

He knew what she meant. He hesitated, then said, 'Not since I walked in your rose garden one day.'

She caught her breath. 'Oh, you know about that.'

They fell silent for a moment, then she said, 'He was a very fine man, Mark.'

'He must have been. He was married to a very fine lady.'

He could have sworn there were tears in her eyes, but he must have been mistaken because a moment later she chuckled – 'Any more compliments like that and we'll actually be flirting. I'll have to look up our contract – I'm sure there's a clause somewhere to put a stop to that sort of thing.'

But when they hugged goodbye they embraced for longer than usual.

'Next year is the big year, Mark,' she said. 'If we can survive 1952 Kenya will be on the rails again – and running in the right direction too.'

He kissed her cheek. 'No Surrender.'

'That's right,' she smiled, 'you tell 'em that at Westminster, from me.'

For the first time in three years, Mark Averdale felt the tiniest twinge of regret as he boarded the aircraft. Of course he was anxious to get home to Kate – his delicious, desirable, wonderful Kate – but his visit had flown this time. So much was happening, so quickly. Next year he would try to get out *three* times, not just twice – make it every four months. He waved through the window to Ziggy. Next year was the big year, she had said – and he had never known her to be wrong. He sighed as he settled into his seat – if Kenya settled down again the future looked better and better. Really, he thought, he had plenty to be happy about.

And Kate was happy too. Sometimes she compared her situation with Jenny's, with whom she still corresponded. Mrs Jennifer Clayton Wells now lived on a USAAF base in Omaha – '*And guess what, I'm pregnant again. Thank heavens everyone is thrilled this time, not like when we had Scott. Clayton even stayed smiling when I told him Ma would come down and stay for the last month. I already told her if it's a girl we shall call her Kate after you. "Why Jenny," she said, "what a lovely idea." She really does think of you as her OTHER daughter, no matter what happened. I'm glad you and she write to each other now. The truth is she's ashamed of the way she behaved at Glossops that time and can't quite admit it. She does worry about you. Only the other day she said – "I hope Kate doesn't waste the best years of her life looking after that Lord Averdale. She should be out enjoying herself, not nursing an old man. After all, she*

634

*is twenty now. It's time she was thinking of getting married."
That's what she said Kate, which is a cowardly way of saying
I'm concerned too. I don't mean to pry (liar) but you never
mention any men in your letters??? Believe me there are
some things in life a girl's got to do – and as Clayton says
"marrying and raising a family beats the hell out of most of
them." I'm so glad now we had Scott when we did. Clayton
says "We didn't start a family too early, we just got married
a mite late." He's always saying things like that. We want
two more after this baby and all before I'm twenty-five. That
way we'll be young enough to enjoy them. As Clayton says
"The family that plays together stays together . . ."'*

Kate read the latest letter and sat for a while studying a
photograph of a very chubby Jenny bouncing Scott on her
knee while an adoring Clayton looked over her shoulder.
They certainly looked happy. Kate was glad, but not
envious. She flicked through the rest of the photographs.
Jenny's clothes were awful. And from what could be seen
the furnishings of their little house were in terrible taste.

Imagine Aunt Alison being called *Ma*. Ma and Pa
Johnstone, as no doubt Clayton would say. Miss Jenkins at
Glossops would positively shudder. Kate giggled . . .
'nursing an old man' indeed. Mark would be furious. She
looked again at the photographs. She had to admit that
Clayton was younger than Mark, in fact he looked younger
than any man she knew – he was a *boy*, not a man.

She shrugged. 'Everyone to their own taste. Clayton is
certainly not mine – and his witty little sayings would drive
me round the bend.'

She put the letter and photographs aside and reached for
the morning papers. But as she glanced at the headlines her
mind was still on Jenny and Clayton Wells. The phrase
'everyone to their own taste' repeated in her mind. Clayton
must be to Jenny's taste, otherwise she wouldn't have
chosen him, but did girls really choose, or did men do the
choosing? She wondered . . . especially about Jenny.

As she turned a page, her eye fell on a face she
recognized. From years ago. It was the ski-instructor for
whom she and Jenny had competed in Switzerland. How
amazing. But as she read the caption she realized she was
wrong.

New York welcomes London newspaperman.
Sean Connors arrives aboard the Queen . . .

Sean Connors? How odd, she had listened to his broadcasts as a child during the war. Goodness, how many times had she heard his announcement – 'This is Sean Connors speaking to you from the heart of Great Britain . . .' They had all listened together – Aunt Alison and Yvette, often misty-eyed, and her and Jenny. Week after week.

Kate held the paper at full-length, squinting slightly to look at the photograph. He was so like that ski-instructor. 'Well Jenny my love,' she mused, 'you certainly had better taste then. No girl could be blamed for choosing someone like that.'

CHAPTER SEVEN

New York! From the moment the *Queen Elizabeth* docked Sean was overwhelmed. He had written to Freddie, and to CBS, and to his agents – making appointments, fixing meetings, planning a schedule – but he had forgotten the great American public. *Seven Days in London* was a thing of the past. The Second World War had been over six years. The world had changed – but Sean's vast wartime listening audience lived on . . . and their welcome astonished him.

Freddie and CBS organized it – or rather originated it, for once the news spread the welcome was hardly 'organized'. It was pandemonium. Every reporter in New York wanted an interview. Microphones were Sean's business but he had never seen so many. Cunard served an ocean of champagne, the party on board lasted three hours – Sean was hoarse from answering questions. His right hand was bruised from being shaken. His back was sore from being slapped. His face ached from smiling into cameras. But most of all, once he had recovered from his vast surprise, he was deeply touched. The welcome brought a lump to his throat.

Hours later (Sean lost sense of time) he found himself with Freddie and Margaret in their New York apartment. They had seen each other throughout that tumultuous day – had hugged and kissed each other hello – but not until late that night were the three of them alone.

Sean slumped, with a glass in his hand and a dazed look on his face. 'I can't believe it. All those marvellous people. Hell, anyone would think I *won* the war. Besides it was all so long ago . . .'

Freddie and Margaret embraced each other, delighted with the entire day. Freddie chuckled gleefully, 'Didn't I always say you had a lot of friends over here?'

Freddie had grown plump, not gross but certainly corpulent – and his hairline had retreated over his scalp. Sean had to make an effort to remember the dapper, brown-haired figure who had stepped into the path of that London taxi all those years before. But Margaret was as lovely as ever – delicate, beautiful and very assured.

They talked for hours – still high on champagne and excitement. Each kept interrupting with – 'Do you remember when . . .'

The room overflowed with laughter and love.

Before Margaret went to bed she made a little speech – 'I'm going to say this once and never again. It's my turn to apologize for all the time we lost, I should have *made* Freddie see sense. But you were always in our hearts, Sean, and now you're here . . . well we're never going to lose you again.'

Then she kissed him goodnight while Freddie sat beaming and nodding his head.

It was more than just Margaret – the whole of New York took to Sean. Cab drivers stared into their mirrors – 'Say buddy, ain't you Sean Connors the broadcaster? Well how about that? It's a pleasure to meet you.'

People stopped him on the sidewalk and waylaid him in elevators – 'Oh brother, I wanna tell you, some of your shows in the war were just something' – and – 'Are you making your career in New York now?' – and – 'Now you let me know if I can do anything for you.'

He was on every chat show and in every newspaper.

Then, after about ten days, it stopped.

Margaret chuckled, 'That's New York. Everyone's said hello – now they figure it's up to you.'

Sean had so many initial impressions. Prosperity, the abundance of food, crowded, well stocked shops, the absence of queues. Freddie took him everywhere and was delighted with his reaction. 'I tell you Sean, old buddy, you should appoint me guide to all the great cities. London in '38, New York now – stick with me pal, I'll show you the world.'

Freddie and Margaret enjoyed themselves hugely. Freddie still behaved towards Margaret as he had in the old days. He fussed over her constantly. 'You want the truth,' he said to Sean one night when she had gone to bed, 'we've been married eleven years, we've got three wonderful kids, and I still can't believe my luck. It's the original fairy story. I'm the stable boy who married a princess. I'm scared to death that one day she'll find out I'm not the prince.'

It was useless to tell him he had been Margaret's prince since before Dunkirk.

Then, on the twelfth day of Sean's visit, Ambassador Kennedy telephoned.

Sean was delighted to hear from him – even though Freddie's dislike of Kennedy was as strong as ever. 'He hasn't changed. He still chases every blonde in town.'

Sean found it hard to blame the Ambassador for that. American women gave Sean his biggest surprise. They were so beautiful, at least those who dined at the Mallons' were. Freddie's friends all seemed to have married film stars. Most were mothers of families, but none looked older than twenty-five. The men showed their age, yet their wives were stunning. American women seemed to have discovered the elixir of youth – no wonder Ambassador Kennedy still chased them.

In fact American womanhood threatened Sean's self-confidence. Interviewing actresses in London was one thing, that was his ground and he asked the questions – for half a dozen beauties to quiz him over dinner every night was a different matter entirely. But he survived, helped by Freddie and Margaret – he even became accustomed to

Margaret inviting an unattached girl as his dinner companion when she gave her little parties. Which is how he met Gloria Farrell from Boston.

Gloria was a journalist who wrote about homes and gardens for one of Freddie's magazines. She was petite, blonde, blue-eyed, pert-nosed and easy to look at. Quick, lively, third generation Irish-American, Catholic and proud of it. She was also something else – Margaret's best hope of rescuing Sean from bachelorhood which she considered to be a miserable state. His description of life in London appalled her – sharing an apartment with two other men, working all round the clock, never going to parties or the theatre – 'But don't you have any friends?' she had asked.

'Hundreds,' Sean grinned.

But there was no *woman* in his life.

Gloria was the third single girl invited to the Mallons' for dinner, and since she and Sean got on so well together Margaret ceased to cast her net wider – in fact she took her strategy a step further – 'Sean, I feel awful about this but I can't take you sightseeing tomorrow. I'm terribly sorry. But I spoke with Gloria. She's working out the most fantastic programme. She'll collect you at nine-thirty in the morning.'

Sean was too bemused to suspect an ulterior motive. American hospitality was overwhelming, people were queuing up to entertain him – if someone dropped out half a dozen others were ready to fill the breach.

So amid a welter of impressions, another sensation seeped into Sean's bloodstream – the almost forgotten pleasure of being in the close company of a good-looking woman – and he liked it. The pace of life in New York was supposedly faster than in London, but not for Sean. He would have worked much harder in London, but as a guest of the Mallons he lived life as they lived it – and if that included candle-lit suppers and entertaining small talk, there was little he could do about it. He adjusted. He began to enjoy himself – for the first time in years he allowed himself the pleasure of admiring slender ankles, plunging necklines and sparkling eyes. He relaxed and found it was fun.

Gloria was certainly fun. They lunched together whenever their schedules permitted. They met two evenings a week, often at Margaret's dinner table, but sometimes Sean and Gloria took Freddie and Margaret out for an evening. By the end of eight weeks when Sean appeared around town people automatically expected to see Gloria on his arm. They were fast becoming 'a couple'.

But, irrespective of what happened in the evenings, Sean's work schedule was crowded, most days were crammed with business meetings – so much so that after consulting their calendars he and Ambassador Kennedy found they had time only to meet each other for lunch.

'It's been a heck of a long time,' said the Ambassador, 'but I'm delighted you finally made it.'

Sean still liked him. Despite Freddie and Margaret, despite the grapevine gossip, there was something about Joe Kennedy that reached out to Sean. 'He is so like the Da,' Sean thought as he listened to a glowing account of Jack's political career – 'he's so proud of his son, so determined to help him every step of the way – the Da would have been like that with me.'

When they parted the Ambassador chuckled, 'We must have a night out before you go home. I know all the right places,' he winked, 'a young man like you needs some fun.'

But Sean was having fun already, and he had met Gloria by then.

At the end of ten weeks Sean's business in New York was complete. He had negotiated UK screening rights to all the American television material he needed – more than one channel could handle in fact. Sean formed another company whose function was to sell material to *every* channel in the UK – and also to buy rights in British-made programmes for sale in the States. Like the Mallon Property Company it started as a sideline but, by the early seventies, it was earning a fortune.

Throughout his visit he had telephoned London every week. All was well. Tubby was on top of things in the property company, Michael O'Hara was running London & Continental with smooth efficiency – Sean could stay a little longer if he liked.

Freddie persuaded him. The old bond had re-emerged

stronger than ever, besides they were doing so much business together that the most profitable part of Sean's trip was just beginning to surface. In a sense they merged their interests. Freddie was planning to launch a version of *Seven Days*, his main magazine, in Europe – 'Why don't we slot London & Continental News into that?' he said to Sean. 'Your boys provide the European coverage, my people give you the American news – between us we've got the whole package. Graft a marketing end on to Michael O'Hara's office in London and we're ready to go.'

The details were more complicated, but that was the principle – Freddie was saved the cost of setting up a London office, and Sean funnelled London & Continental News into The Seven Days Corporation for fifty per cent of the stock. Both Sean and Freddie withheld their other interests – in Freddie's case his specialist magazines, and in Sean's case his sixty per cent holding in the Mallon Property Company and Transatlantic Television, as he had named his new company. Michael O'Hara would be appointed Managing Editor of *Seven Days* for Europe, and Freddie's New York editor, Sam Gittins, would run the American end.

'A perfect marriage,' Margaret pronounced when they told her about it.

Sean and Freddie spent an exciting few days discussing the in-depth political analysis and profiles which the new *Seven Days* would provide – but Freddie wanted more . . .

'Africa,' he said, 'Sean, we must have our own men covering Africa. Have you seen the news-stands? *Time* magazine? Hardly a week goes by without Gichuru on the cover, or Tom Mboya, or . . . what's that guy . . . Kenyatta. I tell you, *Time*'s murdering me on their African coverage. Can you get say three of your boys out there . . . give me some really big spreads, photographs, interviews, you know, "The Emerging Giant" . . . "The Dying Days of the British Raj" . . . that sort of thing.'

The following morning Sean telephoned Michael in London and a week later Jimmy Cross, London & Continental's 'Africa desk' man, was on a flight to Nairobi with instructions to recruit more men when he got there.

Africa fascinated Freddie – 'It's not just me, *everyone's* fascinated. It's starting to dominate the UN. Africa will be where the big stories are in the fifties. I've been in the news business too long to doubt my own hunch.'

But Freddie was expanding on other fronts too. He was buying a number of newspapers across America – 'That's a separate corporation. You can come in if you like. After all, if we've got reporters round the world we need all the outlets we can get.'

So, two weeks after that, Sean set out across America – ostensibly to pay his respects to the many editors who had syndicated his column over the years, but also to conclude negotiations for the purchase of three newspapers whose owners had talked to Freddie in New York.

Wherever Sean went he was interviewed – by the papers themselves, by radio and television. Invariably he achieved a favourable reaction – but then came Chicago – and Chicago was a disaster which was to haunt him for years.

He should have known better. He was an experienced journalist – well used to the ways of the press. He was a successful businessman with an assured, easy manner. He was even a minor celebrity.

But in Chicago he took a mauling.

In fairness he was not feeling well. He had developed a streaming cold. To keep a clear head was impossible. He was running a temperature. It was an effort to stop shivering. And he had suffered a thoroughly bad day.

In New York Freddie had agreed terms on a paper, but when Sean arrived in Chicago a competitive bid was on the table. The asking price had been raised. Sean argued with the owners all morning. Then went back to his hotel to telephone Freddie. He sat on his bed drinking whisky and hot water for his cold, interrupting his conversation with explosive bouts of sneezing into an already sodden handkerchief.

Three more hours at the newspaper that afternoon failed to achieve agreement. Sean limped back to his hotel wanting nothing more than a warm bed and oblivion. He ached all over. His eyes streamed. He *should* have gone directly to bed – instead he worried about a radio interview arranged for six-fifteen. Sean was a journalist himself – he hated the thought of letting a fellow professional down. So he drank more whisky and hot water, rang down for a cab and arrived at the studio. He consoled himself with one thought – that in less than an hour he would be in bed.

But that was before the disaster.

Hugh McIlroy's interview was hostile from the opening question.

'Mr Connors, you first won fame during the war when you called upon Ireland to fight against Hitler. Do you think that was right?'

'It was right to fight Hitler –'

'But Ireland was neutral – a tiny country, poorly equipped – Ireland's involvement wouldn't have made a scrap of difference to the war.'

'If the Allies had been able to operate from Irish ports –'

'Weren't you calling your countrymen cowards?'

'Certainly not. Thousands of Irishmen fought in the British army –'

'Ah! The *good* Irish fought for the British, the *bad* stayed at home. Is that what you're saying?'

Sean was caught off-balance. It was stifling hot in the studio. His eyes were watering. His nose was all blocked-up.

'I'm not saying that. What I mean is –'

'That's how it sounded, Mr Connors. In fact haven't you consistently bad-mouthed your own countrymen? For instance, didn't you call the IRA the scum of the earth?'

Sean was totally unprepared. Other interviewers had asked about Dunkirk and the Blitz . . .

McIlroy opened a file. 'I have the exact quotation here if you'd like to refresh your memory.'

'I haven't *bad-mouthed* anyone –'

'But you did call the IRA the scum of the earth.'

'Well I may have . . . I mean yes . . . I know when you mean, in London, I was beaten up –'

'By the IRA?'

'Well not exactly, but *because* of the IRA –'

'According to the reports, you were beaten up by a gang of London dockers, East End thugs, who not only attacked you but half-killed some other Irish –'

'That's true, but –'

'But instead of blaming the Brits you called the IRA the scum of the earth? Isn't that an odd reaction? It looks like you were currying favour –'

'That's rubbish!' Sean snapped.

His face went dark red. Beads of sweat rose all over his forehead.

McIlroy shrugged. 'Mr Connors, does the name William Joyce mean anything to you?'

'Joyce?' Sean was muzzy-headed, taken aback. 'Joyce? You mean the writer –'

'That was *James* Joyce,' McIlroy smirked, 'every real Irishman knows that.'

Sean tried to clear his nose, but merely spluttered into his handkerchief. Sweat was soaking his shirt. The studio felt like an oven.

McIlroy hurried on, 'The Joyce I mean was better known as Lord Haw-Haw. He was a broadcaster, like yourself in a way, broadcasting from another country during the war, telling his countrymen how mistaken they were. The British called him a traitor and hung a noose round his neck. Weren't you called a traitor in Ireland –'

Sean was furious. 'Not by people whose opinion I respect.'

'You mean you don't respect those who disagree with you –'

'Not necessarily,' Sean glowered, 'but I'll make an exception in your case.'

McIlroy blinked.

Sean rejoiced to have scored a small point. He tried to calm his jangled nerves. He wished his head would clear. His temples throbbed, breathing was difficult. He had stumbled into a minefield but could escape if he kept cool . . . after all he had been in thousands of interviews, none as hostile, but experience would see him through . . .

All such resolutions were forgotten a moment later.

'During the war,' McIlroy persisted, 'you must have realized your patriotism would be called into doubt?'

Sean remembered agonizing over that decision, his bitter argument with Dinny, and his remorse afterwards . . .

He answered carefully, 'I was a reporter doing a job. Those were dark days in 1940 –'

'For the British Empire perhaps, but not for Ireland.'

In temper Sean blurted out, 'I doubt Ireland would be free today if Hitler had –'

'But Ireland is *not* free,' McIlroy pounced, 'the British still rule the north.'

Sean bit his tongue.

'Wasn't your father a famous Irish patriot?' McIlroy asked, shifting his ground.

'He was.'

'In fact he was an IRA hero –'

'He was.'

Sean's face was bone white. He looked sick. But his eyes should have warned McIlroy – his eyes were like chipped ice.

'Didn't your father fight in the Easter Rising? Wasn't he even in the GPO with Pearse and Connolly –'

'He was,' Sean snapped, at the end of his tether, 'times were different –'

'So different that you call the IRA the scum of the earth. Your own father? You condemned your country and your *own father –*'

'That's enough!' Sean snarled furiously. 'Leave my father out of this –'

'You were the one to call him the scum of the earth. I'm surprised –'

Sean's fist exploded on McIlroy's jaw. The microphone was knocked flying. Sean was on his feet, rushing at McIlroy. By the time sound-engineers dashed in from the control room Sean was boring after McIlroy. A swinging right crashed McIlroy against the far wall. Elsewhere in the building programme controllers killed the transmission – but not before listeners heard Sean's outraged rasp – 'You poisonous son of a bitch!'

Fifteen minutes later – still shaking with temper, shivering with cold, muzzy-headed and confused – Sean was ushered into a cab. Whisky on his breath led someone to claim he was drunk.

Back at the hotel he climbed into bed, wishing it was all a bad dream.

But the dream persisted through twelve hours of sleep. It was waiting when he awoke. A newspaper pushed under the door bore the headline – *Drunken Irish brawl heard by millions!*

He felt like death. Room service sent up coffee – with the rest of the papers and a list of phone messages. He groaned aloud. Even the New York papers carried the story – *Sean Connors in Chicago Bust!*

The telephone messages were mostly from reporters – but Gloria and Freddie had called – and so had the newspaper proprietors with whom Sean had spent the previous day. Their message read – '*Can see no purpose in further discussions. Have agreed sale with other party.*'

Freddie was more concerned about Sean's health when they spoke on the phone – 'You sound lousy. Get yourself back to bed. Have the hotel send up a doctor. I'll call you later, OK?'

Sean did as he was told. He ached all over. Sweat flowed from every pore in his skin.

An hour later a Doctor Wharton called Freddie from Sean's bedside – 'Mr Connors has a bad dose of 'flu. He needs to stay warm and in bed for a couple of days.'

Sean slept fitfully, thrashing about on the bed. He dreamt feverishly of his father but it was all mixed up. Ambassador Kennedy kept saying – 'One day my boy's going to run for the White House.' The dream rolled back through the years to the little house in Ballsbridge – Sean was shaking hands with Joe Kennedy Jnr, the Ambassador was laughing in the background – 'Someone should take a picture – the future President of the USA shaking hands with the future Taoiseach of Ireland.' But Jack was going to run for President, not Joe, Joe was dead. So was the Da. And the Widow O'Flynn was laughing – 'Sure you'll be many things in your life but you'll never be Taoiseach.'

When he awoke it was evening. The doctor was back. There was a blonde at his side. The doctor was saying – 'He's still burning up, but the worst should be over by morning. I'll look in before nine . . .'

He dreamt all night. Awful nightmares. At one stage he woke up. It was Val in that chair. They were in the hospital before the war. Any minute now a message would come on

646

the radio . . . *'The police have now named the man believed to have been responsible for last Friday's bomb explosions in Coventry. He is Matthew Riordan, known to be a member of the IRA . . .'*

'Riordan!' Sean shouted.

He sat bolt upright, staring with wild eyes as Val leapt from her chair.

'Hey honey,' Gloria Farrell rushed to the bedside. 'What's the matter? You look like you've seen a ghost?'

Sean clung to her – 'Oh Val, that bastard Riordan just killed the Da!'

Matt Riordan – Matt Lambert as he had become – had fathered two children by that spring of 1952. After the successful operation on his eyes Matt had moved into Hugh Ryan's house in Ballymurphy – first as a lodger, then as Bridie's suitor, and finally as her husband. Hugh still lived with them and although the small house sometimes threatened to burst apart under the impact of three adults and two small children it was a happy enough household for most of the time.

The thought of losing his sight had terrified Matt. Nothing in all the years in the Curragh prison camp, or during the bombing campaign in England – nothing frightened him as much as the prospect of blindness. The shock, the pain, the joy of regaining full sight was a shattering experience which showed him the world through what were almost new eyes – and wherever he looked he saw Bridie.

He had been painfully shy to begin with. He had been at ease in female company once – as a youngster in his father's butcher's shop, even later when he lived with his mother on the Falls – but that was before years spent on the Curragh. Rehabilitation might have been painful but for a fact of which Matt was unaware – that Bridie herself wanted to marry and saw Matt as her last chance.

She had passed her thirty-first birthday. There had been a man once, but he had emigrated to Australia and although he had promised to send for her he never had. There had been no one since, and Bridie's youthful prettiness was fast losing its bloom.

Matt had been grateful for the offer of lodging with the Ryans – after all he had nowhere to go. He was quite alone in the world – especially when Clancy and the boys were arrested and imprisoned in England. And staying with the Ryans helped establish his identity as William Lambert – better known as Matt to his friends.

'Just for a few weeks,' Matt said at the outset, 'then I'll get going again.'

But go where? As Matt peered out myopically from behind the thick lenses of his new spectacles he found only remnants of the IRA. The war, internment north and south of the border, had scattered Republicans like seeds on the wind. The IRA – even in the Falls and Short Strand and Ballymurphy itself – had ceased to exist.

Hugh Ryan argued powerfully for the way things were – 'Give this Labour Government a chance, Matt. They're not in cahoots with the Unionists like the Tories – I've met some of them in London, they've got an open mind about Ireland. Meanwhile we need this Welfare State they talk about – the people *want* it –'

A younger Matt, full of strength, might have resisted Hugh's arguments – but Matt weakened and wearied by years on the Curragh – still recovering from the fright of nearly going blind – Matt in that tired state was more easily discouraged. Besides he had Bridie to contend with by then.

They were often alone in the house – Hugh was married to his work and spent at least three evenings a week at the hospital. Bridie cooked and washed during her own hours away from the hospital, but she was efficient and got things done – there was always time to sit down with Matt in the evenings. After ten weeks as a lodger Matt had kissed her, then found his way to her bed, and seven weeks later they were married.

Bridie was good for him – she had snared him with artful determination, but that never lessened her anxiety to make him happy.

Their first son – Liam Riordan Lambert – was born in 1949. Their second – Fergus Riordan Lambert – was born a year later.

Matt worked as a porter at the hospital, but after a while

found an opening to return to his old trade as a butcher. He worked, he made love to Bridie in their big double bed, he played chess with Hugh – and the time passed. He told himself he was taking a breather. He talked nationalist politics to those who would listen – he read the newspapers, listened to the radio, and watched the world change.

In Belfast it changed for the better. The Labour Party pushed through so many reforms, in health-care, housing, education, social security, and other services, that the spectre of poverty was being forced out of the ghettoes. More men were in work – and even the unemployed were cushioned by the new Welfare State. Large Catholic families were given State allowances for the children, sick benefits, free milk for nursing mothers . . .

But south of the border – in the proud new Republic of Ireland – there were few such benefits. When a Mother and Child Bill was promoted in the Dail, to provide free, State-administered health services for mothers and children, the bill was thrown out by the Catholic Church.

When Catholics in Belfast looked south across the border they saw lower living standards. 'We're better off here,' they told Matt. 'If Dublin wants a united Ireland it will have to do better than that. We're better off with the Prods.'

'Where's your national pride?' Matt asked up and down the Falls. 'What about one nation again?'

But few people listened.

Yet – and Matt clung to the thought – there was change on one level, but life remained constant on another. Unionist MPs fought reform every step of the way at Westminster. And Prod rule was as firm as ever in Belfast. B Specials still marched the streets. The gabled ends of houses were still painted with giant murals of King Billy slaughtering Croppies at the Boyne. 'Fuck the Pope' was still daubed on walls in letters three feet high. And in July – on 'the glorious twelfth' – the Orangemen still took to the streets in vast processions, with their flutes and their drums and their swaggering insult to the Catholic community.

Some things never changed.

Like the old men who sat on their doorsteps in the Falls – 'Who's the bad man?' they shouted to the kids.

'King Billy!' would come the chorus.
'And what does he ride?'
'He rides a white horse.'
'And where is it kept?'
'In the Orange Hall.'
'And what will we do with it?'

'Blow it all up,' came the delighted shrieks. 'We'll blow up King Billy an' his white horse. We'll blow up the Orange Hall and Sandy Row an' all!'

'Aye,' Matt mused as he listened to the street games, 'but *when*? When will we blow them all up?'

And so the time passed. Matt was not consciously unhappy. Bridie kept him well fed and looked after – and Hugh was around often enough for a crack and a game of chess. Meanwhile Matt was forever trying to interest the neighbours in Republican politics. He never gave up, he talked to everyone – but as the years slipped by he felt a growing sense of failure. His mission in life had been thwarted. The IRA was dead, while Lord Averdale for instance was still very much alive, making a name for himself in London. Whenever Matt opened a paper there was Averdale giving some speech, more often about Africa than Ulster. But one day, Matt still promised himself, one day I'll kill that bastard. And one day I'll get myself over to London and hunt down Sean Connors.

But by spring 1952 Matt was beginning to wonder if the day would ever come.

Freddie Mallon used up a few favours in Chicago to sweep the debacle in the radio studio under the carpet. Sean survived the fracas, but wherever he went after that he was asked about Ireland. No matter what people thought in London, or Dublin, or Belfast – plenty of Americans wanted to ask 'the Irish question', especially when there was a chance of an explosive reply. But Sean kept a tight grip on his temper and never allowed himself to be baited again as he had in Chicago.

'And that wouldn't have happened,' he told Gloria, 'if I hadn't felt so lousy.'

She accompanied him for the next eighteen days – acting as secretary, guide and companion as he finished his tour.

She organized appointments, telephoned London, liaised with Freddie and made herself so useful that Sean wondered how he had managed without her.

As for 'the Irish question', Sean tried to bury it. It hardly seemed his business any more – it was a back-number, yesterday's news – he was amazed at the interest. But it was certainly there, especially among people of Irish extraction, most of whom seemed puzzled by his attitude. Even Gloria said – 'Surely you don't *condone* the British staying in Ireland? They should get out. Just as they were kicked out of India. People should be free to run their own affairs.'

'Sure I agree, but there's no chance of the British being kicked out by the Prods in the north.'

'Well of course not – the Prods are British.'

'And Irish,' he reminded her, 'they're Irish too, remember.'

He wondered if he *cared* any more? After all, he had never been back – what was Ireland to him? He was too busy building assets – his life lay in London, and – as seemed increasingly likely – in the US of A – a subject Gloria talked about increasingly often.

'Freddie said he can see you spending a lot of time here in future, Sean.'

He chuckled, excited by the prospect. 'If we tie up as many papers as Freddie talks about – who knows, I could spend six months a year in London and six months over here.'

'My,' she sighed. Her eyes shone. 'And I thought all tycoons were Americans these days.'

It was an exciting tour, crossing America and back again – and Gloria was an unexpected bonus. She was like Val in some ways – of course her accent was different and some of her opinions were quite opposite to Val's – but she was fair-haired and blue-eyed. Sean was enchanted – even though she refused to join him in bed. She did everything else. Her kisses were passionate. She let his hands roam over her body. She seemed to encourage him . . . but then stopped short – 'Oh Sean, let's not get carried away. I don't want to do that until I get married.'

He almost proposed in St Louis. St Louis was a triumph.

After two days of solid negotiation it was agreed that the *St Louis Post* would sell out to Freddie's new corporation for half the sum Freddie thought possible. Sean and Gloria had a celebration supper afterwards. She *almost* joined him in bed, but then – 'Sean, please no, I really am a good Catholic, I would be bitterly ashamed in the morning.'

Sean went lonely to bed, sour with frustration. Part of him wanted to get married – seeing Freddie and Margaret so happy with each other – being married and raising a family would be fun, he was sure about that. And Gloria was a fine-looking woman, he would miss her when he went back to London . . . yet he was still nagged by some indefinable doubt.

So – apart from trying to reach a decision about Gloria, and being dogged by questions about Ireland – it was a successful trip. Sean returned to New York with agreements signed with two newspapers and knowing that others were on the verge of agreement. Freddie was delighted – and Margaret was so pleased that Gloria had taken the chance to show Sean some of America.

The four of them had a celebration dinner that night, and when Sean returned to the Mallon apartment after taking Gloria home he found Freddie still working – on the telephone to another newspaper owner in Detroit.

'He called me,' Freddie grinned, 'word's getting around, Sean. We'll soon have a network coast to coast.'

They sat for a while; talking, planning and discussing the future. At one point Sean said – 'This Irish thing is bigger here than in London. Maybe we ought to have a man in Dublin –'

'Are you kidding? De Valera's been over to Washington, that's all, stirring things up. It will blow over. Forget it, Sean. Africa will be where the news will be – concentrate on Africa.'

Which is what they decided to do.

A week later Sean made his first transatlantic flight to London – a journey which was to become as familiar as a commuter's trip to town. He was still undecided about Gloria. They were not engaged – the actual subject of marriage had not arisen, at least not between Sean and Gloria, but Margaret raised the issue privately, at five-thirty in the afternoon on the day before he left.

'Gloria will be the loneliest girl in New York when you leave. Why not take her with you?'

'I'll be up to my eyes when I get back. It wouldn't be any kind of a holiday –'

'Sure it would. She's never seen London. And you can't work all the time.'

'But that's it – I *do* when I'm in London –'

'That's no way to live. Look at Freddie, he works hard but he still enjoys –'

'That's Freddie and you – it's the way you live – it's right for you.'

'For you too if you give it a chance. Gloria's madly in love with you, anyone can see that – and it's time you were married . . .'

When Sean resisted, Margaret put a hand on his arm. 'Sean, my dear, Val is dead. You must let go. Stop comparing everyone with Val. Gloria is a person in her own right, different, with her own qualities . . .'

Sean was trying to end an embarrassing conversation when Freddie walked in –exactly as Margaret said, 'Sean, I'm only concerned because I love you.'

Freddie gaped. Sean flinched – and Margaret uttered the tiniest gasp.

Then they all saw the funny side of it. Margaret pretended to faint. Sean ducked into a corner – and Freddie burst out laughing – 'What is it with you two? Every time I turn my back –'

But Freddie was firm with Margaret afterwards – *amazingly* firm – 'Now listen honey, you mean well, but will you butt out of Sean's private life. Let him make his own decisions. If you persist in this match-making I'm going to get darned sore. Do you understand that?'

And Margaret answered 'Yes Freddie' so meekly that Sean had to stifle his laughter.

Afterwards, when they were alone, Freddie said, 'I'm sorry old buddy, I guess all women are hooked on wedding bells. But marriage is a big step, don't let anyone stampede you into it.'

That night, Sean's last night in New York, Freddie threw a party to which most of the city seemed invited. Gloria never looked more beautiful. All of Margaret's glamorous friends were there but, in a moulded gown which clung to her body, Gloria outshone everyone. Sean couldn't take his eyes off her, neither could any other man. It was impossible to have a private conversation, Gloria was sought out all evening as the belle of the ball. The most Sean was able to say was, 'I'll only be away for three months.' 'Fine,' she answered, 'look me up when you get back, my number's in the book.' Which struck him as very casual for someone supposedly 'madly in love' with him. In fact, as he looked at the men crowding round he felt he was vacating a lease on a desirable residence – and prospective new tenants were crowding him out even before his bags were packed.

During the long flight back to London he had warm thoughts about Freddie and Margaret, exciting thoughts about business, and very confused, mixed-up thoughts about Gloria.

And so after four months away, Sean returned to London. But he now saw the city differently. It seemed dowdy after New York, and Britain itself tiny, almost puny, after the spacious strength of America. Yet, despite that, it still felt like home to Sean Connors . . . or at least it did to begin with.

The problem was, other people's lives had moved on. Michael O'Hara was on the verge of marrying, his sweetheart from Dublin was over and already replanning the house they had bought in Hampstead. 'The wedding is next month,' Michael told Sean. 'I'm relying on you to be best man, you know that, don't you?'

Consequently Michael was rarely at the flat in Great Cumberland Place. He worked just as hard, or at least almost, but when Sean proposed meetings in the evening, Michael was likely to say – 'Could we make it a bit earlier, Sean, you see I promised Deirdre I'd meet her at eight.'

At least Tubby was still a confirmed bachelor, but even he had taken on outside interests. Of all things he had become Chairman of a London football club.

Sean couldn't understand them. To him business was the most exciting thing on the planet. Nothing was more fun than wheeling and dealing from morning to night – *nothing!*

The atmosphere at Great Cumberland Place was different. Some of the excitement had gone. Sean remembered the early days. They had worked to beyond midnight, risen at dawn and dashed about all day. He was still ready to do that – but it seemed that Michael and Tubby were not.

Sean was disappointed. He had no cause for complaint – certainly he could find no fault with their work. Mallon's chairman, the newly knighted *Sir* George Hamilton, was full of praise for Tubby – 'He's got a nose for the right properties. He underestimates the time things take, but with young Brian Tillet and Jack Thornton tying up the loose ends, I'd back Tubby against any other property developer in England.'

It was the same in Fleet Street. Michael O'Hara ran a tight ship. He had developed a fine team of reporters – and even before Sean returned a great deal of work had been done to prepare for the launch of *Seven Days* throughout Europe.

And Fleet Street itself was agog with the news coming out of Africa. Jimmy Cross was filing reports from Durban and Johannesburg about race riots – it seemed that any day South Africa would explode over the new racial laws.

'Freddie's hunch is paying off,' Sean smiled with satisfaction, 'he always did have a nose for the best stories.'

But it was a frustrating summer. Sean liked *sharing* triumphs. Tubby and Michael were as enthusiastic as ever, but some of their single-mindedness had gone. Tubby even took a holiday, going on a summer tour of Australia with his football club! And Michael married his Deirdre – so Sean was left alone in the flat at Great Cumberland Place. Of course he was busy most days, at least in the week – but the evenings and weekends seemed empty. Sean had ceased to be a journalist and was no longer dashing from one event to the next. The Mallon Property Company only needed him for major decisions. Transatlantic Television was ticking over until the new commercial channels opened up. Sean was left with time on his hands and no social life to fall back on.

London girls seemed drab after the girls of New York. He wrote to Gloria. He telephoned her. He arranged with

Margaret that a dozen red roses be delivered to her every day. And before June was out Sean was on his way back to New York.

They were married at the end of July. As she clung to his arm and looked up at him, Sean felt the happiest, luckiest man in the world. Gloria was beautiful, and she was his wife.

But their honeymoon in Miami was a disaster. She had wept as he made love to her – 'Oh Sean, it hurts, please stop, I can't bear the pain.'

He was as tender and gentle, as patient and as considerate as could be – but whenever he tried it was the same – 'Oh why must we do this – it hurts and I don't like it. Sean, if you really loved me you wouldn't ask me to do it.'

They talked about it. Back in New York he persuaded her to visit a gynaecologist. She did so reluctantly but it seemed to make little difference. Every night she talked of 'an extended period this month' – or – 'it's not the safe time, Sean, we don't want a family just yet' – or – 'not tonight Sean, I think dinner disagreed with me.'

They sailed for England on the *United States* which that year had won the coveted Atlantic Blue Riband. Their state-room was luxurious – the crossing was smooth – they dined at the Captain's table – they danced in the ballroom. Mrs Gloria Connors was admired from one end of the ship to the other. She was fun. Everyone agreed she was charming. 'She's so in love with her handsome husband,' people said as they watched her. And Sean thought so too, as she looked up at him with her big blue-eyed 'you are so masterful' look. He enjoyed being with her. He liked the way heads turned when she entered a room, he was proud of her – but in their state-room it was the same every night.

'I'll get used to it in time, Sean – that's all I need, *time*.'

She hated the flat at Great Cumberland Place.

'So OK, we'll move,' Sean told her, 'I'll get Brian Tillet to show you some of our other flats.'

But she didn't much like those either.

Once a week they tried to make love. Gloria rucked her nightdress up to her waist and spread her legs wide on the bed – but the noises she made were of pain not of passion.

Meanwhile everyone complimented Sean on his beautiful wife. 'Charming,' they all said, 'and so sophisticated, but then these American girls are, aren't they?'

He tried not to think of Val. He tried to forget the pleasure they had found in each other's arms, the naturalness, the shared delight, the joy and the happiness.

He kept telling himself it would get better. Whenever he met her around town – lunch at the Savoy, dinner at The Twenty-One Club, a night out at Churchill's – his heart quickened at the sway of her hips as she walked towards him, her smile, her scent – he wanted her.

But every night she turned her face to the wall.

When they talked about it she said – 'Sean, I love you so much. It's not I don't try . . . I *do*, I try very hard . . . it's just that . . . oh I don't know, let's not make a big thing of it. Let's just enjoy ourselves in other ways, like we did before we married. It will work out, you'll see, give it time.'

By then it was mid-October. They had given it nine weeks. But Sean told himself, 'Sure, give it time, it will work out, it's bound to.'

Preparations for the launch of *Seven Days* throughout Europe were advancing at a rapid rate. Sean spent most days in Fleet Street – although more often as an onlooker, as he was compelled to admit. After all, Michael was Managing Editor – but it was more than just Michael, it was the team he had assembled – a very competent staff who were meshing together into a unit which promised to be brilliant. And nobody outshone Jimmy Cross.

James Cross (as he was called on his byline) had only been in Africa six months but he did possess advantages over most of the journalists who had rushed out from London. James Cross had been born there. He had lived in Southern Rhodesia as a boy, then his restless father had moved the family to Nairobi for two years, after which they had lived in Johannesburg and Cape Town. Jimmy Cross knew parts of Africa like the back of his hand. After the war he had come to England in search of a university education, stayed in London, gravitated to Fleet Street and joined London & Continental. He had been an asset on the 'Africa desk' in London – but he was an asset beyond price in the field.

In six months Jimmy had criss-crossed the continent – but his main base had been at Nairobi. 'When the genie comes out of the bottle,' he wrote to Michael, 'it will come out in Kenya first.'

Michael disagreed. South Africa had to be the flashpoint in his opinion – and most people agreed with Michael.

Jimmy had compromised by appointing a stringer in Jo'burg and another one in Pretoria – then he based himself in Nairobi. Since when some of Jimmy's stories about the Mau Mau had made headlines all over the world. People felt their blood run cold as they read of barbaric initiation ceremonies. They winced at accounts of the sacrificial slaughter of animals – and were revolted to learn that drinking blood and human semen was part of Mau Mau ritual. And throughout it all Jimmy stood by his prediction.

Jimmy was right. In October white homesteads were attacked by Mau Mau. Farmers and their families were terrorized. The Governor declared a State of Emergency.

British troops were rushed out from England. More soldiers flew in from the garrison on Cyprus. In Nairobi, police swooped and arrested hundreds of black African leaders. Detention camps were crammed full . . .

Then, on 10 November, James Cross cabled his most dramatic story of all.

Throughout the world people were stunned at the news.

Lord and Lady Averdale Murdered.

Kenya is sickened and dazed this morning. Cutters Lodge, home of Lord and Lady Averdale, was attacked by black guerrillas last night and burned to the ground. Policemen at the scene have described scenes of unparalleled carnage. Exact details are unknown, but it is believed that many of the Kikuyu labourers employed at Cutters and the nearby Bowley estates went to the aid of Lord and Lady Averdale – and paid for the intervention with their lives. Police experts seem certain that Lady Averdale was trapped in the fire and Lord Averdale lost his life in a courageous rescue attempt . . .

. . . half an hour ago the Governor declared this to be

Kenya's blackest day. Lady Averdale was renowned as an advocate for improving the expectations of the African. Working conditions at Cutters were described as 'a model of multi-racial harmony, an example to every farmer in Africa' by a recent United Nations delegation.

Tributes are pouring into my temporary office here at the Norfolk Hotel. A man stopped me an hour ago and said – 'Mark Averdale was the only Westminster politician who understood Kenya . . . who will speak for us now?' A call from Mombasa quotes Mr Motilal Gungi, a prominent Indian businessman, as saying – 'Lady Averdale was a truly great person . . . her goodness was an example to us all . . . the whole Indian community will mourn her passing . . .'

CHAPTER EIGHT

Kate O'Brien was woken at six in the morning. The Colonial Office was telephoning to say Lord Averdale had been involved in 'an accident'. That was all she knew until two officials arrived at seven-fifteen. She listened in stunned silence. She did not weep, or wring her hands, or cry out – she just sat and stared.

She went back to her bedroom and sat on her bed. She felt so . . . so unbelievably *empty*. Sometimes she had questioned her feelings for him. Her emotions always fell short of those described by the girls at Glossops. She never went 'weak at the knees', or 'turned to jelly' when he kissed her – but she had grown fond of him. She liked him – she liked him a lot. He was pompous at times – and arrogant – and when he lost his temper he could be hurtfully rude, but never with her. He was patient and attentive, kind and considerate. He was her protector, her provider, her tutor . . . quite simply her life.

It was then that she wept – when she realized she had loved him without ever being 'in love'.

The telephone was busy all morning – every paper in Fleet Street wanted to speak to her. Crystal, her maid, took the calls. Kate thought Fleet Street's attitude was callous and intrusive . . . she was dazed and upset . . . she consoled herself with the message that Tim was on his way from Belfast. She thanked God for that. Dear Tim, she thought, thank heavens I have Tim. We shall be all right if we are together.

She ran to him as he came through the door. He was gaunt and ashen-faced. He held her, then pushed her away.

He was shaking with temper – 'There's a crowd of photographers outside. The press are besieging the house!'

'Oh, I didn't know . . . Crystal has been answering –'

'Dozens of them. They're like vultures . . . like . . . jackals!'

Kate choked. She could hear Mark saying, 'Pariahs! That's what they are. Blasted reporters are the bane of my life.'

Tim had been drinking. She smelt alcohol on his breath. And as soon as he threw his coat down he asked for a drink.

'I'll get some coffee,' she said.

'I said a *drink*! Give me some whisky.'

She had never seen him so . . . so belligerent. Whatever she said seemed wrong. He snapped about everything. Of course he was upset – but so was she. She wanted to tell him that she hurt too. She wanted to hold his hand. All morning she had told herself that Tim was on his way – that the awfulness wouldn't be so bad when he got here – but it was worse. He snarled at whatever she said.

She was still in her dressing-gown – eventually she used that as an excuse to flee to her bedroom – to dress – which is what she was doing when Crystal put a call through on the extension. It was the man from the Colonial Office, asking about funeral arrangements . . . were the bodies to be flown to Ulster or buried in Kenya?

Kate's head was a whirl. The man wanted an immediate decision. With all her heart she begged Mark to tell her what to do. What would he want? And Ziggy – what would *she* want? She had never been to Ulster – Ziggy had loved Kenya – she would want to be buried there, Kate felt certain. She caught her breath. The rose garden. Mark had told her about a rose garden, the grave of her husband, her *first* husband. Oh God, would that look awful? Ziggy buried between *two* husbands? Or Ziggy buried elsewhere with Mark? Or Ziggy buried *without* Mark – separately, him in Ulster, her in Kenya? That would be macabre. She couldn't do that.

'Miss O'Brien?' the man persisted.

She wanted to scream, I'm twenty-one – that's all – I don't know what to do!

'We rather thought Ulster,' the man said, 'in view of Lord Averdale's –'

'No,' she said quickly, reaching a decision.

She told him about the rose garden at Cutters. 'I see,' he said, sounding doubtful. In that case the funeral would have to be the day after tomorrow. 'These hot countries, you know.' Should they make travel arrangements for her and her brother?

Kate closed her eyes. Blackness engulfed her. Oh Mark, tell me what to do.

She finished dressing and returned to the drawing-room, not knowing if she would find Tim drunk or sober.

But he was sober. Crystal had served coffee and sandwiches. Kate had not had a thing all day. She poured herself coffee, feeling dazed and lightheaded.

Tim looked at his watch. 'Nearly six,' he said, 'Buckley should be here soon.'

'Buckley?'

'The Averdale solicitor. I tracked him down this morning before I left. He was in Manchester –'

'Oh thank heavens. What a relief. He'll know what to do. There's just so much . . . I mean . . . apparently we have to fly out to Nairobi in twenty-four hours –'

'What for?'

'The funeral. I just had the Colonial Office back –'

'But the funeral will be in Belfast.'

'Oh? Well, actually I told him Kenya . . . it seemed the best –'

'You *what*?' Tim leapt to his feet.

She stared at him. 'They wanted an immediate decision. I didn't think of the solicitor. I've never met him –'

'Who gave you the *right*?'

She sat down hurriedly. 'It's not a *right*. I thought it was best, that's all. If it's wrong we can probably change it –'

'I'll say we will. Good God, what's got into you?'

'I don't understand –'

'Not much you don't. Well we'll see about that. Buckley must have the will.'

She struggled to follow his meaning. 'Will? Oh, you mean Mark might have left instructions . . . oh thank God if he did –'

'I don't mean that. I want to know where I stand, that's what. You think he's left you the lot, don't you? Or do you bloody well *know*? Was that the price? Was that the price for sleeping with him?'

'Oh no,' she whispered, then buried her head in her hands. 'Oh Tim, *no* –'

'*No*? You didn't think I knew, did you? How d'you think I felt when I found out? My own sister – our guardian's whore! How do you think *I* felt? After all the years when it was just him and me in Ulster – all those years you were away in the war with your precious Aunt Alison, and then at Glossops – you never gave him a thought, did you? You never wanted to see him again. Or me. You told me that once. Then it all changed, suddenly, that Christmas, that's when it changed – when he married this other whore in Kenya and came back and took you on holiday. Just you! Not me! It didn't matter that I was alone in Belfast . . . it didn't matter because I'm always there, whenever he needed me I was there. I've always looked after his interests . . . I've worked and worked and . . .'

His voice broke to a sob. He collapsed into a chair, his face contorted with misery.

She flew to his side, kneeling, her arms reaching up to encircle his neck.

'Get away from me!' he spat at her. 'Get away, you bloody whore!'

She lost her balance and sprawled at his feet. He leapt up and stood over her. 'Well?' he shouted, 'I haven't heard a denial! I'm listening – have you *nothing* to say?'

How could she even *begin* to explain? He would never believe Mark would have married her . . .

'Tim –' she started.

He hit her. His open hand cracked across her face. She fell backwards – but he grabbed her wrist and pulled her to her feet. 'Come on,' he snapped, 'I'll even show you proof.'

He dragged her into the hall and along to her bedroom, where he flung her across the bed before crossing to the wood panelling alongside her dressing-room. She knew what he was doing, even as he fumbled to find the concealed catch. A moment later the secret door rolled back to reveal the hidden elevator.

'I found it last time I stayed. Quite by accident. My suit-case was missing. I came in here to see if it had been put here by mistake. Then I leant against the wall – and hey presto!' He swung round to face her. 'So I took a ride in it. We both know where it goes – don't we – you rotten bitch!'

She pulled herself upright on the bed. Her cheek was aflame with the mark of his hand. She was trembling uncontrollably.

'Not that I didn't suspect,' he panted. 'Even before – but I didn't want to believe it. I *couldn't* – not my own sister. And her so full of what it meant to have a brother. I told myself I was wrong – Kate wouldn't do that, Kate hasn't changed him, it's this bloody whore in Kenya, filling him up with stupid ideas –'

'That's enough!' she shrieked. She stood up, hugging herself to stop shaking. 'Ziggy is *dead* –'

'She killed him, the bitch. All her crazy schemes. Averdale steel, I used to remind him of that when he told me about them, Averdale steel is the way to keep the Croppies down. He taught me that as a kid. It's her fault he's dead. If he'd listened to me . . . but she changed him, the cow, she never let up, as soon as he got there she was on at him with her silly bloody ideas –'

'All right, Tim.' Her words were less of a shriek this time.

She took a deep breath. 'You've had your say. Now listen to me. Mark would never have a word spoken against Ziggy. Her ideas may not have been yours, they may have been wrong, I don't know, that doesn't matter – all that matters now is we do what Mark would have expected of us. And he would *not* have expected this screaming match – he would *not* have expected you to call Ziggy a bitch . . . and . . .'

'Whore is the word you're looking for,' he sneered.

Kate went bright red, as red as her hair, so red that the mark on her face was no longer visible. Her eyes blazed, but she was more in control of herself. She had recovered from the fright of being struck and dragged along the corridor.

'We're both upset,' she said, 'and you've been drinking. There's no point in continuing this conversation –'

She was interrupted by a cough – Crystal appeared at the still open door. 'Excuse me, Miss Kate, but Mr Buckley has arrived. I've put him in the drawing-room.'

A stricken look crossed Tim's face. Kate read his expression. Pain and bitterness, and fear. Her heart went out to him. Poor Tim, he must have been so desperately lonely. She had *tried* to reach him – she had invited him to stay whenever Mark went away, but the situation had defeated everyone. She wanted to say, 'Tim, I'm your sister . . . we're all we've got' . . . but Crystal was waiting for an answer.

Crystal had seen the secret elevator. She averted her eyes, but Kate knew.

Kate groaned under her breath – so now your suspicions are confirmed too, she thought wearily

'Thank you, Crystal,' she said. 'Please tell Mr Buckley we shall join him immediately.'

She waited until Crystal left, then crossed to the panelling to close the lift door.

Tim grabbed her arm. 'Buckley must have the will. If you've talked me out of what's rightfully mine –'

'For God's sake! How can you be so . . so despicable. Poor Mark was only killed last night. How could you even think, I didn't even know there *was* a will.'

For a split second they stared at each other, then Kate turned away. 'I'll have to change, you've torn the sleeve of this dress.'

When he left she felt faint and a little bit sick. She wanted to cry but steeled herself. She changed and brushed her hair, then powdered her face to conceal the mark of Tim's blow. She forced herself to take time, needing to collect herself after the awful scene. What had made Tim so bitter . . . her for sleeping with Mark . . . Mark for neglecting him

. . . or fear that Mark might not have bequeathed everything to him? She shuddered. She had been stunned . . . even to think of that . . . but Tim had thought . . . that's what made it so horrible . . . Tim had thought. She had wanted to cry out – 'Tim dear, we're orphans, nothing is *rightfully ours*', but he had looked at her so coldly that she had been lost for words.

Eventually she pulled herself together. She was ready to face the solicitor. When she entered the room Tim was in the middle of saying something. He broke off and swung round to face her – 'Ah, so you've deigned to honour us after all.'

She could have said that he had made it necessary for her to change her dress – but instead she shook hands with the solicitor and sat down in the nearest chair.

'Mr Buckley agrees with me,' Tim blurted out, unable to conceal his triumph, 'the funeral should take place in Belfast. You should never have said that to the Colonial Office.'

'I see,' Kate stared down at her hands clasped in her lap.

The solicitor cleared his throat. He was short and fat, with a red face full of broken veins, and black hair sprinkled with grey. Suddenly Kate realized that he had known Tim for years – every visit Tim had made to Glossops had been incorporated into a trip to London to see the Averdale solicitor. Mr Buckley and Tim were *old friends*.

Buckley began with expressions of sympathy – then he seemed to reprimand Tim, 'What I actually said was the Colonial Office was wrong to ask you for instructions –'

Kate's heart rose, only to fall again as Buckley continued – 'after all, you were shocked and distressed, how could you be expected to think rationally.'

True, but she had *tried* to do what Mark would have wanted.

'Did . . . did he leave any instructions?'

'Not specifically, no – as a matter of fact this will was only made six months ago. I think all that flying was beginning to worry him – but my dear, *all* Averdales are buried in Ulster. Anywhere else would be quite inappropriate. And

665

after what happened, surely Kenya would be the last place . . .'

'And Ziggy – Lady Averdale?'

'Naturally will be laid to rest beside him. As husband and wife . . .' he smiled, 'I'm sure you understand, now you've had a chance to reflect on the matter.'

Kate began to marshal her arguments – but how could she explain that Ziggy would have wanted to be buried in her rose garden, no matter what – or that Mark would have been the last person in the world to oppose her wishes? How could she possibly explain that?

Buckley cleared his throat again. 'As a matter of fact I telephoned the Colonial Office while we were waiting. Tim had a brief word with them too. The . . . um, the misunderstanding has been completely cleared up . . . there's nothing for you to worry about.'

Kate shook with temper. Words poured out . . . if Mark had left specific instructions, that would have been one thing, she said . . . but in the absence of such neither Tim nor Mr Buckley had the right to make such an arbitrary decision. If anyone knew what Mark and Ziggy would have wanted Kate was in the best position to judge.

Buckley was taken aback. He had not expected opposition. He did his best to transfer the blame for 'this misunderstanding' to the Colonial Office for their thoughtlessness in asking Kate, but he refused to reconsider his decision. The matter was closed, that was an end to it.

Kate prayed that Mark would forgive her. At least she had tried. And perhaps she *was* wrong . . . after all, she couldn't be sure . . . she was just so confused and upset and hating every minute of this meeting. She wanted to flee to her room. Vaguely she heard Buckley going on about the funeral arrangements in Belfast, and about reading the will formally afterwards, then he said, 'But there is something I should give you before I go.'

He fumbled in his briefcase and withdrew two large envelopes.

'Lord Averdale wanted you to have these as soon as possible, in the event of, well, a tragedy like this. I've no idea what they contain –'

666

'The will,' Tim blurted out, 'why wait until –'

'These matters must take their proper course,' Buckley said, with a sharp look at Tim. Then he softened, 'As I was saying, I've no idea what these contain, but perhaps they will put your mind at rest on . . . well, your expectations.'

Tim stared at the envelope, confusion on his face, mingled with fear, mingled with hope.

Buckley closed his briefcase and stood up. 'Now, if you will excuse me . . .'

'I'll see you in Belfast tomorrow,' Tim said, still staring at the envelope. 'If you catch the morning flight I'll have someone meet you at Aldergrove. I'll get back there tonight –'

'I'll come,' Kate said in a despairing attempt to bridge the chasm which had opened between them. 'The two of us together –'

'No,' Tim shook his head. 'If Mr Buckley gets over tomorrow we'll do everything that needs to be done.'

They were shutting her out. They even left together, as if neither of them wanted to be alone with her.

Crystal came in afterwards – with a bowl of soup on a tray – 'You must eat, Miss Kate . . .'

But Kate could not face it. She looked at the long list of telephone messages and couldn't face that either. Finally she picked up the envelope, addressed simply to 'Kate' in Mark's handwriting, and took it to her room. She had never felt more alone in her life.

Sean Connors had been working on the Averdale story all day – ever since Freddie Mallon telephoned from New York that morning – 'Wasn't Averdale the guy you knew? Wasn't he the guy who sold you the *Dublin Gazette*?'

All those years ago.

'Listen, Sean. This has got to be the first cover story. It's a natural. It's world wide – "British Peer slain by African terrorists" – Sean, it's made for us.'

It was ten days before publication – ten days before the European launch of the international edition of *Seven Days*.

'Sean, listen to me. We've got an inside track. For Chrissakes, you even *knew* the guy. Then there's . . . what's his name, Jimmy Cross, on the spot with his big local connection . . . then there's Ulster and the Irish end. Once you tick off the African interest, the United Nations angle – my people are already working on that – then there's Averdale being a famous Westminster politician . . . hell this story's got everything we need for the first issue.'

'He's right,' Michael O'Hara said afterwards, 'there's even another angle – a beautiful girl.'

Sean looked at him.

'You remember asking me to go to one of Averdale's press briefings? Well I went. Dear God, you should see this Kate O'Brien. If Deirdre hadn't been in London already, and me about to get married . . . well I've never seen a more beautiful creature in my life.'

'That's what Jimmy Cross said.'

'He was never more right. God knows how she got stuck with Averdale.'

'She's his ward, isn't she – I mean she was.'

'So they told me – but the way he looked at her . . .' Michael shrugged. 'Ah, 'tis probably just my dirty mind. There wasn't a man in the room not looking at her the same way.'

Two hours later Sean spoke to Jimmy Cross in Nairobi. Jimmy was thrilled. His story was to be the lead in the special inaugural edition of *Seven Days*. Ten thousand words on the political ferment in Africa. Local profiles on the Governor, the Officer Commanding British Forces in Kenya, black politicians – everything and everyone. But he was less thrilled to hear about Kate O'Brien.

'You want me to call her from *here*? But –'

'She's not taking any calls. We can't get through to her. And the butler at the main house called in the police – now there's constables front, back and sideways, all hemmed in by reporters and cameramen –'

'I'm not sure she'll speak to me either –'

'You were a regular at her little soirées weren't you? Besides, just calling from Nairobi might help. Give her the usual spiel –'

'Sir . . . Mr Connors . . . she's a very nice girl –'

'So? Tell her we'll protect her. And get her to call me.'

Immediately afterwards Sean telephoned Gloria at

668

home – 'I'm working tonight, God knows when I'll be through. No, don't wait up, expect me when you see me.' He replaced the receiver with a great surge of relief – whether because he was working flat-out again or because he was not going home to Gloria was something he was unable to answer.

But he soon realized that it would not be easy to revert to the role of full-time journalist. Michael's team was already in action. The first international edition of *Seven Days* would feature the Averdale murders, but the combined articles amounted to a total assessment of Britain's abilities to preserve her role as a Colonial power. Reportage would discuss not only troubles in Kenya and Africa but other flashpoints, the West Indies, the Mediterranean, and South-East Asia. In New York Freddie's team were scouring the UN building, while in London major interviews were scheduled with the Foreign Secretary and Oliver Lyttleton, the new Secretary for the Colonies.

Most of the material for the rest of the magazine was ready. Sean flicked through dummy pages of the specially commissioned articles – theatre, books, cinema, the arts, medicine, education, big business, small business, trade unions ...

'It ain't called *Seven Days* for nothing,' Michael cracked, 'it'll take 'em seven days to read it.'

It was a very long way from the old *Dublin Gazette*. And yet, Sean mused, it all started from there, from the day he bought the paper from Lord Averdale all those years ago. Now, by a curious twist of fate, Averdale himself would be featured posthumously in the new magazine.

'Your car is ready, Mr Connors.'

He struggled into his overcoat. He had agreed to meet Herbert Morrison and some other Labour front-benchers. The House would rise early as a tribute to Lord Averdale, which in turn meant some of the Labour Party crowd would dine with Sean later and give him their views on the Colonies, especially Kenya.

Meeting Morrison generally evoked memories of Val – but that night, as the car bowled along Whitehall towards Parliament Square, Sean's thoughts strayed back to this girl Kate O'Brien. He wondered if Jimmy Cross had spoken to her? She had not called the office. Her story might be useful . . .

Kate barely slept that night. By dawn the next morning she had read, re-read, and wept over Mark's letter until she knew passages by heart.

'I hope to God you never read this, my darling. I wanted to look after you for so much longer. I wanted you for the rest of my life – but if you read this I suppose that wish will have been granted. I dreamt of you for so many years, but you are so much more than I dreamt of . . .'

She felt unworthy. Throughout most of her life she had yearned to be loved – and when it had come the avalanche of his feelings had swamped her. But – she clung to the thought – she was glad to have pleased him – *glad, glad, glad* – no matter that her brother called her a whore, no matter that there was so much the world would never understand.

Mark had left her everything in London.

'. . . the house, the paintings, various bank accounts, Buckley will have the details. Don't worry, my darling, business will never become a burden, your monthly needs will be paid as a matter of routine . . . you need only consult your trustees on exceptional items – and having suffered trustees myself in the past I am giving you two from whom you will receive every help – your dear brother Tim, who has matured so well – and Ronald Buckley . . .'

She flinched. She had crossed swords with Buckley already, and Tim in his present mood was unlikely to provide 'every help'.

Mark had left the Bowley estates to Ziggy . . .

'. . . for reasons almost too complicated to explain – I could say because Africa is neither your world nor Tim's, and although that is true it does not explain what Ziggy has come to mean to me. I hope you will visit her, Kate – the thought of you two together is a fond one of mine, for you have both given me so much in such different ways . . .'

Everything else was left to Tim.

'. . . sometimes I think he has become more of an Averdale than I am.'

670

There were many more pages in which he expressed his love for her. She wept as she read them. She had never expected a will. She had not thought of a future without Mark, not since that Christmas four years before, and now he had gone.

'. . . *but I shall always be with you Kate, just as you will always be mine. You were mine before you were born, and you must remain mine even after my death. It is the way things are. Of course you must never marry. My possessions are yours as long as I possess you – but should you ever marry, everything Averdale will be stripped from you and given to Tim. It is the Averdale way.*'

The proviso hardly registered, she was too upset, too dazed by events.

She dozed from time to time – then woke with a start – and the whole nightmare flooded back – Mark and Ziggy killed, and Tim who seemed suddenly to hate her. She wondered what she would do. The future seemed so empty . . .

At eight o'clock the telephone started ringing again . . . mostly reporters wanting some sort of comment . . . but Buckley called to say the funeral would take place in Belfast in three days' time . . . and Tim rang to say he was trying to get hold of Buckley. Tim was furious, 'That conniving bitch! Well she's dead too. That must invalidate this nonsense about the Bowley estates. We must oppose it, Kate, we *must*! God knows what the legal complications are, I've been trying to speak to Buckley –'

'No Tim, no,' she almost sobbed into the telephone.

'Listen. You'll need me in the future. I'm your trustee –'

She hung up. Oh Tim, she thought, I need you *now*, not in the future – and not so hatefully callous.

Half an hour later the newspapers arrived. Kate no longer had to search out items for Ziggy. Ziggy and Mark were on the front pages. Descriptions of Mark tore a gasp of pain from Kate – he was called 'arrogant' . . . 'self-opinionated' . . . 'domineering' . . . which perhaps was true but he was other things too. And Kate searched in vain for a proper tribute to Ziggy. Not one paper gave a full account of what she had been trying to do in Kenya. Reading them

671

Kate was reminded of the farmers she had shown around London – 'Heck Kate, once upon a time Britain was proud of the Colonies – now we're looked on as cut-throats and bandits.'

Crystal stood over her while she ate some toast, the first food Kate had eaten in twenty-four hours. And it was Crystal who persuaded her to speak to Jimmy Cross when he called from Nairobi – 'He's phoned four times already. He knows you don't want to be disturbed, but he says he's calling from Africa to help you.'

'Jimmy?' Kate said into the receiver, 'Jimmy, is that you?'

They had only met a dozen times. She was careful not to have favourites, her professional relationship with Jimmy Cross was no stronger than with half a dozen Fleet Street reporters, but it was such a relief to hear a friendly voice . . .

Jimmy expressed condolences, he was kind and considerate – but then he presented his argument, that the best way to disperse the crowd outside her door was to grant an exclusive interview to one paper – 'once we spread the word most of the boys will leave you alone.'

'But I've nothing to say, I'm shocked and upset –'

'Kate,' he said firmly, 'that crowd outside won't be your usual polite lobby correspondents. You've got the monkeys out there, the *paparazzi* – believe me, all sorts of things will be printed. Some you won't like. Do it my way and you'll have a chance to tell the world what the man was *really* like.'

She owed Mark that. She had read some of the things . . .

'It's the background they want, Kate. What were his ambitions for Kenya? What happens to the "Britain in Africa" campaign now? What –'

'I don't know,' Kate cried. She felt desperate.

'Do one thing for me Kate, will you – phone Sean Connors for me.'

'Sean Connors the broadcaster?'

Jimmy's exclamation was muffled. 'These days he's a lot more than that. Among other things he's my boss. Here's the number. Will you call him right away?'

'I don't know.'

'Please, Kate.'

So she did. She was confused and a little light-headed. She was sick about Tim. She had barely slept a wink through the night.

She announced herself to a telephonist – and then she was through to him.

'This is Sean Connors speaking.'

She trembled at the sound of his voice. She knew it so well. It brought back so many memories . . . listening to the radio with Uncle Ned in Dayton, Ohio . . . and later, listening with Aunt Alison and Jenny and Yvette . . . tuning in week after week for news of the war.

'Hello,' he said again. 'This is Sean Connors speaking –'

'From London,' she whispered huskily. 'This is Sean Connors speaking from London – bringing you the news from the heart of Great Britain – the country that now stands alone.'

He caught his breath, then said, 'That's a very nice compliment, Miss O'Brien, especially at a time of great personal sadness. May I express my sympathy and apologize for intruding.'

She was weeping silently. Tears filled her eyes and ran down her cheeks. She remembered Yvette weeping when Paris was liberated in the war – and Aunt Alison crossing the room to take her in her arms. She remembered all the love in that Washington apartment and her heart ached.

She heard his voice more than his words. She had always liked his voice – the warm timbred tones, the accent which was a strange mixture of Irish brogue, British crisp and American drawl. She felt she had known him all her life.

He was telling her what he wanted. Background for an article he was writing on Lord Averdale . . . 'Naturally I don't want to intrude now,' he said, 'but I could meet you in a few days' time . . .'

All my life, she kept thinking, I feel as though I've known him all my life. He sounded so safe, so reliable, so trustworthy. He sounded like a *friend* – which was the exact word he used a moment later – 'May I make a suggestion, Miss O'Brien. Haven't you a friend you could stay with –

I can imagine what it's like, with everyone pestering you . . .'

A friend? Aunt Alison in Washington – Jenny in Omaha – Yvette in Paris. She had more than a friend twenty-four hours ago, she had her own brother . . .

'Failing that,' he was saying, 'I could arrange for you to be spirited away for a few days. It would give you time by yourself – time to recover from the shock, a chance to think . . .'

It sounded idyllic . . . to get away from everyone, Tim, this apartment with its memories and incessantly ringing telephone . . .

She told him about the funeral in Belfast.

'We'll take care of that too,' he said calmly, 'we'll get you there and take you away afterwards.'

But why would he be so kind?

'And when it's all over,' he said easily, 'perhaps you'll grant me my interview.'

It was such a relief to let someone take over. She didn't even ask where she was going, or who would go with her – she just *knew* he would take care of her. Yes, she said, she could be ready in two hours – yes, there was a back way into the apartment, up the fire-escape from the mews behind the building . . .

Three hours later she was being driven up the Great North Road and out of London. Mr Connors had sent two people to look after her – a chauffeur and a very competent secretary from his office who seemed determined to mother her – 'You look tired out, Miss O'Brien. Why not doze for a while. I'll wake you up when we get there.'

Even then Kate failed to ask where they were going.

'Chester,' Sean said to Michael, 'she can spend the two days there, fly over to Belfast for the funeral, fly back and stay at Chester that night. Then Arthur will drive her back down to London on Friday and I'll interview her on Saturday.'

'That's three days before we publish. We print on Monday.'

'So? Just save me half a page, we won't need more . . .' he hesitated, 'unless I can get her to show me over

674

Averdale's mansion. Herbert Rice was saying that Averdale's art collection is one of the best in Europe. We could do a feature on how the man lived, maybe a double-page spread of interior shots.'

Kate needed those two days. She was so shattered when she arrived at Chester that she went straight to bed. Emily Jones, her chaperone, had arranged everything with the hotel – 'My room is one side of you and Arthur is on the other. He was born in these parts, he'll be happy to show you round tomorrow if you feel up to it. Meanwhile you get a good night's sleep, that's the best medicine I know.'

Kate was so exhausted that she slept soundly. The previous thirty-six hours had drained her, she was nearer collapse than she realized. But she awoke the next morning refreshed, stronger, more able to cope.

Emily Jones herself delivered breakfast on a tray. 'It's a nice morning, why not let Arthur take you for a drive, it'll be better than sitting in your room?'

She dressed and they went out. Emily sat in front with Arthur. Neither said much, as if they realized she was better left to her thoughts – in fact when Arthur reached Rhyl he suggested she go for a walk along the beach – 'Not if you don't want to of course Miss, but sometimes a breath of sea air . . .'

So she walked, to please them to begin with, although they stayed in the car. Once she got going, with her hands thrust deep in her pockets and the collar turned up – she walked miles, lost in thought. The breeze helped clear her mind. She saw things more clearly. She had been dreadfully shocked about poor Mark and Ziggy, but it was Tim who had driven her to the edge of hysteria. His attitude, his manner. Of course he was upset, she made allowances – she could even understand his jealousy, after all he and Mark must have grown close during the war. And he must have been shocked about her sleeping with Mark. She could *understand* – but none of it justified hostility verging on hatred, she did not deserve that. And his avarice – his disgusting anxiety about the will – Kate would never forgive him . . .

But it was the second day, again as she walked the beach

at Rhyl, that she began to think of her future. What would she do? She had to do *something*. . . her life had a pattern before, meeting journalists, politicians, artists, but that was as an adjunct to Mark – she lacked a separate existence.

Dealing with her trustees would be awful. Tim had threatened her already.

She would go to Paris, to Yvette, as soon as she could. Just for a while, until she sorted herself out. And after that, perhaps she would start a little business, a shop or something.

That evening she dined with Arthur and Emily, 'my new friends' as she called them when she had telephoned Tim before she left London – 'I'm going away, to stay with friends until the funeral.'

'Stay with who you bloody well like,' he had snapped.

After dinner she washed her hair and went early to bed again, dreading the funeral the next day, yet wanting it over, both at the same time.

The event was as grim as she had imagined.

Everyone in Belfast seemed to be at the funeral – and not just Belfast, Westminster politicians of all parties walked in the procession to pay their respects. Kate smiled inwardly as she imagined Mark's reaction – 'All those jumped up clerks from the Labour Party! Good grief Kate, the world's gone mad!'

Poor Mark.

The funeral was only for him. Ziggy's lawyers in Nairobi had stepped in at the last minute. Apparently she had left specific instructions in her own will, asking to be buried in her rose garden. There had been an awful row. The matter had been taken to the Governor. But, after an embarrassing wrangle, Ziggy's wishes had been observed.

Twelve hundred people followed the cortege through the streets and at least eight hundred sipped sherry and chewed smoked salmon sandwiches afterwards. All either thought it or said it – 'Damn odd, Averdale and his wife being buried separately.' Kate felt their eyes throughout the entire day. It made the ordeal even worse.

She whispered goodbye at the graveside, but shed no more tears.

Tim was as remote as ever. She had promised herself that she would make another attempt to reach him, but his eyes remained cold and his manner was barely civil.

'Mark Averdale was the last of his line,' Buckley told Tim in Kate's hearing, 'so the title dies with him. I just thought you'd like to know. Put your mind at rest about some bloody lumberjack in Canada turning up to claim the title. Don't worry, it can't happen.'

The very last Averdale. Nine generations. Kate was to have provided the tenth – Mark had told her ·as much . . .

The very last Averdale.

Then it was all over, and she was on the aircraft looking down at the Irish Sea – wondering if she would ever go to Ulster again. She hoped not. She hated the place. Arthur ordered her a brandy and Emily gave her an encouraging smile. Kate thanked them both – she would have been lost without them. She owed Mr Connors more than his interview. She would never be able to thank him enough

CHAPTER NINE

Seven Days was a journalistic triumph. It dominated the news-stands. Everything was praised; the writing, the photographs, even the printing. Issue number one bore Lord Averdale's picture on the cover with the caption 'End of an Empire?' Inside questions were posed not just about the survival of the Averdale interests, but the stability of the British Empire itself. Reporter after reporter told the same story – growing unrest in the Colonies and indecision at Westminster.

The issue became a collector's item, and not just for the political news. Few readers failed to admire the full-colour portrait on page forty-eight, showing Kate O'Brien in the drawing-room of the Belgrave Square mansion. She was unsmiling and looking at a painting not the camera, but her elegance drew the eye more than the contrived poses of the professional models adorning the advertisement pages.

And the article itself – 'The other side of Lord Averdale' – went a long way towards a public reassessment of the murdered peer. 'Lord Averdale,' Miss O'Brien was quoted as saying, 'was too shy to express his ideals – but he was a very fine person, once you got to know him.'

Not everyone agreed but most men were willing to bet the description fitted Kate O'Brien herself – she was obviously 'a very fine person' but getting to know her was a challenge, as Sean Connors found out.

She was more self-assured than he had expected. Their telephone conversation had led him to imagine a tremulous girl, liable to dissolve into tears. Instead he found a calm, assured young woman who was not only exceptionally attractive but as confident as any female he'd met in New York.

As for Kate, those precious two days walking the beach at Rhyl had given her a chance to collect herself. She was able to hide behind the sophistication she had worked so hard to develop. The biggest dent to her self-assurance was Sean Connors himself. As soon as she saw him she realized he was much better-looking than that ski instructor. Taller, broader, more polished, and possessing infinitely more presence.

The interview went well. Kate thanked him for 'spiriting her away' for a few days and he responded by expressing his sympathy for her involvement in the Averdale tragedy. Kate listened gravely, with her eyes downcast in case he should read what was going through her mind. She fought the urge to blurt out – 'I've known you all the days of my life, you should have been here when I needed you.'

And Sean asked questions in a calm, level voice, while all the time thinking – 'Why do I feel so bloody protective, so anxious not to hurt her? I'm just here for a story, that's all. I'll never see her again. Just get the story . . .'

Kate had given much thought to 'the story'. It was her one chance to square her account with Mark and poor Ziggy. Do this now, she told herself, render this last service, then you can flee to Yvette in Paris. She rehearsed her argument one last time, took a deep breath, and began to tell him, began to *sell* him 'the story'.

She showed him the Averdale collection – 'Someone

described Lord Averdale as selfish,' she said. 'What nonsense. He assembled one of Europe's most important art collections for the benefit of the public. His intention was to put everything on permanent exhibition . . .'

She talked of the left-wing press which had labelled him 'reactionary'. 'How can that be true?' she asked, 'the best working conditions in Africa were found on his estates. Was it reactionary to help Africans buy land? Was it reactionary to start work on a model housing settlement? Or to fund schools and hospitals? I wonder at times if the men on the *Daily Worker* understand what the word means. Most people would call such actions progressive. But they have such closed minds on the *Worker* that they cannot admit anyone named *Lord* Averdale could be progressive about anything.'

It was quite a performance. Her green eyes flashed with temper, and although she showed her inexperience by hectoring at times, Sean Connors wrote it all down. It was hard to reconcile her description with the man from whom he had bought the *Dublin Gazette* but he said nothing about that. He never even admitted to meeting the man. Instead he asked gentle questions and tried to get to know her. He felt a great need to do that. Professional curiosity, he told himself, but it was more than that and deep in his heart he knew it.

So Sean Connors got his story. *Seven Days* was the only journal to interview Miss Kate O'Brien, just as it was alone in presenting 'The other side of Lord Averdale'. But there was more than professional interest in Sean's closing question-- 'And what about you, Miss O'Brien? Have you had a chance to think about your own life?'

'Not really. I'm going to stay with a very old friend in Paris for a few weeks, perhaps even a few months, I don't honestly know. I need somewhere quiet to sort myself out.'

He gave her his card. 'I hope you'll call me when you get back, if you think I might be able to help in any way.'

Then he left. She watched from the window. 'All the days of my life,' she whispered, 'I feel I've known you all the days of my life.'

Four weeks later it was Christmas. Sean gave a series of

parties in his new house in Hill Street, in fact Christmas seemed one long party. All of his friends were there – Michael and Deirdre, Tubby, Sir George and Lady Cynthia Hamilton – and, a marvellous surprise, Freddie and Margaret flew over from New York, complete with their family. The house was greatly admired and Gloria was much praised for capturing the latest vogue in interior decorating. Sean felt warm and happy, surrounded by the people important in his life. And he sensed something else – he sensed his success. For the first time it seemed tangible. He had assets. His businesses brought him wealth and prestige. He owned this wonderful house and everything in it. His suits were tailored in Savile Row, he bought handmade shirts in Jermyn Street – and his reputation had so soared since the launch of *Seven Days* that people in the Savoy Grill were as likely to point him out as the celebrities he accompanied. The name Seán Connors was beginning to mean something . . . and yet . . . happy though he was, hugely successful though he was becoming – the taste of success was less sweet than he had imagined.

He wondered why? After all, everything was perfect – his bank account, his house, his wife, *especially* his wife. When George had met her the first time he couldn't wait to take Sean aside – 'She's a jewel!' And Cynthia approved too – 'Sean darling, she's an absolute *angel*!' Everyone admired her. She was so incredibly competent. She organized a houseful of guests with the effortless skill of an Elsa Maxwell. The Mallon kids saw the pantomime at the Palladium and the circus at Olympia – the adults went racing on Boxing Day and enjoyed the theatre in the evening. The Christmas tree in the hall was a work of art. Everyone received a superbly chosen gift that was just right for them – never had people said 'Oh darling, it's *exactly* what I wanted' with such genuine enthusiasm. And throughout it all Gloria shone like the star of Bethlehem. When the Mallon children quarrelled it was Gloria, not their nurse, who reached them first – 'Hey gang, did I tell you the treat planned for you this afternoon?' When Deirdre got hiccups over dinner it was Gloria who knew the instant cure. And never once was there a curl out of place, a crook in her stockings, or a crease in her dress.

It was the same after Christmas. The Mallons returned to New York and the newly established household at Hill Street settled down to what was to become normal routine. Sean never had cause for complaint. Shirts were always freshly laundered. Suits were cleaned in rotation. Shoes were treed. If he and Gloria were going out that evening a change of clothing was laid out ready for him – if they were staying at home ice was stirred into his whisky as he came through the door. And Gloria was always waiting to greet him – as spick and span, as clean and shining, as a surgeon's knife.

The house ran with the noiseless efficiency of the clock in a Rolls-Royce. Other husbands may have arrived home to tales of woe – about the milkman who failed to leave merchandise on the back step, or the dustman who did. If such domestic mishaps occurred in Hill Street Sean never heard about them. Gloria organized everything with the help of a Spanish maid who lived in, a daily char who lived out, a woman who cooked on special occasions, and an odd-job man who called every Friday.

When they had people in, Gloria was the perfect hostess. When they went to people she was the perfect guest. Small talk, as practised by Gloria, was a minor art form. She could discourse for hours on the latest fashions, on so-and-so's new novel, on the British theatre (which she loved) and British films (which she hated). To maintain three conversations at once took no effort, four was no problem and only when five were running simultaneously did she have to concentrate.

Not only that but she looked good. When they were in company it was rare for another woman to be judged more attractive, and *never* better groomed. Grooming was something at which Gloria excelled. Everything she wore was crisply fresh. The tiniest smudge on a blouse would require her to change. If cleanliness was next to godliness then Gloria was truly saintly.

And yet . . .

By March Sean had defined at least one 'and yet'. They never talked to each other. Not really talked, not about anything important. Her conversation was no different with him than with anyone else – Freddie, for instance, or Michael. She conducted the same light-hearted, good-humoured banter with everyone. Small-talk. Background chatter. She refused to discuss anything serious. 'It's so boring,' she said when he tried, 'and people talking politics or religion always end up having an argument. I ask you, who wants to argue?'

He did. He liked arguing. He and Val had argued all the time . . . about Catholicism, Fascism, Democracy, the Labour Party, the state of the nation, the state of the world . . . they could argue about anything, at least until bedtime, and bedtime could be at midday if the mood struck them.

But bedtime with Gloria was another 'and yet'. Nothing worked – not candle-lit suppers, soft violins, extravagant compliments, expensive presents, nothing. Even when they did make love it was never the uncomplicated coupling he had enjoyed with Val. Gloria sent out subtle unspoken signals with which he tried to comply. As month followed month he learned it was useless to try unless he bathed first, it was essential to be spotlessly clean when he lay down beside her. Clean and fresh-smelling – which meant dousing himself in eau de cologne, and not only brushing his teeth but gargling with a mouth wash. Copulation for Gloria remained a distasteful business, only bearable when conducted under sanitized, sterilized, disinfectant-reeking, laboratory conditions.

Sean made the effort less and less and got little joy from it when he did. More often it filled him with painful reminders – his union with Gloria was a sham compared to the love he had once known with Val.

But, apart from his marriage, life for Sean was full and exciting. The circulation of *Seven Days* rose with every issue, advertisers queued up to buy space, and Jimmy Cross was voted 'Reporter of the Year' by Fleet Street for his vivid accounts of Mau Mau atrocities in Kenya. By that autumn, 1953, whole battalions of British soldiers were engaged in battles against strong guerilla groups. Eighty thousand Kikuyu were held in concentration camps. The gallows in Nairobi crashed away at a rate never seen before on British soil. And as Sean read the despatches his mind often turned to that beautiful red-haired girl who had

682

talked so earnestly of Lady Averdale's predictions.

'Unless we succeed in creating partnerships,' Lady Averdale had said, 'the soil of Kenya will run red with blood.'

And now it was happening.

Yvette Lefarge had welcomed Kate with open arms. Kate's instincts had been sound. Of all the substitute mothers she had clung to over the years none loved her in such an uncomplicated fashion as the elderly Frenchwoman, nor would have accepted her relationship with Mark Averdale with such understanding – Eleanor Bleakley might have fainted on the spot, Alison Johnstone would have been shocked to the core, but Yvette was much wiser than that.

Not that the 'relationship' was discussed to begin with – December passed with Kate making only guarded references to her life with Mark Averdale. Yvette was unconcerned. She enjoyed Kate's company and was content to let time heal the shock. It was only in January, when Kate was beginning to wonder 'What am I going to do with my life?' that Yvette learned the entire story.

'Should I say I knew about your *affaire* without needing to be told?' Yvette smiled. 'Or should I pretend to be shocked? Which reaction would you prefer? Tell me and I'll try to oblige.'

They talked for hours after that – not as mother and daughter, a mother might have been censorious and Yvette was never that, but perhaps as grandmother and granddaughter, or perhaps just as friends.

Seeing Kate's troubled expression Yvette said, 'Do you remember when you used to sketch as a child? All those problems with perspective. Isn't it the same now?'

Kate frowned.

'So you've had your first lover. You were lucky, were you not? He loved you, he was kind, bought you presents, gave you a good time. What is there to regret?'

'Aunt Alison would say I've ruined my life.'

Yvette chuckled, 'Yes, she might, but she also said that when she thought you were nursing an old man. Dear Alison sees everything in such simple terms. What she wants is you to have a big white wedding and lots of babies.'

'You make it sound wrong.'

'Wrong? It's not wrong. Or right. It's irrelevant. The only thing which counts is what you want.'

But defining that was difficult. In the short term Kate wanted a reconciliation with Tim. She was bitterly hurt by his attitude. They were brother and sister, orphans, they should remain close, always, for the rest of their lives. So she told Yvette everything – the details of Mark's letter and his subsequent will – and Tim's bitterness. She even described the scene in her apartment.

'He called me a whore!'

'What does he know about such things? He called Ziggy a whore too, didn't he? Your brother was behaving like a jealous woman, and using spiteful woman's language.'

'Oh Yvette,' Kate hugged her. 'It's such a relief to talk to you. I was so terrified you would disapprove.'

'Approve, disapprove, what does it matter? I only want you to be happy.'

'Can a whore be happy?'

Yvette laughed, 'Will you stop using that silly word. You haven't seen enough life yet, my child, to understand what the word means.'

'But to . . . to have sex outside marriage –'

'Oh, marriage. A wife wants a fur coat. So what does she do? She withholds her favours in bed, or she teases, or gives herself according to how well she understands her husband. Eh? That happens every night of the week. Is she a whore? To be a whore is a state of mind. It has nothing to do with marriage.'

And so Yvette taught Kate 'perspective' for the second time in their lives. But the conversation often turned back to Tim. What was Kate to do about him?

Yvette shrugged, 'He is upset because of what you took. First you took Mark's time. Well, there wasn't a thing you could do about that – and it's too late to worry now. Then you took some of Mark's possessions. So, if your brother believes they are his, and if you believe that too, give them to him. See if that makes him happy.'

'But . . . how would I live –'

'Perhaps your brother loves you enough to give everything back.'

'Well that's just it, I don't think he does –'

'So where is the problem? If you don't think he loves you, then don't do it. Keep the possessions. Mark wanted you to have them.'

'But then Tim –'

'Still won't love you. So what have you proved? That you can't buy love?' Yvette smiled. 'There you are, you've learned two important lessons in one day. I think your old tutor deserves to be taken out to lunch for that.'

And so they went. In fact they went out quite a lot. Kate loved Paris and Yvette was proud of her city. They made a striking couple; Kate, tall and slim, with her vivid red hair: Yvette, petite, ram-rod straight and as nimble as a cat despite her years. They both dressed well. Yvette was now quite comfortably off. The two houses her family had owned had been blitzed to rubble in the war and German reparation payments enabled her to live in a pleasant apartment. She led a cosy middle-class existence which included meeting her friends in various cafés, visits to the ballet and the cinema, holidays – she even, to Kate's amused surprise, had two ardent admirers, each of whom took her out to dinner once a week. Both were retired widowers, and both had proposed marriage.

'What do I want with marriage?' Yvette chuckled throatily, 'I am comfortable as I am. Besides I can see them both this way. If I married Henri he would forbid me to see Gerard and vice versa. What a ridiculous waste that would be.'

So two nights a week Yvette went out to dinner with her admirers and Kate stayed at home – at least she did until the end of January, by which time she had admirers of her own. They were just casual dinner dates whose company she enjoyed and the amusing young men knew it. They struck poses and made her laugh, but provoked no excitement. Being young they lacked . . . she struggled for the right word . . . and then defined it as presence.

'Ah, presence!' Yvette said. 'An inner confidence born of success. Pierre and the others are too young to have acquired that. Perhaps they never will, only time will tell.'

Which reminded Kate of Sean Connors, simply because he had more presence than any man she knew – 'He

685

suggested I telephone him when I go back.'

'And will you?'

Kate thought about that. 'I'd like to see him again – but no, I don't think so, at least not until I've decided what to do with my life.'

And that was a constant topic of conversation.

'Why do anything?' Yvette asked one day. 'You have a big house, servants, an allowance. Why not just spend time with your artist friends and listen to them talk about life? You might find it amusing, perhaps even instructive.'

'No. I don't think I want to live in that house again. Not even in the apartment.'

'Good! Then you can stay here with me.'

But they both knew that was not the answer. Yvette enjoyed having Kate to visit but a permanent arrangement would have been a strain – and they both knew it. Yvette had come to cherish her independence.

'You're a lot like Ziggy,' Kate said one day. 'I know I never met her but we wrote to each other all the time, and Mark used to talk about her. She was remarkable. She dealt with life on her own terms and relied on no one. She must have been very strong.'

Yvette seemed lost in thought, then she said, 'Kate my darling, I remember you as a child. You tried so hard to please. Always spinning your little schemes, so anxious for everyone to form a high opinion of you. But at times you cannot please people. Look at Tim. Give him your inheritance if you like, he will still resent you because Mark was your lover. There is nothing you can do. Ziggy sounds to have been a wise woman, but her secret was very simple. She never made herself a slave to other people's opinions.' Yvette laid a hand on her heart. 'It's what you feel here that's important, that's all that matters. Remember that and you'll be every bit as strong as your friend Ziggy.'

Kate never forgot that advice, no more than she forgot so many of the lessons Yvette taught her. Few people who knew Kate, the journalists in London, or her dinner dates in Paris, or Yvette's friends, most of whom Kate had met by February – few if any suspected the fragility of her self-confidence. They were blinded by her poise, her dazzling smile, the flash of silk-clad legs as she alighted from a taxi.

686

But Yvette was not blind. Kate had been deeply hurt when her brother called her a whore – as Yvette realized, which is why she worked hard to restore Kate's self-esteem.

By the end of February Kate could even joke about it. 'I'll have to come over every so often for you to boost my morale, you know that don't you.'

But Yvette shook her head. 'Just take a quiet moment now and then to question your opinion of yourself. Remember, even your friend Ziggy had her rose garden.'

So by the middle of March Kate felt able to cope again, which was fortunate because it was then that she met Marcel Crispin in the *Café de la Paix*. Sunday lunch at the *Café de la Paix* was part of Yvette's way of life, a pleasure Kate had come to share. They always sat at the same huge oval table with a dozen or so friends, the number swelling occasionally to include someone's relative from out of town. Everyone talked at once on every subject under the sun – politics, the newspapers, the latest scandal, food, wine – reputations were attacked, opinions were argued, the conversation was boisterous, amusing and fun. Kate had never known anything like it. The atmosphere was that of a large, happy family. People hugged when they met as if they had been parted for years. They began at noon and the long leisurely meal rarely ended before four. Even before March Kate had realized she would miss Sunday lunch at the *Café de la Paix* when she returned to London – and then, on the third Sunday in March, Pierre Dreher introduced Marcel Crispin.

'He's not from out of town,' Pierre explained to the gathering, 'but he has a very special reason for wanting to join us for lunch.' But before the reason was revealed a heated discussion broke out on French politics which embroiled everyone at the table – Crispin included, who argued so good-humouredly that he might have eaten at the *Café de la Paix* every day.

Later Kate looked up and caught him watching her. Pierre had embarked on a story and most people were looking at him – but Crispin's eyes were on Kate. She smiled and turned back to Pierre – but knew Crispin was still watching her. Then everyone was laughing at Pierre's story and Kate forgot about it – at least she did until the end of the meal.

Pierre tapped the rim of his glass and called for attention. 'And now,' he said, 'Marcel will explain why he was so insistent on joining us today.'

All attention focused on Crispin. To Kate's surprise he looked directly at her and began to address her in very poor English.

Pierre shouted, 'For God's sake, say it in French. Kate's French is perfect. We'll never understand your attempts to speak English.'

Which brought a shout of approval from everyone.

Pierre beamed around the table, 'Marcel wants to put a proposition to Kate . . .' He was interrupted by shouts of 'Oh la la!' and minutes elapsed before order was restored, 'But I told him,' Pierre continued, 'that as we are Kate's friends and advisors, he should put his proposal to her in our presence.'

Kate cast an astonished look at Yvette but met only an amused twinkle in reply . . . and a moment later Crispin was taking a magazine from his inside pocket. It was a copy of *Seven Days*. The first issue. Kate glimpsed Mark's face on the cover. But Crispin quickly turned to an inside page – it was the photograph of Kate in the drawing-room of Belgrave Square.

Crispin apologized for his inability to address her in English, then went on to introduce himself as an advertising agent. One of his clients was a perfumier and – 'We have a new perfume, soon to be launched. The advertising campaign will be massive, the biggest ever in France.'

Everyone at the table hung on his every word.

'And we need a face,' Crispin continued, 'of course we have looked. We have scoured France. Hundreds, thousands of photographs have been studied. But we wanted a new face, not known to the public. Our top models here, they do everything, you understand – clothes, cars, wine – well that is not good. Our face must be exclusive to us, as exclusive as our perfume.'

They wanted Kate.

Crispin waved the magazine, 'Our president came across

this. He took one look and said this is the girl. Find me this girl. We must have her.'

The magazine was passed down the table. People exclaimed over it. Paul Lemercier even took it to the door to examine the photograph in a better light. He returned smiling broadly to blow kisses down the table to Kate.

'But I'm not a model,' she kept telling Crispin.

He threw up his hands, 'That is the whole point. Here is this beautiful woman, so different, so unspoiled . . . and so unknown in France. She is a woman of mystery, you see the intrigue . . .'

It developed into a riotous party. Pierre and Paul Lemercier insisted on acting as Kate's agents. What was the fee, they demanded. Crispin implored them to be sensible – 'Besides you know nothing of advertising. Pierre, you are a lawyer –'

'And I am a businessman,' Paul interrupted, 'Kate could not be in better hands.'

They adjourned to Yvette's apartment, Pierre and Lemercier still arguing about Kate's fee. It was taken for granted that she would do it – why not, she was the most beautiful girl they knew. 'But the money must be right,' Pierre said, wagging a finger under Crispin's nose, 'and if you want her exclusively it will be very expensive for you.'

They drank wine and coffee and cognac – and whenever Kate asked a question she was told to be quiet – 'Leave this to us,' Paul said firmly. The atmosphere was so full of laughter and argument that she suspected an elaborate joke – but when she went out to the kitchen to help prepare supper Yvette was positively aglow – 'Isn't it marvellous! Your face will be the most famous in France –'

'But I haven't said I'll do it –'

'Of course you will. It's exactly right. You will be famous and rich . . .'

Rich by Averdale standards was out of the question, but Pierre and Paul struck a hard bargain. When they joined Kate in the kitchen they had negotiated a fee equal to her allowance – not only that but – 'If the promotion goes well the contract extends another three years, for *twice* as much money!'

And so Kate agreed to become a model, but not without

adding a condition of her own – although she did not broach the subject until the next day. She had slept on it by then – besides the mood in Marcel Crispin's office on the Monday was a good deal less frenzied than in Yvette's apartment.

Kate presented her argument well . . . but, as she admitted to Yvette afterwards the idea merely needed a launch-pad. And Marcel Crispin, Kate decided, made a perfect launch-pad.

The modelling assignment would be finalized by May – which left her with time on her hands for most of the year. Of course she would take holidays and spend time with Yvette – but she wanted more from life . . .

Crispin frowned and wondered where it was leading. He had been delighted to capture Kate for his perfumier. The perfume account was huge. The agency would make a great deal of money. He wanted no complications now.

Kate described the 'Britain in Africa' campaign. She had enjoyed herself with the journalists. She had established a rapport with them. When they published stories sympathetic to the cause she had been delighted – 'You can't imagine the hostility we had to overcome.'

Crispin remembered *Seven Days*. Kate had certainly obtained some very favourable press comment for the late Lord and Lady Averdale.

'Well,' Kate summed up, 'I've been thinking. You must have clients who export to Britain. How about me running a press office in London on their behalf?'

Crispin was intrigued. and relieved. Most models wanted to become actresses but since few had talent they invariably complicated their lives, and his. He promised to discuss the matter with his President that very evening.

A week later, after Kate had lunched with the President, the idea was taken a step further. The agency was planning a London office – 'Not immediately, you understand, but at the end of the year. Perhaps when you finish your modelling engagement you could work in our Paris office for a while, learning the ropes – then, who knows, perhaps you could take charge of Public Relations in London.'

The challenge gave Kate a much greater thrill than becoming 'the most famous face in France'.

690

Then a letter from Tim arrived which seemed to crystallize everything. She had written to him twice, long chatty letters, full of her life in Paris and asking concerned questions about him. But his single reply was coldly unyielding. He said it was unfair to expect the Averdale estate to provide her with a mansion in London if she spent so much time away – *'Not only that but staff wages, heating bills, rates all mount up – and the cost of insuring those paintings is a scandal. The whole lot should be sold off as soon as possible.'*

'Well,' Yvette said when she read it, 'what do you intend to do about that?'

'He can sell the house,' Kate said happily, 'and the apartment. In fact everything except the paintings. They are the Averdale Collection. I shall arrange to loan them to the Tate, or perhaps even the National for public exhibition.'

A tiny smile lit Yvette's face. 'And you? Where will you live in London – when you take up this very important post as a Public Relations consultant?'

'My trustees can buy me a little mews cottage. I'll pay them back, so much every month from my earnings.'

'Bravo!' Yvette clapped her hands. 'Vive la Independence. But you will still have your allowance – that is, unless you plan to marry?'

Kate shook her head, 'No, I won't need the allowance. I shall support myself. As for marriage,' she mimicked Yvette's scornful tone, 'what do I want with marriage? I shall be comfortable as I am. I'll find an Henri to take me to dinner on Tuesdays, and a Gerard for Thursdays – and I shall have long lingering lunches with my journalists – just like you at the *Café de la Paix*.'

'Ah,' Yvette shook her head in smiling admiration. 'This whole conversation reminds me of your friend Ziggy Beck – someone dealing with life on her own terms, relying on no one.'

Kate just smiled. For the first time in her life she felt free.

Sean Connors felt anything but free. His marriage had turned sour and his wife was pregnant. How was a source of amazement – their sexual couplings had been so clinical that pregnancy constituted a miracle birth. In a moment of wry humour Sean imagined the baby being born wearing a surgical mask and already in diapers. Not that he shared the joked with Gloria – in fact sharing anything had become rare.

Of course they shared the obvious – the house in Hill Street and a king-sized bed, so large that Gloria could turn in the night without even brushing him. It was a token bed, purpose built for a token marriage. In fact, Sean realized, it was exactly what Gloria wanted – a symbol of marriage without the messy reality. She wanted to be known as 'Mrs Sean Connors, wife of the international tycoon'. That was how she saw herself – she even used the word. He overheard her on the phone once to a girlfriend over from New York – 'Of course Sean's into everything these days, real-estate over here, papers over there – these international tycoons never stop, you know.'

The worst part, he mused, was she really believed she was the perfect wife. Nobody ran a cleaner home – or organized a better dinner party – or cared more for her husband's clothes. But all it amounted to was a little girl playing in her doll's house – and he was the doll.

She discovered she was pregnant in November, four days before they were due in New York. 'I can't possibly fly now,' she told Sean, 'we shall have to sail next week on the *Queen Mary*.'

After that she was sick every morning. Crossing the Atlantic was ghastly.

But New York cheered her up. Freddie and Margaret were there to greet them, along with what seemed like a hundred of Gloria's friends. She told everyone of her mother-to-be status within ten minutes of meeting them. She even seemed excited about her condition but, as Sean realized, she could hardly grumble 'I told you we were doing it too often' when talking to Freddie.

Within days of arriving Gloria was saying – 'Gee, New York's terrific! London's quaint but not in the same league.'

And a day after that she said, 'The baby *must* be born here. Those London hospitals are positively primitive. I wouldn't feel able to trust them.'

The next day she was talking about buying a house. 'After all, you said we'd spend six months in every twelve over here. We can't stay with Freddie all the time. Besides I *need* a house for the baby.'

She found the house in Scarsdale a week before Christmas. 'Sean, can you take time out to look at it tomorrow? You'll just love it. Scarsdale's cute. It will be just perfect for when I have the baby.'

On Christmas Eve he agreed to buy the house.

On New Year's Eve he agreed that she should stay behind when he returned to London at the end of January.

'There's so much to do, Sean. Decorators to organize, furnishings to buy. These things all take so much time. Once I get all bloated I won't want to be bothering with pattern books and things . . . it makes sense for me to stay . . .'

He did not really mind. After all, he was unlikely to be inconvenienced. Consuela, their Spanish maid, had just married and her new husband had joined the household as a manservant. Even now Consuela's rooms in Hill Street were being converted into a staff flat . . . so by the time Sean returned the house would be running along the well oiled tracks laid down by Gloria.

As for more basic needs . . . 'Sean, how could you even *think* of it? It wouldn't be right . . . not for a woman in my condition.'

It was a relief in a way. Sean's previous lovemaking had been with enthusiastic partners. The act had been so mutually satisfying that he had imagined all women had the same needs.

As usual Sean lost himself in work. The economy of the United States under Eisenhower's Presidency grew ever stronger. Business was booming. During the nine or ten weeks of his visit, Sean drove himself hard. In fact he saw little of Gloria. She linked up with some of her old girlfriends and spent most days with them – more time with them than with Margaret. When Sean and Freddie were in New York the two couples dined together – they took in a show one weekend – but more often than not Sean was away working on his business interests. So when January

693

ended Sean was still unsure how long Gloria planned to stay in New York.

'I guess it depends how I feel,' she said, 'maybe I'll come over in the spring, if everything is finished with the house – why don't we see how it goes.'

Sean had intended to fly back to London until he met Bill Hartley. Hartley owned a newspaper in Wisconsin, not a big one but big enough for Freddie to want to buy. Hartley was on the verge of retiring. 'My wife died a few years back. It reminded me, there's a big wide world out there I've hardly seen.' So he was going to Europe on vacation. 'Sailing on the *Queen Mary* next week. If you're going to London why not come on the boat – we could talk business during the voyage.'

So Sean chose not to fly.

Hartley was a youthful-looking fifty-five and when he walked into the bar on the first night out from New York he clearly intended to start his vacation without further delay. 'Sean, there's some people I just met. I suggested they join us for dinner. They might be fun. Maybe we should leave our business talk over until the morning.'

Which was how Sean met Eloise. She was a thirty-year-old divorcee from Denver, Colorado, who was just 'knocked all of a heap to meet Sean Connors, the broadcaster'. She had chestnut hair, blue eyes, an appealing smile and cheeks full of dimples. After dinner they danced in the nightclub, and after that she joined him in his state-room for a nightcap. 'Just one teeny-weeny little drink,' she said, but they both knew she was joking by then.

Eloise's dimples were not confined to her face. Her deliciously rounded little body abounded with them. 'I know,' she sighed, 'it's the sign of a happy person.'

She was happy all night. So was Sean. They made love and dozed, until she aroused him again. She groaned softly, 'Oh Sean, that's so good. It feels like . . . like when you've been away a long time, and you come home. You know what I mean?'

And Sean knew exactly.

By the time the *Queen Mary* docked in Southampton Sean was committed to rather more than just buying Bill Hartley's newspaper.

694

'You mean it?' Eloise asked breathlessly. 'If I stay over a month you'll really show me round? Honestly? My, imagine that, being shown London by Sean Connors. I mean, I'm supposed to go on to Rome but the tour guide would have to be Julius Caesar to match that.'

She returned to the States in the middle of March. Sean was sorry and glad to see her go – sorry because he had enjoyed her so much – but relieved because she had cut into his working days more than he had intended. Some aspects of his business had been neglected.

Gloria wrote to say she did not feel up to travelling, and the new house was only half-finished – '*Anyway, by the time I get there I guess you'll be ready to come back to New York. Do you realize BABY DAY is only twelve weeks away. I saw the Doctor yesterday and everything's fine, so you're not to worry . . .*'

Sean had not been worrying at all, as he guiltily realized.

Without Eloise to distract him he plunged happily back into business. The London office building boom was under way. The Mallon Property Company discarded residential developments in favour of a move into the business sector. As the projects grew the amounts of money escalated to gigantic figures. Sir George Hamilton, Sean and Tubby found themselves in endless negotiations with banks, insurance companies, and pension funds. The scale of the business was now so huge that it seemed impossible for the whole thing to have come about as a result of Tubby's problems at Rutland Gate.

And Transatlantic Television was building up too. As commercial television got under way the situation Sean had foreseen began to emerge – the independent contractors needed to win a big share of the BBC's audience, but they lacked the capacity to produce enough programmes. Sean had the best American programmes . . . and began to do business.

Meanwhile *Seven Days* was becoming famous for spotting a trend, and no better illustration of that existed than in its coverage of events in British Colonial Africa. James Cross had been writing for a long time of the need to form multi-racial partnerships, and in 1954 this theme was picked up by the new Colonial Secretary, Alan

Lennox-Boyd. In the light of Mau Mau in Kenya, the British Government was shifting its ground. An experiment with self-government was started in the Sudan. The Rhodesias merged with Nyasaland. And in Salisbury black politicians sat down with their white counterparts in a new parliament for the first time. Colonial Secretary Lennox-Boyd talked endlessly of the exciting prospects which lay ahead for multi-racial partnerships. In the House of Commons his approach was thought to represent radical new thinking, but regular readers of *Seven Days* knew better than that. They could recall that the murdered Lady Averdale had called for the very same thing.

Sean followed the Kenya story with professional interest, but never without being reminded of Kate O'Brien. She had not telephoned as he had hoped. He blamed himself. He should have been more positive, made some excuse – a follow-up interview perhaps. He telephoned her apartment in Belgrave Square. The number had been disconnected. He tried the main house itself, only to learn it had been sold. He wondered where she was and what she was doing. And sometimes, as he sat alone in Hill Street, drinking a last whisky before going to bed, he was saddened by the thought that he might never see her again.

They did meet again, but surprisingly not until 1957 – almost five years after the Averdale murders. Surprisingly for a number of reasons – they both owned houses in London, within three miles of each other, and they were both bound up with the communications industry. But against that Sean was in the States a good deal, and Kate was back and forth to France – they led busy lives – lives which, like most others, saw success and failure, happiness and sadness.

Sean's biggest failure was his marriage. Gloria almost lost her life giving birth to their son. She was in labour twenty-seven hours, and only an emergency Caesarian operation saved her life and that of her child. After that the marriage was over from a physical point of view. Gloria had found the sex act distasteful before, but after giving birth to Patrick, the very thought of sexual intercourse

696

terrified her. She refused to sleep in the same bed as Sean, in fact she even refused to sleep in the same room.

To begin with he tried to be a dutiful husband – after what Gloria had been through it was easy to understand how frightened she was – and he *did* understand, he tried to make every allowance, but fate was against him by then. He was mixing with glamorous people. As a rich, successful and influential man he was invited to all sorts of functions – and when Gloria preferred to stay at home, Sean went to parties alone. Mostly they were to do with his business interests, but that never lessened the number of attractive women in attendance. In fact as Sean's television interests burgeoned actresses and starlets made a beeline for him when he entered a room. Eloise Summers, the pretty divorcee from Denver, was merely the first of a number of girlfriends.

As for Gloria, she built a shell around herself. If rumour reached her of her husband's *affaires* she turned a deaf ear. She seemed to accept it. Perhaps just as Sean had tried to understand her, she understood him. There was much in her life to compensate. She loved her house in Scarsdale, she had all the money she needed. She became one of the girls – coffee mornings, charity committee meetings – she was a born organizer, the young matrons of Scarsdale quickly adopted her as their leader. Many had husbands like Sean – away on business, on trips overseas – and even when some husbands were home there were always enough grass widows for an evening of bridge or canasta. Gloria Connors was looked up to locally, after all she was the wife of an international tycoon, and if Sean was away more often than most it was because he was that much richer and more successful. If Gloria *was* ever concerned with the rumours of Sean's various dalliances she consoled herself with the thought that he was out 'on loan', that was all, for a night or a week – but thanks to a good Catholic marriage he was hers for life and she would never let go.

She remained in Scarsdale. Her attachment to London was always minimal. She had no desire to see Hill Street again. It was enough to know that Sean had a comfortable home on both sides of the Atlantic, and she had furnished them both. Her identity was stamped on them as clearly as a portrait signed by the artist.

Initially she used her frail strength as an excuse not to accompany Sean back to London – but in the second year she claimed it would upset the baby, and in the third said much the same – with the added proviso that her social commitments to the girls were now so extensive that she would let them down by going away.

Sean disliked Scarsdale – but then he was a big-city boy who liked to be in the middle of things. That was where it happened – not on the edge – and people who lived on the edge seemed pompous and pretentious to him, whether it was Scarsdale, New York or Rickmansworth, London.

So when he was in New York he often called Gloria to say he was working late and he would stay over at Freddie's – 'But tomorrow looks an easier day, I'll be home in time for dinner.'

And so the pattern of their lives became established.

If his friends saw what was happening few said anything. Nobody in London really spoke out and even Sean's best friends, Freddie and Margaret in New York, were careful – their usual tack was to criticize the Kennedys, and so get at Sean through them. Sean was seeing an ever increasing amount of the Kennedys. He was never one of the Clan, but he spent a number of weekends at Hyannis Port and knew the whole family. His favourite remained the Ambassador. He and old Joe Kennedy had a soft spot for each other, a throwback to those pre-war days when the Ambassador had extended a helping hand and in return Sean had been uncritically loyal. As for the rest of the family, he liked Jack, was watchful of Jackie, careful with Bobby, and felt slightly sorry for Teddy who seemed overshadowed by his older brothers. Most of all he admired their togetherness, their fierce loyalty to each other. But the Kennedys were raising eyebrows for their non-political activities, as Freddie was always quick to point out.

The Ambassador telephoned Sean at the Mallon apartment once, interrupting supper, and when Sean returned to the table Freddie growled – 'You know what that old devil's up to? Trying to hi-jack the White House for Jack. Well he won't get away with it, not in a million

698

years. Jack's too young for a start. The Old Man is grooming him to run in '60. Jack will only be forty-two, forty-three even then. No one that age ever made President. Second reason, none of the big name Democrats have any time for him – Truman hates his guts, so does Sam Rayburn, Lyndon Johnson doesn't trust him, nor does Eleanor Roosevelt – so if they hate the Old Man they'll never buy his son. And third, the biggest reason of all, he's Catholic and that's the kiss of death –'

'Freddie,' Margaret looked embarrassed, 'Sean's Catholic too, remember.'

'Oh Sean's the one who got away,' Freddie grinned. 'His father taught him that.'

They talked about Sean's father for a while after that, and then Margaret said, 'He sounds wonderful.'

'He was. Perhaps that's why I like Old Man Kennedy so much. He reminds me of the Da in some ways.'

'I'm sure your father was a much nicer man,' Margaret said quickly.

Sean cocked an eyebrow, 'Oh? You don't like Kennedy either?'

'I only met him once –'

'*And* he made a pass at her,' Freddie scowled. 'I tell you, that man should be castrated!'

'Freddie,' Margaret's hand moved across the table to cover his. She smiled at Sean. 'It's a reflex action with Kennedy, he makes a grab for anything in skirts, I'm sure I wasn't singled out, after all he's usually surrounded by a dozen blondes.' Her smile faded as she concentrated, 'No Sean, I don't like your friend the Ambassador. He's a man of strong will and low tastes. He's anti-semitic, anti-black, anti-liberal, in other words a bigot. How his wife copes is a mystery, that's her business, but frankly I think he is everything bad in American public life. To imagine him anywhere near the White House frightens me silly. His attitude towards women is not just a scandal . . . it's, well, downright *un-American*!' She flushed. 'In the main American men are kind and generous and chivalrous, I should know, I married one, and thank God he's not like Kennedy at all.'

Freddie sat back and applauded. Then he leant across

the table to kiss her. Margaret blushed and glanced anxiously at Sean, 'I'm sorry, I ought not to have said that –'

'In America?' Sean grinned. 'What happened to free speech?'

She smiled and gave him a long look. He knew why. She wasn't just talking about Kennedy, she meant him too. She was saying the rumours had reached her and she disapproved.

They meant well. Sean knew that both Freddie and Margaret were concerned about him. But they had each other, and Sean's bed was empty.

Kate's bed remained empty too – though in her case from choice. Over the years she had discovered that some photographers thought no session in the studio could commence until – 'We get to know each other. After all, we are artists you and I. The camera must make love to you, *oui*? And so must the man behind the view-finder. We must make music . . . and afterwards, you will see . . . it will show in our work.'

The first time she heard that line she was embarrassed. The second time she was prepared. She rummaged through her work-bag and produced an harmonica. 'I'll sing if you play,' she smiled. For the man who talked of 'making chemistry' she carried a small bunsen-burner and a microscope – and those who talked of 'sharing a beautiful experience' were handed tickets to the local art gallery.

It was the same with the journalists in London. Kate went to enormous lengths to win press coverage for her clients. Many reporters became firm friends, but those who wanted to go further were told – 'Harry' or 'Bob' or 'David' – 'I'd love to go to bed with you, believe me, a good-looking man like you, a girl would be crazy to miss an opportunity like that – but what would it do to your reputation? Imagine when you write about my clients. People will scream you only wrote it because, well, you know. And if you don't write about my clients *I* will scream. You'll be caught in the middle. Darling it would be too awful for you. You can't make the sacrifice, I won't let you.'

700

She joked her way out of endless situations while smoothing their egos and retaining their friendship. Some were more difficult to dissuade than others, but once Kate made them grin she knew she was safe.

In France her face smiled down from hoardings from Marseilles to Dieppe. In Paris it brightened the Metro and lent beauty to the news-stands. At the end of the first year her contract was renewed at twice the fee – exactly as Pierre and Paul had negotiated.

In London her flair for winning the right sort of publicity for clients brought more work than she could handle. She chose carefully, restricting herself to products she liked and could believe in, and rejecting all others. She turned her back on all offers of political work – political campaigns, she decided, were just too dangerous. The 'Britain in Africa' programme was the last of its kind she ever wanted to be associated with . . . and that, she said firmly, was her last word on the subject.

She worked hard but played hard as well. Most nights she had a date – dinner, the theatre, a preview at an art gallery – sometimes they were 'working evenings' spent with clients, but often they were just a few precious hours spent relaxing with friends.

She had become a successful and independent young woman.

She was proud of herself.

Whenever uncertainties plagued her she remembered Yvette's advice – 'It's your opinion of yourself that matters' and Kate had grown confident enough to believe she had little with which to reproach herself – although she was sometimes concerned about Tim.

They had achieved a grudging reconciliation. He had been pleased with her decision to sell the mansion – but angry about her arrangements to put the Averdale Collection on permanent display at the Tate. Pleased with her determination to provide for herself – but angry when she denied him access to Mark's money.

'God dammit,' he had raged, 'I could put that to use in Ulster. Every business we've got is starved of capital. Yet you leave all that money in the bank collecting interest. What for, if you're not going to use it?'

'I can't use it,' she pointed out, 'without my trustees' permission.'

'So – Buckley and I will listen to anything reasonable. What do you want to do with it?'

'I don't know, but maybe one day I shall.'

She wasn't being deliberately difficult. She just felt that the money had been left with her, and it should stay with her – for the time being. Besides she had a nagging doubt that Tim might not bother to see her again if she let him have the money. As things were he generally called when he was in London, about once every three months. She told herself they were growing closer – that they were brother and sister – they were the only 'real family' each other had. It was still important to her – no matter how independent she became.

Then, in the autumn of '57, she met Sean Connors again, and suddenly independence ceased to be the biggest thing in her life.

They met professionally. *Seven Days* was preparing an important series of articles on the soon-to-be formed EEC. Kate was interested as soon as she heard – after all she represented seven large French companies by then – she had her clients' interests to think about. *Seven Days* was the biggest platform her clients could have. But . . . and she was conscious of the but, she felt a stir of excitement at the prospect of seeing Sean Connors again. She had wanted to telephone him so often, but lacked a valid excuse. Now that she had one she didn't hesitate – she just hoped he was in London.

'Hello,' he said when he answered the phone, 'this is Sean Connors speaking.'

'If I were to say this is Sean Connors, speaking from London, the heart of Great Britain, the country that now stands alone . . . could you guess who was calling?'

'Where the devil have you been?'

He knew! He still remembered!

They met for lunch the same day. She almost trembled when she shook hands. Then he was guiding her to a corner table and she was telling herself – 'I've done this hundreds of times. It's just lunch with a newspaperman, that's all, nothing to get excited about.'

702

He was so staggered about her being in the PR business. 'And in London,' he kept saying, 'why on earth didn't you call me before?'

'You weren't running a big series on France before –'

'But you didn't have to wait for that. I wanted to see you –'

'What about?'

'Well, just to make sure you were all right, to see if I could help . . .'

'Well now you can,' she said, laughing, and he was laughing too, his hand reaching across the table to clasp hers. 'It's just so marvellous to see you again,' he said.

He told himself it was crazy, to feel this excited, after all, I hardly know her.

They talked and talked and talked. At half past three every waiter in the restaurant seemed to be hovering around their table. The restaurant was closed, the staff wanted to go home.

'Can we meet for dinner tonight?' he asked.

She hesitated.

'I want to hear all about your clients,' he said, 'maybe we could include something about them . . .'

So she said yes.

'It's just a working dinner,' she told herself as she bathed and changed for the evening, 'I have at least one every week. It's not a big deal.'

He picked her up from her little house at eight o'clock. They had a drink first. He praised her taste in furnishings and paintings and just about everything. It seemed so natural for him to be there. She wore her Givenchy original, black lace, bare shoulders, bare-backed but high at the front. 'It's too dressy for a working dinner' she had told herself earlier . . . but the dress was on by then.

CHAPTER TEN

Kate never felt more alive, more vital, more . . . joyous! She woke every morning with a smile on her face. Orange-juice tasted like champagne. The simplest things gave her pleasure. She had an insane urge to hug passers-by on the street. She was wildly extravagant, she spent a fortune on clothes – she overtipped cabbies and doormen and hairdressers.

She was head over heels in love.

She telephoned him all the time – at all hours, day and night. She played games, ridiculous, mad, insane games . . . she lowered her voice when she called him in an absurd attempt to mimic his accent – 'Hello. This is Sean Connors speaking from London, heart of Great Britain, the country that now stands alone – '

'Kate? What's the time . . . oh my God, it's *three* in the morning!'

'So? Why aren't you here in my bed?'

'I only just left it – '

'And drove straight home and went to sleep. Humph!' She tossed her head, 'I don't think much of that. Why aren't you pacing the floor, saying over and over again "I love that woman, that marvellous, fantastic – "'

'*Crazy* – '

' – adorable woman – '

'I did, I swear, before I rolled into bed. I said all those things – '

'To yourself? That's no good! Tell *me* . . . I'm listening . . . Sean, *tell me!*'

They tried to be discreet, but it happened so quickly. They had no time to lay down ground rules, no time to invent alibis. It just exploded. Seventy-five hours after their first lunch together. The second time he took her out to dinner. He took her home and they were barely inside the door when she was in his arms. They were both trembling so violently, undressing took ages.

704

But after . . . when he left at five in the morning . . . the names she called herself? She wept. She could hardly believe it. Her of all people. All the clever ploys she had invented for fending men off, for keeping them at bay, all the strategies, she hadn't used one of them, nor had she wanted to.

'Tim was right. I'm a whore, a tramp. Oh what must he think of me!'

But then *he* telephoned – 'Kate, darling, I must see you again, lunch today, dinner tonight . . .'

Her heart soared. She gloried at the sound of his voice. When she opened the door to him she was vibrant and happy and smiling . . .

He took her to the country that weekend, and the next, and the one after.

She kept telling herself – 'He's married. He has a wife and child in America. Pull yourself together!' She told herself that a hundred times. But it made no difference. When he telephoned, smiled, made love to her, nothing else mattered . . .

Until the misery of that first awful Christmas when he went to New York. Fourteen entire days and nights without seeing him. Fourteen days and nights when he was with his wife and child and smart American friends. Three hundred and thirty-six hours when she went out of her mind, twenty-three thousand minutes of torment . . .

But he loved her!

Oh the joy, the delirious, heart-bursting, blood-bubbling intoxication of hearing him say over and over again – 'Kate, I love you.'

Sean was just as afflicted. Gourmet meals were tasteless unless Kate was there to share them. Days were grey unless he saw her. He rarely laughed outside of her company. Even business was less exciting – long negotiations were almost impossible to sustain, concentration proved difficult, his attention kept wandering. He told himself he was behaving like a schoolboy . . .

But she loved him.

It took them months to come to their senses. The spring of '58 passed in a blur of apple-blossom and candle-lit suppers, of holding hands in the moonlight, of small country hotels nestled in the folds of the Hampshire hills...

Sean had known love before, with Val. He had never felt for Gloria in the same way – not even at the outset. He thought the difference was that he had grown up – that he could cope with relationships without losing his head. He told himself that about his marriage and *affaires* with half a dozen women. 'I'm a man-of-the-world – of course I don't react like a kid any more.' But he did with Kate. She made his pulse race and his eyes sparkle, and turned every day into a holiday.

But Kate had never been in love. For the first time all the corny, hackneyed, banal expressions overheard at Glossops made sense. She did 'go weak at the knees'... she really did 'melt in his arms'... and most certainly she 'longed for his kiss'.

As spring turned into summer the pattern of their lives changed completely. Most weekends were spent together, generally out of town to lessen the risk of meeting people they knew. During the week they met for lunch or dinner when they could, and Sean often spent most of the night at Kate's place. She never set foot in Hill Street. She refused to stop by even for a drink, despite the convenience it offered at times. Hill Street belonged to Sean's wife in Kate's eyes... which was not a subject she liked thinking about.

By the autumn of '58 they had been lovers for a whole year.

'It doesn't seem possible,' she sighed, 'a year ago I thought I was happy. I had everything I wanted. Dammit I *was* happy. My life was under control, uncomplicated...'

He kissed her.

'And empty,' she said a long time later.

By the end of that year each knew the other's life history. Kate made him laugh with tales of Glossops and accounts of *Pygmalion*... and of Aunt Alison in Washington and Jenny in Omaha. But mostly, when she talked of the past, it was the immediate past – dear Yvette and her friends in Paris, her work in France as a model, and her public relations career in London.

Sean talked of Tubby and the property company, and

ow he and Freddie had put *Seven Days* together. He told
her about Transatlantic Television, his contacts with show
business, the Kennedys, his interest in politics . . . he told
her so much about his life.

They never lied to each other, not once.

And yet . . . some aspects of the past were brushed over
lightly. For example Sean often talked of his boyhood in
Dublin but made no reference to the Widow O'Flynn. And
when he talked of his early days in London it was Freddie
this and Freddie that . . . almost as if Val Hamilton had
never existed. It was hard. Sometimes he *wanted* to talk
about Val – it was so long ago, a different world – he longed
to describe his life as it had been. But he remembered
Kate's expression when Gloria's name cropped up, he had
seen the pain in her eyes. To admit to Gloria was bad
enough, to reveal his feelings for Val would be a thousand
times worse. So no mention of Val passed Sean's lips.

Kate did the same. When she learned that Sean's father
had been an IRA hero, she 'adjusted' her account of the
death of her parents. It was easily done. After all she had
no clear idea . . . during her childhood she believed they
had died in an accident. It was only at Glossops that Tim
told her otherwise, and she had been so horrified that even
that memory was garbled. She had a vague picture of her
father marching into battle against the IRA, but that was
all. If Sean's father had fought on the other side it seemed
insensitive to mention it. So she simply said her parents had
died in an accident. Besides, she was more worried about
explaining what happened *after* she became Mark
Averdale's ward. She was worried sick about that. She had
become Sean's mistress so easily that he might think she
made a habit of it. She was terrified it would reduce her in
his eyes, petrified he would change his opinion of her.
Sean's opinion was the most important thing in her life.
So she emphasized how hard she had worked for Lord
and *Lady* Averdale. She talked of her contacts with Ziggy,
how much she admired Ziggy . . . and of Mark's long
absences in Nairobi, and his obvious affection for his
wife . . .

Sean told Kate the truth – in the main Kate told Sean the
truth – certainly neither told a lie, but they held some things

back for fear of hurting the other – and in that they were no different from lovers the world over. Ghosts belong to the past, not the sunlit, brightly coloured world of people in love.

But for the most part their conversation was of other things. Kate's work in public relations had given her many friends in Fleet Street. She and Sean knew some of the same people . . . they shared interests in common . . . there was too much to talk about in the present to spend time on the past.

They did try to be discreet, at least to begin with – but it was not long before most of their friends knew. Not everyone approved. Michael O'Hara was captivated by Kate, but his own Catholicism filled him with reservations and his wife Deirdre filled him with more. The Hamiltons worried, and even Freddie fretted when he came face to face with the relationship on a visit to London – 'It can only lead to trouble,' he muttered, expressing the concern of Sean's friends.

But the lovers were blinded by the stars in their eyes.

For eighteen months just being in love was enough. They dove-tailed their busy working schedules to fit each other's plans. When Sean went to New York, Kate went to Paris. If she was taking a party of journalists around the vineyards of Bordeaux, Sean used the opportunity to go to Manchester to negotiate on some property. But wherever they were not a day passed without them telephoning each other – and not a month passed without them celebrating some anniversary – 'our first trip to Scotland' – 'that weekend in Wales'.

When they were together they were ecstatically happy. When they were apart they counted the hours.

But they suffered. Pain. Moments of doubt. And fear. Kate was stricken every time Sean went to New York. She agonized about her 'mistress' status. Always a mistress, never a wife. Old childhood insecurities returned to haunt her. All the days of her life she had longed for clear-cut unequivocal relationships. She had hated being an orphan. Countless times she had longed to introduce the Johnstones not as 'my Aunt and Uncle' but as 'my mother and father'. And how wonderful it would be to introduce

708

ean as 'my husband'. How proud she would be . . . and
ow secure she would feel.

Sean's absences in the States were not the only cause of
Kate's insecurity. Her brother Tim was a nightmare. She
till loved him, after all he was the only real family she had
. . and yet. He would no more understand about Sean than
e had about Mark. He would call her a whore. He might
ven . . . if he ever met Sean . . . reveal her past relationship
vith Mark! That was a terrifying prospect. Kate would do
nything to avoid that. Thankfully Tim was rarely in
London so the chance of him meeting Sean was remote, but
he possibility that he *might* played on Kate's mind. Tim,
he decided, was a matter best left for the future . . . for
vhen she felt more able to cope.

Few doubted that Sean would cope. His breezy self-
onfidence surmounted most problems. But in one matter
e was helpless. His Catholic marriage to Gloria. Divorce
vas out of the question – not only did the Church make
lissolving the union impossible, but Gloria had no wish to
hange her status. Why should she? She had all she wanted
– a smart house in Scarsdale, money, the cachet of
narriage (wife of an international tycoon) . . . and most
mportant of all, her niche as the local Queen Bee.
Contentment was reflected in her figure which plumped out
o matronly size. She was safe and secure, a good Catholic
vife protected by a good Catholic marriage.

Sean told her there was 'another woman' early in 1959.
His trips to New York had become more frequent, because
e stayed for shorter periods and hence was compelled to
o more often. If Gloria realized that more than his
chedule had changed, she said nothing – perhaps she was
leased by his absences. But she was certainly not pleased
y his announcement.

'There have been women before,' she said, 'but you've
ever chosen to tell me about them.'

Her cold reminder of past betrayals tugged at Sean's
onscience. Guilt made him defensive. He wanted to say
he failure of the marriage was as much her fault as his –
e even started to frame the words, then stopped himself,
ware of the futility. 'It's different this time,' he said, 'I
ant this relationship to last.'

'How sweet – and how tiresome for you to be encumbered by a wife and child.'

Her tone was only slightly malicious, just as her eyes were cool, not cold with temper or outrage. The impersonal interest echoed in her voice when she asked – 'What's she like? Young I suppose, and passionate in bed.'

Sean remained silent. How could he explain that Kate made him laugh, made him feel young – that sometimes just talking to her, answering her quick questions, seeing the love in her eyes, was like coming in from the cold to be warmed by a fire.

Afterwards, dozing through the long flight to London, he wondered why he had even bothered to tell Gloria. It had accomplished nothing. In fact she had cut the conversation short to go to a bridge-party. They hadn't even had a row. Her parting comment summed up her attitude – 'How you behave in London is your business. I only hope you don't make a fool of yourself in public, that's all. It might make the papers back here.'

Sean was reminded of his father's rules. 'If you make a mistake,' the Da had said, 'always be ready to pay for it.' Sean was, but other people would pay too. Kate mostly, of course, but also Patrick his son. Sean remembered his own upbringing with Brigid and Tomas, Maureen and Michael . . . and always the Da. How close they had been. How much closer than Sean was to Patrick.

In London Kate listened quietly to an account of his conversation with Gloria.

'Don't look so sad,' she said, 'nothing matters as long as we are together.'

But it did. The Permissive Society was more catch phrase than reality in 1960. Attitudes had changed by the end of the decade, but to begin with eyebrows were raised when a married man on the edge of public life was so often seen with the same vivacious redhead. Sean and Kate were careful not to flaunt their relationship, but concealing it was impossible. Most of the gossip-columnists knew but – thankfully perhaps – professionals have a way of looking after their own, so when Kate's face appeared in the *Express* or the *Mail* she was never noticeably accompanied by Sean Connors.

'I sometimes think we live in a goldfish bowl,' Kate once said sadly.

But they escaped at weekends. Sean bought a cottage near Cookham and most Friday evenings found the lovers fleeing from London for two days of blissful anonymity. Kate cooked and kept house and pretended she was married – while Sean mended the roof and even raised vegetables. They ate and drank, lazed and talked – and fell ever deeper in love. Weekends were a magical interlude in their very busy lives, for from Monday to Friday the world moved on – and Sean's businesses moved with it.

Seven Days burst all circulation records. The whole planet read about itself in the magazine's pages. In the States Joe Kennedy (to Sean's delight and Freddie's chagrin) was wheeling and dealing his son into the White House. Sean saw the Ambassador whenever he went to New York, and was often in the room when Jack telephoned from somewhere on the campaign trail. The old man would snort and grunt as Jack related some setback, then he would say – 'Jack, this could be the best thing ever to happen to you. Let's play it this way . . .' And after he would say, 'Sean, give me a minute, I need to make a few calls for Jack . . .' and Sean would listen as the old campaigner soft-talked a favour or strong-armed an obligation to get what he wanted.

So like the Da, Sean always thought.

But *Seven Days* covered more than the race for the White House. As a new decade began few people would have disagreed with Freddie's prediction – 'Sean, we need men in Africa – that's where the stories will come from.'

And come they had, in a never ending stream which built to a flood.

By 1960 not even the promise of 'a multi-racial society' could stem the rising tide of nationalism. Black Africans wanted their continent and wanted it *now*. Already Nkrumah had won independence for the Gold Coast and renamed it Ghana. Elsewhere De Gaulle was embarking on a programme of independence for French West Africa – and Belgium did the swiftest about-turn of all by agreeing that the Congo should not wait thirty years as had been said all along, but could go free in *seven months*! As the year opened the British Prime Minister left London for a six week tour of the continent. Wherever he went Macmillan met ambitious young locals jostling for control of their native lands. The movement towards independence was irresistible and Macmillan knew it. Towards the end of his tour he reached the bastion of white supremacy in Africa and told an audience in Cape Town – '*The wind of change is blowing through the continent . . .*'

Writing in *Seven Days* James Cross called Macmillan's speech the greatest ever made by a British leader on the subject of the British Empire. It was a speech which finally and irrevocably surrendered the British Imperial dream.

Matt Riordan sneered when he read it. 'Finally surrendered the British Imperial dream. The British might be surrendering in Africa but the buggers are hanging on here.'

Matt was active in the IRA again – when he could find the IRA. Rekindling enthusiasm for a physical force movement was not easy in the north – Catholics turned deaf ears to Matt's arguments for a united Ireland. There was real poverty in the south, but thanks to the Welfare State much hardship had been alleviated north of the border.

'It's no bloody paradise,' people told Matt, 'but it's maybe the best deal going in Ireland.'

Of course he said they were wrong. Prods in Stormont were manipulating the Welfare State to suit themselves – Prods still got the best houses and the best jobs. Matt told his listeners over and over again – but most people just shrugged.

Matt had recovered some of his old strength. Bridie had nursed him through the worst of his ills. She had made him a comfortable home and borne him two fine sons and three daughters – and helped establish his identity as William Lambert, known as Matt to his friends in Ballymurphy.

'Doctor Hugh', Bridie's brother, had moved out in '53 when the first of the girls was born. Hugh Ryan's departure had been a relief for Matt. He liked him, he was grateful to the man, without Hugh's help Matt might have lost his sight and well he knew it. But having Hugh around all the time was a constant restraint. Hugh was so strongly opposed to force that there was no telling what he would do if he knew Matt was getting involved again . . .

It began with a visit to Dublin. The IRA was still outlawed on both sides of the border, but attitudes were different in the south. After all, every politician in the Dail was a Republican who believed in a united Ireland. So blind eyes were turned. Special Branch detectives kept tabs on known members of the IRA, but there was no harassment as during the war. In fact Special Branch men and the IRA boys greeted each other with a friendly 'Hello' when they met on the streets.

Gradually Matt made contacts. The movement was still alive – starved of cash, fragmented, lacking organization – but thanks be to God there were still men ready to die for Ireland.

Back and forth Matt went, all during the Border Campaign of the late fifties when IRA columns struck across the border to raid army camps for arms. Small arsenals were gathered and transported back to hideouts in the south. A big camp was established at Ballinascorney above Bohernebreena in the Dublin Mountains. Matt began training groups of seventy men at a time – men who would return to their homes and train volunteers in their areas. The IRA was growing again.

But never fast enough. The attacks across the border were repulsed. Men were killed and others locked up. The north was as impregnable as ever.

Matt remembered his father's advice. 'The answer lies in America,' he told his men in the Dublin Mountains. American support had been neglected. Public opinion in the States was confused . . .

By the start of the sixties Matt was running a propaganda campaign to win dollars and guns from America. Every month he travelled south to shoot film of the IRA training in the Dublin Mountains. They made a great deal of noise – blasting away with Bren guns and Thompsons and Lee Enfields – but the Special Branch men who came to investigate were never a problem, some even offered to help. Matt grinned. With the Dail turning a blind eye and

Special Branch lending a hand, all he needed now was money and guns.

Matt stepped up the campaign. Posters were sent to America showing a starving, sad-eyed child peering through barbed wire – '*This child's father is in a concentration camp in occupied Ireland*' ran the caption.

There were no concentration camps, north or south, but that never bothered Matt – 'There will be,' he said grimly, 'once we get going again.'

Matt never gave up.

And the Americans began to respond – especially when Jack Kennedy became President. An Irish-American in the White House! Matt was jubilant. He redoubled his efforts. There were splits and arguments within the IRA but Matt never bothered his American audience with that – 'Sure we'll only confuse them and they'll stop sending money.'

Matt was busy again, planning the downfall of his enemies.

Sean's biggest enemy was time, time to cram fifteen hours work into a business day in order to spend time with Kate . . . not because it was asked of him but simply because it was what he wanted from life. In a changing world the most constant thing was their love.

By 1963 they could look back and laugh . . . to the time in '59 when Kate, cornered at a cocktail party, was called a 'worthless home-wrecker' by an indignant wife who had learned of Kate's *affaire* with Sean. Or 1961 when Sean was invited to a reception at Number Ten but discreetly asked to 'come unaccompanied'. Kate could laugh at the spiteful powder-room stories which circulated about her – Sean could smile at the fact that although he and Michael O'Hara were as friendly as ever, Michael's wife Deirdre never disguised her hostility towards Kate.

They could laugh, though sadly at times, at snubs and slights which had come their way. Attitudes were changing but change was gradual and – as Kate reflected ruefully – 'damn painful at times'.

But their love was indestructible.

'So it should be,' Sean joked, 'it's been baptized in fire and brimstone.'

714

Which is how it seemed at times. Sean and Kate were frequently hurt – by Margaret Mallon for instance. She snubbed Kate from the outset. In London Margaret arrived at a restaurant once to find Sean and Kate already at a corner table. Margaret walked out – but not before Sean caught her arm – 'I'd like you to meet Kate.' But Margaret refused. True, Freddie tried to make up for it the next day by inviting Sean and Kate for drinks at the Savoy, then taking them to dinner and on to a club – making sure as many people as possible saw them together. From that day on Freddie always dined with them when he was in London – but Margaret never did.

Kate was saddened to the point of tears. She even contemplated ending the *affaire* – or at least trying to – 'Perhaps I should move away. Go and live in Paris perhaps. Darling, I can't stand by and watch your whole world turned upside down because of me.'

'Rubbish,' Sean snapped angrily. 'Besides, it's a bloody sight worse for you – don't you think I know how you get hurt at times?'

But later he calmed down – 'Besides, how the hell could I run my businesses from Paris?'

She clung to him – 'And how could I ever live without you?'

But it was not only friends who caused Sean concern – what fretted him most was his son. Every time Sean went to New York he spent time with Patrick. Birthdays were always remembered, no Christmas passed without a lavish gift, no holiday ended without some special treat. Sean worked hard to preserve a bond between them. Gloria raised no objections. She had become so immersed in her own social world that she rarely spent time with the child – but she was adamant about one thing – Patrick stayed firmly with her.

Sean's eyes were often dark with sadness when he returned to London. Kate knew why without being told. She suffered with him. It was part of the price they paid for their happiness.

Then, in 1964, came a big change in their lives, though the catalyst was sparked the previous November. Sean was in the *Seven Days* London office when the news came through from Dallas. Jack Kennedy had been shot! Nobody could believe it. The most popular President of modern times . . . shot, perhaps fatally? It defied credibility. Michael O'Hara kept five telephone lines open to *Seven Days* in New York. The air was full of garbled conversation – then Freddie came on, confirming the story. The President had been assassinated. Jack Kennedy was dead!

Sean flew over for the funeral, still shocked. He had met Jack on exactly eight occasions during his Presidency and liked him more every time. Even Freddie, no admirer of the Kennedys and a staunch Republican, had been heard to admit – 'He's developing into a great leader . . .' But tragically Jack would develop no more, to the loss of America and perhaps the whole world.

Sean's heart went out to the old Ambassador. Now so crippled by a stroke that even speech was impossible, old Joe was too sick to attend the state funeral. He watched it on television, propped up in his bed at Hyannis Port. Sean did not see him at all during his visit, in fact he never saw him again – but he thought of him often.

Sadly such events sell newspapers. Freddie's team produced an issue of *Seven Days* which sold more copies than any edition before or since – a chilling reminder that people derive a vicarious thrill from tragedy, perhaps simply because, for them, life still goes on. Few people leave a funeral without experiencing the wish to live to the full the time left to them.

Not that Sean lived life any other way. That Christmas he and Kate went to Switzerland where she taught him to ski. Kate had taught him much by that Christmas – about art and books, food and drink, and taking time out to simply enjoy himself. Despite the problems, after six years they were more in love than ever. Strangers swore they were a honeymoon couple and looked for a ring on Kate's hand. But that could never be with Gloria alive and Kate knew it. Not that she wept any more, or wished Gloria harm, or cursed her own rotten luck. But Kennedy's death affected Kate deeply. It was a reminder that life is fleeting. So when Sean went to Germany for a week on business, Kate went too. In May when he went to Italy she went with him. And in June, when he announced a trip to Australia she finally gave up her work with the PR agency.

She travelled to Paris to tell a surprised and disappointed Marcel Crispin. He tried hard to persuade her against it, but Kate's mind was made up – as she told Yvette afterwards. 'I'm sorry, I know you disapprove, but you taught me to do what I feel is right.'

'So I did,' Yvette agreed, 'but, my dear, without your own income you are so vulnerable. Especially after your arrangements with Tim.'

'Ah, Tim.'

Tim had continued to cast a shadow. Kate had succeeded in keeping him and Sean from meeting – mostly because Tim was so rarely in London. Kate was glad. She would never forget Tim's vicious language when Mark was killed and feared a similar scene if Tim ever discovered she had a new lover. Yet Tim was still her brother . . . and when he wrote saying he needed money for the expansion of his businesses she had loaned him her entire Averdale inheritance.

'It was just sitting in the bank, Yvette. I don't need it. And if it makes Tim happy and keeps him from interfering in my life . . . well, I can't think of a better use for it.'

'That's all very well when you are earning your own living . . . but now –'

'Where's my *security*?' Kate laughed and threw up her hands. 'Oh you French are so cautious about money. Sean's a millionaire. He's got all the money in the world –'

'And a wife in America.'

'I don't care if he's got six wives. He loves me, and I want to spend the rest of my life with him. Oh Yvette, can't you see, it's such a waste otherwise.'

Yvette sighed, 'But you enjoy your work –'

'I do, I did – but I enjoy Sean's company more. He can set me to work if he wants to. He's involved in so many things. I can be a sort of personal assistant –'

'For a salary?'

'Oh darling Yvette – please understand. I tried being like you and Ziggy, I enjoyed it, really I did. Independence is wonderful, it was what I needed for a while. The experience was good for me . . . but well I've been thinking. Sean is forty-one now and I'm over thirty! No, don't laugh, I know you think we're still babies – let's hope we've a million years left together – but however long it is I want to share every minute with Sean.'

Kate laughed when she hugged the frail old lady goodbye – 'Don't worry Yvette, please. I know what I'm doing, really I do. Sean will never let me down.'

Yet, as she flew back to London her confidence faded. She was throwing herself at him. Perhaps he *preferred* things as they were – spending weekends and holidays with her, seeing her for dinner, spending two illicit nights a week in her tiny mews cottage. Perhaps that was how Sean wanted her – always a mistress, never a wife.

By the time she met him that evening she was panicky with nerves. What a fool she had been not to discuss it before. Why had she so stupidly assumed he would be delighted?

But he was!

Oh the relief, when she saw that look on his face.

'You mean it?' he asked, wide-eyed and incredulous, 'Throw everything up and just move in with me? Live with me, all the time?'

'If you want me –'

'If I want you! Kate, I can't *marry* you –'

'I know –'

'But aren't you worried?'

'That people will talk?' She laughed, 'Sean, it's 1964! The permissive society has arrived. Don't you read your own newspapers? Besides, people talk *now*. What more can they say? Anyway I don't care. It's what I feel here that matters,' she put her hand on her heart, 'and what you think of me. That's all I care about.'

He crushed her to him until she was breathless. In his mind the decision had to be hers, and now she had made it he was overjoyed.

By the time they set out for Australia Sean had put Hill Street on the market – 'When we get back *you* can find us a new house!' he said proudly.

The voyage to Australia was long and relaxing and wonderful.

718

'About time we had a honeymoon,' Sean said.

Kate had never felt more secure. She would have dismissed any thoughts that Sean's love was less deep than hers. But in Sydney she had a terrible fright.

It was during the third week of their stay. Sean had negotiated the purchase of a newspaper, and expanded his television interests. Everything was fine. They were planning to spend their last few days sightseeing – when Michael O'Hara telephoned from London with some terrible news. Dinny Macaffety had died in his sleep the night before.

Sean was grief-stricken. He made frantic calls to the airlines, but it was impossible to reach Dublin in time for the funeral. He felt so . . . so guilty. 'I owed him so much,' he told Kate sadly, 'Dinny and the Da between them . . . oh I dunno Kate, I've ignored so many obligations. All these years I've said to myself there's time for that tomorrow, do this now, it's more important, leave that . . . and now tomorrow's too late.'

She was thankful to be there. It would have destroyed her to be the other side of the world, unable to comfort him. They talked through the night . . . mostly Sean talking, and drinking and smoking . . . telling her about Dinny and the *Dublin Gazette*. Then, at dawn, he dozed for a while . . . and when he awoke he talked of his son.

'You know,' he said, 'it doesn't seem possible but Pat is nine already. I hardly know him. Nine years old! When I think of the Da . . . when I was that age, we were so close Kate, you can't imagine.' He put his head in his hands and groaned, 'Oh Christ, I've been so bloody selfish.'

His words terrified her. His sense of regret. Blaming himself about wrong decisions. Only one interpretation was possible. He was going back to his wife!

Kate held his hand and prayed she was wrong. She told herself to stay quiet. I must not plead, mustn't say I love him too much to live without him . . . oh God give me strength!

He drew her to him – 'Kate darling, I don't know how to say this . . .'

Her heart stopped. She closed her eyes. God give me strength.

'It's such a hard thing to explain . . .'

It was over, she knew it. All over. She choked, unable to breathe.

'We've been so happy . . . I mean, I don't even know if I can do this . . .'

She resolved to catch the first flight to Paris. No, she would kill herself – go down to the beach and swim out as far as she could . . . swim and swim . . . he wouldn't know . . . not until after . . .

'I don't even know if Gloria will agree. But if I can persuade her . . . what I mean is, could you love my son too? I know it would be . . . well another woman's child and all that . . . but you'll love him in time . . .'

Her ears buzzed. She could hardly hear what he was saying.

'Of course he'd be away at school most of the time, but if he came to England – well we could take him on holidays and things.'

She wept for fully ten minutes.

They flew to the States direct from Sydney.

In New York Kate stayed in the suite at the Waldorf-Astoria, pacing up and down, smoking endless cigarettes – asking herself again and again if they were doing the right thing. She remembered her own childhood. Pulled one way, then the other. Not that Sean had neglected his son, but Gloria was the boy's mother.

'I know that,' Sean had snapped. 'If she were a *real* mother, maybe it would be different. But he's just another symbol to her. I don't know what it is about Gloria but she's screwed up emotionally. People are as possessions to her, adjuncts to her own importance.'

But most days Sean was downtown with his lawyers – and Kate waited alone.

Then, unexpectedly, Freddie Mallon called to see her at the hotel.

Kate was surprised, 'Oh,' she said, 'Sean's not here. He's –'

'With the lawyers, I know. I wondered if you would have lunch with me.'

She liked Freddie. She would have liked Margaret if Margaret had let her. Freddie and Margaret were Sean's

720

oldest friends, and Kate would have liked anyone on that basis. Even so she couldn't resist a smile as she walked into the dining-room. 'Aren't you afraid someone will see us? If your wife heard you were lunching with a notorious *femme fatale . . .*'

Freddie chuckled, 'She wouldn't turn a hair. I'm the jealous one in our family.'

But despite his rueful laughter he seemed ill at ease. He ordered the meal, then gave a little grin to hide his embarrassment. 'About Margaret,' he said, 'you don't understand. She put a lot of work into Sean's marriage. She was wrong, but that's not the issue. She thought she was acting for the best,' he shrugged, 'then things didn't work out and she's got a conscience about it. Her easiest way out is to blame you. I don't say she rationalizes it – but that's what it boils down to. Now she's all mixed up and doesn't know what to do.' His embarrassment deepened, 'Don't get me wrong, I'm not apologizing for my wife – but, well Margaret is so special to me it upsets me for someone to think badly of her.'

Kate was unsure of how to respond. Of course it *was* an apology and she was grateful. She thought Freddie was one of the kindest men she had ever met.

He scowled. 'That's not why I wanted to have lunch, but I just thought I'd say it.'

'It's not why I came either,' she smiled, 'I was just pleased to see someone I always think of as a friend – and he just proved it.'

Freddie relaxed a notch after that. Then he said – 'Sean's going about things the wrong way. Gloria's got the law on her side. Sean's only chance is to make a deal with her, not attack her through the courts.'

Kate thought so too. In fact she had said so to Sean. She sighed – 'I know, but be fair – Sean *did* go and see her –'

'And they had a furious row,' Freddie nodded, 'I know, I heard about it.' He gave her a searching look. 'Tell me Kate, how do *you* feel about Patrick living in England?'

She had asked herself that a thousand times. She was afraid – afraid of anything that might mar her happiness. On the other hand she wondered if Sean would ever be truly happy with his child on his conscience.

'Well?' Freddie said.

She took a deep breath, 'I want whatever Sean wants. If he wanted to go and live in Timbuctoo it would be all right with me. If he wants me to make a home for his son, that's all right too . . . but it won't be easy. Patrick might resent me, he mightn't like me, but if he gives me half a chance I swear I'll do everything in my power to make him happy.'

Freddie sat looking at her for a long time. Then, to her utter amazement, he said – 'OK, I believe you. Tell Sean it's all fixed.'

She gaped. Her mind reeled as she listened. Freddie had arranged everything. He chuckled at her expression – 'Really it wasn't that difficult. All you've got to do is understand Gloria. What she really wants in life is recognition – so I made her an offer she couldn't refuse. She's going to be the new Dorothy Parker. She's going to write a column on Hollywood, starting next month. The Gloria Connors page. It's to be syndicated coast to coast. Of course she'll have to live out there –'

'She's leaving *Scarsdale*?'

'She's going to be very busy, too busy to devote time to young Pat – so she has agreed, he can go to England with his father –'

'Oh Freddie!' Kate clasped his hand across the table. 'Sean will be delirious! How can I ever thank you –'

'By making the son happy,' Freddie said firmly, 'as well as the father.'

She was too excited to eat. When Freddie left she sat in a fever of impatience waiting for Sean. He returned at half past three, grey and tired from his meeting with the lawyers. 'Bloody hopeless,' he said bitterly – and then she told him.

In all the time she had known him she had never seen him so happy. His joy overflowed on to her – but not enough to douse all of her worries – 'Oh God, Sean, I hope he likes me. Supposing –'

'Darling he'll *love* you!'

And so it turned out. When Patrick arrived in London a month later Kate took him everywhere. The Tower

722

Buckingham Palace, Westminster Abbey – she retrod the path she had travelled with Jenny and Aunt Alison so many years before. She and Pat got on well, although he was more reserved than she had expected of Sean's son. But gradually Kate broke the barriers down. Sometimes she wondered what his mother had told him about her – but never dared ask.

They moved into a large house in Hampstead. Kate was ever busier – but she always made time for Pat.

The months flew past to the end of the year. *Seven Days* continued to report on a changing world. The war escalated in Vietnam. Lyndon Johnson struggled to run Washington in the wake of the Kennedy legend. And the British Empire shrank like a snowball on a bonfire. Giving independence to the colonies became almost routine. Jomo Kenyatta was elected Prime Minister of a self-governing Kenya. Zanzibar achieved internal rule. Nigeria became a republic, Nyasaland a self-governing protectorate. Macmillan's 'wind of change' swept through the continent. The colonies were going but, as *Seven Days* noted, they were leaving with British goodwill. In Lancaster House and the Colonial Office, even in the House of Commons itself, Michael O'Hara's reporters told the same story – 'It's like the kids growing up and leaving home, Westminster seems sad and proud about it both at the same time.'

Changes were taking place on Westminster's own doorstep. In Northern Ireland Lord Brookeborough at last stepped down from office. In twenty years as Prime Minister he had never once crossed the border to Dublin, never once visited a Catholic school, or even attended a civic reception in a Catholic town. His successor, Terence O'Neill, promised changes – and Belfast soon realized that he meant. When Pope John died O'Neill sent a message of condolence to Cardinal Conway in Armagh, but allowed it to be published. Belfast gasped at the headline – '*The Pope: Ulster Premier's Message of Sympathy*' – and Belfast gasped again when flags were lowered to half-mast over Stormont.

'Oh dear,' Kate smiled when she read the papers. 'Poor Tim will not approve at all.' 'The wind of change indeed,' she said, looking at pictures of O'Neill visiting Catholic schools.

But Kate paid only a passing interest. Her life was full of her new house, and of Sean and Pat Connors. When Pat went to school Kate wrote every week, and sent him hampers from Fortnums and books from Hatchards. Sean wrote too, but his contributions were often a scrawled P.S. on Kate's long letters. He did get down to the school for sports day, however, and at half-term he did take Pat to watch Tubby's football team play in a cup tie. He did *care* ... he was just so damn busy. Sir George Hamilton retired, Brian Tillet was smashed up in a car crash, Thornton had a blazing row with the new Chairman and walked out ... 'But once I get that sorted out we'll spend more time together,' he promised his son, 'meanwhile if you want anything, Kate will take care of it.'

And Kate did. When Pat was struck down with chicken pox Kate rushed down to the school to sit at his bedside. When Pat broke his arm in the gym, it was Kate who arrived bearing gifts and messages of sympathy ...

Pat grew used to it. He knew his father was a busy man. Besides Kate's visits were greatly welcomed. Other boys were visited by middle-aged mums, nobody had anyone as glamorous as Kate. 'Is she your father's girlfriend?' Tommy Hillary wanted to know. 'She's his mistress,' Pat said proudly, 'international tycoons don't have girl friends.'

Kate guessed what was said but paid it no heed. 'So long as he doesn't resent me,' she told herself, 'I can cope.'

She coped, more and more with every passing year. She could cope with anything as long as Sean loved her. And he did. He told her so every day.

So Kate did more than survive, she triumphed – but her happiness was never easily won. No mention is made in *The Power in the Back Room* of the snubs and the slights and the spitefulness with which she had to contend. Nor of her devotion to young Patrick.

Her contact with Tim was minimal. He was never in London. Kate sent him cards on his birthday, and wrote now and then, but rarely received a reply. So as time passed whole weeks slipped by without her even thinking of Tim.

eland, north or south, was light years away from Kate's
fe in Swinging London.

But as those golden years gathered pace, Ireland became
ery much more in the news – until Kate was not just
eminded of Tim, she *saw* him, staring up at her from the
ages of a newspaper or bellowing from the television
creen. Tim was making a name for himself.

CHAPTER ELEVEN

eople said Tim O'Brien was more of an Averdale than
Mark ever was – but then Tim's life was never complicated
y anyone like Ziggy Beck. Tim saw events in
ncompromising black and white, especially when it came
o politics. In his view Prime Minister O'Neill was
etraying the first tenet of Unionism, that of 'No
urrender' – and when O'Neill invited the Taoiseach of the
ish Republic to lunch in Belfast Tim erupted with anger.
'Neill had been nothing but trouble since he took office
forever encouraging Catholics to expect more than their
ue – 'Good grief, isn't it enough we give them grants for
eir schools, subsidize their housing and pay them
nemployment benefits. Money for this and for that . . . I
on't know what O'Neill thinks he's doing, but he's a
loody disgrace to the Unionist Party!'

And a growing number of Unionists agreed with him.

In the years after Mark Averdale's death Tim's energies
ad been devoted exclusively to business. The Averdale
mpire was still substantial. But many Averdale interests
ere losing money. Shipbuilding was a disaster. The linen
dustry was in decline. Tim drove himself hard. In a series
f shrewd moves he expanded on other fronts. He switched
om linen to synthetic fibres, he invested heavily in carpet
anufacture, he built up a controlling interest in a whisky
istillery. It all took time and a great deal of money. Tim
orrowed from the banks and when they protested he
ised more cash by borrowing from Kate. He had no
ualms about that. The money was rightfully his anyway.

It *would* have been his but for his guardian's infatuation. What irked Tim most was the matter of the paintings. He had wanted to sell them outright but Kate had insisted on loaning them to the Tate. Tim fumed.

He lacked time to be curious about Kate. Throughout the early sixties he had worked an eighteen-hour day to salvage his inheritance. Every ounce of his dogged tenacity was applied to achieving business success – and by the time that policy was paying dividends Captain Terence Blood O'Neill had come to office and was threatening to shake Stormont to its very foundations.

Unionists took to the streets in protest. Protestants throughout the whole of Ulster were alarmed that O'Neill was going too far. In Belfast photographs of O'Neill talking to nuns were burned on street corners. A fiery new orator, Ian Paisley, railed and ranted at mass meetings – and always in support was Tim O'Brien.

But Ulster's Catholics were organizing their own protest marches and spawning a spate of new organizations, all committed to winning a better deal for the Catholic minority.

Protestants reacted by assembling the Ulster Protestant Volunteers. Paisley published a virulent campaign in his newspaper, the *Protestant Telegraph*, urging that the Specials be mobilized to put down an imminent Catholic uprising.

And Tim O'Brien went on television to preach the same message.

In the spring of '66 Catholics were attacked by petrol bombs . . .

In May a woman died when the Catholic-owned pub next to her house was hit . . .

In June, three Catholic barmen were shot as they left a Protestant pub . . .

In London few people paid much heed to Northern Ireland. Michael O'Hara's reporters monitored the story as a matter of routine – but nobody at Westminster seemed greatly concerned. Harold Wilson's Labour Government was predictably cagey . . . the internal rule of Northern Ireland was traditionally left in Stormont's hands . . . which

726

s where it should stay according to a Labour spokesman. Few people seemed really interested. But the men from *Seven Days* dug deep. In the House of Commons Gerry Fitt, a Republican Socialist MP for the Dock seat in Belfast, had a good deal to say about Stormont – and none of it complimentary. A handful of Labour MPs were beginning to get restless – it seemed incredible to them that the principle of 'one man, one vote' did not apply to every part of the United Kingdom – a surprise shared with others when *Seven Days* reported the fact later that week.

But generally there was little interest. Fleet Street headlined other stories and banished Northern Ireland to an inside page.

Yet, perversely perhaps, the men from *Seven Days* kept the story alive. In August, when the Northern Ireland Prime Minister was in London to meet Wilson and Home Secretary Roy Jenkins, *Seven Days* reporters were disinclined to believe that the talks were merely routine. Backbench MPs were quizzed . . . civil servants were questioned . . . rumours were sifted, two was added to two until it made four . . . and then a theory emerged.

Michael O'Hara listened carefully when it was explained to him.

'Wilson doesn't want to know. According to him any politician who gets involved with Ulster needs his head examined. But some of his backbenchers are getting restless, so he'll have to do something . . . and that means he will push O'Neill to go faster on reforms.'

'Go on,' Michael O'Hara said.

'The situation stinks over there. A quarter of a million Catholics are disqualified from voting in local elections, and things like housing allocations are a farce. Something has to be done, and Wilson can only go one way. He and Jenkins will shove O'Neill to go faster.'

'And then?'

'Well it's bloody obvious. O'Neill is already in trouble with his party. Most of them are up in arms. Paisley is roaming the streets and this other fellow, what's his name – Tim O'Brien – was on the box the other night talking about a Protestant backlash.'

But Michael O'Hara remained sceptical. 'It's not big

727

enough to warrant special coverage, but maybe keep an eye on it.' He grinned, 'Sure you've got to be Irish yourself to know these things often blow over in five minutes.'

Even so, as Michael drove home later, he thought it would be something to talk to Sean about when he got back from the States.

But Michael did not mention Northern Ireland when Sean returned from America. He hardly had time. Sean and Kate were only in London for a month before setting off for Australia to pursue Sean's television interests. During a frantic four weeks Sean attended nine board meetings, opened three new office blocks built by the Mallor Property Company, spent days negotiating with the television companies, sanctioned the take-over of two building contractors . . . and devoted hours to meetings in the City with institutional investors.

Kate was busy too – but never too busy for Patrick. In fact Pat provoked a rare argument with Sean.

'I don't care how busy you are, Sean, that boy is a darned sight more important than improving your balance sheet!'

After which Sean spent a weekend with his son, messing about with boats on the river. It did not satisfy Kate – 'I'm leaving you, Sean, next Friday!'

'You're *what*?'

The horror in his face did her heart good. She smiled, 'I'm sorry darling. I'm going to Paris for a week, with a much younger man.'

She took Patrick – and they had fun. Whatever he wanted to see, they saw – including the floor-show at the Lido. 'Heck Kate, the boys at school will never believe this. Can we go to that other place, the Crazy Horse, tomorrow night? Someone said the girls there hardly wear anything at all!'

Yvette flattered him outrageously – 'Another year or two and every young girl in Paris will be waiting when you arrive.'

Pat's chest expanded a good two inches and he felt seven foot tall.

Kate telephoned Sean every night. It was the first time they had been parted since she had resigned from running

728

Crispin's office in London. She missed him desperately – and he missed her – 'Do you realize what this is doing to me? I'm not eating properly, I can't sleep at nights . . .'

'Get used to it, darling. I'm going on a cruise with Pat when we get back –'

'A cruise –'

'To Australia.'

'But Kate, we're *flying* to Australia. Going by ship takes too long.'

Kate had her way. When they left for Australia at the end of that month, all three of them sailed on the *Ocean Queen*. Pat and Sean spent twenty-seven wonderful days together – swimming in the pool, playing deck games, sightseeing at ports of call. They were the best-looking 'family' aboard ship. Kate never felt more proud in her life. When Pat left the ship at Hong Kong to fly back to London and school he squeezed her arm in a grown-up way. 'You're the best pal a boy ever had, Kate. Not only that, I bet no one ever had a pal who looks as good as you in a swimsuit.'

'Cheeky young bugger,' Sean growled afterwards. 'Another few years and I'll be fighting him off for your favours.'

'Oh I don't know,' Kate mused, 'I hope I don't have to wait anything like as long as a few years.'

Kate was never happier. She belonged. She loved and was loved in return. In a way, she had come to symbolize the sixties. Old taboos were giving ground in the face of a social, and sexual, revolution. Not that Kate saw herself as a revolutionary – she merely lived her life according to the advice Yvette had given her – 'Always remember,' Yvette had said, 'it's what you feel in your heart that matters.'

As for Sean, 1966 was a glittering year. Everything he touched turned to gold. And with Kate at his side his world was just perfect.

Except . . . well there was one thing . . . two really, small incidents which marred his last trip to New York. His hotel was picketed by a group calling themselves 'The Friends of Ireland'. Placards were waved below his window. One said simply – 'Brits get out of Ireland' but another read – 'Pat

Connors was an Irish hero, Sean Connors is a British stooge.'

A rival magazine had published a piece on him, based on the disastrous interview he had given in Chicago all those years earlier.

Freddie told him not to worry – 'It stirred up a few cranks, that's all. Don't let it get under your skin.'

But it did – then something else cropped up. Sean was at a party with an Irish-American he had met through Ambassador Kennedy. A collection was being taken up for the IRA – and when Sean refused to give even a dime he found himself criticized by everyone in the room. He had left shortly after – and of course Kate told him to forget it – but now and then it crept back into his mind.

Thankfully his life was too crowded to dwell on it. His businesses were now so far flung that the whole world was his oyster. Ireland was deep in the past, along with bad memories like Matt Riordan.

But while Matt Riordan was a fading image in the mind of Sean Connors, that was never the case in reverse. Matt's hatred lived on. He clung to it. It was his life-raft through a sea of failure. Matt's existence had never been sweetened by the taste of success. Matt knew only the bitterness of defeat, the heartache of setbacks – but he never gave up. Often down but never counted out, he always got up and fought on. Hatred bolstered his self-respect. He was forever telling himself that he would settle with Connors and all enemies of Ireland one day . . . one fine day in the future.

The going was hard most of the time. Matt had initiated a propaganda campaign that was beginning to capture Irish-American interest – but the IRA still struggled to find support in the north. It sickened Matt. Catholics were protesting about injustice as never before, but few were prepared to fight for a united Ireland – 'All we want is equal rights with the Prods.'

Matt exploded with temper – 'You're fighting the wrong bloody war. We want the Brits out of Ireland.'

But not all Catholics agreed. Many had relatives on the mainland, who enjoyed a good living, free of religious discrimination. 'If we could only get that,' they told Matt, 'we'll talk about the border some other day.'

Matt groaned as the peaceful Civil Rights movement gathered momentum and the IRA languished further behind. Frustration made him angry, but he encouraged himself with the thought that the seeds were there – 'It's confrontation on the streets we want. One bloody big riot and O'Neill's fine talk will go up in smoke. Then the people will turn to the IRA.'

But where was the IRA? Even in the south it was in tatters again – divided by arguments.

Matt was often in Dublin. IRA leaders seemed more left-wing every time he met them. He told them bitterly, 'Will you stop yapping about a Marxist society, for God's sake! It sounds like another Cuba. Can you imagine the reaction to that in the States? We'll not get a penny from America that way.'

A lesser man might have given up. Many Irishmen *did* give up. The communist atheism spouted by IRA leaders sounded discordant to Catholic ears. But Matt could no more give up than fly through the air. Liam Riordan would have been proud of his son. Prod shouts of 'No Surrender!' struck an answering chord in Matt's heart – he would *never* surrender, he would fight all the days of his life.

So the months dragged by. He was often away for weeks at a time. His marriage suffered. When he was home conversation with Bridie withered and died. His children grew watchful of his moods. Matt was stern-faced and tight-lipped, like his father before him.

Sometimes in Dublin he took a rare hour off from IRA business to ask around the pubs for news of Sean Connors. But few people had even heard of Sean Connors – or at least not the Sean Connors Matt was seeking. Now and then he met an old feller who said the man Matt was after was living in the States – or in London – or in Australia. One thing was sure, he wasn't in Dublin.

If the news was disappointing, few would have guessed from Matt's expression. His face remained impassive. He stared through the thick lenses of his glasses, his eyes cold and unblinking. 'Sure he was a watchful old devil,' someone once said, 'lonely. Even in a crowd with people around·him, he was involved but somehow apart.'

Involved but somehow apart summed up Matt's relationship with the IRA leadership. Clashes occurred frequently throughout 1967. Matt was sick and tired of listening to Marxist arguments. Catholic restlessness in Belfast could be channelled into an uprising. 'Every week there's some incident. If we got hold of it, fanned the flames, I tell you, the Prods have never been edgier.'

But Matt won little support in Dublin.

Once again he returned to Belfast. Nobody gave him a second glance as he walked down the train in search of a seat. His appearance had become even less noteworthy. Thin, gaunt-faced with large spectacles, untidily dressed, he looked too mild-mannered to be a fanatic, too frail for a terrorist. But, as Matt had learned from Ferdy Malloy years before – appearances can be deceptive.

As the train rolled north Matt read the periodicals he had bought at the station. The *Irish Times* and the *Independent* were swiftly dealt with, after which he read *Seven Days* from cover to cover. No more than a few paragraphs were devoted to Northern Ireland. Matt swore softly. To his mind the injustices done to Catholics deserved banner headlines all over the world. He stared at the folded magazine in his lap. The publisher's name caught his eye – 'The Seven Days Corporation Inc.' It meant nothing to him, some fat cat American businessman, he imagined, who cared only about profits – but then he focused on the next line – 'European Editor, Michael O'Hara' – and that made him angry. 'A name like that,' he whispered under his breath, 'wouldn't you think a feller called O'Hara would take more interest in Ireland.'

Yet Michael O'Hara could hardly be blamed. *Seven Days* was an international magazine with an international audience. Stories from all over the world competed for space – for instance, from Africa, from Kenya, where President Kenyatta was showing open contempt for Ziggy Beck's dream of a multi-racial society. Africa now belonged to Africans, which gave Kenyatta *carte blanche* to discriminate against *non*-Africans – especially those of Indian origin. Kenyan Asians fled in their thousands. But those who escaped to Britain failed to find a multi-racial society there. Enoch Powell frightened people silly with his nightmarish vision of the consequences of mass immigration – so brown men were shunned by white and black men alike. Ziggy Beck would have wept.

But Ziggy might have been encouraged by other stories – people *were* protesting against injustice. Young people were changing the order of things. Student power was growing. *Seven Days* told of campus unrest from Berkeley, California, to London's LSE. Youth everywhere, it seemed, was impatient and distrustful of political leaders . . . whether they be Charles de Gaulle, Lyndon Johnson or Harold Wilson. Young people took to the streets to demonstrate for change – and in that respect the young of Northern Ireland were no different – but the consequences were.

Even so, when clashes occurred in Belfast, those in power at Westminster seemed as unconcerned as ever.

'Leave it to Stormont,' was Prime Minister Wilson's attitude – and Roy Jenkins echoed the theme – 'Ireland has been the political graveyard of many a politician,' he sighed.

Even his successor, Jim Callaghan, paid little attention to the Province. Later he said – 'I had no occasion . . . to look at the problems of Northern Ireland unless they forced themselves on me.'

But the problems *were* forced on him in October.

It happened in Londonderry – the 'Maiden City' as Loyalists call it. Republicans don't call it that – they still call it Derry, the name it had before the Plantation.

The clash in Derry was the answer to Matt Riordan's prayers.

It was a spark which fanned into flames.

Yet things were peaceful to begin with – the Civil Rights movement were conducting an orderly march. Banners protested about poor housing, and unemployment ten times worse than on the mainland. Led by Gerry Fitt and two other Westminster MPs, two thousand people set off to walk to the centre of the city. Then, at the approach to Craigavon Bridge, they were stopped by a phalanx of RUC men. The marchers halted. Their leaders accepted the police order to go no further. They held their meeting where they stood, and were about to disperse when they realized that the police had sealed the street. RUC men were advancing from both ends – then the police unsheathed batons – and charged!

The next day every front page in Britain carried the same picture – Gerry Fitt, a Westminster MP, with blood streaming down his head from a gash opened by a policeman's club.

Ninety-five people were injured.

Thirty-six were arrested.

Rioting broke out in the Bogside that night and continued the next day.

At last, the Catholic minority was fighting back – and Matt Riordan's prayers had been answered.

The *Seven Days* office discussed the theory of a gathering storm. Especially when Prime Minister O'Neill was summoned to Downing Street. Lips were sealed after the meeting, but the message was clear. Outraged backbenchers and a horrified British public had finally goaded Wilson into action – O'Neill had been told to accelerate reforms.

Michael O'Hara's men said – 'O'Neill is between a rock and a hard place. The Unionists won't let him go forward, now Wilson won't let him go back.'

This time Michael thought they were right. Northern Ireland was building up into a major story. He would have liked to discuss it with Sean – but Sean was in America again, involved with his television interests.

Michael made his decision the next morning. He sent James Cross to Belfast – the same James Cross who had reported the death of the Averdales in Kenya and who, since then, had covered many other trouble-spots around the world.

In a way, by sending Jimmy Cross to Belfast, Michael O'Hara acknowledged the inevitability of an explosion, but Michael's decision was much more than that. It triggered off a chain of events which was to lead to another strand in the Irish tragedy, but no one was to know that at the time. Besides, when Sean telephoned from New York he approved – 'That's a good move, Michael. Ulster is getting a lot of headlines over here right now.'

To begin with it was just another story. But as the months passed – and Jimmy Cross wrote of one violent incident after the other – the whole thing began to play on Sean's mind. Ireland came into conversation more, wherever he was in the world. 'Say Sean, just what the hell is going on in Ulster?'

Of course nothing happened overnight. Christmas found him in Switzerland with Kate – and Pat came over from school to join them for the holiday. Sean was too happy to worry about a miserable subject like Ireland. 'Besides it's a complicated issue,' as he once told a friend, 'especially for someone like me. Well look at my life. I've never been back since I left. Most of my friends are English or American. Deep in my heart I believe in a united Ireland, but the truth is London has been kind to me. I've nothing against anyone in England, in fact I've a lot of people to thank.'

Yet the subject nagged away at the back of his mind.

It played on Kate's mind too, for quite different reasons. For instance she was in Paris the following April, when Terence O'Neill was forced to resign as Prime Minister of Northern Ireland. Yvette had been taken ill and Kate spent a worrying fortnight hurrying back and forth between her hotel and the nursing home. Business had called Sean to New York.

Thankfully Yvette responded to treatment and began to recover. One afternoon she smiled up from her pillow – 'You know, I was wrong to worry about Sean. He makes you very happy, anyone with half an eye can see that.'

'I haven't a worry in the world, except making sure you get better.'

That was not entirely true and Kate knew it. She was increasingly worried about Sean. This Irish thing was beginning to get to him. Even the night he left for New York he had been fretting about it.

'Did I ever tell you,' he said, 'the Da always wanted me to go into politics. He wanted me to be Taoiseach, can you imagine? I think I wanted it too for a time. Then I got this

735

bee in my bonnet about getting some assets together, and
after that, well –'

'You made your fortune, got married – and then you met
me.'

She was bright and jokey in a deliberate attempt to
change the subject. But his mood persisted, 'He had such
high hopes of me . . . the Da I mean . . . he –'

'Darling, you make yourself sound like a failure! Good
heavens, look at all you've done. What did *Fortune*
magazine say – "Sean Connors, a new breed of
businessman –"'

'The Da wouldn't have been impressed.'

'Well everyone else is. I'm impressed out of my mind. I
think you're quite, quite wonderful.'

At least he smiled then – and kissed her – but later in bed
he said, 'I ought to do something, Kate. For Ireland I mean.
God knows what, but take Freddie during the war. He threw
up his career to go stomping across the States telling them
they should be in the war. It wasn't popular . . . it took guts
. . . but Freddie did what he believed was right.'

He fell asleep shortly after, but Kate was awake for
hours. She hated Ireland, despite the Scots-Irish blood in
her veins. To her mind it was a cruel place where cruel
things happened. She had not been back since Mark's
funeral. Her parents had been murdered in Ireland, or at
least Tim said so . . . and so had Sean's father, she knew
that without knowing the details. She had not asked. That
all belonged in the past. She had the future to look forward
to – with Sean. She snuggled into his side. 'Please God,' she
prayed, 'let our happiness last forever – and make the
Troubles in Ireland go away.'

But the Troubles did not go away – they multiplied with
bewildering speed.

In August rioting broke out all across Northern Ireland.
Protestant mobs stormed the Falls Road determined to
burn every house to the ground – and might have
succeeded but for the courage of one man. Armed with a
tommy-gun and moving like a cat across the rooftops, Matt
Riordan held the crowd at bay while barricades were
raised. Three hundred houses went up in flames. Six people

ere killed. But without Matt Riordan the slaughter would
ave been wholesale.

Matt was hailed as a saviour, but Catholics elsewhere
vere less lucky. There was no Matt Riordan in Derry – no
RA at the moment of peril. Graffiti on the walls said it
lainly – 'IRA means I Ran Away'. Catholics could only
ope that help would come from south of the border.

And help did come. In Dublin, Taoiseach Jack Lynch,
ppalled by the violence, announced that units of the Irish
rmy had moved up to the border and were opening field
ospitals to treat Catholic wounded.

Lynch's televised speech stuck terror into Ulster
rotestants. Rumour spread that Irish troops had *crossed*
he border. In London Home Secretary Callaghan feared
hat 'within twenty-four hours we might face civil war in the
orth and an invasion from the south'.

The order was given – and British troops poured into
orthern Ireland.

But the *Seven Days* team was convinced that further
trife was inevitable. 'The only chance of peace,' they told
Michael O'Hara, 'is for Stormont to be suspended, which
Callaghan either won't or can't do.'

Instead Callaghan flew to Northern Ireland and told
ubilant Catholics that social reforms would be granted in
ull.

'It won't happen,' Jim Cross insisted on the phone from
Belfast, 'Stormont will resist every inch of the way.'

And so they did – even though Chichester-Clark,
O'Neill's successor, struggled to find a middle path
etween Westminster's insistence on reform and the
Unionist battlecry of 'No Surrender!'

'He's between a rock and a hard place,' the *Seven Days*
eam continued to tell Michael O'Hara. 'All he can do is
ang on and hope Wilson loses the general election. If the
ories get back they might not push so hard.'

And the Tories did get back. Ted Heath was the new
rime Minister in London, Reginald Maudling was Home
ecretary. Maudling spent a day in the troubled Province,
 the end of which, baffled by conflicting arguments, he
imbed back on board his aircraft – 'Give me a large
otch,' he groaned, 'God, what a bloody awful country.'

'That sums up Westminster opinion,' Michael O'Har said when the remark was reported to him, 'Heath's crow won't do anything. They'll put Northern Ireland on th back burner and hope the Troubles die down.'

But the Troubles did not die down.

In Belfast Matt Riordan was raising an army. This wa to be his finest hour and he knew it. All the days of his lif seemed to have been leading to this. Some Catholics sti clung to the Civil Rights cry of non-violence, but othe were ready to fight. And Matt was ready to lead. H travelled to Dublin in search of money and arms. He g more help from the Dail than the IRA. Matt fumed an raged, but the IRA seemed more anxious to talk Marxi theory than Irish reality.

'To hell with you,' Matt roared, 'we'll fight on our ow without your help.'

Back in Belfast Matt formed a Northern Comman which renamed itself the *Provisional IRA* within week Soon they were training recruits as never before. Ma seemed everywhere . . . organizing, encouragin planning. His American connection began to pay off – th supply of money and guns reaching Belfast from the Unite States reached record proportions.

For Matt it was the realization of a lifelong dream.

But Matt's dream was Tim O'Brien's nightmare. Ti cursed Terence O'Neill – 'That man wrecked the Unioni Party.' And so it seemed. The once monolithic Unioni Party burst apart under the strain of the times. Like th IRA it split in half. Ian Paisley formed the Democrat Unionist Party and took much Protestant support with hi – including the backing of Tim O'Brien – 'Nine generatio of Averdales built an empire in Ulster. It's my inheritanc By God, I'll defend it to the last drop of my blood.'

No Surrender!

Tim O'Brien was not the only Protestant ready to she blood. As the Provos grew in strength, so did the opposin Ulster Volunteer Force.

Bewildered British soldiers kept Northern Ireland fro plunging into a bloodbath – but not even an army cou preserve the peace. As violence escalated, a skeletal han

ached out around the world to touch everyone with Irish
blood in their veins – Sean Connors and Kate O'Brien
included.

Kate resisted. She wanted no more than her blissful
existence with Sean. But Sean was troubled. Life had been
kind to him. He had acquired wealth and success beyond
his dreams. He had found a perfect partner in Kate. He
lacked nothing – except peace from his conscience.
Memories of his father plagued him. It had been easy once
he had told himself that he would build assets first, *then*
he would do something for Ireland. Besides the Troubles
had seemed to fade away. But now Sean had assets, and
Ireland's Troubles grew worse every day. He had to do
something.

'I owe it to the Da,' he told Kate.

'But you're not a politician. What on earth *can* you do?'

'I don't know,' Sean shook his head glumly, 'but I must
do something. I've always believed in one Ireland. People
have a right to run their own affairs.'

'The people in the north want to stay part of Britain –'

'The *Protestants* in the north –'

'The majority in the north.'

They backed away, not wanting to argue. In truth, Kate
cared nothing for Ireland. She just hated the idea of Sean
becoming involved. Instinctively she felt no good would
come of it. 'Besides,' she said, 'you hate the IRA. I've
heard you in New York –'

'I know, I *do* hate the IRA but . . . oh it's hard to explain.
When I first came to London the British Empire spanned
the world. All the atlases were smothered in red. But when
people wanted to go free there was no British outcry to
keep them by force, they just let them go. Why should
Ireland be different?'

Kate said nothing.

'It started in Dublin,' Sean mused, 'the break-up of the
Empire. 1916 and all that – the Da fighting alongside
Pearse and Connolly in the Post Office. The Irish were *first*,
yet all these years later Ireland is still divided –'

'It's not your concern –'

'I must do *something*. It's bad enough being called a
traitor every time I go to the States. I believed I was right

739

when I spoke out during the war. I spoke out then and I must speak out now.'

The idea terrified her. The papers were full of terrorist killings . . .

Jim Cross's despatches from Belfast grew more lurid every week. *Seven Days* expanded its coverage of the Troubles from half a column to a regular page, sometimes more according to the number of sectarian killings.

Then, at the end of July, Jim Cross came over from Belfast for one of their regular meetings. Sean and Michael spent the day with him – and by the end of the afternoon Sean was outlining one of the most ambitious projects of his life.

'It will be colossal if we pull if off,' Michael said.

'Can we guarantee television coverage?' asked Jimmy Cross.

Sean nodded, 'I'll get the coverage, if you get the right people on camera.'

All three were excited by the prospect. *Seven Days* would produce a special issue on the Troubles, and Transatlantic Television would make a documentary for screening coast to coast across the States.

'Not just the States,' Sean added, 'Australia will buy it, so will the Canadians – interest in Ireland has really built up. The programme will have an audience of millions, all over the world.'

Sean wanted every point of view represented.

Jimmy frowned, 'If we include the para-militaries we'll have the law on our backs. The RUC will call it an incitement to riot –'

'Rubbish! We merely want to include all shades of opinion.'

Jimmy shrugged, 'I'm just warning you. The Ulster Volunteers and the IRA are illegal organizations. The RUC will squeal like stuck pigs.'

But Sean was determined – 'We'll handle the RUC as best we can. God knows I hold no brief for the IRA, or the other lot – but we've got to include them to show the whole problem. The point is, can you persuade them to put up some spokesmen?'

Jimmy thought he could. After months in Belfast he

ad come to know most of the participants, legal and
therwise. 'The Provos might put up a man called Matt
Lambert. He seems to be their propaganda chief. If he
thinks he'll get big coverage in the States, I'm sure he'll buy
t.'

'And the UVF?'

'More difficult,' Jimmy admitted. 'Paisley pretends to
ave no truck with them, so he won't speak their piece –
ut he will spiel for hours on the Democratic Unionists.
This fellow O'Brien might do it though. He won't admit
eing involved with the UVF either, but I'm bloody sure
e is. And if I tell him the IRA will get their message across
'm damn sure he will want a rebuttal.'

'Tim O'Brien?' Sean asked to be sure.

'That's right. Why, do you know him?'

Sean smiled, 'I've never met him, but he's Kate's
brother.'

Kate was terrified. It was hard to say which frightened her
most – Sean going to Belfast to make a television
documentary, or Sean meeting her brother.

'I don't want you involved,' she said flatly. 'Why do *you*
have to go?'

'We're involved already. Jim Cross has been filing stories
or ages. It's news Kate, that's all. I'm in the news
business.'

'No. It's more than that for you. It's Ireland. It's your
father and all the things you were taught as a boy. It's
marches and banners and violence . . .'

He tried to calm her, 'Kate, there's no reason to get
upset –'

'Why do you have to go? There's Michael and Jimmy
Cross . . . and all the others. Why you?'

Then she dissolved into tears.

Later, when she recovered, she tried to explain . . . but
explaining a premonition proved impossible – 'I know it
sounds stupid, irrational . . . but Ireland frightens me. I
don't want you mixed up in Irish politics –'

'We're making a documentary, that's all –'

She wanted to explain about Tim – but shied away from
putting thoughts into words. Tim could be so spiteful at

741

times. If he found out about her and Sean . . . if he dragge
up her past! Oh why hadn't she told Sean about Mar
. . . why had she kept putting it off? There had seemed n
need . . . they had been so happy . . .

'Honestly darling, there's nothing to worry about,' Sea
reassured her. 'We'll be in and out of Belfast in a coupl
of days. People will hardly know we are there.'

But Sean's hopes of slipping quietly across to Belfast wer
dashed completely three weeks later. It was inevitabl
really. Sean's staff had worked discreetly, but too man
people were involved for the operation to be mounte
unnoticed.

In Belfast itself, Jim Cross met not only legitimat
politicians, but held clandestine meetings with the IRA an
UVF. A house on the outskirts of the city was rented an
turned into a small studio. Transatlantic Televisio
technicians arrived with a mass of equipment . . .

In New York deals were struck with the network
for screening three programmes called *Spotlight o
Ireland*.

At Westminster, *Seven Days*' reporters recorde
comments from everyone short of the Speaker.

In Dublin, Deputies in the Dail were interviewed.

In Washington, Congressmen pronounced judgemen
on the subject . . . and in Sydney, Australians read abou
the forthcoming television series in one of Sean's ow
papers . . .

Yet none of that might have mattered but for events i
Fleet Street itself. As rumours grew that *Seven Days* an
Transatlantic TV were about to produce major features o
Northern Ireland, a rival newspaper editor decided t
publish the story behind the story. '*The Rise and Rise o
Sean Connors*' ran the headline, below which was a résum
of Sean's career, complete with old photographs taken a
the CBS studio during the war. Not only that but mor
recent photographs pictured him with '. . . *the glamorou
Kate O'Brien, who has been his constant companion fo
years . . .*'

Tim O'Brien could scarcely believe his eyes. He read th

742

rticle again and again. He stared at the face and knew he as right . . .

Years fell away. Even in the more recent photographs here was a resemblance, the same square jaw and thick lack hair . . . but the earlier pictures were positive proof. Ie *knew* that face. It was imprinted on his memory. If he losed his eyes he could still see the man running up the ane at Keady, brandishing a revolver . . . he could still hear he gunfire and feel the pain in his legs. It was the face he ad seen in the lane at Keady, all those years before . . . *he man who murdered his parents!*

Tim caught his breath, struck by another memory. On train, as a boy, catching a glimpse of that face in another aper . . . with '*Irish journalist leaves hospital*' daubed on placard. Unable to see the name . . . just the face . . . *that* ace. Now he had a name to go with it – Sean Connors! After all this time . . . but the shock went even deeper. Sean Connors and Kate! '. . . *the glamorous Kate O'Brien, who as been his constant companion for years . . .*'

Tim swore aloud. The *whore*! The filthy, disgusting . . .

He went rigid as the full implication hit him.

His sister slept with the man who had murdered their arents!

im O'Brien's anger was nothing compared to Matt Riordan's reaction. Matt was shattered. He had agreed to he documentary because of the promised American xposure – but there had been no mention of Connors. Cross, Jim Cross . . . never said a word about Connors. Just ransatlantic TV and *Seven Days*. Now it turned out that ean Connors owned them both!

Matt read the article again. He reached for a cigarette vith a shaking hand. Connors was rich – with big houses nd fancy cars no doubt, and holidays in the sun with this ancy woman . . .

A life-style beyond Matt's comprehension. He tried to nagine it. But comparison was impossible. A life of luxury ompared to one dedicated to the cause.

He remembered brave men he had known – Ferdy Malloy and so many others – all dead, killed fighting for reland. And his own father – Granite Liam Riordan –

murdered at Keady by this bastard Sean Connors

It took time for the shock to wear off but when it did
Matt realized the full implications, Connors was coming
back to Ireland. They would meet face to face. After all
these years. The realization of Matt's impossible dream!

'*Now*,' the article concluded, '*Sean Connors – whose
own father was an IRA hero – breaks new ground by
combining his television and magazine interests for an in
depth investigation into the problems facing Belfast. Sean
Connors takes his own empire back to Ireland. It could be
a historic reunion.*'

CHAPTER TWELVE

And so Sean Connors returned to Ireland. He and Kate
arrived in Belfast at noon and Jimmy Cross met them at the
airport.

Jimmy could hardly wait to get to the car. 'That bloody
newspaper story is all over town. The *Telegraph* expanded
on it this morning. The Prods are pulling their hair out
about your old man being in the IRA. They reckon you will
be biased against them. You can imagine the line. Can we
trust this man to be fair – that sort of stuff. Will he provide
more propaganda for the IRA –'

'Rubbish. I'm accused of the opposite in New York.
They call me a British stooge.'

Jimmy smiled grimly, 'You can't win, but neither can
anyone else over here.'

'What about the people who have promised us
interviews? Has anyone pulled out?'

'Not that I've heard. This guy Matt Lambert is lined up
for the morning . . . then O'Brien in the afternoon. But you
haven't heard all the bad news yet. The RUC are waiting
at the hotel. If they have their way we won't interview
anyone . . .'

Kate was only half listening. She stared out of the
window. Mostly she was thinking of that awful line in the
paper about her being Sean's 'constant companion'. Tim

must have read it by now. She braced herself against the lash of his tongue. Not that she minded what he called her . . . as long as he kept quiet about Mark. Sean would be so hurt. How could she explain she had been a girl fresh out of school . . .

The car slowed down at a road block. Soldiers waved them on. Soldiers carrying guns. Kate shuddered.

She had to reach Tim first, before he saw Sean. Make him promise to keep quiet. It was all she could do. She thanked heaven for the Averdale Collection. If need be she would sell the paintings . . . Tim could have the money . . . he could have *everything*. Oh God they had been so happy . . .

She had pleaded with Sean, begged him to stay in London. But he had been adamant – 'No Kate, maybe it's only symbolic me being there, but I owe it to the Da to make sure we do a good job.'

She was sick of 'the Da'. *Sick, sick sick!* What was it that made the Irish cling to the past? What did she care that 'the Da' was an IRA hero? Besides Sean hated the IRA. How could he be so damned ambivalent . . .

He had urged her to stay in London – 'I'll only be away three or four days.'

How could she stay behind while Tim wrecked her whole life?

'No,' she had said, 'if you go, I'll go with you.'

And here she was.

The car stopped at traffic lights. She stared at graffiti scrawled on the wall. Only as the car moved off did she realize the four foot high letters said 'Fuck the Pope'.

'That's the hotel,' Jimmy was saying, 'we'll go in the back way, in case some of the opposition are in the front lobby.'

But *the opposition* were in the back lobby too. Flashbulbs burst as Kate stepped from the car. 'Miss O'Brien – look this way please.'

She turned a stunned face.

'Is it true Tim O'Brien is your brother?'

She gasped.

Suddenly the air was full of questions – 'Can we have your comments on the situation, Miss O'Brien?' – 'What about your brother's political future?'

'Okay boys,' Sean shouted, 'let Miss O'Brien through
I'll be back down in ten minutes. We'll have a drink in th
bar. I'll give you a statement then. Let Miss O'Brie
through.'

They jostled her from every side. Cameras whirred an
clicked into her face . . .

But Sean was not 'back down in ten minutes'. Half an hou
later he was still arguing with Inspector Carstairs of th
RUC.

'Now look Inspector,' Sean said, his voice full of temper
'I'm sorry but your people cannot be present durin
filming. I want people to speak freely, without any pressur
or intimidation –'

'That's not good enough,' Carstairs said testily. He wa
a ginger-haired man whose ruddy complexion becam
more so as he became angry. 'The very least I'll settle fo
is a list of the people you intend to interview.'

'For God's sake, this is a free country –'

'And a dangerous one, if you mix with subversiv
elements.'

'Mr Cross has interviewed subversives all over the world
Mau Mau, Enosis, Viet-Cong –'

'Not on *my* patch!' Carstairs fairly bristled. Then he said
'This place at Lisburn that you're using for a studio. I giv
you fair warning. I've placed it under surveillance. If we se
any wanted criminal enter or leave we shall arrest everyon
concerned.'

That was a body blow and Sean knew it. 'Polic
harassment,' he snapped, then relented in an effort t
reach agreement. 'Look Inspector, we want to make th
film totally objective. Our only concern –'

'*My* only concern,' Carstairs said as he walked to th
door, 'is to maintain the peace in this city.'

He slammed the door behind him.

'Damn and blast,' Sean turned to Jimmy, 'unde
surveillance. Will that affect anything?'

Jimmy groaned, 'God knows. The para-militaries won
like it. This guy Lambert in the morning, he's not on th
run exactly, but he treads a bloody thin line.'

It was a very bad start. Sean groaned, 'Imagine th

outcry if someone is arrested because of us? If an IRA man gets picked up people in New York will swear I set him up.'

They discussed the possibility of moving the studio, but the complications of shifting so much equipment defeated them. 'Besides,' Jimmy said, 'if the police are watching they will just follow us.'

It was obviously true. Finally Sean said, 'You'd better warn this Lambert, just in case.'

But even that was far from easy. Jimmy shook his head. He's not exactly the type you ring up. I generally leave a message in a certain pub and he calls me a day or so later.'

It was possible that Matt Lambert would not receive a warning in time. Lambert could walk into a trap!

Jimmy left the message at the pub, and returned to spend an uncomfortable afternoon reviewing options. To abandon the project was inconceivable, Sean was in too deep to pull out. 'We shall just have to go ahead,' he said, 'and hope for a few lucky breaks.'

Later, over dinner, they listed the responses they would seek to elicit in the interviews. Kate generally enjoyed such sessions – she had made contributions to such meetings in Los Angeles and London and Rome – but that night in Belfast she barely said a word.

Jimmy was taking about her brother. 'O'Brien will take the line that Provo aggression brought the UVF into being. He won't admit to being part of it. He will call it an understandable reaction to Catholic violence. My guess is . . .' Jimmy broke off with an apologetic look in her direction, 'I'm sorry Kate, I keep forgetting he's your brother –'

'That's all right,' she said quietly, 'it was bound to come out sooner or later.'

She hoped nothing else would 'come out'.

She left them shortly after – 'I'm sorry, but I'm tired. I'll have an early night, if you'll excuse me . . .'

She declined Sean's offer to escort her upstairs – 'Don't be silly, you and Jimmy have work to do.'

Once in her suite she telephoned Tim. She had called him from London without success. Now, yet again, his housekeeper informed her he was out at a meeting.

'It's very urgent that I speak to him.'

'Shall I ask him to call you back later?'

Kate hesitated. Sean might be with her later. She too[k] a deep breath, 'No, but will you tell him I shall call roun[d] in the morning, before he meets the Transatlanti[c] Television people. I'll be there at about eleven.'

'At about eleven,' she repeated as she hung up. Th[e] eleventh hour. How appropriate. But it was the onl[y] possible time. Sean would be at his studio, involved wit[h] his interviews . . . she could offer to bring Tim along to th[at] place Osprey House at Lisburn . . . it will all look ver[y] natural . . .

'It will all look very natural,' Matt Riordan said, 'just driv[e] up to the hotel at nine-thirty in the morning, wait for hi[m] to come out, open the back door for him, and then driv[e] him slowly away.'

The man in the peaked cap licked his lips. 'Suppose he'[s] late? You know what the police are like. They'll move m[e] on –'

Matt shook his head. 'Just park the car and go to th[e] desk. Say you're the chauffeur for Mr Sean Connors, com[e] to take him to Lisburn. If he's not in the lobby they'll rin[g] up to his room.'

'And he'll be alone. You're *sure* he'll be alone?'

Matt flicked the schedule on the table in front of him. [It] was a list of the fleet of cars hired by Transatlanti[c] Television – six vehicles in all which would ferry peopl[e] back and forth from the city centre to the studio at Lisbur[n] 'Look for yourself,' Matt said. 'Technical staff to b[e] collected at eight-thirty. Mr James Cross at nine, and M[r] Sean Connors nine-thirty. The only one left in the hotel i[s] this fancy woman of his, and if she's with him, well . . . on[e] wee girl won't trouble you.'

The man smiled sheepishly.

'Don't forget,' Matt reminded him, 'I'll be watchin[g] every move.'

The man nodded, aware of the edge in Matt's voice. [A] lot of trouble was being taken about Mr Sean Connors an[d] the man wondered why.

Matt read the question in his eyes. 'It goes back a lon[g] way. All the days of my life. But you've no need to worry

748

Do your part and you'll be safe enough. Meanwhile you'd best get some sleep . . . it won't be long until morning.'

Morning came early for Kate O'Brien. She was awake at five, and again at six. Finally at seven she abandoned all hope of sleep. She rose and ran a bath, sinking into the scented water in the hope it might relax her. The prospect of facing Tim knotted every nerve in her body.

Sean came into the bathroom and kissed her. He leant over the bath, one hand cupping her breast while he nuzzled her ear. 'Couldn't you sleep?'

She blurted out – 'Darling let's go home. Jimmy and the others will do a good job. Really there's no need for you to be here. Let's catch the first flight back to London. We could collect Pat from school and spend a few –'

'Hey . . . what's come over you? Kate, this will only take three or four days.'

It was useless and she knew it.

She watched him shave. She liked to watch him.

He said, 'I'm up so early I could go in with Jimmy.'

'Don't rush off,' she said quickly. 'Let's just have a nice leisurely breakfast together.'

He shrugged, 'OK, if that makes you happy.'

They dressed and went down to the dining-room. Jimmy was already finishing his breakfast. Sean waved and might have joined him, but Kate steered them to a table near the window – 'No shop talk,' she said, 'you've got the rest of the day for that.'

'You *are* in a funny mood. Let me at least get the papers.'

That was a mistake. As soon as she saw the headlines her stomach knotted up again. '*Sean Connors of Transatlantic TV arrives in Belfast with Miss Kate O'Brien . . .*'

'Well,' Sean said, 'at least the *Telegraph*'s got a good picture of you.'

She managed a smile, thinking Tim would be blind to miss that.

Sean attacked breakfast with his usual gusto. 'What are you doing today?' he asked, 'you coming down to the studio?'

'Later. I promised Tim I'd call round this morning.'

'Great, why not come down with him? Don't make him late though. He's scheduled for two-thirty.'

She nodded.

'Do you want me to arrange a car?'

'No, I've got the address – Osprey House, Lisburn. Tim probably knows where it is. We'll find it. No problem.'

'I'm looking forward to meeting him. Funny, us not meeting until now.'

Jimmy was leaving. He waved from the door. Sean dabbed his mouth with a napkin, looked at his watch, then called, 'I'll be along in half an hour, OK.'

Kate stared after Jimmy's retreating back. She cleared her throat, uncertain of the words she would use, but knowing she had to prepare the ground in case Tim proved impossible. 'He can be difficult, my brother,' she said in a rush, 'spiteful at times. We haven't always got on.'

Sean swallowed some coffee and shot another look at his watch.

'He . . .' she swallowed, 'he won't understand about us for instance.'

Sean grinned, 'Neither would I if I were your brother. You're too good for me, do you think I don't know that?'

She wanted to say oh God Sean, don't put me on a pedestal, I don't deserve it. It will make it harder when Tim tells you about Mark. She wanted to say that, but the words wouldn't come.

'Listen,' he said, reaching for her hand, 'that's a good idea of yours, about taking a break with Pat. Why not call the school. Say we'll pick Pat up first thing Saturday. Then we'll go off for a few days. You look a bit peaky. A break will do you good.'

She nodded, then tried again, 'Sean, if Tim says something about me . . . . it couldn't make any difference to us could it?'

He frowned. 'You mean he'll tell me to stop seeing you? Something crazy like that? Don't be silly, darling. Maybe I can't marry you, but I'll cherish you all the days of my life. That ought to be good enough for any brother.'

That wasn't what she meant at all. And she was gathering her courage for a final try when the head waiter hurried over to their table.

750

'Excuse me, Mr Connors,' he said, 'but your chauffeur is at the desk. He's come to take you to Lisburn.'

From a car across the street, Matt Riordan watched as Sean Connors descended the steps from the hotel and climbed into the back of the hired car. The chauffeur closed the door and hurried round to the front.

Matt removed his spectacles and polished them with the end of his tie. He blinked myopically, unable to focus without his glasses. Not that he needed to at that moment. His mind was busy with other scenes – scenes from the past, crystal clear in his memory. He closed his eyes and watched tongues of flame shoot up from his father's pub. He saw the glass front of his mother's drapery cascade across the street and the butcher's shop under a pall of smoke. But most vividly of all he remembered the day at Keady when Granite Liam Riordan was cut down by bullets.

'Funny,' he said, replacing his glasses, 'they say a man's past life flashes before him when he's at the point of death. I must ask Connors if it's true.'

The car across the street was edging out into traffic. Matt gave a sigh of satisfaction. He had never felt so relaxed, so at peace with himself. He glanced at his watch. Nine-thirty-five. Everything was going to plan.

Little was going to plan for Jimmy Cross. He was having a disastrous morning. From the moment he arrived at the studio the telephone had delivered bad news. They were all pulling out. First the Unionist Party, then the Democratic Unionists, then the Orange Order, now the Ulster Defence Association. The entire Protestant community was boycotting the programme – and all because of that newspaper article about Sean's father being in the IRA.

Jimmy pleaded on the telephone – 'Sean Connors has no sympathy for the IRA or any other para-military group. He is a respected international journalist. Besides, I shall be conducting most interviews – not him.'

But his pleas fell on deaf ears.

Jimmy checked through his schedules again. The Alliance Party was still due to send a spokesman. The

Trade Unions hadn't pulled out. Sinn Fein was sending someone up from Dublin in the morning – but the programme was losing its balance. The whole point was to present *all* shades of opinion.

By ten-fifteen Jimmy was frantic. Sean was late. And there was no sign of Matt Lambert.

Jimmy wondered if the IRA had decided on a boycott too.

He snatched up the telephone and spoke to the front desk. 'Has Mr Lambert arrived yet?'

'No sir, I'll buzz you immediately he sets foot through the door.'

Jimmy tried to curb his impatience. He smoked another cigarette. Sean *must* be here soon. It was only half an hour from the hotel.

But at ten-forty-five Sean had still not arrived.

Jimmy told the girl to phone the hotel – 'See if Mr Connors has been delayed for some reason. If you can't get hold of him I'll speak to Miss O'Brien.'

But Mr Connors had left the hotel – 'At nine-thirty. And Miss O'Brien drove off in a cab five minutes ago.'

Kate gazed out of the cab window as an armoured Saracen personnel carrier turned into a side street. It seemed impossible to believe this was Britain. Troops on the streets. Soldiers in flak-jackets, with plastic visors and riot shields. People searched for weapons or bombs as they went into shops. Even in the hotel everyone had been searched . . . heavens, what a place!

She rehearsed her meeting with Tim yet again. She would make him a straight offer . . . the Averdale Collection for his silence. Two million pounds worth of paintings . . . two million good reasons for him not to make a mess of her life. It was such a good offer he was bound to accept.

And yet she was nervous when the cab dropped her outside his door . . . and even more so ten minutes later when she was shown into her brother's study. The housekeeper withdrew, closing the double doors behind her. The room was in semi-darkness. Curtains covered part of the windows, most of the light was provided by the fire n the hearth. He sat in an armchair, not rising to greet her, n fact not even looking at her.

'Hello, Tim.'

She thought he was going to remain silent, but then his words lashed her – 'I don't know how you've the brazen ffrontery to come to Belfast, let alone call at my house. The name O'Brien is respected in this city. It stands for omething fine and brave, like the name Averdale. You're disgrace to them both.'

She had no immediate answer. He had not offered her chair. He had not as much as looked up. She remained tanding in the middle of the room.

'I knew you'd come,' he said, staring into the fire.

She took a deep breath, 'Then you can guess why.'

He laughed, a bitter mocking sound. 'Not to tell me ou're a whore. Everyone in Ulster knows that after this orning's papers.'

She bit her lip.

'Well?' he sneered.

'I've come to offer you the Averdale Collection. You can ell the paintings. That's what you want isn't it? To sell em. You can have all the money.'

He threw his head back and laughed. His elbow knocked table beside him. Whisky slopped back and forth in a mbler. He stopped laughing and asked, 'So that's our game. What's it worth . . . how many pieces of lver –'

'About two million pounds. Maybe more now –'

'Two million pounds,' he mimicked.

He swung round to face her for the first time. 'Well it's ot enough. *Ten* million isn't enough. So what now, hore? What's your next offer? Your body? It's always orked in the past –'

'Don't be so despicable –'

'*Me!*' he pointed a finger at himself, 'Me despicable?'

Even in that dim light the look in his eyes frightened her. e retreated a step. Nothing she said would have the ghtest effect, she had fooled herself. She called upon her urage, Ziggy's courage, Yvette's courage. Very well. e had no intention of pleading. She would do what she ould have done years ago. Tell Sean herself . . .

753

'Where are you going?' His voice cracked as she turned for the door.

'Does it matter? I came here to –'

'Buy me. That's why you came. Well I can't be bought. Not where my parents are concerned. Honour thy parents. That's what they teach in good Protestant schools. Well I do honour mine –'

'I don't know what you're talking about.'

'No, you don't. You never have. I tried to tell you once. I *did* tell you, so my conscience is clear. But you . . .'

He stood up with his back to the fire. It was difficult to read his expression, but his whole stance conveyed gloating triumph which mystified her.

She took another step to the door.

'Wait,' he snapped. 'There's something you should know before you go.'

'I don't see why I should listen to your insults. I don't deserve them.'

'Oh?' He laughed. 'Well I shall let you be the judge of that – when I tell you something about yourself –'

'You know very little of my life.'

'I know enough,' he scowled, 'I know a secret that will destroy you.'

Her eyes went to the whisky glass. She wondered if he were drunk.

'Don't let that fool you,' he chuckled, 'merely a celebratory drink on an auspicious occasion.'

She stared at him.

'You may as well sit down,' he said, 'you won't leave before I tell you my secret.'

For a split second she was undecided. Then she crossed to a sofa near the window.

He reached for his glass and raised it in a toast. 'Ironic how life works out. For you to come back to Belfast in September. You should have been here a few weeks ago on the second. Now that would have been rich. The second of September. It means nothing to you I suppose?'

She thought. 'No, should it?'

'It was the date our parents were murdered. When they were shot down in cold blood.'

She caught her breath, 'Oh dear, all those years ago.'

'As you say,' he grunted as he sat down again. 'I was
hat . . . about nine . . . and you were six or seven. We
ent to London to live in our guardian's big house.
rphans, facing the great unknown.'

Bitterness crept back into his voice. 'Our paths parted
en. You became the household pet. Everyone made a
ass of you. I was the cripple boy nobody wanted to know.
h I used to watch you go off with your nurse for walks and
utings. But I had to work. God how I worked. You've no
dea of the pain, the suffering – day after grinding day with
nly Williams to give me encouragement. You never asked
out me, nor did anyone else. I remember Fridays most,
hen our guardian arrived home. First thing he did was
nd for your nurse. Then you arrived, all prettied up in
od clothes – to prance up and down, twirling your
irts.'

He broke off to sip from his glass. 'I used to watch,' he
id. 'I couldn't walk, so I dragged myself along the landing
look down into the hall. Sometimes the study door was
pen. I could see you sitting in his lap, hugging him and
rieking with excitement. Then Williams would go into
e study and I'd drag myself back to my room as fast as
could – always thinking it would be my turn next, that our
ardian would come up and see me. But he never did. It
as always you. You were a princess. I was a cripple.'

She felt uncomfortable, even a little ashamed. It was all
ue, she knew it was true.

'One thing kept me going. A face. I used to have
ghtmares about it. Night after night. I woke up
reaming, covered in sweat. It was the murderer, coming
get me. I couldn't walk, let alone run away. I had to just
ay in that sweat-soaked bed and wait for him to come out
f the darkness. Always the same face. I knew it by heart
nose, ears, mouth, eyes, hair, everything. It was the face
f the man who murdered our parents, the man I saw in the
ne at Keady, the man with the gun.

'I was afraid of the dark – terrified to go to sleep. I
egged Williams to leave the light on, I told him about the
eam, about that man's face. All he said was – "Good,
ou'll remember that face all the days of your life. One day
ou'll find him and take your revenge." I would scream,

755

"How can I? I'm a cripple. I can't walk." And he'd shou
at me, "Make yourself walk."'

Kate listened in horror. 'Tim . . . I'm so sorry.'

'Sorry?' He looked at her angrily. 'I don't want your pit·
I want you to *understand*. Suppose it happened to you
Suppose you endured those nightmares every night, fo
years and years? Do you think you would forget that face
Ever? Do you?'

'No . . . I don't suppose –'

'*Suppose!*' His eyes blazed. 'Suppose nothing. Woul
you or wouldn't you?'

Whisky slopped over the rim of his glass.

'No,' she said hurriedly, 'I mean yes, I'm sure I'
remember it.'

'Every day of your life?'

'Yes, every day of my life. I could never forg·
something so awful.'

He smiled abruptly, and the sudden grin lent an almo·
insane cast to his face. Then he gave a satisfied grunt an
turned away.

'Quite right,' he muttered, 'something so awful, as yc
say, anyone would be the same, that face would hau·
every day of their life.'

He was silent for a moment, then he said, 'I made myse
walk all right. Exercising every day. So tired at times th.
I collapsed. Williams left me on the floor. "Make yourse
walk," he would jeer. So I did. Then a wonderful thir
happened. Our guardian was really nice to me, so kind th
I used to cry with happiness. You were still his favourit·
but there was room for me too. When the war came a·
you were sent to America, and it was just him and me.
thought I was the luckiest boy on God's earth.

'Then I saw that face again. I was on a train, looking o·
of the window. We were in the station, opposite
bookstall. There was this face, on the front page of
newspaper. My murderer was headline news. He was som
kind of hero, coming out of hospital. I couldn't see h
name, just the face. The train moved off and the paper w
gone. But as you said, something like that stays with yc
every day of your life.'

He looked at her, again with that queer grin. It made h

feel uneasy. She was glad when he turned back to the fire.

'The war years were good,' he said, 'it was just him and me. I was determined to make him proud, so I worked harder than ever to pass my exams. Sometimes he sat and talked about "after the war, when Kate comes home". We would all live together at Brackenburn. I worried about that, but not often. You see I planned to be an important man by then, running the Averdale businesses, perhaps even going into Stormont. Besides, I wanted to do something else to make him proud of me. I planned to kill the man who murdered my parents.'

A shiver ran up her spine.

'At one stage,' he continued, 'I even stole a gun from the armoury, ready for the day when I confronted the murderer. Meanwhile I remembered that face.' He shrugged. 'As you say, something like that stays in your mind all the days of your life.'

He finished the whisky in his glass. 'Then the war ended and you came home. You can't imagine the excitement, the princess was returning from exile. I half expected a civic reception – but instead he was bleak with disappointment. You weren't what he expected, were you?'

There was no mistaking his malice. Kate looked away. He poured himself another whisky, without offering her any kind of drink, not even coffee.

'I felt sorry for you,' he said. 'After all, I knew the pain of rejection. So when he went to Africa I visited you at school when I could. Before, when I was crippled, I had hated you, but by then our roles had reversed. I was the success, you were the failure. Then I realized you hated me. You hated us both. You never wanted to come back, you preferred your precious friends in America –'

'That was wrong of me,' she burst out, 'I said I was wrong. I was sorry –'

'Sorry! Again you use that word. You were so sorry that when I told you about the man who killed our parents you didn't want to know. I even described him to you –'

'It wasn't that. I was upset. I couldn't see the good of dwelling on the past.'

'Couldn't you! Well by God you soon will!'

She stared, without comprehension.

'You know most of the story after that,' he shrugged, 'some of it better than I do. For instance I don't know when you first became a whore, but it was early on, you and tha — that Jenny person. But she was less clever than you. She got pregnant didn't she?'

Kate was shocked, 'How did you know?'

'He told me. That Christmas. He came home for a couple of days, remember? When I asked about you he said you were upset about Jenny getting into trouble with some man – so he was giving you a special Christmas treat. Ha, and to think I believed it! Good God, he guessed what you were like even then.'

Kate flushed bright red. 'It . . . it wasn't like that at all –'

'Not much! And all the time he was screwing you I was up to my eyes in work. I worked like a dog to save the Averdale business – but all he wanted was money for his bloody art collection, and to take his fancy whore all over Europe –'

She jumped up and started across the room. He sprang from his chair and reached her at the door, gripping her wrist and pulling her round to face him.

'Damn you!' he shouted. 'You stay and listen to me!'

They were both trembling. His grip was a vice. She tried to pull away, but he laughed – 'What will you do? Scream rape? Nobody will believe you.'

She slapped his face with every ounce of her strength.

'All right,' he panted, 'forget your past. I'll just tell you the secret, then you can go.'

'I don't want to hear!'

'It's the face. I've seen it! The murderer. He's in Belfast.'

'I don't understand,' she said weakly, 'I don't know what you mean.'

'The man who killed our parents is here. He knows you and you know him.'

He released her arm. She rubbed her wrist, still staring at him. 'Well . . . hadn't you better tell someone . . . the police –'

'All I had was a face, remember. When I saw it in the papers last week I could hardly believe it. I had to make sure it was the same as I saw from the train, all those years

758

go. I called Buckley in London and told him to dig back through the archives in Fleet Street. And he found it, the exact picture. This man, with his arm in a sling, being helped down some hospital steps.'

He grinned triumphantly. 'Buckley even got a copy of the photograph. Would you like to see it? The man who made you an orphan, all those years ago.'

She hesitated . . . distracted by his gloating manner.

Tim crossed the room to his desk. She followed, her legs quaking, a sick dread numbing her mind. Tim waved a newspaper in front of her. She saw the headline – '*The rise and rise of Sean Connors.*' The wartime photograph of Sean had been outlined in red ink. Clipped next to it was another photograph – Sean with his arm in a sling, being helped down some steps.

Tim was laughing, 'Judge yourself, that's what I said when you challenged my insults. Well – what do you call a woman who sleeps with the murderer of her parents?'

'It can't be,' she said weakly. 'You must be wrong–'

'You'd remember. That's what you said. And I did. I even described that face to you at Glossops. Square jaw, black hair and – it doesn't show it here – but his eyes are vivid blue.'

Kate clutched the desk for support.

'A murderer's whore!' Tim shouted. 'Whore . . . whore . . . whore . . .'

'It's a mistake,' she whimpered, 'some kind of terrible mistake.'

'No! He was at Keady, in the lane, I saw him!'

She turned blindly for the door.

'Justice,' Tim screamed, 'don't you see. Justice. I've settled with you both.'

The door was jammed. Or locked. She fought and struggled with the handle.

'Whore . . . whore . . . whore . . .'

The door gave way. She stumbled into the hall. The passage stretched before her. He followed her, screaming all the time – 'Whore . . . bloody whore.'

She reached the front door. Street noises erupted as she stood on the steps. A troop carrier rumbled past – some soldiers whistled at her. She stumbled on the pavement and

almost fell. Her legs walked with a will of their own. He
mind was still in that house, with Tim leering an
gibbering. She stepped into the road. A car squealed to
halt. Someone shouted. People looked and stared. Sh
kept telling herself it can't be true. It was more of Tim's lie
. . . spiteful, horrible lies . . .

She came upon a taxi-rank. Dazed and shocked, sh
gave the man her London address – and was baffled by h
blank face. He asked if she were ill. Finally she understoo
– and told him to take her to the hotel.

The ride only took five minutes – but years of her li
passed through her mind. Sean? Could it have been Sea
. . . all those years ago? Sean . . . did you make me a
orphan?

Something was happening at the hotel.

Men with cameras were all over the front steps . . . an
policemen . . . and soldiers.

Jimmy Cross was pushing everyone aside to open th
door of her cab. Poor Jimmy looked sick. As white as sh
was, as if he were in shock.

He took one look at her face and said, 'My God, yo
know.'

'Know? No I don't. Not until I see Sean. It's all
mistake. Tim is telling lies. Sean will sort it all out, Sea
always does.'

She was blinded by flashbulbs. Jimmy was steering he
through the mob at the entrance. The lobby was crowde
too, a great crush of people centred round that RU
Inspector who was so difficult with Sean . . . Carstairs o
something . . . he was reading out a statement . . . othe
were writing it down, she heard snatches as Jimm
shouldered ahead of her through the throng.

'. . . abducted at approximately nine-thirty by a ma
posing as a chauffeur . . . taken to a house in Ballymurph
. . . was shot in both knees, then killed by a bullet in th
back of the head . . . the IRA have already claime
responsibility . . .'

Kate closed her eyes in horror. Someone had bee
killed. How awful. Oh God, what a terrible place.

Two British soldiers craned their necks above the crow
Jimmy pushed past them, and as Kate squeezed alor

ne soldier asked the other – 'Who they got this time?'

'Some bloke called Connors by the sound of it . . . Sean Connors.'

The other one groaned, 'Christ – when will these stupid Irish bastards stop killing each other.'

EPILOGUE

We buried my father in London. Jimmy Cross took th
decision after calling Freddie Mallon in New York
Michael O'Hara had a say in it too, but whoever decide
I am sure it was right, because as Freddie said at the funera
– 'During the war Sean Connors *was* London for million
of people.' It was meant as a tribute but the IRA used i
for their own ends – the label 'British stooge' followed m
father to his grave, which was ironic when hardline Prod
were boycotting him as an IRA sympathizer at the ver
time of his death. Yet somehow that kind o
misunderstanding is symbolic of the whole Irish tragedy.

I was young at the time and not much help to anyone
In fact the reverse. The problems started when Freddie an
Margaret flew in for the funeral, complete with my mother
Of course, it was all they could do – after all she had a righ
to be there – but her presence automatically exclude
Kate, and that upset me. Kate had given my father so mucl
happiness that for her to be displaced by someone who ha
looked on him as a meal ticket seemed wrong to me – an
being young I said so. Not only that but I refused to atten
the ceremony without Kate, which caused a hell of a row
Finally Kate persuaded me to go to the service without her
I am glad I went, and sorry about the scene I cause
beforehand . . . but of course it is too late to do anythin
about that now. The day after the funeral I took Kate t
the graveside and left her to say her goodbyes – but in trutl
she no more said goodbye then than she has now.

We simply had to try to pick up the pieces and get on witl
our lives. I finished school and went on to university – an
Kate lived in Paris with her friend Yvette for a while.
ought to have explained that my father left Kate a wealth
woman. (My mother was well provided for too, I hasten t
add.) Not that money could compensate for the loss of m
father. Kate's behaviour was strained to the point of bein;
positively strange after that awful day in Belfast. Of cours

762

put it down to my father's death . . . which it was . . . but something else plagued her, of which I knew nothing at the time.

Anyway, I spent most holidays in Paris with Kate, and thankfully the special closeness between us remained as firm as ever. Kate has been a combination of mother and big sister and 'the kind of woman I would like to marry' for as long as I can remember. I love her very much, so I was worried sick when she showed no signs of recovering from the death of my father. She nursed Yvette and took an interest in me – but apart from us she shut out the rest of the world. Not only that but when we talked of my father something more than love showed in her eyes – a guarded, almost haunted look which made no sense at all – as if she kept a secret about him from everyone, but especially from me.

Well when Yvette died Kate came back to England to live. Not in London, she bought a small house in Cornwall, on the coast near St Ives, where she lived quite alone save for her dog. I had started on *Seven Days* by then, but I went down to see Kate every third weekend. I was the only company she had, apart from her dog – but we were all she wanted, because she firmly rejected any suggestion of living in London or seeing any of her old friends.

Then Paul Thompson published a book about my father called *The Power in the Back Room*. We all hated it. Freddie Mallon even issued a writ. According to Thompson (who had once worked on *Seven Days* as a junior reporter) Sean Connors was nothing more than a glib Irishman with friends in high places. Much was made of 'the Kennedy connection' in the States and Sir George Hamilton's influence in London. What was worse, he had an awful lot to say about Kate being my father's mistress. He even suggested that my mother had been left abandoned in New York. Generally it was a hatchet job. As soon as I calmed down I was determined to write the real story of my father's life. Freddie Mallon and Tubby Reynolds urged me on, and since they were both on the verge of retirement they wanted me to start right away.

Kate was the problem.

I had expected *The Power in the Back Room* to upset her

as much as it had everyone else – but to my surprise she seemed quite unmoved about the book. 'It doesn't matter what they say about me,' she said, then she laughed 'Funny that. Once upon a time other people's opinion were all I cared about.'

She wasn't even too upset by what Thompson wrot about my father. 'Sean wasn't anything like that. We kne what he was really like, and we loved him.'

But when I told her about my book she became ver agitated, even frightened. I had planned to ask her to hel with research. She not only refused, but when I persiste she burst into tears. I said – 'Kate, my father adore you and so do I, nothing in my book will hurt you, promise.'

It was then that I learned of her meeting with Tim, o the morning of my father's death. I was horrified. Poo Kate. She had tried to reject her brother's story but ha never been able to discuss it with anyone else. For years sh had lived with that awful secret, in constant fear tha someone would accuse my dead father of having murdere her parents. Yet – amazingly – her concern was more fo me than herself – 'I didn't want anything to spoil you memory of him.'

No wonder she had taken Thompson's book in her strid – she had expected Sean Connors to be accused of muc worse.

I made her tell me the whole story then, everything tha Tim had told her. I certainly did not believe it, and I don think she did, but by then she had tortured herself with th story for so long that she didn't know what to believe. Sh kept insisting that Tim had been so *sure* – 'He carried tha face in his mind every day of his life.'

It upset her to tell me, but I've no doubt it helped he to share her burden. So much so that when she had calme down the following day she agreed that I should do th book – she would even help – on condition that if discovered any truth in Tim O'Brien's allegations I woul not publish a word. I accepted the proviso to humour he as much as anything, for I never could believe anything ba of my father.

The following day I telephoned Michael O'Hara an

sked him point blank – 'Where was my grandfather illed?'

After a while he remembered. 'Keady,' he said, 'it's a ttle place just over the border.'

I felt sick. Keady was where Kate's parents were urdered.

I flew over to Dublin and started digging from there. It id not take long. The National Library has copies of ewspapers back to the year dot. And I found out the truth that my grandfather was killed in the Killing at Keady – the very same 'incident' in which Kate's parents were hot. Not only that but my father was there when it appened. I nearly abandoned the project – but I was apped by then – to quit would almost be an admission of y father's guilt. I could never live with that, and it would estroy Kate. So I had to go on.

Well, you know most of the rest. The last link – that of latt Riordan – might have remained hidden but for a iend who knew I was doing research for this book. One ay he phoned me from Belfast to say that the Ulster olunteer Force had killed a man known as Matt Lambert. had never heard of Lambert. 'Well I hadn't either,' said y friend, 'but the RUC seem to think he was the man who illed your father.' So I flew to Belfast and started again.

All told the project has been exhausting. When my ather was killed everyone thought it was just another IRA illing. No one guessed at the truth – of those strands in my ather's life which had become so tangled with the iordans and the O'Briens and even Lord Averdale. Now is finished I am glad the full story can be told at last . . sad and terrible though it is, but then so is the history f Ireland.

Kate agrees with everything I have written – in fact the ost important aspect of this book is what it has done for ate. Proving my father's innocence lifted a shadow from er eyes. Her reaction was one of overwhelming relief – Now nobody can ever tarnish Sean's name.'

I hope that is true. Certainly Kate remains untarnished. he is still beautiful. Her life in St Ives is less solitary these ays. Some time ago, when we finally established what appened at the Killing at Keady, she took up painting –

and these days she paints well enough for London galleries to take her work. It brings her up to town once a month and of course we meet for dinner. There is no man in her life, unless you count me, but at least she mixes with people again and has come to terms with her life.

The remarkable Maeve Tully is still alive although no longer living in Dublin. Molly Oakes too is thriving, married now, with a grown-up family in Australia. May I take this opportunity of thanking them both for their generous help with their parts of this story.

Tim O'Brien died last year, so Kate is not merely the only survivor of the Killing at Keady, but the sole survivor of that terrible day in Belfast when the paths of Sean Connors and Matt Riordan crossed for the last time – the day Kate and I will always remember as THE KILLING ANNIVERSARY. Now, as the violence in Northern Ireland makes headlines every day, we often wonder how many old feuds are being settled, or – even worse – how many new ones are being started. And we pray for peace to come to the troubled land of our fathers.

Patrick Connors.
1984.

Gerald Seymour

writes internationally best-selling thrillers

'Not since Le Carré has the emergence of an international suspense writer been as stunning as that of Gerald Seymour.' *Los Angeles Times*

HARRY'S GAME   £1.75
THE GLORY BOYS   £1.95
KINGFISHER   £1.75
RED FOX   £1.95
THE CONTRACT   £1.75
ARCHANGEL   £1.95
IN HONOUR BOUND   £1.95

FONTANA PAPERBACKS

Fontana Paperbacks: Fiction

Fontana is a leading paperback publisher of both non-fiction, popular and academic, and fiction. Below are some recent fiction titles.

- ☐ COMING TO TERMS Imogen Winn £2.25
- ☐ TAPPING THE SOURCE Kem Nunn £1.95
- ☐ METZGER'S DOG Thomas Perry £2.50
- ☐ THE SKYLARK'S SONG Audrey Howard £1.95
- ☐ THE MYSTERY OF THE BLUE TRAIN Agatha Christie £1.75
- ☐ A SPLENDID DEFIANCE Stella Riley £1.95
- ☐ ALMOST PARADISE Susan Isaacs £2.95
- ☐ NIGHT OF ERROR Desmond Bagley £1.95
- ☐ SABRA Nigel Slater £1.75
- ☐ THE FALLEN ANGELS Susannah Kells £2.50
- ☐ THE RAGING OF THE SEA Charles Gidley £2.95
- ☐ CRESCENT CITY Belva Plain £2.75
- ☐ THE KILLING ANNIVERSARY Ian St James £2.95
- ☐ LEMONADE SPRINGS Denise Jefferies £1.95
- ☐ THE BONE COLLECTORS Brian Callison £1.95

You can buy Fontana paperbacks at your local bookshop or newsagent. Or you can order them from Fontana Paperbacks, Cash Sales Department, Box 29, Douglas, Isle of Man. Please send a cheque, postal or money order (not currency) worth the purchase price plus 15p per book for postage (maximum postage is £3.00 for orders within the UK).

NAME (Block letters) _____

ADDRESS _____

_____

While every effort is made to keep prices low, it is sometimes necessary to increase them at short notice. Fontana Paperbacks reserve the right to show new retail prices on covers which may differ from those previously advertised in the text or elsewhere.